THE MATT SCUDDER

ALSO BY LAWRENCE BLOCK

THE MATT SCUDDER MYSTERIES 2

A STAB IN THE DARK

EIGHT MILLION WAYS TO DIE

WHEN THE SACRED GINMILL CLOSES

Lawrence Block

ORION

This edition first published in Great Britain in 1997 by
Orion
An imprint of Orion Books Ltd
Orion House, 5 Upper St Martin's Lane
London WC2H 9EA

A CIP catalogue record for this book is available
from the British Library

ISBN: (Csd) 0 75280 540 1
(Ppr) 0 75280 539 8

Printed and bound in Great Britain by
Clays Ltd, St Ives plc.

CONTENTS

A STAB IN THE DARK

FOR PATRICK TRESE

ONE

I didn't see him coming. I was in Armstrong's at my usual table in the rear. The lunch crowd had thinned out and the noise level had dropped. There was classical music on the radio and you could hear it now without straining. It was a gray day out, a mean wind blowing, the air holding a promise of rain. A good day to be stuck in a Ninth Avenue saloon, drinking bourbon-spiked coffee and reading the *Post*'s story about some madman slashing passersby on First Avenue.

'Mr Scudder?'

Sixty or thereabouts. High forehead, rimless eye-glasses over pale blue eyes. Graying blond hair combed to lie flat on the scalp. Say five-nine or -ten. Say a hundred seventy pounds. Light complexion. Cleanshaven. Narrow nose. Small thin-lipped mouth. Gray suit, white shirt, tie striped in red and black and gold. Briefcase in one hand, umbrella in the other.

'May I sit down?'

I nodded at the chair opposite mine. He took it, drew a wallet from his breast pocket and handed me a card. His hands were small and he was wearing a Masonic ring.

I glanced at the card, handed it back. 'Sorry,' I said.

'But—'

'I don't want any insurance,' I said. 'And you wouldn't want to sell me any. I'm a bad risk.'

He made a sound that might have been nervous laughter. 'God,' he said. 'Of course you'd think that, wouldn't you? I didn't come to sell you anything. I can't remember the last time I wrote an individual policy. My area's group policies for corporations.' He placed the card on the blue-checked cloth between us. 'Please,' he said.

The card identified him as Charles F. London, a general agent with Mutual Life of New Hampshire. The address shown was 42 Pine Street, downtown in the financial district. There were two telephone numbers, one local, the other with a 914 area code. The northern suburbs, that would be. Westchester County, probably.

I was still holding his card when Trina came over to take our order. He asked for Dewar's and soda. I had half a cup of coffee left. When she was out of earshot he said, 'Francis Fitzroy recommended you.'

'Francis Fitzroy.'

'Detective Fitzroy. Eighteenth Precinct.'

'Oh, Frank,' I said. 'I haven't seen him in a while. I didn't even know he was at the Eighteenth now.'

'I saw him yesterday afternoon.' He took off his glasses, polished their lenses with his napkin. 'He recommended you, as I said, and I decided I wanted to sleep on it. I didn't sleep much. I had appointments this morning, and then I went to your hotel, and they said I might find you here.'

I waited.

'Do you know who I am, Mr Scudder?'

'No.'

'I'm Barbara Ettinger's father.'

'Barbara Ettinger. I don't – wait a minute.'

Trina brought his drink, set it down, slipped wordlessly away. His fingers curled around the glass but he didn't lift it from the table.

I said, 'The Icepick Prowler. Is that how I know the name?'

'That's right.'

'Must have been ten years ago.'

'Nine.'

'She was one of the victims. I was working over in Brooklyn at the time. The Seventy-eighth Precinct, Bergen and Flatbush. Barbara Ettinger. That was our case, wasn't it?'

'Yes.'

I closed my eyes, letting the memory come back. 'She was one of the last victims. The fifth or sixth, she must have been.'

'The sixth.'

'And there were two more after her, and then he went out of business. Barbara Ettinger. She was a schoolteacher. No, but it was something like that. A day-care center. She worked at a day-care center.'

'You have a good memory.'

'It could be better. I just had the case long enough to determine it was the Icepick Prowler again. At that point we turned it over to whoever had been working that case all along.

2

Midtown North, I think it was. In fact I think Frank Fitzroy was at Midtown North at the time.'

'That's correct.'

I had a sudden rush of sense memory. I remembered a kitchen in Brooklyn, cooking smells overladen with the reek of recent death. A young woman lay on the linoleum, her clothing disarrayed, innumerable wounds in her flesh. I had no memory of what she looked like, only that she was dead.

I finished my coffee, wishing it were straight bourbon. Across the table from me, Charles London was taking a small tentative sip of his scotch. I looked at the Masonic symbols on his gold ring and wondered what they were supposed to mean, and what they meant to him.

I said, 'He killed eight women within a period of a couple months. Used the same MO throughout, attacked them in their own homes during daylight hours. Multiple stab wounds with an icepick. Struck eight times and then went out of business.'

He didn't say anything.

'Then nine years later they catch him. When was it? Two weeks ago?'

'Almost three weeks.'

I hadn't paid too much attention to the newspaper coverage. A couple of patrolmen on the Upper West Side had stopped a suspicious character on the streets, and a frisk turned up an icepick. They took him into the station house and ran a check on him, and it turned out he was back on the streets after an extended confinement in Manhattan State Hospital. Somebody took the trouble to ask him why he was toting an icepick, and they got lucky the way you sometimes do. Before anybody knew what was happening he'd confessed to a whole list of unsolved homicides.

'They ran his picture,' I said. 'A little guy, wasn't he? I don't remember the name.'

'Louis Pinell.'

I glanced at him. His hands rested on the table, fingertips just touching, and he was looking down at his hands. I said that he must have been greatly relieved that the man was in custody after all these years.

'No,' he said.

The music stopped. The radio announcer hawked subscriptions to a magazine published by the Audobon Society. I sat and waited.

'I almost wish they hadn't caught him,' Charles London said.

3

'Why?'

'Because he didn't kill Barbara.'

Later I went back and read all three papers, and there'd been something to the effect that Pinell had confessed to seven Icepick Prowler slayings while maintaining he was innocent of the eighth. If I'd even noted that information first time around, I hadn't paid it any mind. Who knows what a psychotic killer's going to remember nine years after the fact?

According to London, Pinell had more of an alibi than his own memory. The night before Barbara Ettinger was murdered, Pinell had been picked up on the complaint of a counterman at a coffee shop in the east twenties. He was taken to Bellevue for observation, held two days and released. Police and hospital records made it quite clear that he was in a locked ward when Barbara Ettinger was killed.

'I kept trying to tell myself there was a mistake,' London said. 'A clerk can make a mistake recording an admission or release date. But there was no mistake. And Pinell was very adamant on the subject. He was perfectly willing to admit the other murders. I gather he was proud of them in some way or other. But he was genuinely angry at the idea that a murder he hadn't committed was being attributed to him.'

He picked up his glass but put it down without drinking from it. 'I gave up years ago,' he said. 'I took it for granted that Barbara's murderer would never be apprehended. When the series of killings stopped so abruptly, I assumed the killer had either died or moved away. My fantasy was that he'd had a moment of awful clarity, realized what he'd done, and killed himself. It made it easier for me if I was able to believe that, and from what a police officer told me, I gathered that that sort of thing occasionally happens. I came to think of Barbara as having been the victim of a force of nature, as if she'd died in an earthquake or a flood. Her killing was impersonal and her killer unknown and unknowable. Do you see what I mean?'

'I think so.'

'Now everything's changed. Barbara wasn't killed by this force of nature. She was murdered by someone who tried to make it look as though her death was the work of the Icepick Prowler. Hers was a very cold and calculating murder.' He closed his eyes for a moment and a muscle worked in the side of his face. 'For years I thought she'd been killed for no reason at all,' he said, 'and that was horrible, and now I can see that she was killed for a reason, and that's worse.'

4

'Yes.'

'I went to Detective Fitzroy to find out what the police were going to do now. Actually I didn't go to him directly. I went to one place and they sent me to another place. They passed me around, you see, no doubt hoping I'd get discouraged somewhere along the way and leave them alone. I finally wound up with Detective Fitzroy, and he told me that they're not going to do anything about finding Barbara's killer.'

'What were you expecting them to do?'

'Reopen the case. Launch an investigation. Fitzroy made me see my expectations were unrealistic. I got angry at first, but he talked me through my anger. He said the case was nine years old. There weren't any leads or suspects then and there certainly aren't any now. Years ago they gave up on all eight of those killings, and the fact that they can close their files on seven of them is simply a gift. It didn't seem to bother him, or any of the officers I talked to, that there's a killer walking around free. I gather that there are a great many murderers walking around free.'

'I'm afraid there are.'

'But I have a particular interest in this particular murderer.' His little hands had tightened up into fists. 'She must have been killed by someone who knew her. Someone who came to the funeral, someone who pretended to mourn her. God, I can't stand that!'

I didn't say anything for a few minutes. I caught Trina's eye and ordered a drink. The straight goods this time. I'd had enough coffee for a while. When she brought it I drank off half of it and felt its warmth spread through me, taking some of the chill out of the day.

I said, 'What do you want from me?'

'I want you to find out who killed my daughter.'

No surprise there. 'That's probably impossible,' I said.

'I know.'

'If there was ever a trail, it's had nine years to go cold. What can I do that the cops can't?'

'You can make an effort. That's something they can't do, or at least it's something they *won't* do, and that amounts to the same thing. I'm not saying they're wrong not to reopen the case. But the thing is that I want them to do it, and I can't do anything about it, but in your case, well, I can hire you.'

'Not exactly.'

'I beg your pardon?'

'You can't hire me,' I explained. 'I'm not a private investigator.'

'Fitzroy said—'

'They have licenses,' I went on. 'I don't. They fill out forms, they write reports in triplicate, they submit vouchers for their expenses, they file tax returns, they do all those things and I don't.'

'What do you do, Mr Scudder?'

I shrugged. 'Sometimes I'll do a favor for a person,' I said, 'and sometimes the person will give me some money. As a favor in return.'

'I think I understand.'

'Do you?' I drank the rest of my drink. I remembered the corpse in that Brooklyn kitchen. White skin, little beads of black blood around the puncture wounds. 'You want a killer brought to justice,' I said. 'You'd better realize in front that that's impossible. Even if there's a killer out there, even if there's a way to find out who he is, there's not going to be any evidence lying around after all these years. No bloodstained icepick in somebody's hardware drawer. I could get lucky and come up with a thread, but it won't turn into the kind of thing you can spread out in front of a jury. Somebody killed your daughter and got away with it and it galls you. Won't it be more frustrating if you know who it is and there's nothing you can do about it?'

'I still want to know.'

'You might learn things you won't like. You said it yourself – somebody probably killed her for a reason. You might be happier not knowing the reason.'

'It's possible.'

'But you'll run that risk.'

'Yes.'

'Well, I guess I can try talking with some people.' I got my pen and notebook from my pocket, opened the notebook to a fresh page, uncapped the pen. 'I might as well start with you,' I said.

We talked for close to an hour and I made a lot of notes. I had another double bourbon and made it last. He had Trina take away his drink and bring him a cup of coffee. She refilled it twice for him before we were finished.

He lived in Hastings-on-Hudson in Westchester County. They'd moved there from the city when Barbara was five and her younger sister Lynn was three. Three years ago, some six years after Barbara's death, London's wife Helen had died of cancer.

6

He lived there alone now, and every once in a while he thought about selling the house, but so far he hadn't gotten around to listing it with a realtor. He supposed it was something he'd do sooner or later, whereupon he'd either move into the city or take a garden apartment somewhere in Westchester.

Barbara had been twenty-six. She'd be thirty-five now if she had lived. No children. She had been a couple of months' pregnant when she died, and London hadn't even known that until after her death. Telling me this, his voice broke.

Douglas Ettinger had remarried a couple of years after Barbara's death. He'd been a caseworker for the Welfare Department during their marriage, but he'd quit that job shortly after the murder and gone into sales. His second wife's father owned a sporting goods store on Long Island and after the marriage he'd taken in Ettinger as a partner. Ettinger lived in Mineola with his wife and two or three children – London wasn't sure of the number. He had come alone to Helen London's funeral and London hadn't had any contact with him since then, nor had he ever met the new wife.

Lynn London would be thirty-three in a month. She lived in Chelsea and taught fourth-graders at a progressive private school in the Village. She'd been married shortly after Barbara was killed, and she and her husband had separated after a little over two years of marriage and divorced not long after that. No children.

He mentioned other people. Neighbors, friends. The operator of the day-care center where Barbara had worked. A coworker there. Her closest friend from college. Sometimes he remembered names, sometimes not, but he gave me bits and pieces and I could take it from there. Not that any of it would necessarily lead anywhere.

He went off on tangents a lot. I didn't attempt to rein him in. I thought I might get a better picture of the dead woman by letting him wander, but even so I didn't develop any real sense of her. I learned she was attractive, that she'd been popular as a teenager, that she'd done well in school. She was interested in helping people, she liked working with children, and she'd been eager to have a family of her own. The image that came through was of a woman of no vices and the blandest virtues, wavering in age from childhood to an age she hadn't lived to attain. I had the feeling that he hadn't known her terribly well, that he'd been insulated by his work and by his role as her father from any reliable perception of her as a person.

7

Not uncommon, that. Most people don't really know their children until the children have become parents themselves. And Barbara hadn't lived that long.

When he ran out of things to tell me I flipped through my notes, then closed the book. I told him I'd see what I could do.

'I'll need some money,' I said.

'How much?'

I never know how to set a fee. What's too little and what's too much? I knew I needed money – a chronic condition, that – and that he probably had it in fair supply. Insurance agents can earn a lot or a little, but it seemed to me that selling group coverage to corporations was probably quite lucrative. I flipped a mental coin and came up with a figure of fifteen hundred dollars.

'And what will that buy, Mr Scudder?'

I told him I really didn't know. 'It'll buy my efforts,' I said. 'I'll work on this until I come up with something or until it's clear to me that there's nothing to come up with. If that happens before I figure I've earned your money you'll get some back. If I feel I have more coming I'll let you know, and you can decide then whether or not you want to pay me.'

'It's very irregular, isn't it?'

'You might not be comfortable with it.'

He considered that but didn't say anything. Instead he got out a checkbook and asked how he should make the check payable. To Matthew Scudder, I told him, and he wrote it out and tore it out of the book and set it on the table between us.

I didn't pick it up. I said, 'You know, I'm not the only alternative to the police. There are big, well-staffed agencies who operate in a much more conventional manner. They'll report in detail, they'll account for every cent of fees and expenses. On top of that, they've got more resources than I do.'

'Detective Fitzroy said as much. He said there were a couple of major agencies he could recommend.'

'But he recommended me?'

'Yes.'

'Why?' I knew one reason, of course, but it wasn't one he'd have given London.

London smiled for the first time. 'He said you're a crazy son of a bitch,' he said. 'Those were his words, not mine.'

'And?'

'He said you might get caught up in this in a way a large agency wouldn't. That when you get your teeth in something

8

you don't let go. He said the odds were against it, but you just might find out who killed Barbara.'

'He said that, did he?' I picked up his check, studied it, folded it in half. I said, 'Well, he's right. I might.'

TWO

It was too late to get to the bank. After London left I settled my tab and cashed a marker at the bar. My first stop would be the Eighteenth Precinct, and it's considered bad manners to show up empty-handed.

I called first to make sure he'd be there, then took a bus east and another one downtown. Armstrong's is on Ninth Avenue, around the corner from my Fifty-seventh Street hotel. The Eighteenth is housed on the ground floor of the Police Academy, a modern eight-story building with classes for recruits and prep courses for the sergeants' and lieutenants' exams. They've got a pool there, and a gym equipped with weight machines and a running track. You can take martial arts courses, or deafen yourself practicing on the pistol range.

I felt the way I always do when I walk into a station house. Like an impostor, I suppose, and an unsuccessful one at that. I stopped at the desk, said I had business with Detective Fitzroy. The uniformed sergeant waved me on. He probably assumed I was a member in good standing. I must still look like a cop, or walk like one, or something. People read me that way. Even cops.

I walked on through to the squad room and found Fitzroy typing a report at a corner desk. There were half a dozen Styrofoam coffee cups grouped on the desk, each holding about an inch of light coffee. Fitzroy motioned me to a chair and I sat down while he finished what he was typing. A couple of desks away, two cops were hassling a skinny black kid with eyes like a frog. I gather he'd been picked up for dealing three-card monte. They weren't giving him all that hard of a time, but then it wasn't the crime of the century, either.

Fitzroy looked as I remembered him, maybe a little older and a little heavier. I don't suppose he put in many hours on the running track. He had a beefy Irish face and gray hair cropped close to his skull, and not too many people would have taken him for an accountant or an orchestra conductor or a cabbie. Or a stenographer – he made pretty good time on his typewriter, but he only used two fingers to do it.

He finished finally and pushed the machine to one side. 'I swear the whole thing's paperwork,' he said. 'That and court appearances. Who's got time left to detect anything? Hey, Matt.' We shook hands. 'Been a while. You don't look so bad.'

'Was I supposed to?'

'No, course not. How about some coffee? Milk and sugar?'

'Black is fine.'

He crossed the room to the coffee machine and came back with another pair of Styrofoam cups. The two detectives went on ragging the three-card dealer, telling him they figured he had to be the First Avenue Slasher. The kid kept up his end of the banter reasonably well.

Fitzroy sat down, blew on his coffee, took a sip, made a face. He lit a cigarette and leaned back in his swivel chair. 'This London,' he said. 'You saw him?'

'Just a little while ago.'

'What did you think? You gonna help him out?'

'I don't know if that's the word for it. I told him I'd give it a shot.'

'Yeah, I figured there might be something in it for you, Matt. Here's a guy looking to spend a few dollars. You know what it's like, it's like his daughter up and died all over again and he's got to think he's doing something about it. Now there's nothing he *can* do, but if he spends a few dollars he'll maybe feel better, and why shouldn't it go to a good man who can use it? He's got a couple bucks, you know. It's not like you're taking it from a crippled newsie.'

'That's what I gathered.'

'So you'll give it a shot,' he said. 'That's good. He wanted me to recommend somebody to him and right off I thought of you. Why not give the business to a friend, right? People take care of each other and that makes the world go on spinning. Isn't that what they say?'

I had palmed five twenties while he was getting the coffee. Now I leaned forward and tucked them into his hand. 'Well, I can use a couple days work,' I said. 'I appreciate it.'

'Listen, a friend's a friend, right?' He made the money disappear. A friend's a friend, all right, but a favor's a favor and there are no free lunches, not in or out of the department. And why should there be? 'So you'll chase around and ask a few questions,' he went on, 'and you can string him for as long as he wants to play, and you don't have to bust your hump over it. Nine years, for Christ's sake. Wrap this one up and we'll fly you down to Dallas, let you figure out who killed J.F.K.'

'It must be a pretty cold trail.'

'Colder'n Kelsey's legendary nuts. If there was any reason at the time to think she wasn't just one more entry in the Icepick Prowler's datebook, then maybe somebody would of done a little digging at the time. But you know how those things work.'

'Sure.'

'We got this guy now over here on First Avenue taking whacks at people on the street, swinging at 'em with a butcher knife. We got to figure they're random attacks, right? You don't run up to the victim's husband and ask him was she fucking the mailman. Same with what's-her-name, Ettinger. Maybe she *was* fucking the mailman and maybe that's why she got killed, but there didn't look to be any reason to check it out at the time and it's gonna be a neat trick to do it now.'

'Well, I can go through the motions.'

'Sure, why not?' He tapped an accordion-pleated manila file. 'I had them pull this for you. Why don't you do a little light reading for a few minutes? There's a guy I gotta see.'

He was gone a little better than half an hour. I spent the time reading my way through the Icepick Prowler file. Early on, the two detectives popped the three-card dealer into a holding cell and rushed out, evidently to run down a tip on the First Avenue Slasher. The Slasher had done his little number right there in the Eighteenth, just a couple of blocks from the station house, and they were evidently pretty anxious to put him away.

I was done with the file when Frank Fitzroy got back. He said, 'Well? Get anything?'

'Not a whole lot. I made a few notes. Mostly names and addresses.'

'They may not match up after nine years. People move. Their whole fucking lives change.'

God knows mine did. Nine years ago I was a detective on the NYPD. I lived on Long Island in a house with a lawn and a backyard and a barbecue grill and a wife and two sons. I had moved, all right, though it was sometimes difficult to determine the direction. Surely my life had changed.

12

I tapped the file folder. 'Pinell,' I said. 'How sure is it he didn't kill Barbara Ettinger?'

'Gilt-edged, Matt. Bottled in bond. He was in Bellevue at the time.'

'People have been known to slip in and out.'

'Granted, but he was in a straitjacket. That hampers your movement a little. Besides, there's things that set the Ettinger killing apart from the others. You only notice them if you look for them, but they're there.'

'Like what?'

'Number of wounds. Ettinger had the lowest number of wounds of all eight victims. The difference isn't major but maybe it's enough to be significant. Plus all the other victims had wounds in the thighs. Ettinger had nothing in the thighs or legs, no punctures. Thing is, there was a certain amount of variation among the other victims. He didn't stamp out these murders with a cookie cutter. So the discrepancies with Ettinger didn't stand out at the time. The fewer wounds and the no wounds in the thighs, you can look at it that he was rushed, he heard somebody or thought he heard somebody and he didn't have time to give her the full treatment.'

'Sure.'

'The thing that made it so obvious that it was the Icepick guy who cooled her, well, you know what that was.'

'The eyes.'

'Right.' He nodded approval. 'All of the victims were stabbed through the eyes. One shot through each eyeball. That never made the papers. We held it back the way you always try and hold one or two things back to keep the psychos from fooling you with false confessions. You wouldn't believe how many clowns already turned themselves in for the slashings down the street.'

'I can imagine.'

'And you have to check 'em all out, and then you have to write up each interrogation, and that's the real pain in the ass. Anyway, getting back to Ettinger. The Icepick guy always went for the eyes. We kept the wraps on that detail, and Ettinger got it in the eye, so what are you going to figure? Who's gonna give a shit if she got it in the thighs or not when you've got an eyeball puncture to run with?'

'But it was only one eye.'

'Right. Okay, that's a discrepancy, but it lines up with the

13

fewer punctures and the no wounds in the thighs. He's in a hurry. No time to do it right. Wouldn't you figure it that way?'

'Anybody would.'

'Of course. You want some more coffee?'

'No thanks.'

'I guess I'll pass myself. I've had too much already today.'

'How do you figure it now, Frank?'

'Ettinger? What do I figure happened?'

'Uh-huh.'

He scratched his head. Vertical frown lines creased his forehead on either side of his nose. 'I don't think it was anything complicated,' he said. 'I think somebody read the papers and watched television and got turned on by the stories about the Icepick guy. You get these imitators every now and then. They're psychos without the imagination to think up their own numbers so they hitch a ride on somebody else's craziness. Some loony watched the six o'clock news and went out and bought an icepick.'

'And happened to get her in the eye by chance?'

'Possible. Could be. Or it could be it just struck him as a good idea, same as it did Pinell. Or something leaked.'

'That's what I was thinking.'

'Far as I can remember, there was nothing in the papers or on the news. Nothing about the eye wounds, I mean. But maybe there was and then we squelched it but not before this psycho read it or heard it and it made an impression. Or maybe it never got into the media but the word was around. You got a few hundred cops who know something, plus everybody who's around for the postmortems, plus everybody who sees the records, all the clerks and all, and each of them tells three people and those people all talk, and how long does it take before a lot of people know about it?'

'I see what you mean.'

'If anything, the business with the eyes makes it look like it was just a psycho. A guy who tried it once for a thrill and then let it go.'

'How do you figure that, Frank?'

He leaned back, interlaced his fingers behind his head. 'Well, say it's the husband,' he said. 'Say he wants to kill her because she's fucking the mailman, and he wants to make it look like the Icepick Prowler so he won't carry the can for it himself. If he knows about the eyes, he's gonna do both of them, right? He's not taking any chances. A nut, he's something else again. He does one eye because it's something to do, and then maybe he's bored with it so he doesn't do the other one. Who knows what goes through their fucking heads?'

'If it's a psycho, then there's no way to tag him.'

'Of course there isn't. Nine years later and you're looking for a killer without a motive? That's a needle in a haystack when the needle's not even there. But that's all right. You take this and play with it, and after you've run the string you just tell London it must have been a psycho. Believe me, he'll be happy to hear it.'

'Why?'

'Because that's what he thought nine years ago, and he got used to the idea. He accepted it. Now he's afraid it's somebody he knows and that's driving him crazy, so you'll investigate it all for him and tell him everything's okay, the sun still comes up in the east every morning and his daughter was still killed by a fucking Act of God. He can relax again and go back to his life. He'll get his money's worth.'

'You're probably right.'

'Course I'm right. You could even save yourself running around and just sit on your ass for a week and then tell him what you'll wind up telling him anyway. But I don't suppose you'll do that, will you?'

'No, I'll give it my best shot.'

'I figured you'd at least go through the motions. What it is, you're still a cop, aren't you, Matt?'

'I suppose so. In a way. Whatever that means.'

'You don't have anything steady, huh? You just catch a piece of work like this when it comes along?'

'Right.'

'You ever think about coming back?'

'To the department? Not very often. And never very seriously.'

He hesitated. There were questions he wanted to ask, things he wanted to say to me, but he decided to leave them unsaid. I was grateful for that. He got to his feet and so did I. I thanked him for the time and the information and he said an old friend was an old friend and it was a pleasure to be able to help a pal out. Neither of us mentioned the hundred dollars that had changed hands. Why should we? He'd been glad to get it and I was glad to give it. A favor's no good unless you pay for it. One way or the other, you always do.

15

THREE

It had rained a little while I was with Fitzroy. It wasn't raining when I got back outside, but it didn't feel as though it was through for the day. I had a drink around the corner on Third Avenue and watched part of the newscast. They showed the police artist's sketch of the Slasher, the same drawing that was on the front page of the *Post*. It showed a round-faced black man with a trimmed beard and a cap on his head. Mad zeal glinted in his large almond-shaped eyes.

'Imagine that comin' up the street at you,' the bartender said. 'I'll tell you, there's a lot of guys gettin' pistol permits on the strength of this one. I'm thinkin' about fillin' out an application myself.'

I remember the day I stopped carrying a gun. It was the same day I turned in my shield. I'd had a stretch of feeling terribly vulnerable without that iron on my hip, and now I could hardly recall how it had felt to walk around armed in the first place.

I finished my drink and left. Would the bartender get a gun? Probably not. More people talked about it than did it. But whenever there's the right kind of nut making headlines, a Slasher or an Icepick Prowler, a certain number of people get pistol permits and a certain number of others buy illegal guns. Then some of them get drunk and shoot their wives. None of them ever seems to wind up nailing the Slasher.

I walked uptown, stopped at an Italian place along the way for dinner, then spent a couple of hours at the main library on Forty-second Street, dividing my time between old newspapers on microfilm and new and old Polk city directories. I made some notes, but not many. I was mostly trying to let myself sink into the case, to take a few steps backward in time.

By the time I got out of there it was raining. I took a cab to Armstrong's, got a stool at the bar and settled in. There were people to talk to and bourbon to drink, with enough coffee to keep fatigue at bay. I didn't hit it very hard, just coasted along, getting by, getting through. You'd be surprised what a person can get through.

The next day was Friday. I read a paper with breakfast. There'd been no slashings the previous night, but neither had there been any progress in the case. In Ecuador, a few hundred people had died in an earthquake. There seemed to be more of those lately, or I was more aware of them.

I went to my bank, put Charles London's check in my savings account, drew out some cash and a money order for five hundred dollars. They gave me an envelope to go with the money order and I addressed it to Ms Anita Scudder in Syosset. I stood at the counter for a few minutes with the bank's pen in my hand, trying to think of a note to include, and wound up sending the money order all by itself. After I'd mailed it I thought about calling to tell her it was in the mail, but that seemed like even more of a chore than thinking of something to put in a note.

It wasn't a bad day. Clouds obscured the sun, but there were patches of blue overhead and the air had a tang to it. I stopped at Armstrong's to cover my marker and left without having anything. It was a little early for the day's first drink. I left, walked east a long block to Columbus Circle, and caught a train.

I rode the D to Smith and Bergen and came out into sunshine. For a while I walked around, trying to get my bearings. The Seventy-eighth Precinct, where I'd served a brief hitch, was only six or seven blocks to the east, but that had been a long time ago and I'd spent little time in Brooklyn since. Nothing looked even faintly familiar. I was in a part of the borough that hadn't had a name until fairly recently. Now a part of it was called Cobble Hill and another chunk was called Boerum Hill and both of them were participating wholeheartedly in the brownstone renaissance. Neighborhoods don't seem to stand still in New York. They either improve or deteriorate. Most of the city seemed to be crumbling. The whole South Bronx was block after block of burned-out buildings, and in Brooklyn the same process was eroding Bushwick and Brownsville.

These blocks were going in the other direction. I walked up one street and down another and found myself becoming aware of changes. There were trees on every block, most of them planted within the past few years. While some of the brown-stones and brickfronts were in disrepair, more sported freshly painted trim. The shops reflected the changes that had been

17

going on. A health food store on Smith Street, a boutique at the corner of Warren and Bond, little up-scale restaurants tucked in all over the place.

The building where Barbara Ettinger had lived and died was on Wyckoff Street between Nevins and Bond. It was a brick tenement, five stories tall with four small apartments on each floor, and it had thus escaped the conversion that had already turned many of the brownstones back into the one-family houses they had originally been. Still, the building had been spruced up some. I stood in the vestibule and checked the names on the mailboxes, comparing them to those I'd copied from an old city directory. Of the twenty apartments, only six held tenants who'd been there at the time of the murder.

Except you can't go by names on mailboxes. People get married or unmarried and their names change. An apartment gets sublet to keep the landlord from raising the rent, and the name of a long-dead tenant stays on the lease and on the mailbox for ages. A roommate moves in, then stays on when the original leaseholder moves out. There are no shortcuts. You have to knock on all the doors.

I rang a bell, got buzzed in, went to the top floor and worked my way down. It's a little easier when you have a badge to flash but the manner's more important than the ID, and I couldn't lose the manner if I tried. I didn't tell anyone I was a cop, but neither did I try to keep anyone from making the assumption.

The first person I talked to was a young mother in one of the rear apartments on the top floor. Her baby cried in the next room while we talked. She'd moved in within the past year, she told me, and she didn't know anything about a murder nine years previously. She asked anxiously if it had taken place in that very apartment, and seemed at once relieved and disappointed to learn it had not.

A Slavic woman, her hands liver-spotted and twisted with arthritis, gave me a cup of coffee in her fourth-floor front apartment. She put me on the couch and turned her own chair to face me. It had been positioned so she could watch the street.

She'd been in that apartment for almost forty years, she told me. Up until four years ago her husband had been there, but now he was gone and she was alone. The neighborhood, she said, was getting better. 'But the old people are going. Places I shopped for years are gone. And the price of everything! I don't believe the prices.'

She remembered the icepick murder, though she was surprised it had been nine years. It didn't seem that long to her. The woman who was killed was a nice woman, she said. 'Only nice people get killed.'

She didn't seem to remember much about Barbara Ettinger beyond her niceness. She didn't know if she had been especially friendly or unfriendly with any of the other neighbors, if she'd gotten on well or poorly with her husband. I wondered if she even remembered what the woman had looked like, and wished I had a picture to show her. I might have asked London for one if I'd thought of it.

Another woman on the fourth floor, a Miss Wicker, was the only person to ask for identification. I told her I wasn't a policeman, and she left the chain lock on the door and spoke to me through a two-inch opening, which didn't strike me as unreasonable. She'd only been in the building a few years, did know about the murder and that the Icepick Prowler had been recently apprehended, but that was the extent of her information.

'People let anyone in,' she said. 'We have an intercom here but people just buzz you in without determining who you are. People talk about crime but they never believe it can happen to them, and then it does.' I thought of telling her how easy it would be to snap her chain lock with a bolt cutter, but I decided her anxiety level was high enough already.

A lot of the tenants were out for the day. On the third floor, Barbara Ettinger's floor, I got no response from one of the rear apartments, then paused in front of the adjoining door. The pulse of disco music came through it. I knocked, and after a moment the door was opened by a man in his late twenties. He had short hair and a mustache, and he was wearing nothing but a pair of blue-striped white gym shorts. His body was well-muscled, and his tanned skin glistened with a light coating of sweat.

I told him my name and that I'd like to ask him a few questions. He led me inside, closed the door, then moved past me and crossed the room to the radio. He lowered the volume about halfway, paused, turned it off altogether.

There was a large mat in the center of the uncarpeted parquet floor. A barbell and a pair of dumbbells reposed on it, and a jump rope lay curled on the floor alongside. 'I was just working out,' he said. 'Won't you sit down? That chair's the comfortable one. The other's nice to visit but you wouldn't want to live there.'

I took the chair while he sat on the mat and folded his legs tailor-fashion. His eyes brightened with recognition when I mentioned the murder in 3-A. 'Donald told me,' he said. 'I've only been here a little over a year but Donald's been living here for ages. He's watched the neighborhood become positively chic around him. Fortunately this particular building retains its essential tackiness. You'll probably want to talk to Donald but he won't be home from work until six or six thirty.'

'What's Donald's last name?'

'Gilman.' He spelled it. 'And I'm Rolfe Waggoner. That's Rolfe with an e. I was just reading about the Icepick Prowler. Of course I don't remember the case. I was in high school then. That was back home in Indiana – Muncie, Indiana – and that was a long ways from here.' He thought for a moment. 'In more ways than one,' he said.

'Was Mr Gilman friendly with the Ettingers?'

'He could answer that better than I can. You've caught the man who did it, haven't you? I read that he was in a mental hospital for years and nobody ever knew he killed anybody, and then he was released and they caught him and he confessed or something?'

'Something like that.'

'And now you want to make sure you have a good case against him.' He smiled. He had a nice open face and he seemed quite at ease, sitting on a mat in his gym shorts. Gay men used to be so much more defensive, especially around cops. 'It must be complicated with something that happened so many years ago. Have you talked with Judy? Judy Fairborn, she's in the apartment where the Ettingers used to live. She works nights, she's a waitress, so she'll be home now unless she's at an audition or a dance class or shopping or – well, she'll be home unless she's out, but that's always the case, isn't it?' He smiled again, showing me perfectly even teeth. 'But maybe you've already spoken with her.'

'Not yet.'

'She's new. I think she moved in about six months ago. Would you want to talk to her anyway?'

'Yes.'

He uncoiled, sprang lightly to his feet. 'I'll introduce you,' he said. 'Just let me put some clothes on. I won't be a minute.'

He reappeared wearing jeans and a flannel shirt and running shoes without socks. We crossed the hall and he knocked on the door of Apartment 3-A. There was silence, then footsteps and a woman's voice asking who it was.

'Just Rolfe,' he said. 'In the company of a policeman who'd like to grill you, Ms Fairborn.'

'Huh?' she said, and opened the door. She might have been Rolfe's sister, with the same light brown hair, the same regular features, the same open Midwestern countenance. She wore jeans, too, and a sweater and penny loafers. Rolfe introduced us and she stepped aside and motioned us in. She didn't know anything about the Ettingers, and her knowledge of the murder was limited to the fact that it had taken place there. 'I'm glad I didn't know before I moved in,' she said, 'because I might have let it spook me, and that would have been silly, wouldn't it? Apartments are too hard to find. Who can afford to be superstitious?'

'Nobody,' Rolfe said. 'Not in this market.'

They talked about the First Avenue Slasher, and about a recent wave of local burglaries, including one a week ago on the first floor. I asked if I could have a look at the kitchen. I was on my way there as I asked the question. I think I'd have remembered the layout anyway, but I'd already been in other apartments in the building and they were all the same.

Judy said, 'Is this where it happened? Here in the kitchen?'

'Where did you think?' Rolfe asked her. 'The bedroom?'

'I guess I didn't think about it.'

'You didn't even wonder? Sounds like repression.'

'Maybe.'

I tuned out their conversation. I tried to remember the room, tried to peel off nine years and be there once again, standing over Barbara Ettinger's body. She'd been near the stove then, her legs extending into the center of the small room, her head turned toward the living room. There had been linoleum on the floor and that was gone, the original wood floor restored and glossy with polyurethane. And the stove looked new, and plaster had been removed to expose the brick exterior wall. I couldn't be sure the brick hadn't been exposed previously, nor could I know how much of my mental picture was real. The memory is a cooperative animal, eager to please; what it cannot supply it occasionally invents, sketching carefully to fill in the blanks.

Why the kitchen? The door led into the living room, and she'd let him in either because she knew who he was or in spite of the fact that she didn't, and then what? He drew the icepick and she tried to get away from him? Caught her heel in the linoleum and went sprawling, and then he was on her with the pick?

The kitchen was the middle room, separating the living room

and bedroom. Maybe he was a lover and they were on their way to bed when he surprised her with a few inches of pointed steel. But wouldn't he wait until they got where they were going?

Maybe she had something on the stove. Maybe she was fixing him a cup of coffee. The kitchen was too small to eat in but more than large enough for two people to stand comfortably waiting for water to boil.

Then a hand over her mouth to muffle her cries and a thrust into her heart to kill her. Then enough other thrusts of the icepick to make it look like the Icepick Prowler's work.

Had the first wound killed her? I remembered beads of blood. Dead bodies don't bleed freely, but neither do most puncture wounds. The autopsy had indicated a wound in the heart that had been more or less instantly fatal. It might have been the first wound inflicted or the last, for all I'd seen in the Medical Examiner's report.

Judy Fairborn filled a teakettle, lit the stove with a wooden match, and poured three cups of instant coffee when the water boiled. I'd have liked bourbon in mine, or instead of mine, but nobody suggested it. We carried our cups into the living room and she said, 'You looked as though you saw a ghost. No, I'm wrong. You looked as though you were looking for one.'

'Maybe that's what I was doing.'

'I'm not sure if I believe in them or not. They're supposed to be more common in cases of sudden death when the victim didn't expect what happened. The theory is that the soul doesn't realize it died, so it hangs around because it doesn't know to pass on to the next plane of existence.'

'I thought it walked the floors crying out for vengeance,' Rolfe said. 'You know, dragging chains, making the boards creak.'

'No, it just doesn't know any better. What you do, you get somebody to lay the ghost.'

'I'm not going to touch that line,' Rolfe said.

'I'm proud of you. You get high marks for restraint. That's what it's called, laying the ghost. It's a sort of exorcism. The ghost expert, or whatever you call him, communicates with the ghost and lets him know what happened, and that he's supposed to pass on. And then the spirit can go wherever spirits go.'

'You really believe all this?'

'I'm not sure what I believe,' she said. She uncrossed her legs, then recrossed them. 'If Barbara's haunting this apartment, she's being very restrained about it. No creaking boards, no midnight apparitions.'

'Your basic low-profile ghost,' he said.

'I'll have nightmares tonight,' she said. 'If I sleep at all.'

I knocked on all the doors on the two lower floors without getting much response. The tenants were either out or had nothing useful to tell me. The building's superintendent had a basement apartment in a similar building on the next block, but I didn't see the point in looking him up. He'd only been on the job for a matter of months, and the old woman in the fourth-floor-front apartment had told me there had been four or five supers in the past nine years.

By the time I got out of the building I was glad for the fresh air, glad to be on the street again. I'd felt something in Judy Fairborn's kitchen, though I wouldn't go so far as to call it a ghost. But it had felt as though something from years past was pulling at me, trying to drag me down and under.

Whether it was Barbara Ettinger's past or my own was something I couldn't say.

I stopped at a bar on the corner of Dean and Smith. They had sandwiches and a microwave oven to heat them in but I wasn't hungry. I had a quick drink and sipped a short beer chaser. The bartender sat on a high stool drinking a large glass of what looked like vodka. The other two customers, black men about my age, were at the far end of the bar watching a game show on TV. From time to time one of them was talking back to the set.

I flipped a few pages in my notebook, went to the phone and looked through the Brooklyn book. The day-care center where Barbara Ettinger had worked didn't seem to be in business. I checked the Yellow Pages to see if there was anything listed under another name at the same address. There wasn't.

The address was on Clinton Street, and I'd been away from the neighborhood long enough so that I had to ask directions, but once I'd done so it was only a walk of a few blocks. The boundaries of Brooklyn neighborhoods aren't usually too well defined – the neighborhoods themselves are often largely the invention of realtors – but when I crossed Court Street I was leaving Boerum Hill for Cobble Hill, and the change wasn't difficult to see. Cobble Hill was a shade or two tonier. More trees, a higher percentage of brownstones, a greater proportion of white faces on the street.

23

I found the number I was seeking on Clinton between Pacific and Amity. There was no day-care center there. The ground floor storefront offered supplies for knitting and needlepoint. The proprietor, a plump Earth Mother with a gold incisor, didn't know anything about a day-care center. She'd moved in a year and a half ago after a health food restaurant had gone out of business. 'I ate there once,' she said, 'and they *deserved* to go out of business. Believe me.'

She gave me the landlord's name and number. I tried him from the corner and kept getting a busy signal so I walked over to Court Street and climbed a flight of stairs. There was just one person in the office, a young man with his sleeves rolled up and a large round ashtray full of cigarette butts on the desk in front of him. He chainsmoked while he talked on the phone. The windows were closed and the room was as thick with smoke as a nightclub at four in the morning.

When he got off the phone I caught him before it could ring again. His own memory went back beyond the health food restaurant to a children's clothing store that had also failed in the same location. 'Now we got needlepoint,' he said. 'If I were gonna guess I'd say she'll be out in another year. How much can you make selling yarn? What happens, somebody has a hobby, an interest, so they open up a business. Health food, needlepoint, whatever it is, but they don't know shit about business and they're down and out in a year or two. She breaks the lease, we'll rent it in a month for twice what she pays. It's a renter's market in an upscale neighborhood.' He reached for the phone. 'Sorry I can't help you,' he said.

'Check your records,' I said.

He told me he had lots of important things to do, but halfway through the statement changed from an assertion to a whine. I sat in an old oak swivel chair and let him fumble around in his files. He opened and closed half a dozen drawers before he came up with a folder and slapped it down on his desk.

'Here we go,' he said. 'Happy Hours Child Care Center. Some name, huh?'

'What's wrong with it?'

'Happy hour's in a bar when the drinks are half price. Hell of a thing to call a place for the kiddies, don't you think?' He shook his head. 'Then they wonder why they go out of business.'

I didn't see anything the matter with the name.

'Leaseholder was a Mrs Corwin. Janice Corwin. Took the place on a five-year lease, gave it up after four years. Quit the premises eight years ago in March.' That would have been a year after Barbara Ettinger's death. 'Jesus, you look at the rent and you can't believe it. You know what she was paying?'

I shook my head.

'Well, you saw the place. Name a figure.' I looked at him. He stubbed out a cigarette and lit another. 'One and a quarter. Hundred and twenty-five dollars a month. Goes for six now and it's going up the minute the needlework lady goes out, or when her lease is up. Whichever comes first.'

'You have a forwarding address for Corwin?'

He shook his head. 'I got a residential address. Want it?' He read off a number on Wyckoff Street. It was just a few doors from the Ettingers' building. I wrote down the address. He read off a phone number and I jotted that down, too.

His phone rang. He picked it up, said hello, listened for a few minutes, then talked in monosyllables. 'Listen, I got someone here,' he said after a moment. 'I'll get back to you in a minute, okay?'

He hung up and asked me if that was all. I couldn't think of anything else. He hefted the file. 'Four years she had the place,' he said. 'Most places drop dead in the first year. Make it through a year you got a chance. Get through two years and you got a good chance. You know what's the problem?'

'What?'

'Women,' he said. 'They're amateurs. They got no need to make a go of it. They open a business like they try on a dress. Take it off if they don't like the color. If that does it, I got calls to make.'

I thanked him for his help.

'Listen,' he said, 'I always cooperate. It's my nature.'

I tried the number he gave me and got a woman who spoke Spanish. She didn't know anything about anybody named Janice Corwin and didn't stay on the line long enough for me to ask her much of anything. I dropped another dime and dialed again on the chance that I'd misdialed the first time. When the same woman answered I broke the connection.

When they disconnect a phone it's close to a year before they reassign the number. Of course Mrs Corwin could have changed her number without moving from the Wyckoff Street address. People, especially women, do that frequently enough to shake off obscene callers.

Still, I figured she'd moved. I figured everyone had moved, out of Brooklyn, out of the five boroughs, out of the state. I started to walk back toward Wyckoff Street, covered half a block, turned, retraced my steps, started to turn again.

I made myself stop. I had an anxious sensation in my chest and stomach. I was blaming myself for wasting time and starting to wonder why I'd taken London's check in the first place. His daughter was nine years in the grave, and whoever killed her had probably long since started a brand-new life in Australia. All I was doing was spinning my goddamned wheels.

I stood there until the intensity of the feeling wound itself down, knowing that I didn't want to go back to Wyckoff Street. I'd go there later, when Donald Gilman got home from work, and I could check Corwin's address then. Until then I couldn't think of anything I felt like doing about the Ettinger murder. But there was something I could do about the anxiety.

One thing about Brooklyn – you never have to walk very far before you encounter a church. They're all over the place throughout the borough.

The one I found was at the corner of Court and Congress. The church itself was closed and the iron gate locked, but a sign directed me to St Elizabeth Seton's Chapel right around the corner. A gateway led to a one-story chapel tucked in between the church and the rectory. I walked through an ivy-planted courtyard which a plaque proclaimed to be the burial site of Cornelius Heeney. I didn't bother reading who he was or why they'd planted him there. I walked between rows of white statues and into the little chapel. The only other person in it was a frail Irishwoman kneeling in a front pew. I took a seat toward the back.

It's hard to remember just when I started hanging out in churches. It happened sometime after I left the force, sometime after I moved out of the house in Syosset and away from Anita and the boys and into a hotel on West Fifty-seventh. I guess I found them to be citadels of peace and quiet, two commodities hard to come by in New York.

I sat in this one for fifteen or twenty minutes. It was peaceful, and just sitting there I lost some of what I'd been feeling earlier.

Before I left I counted out a hundred fifty dollars, and on my way out I slipped the money into a slot marked 'For the Poor.' I started tithing not long after I began spending odd moments in churches, and I don't know why I started or why I've never stopped. The question doesn't plague me much. There are no end of things I do without knowing the reason why.

I don't know what they do with the money. I don't much care. Charles London had given me fifteen hundred dollars, an act which didn't seem to make much more sense than my passing on a tenth of that sum to the unspecified poor.

There was a shelf of votive candles, and I stopped to light a couple of them. One for Barbara London Ettinger, who had been dead a long time, if not so long as old Cornelius Heeney. Another for Estrellita Rivera, a little girl who had been dead almost as long as Barbara Ettinger.

I didn't say any prayers. I never do.

FOUR

Donald Gilman was twelve or fifteen years older than his roommate, and I don't suppose he put in as many hours with the dumbbells and the jump rope. His neatly combed hair was a sandy brown, his eyes a cool blue through heavy horn-rimmed glasses. He was wearing suit pants and a white shirt and tie. His suit jacket was draped over the chair Rolfe had warned me about.

Rolfe had said Gilman was a lawyer, so I wasn't surprised when he asked to see my identification. I explained that I had resigned from the police force some years earlier. He raised an eyebrow at this news and flicked a glance at Rolfe.

'I'm involved in this at the request of Barbara Ettinger's father,' I went on. 'He's asked me to investigate.'

'But why? The killer's been caught, hasn't he?'

'There's some question about that.'

'Oh?'

I told him that Louis Pinell had an unbreakable alibi for the day of Barbara Ettinger's murder.

'Then someone else killed her,' he said at once. 'Unless the alibi turns out to be unfounded. That would explain the father's interest, wouldn't it? He probably suspects – well, he could suspect anyone at all. I hope you won't take it amiss if I call him to confirm that you're here as his emissary?'

'He may be hard to reach.' I had kept London's card and I got it out of my wallet. 'He's probably left the office by now, and I wouldn't think he's arrived home yet. He lives alone, his wife died a couple years ago, so he most likely takes his meals at restaurants.'

Gilman looked at the card for a moment, then handed it back. I watched his face and could see him make up his mind. 'Oh, well,' he said. 'I can't see the harm in talking with you, Mr Scudder. It's not as though I knew anything substantial. It was all a fair amount of years ago, wasn't it? A lot of water under the bridge since then, or over the dam, or wherever it goes.' His blue eyes brightened. 'Speaking of liquid, we generally have a drink about now. Will you join us?'

'Thank you.'

'We generally mix up some martinis. Unless there's something else you'd prefer?'

'Martinis hit me a little hard,' I said. 'I think I'd better stick with whiskey. Bourbon, if you've got it.'

Of course they had it. They had Wild Turkey, which is a cut or two better than what I'm used to, and Rolfe gave me five or six ounces of it in a cut-crystal Old Fashioned glass. He poured Bombay gin into a pitcher, added ice cubes and a spoonful of vermouth, stirred gently and strained the blend into a pair of glasses that were mates to mine. Donald Gilman raised his glass and proposed a toast to Friday, and we drank to that.

I wound up sitting where Rolfe had had me sit earlier. Rolfe sat as before on the rug, his knees drawn up and his arms locked around them. He was still wearing the jeans and shirt he'd put on to introduce me to Judy Fairborn. His weights and jump rope were out of sight. Gilman sat on the edge of the uncomfortable chair and leaned forward, looking down into his glass, then looking up at me.

'I was trying to remember the day she died,' he said. 'It's difficult. I didn't come home from the office that day. I had drinks with someone after work, and then dinner out, and I think I went to a party in the Village. It's not important. The point is that I didn't get home until the following morning. I knew what to expect when I got here because I read the morning paper with my breakfast. No, that's wrong. I remember that I bought the *News* because it's easier to manage on the train, the business of turning the pages and all. The headline was *Icepick Killer Strikes in Brooklyn*, or words to that effect. I believe there had been a previous killing in Brooklyn.'

'The fourth victim. In Sheepshead Bay.'

'Then I turned to page three, I suppose it must have been, and there was the story. No photograph, but the name and address, of course, and that was unmistakable.' He put a hand to his chest. 'I remember how I felt. It was incredibly shocking. You don't expect that sort of thing to happen to someone you know. And it made me feel so vulnerable myself, you know. It happened in this building. I felt that before I felt the sense of loss one feels over the death of a friend.'

'How well did you know the Ettingers?'

'Reasonably well. They were a couple, of course, and most of their social interaction was with other couples. But they were right across the hall and I'd have them in for drinks or coffee from time to time, or they'd ask me over. I had one or two parties that they came to, but they didn't stay very long. I think they were comfortable enough with gay people, but not in great quantity. I can understand that. One doesn't like to be overwhelmingly outnumbered, does one? It's only natural to feel self-conscious.'

'Were they happy?'

The question pulled him back to the Ettingers and he frowned, weighing his answer. 'I suppose he's a suspect,' he said. 'The spouse always is. Have you met him?'

'No.'

' "Were they happy?" The question's inevitable, but who can ever answer it? They seemed happy. Most couples do, and most couples ultimately break up, and when they do their friends are invariably surprised because they *seemed* so bloody happy.' He finished his drink. 'I think they were happy enough. She was expecting a child when she was killed.'

'I know.'

'I hadn't known it. I only learned after her death.' He made a little circle with the empty glass, and Rolfe got gracefully to his feet and replenished Gilman's drink. While he was up he poured me another Wild Turkey. I was feeling the first one a little bit so I took it easy on the second.

Gilman said, 'I thought it might have steadied her.'

'The baby?'

'Yes.'

'She needed steadying?'

He sipped his martini. '*De mortuis* and all that. One hesitates to speak candidly of the dead. There was a restlessness in Barbara. She was a bright girl, you know. Very attractive, energetic, quick-witted. I don't recall where she went to school, but it was a good school. Doug went to Hofstra. I don't suppose there's anything the matter with Hofstra, but it's less prestigious than Barbara's alma mater. I don't know why I can't remember it.'

'Wellesley.' London had told me.

'Of course. I'd have remembered. I dated a Wellesley girl during my own college career. Sometimes self-acceptance takes a certain amount of time.'

'Did Barbara marry beneath herself?'

'I wouldn't say that. On the surface, she grew up in Westchester and went to Wellesley and married a social worker who grew up in Queens and went to Hofstra. But a lot of that is just a matter of labels.' He took a sip of gin. 'She may have thought she was too good for him, though.'

'Was she seeing anybody else?'

'You do ask direct questions, don't you? It's not hard to believe you were a policeman. What made you leave the force?'

'Personal reasons. Was she having an affair?'

'There's nothing tackier than dishing the dead, is there? I used to hear them sometimes. She would accuse him of having sex with women he met on the job. He was a welfare caseworker and that involved visiting unattached women in their apartments, and if one's in the market for casual sex the opportunity's certainly there. I don't know that he was taking advantage of it, but he struck me as the sort of man who would. And I gather she thought he was.'

'And she was having an affair to get even?'

'Quick of you. Yes, I think so, but don't ask me with whom because I've no idea. I would sometimes be home during the day. Not often, but now and then. There were times when I heard her coming up the stairs with a man, or I might pass her door and hear a man's voice. You have to understand that I'm not a busybody, so I didn't try to catch a peek of the mystery man, whoever he was. In fact I didn't pay the whole business a great deal of attention.'

'She would entertain this man during the day?'

'I can't swear she was entertaining anybody. Maybe it was the plumber come to repair a leaky faucet. Please understand that. I just had the feeling that she might have been seeing someone, and I knew she had accused her husband of infidelity, so I thought she might be getting a bit of sauce for the goose.'

'But it was during the day. Didn't she work days?'

'Oh, at the day-care center. I gather her schedule was quite flexible. She took the job to have something to do. Restlessness, again. She was a psychology major and she'd been in graduate school but gave it up, and now she wasn't doing anything, so she started helping out at the day-care center. I don't think they paid her very much and I don't suppose they objected if she took the odd afternoon off.'

'Who were her friends?'

'God. I met people at their apartment but I can't remember

any of them. I think most of their friends were his friends. There was the woman from the day-care center, but I'm afraid I don't remember her name.'

'Janice Corwin.'

'Is that it? It doesn't even ring a muted bell. She lived nearby. Just across the street, if I'm right.'

'You are. Do you know if she's still there?'

'No idea. I can't remember when I saw her last. I don't know that I'd recognize her anyway. I think I met her once, but I may just recall her because Barbara talked about her. You say the name was Corwin?'

'Janice Corwin.'

'The day-care center's gone. It closed years ago.'

'I know.'

The conversation didn't go much further. They had a dinner date and I'd run out of questions to ask. And I was feeling the drinks. I'd finished the second one without being aware of it and was surprised when I found the glass empty. I didn't feel drunk but I didn't feel sober either, and my mind could have been clearer.

The cold air helped. There was a wind blowing. I hunched my shoulders against it and walked across the street and down the block to the address I had for Janice Corwin. It turned out to be a four-story brick building, and a few years back someone had bought it, turned out the tenants as soon as their leases expired, and converted it for single-family occupancy.

According to the owner, whose name I didn't bother catching, the conversion process was still going on. 'It's endless,' he said. 'Everything's three times as difficult as you figure, takes four times as long, and costs five times as much. And those are conservative figures. Do you know how long it takes to strip old paint off door jambs? Do you know how many doorways there are in a house like this?'

He didn't remember the names of the tenants he'd dispossessed. The name Janice Corwin was not familiar to him. He said he probably had a list of the tenants somewhere but he didn't even know where to start looking for it. Besides, it wouldn't have their forwarding addresses. I told him not to bother looking.

I walked to Atlantic Avenue. Among the antique shops with their Victorian oak furniture and the plant stores and the Middle Eastern restaurants I managed to find an ordinary coffee shop with a Formica counter and red leatherette stools. I wanted a drink more than I wanted a meal, but I knew I'd be in trouble if I didn't have something to eat. I had Salisbury steak and mashed potatoes and green beans and made myself eat everything. It wasn't bad. I drank two cups of so-so coffee and paused on my way out to look up Corwin in the phone book. There were two dozen Corwins in Brooklyn, including a J. Corwin with an address that looked to be in Bay Ridge or Bensonhurst. I tried the number but nobody answered.

No reason to think she'd be in Brooklyn. No reason to think she'd be listed under her own name, and I didn't know her husband's name.

No point checking the post office. They don't hold address changes longer than a year, and the building on Wyckoff Street had changed hands longer ago than that. But there would be ways to trace the Corwins. There generally are.

I paid the check and left a tip. According to the counterman, the nearest subway was a couple blocks away on Fulton Street. I was on the train heading for Manhattan before I realized that I hadn't even bothered to walk over to Bergen and Flatbush and take a look at the station house of the Seventy-eighth Precinct. Somehow I hadn't thought of it.

FIVE

I stopped at the desk when I got back to my hotel. No mail, no messages. Upstairs in my room I cracked the seal on a bottle of bourbon and poured a few fingers into a glass. I sat there for a while skipping around in a paperback edition of *The Lives of the Saints*. The martyrs held a curious fascination for me. They'd found such a rich variety of ways of dying.

Couple of days earlier there'd been an item in the paper, a back-pages squib about a suspect arrested for the year-old murder of two women in their East Harlem apartment. The victims, a mother and daughter, had been found in their bedroom, each with a bullet behind the ear. The report said the cops had stayed on the case because of the unusual brutality of the murders. Now they'd made an arrest, taking a fourteen-year-old boy into custody. He'd have been thirteen when the women were killed.

According to the story's last paragraph, five other persons had been killed in or around the victims' building in the year since their murder. There'd been no indication whether those five murders were solved, or whether the kid in custody was suspected of them.

I let my mind slip off on tangents. Now and again I'd put the book aside and find myself thinking about Barbara Ettinger. Donald Gilman had started to say that her father probably suspected someone, then caught himself and left the name unsaid.

The husband, probably. The spouse is always the first suspect. If Barbara hadn't apparently been one of a series of victims, Douglas Ettinger would have been grilled six ways and backwards. As it was, he'd been interrogated automatically by detectives from Midtown North. They could hardly have done otherwise. He was not only the husband. He was also the person who had discovered the body, coming upon her corpse in the kitchen upon returning from work.

I'd read a report of the interrogation. The man who conducted it had already taken it for granted that the killing was the work of the Icepick Prowler, so his questions had concentrated on Barbara's schedule, on her possible propensity for opening the door for strangers, on whether she might have mentioned anyone following her or behaving suspiciously. Had she been bothered recently by obscene telephone calls? People hanging up without speaking? Suspicious wrong numbers?

The questioning had essentially assumed the subject's innocence, and the assumption had certainly been logical enough at the time. Evidently there had been nothing in Douglas Ettinger's manner to arouse suspicion.

I tried, not for the first time, to summon up a memory of Ettinger. It seemed to me that I must have met him. We were on the scene before Midtown North came to take the case away from us, and he'd have had to be somewhere around while I was standing in that kitchen eyeing the body sprawled on the linoleum. I might have tried to offer a word of comfort, might have formed some impression, but I couldn't remember him at all.

Perhaps he'd been in the bedroom when I was there, talking with another detective or with one of the patrolmen who'd been first on the scene. Maybe I'd never laid eyes on him, or maybe we'd spoken and I'd forgotten him altogether. I had by that time spent quite a few years seeing any number of recently bereaved. They couldn't all stand out in sharp relief in the cluttered warehouse of memory.

Well, I'd see him soon enough. My client hadn't said whom he suspected, and I hadn't asked, but it stood to reason that Barbara's husband headed the list. London wouldn't be all that upset by the possibility that she'd died at the hands of someone he didn't even know, some friend or lover who meant nothing to him. But for her to have been killed by her own husband, a man London knew, a man who had been present years later at London's wife's funeral –

There's a phone in my room but the calls go through the switchboard, and it's a nuisance placing them that way even when I don't care if the operator listens in. I went down to the lobby and dialed my client's number in Hastings. He answered on the third ring.

35

'Scudder,' I said. 'I could use a picture of your daughter. Anything as long as it's a good likeness.'

'I took albums full of pictures. But most of them were of Barbara as a child. You would want a late photograph, I suppose?'

'As late as possible. How about a wedding picture?'

'Oh,' he said. 'Of course. There's a very good pictue of the two of them, it's in a silver frame on a table in the living room. I suppose I could have it copied. Do you want me to do that?'

'If it's not too much trouble.'

He asked if he should mail it and I suggested he bring it to his office Monday. I said I'd call and arrange to pick it up. He asked if I'd had a chance to begin the investigation yet and I told him I'd spent the day in Brooklyn. I tried him on a couple of names – Donald Gilman, Janice Corwin. Neither meant anything to him. He asked, tentatively, if I had any leads.

'It's a pretty cold trail,' I said.

I rang off without asking him who he suspected. I felt restless and went around the corner to Armstrong's. On the way I wished I'd taken the time to go back to my room for my coat. It was colder, and the wind had an edge to it.

I sat at the bar with a couple of nurses from Roosevelt. One of them, Terry, was just finishing up her third week in Pediatrics. 'I thought I'd like the duty,' she said, 'but I can't stand it. Little kids, it's so much worse when you lose one. Some of them are so brave it breaks your heart. I can't handle it, I really can't.'

Estrellita Rivera's image flashed in my mind and was gone. I didn't try to hold onto it. The other nurse, glass in hand, was saying that all in all she thought she preferred Sambucca to Amaretto. Or maybe it was the other way around.

I made it an early night.

SIX

Even if I couldn't recall meeting Douglas Ettinger, I had a picture of him in my mind. Tall and raw-boned, dark hair, pallid skin, knobby wrists, Lincolnesque features. A prominent Adam's apple.

I woke up Saturday morning with his image firmly in mind, as if it had been imprinted there during an unremembered dream. After a quick breakfast I went down to Penn Station and caught a Long Island Railroad local to Hicksville. A phone call to his house in Mineola had established that Ettinger was working at the Hicksville store, and it turned out to be a $2.25 cab ride from the station.

In an aisle lined with squash and racquet-ball equipment I asked a clerk if Mr Ettinger was in. 'I'm Doug Ettinger,' he said. 'What can I do for you?'

He was about five-eight, a chunky one-seventy. Tightly curled light brown hair with red highlights. The plump cheeks and alert brown eyes of a squirrel. Large white teeth, with the upper incisors slightly bucked, consistent with the squirrel image. He didn't look remotely familiar, nor did he bear any resemblance whatsoever to the rail-splitter caricature I'd dreamed up to play his part.

'My name's Scudder,' I said. 'I'd like to talk to you privately, if you don't mind. It's about your wife.'

His open face turned guarded. 'Karen?' he said. 'What about her?'

Christ. 'Your first wife.'

'Oh, Barbara,' he said. 'You had me going for a second there. The serious tone and all, and wanting to talk to me about my wife. I don't know what I thought. You're from the NYPD? Right this way, we can talk in the office.'

His was the smaller of the two desks in the office. Invoices and correspondence were arranged in neat piles on it. A Lucite

37

photo cube held pictures of a woman and several young children. He saw me looking at it and said, 'That's Karen there. And the kids.'

I picked up the cube, looked at a young woman with short blonde hair and a sunny smile. She was posed next to a car, with an expanse of lawn behind her. The whole effect was very suburban.

I replaced the photo cube and took the chair Ettinger indicated. He sat behind the desk, lit a cigarette with a disposable butane lighter. He knew the Icepick Prowler had been apprehended, knew too that the suspect denied any involvement in his first wife's murder. He assumed Pinell was lying, either out of memory failure or for some insane reason. When I explained that Pinells's alibi had been confirmed, he seemed unimpressed.

'It's been years,' he said. 'People can get mixed up on dates and you never know how accurate records are. He probably did it. I wouldn't take his word that he didn't.'

'The alibi looks sound.'

Ettinger shrugged. 'You'd be a better judge of that than I would. Still, I'm surprised that you guys are reopening the case. What can you expect to accomplish after all this time?'

'I'm not with the police, Mr Ettinger.'

'I thought you said –'

'I didn't bother to correct your impression. I used to be in the department. I'm private now.'

'You're working for somebody?'

'For your former father-in-law.'

'Charlie London hired you?' He frowned, taking it all in. 'Well, I guess it's his privilege. It's not going to bring Barbie back but I guess it's his right to feel like he's doing something. I remember he was talking about posting a reward after she was murdered. I don't know if he ever got around to it or not.'

'I don't believe he did.'

'So now he wants to spend a few dollars finding the real killer. Well, why not? He doesn't have much going for him since Helen died. His wife, Barbara's mother.'

'I know.'

'Maybe it'll do him good to have something he can take an interest in. Not that work doesn't keep him busy, but, well –' He flicked ashes from his cigarette. 'I don't know what help I can give you, Mr Scudder, but ask all the questions you want.'

I asked about Barbara's social contacts, her relationships with people in the building. I asked about her job at the day-care center. He remembered Janice Corwin but couldn't supply her husband's name. 'The job wasn't that important,' he said. 'Basically it was something to get her out of the house, give her a focus for her energy. Oh, the money helped. I was dragging a briefcase around for the Welfare Department, which wasn't exactly the road to riches. But Barbie's job was temporary. She was going to give it up and stay home with the baby.'

The door opened. A teenage clerk started to enter the office, then stopped and stood there looking awkward. 'I'll be a few minutes, Sandy,' Ettinger told him. 'I'm busy right now.'

The boy withdrew, shutting the door. 'Saturday's always busy for us,' Ettinger said. 'I don't want to rush you, but I'm needed out there.'

I asked him some more questions. His memory wasn't very good, and I could understand why. He'd had one life torn up and had had to create a new one, and it was easier to do so if he dwelled on the first life as little as possible. There were no children from that first union to tie him into relations with in-laws. He could leave his marriage to Barbara in Brooklyn, along with his caseworker's files and all the trappings of that life. He lived in the suburbs now and drove a car and mowed a lawn and lived with his kids and his blonde wife. Why sit around remembering a tenement apartment in Boerum Hill?

'Funny,' he said. 'I can't begin to think of anyone we knew who might be capable of ... doing what was done to Barbie. But one other thing I could never believe was that she'd let a stranger into the apartment.'

'She was careful about that sort of thing?'

'She was always on guard. Wyckoff Street wasn't the kind of neighborhood she grew up in, although she found it comfortable enough. Of course we weren't going to stay there forever.' His glance flicked to the photo cube, as if he was seeing Barbara standing next to a car and in front of a lawn. 'But she got spooked by the other icepick killings.'

'Oh?'

'Not at first. When he killed the woman in Sheepshead Bay, though, that's when it got to her. Because it was the first time he'd struck in Brooklyn, you see. It freaked her a little.'

'Because of the location? Sheepshead Bay's a long ways from Boerum Hill.'

'But it was Brooklyn. And there was something else, I think, because I remember she identified pretty strongly with the woman who got killed. I must have known why but I can't remember. Anyway, she got nervous. She told me she had the feeling she was being watched.'

'Did you mention that to the police?'

'I don't think so.' He lowered his eyes, lit another cigarette. 'I'm sure I didn't. I thought at the time that it was part of being pregnant. Like craving odd foods, that sort of thing. Pregnant women get fixated on strange things.' His eyes rose to meet mine. 'Besides, I didn't want to think about it. Just a day or two before the murder she was talking about how she wanted me to get a police lock for the door. You know those locks with a steel bar braced against the door so it can't be forced?'

I nodded.

'Well, we didn't get a lock like that. Not that it would have made any difference because the door wasn't forced. I wondered why she would let anyone in, as nervous as she was, but it was daytime, after all, and people aren't as suspicious in the daytime. A man could pretend to be a plumber or from the gas company or something. Isn't that how the Boston Strangler operated?'

'I think it was something like that.'

'But if it was actually someone she knew –'

'There are some questions I have to ask.'

'Sure.'

'Is it possible your wife was involved with anyone?'

'Involved with – you mean having an affair?'

'That sort of thing.'

'She was pregnant,' he said, as if that answered the question. When I didn't say anything he said, 'We were very happy together. I'm sure she wasn't seeing anyone.'

'Did she often have visitors when you were out?'

'She might have had a friend over. I didn't check up on her. We trusted each other.'

'She left her job early that day.'

'She did that sometimes. She had an easygoing relationship with the woman she worked for.'

'You said you trusted each other. Did she trust you?'

'What are you driving at?'

'Did she ever accuse you of having affairs with other women?'

'Jesus, who've you been talking to? Oh, I bet I know where this is coming from. Sure. We had a couple of arguments that somebody must have heard.'

'Oh?'

40

'I told you women get odd ideas when they're pregnant. Like food cravings. Barbie got it into her head that I was making it with some of my cases. I was dragging my ass through tenements in Harlem and the South Bronx, filling out forms and trying not to gag on the smell and dodging the crap they throw off the roof at you, and she was accusing me of getting it on with all of those damsels in distress. I came to think of it as a pregnancy neurosis. I'm not Mr Irresistible in the first place, and I was so turned off by what I saw in those hovels that I had trouble performing at home some of the time, let alone being turned on while I was on the job. The hell, you were a cop, I don't have to tell you the kind of thing I saw every day.'

'So you weren't having an affair?'

'Didn't I just tell you that?'

'And you weren't romancing anybody else? A woman in the neighborhood, for example?'

'Certainly not. Did somebody say I was?'

I ignored the question. 'You remarried about three years after your wife died, Mr Ettinger. Is that right?'

'A little less than three years.'

'When did you meet your present wife?'

'About a year before I married her. Maybe more than that, maybe fourteen months. It was in the spring, and we had a June wedding.'

'How did you meet?'

'Mutual friends. We were at a party, although we didn't pay any attention to each other at the time, and then a friend of mine had both of us over for dinner, and –' He broke off abruptly. 'She wasn't one of my ADC cases in the South Bronx, if that's what you're getting at. And she never lived in Brooklyn, either. Jesus, I'm stupid!'

'Mr Ettinger –'

'I'm a suspect, aren't I? Jesus, how could I sit here and not have it occur to me? I'm a suspect, for Christ's sake.'

'There's a routine I have to follow in order to pursue an investigation, Mr Ettinger.'

'Does he think I did it? London? Is that what this whole thing is about?'

'Mr London hasn't told me who he does or doesn't suspect. If he's got any specific suspicions, he's keeping them to himself.'

'Well, isn't that decent of him.' He ran a hand over his forehead. 'Are we about through now, Scudder? I told you we're busy on Saturdays. We get a lot of people who work hard all week and Saturday's when they want to think about sports. So if I've answered all your questions –'

'You arrived home about six thirty the day your wife was murdered.'

'That sounds about right. I'm sure it's in a police report somewhere.'

'Can you account for your time that afternoon?'

He stared at me. 'We're talking about something that happened nine years ago,' he said. 'I can't distinguish one day of knocking on doors from another. Do you remember what *you* did that afternoon?'

'No, but it was a less significant day in my life. You'd remember if you took any time away from your work.'

'I didn't. I spent the whole day working on my cases. And it was whatever time I said it was when I got back to Brooklyn. Six thirty sounds about right.' He wiped his forehead again. 'But you can't ask me to prove any of this, can you? I probably filed a report but they only keep those things for a few years. I forget whether it's three years or five years, but it's certainly not nine years. Those files get cleaned out on a regular basis.'

'I'm not asking for proof.'

'I didn't kill her, for God's sake. Look at me. Do I look like a killer?'

'I don't know what killers look like. I was just reading the other day about a thirteen-year-old boy who shot two women behind the ear. I don't know what he looks like, and I don't imagine he looks like a killer.' I took a blank memo slip from his desk, wrote a number on it. 'This is my hotel,' I said. 'You might think of something. You never know what you might remember.'

'I don't want to remember anything.'

I got to my feet. So did he.

'That's not my life anymore,' he said. 'I live in the suburbs and I sell skis and sweatsuits. I went to Helen's funeral because I couldn't think of a decent way to skip it. I should have skipped it. I –'

I said, 'Take it easy, Ettinger. You're angry and you're scared but you don't have to be either one. Of course you're a suspect. Who would investigate a woman's murder without checking out the husband? When's the last time you heard of an investigation like that?' I put a hand on his shoulder. 'Somebody killed her,' I said, 'and it may have been somebody she knew. I probably

42

won't be able to find out much of anything but I'm giving it my best shot. If you think of anything, call me. That's all.'

'You're right,' he said. 'I got angry. I –'

I told him to forget it. I found my own way out.

SEVEN

I read a paper on the train ride back to the city. A feature article discussed the upturn in muggings and suggested ways for the reader to make himself a less attractive target. Walk in pairs and groups, the reporter advised. Stick to well-lighted streets. Walk near the curb, not close to buildings. Move quickly and give an impression of alertness. Avoid confrontations. Muggers want to size you up and see if you'll be easy. They ask you the time, ask for directions. Don't let them take advantage of you.

It's wonderful how the quality of urban life keeps getting better. *'Pardon me, sir, but could you tell me how to get to the Empire State Building?' 'Fuck off, you creep.'* Manners for a modern city.

The train took forever. It always felt a little strange going out to Long Island. Hicksville was nowhere near where Anita and the boys lived but Long Island is Long Island and I got the vaguely uncomfortable feeling I always get when I go there. I was glad to get to Penn Station.

By then it was time for a drink, and I had a quick one in a commuters' bar right there in the station. Saturday might be a busy day for Douglas Ettinger but it was a slow one for the bartender at the Iron Horse. All his weekday customers must have been out in Hicksville buying pup tents and basketball shoes.

The sun was out when I hit the street. I walked across Thirty-fourth, then headed up Fifth to the library. Nobody asked me what time it was, or how to get to the Holland Tunnel.

Before I went into the library I stopped at a pay phone and called Lynn London. Her father had given me her number and I checked my notebook and dialed it. I got an answering machine with a message that began by repeating the last four digits of the number, announced that no one could come to the phone, and

44

invited me to leave my name. The voice was female, very precise, just the slightest bit nasal, and I supposed it belonged to Barbara's sister. I rang off without leaving a message.

In the library I got the same Polk directory for Brooklyn that I'd used earlier. This time I looked up a different building on Wyckoff Street. It had held four apartments then, and one of them had been rented to a Mr and Mrs Edward Corwin.

That gave me a way to spend the afternoon. In a bar on Forty-first and Madison I ordered a cup of coffee and a shot of bourbon to pour into it and changed a dollar into dimes. I started on the Manhattan book, where I found two Edward Corwins, an E. Corwin, an E. J. Corwin and an E. V. Corwin. When none of those panned out I used Directory Assistance, getting the Brooklyn listings first, then moving on to Queens, the Bronx and Staten Island. Some of the numbers I dialed were busy, and I had to try them four or five times before I got through. Others didn't answer.

I wound up getting more dimes and trying all the J. Corwins in the five boroughs. Somewhere in the course of this I had a second cup of coffee with a second shot of bourbon in it. I used up quite a few dimes to no discernible purpose, but most investigatory work is like that. If she just roots around enough, even a blind sow gets an acorn now and then. Or so they tell me.

By the time I left the bar, some two-thirds of my phone numbers had check marks next to them indicating I'd reached the party and he or she was not the Corwin I was looking for. I'd call the rest of them in due course if I had to, but I didn't feel very hopeful about them. Janice Corwin had closed a business and given up an apartment. She might have moved to Seattle while she was at it. Or she and her husband could be somewhere in Westchester or Jersey or Connecticut, or out in Hicksville pricing tennis rackets. There was a limit to how much walking my fingers could do, in the white or yellow pages.

I went back to the library. I knew when she'd closed up shop at the Happy Hours Child Care Center; I'd learned that much from her landlord. Had she and her husband moved out of Boerum Hill at about the same time?

I worked year by year through the Polk directories and found the year the Corwins dropped out of the brick building on Wyckoff Street. The timing was right. She had probably closed the day-care center as a prelude to moving. Maybe they'd gone to the suburbs, or his company transferred him to Atlanta. Or they split up and went separate ways.

I put the directory back, then got an intelligent thought for a change and went back to reclaim it. There were three other tenants in the building who'd remained there for a few years after the Corwins moved out. I copied their names in my notebook.

This time I made my calls from a bar on Forty-second Street, and I bypassed the Manhattan book and went straight to Brooklyn information. I got lucky right away with the Gordon Pomerances, who had stayed in Brooklyn when the Wyckoff Street building was sold out from under them. They'd moved a short mile to Carroll Street.

Mrs Pomerance answered the phone. I gave my name and said I was trying to reach the Corwins. She knew at once who I was talking about but had no idea how I could reach them.

'We didn't keep in touch. He was a nice fellow, Eddie, and he used to bring the children over for dinner after she moved out, but then when he moved we lost contact. It's been so many years. I'm sure we had his address at one point but I can't even remember the city he moved to. It was in California, I think Southern California.'

'But she moved out first?'

'You didn't know that? She left him, left him flat with the two kids. She closed the whatchamacallit, the day-care center, and the next thing you know he's got to find a day-care center for his own children. I'm sorry, but I can't imagine a mother walking out on her own children.'

'Do you know where she might have gone?'

'Greenwich Village, I suppose. To pursue her art. Among other things.'

'Her art?'

'She fancied herself a sculptor. I never saw her work so for all I know she may have had some talent. I'd be surprised if she did, though. There was a woman who had everything. A nice apartment, a husband who was an awfully sweet guy, two beautiful children, and she even had a business that wasn't doing too badly. And she walked away from it, turned her back and walkd away.'

I tried a long shot. 'Did you happen to know a friend of hers named Barbara Ettinger?'

'I didn't know her that well. What was that name? Ettinger? Why is that name familiar to me?'

'A Barbara Ettinger was murdered down the block from where you lived.'

46

'Just before we moved in. Of course. I remember now. I never knew her, naturally, because as I said it was just before we moved in. She was a friend of the Corwins?'

'She worked for Mrs Corwin.'

'Were they that way?'

'What way?'

'There was a lot of talk about the murder. It made me nervous about moving in. My husband and I told each other we didn't have to worry about lightning striking twice in the same place, but privately I was still worried. Then those killings just stopped, didn't they?'

'Yes. You never knew the Ettingers?'

'No, I told you.'

An artist in Greenwich Village. A sculptor. Of the J. Corwins I'd been unable to reach, had any lived in the Village? I didn't think so.

I said, 'Would you happen to remember Mrs Corwin's maiden name?'

'Remember it? I don't think I ever knew it in the first place. Why?'

'I was thinking she might have resumed it if she's pursuing an artistic career.'

'I'm sure she did. Artistic career or not, she'd want her own name back. But I couldn't tell you what it was.'

'Of course she could have remarried by now –'

'Oh, I wouldn't count on it.'

'I beg your pardon?'

'I don't think she remarried,' Mrs Pomerance said. There was a sharpness to her tone and I wondered at it. I asked her what made her say that.

'Put it this way,' she said. 'Sculpture or no sculpture, she'd probably live in Greenwich Village.'

'I don't understand.'

'You don't?' She clicked her tongue, impatient with my obtuseness. 'She left her husband – *and* two children – but not to run off with another man. She left him for another woman.'

Janice Corwin's maiden name was Keane. It took a subway ride to Chambers Street and a couple of hours in various offices of the Department of Records and Informations Services to supply this kernel of information. Most of the time was spent getting clearance. I kept needing the permission of someone who didn't come in on Saturdays.

I tried marriage licenses first, and when that failed to pan out I had a shot at birth certificates. Mrs Pomerance had been a little hazy on the names and ages of the Corwin children, but she was pretty sure the youngest's name was Kelly and that she'd been five or six when her mother left. She'd been seven, it turned out; she'd be around fifteen now. Her father was Edward Francis Corwin, her mother the former Janice Elizabeth Keane.

I wrote the name in my notebook with a sense of triumph. Not that there was much likelihood that it would slip my mind, but as a symbol of accomplishment. I couldn't prove that I was an inch closer to Barbara Ettinger's killer than I'd been when Charles London sat down across from me at Armstrong's, but I'd done some detecting and it felt good. It was plodding work, generally pointless work, but it let me use muscles I didn't get to use all that often and they tingled from the exertion.

A couple of blocks from there I found a Blarney Stone with a steam table. I had a hot pastrami sandwich and drank a beer or two with it. There was a big color set mounted over the bar. It was tuned to one of those sports anthology shows they have on Saturday afternoons. A couple of guys were doing something with logs in a fast-moving stream. Riding them, I think. Nobody in the place was paying much attention to their efforts. By the time I was done with my sandwich the log-riders were through and a stock-car race had replaced them. Nobody paid any attention to the stock cars, either.

I called Lynn London again. This time when her machine picked up I waited for the beep and left my name and number. Then I checked the phone book.

No Janice Keanes in Manhattan. Half a dozen Keanes with the initial J. Plenty of other variations of the name – Keene, Keen, Kean. I thought of that old radio show, *Mr Keene, Tracer of Lost Persons*. I couldn't remember how he spelled it.

I tried all the J. Keanes. I got two that failed to answer, one persistent busy signal, and three people who denied knowing a Janice Keane. The busy signal lived on East Seventy-third Street and I decided that was no address for a lesbian sculptor from Boerum Hill. I dialed Directory Assistance, all set to go through my routine again for the other four boroughs, but something stopped me.

She was in Manhattan. Damn it, I knew she was in Manhattan.

I asked for a Janice Keane in Manhattan, spelled the last name, waited a minute, and was told the only listing in Manhattan

48

under that name and with that spelling was unpublished. I hung up, called back again to get a different operator, and went through the little ritual that a cop uses to obtain an unlisted number. I identified myself as Detective Francis Fitzroy, of the Eighteenth Precinct. I called it the One-Eight Precinct because, although cops don't invariably talk that way, civilians invariably think they do.

I got the address while I was at it. She was on Lispenard Street, and that was a perfectly logical place for a sculptor to be living, and not too long a walk from where I was.

I had another dime in my hand. I put it back in my pocket and went back to the bar. The stock cars had given way to the feature of the program, a couple of black junior-middleweights topping a fight card in some unlikely place. Phoenix, I think it was. I don't know what a junior-middleweight is. They've added all these intermediate weight classes so that they can have more championship fights. Some of the patrons who'd passed up the log-rollers and the stock cars were watching these two boys hit each other, which was something they weren't doing very often. I sat through a few rounds and drank some coffee with bourbon in it.

Because I thought it would help if I had some idea how I was going to approach this woman. I'd been tracking her spoor through books and files and phone wires, as if she held the secret to the Ettinger murder, and for all I knew Barbara Ettinger was nothing to her beyond a faceless lump who put the alphabet blocks away when the kids were done playing with them.

Or she was Barbara's best friend. Or her lover – I remembered Mrs Pomerance's questions: 'She was a friend of the Corwins? Were they that way?'

Maybe she had killed Barbara. Could they have both left the day-care center early? Was that even possible, let alone likely?

I was spinning my wheels and I knew it but I let them spin for a while anyway. On the television screen, the kid with the white stripe on his trunks was finally beginning to use his jab to set up right hands to the body. It didn't look as though he was going to take his man out in the handful of rounds remaining, not like that, but he seemed a safe shot for the decision. He was wearing his opponent down, grinding away at him. Jabbing with the left, hooking the right hand to the rib section. The other boy couldn't seem to find a defense that worked.

I knew how both of them felt.

I thought about Douglas Ettinger. I decided he didn't kill his wife, and I tried to figure out how I knew that, and decided I knew it the same way I'd known Janice Keane was in Manhattan. Chalk it up to divine inspiration.

Ettinger was right, I decided. Louis Pinell killed Barbara Ettinger, just as he'd killed the other seven women. Barbara had thought some nut was stalking her and she was right.

Then why'd she let the nut into her apartment?

In the tenth round, the kid who'd been getting his ribs barbecued summoned up some reserve of strength and put a couple of combinations together. He had the kid with the stripe on his trunks reeling, but the flurry wasn't enough to end it and the kid with the stripe hung on and got the decision. The crowd booed. I don't know what fight they thought they were watching. The crowd in Phoenix, that is. My companions in the Blarney Stone weren't that involved emotionally.

The hell with it. I went and made my phone call.

It rang four or five times before she answered it. I said, 'Janice Keane, please,' and she said she was Janice Keane.

I said, 'My name's Matthew Scudder, Ms Keane. I'd like to ask you some questions.'

'Oh?'

'About a woman named Barbara Ettinger.'

'Jesus.' A pause. 'What about her?'

'I'm investigating her death. I'd like to come over and talk with you.'

'You're investigating her death? That was ages ago. It must have been ten years.'

'Nine years.'

'I thought it was the Mounties who never gave up. I never heard that about New York's Finest. You're a policeman?'

I was about to say yes, but heard myself say, 'I used to be.'

'What are you now?'

'A private citizen. I'm working for Charles London. Mrs Ettinger's father.'

'That's right, her maiden name was London.' She had a good telephone voice, low-pitched and throaty. 'I can't make out why you're starting an investigation now. And what could I possibly contribute to it?'

'Maybe I could explain that in person,' I said. 'I'm just a few minutes away from you now. Would it be all right if I come over?'

'Jesus. What's today, Saturday? And what time is it? I've been

50

working and I tend to lose track of the time. I've got six o'clock. Is that right?'

'That's right.'

'I'd better fix something to eat. And I have to clean up. Give me an hour, okay?'

'I'll be there at seven.'

'You know the address?' I read it off as I'd received it from Information. 'That's it. That's between Church and Broadway, and you ring the bell and then stand at the curb so I can see you and I'll throw the key down. Ring two long and three short, okay?'

'Two long and three short.'

'Then I'll know it's you. Not that you're anything to me but a voice on the phone. How'd you get this number? It's supposed to be unlisted.'

'I used to be a cop.'

'Right, so you said. So much for unlisted numbers, huh? Tell me your name again.'

'Matthew Scudder.'

She repeated it. Then she said, 'Barbara Ettinger. Oh, if you knew how that name takes me back. I have a feeling I'm going to be sorry I answered the phone. Well, Mr Scudder, I'll be seeing you in an hour.'

EIGHT

Lispenard is a block below Canal Street, which puts it in that section known as Tribeca. Tribeca is a geographical acronym for *Triangle Below Canal*, just as SoHo derives from *South of Houston* Street. There was a time when artists began moving into the blocks south of the Village, living in violation of the housing code in spacious and inexpensive lofts. The code had since been modified to permit residential loft dwelling and SoHo had turned chic and expensive, which led loft seekers further south of Tribeca. The rents aren't cheap there either now, but the streets still have the deserted quality of SoHo ten or twelve years ago.

I stuck to a well-lighted street. I walked near the curb, not close to buildings, and I did my best to move quickly and give an impression of alertness. Confrontations were easily avoided in those empty streets.

Janice Keane's address turned out to be a six-story loft building, a narrow structure fitted in between two taller, wider and more modern buildings. It looked cramped, like a little man on a crowded subway. Floor-to-ceiling windows ran the width of the facade on each of its floors. On the ground floor, shuttered for the weekend, was a wholesaler of plumber's supplies.

I went into a claustrophobic hallway, found a bell marked Keane, rang it two long and three short. I went out to the sidewalk, stood at the curb looking up at all those windows.

She called down from one of them, asking my name. I couldn't see anything in that light. I gave my name, and something small whistled down through the air and jangled on the pavement beside me. 'Fifth floor,' she said. 'There's an elevator.'

There was indeed, and it could have accommodated a grand piano. I rode it to the fifth floor and stepped out into a spacious loft. There were a lot of plants, all deep green and thriving, and relatively little in the way of furniture. The doors were oak, buffed to a high sheen. The walls were exposed brick. Overhead track lighting provided illumination.

She said, 'You're right on time. The place is a mess but I won't apologize. There's coffee.'

'If it's no trouble.'

'None at all. I'm going to have a cup myself. Just let me steer you to a place to sit and I'll be a proper hostess. Milk? Sugar?'

'Just black.'

She left me in an area with a couch and a pair of chairs grouped around a high-pile rug with an abstract design. A couple of eight-foot-tall bookcases reached a little more than halfway to the ceiling and helped screen the space from the rest of the loft. I walked over to the window and looked down at Lispenard Street but there wasn't a whole lot to see.

There was one piece of sculpture in the room and I was standing in front of it when she came back with the coffee. It was the head of a woman. Her hair was a nest of snakes, her face a high-cheekboned, broad-browed mask of unutterable disappointment.

'That's my Medusa,' she said. 'Don't meet her eyes. Her gaze turns men to stone.'

'She's very good.'

'Thank you.'

'She looks so disappointed.'

'That's the quality,' she agreed. 'I didn't know that until I'd finished her, and then I saw it for myself. You've got a pretty good eye.'

'For disappointment, anyway.'

She was an attractive woman. Medium height, a little more well-fleshed than was strictly fashionable. She wore faded Levi's and a slate-blue chamois shirt with the sleeves rolled to the elbows. Her face was heart-shaped, its contours accentuated by a sharply defined widow's peak. Her hair, dark brown salted with gray, hung almost to her shoulders. Her gray eyes were large and well-spaced, and a touch of mascara around them was the only makeup she wore.

We sat in a pair of chairs at right angles to one another and set our coffee mugs on a table made from a section of tree trunk and a slab of slate. She asked if I'd had trouble finding her address and I said I hadn't. Then she said, 'Well, shall we talk about Barb Ettinger? Maybe you can start by telling me why you're interested in her after all these years.'

53

She'd missed the media coverage of Louis Pinell's arrest. It was news to her that the Icepick Prowler was in custody, so it was also news that her former employee had been killed by someone else.

'So for the first time you're looking for a killer with a motive,' she said. 'If you'd looked at the time –'

'It might have been easier. Yes.'

'And it might be easier now just to look the other way. I don't remember her father. I must have met him, after the murder if not before, but I don't have any recollection of him. I remember her sister. Have you met her?'

'Not yet.'

'I don't know what she's like now, but she struck me as a snotty little bitch. But I didn't know her well, and anyway it was nine years ago. That's what I keep coming back to. Everything was nine years ago.'

'How did you meet Barbara Ettinger?'

'We ran into each other in the neighborhood. Shopping at the Grand Union, going to the candy store for a paper. Maybe I mentioned that I was running a day-care center. Maybe she heard it from someone else. Either way, one morning she walked into the Happy Hours and asked if I needed any help.'

'And you hired her right away?'

'I told her I couldn't pay her much. The place was just about making expenses. I started it for a dumb reason – there was no convenient day-care center in the neighborhood, and I needed a place to dump my own kids, so I found a partner and we opened the Happy Hours, and instead of dumping my kids I was watching them and everybody else's, and of course my partner came to her senses about the time the ink was dry on the lease, and she backed out and I was running the whole show myself. I told Barb I needed her but I couldn't afford her, and she said she mostly wanted something to do and she'd work cheap. I forget what I paid her but it wasn't a whole lot.'

'Was she good at her work?'

'It was essentially baby-sitting. There's a limit to how good you can be at it.' She thought for a moment. 'It's hard to remember. Nine years ago, so I was twenty-nine at the time, and she was a few years younger.'

'She was twenty-six when she died.'

'Jesus, that's not very old, is it?' She closed her eyes, wincing at early death. 'She was a big help to me, and I guess she was

54

good enough at what she did. She seemed to enjoy it most of the time. She'd have enjoyed it more if she'd been a more contented woman generally.'

'She was discontented?'

'I don't know if that's the right word.' She turned to glance at her bust of Medusa. 'Disappointed? You got the feeling that Barb's life wasn't quite what she'd had in mind for herself. Everything was okay, her husband was okay, her apartment was okay, but she'd hoped for something more than just okay, and she didn't have it.'

'Someone described her as restless.'

'Restless.' She tasted the word. 'That fits her well enough. Of course that was a time for women to be restless. Sexual roles were pretty confused and confusing.'

'Aren't they still?'

'Maybe they always will be. But I think things are a little more settled now than they were for a while there. She was restless, though. Definitely restless.'

'Her marriage was a disappointment?'

'Most of them are, aren't they? I don't suppose it would have lasted, but we'll never know, will we? Is he still with the Welfare Department?'

I brought her up to date on Douglas Ettinger.

'I didn't know him too well,' she said. 'Barb seemed to feel he wasn't good enough for her. At least I got that impression. His background was low-rent compared to hers. Not that she grew up with the Vanderbilts, but I gather she had a proper suburban childhood and a fancy education. He worked long hours and he had a dead-end job. And yes, there was one other thing wrong with him.'

'What was that?'

'He fucked around.'

'Did he really or did she just think so?'

'He made a pass at me. Oh, it was no big deal, just a casual, offhand sort of proposition. I was not greatly interested. The man looked like a chipmunk. I wasn't much flattered, either, because one sensed he did this sort of thing a lot and that it didn't mean I was irresistible. Of course I didn't say anything to Barb, but she had evidence of her own. She caught him once at a party, necking in the kitchen with the hostess. And I gather he was dipping into his welfare clients.'

'What about his wife?'

'I gather he was dipping into her, too. I don't –'

55

'Was she having an affair with anybody?'

She leaned forward, took hold of her coffee mug. Her hands were large for a woman, her nails clipped short. I suppose long nails would be an impossible hindrance for a sculptor.

She said, 'I was paying her a very low salary. You could almost call it a token salary. I mean, high-school kids got a better hourly rate for baby-sitting, and Barb didn't even get to raid the refrigerator. So if she wanted time off, all she did was take it.'

'Did she take a lot of time off?'

'Not all that much, but I had the impression that she was taking an occasional afternoon or part of an afternoon for something more exciting than a visit to the dentist. A woman has a different air about her when she's off to meet a lover.'

'Did she have that air the day she was killed?'

'I wished you'd asked me nine years ago. I'd have had a better chance of remembering. I know she left early that day but I don't have any memory of the details. You think she met a lover and he killed her?'

'I don't think anything special at this stage. Her husband said she was nervous about the Icepick Prowler.'

'I don't think . . . wait a minute. I remember thinking about that afterward, after she'd been killed. That she'd been talking about the danger of living in the city. I don't know if she said anything specific about the Icepick killings, but there was something about feeling as though she was being watched or followed. I interpreted it as a kind of premonition of her own death.'

'Maybe it was.'

'Or maybe she was being watched and followed. What is it they say? "Paranoiacs have enemies, too." Maybe she really sensed something.'

'Would she let a stranger into the apartment?'

'I wondered about that at the time. If she was on guard to begin with –'

She broke off suddenly. I asked her what was the matter.

'Nothing.'

'I'm a stranger and you let me into your apartment.'

'It's a loft. As if it makes a difference. I –'

I took out my wallet and tossed it onto the table between us. 'Look through it,' I said. 'There's an ID in it. It'll match the name I gave you over the phone, and I think there's something with a photograph on it.'

'That's not necessary.'

'Look it over anyway. You're not going to be very useful as a subject of interrogation if you're anxious about getting killed. The ID won't prove I'm not a rapist or a murderer, but rapists and murderers don't usually give you their right names ahead of time. Go ahead, pick it up.'

She went through the wallet quickly, then handed it back to me. I returned it to my pocket. 'That's a lousy picture of you,' she said. 'But I guess it's you, all right. I don't think she'd let a stranger into her apartment. She'd let a lover in, though. Or a husband.'

'You think her husband killed her?'

'Married people always kill one another. Sometimes it takes them fifty years.'

'Any idea who her lover may have been?'

'It may not have been just one person. I'm just guessing, but she could have had an itch to experiment. And she was pregnant so it was safe.'

She laughed. I asked her what was so funny.

'I was trying to think where she would have met someone. A neighbor, maybe, or a male half of some couple she and her husband saw socially. It's not as though she could have met men on the job. We had plenty of males there, but unfortunately none of them were over eight years old.'

'Not very promising.'

'Except that's not altogether true. Sometimes fathers would bring the kids in, or pick them up after work. There are situations more conducive to flirtation, but I had daddies come on to me while they collected their children, and it probably happened to Barbara. She was very attractive, you know. And she didn't wrap herself up in an old Mother Hubbard when she came to work at the Happy Hours. She had a good figure and she dressed to show it off.'

The conversation went on a little longer before I got a handle on the question. Then I said, 'Did you and Barbara ever become lovers?'

I was watching her eyes when I asked the question, and they widened in response. 'Jesus Christ,' she said.

I waited her out.

'I'm just wondering where the question came from,' she said. 'Did somebody say we were lovers? Or am I an obvious dyke or something?'

'I was told you left your husband for another woman.'

'Well, that's close. I left my husband for thirty or forty

reasons, I suppose. And the first relationship I had after I left him *was* with a woman. Who told you? Not Doug Ettinger. He'd moved out of the neighborhood before that particular shit hit the fan. Unless he happened to talk to somebody. Maybe he and Eddie got together and cried on each other's shoulder about how women are no good, they either get stabbed or they run off with each other. Was it Doug?'

'No. It was a woman who lived in your building on Wyckoff Street.'

'Someone in the building. Oh, it must have been Maisie! Except that's not her name. Give me a minute. Mitzi! It was Mitzi Pomerance, wasn't it?'

'I didn't get her first name. I just spoke with her on the telephone.'

'Little Mitzi Pomerance. Are they still married? Of course, they'd have to be. Unless he left, but nothing would propel her away from hearth and home. She'd insist her marriage was heaven even if it meant systematically denying every negative emotion that ever threatened to come to the surface. The worst thing about going back to visit the kids was the look on that twit's face when we passed on the stairs.' She sighed and shook her head at the memory. 'I never had anything going with Barbara. Strangely enough, I never had anything going with anybody, male or female, before I split with Eddie. And the woman I got together with afterward was the first woman I ever slept with in my life.'

'But you were attracted to Barbara Ettinger.'

'Was I? I recognized that she was attractive. That's not the same thing. Was I specifically attracted to her?' She weighed the notion. 'Maybe,' she conceded. 'Not on any conscious level, I don't think. And when I did begin to consider the possibility that I might find it, oh, interesting to go to bed with a woman, I don't think I had any particular woman in mind. As a matter of fact, I don't even think I entertained the fantasy while Barbara was alive.'

'I have to ask these personal questions.'

'You don't have to apologize. Jesus, Mitzi Pomerance. I'll bet she's fat, I'll bet she's a plump little piglet by now. But you only spoke to her over the phone.'

'That's right.'

'Is she still living in the same place? She must be. You wouldn't get them out of there with a crowbar.'

'Somebody did. A buyer converted the house to one-family.'

'They must have been sick. Did they stay in the neighbor-hood?'

'More or less. They moved to Carroll Street.'

'Well, I hope they're happy. Mitzi and Gordon.' She leaned forward, searched my face with her gray eyes. 'You drink,' she said. 'Right?'

'Pardon?'

'You're a drunk, aren't you?'

'I suppose you could call me a drinking man.'

The words sounded stiff, even to me. They hung in the air for a moment and then her laughter cut in, full-bodied and rich. ' "I suppose you could call me a drinking man." Jesus, that's wonderful. Well, I suppose you could call me a drinking woman, Mr Scudder. People have called me a good deal worse, and it's been a long day and a dry one. How about a little something to cut the dust?'

'That's not a bad idea.'

'What'll it be?'

'Do you have bourbon?'

'I don't think so.' The bar was behind a pair of sliding doors in one of the bookcases. 'Scotch or vodka,' she announced.

'Scotch.'

'Rocks? Water? What?'

'Just straight.'

'The way God made it, huh?' She brought back a pair of rocks glasses filled about halfway, one with Scotch, the other with vodka. She gave me mine, looked into her own. She had the air of someone trying to select a toast, but evidently she couldn't think of one. 'Oh, what the hell,' she said, and took a drink.

'Who do you think killed her?'

'Too early to tell. It could have been somebody I haven't heard of yet. Or it could have been Pinell. I'd like ten minutes with him.'

'You think you could refresh his memory?'

I shook my head. 'I think I might get some sense of him. So much detection is intuition. You gather details and soak up impressions, and then the answer pops into your mind out of nowhere. It's not like Sherlock Holmes, at least it never was for me.'

'You make it sound almost as though there's a psychic element to the process.'

'Well, I can't read palms or see the future. But maybe there is.'

59

I sipped Scotch. It had that medicinal taste that Scotch has but I didn't mind it as much as I usually do. It was one of the heavier Scotches, dark and peaty. Teacher's, I think it was. 'I want to get out to Sheepshead Bay next,' I said.

'Now?'

'Tomorrow. That's where the fourth Icepick killing took place, and that was the one that's supposed to have spooked Barbara Ettinger.'

'You think the same person –'

'Louis Pinell admits to the Sheepshead Bay murder. Of course that doesn't prove anything, either. I'm not sure why I want to go out there. I guess I want to talk to somebody who was on the scene, someone who saw the body. There were some physical details about the killings that were held back from the press coverage, and they were duplicated in Barbara's murder. Imperfectly duplicated, and I want to know if there was any parallel in the other Brooklyn homicide.'

'And if there was, what would it prove? That there was a second killer, a maniac who confined himself to Brooklyn?'

'And who conveniently stopped at two killings. It's possible. It wouldn't even rule out someone with a motive for killing Barbara. Say her husband decided to kill her, but he realized the Icepick Prowler hadn't been to Brooklyn yet, so he killed some stranger in Sheepshead Bay first to establish a pattern.'

'Do people do things like that?'

'There's nothing you can imagine that somebody hasn't done at one time or another. Maybe somebody had a motive for killing the woman in Sheepshead Bay. Then he was worried that the murder would stand out as the only one of its kind in Brooklyn, so he went after Barbara. Or maybe that was just his excuse. Maybe he killed a second time because he'd found out that he enjoyed it.'

'God.' She drank vodka. 'What was the physical detail?'

'You don't want to know about it.'

'You protecting the little woman from the awful truth?'

'The victims were stabbed through the eyes. An icepick, right through the eyeballs.'

'Jesus. And the … what did you call it? Imperfect duplication?'

'Barbara Ettinger just got it in one eye.'

'Like a wink.' She sat for a long moment, then looked down at her glass and noticed that it was empty. She went to the bar and came back with both bottles. After she'd filled our glasses she left the bottles on the slate-topped table.

'I wonder why he would do a thing like that,' she said.

'That's another reason I'd like to see Pinell,' I said. 'To ask him.'

The conversation turned this way and that. At one point she asked whether she should call me Matt or Matthew. I told her it didn't matter to me. She said it mattered to her that I call her not Janice but Jan.

'Unless you're uncomfortable calling murder suspects by their first names.'

When I was a cop I learned always to call suspects by their first names. It gave you a certain amount of psychological leverage. I told her she wasn't a suspect.

'I was at the Happy Hours all that afternoon,' she said. 'Of course it would be hard to prove after all these years. At the time it would have been easy. Alibis must be harder to come by for people who live alone.'

'You live alone here?'

'Unless you count the cats. They're hiding somewhere. They steer clear of strangers. Showing them your ID wouldn't impress them much.'

'Real hard-liners.'

'Uh-huh. I've always lived alone. Since I left Eddie, that is. I've been in relationships but I always lived alone.'

'Unless we count the cats.'

'Unless we count the cats. I never thought at the time that I'd be living by myself for the next eight years. I thought a relationship with a woman might be different in some fundamental way. See, back then was consciousness-raising time. I decided the problem was men.'

'And it wasn't?'

'Well, it may have been one of the problems. Women turned out to be another problem. For a while I decided I was one of those fortunate people who are capable of relationships with both sexes.'

'Just for a while?'

'Uh-huh. Because what I discovered next was that I may be capable of relationships with men and women, but what I mostly am is not very good at relationships.'

'Well, I can relate to that.'

'I figured you probably could. You live alone, don't you, Matthew?'

'For a while now.'

'Your sons are with your wife? I'm not psychic. There's a picture of them in your wallet.'

'Oh, that. It's an old picture.'

'They're handsome boys.'

'They're good kids, too.' I added a little Scotch to my glass. 'They live out in Syosset. They'll take the train in now and then and we catch a ball game together, or maybe a fight in the Garden.'

'They must enjoy that.'

'I know I enjoy it.'

'You must have moved out a while ago.'

I nodded. 'Around the time I left the cops.'

'Same reason?'

I shrugged.

'How come you quit the cops? Was it this stuff?'

'What stuff?'

She waved a hand at the bottles. 'You know. The booze.'

'Oh, hell, no,' I said. 'I wasn't even that heavy a hitter at the time. I just reached a point where I didn't feel like being a cop anymore.'

'What did it? Disillusionment? A lack of faith in the criminal justice system? Disgust with corruption?'

I shook my head. 'I lost my illusions early in the game and I never had much faith in the criminal justice system. It's a terrible system and the cops just do what they can. As far as corruption goes, I was never enough of an idealist to be bothered by it.'

'What then? Mid-life crisis?'

'You could call it that.'

'Well, we won't talk about it if you don't want to.'

We fell silent for a moment. She drank and then I drank, and then I put my glass down and said, 'Well, it's no secret. It's just not something I talk about a lot. I was in a tavern up in Washington Heights one night. It was a place where cops could drink on the arm. The owner liked having us around so you could run a tab and never be asked for payment. I had every right to be there. I was off-duty and I wanted to unwind a little before I drove back out to the island.'

Or maybe I wouldn't have gone home that night anyway. I didn't always. Sometimes I caught a few hours' sleep in a hotel room to save driving back and forth. Sometimes I didn't have to get a hotel room.

'Two punks held up the place,' I went on. 'They got what was in the register and shot the bartender on the way out, shot him dead just for the hell of it. I ran out into the street after them. I was in plainclothes but of course I was carrying a gun. You always carry it.

'I emptied the gun at them. I got them both. I killed one of them and crippled the other. Left him paralyzed from the waist down. Two things he'll never do again are walk and fuck.'

I'd told this story before but this time I could feel it all happening again. Washington Heights is hilly and they'd taken off up an incline. I remembered bracing myself, holding the gun with both hands, firing uphill at them. Maybe it was the Scotch that was making the recollection so vivid. Maybe it was something I responded to in her big unwavering gray eyes.

'And because you killed one and crippled another –'

I shook my head. 'That wouldn't have bothered me. I'm only sorry I didn't kill them both. They murdered that bartender for no good reason on God's earth. I wouldn't lose a dime's worth of sleep over those two.'

She waited.

'One of the shots went wide,' I said. 'Shooting uphill at a pair of moving targets, hell, it's remarkable I scored as well as I did. I always shot Expert on the police range, but it's different when it's real.' I tried to draw my eyes away from hers but couldn't manage it. 'One shot missed, though, and it ricocheted off the pavement or something. Took a bad hop. And there was a little girl walking around or standing around, whatever the hell she was doing. She was only six years old. I don't know what the hell she was doing out at that hour.'

This time I looked away. 'The bullet went into her eye,' I said. 'The ricochet took off some of its steam so if it had been an inch to the side one way or the other it probably would have glanced off bone, but life's a game of inches, isn't it? There was no bone to get in the way and the bullet wound up in her brain and she died. Instantly.'

'God.'

'I didn't do anything wrong. There was a departmental investigation because that's standard procedure, and it was agreed unanimously that I hadn't done anything wrong. As a matter of fact I received a commendation. The child was Hispanic, Puerto Rican, Estrellita Rivera her name was, and sometimes the press gets on you when there's a minority group casualty like that, or you get static from community groups, but

63

there was none of that in this case. If I was anything I was a fast-acting hero cop who had a piece of bad luck.'

'And you quit the police force.'

The Scotch bottle was empty. There was maybe half a pint of vodka in the other bottle and I poured a few ounces of it into my glass. 'Not right away,' I said, 'but before too long. And I don't know what made me do it.'

'Guilt.'

'I'm not sure. All I know is that being a cop didn't seem to be fun anymore. Being a husband and a father didn't seem to work, either. I took a leave of absence from both, moved into a hotel a block west of Columbus Circle. Somewhere down the line it became clear that I wasn't going back, not to my wife, not to the department.'

Neither of us said anything for a while. After a moment she leaned over and touched my hand. It was an unexpected and slightly awkward gesture and for some reason it touched me. I felt a thickening in my throat.

Then she had withdrawn her hand and was on her feet. I thought for a moment that she meant for me to leave. Instead she said, 'I'm going to call the liquor store while they're still open. The nearest place is on Canal and they close early. Do you want to stick with Scotch or would you rather switch to bourbon? And what brand of bourbon?'

'I should probably be going soon.'

'Scotch or bourbon?'

'I'll stay with the Scotch.'

While we waited for the liquor delivery she took me around the loft and showed me some of her work. Most of it was realistic, like the Medusa, but a few pieces were abstract. There was a lot of strength in her sculpture. I told her I liked her work.

'I'm pretty good,' she said.

She wouldn't let me pay for the liquor, insisting that I was her guest. We sat in our chairs again, opened our respective bottles, filled our glasses. She asked me if I really liked her work. I assured her that I did.

'I'm supposed to be good,' she said. 'You know how I got into this? Playing with clay with the kids at the day-care center. I wound up taking the clay home, that yellow modeling clay, and working with it by the hour. Then I took a night course at Brooklyn College, an adult-ed class, and the instructor told me I had talent. He didn't have to tell me. I knew it.

'I've had some recognition. I had a show at the Chuck Levitan

Gallery a little over a year ago. You know the gallery? On Grand Street?' I didn't. 'Well, he gave me a one-man show. A one-woman show. A one-person show. Shit, you have to think before you talk nowadays, have you noticed?'

'Uh-huh.'

'And I had an NEA grant last year. National Endowment for the Arts. Plus a smaller grant from the Einhoorn Foundation. Don't pretend you heard of the Einhoorn Foundation. I never heard of it before I got the grant. I've got pieces in some fairly decent collections. One or two in museums. Well, one, and it's not MOMA, but it's a museum. I'm a sculptor.'

'I never said you weren't.'

'And my kids are in California and I never see them. He has full custody. The hell, I moved out, right? I'm some kind of unnatural woman in the first place, some dyke who deserts husband and kids, so of course he gets custody, right? I didn't make an issue of it. Do you want to know something, Matthew?'

'What?'

'I didn't *want* custody. I was done with day care. I had fucking had it with kids, my own included. What do you make of that?'

'It sounds natural enough.'

'The Maisie Pomerances of the world wouldn't agree with you. Excuse me, I mean Mitzi. Gordon and Mitzi Fucking Pomerance. Mr and Mrs High-School Yearbook.'

I was able to hear the vodka in her voice now. She wasn't slurring her words any but there was a timbre to her speech that the alcohol had provided. It didn't surprise me. She had matched me drink for drink and I was hitting it pretty good myself. Of course I'd had a head start on her.

'When he said he was moving to California I threw a fit. Yelled that it wasn't fair, that he had to stay in New York so I could visit them. I had visitation rights, I said, and what good were my visitation rights if they were three thousand miles away? But do you know something?'

'What?'

'I was relieved. Part of me was glad they were going, because you wouldn't believe what it was like, traipsing out there on the subway once a week, sitting in the apartment with them or walking around Boerum Hill and always risking blank stares from Maisie Pomerance. Goddamn it, why can't I even get that goddamned woman's name right? Mitzi!'

'I've got her number written down. You could always call her up and tell her off.'

She laughed. 'Oh, Jesus,' she said. 'I gotta pee. I'll be right back.'

When she came back she sat on the couch. Without preamble she said, 'You know what we are? Me with my sculpture and you with your existential angst, and what we are is a couple of drunks who copped out. That's all.'

'If you say so.'

'Don't patronize me. Let's face it. We're both alcoholics.'

'I'm a heavy drinker. There's a difference.'

'What's the difference?'

'I could stop anytime I want to.'

'Then why don't you?'

'Why should I?'

Instead of answering the question she leaned forward to fill her glass. 'I stopped for a while,' she said. 'I quit cold for two months. More than two months.'

'You just up and quit?'

'I went to AA.'

'Oh.'

'You ever been?'

I shook my head. 'I don't think it would work for me.'

'But you could stop anytime you want.'

'Yeah, if *I* wanted.'

'And anyway you're not an alcoholic.'

I didn't say anything at first. Then I said, 'I suppose it depends on how you define the word. Anyway, all it is is a label.'

'They say you decide for yourself if you're an alcoholic.'

'Well, I'm deciding that I'm not.'

'I decided I was. And it worked for me. The thing is, they say it works best if you don't drink.'

'I can see where that might make a difference.'

'I don't know why I got on this subject.' She drained her glass, looked at me over its rim. 'I didn't mean to get on this goddamned subject. First my kids and then my drinking, what a fucking down.'

'It's all right.'

'I'm sorry, Matthew.'

'Forget it.'

'Sit next to me and help me forget it.'

I joined her on the couch and ran a hand over her fine hair. The sprinkling of gray hair enhanced its attractiveness. She

66

looked at me for a moment out of those bottomless gray eyes, then let the lids drop. I kissed her and she clung to me.

We necked some. I touched her breasts, kissed her throat. Her strong hands worked the muscles in my back and shoulders like modeling clay.

'You'll stay over,' she said.

'I'd like that.'

'So would I.'

I freshened both our drinks.

NINE

I awakened with church bells pealing in the distance. My head was clear and I felt good. I swung my legs over the side of the bed and met the eyes of a long-haired cat curled up at the foot of the bed on the other side. He looked me over, then tucked his head in and resumed napping. Sleep with the lady of the house and the cats accept you.

I got dressed and found Jan in the kitchen. She was drinking a glass of pale orange juice. I figured there was something in it to take the edge off her hangover. She'd made coffee in a Chemex filter pot and poured me a cup. I stood by the window and drank it.

We didn't talk. The church bells had taken a break and the Sunday morning silence stretched out. It was a bright day out, the sun burning away in a cloudless sky. I looked down and couldn't see a single sign of life, not a person on the street, not a car moving.

I finished my coffee and added the cup to the dirty dishes in the stainless-steel sink. Jan used a key to bring the elevator to the floor. She asked if I was going out to Sheepshead Bay and I said I guessed I was. We held onto each other for a moment. I felt the warmth of her fine body through the robe she was wearing.

'I'll call you,' I said, and rode the oversized elevator to the ground.

An Officer O'Byrne gave me directions over the phone. I followed them, riding the BMT Brighton Line to Gravesend Neck Road. The train came up above ground level at some point after it crossed into Brooklyn, and we rode through some neighborhoods of detached houses with yards that didn't look like New York at all.

The station house for the Sixty-first Precinct was on Coney Island Avenue and I managed to find it without too much trouble. In the squad room I played do-you-know with a wiry,

long-jawed detective named Antonelli. We knew enough of the
same people for him to relax with me. I told him what I was
working on and mentioned that Frank Fitzroy had steered it my
way. He knew Frank, too, though I didn't get the impression
that they were crazy about each other.

'I'll see what our file looks like,' he said. 'But you probably
saw copies of our reports in the file Fitzroy showed you.'

'What I mostly want is to talk with somebody who looked at
the body.'

'Wouldn't the names of officers on the scene be in the file you
saw in Manhattan?'

I'd thought of that myself. Maybe I could have managed all
this without coming out to the ass end of Brooklyn. But when
you go out and look for something you occasionally find more
than you knew you were looking for.

'Well, maybe I can find that file,' he said, and left me at an old
wooden desk scarred with cigarette burns along its edges. Two
desks over, a black detective with his sleeves rolled up was
talking on the phone. It sounded as though he was talking to a
woman, and it didn't sound much like police business. At
another desk along the far wall a pair of cops, one uniformed and
one in a suit, were questioning a teenager with a mop of unruly
yellow hair. I couldn't hear what they were saying.

Antonelli came back with a slim file and dropped it on the
desk in front of me. I went through it, pausing now and then to
make a note in my notebook. The victim, I learned, was a Susan
Potowski of 2705 Haring Street. She'd been a twenty-nine-year-
old mother of two, separated from her husband, a construction
laborer. She lived with her kids in the lower flat of a two-family
semi-detached house, and she'd been killed around two o'clock
on a Wednesday afternoon.

Her kids found her. They came home from school together
around three thirty, a boy of eight and a girl of ten, and they
found their mother on the kitchen floor, her clothing partly
removed, her body covered with stab wounds. They ran around
the street screaming until the beat cop turned up.

'Finding anything?'

'Maybe,' I said. I copied down the names of the first cop on the
scene, added those of two detectives from the Six-One who'd
gone to the Haring Street house before switching the case to
Midtown North. I showed the three names to Antonelli. 'Any of
these guys still work out of here?'

'Patrolman Burton Havermeyer, Detective Third-Grade Kenneth Allgood, Detective First-Grade Michael Quinn. Mick Quinn died two, maybe three years ago. Line of duty. He and a partner had a liquor store staked out on Avenue W and there were shots exchanged and he was killed. Terrible thing. Lost a wife to cancer two years before that, so he left four kids all alone in the world, the oldest just starting college. You must have read about it.'

'I think I did.'

'Guys who shot him pulled good long time. But they're alive and he's dead, so go figure. The other two, Allgood and Havermeyer, I don't even know the names, so they've been off the Six-One since before my time, which is what? Five years? Something like that.'

'Can you find out where they went?'

'I can probably find out something. What do you want to ask 'em, anyway?'

'If she was stabbed in both eyes.'

'Wasn't there an ME's report in the file whats-his-name showed you? Fitzroy?'

I nodded. 'Both eyes.'

'So?'

'Remember that case some years ago? They pulled some woman out of the Hudson, called it death by drowning? Then some genius in the Medical Examiner's office took the skull and started using it for a paperweight, and there was a scandal about that, and because of all the heat somebody finally took a good look at the skull for the first time and found a bullet hole in it.'

'I remember. She was some woman from New Jersey, married to a doctor, wasn't she?'

'That's right.'

'I got a rule-of-thumb. When a doctor's wife gets killed, he did it. I don't give a shit about the evidence. The doc always did it. I don't remember whether this one got off or not.'

'Neither do I.'

'I take your point, though. The ME's report isn't something you want to run to the bank with. But how good is a witness to something that happened nine years ago?'

'Not too good. Still –'

'I'll see what I can see.'

He was gone a little longer this time, and he had a funny expression on his face when he returned. 'Bad luck case,' he said.

'Allgood's dead, too. And the patrolman, Havermeyer, he left the department.'

'How did Allgood die?'

'Heart attack, about a year ago. He got transferred out a couple of years back. He was working out of Centre Street headquarters. Collapsed at his desk one day and died. One of the guys in the file room knew him from when he worked here and happened to know how he died. Havermeyer could be dead, too, for all I know.'

'What happened to him?'

He shrugged. 'Who knows? He put in his papers just a few months after the Icepick thing. Cited unspecified personal reasons for returning to civilian life. He'd only been in for two, three years. You know what the drop-out rate's like for the new ones. Hell, you're a drop-out yourself. Personal reasons, right?'

'Something like that.'

'I dug up an address and a number. He probably moved six times between then and now. If he didn't leave a trail, you can always try downtown. He wasn't here long enough to have any pension rights but they usually keep track of ex-cops.'

'Maybe he's still in the same place.'

'Could be. My grandmother's still living in three little rooms on Elizabeth Street, same apartment she's been in since she got off the boat from Palermo. Some people stay put. Others change their houses like they change their socks. Maybe you'll get lucky. Anything else I can do for you?'

'Where's Haring Street?'

'The murder scene?' He laughed. 'Jesus, you're a bloodhound,' he said. 'Want to get the scent, huh?'

He told me how to walk there. He'd given me a fair amount of his time but he didn't want any money for it. I sensed that he probably didn't – some do and some don't – but I made the offer. 'You could probably use a new hat,' I said, and he came back with a tight grin and assured me that he had a whole closetful of hats. 'And I hardly ever wear a hat these days,' he said. I'd been offering him twenty-five dollars, cheap enough for the effort he'd expended. 'It's a slow day at a quiet precinct,' he said, 'and how much mileage can you get out of what I just gave you? You got anybody in mind for that Boerum Hill killing?'

'Not really.'

'Like hunting a black cat in a coal mine,' he said. 'Do me one favor? Let me know how it comes out. *If* it comes out.'

I followed his directions to Haring Street. I don't suppose the neighborhood had changed much in nine years. The houses were well kept up and there were kids all over the place. There were cars parked at the curb, cars in most of the driveways. It occurred to me that there were probably a dozen people on the block who remembered Susan Potowski, and for all I knew her estranged husband had moved back into the house after the murder and lived there now with his children. They'd be older now, seventeen and nineteen.

She must have been young when she had the first one. Nineteen herself. Early marriage and early childbirth wouldn't have been uncommon in that neighborhood.

He probably moved away, I decided. Assuming he came back for the kids, he wouldn't make them go on living in the house where they found their mother dead on the kitchen floor. Would he?

I didn't ring that doorbell, or any other doorbells. I wasn't investigating Susan Potowski's murder and I didn't have to sift her ashes. I took a last look at the house she'd died in, then turned and walked away.

The address I had for Burton Havermeyer was 212 St Marks Place. The East Village wasn't that likely a place for a cop to live, and it didn't seem terribly likely that he'd still be there nine years later, on or off the force. I called the number Antonelli had given me from a drugstore phone booth on Ocean Avenue.

A woman answered. I asked if I could speak to Mr Havermeyer. There was a pause. 'Mr Havermeyer doesn't live here.'

I started to apologize for having the wrong number but she wasn't through. 'I don't know where Mr Havermeyer can be reached,' she said.

'Is this Mrs Havermeyer?'

'Yes.'

I said, 'I'm sorry to disturb you, Mrs Havermeyer. A detective at the Sixty-first Precinct where your husband used to work supplied this number. I'm trying to –'

'My former husband.'

There was a toneless quality to her speech, as if she was deliberately detaching herself from the words she was speaking. I had noted a similar characteristic in the speech of recovered mental patients.

'I'm trying to reach him in connection with a police matter,' I said.

'He hasn't been a policeman in years.'

'I realize that. Do you happen to know how I can get hold of him?'

'No.'

'I gather you don't see him often, Mrs Havermeyer, but would you have any idea –'

'I never see him.'

'I see.'

'Oh, do you? I never see my former husband. I get a check once a month. It's sent directly to my bank and deposited to my account. I don't see my husband and I don't see the check. Do you see? Do you?'

The words might have been delivered with passion. But the voice remained flat and uninvolved.

I didn't say anything.

'He's in Manhattan,' she said. 'Perhaps he has a phone, and perhaps it's in the book. You could look it up. I know you'll excuse me if I don't offer to look it up for you.'

'Certainly.'

'I'm sure it's important,' she said. 'Police business always is, isn't it?'

There was no Manhattan telephone book at the drugstore so I let the Information operator look for me. She found a Burton Havermeyer on West 103rd Street. I dialed the number and no one answered.

The drugstore had a lunch counter. I sat on a stool and ate a grilled cheese sandwich and a too-sweet piece of cherry pie and drank two cups of black coffee. The coffee wasn't bad, but it couldn't compare with the stuff Jan had brewed in her Chemex filter pot.

I thought about her. Then I went to the phone again and almost dialed her number, but tried Havermeyer again instead. This time he answered.

I said, 'Burton Havermeyer? My name's Matthew Scudder. I wondered if I could come around and see you this afternoon.'

'What about?'

'It's a police matter. Some questions I'd like to ask you. I won't take up much of your time.'

'You're a police officer?'

Hell. 'I used to be one.'

'So did I. Could you tell me what you want with me, Mr –?'

'Scudder,' I supplied. 'It's ancient history, actually. I'm a detective now and I'm working on a case you were involved with when you were with the Six-One.'

'That was years ago.'

'I know.'

'Can't we do this over the phone? I can't imagine what information I could possibly have that would be useful to you. I was a beat patrolman, I didn't work on cases. I –'

'I'd like to drop by if it's all right.'

'Well, I –'

'I won't take up much of your time.'

There was a pause. 'It's my day off,' he said, in what was not quite a whine. 'I just figured to sit around, have a couple of beers, watch a ball game.'

'We can talk during the commercials.'

He laughed. 'Okay, you win. You know the address? The name's on the bell. When should I expect you?'

'An hour, hour and a half.'

'Good enough.'

The Upper West Side is another neighborhood on the upswing, but the local renaissance hasn't crossed Ninety-sixth Street yet. Havermeyer lived on 103rd between Columbus and Amsterdam in one of the rundown brownstones that lined both sides of the street. The neighborhood was mostly Spanish. There were a lot of people sitting on the stoops, listening to enormous portable radios and drinking Miller High Life out of brown paper bags. Every third woman was pregnant.

I found the right building and rang the right bell and climbed four flights of stairs. He was waiting for me in the doorway of one of the back apartments. He said, 'Scudder?' and I nodded. 'Burt Havermeyer,' he said. 'Come on in.'

I followed him into a fair-sized studio with a Pullman kitchen. The overhead light fixture was a bare bulb in one of those Japanese paper shades. The walls were due for paint. I took a seat on the couch and accepted the can of beer he handed me. He popped one for himself, then moved to turn off the television set, a black and white portable perched on top of an orange crate that held paperback books on its lower two shelves.

He pulled up a chair for himself, crossed his legs. He looked to be in his early thirties, five-eight or -nine, pale complected, with narrow shoulders and a beer gut. He wore brown gabardine slacks and a brown and beige patterned sportshirt. He had deep-set brown eyes, heavy jowls and slicked-down dark brown hair,

74

and he hadn't shaved that morning. Neither, come to think of it, had I.

'About nine years ago,' I said. 'A woman named Susan Potowski.'

'I knew it.'

'Oh.'

'I hung up and thought, why's anybody want to talk with me about some case nine or ten years old? Then I figured it had to be the icepick thing. I read the papers. They got the guy, right? They made a lap and he fell in it.'

'That's about it.' I explained how Louis Pinell had denied a role in the death of Barbara Ettinger and how the facts appeared to bear him out.

'I don't get it,' he said. 'That still leaves something like eight killings, doesn't it? Isn't that enough to put him away?'

'It's not enough for the Ettinger woman's father. He wants to know who killed his daughter.'

'And that's your job.' He whistled softly. 'Lucky you.'

'That's about it.' I drank a little beer from the can. 'I don't suppose there's any connection between the Potowski killing and the one I'm investigating, but they're both in Brooklyn and maybe Pinell didn't do either of them. You were the first police officer on the scene. You remember that day pretty well?'

'Jesus,' he said. 'I ought to.'

'Oh?'

'I left the force because of it. But I suppose they told you that out in Sheepshead Bay.'

'All they said was unspecified personal reasons.'

'That right?' He held his beer can in both hands and sat with his head bowed, looking down at it. 'I remember how her kids screamed,' he said. 'I remember knowing I was going to walk in on something really bad, and then the next memory I have is I'm in her kitchen looking down at the body. One of the kids is hanging onto my pants leg the way kids do, you know how they do, and I'm looking down at her and I close my eyes and open 'em again and the picture doesn't change. She was in a whatchacallit, a housecoat. It had like Japanese writing on it and a picture of a bird, Japanese-style art. A kimono? I guess you call it a kimono. I remember the color. Orange, with black trim.

He looked up at me, then dropped his eyes again. 'The housecoat was open. The kimono. Partially open. There were these dots all over her body, like punctuation marks. Where he got her with the icepick. Mostly the torso. She had very nice

75

breasts. That's a terrible thing to remember but how do you quit remembering? Standing there noticing all the wounds in her breasts, and she's dead. And still noticing that she's got a first-rate pair of tits. And hating yourself for thinking it.'

'It happens.'

'I know, I know, but it sticks in your mind like a bone caught in your throat. And the kids wailing, and noises outside. At first I don't hear any of the noise because the sight of her just blocks everything else. Like it deafens you, knocks out the other senses. Do you know what I mean?'

'Yes.'

'Then the sound comes up, and the kid's still hanging on my pants leg, and if he lives to be a hundred that's how he's gonna remember his mother. Myself, I never saw her before in my life, and I couldn't get that picture out of my head. It repeated on me night and day. When I slept it got in my nightmares and during the day it would come into my mind at odd moments. I didn't want to go in anyplace. I didn't want to risk coming up on another dead body. And it dawned on me finally that I didn't want to stay in a line of work where when people get killed it's up to you to deal with it. "Unspecified personal reasons." Well, I just specified. I gave it a little time and it didn't wear off and I quit.'

'What do you do now?'

'Security guard.' He named a midtown store. 'I tried a couple of other things but I've had this job for seven years now. I wear a uniform and I even have a gun on my hip. Job I had before this, you wore a gun but it wasn't loaded. That drove me nuts. I said I'd carry a gun or not carry a gun, it didn't matter to me, but don't give me an unloaded gun because then the bad guys think you're armed but you can't defend yourself. Now I got a loaded gun and it hasn't been out of the holster in seven years and that's the way I like it. I'm a deterrent to robbery and shoplifting. Not as much of a deterrent to shoplifting as we'd like. Boosters can be pretty slick.'

'I can imagine.'

'It's dull work. I like that. I like knowing I don't have to walk into somebody's kitchen and there's death on the floor. I joke with other people on the job, I hook a shoplifter now and then, and the whole thing's nice and steady. I got a simple life, you know what I mean? I like it that way.'

'A question about the murder scene.'

'Sure.'

'The woman's eyes.'

'Oh, Christ,' he said. 'You had to remind me.'

'Tell me.'

'Her eyes were open. He stabbed all the victims in the eyes. I didn't know that. It was kept out of the papers, the way they'll hold something back, you know? But when the detectives got there they saw it right away and that cinched it, you know, that it wasn't our case and we could buck it on up to some other precinct. I forget which one.'

'Midtown North.'

'If you say so.' He closed his eyes for a moment. 'Did I say her eyes were open? Staring up at the ceiling. But they were like ovals of blood.'

'Both eyes?'

'Pardon?'

'Were both of her eyes the same?'

He nodded. 'Why?'

'Barbara Ettinger was only stabbed in one eye.'

'It make a difference?'

'I don't know.'

'If somebody was going to copy the killer, they'd copy him completely, wouldn't they?'

'You'd think so.'

'Unless it *was* him and he was rushed for a change. Who knows with a crazy person, anyway? Maybe this time God told him only stab one eye. Who knows?'

He went for another beer and offered me one but I passed. I didn't want to hang around long enough to drink it. I had really only had one question to ask him and his answer had done nothing but confirm the medical report. I suppose I could have asked it over the phone, but then I wouldn't have had the same chance to probe his memory and get a real sense of what he'd found in that kitchen. No question now that he'd gone back in time and seen Susan Potowski's body all over again. He wasn't guessing that she'd been stabbed in both eyes. He had closed his own eyes and seen the wounds.

He said, 'Sometimes I wonder. Well, when I read about them arresting this Pinell, and now with you coming over here. Suppose I wasn't the one walked in on the Potowski woman? Or suppose it happened three years later when I had that much more experience? I can see how my whole life might have been different.'

'You might have stayed on the force.'

'It's possible, right? I don't know if I really liked being a cop or if I was any good at it. I liked the classes at the Academy. I liked wearing the uniform. I liked walking the beat and saying hello to people and having them say hello back. Actual police work, I don't know how much I liked it. Maybe if I was really cut out for it I wouldn't have been thrown for a loop by what I saw in that kitchen. Or I would have toughed it out and gotten over it eventually. You were a cop yourself and you quit, right?'

'For unspecified personal reasons.'

'Yeah, I guess there's a lot of that going around.'

'There was a death involved,' I said. 'A child. What happened, I lost my taste for the work.'

'Exactly what happened to me, Matt. I lost my taste for it. You know what I think? If it wasn't that one particular thing it would have been something else.'

Could I say the same thing? It was not a thought that had occurred to me previously. If Estrellita Rivera had been home in bed where she belonged, would I still be living in Syosset and carrying a badge? Or would some other incident have given me an inevitable nudge in a direction I had to walk?

I said, 'You and your wife separated.'

'That's right.'

'Same time you put in your papers?'

'Not too long after that.'

'You move here right away?'

'I was in an SRO hotel a couple blocks down on Broadway. I stayed there for maybe ten weeks until I found this place. Been here ever since.'

'Your wife's still in the East Village.'

'Huh?'

'St Marks Place. She's still living there.'

'Oh. Right.'

'Any kids?'

'No.'

'Makes it easier.'

'I guess so.'

'My wife and sons are out on Long Island. I'm in a hotel on Fifty-seventh Street.'

He nodded, understanding. People move and their lives change. He'd wound up guarding cashmere sweaters. I'd wound up doing whatever it is I do. Looking in a coal mine for a black cat, according to Antonelli. Looking for a cat that wasn't even there.

TEN

When I got back to my hotel there was a message from Lynn London. I called her from the pay phone in the lobby and explained who I was and what I wanted.

She said, 'My father hired you? It's funny he didn't say anything to me. I thought they had the man who killed my sister. Why would he suddenly – well, let's let it ride for now. I don't know what help I could be.'

I said I'd like to meet with her to talk about her sister.

'Not tonight,' she said briskly. 'I just got back from the mountains a couple of hours ago. I'm exhausted and I've got to do my lesson plans for the week.'

'Tomorrow?'

'I teach during the day. I've got a dinner date and I'm going to a concert after that. Tuesday's my group therapy night. Maybe Wednesday? That's not terribly good for me either. Hell.'

'Maybe we could –'

'Maybe we could handle it over the phone? I don't really know very much, Mr Scudder, and God knows I'm beat at the moment, but perhaps I could deal with, say, ten minutes' worth of questions right now, because otherwise I honestly don't know when we could get together. I don't really know very much, it was a great many years ago and –'

'When do you finish your classes tomorrow afternoon?'

'Tomorrow afternoon? We dismiss the children at three fifteen, but –'

'I'll meet you at your apartment at four.'

'I told you. I have a dinner date tomorrow.'

'And a concert after it. I'll meet you at four. I won't take that much of your time.'

She wasn't thrilled, but that's how we left it. I spent another dime and called Jan Keane. I recapped the day and she told me she was in awe of my industriousness. 'I don't know,' I said.

'Sometimes I think I'm just putting in time. I could have accomplished the same thing today with a couple of phone calls.'

'We could have handled our business over the phone last night,' she said. 'As far as that goes.'

'I'm glad we didn't.'

'So am I,' she said. 'I think. On the other hand, I was planning on working today and I couldn't even look at clay. I'm just hoping this hangover wears off by bedtime.'

''I had a clear head this morning.'

'Mine's just beginning to clear now. Maybe my mistake was staying in the house. The sun might have burned off some of the fog. Now I'm just sitting around until it's a reasonable hour to go to sleep.'

There might have been an unspoken invitation in that last sentence. I probably could have invited myself over. But I was already home, and a short and quiet evening had its appeal. I told her I'd wanted to say how I'd enjoyed her company and that I'd call her.

'I'm glad you called,' she said. 'You're a sweet man, Matthew.' A pause, and then she said, 'I've been thinking about it. He probably did it.'

'He?'

'Doug Ettinger. He probably killed her.'

'Why?'

'I don't know why. People always have motives to kill their spouses, don't they? There was never a day when I didn't have a reason to kill Eddie.'

'I meant why do you think he did it.'

'Oh. What I was thinking, I was thinking how devious you would have to be to kill someone and imitate another murder. And I realized what a devious man he was, what a sneak. He could plan something like that.'

'That's interesting.'

'Listen, I don't have any special knowledge. But it's what I was thinking earlier. And now he's doing what? Selling sporting goods? Is that what you said?'

I sat in my room and read for a while, then had dinner around the corner at Armstrong's. I stayed there for a couple of hours but didn't have very much to drink. The crowd was a light one, as it usually is on a Sunday. I talked to a few people but mostly

80

sat alone and let the events of the past two days thread their way in and out of my consciousness.

I made it an early night, walked down to Eighth Avenue for the early edition of Monday's *News*. Went back to my room, read the paper, took a shower. Looked at myself in the mirror. Thought about shaving, decided to wait until morning.

Had a nightcap, a short one. Went to bed.

I was deep in a dream when the phone rang. I was running in the dream, chasing someone or being chased, and I sat up in bed with my heart pounding.

The phone was ringing. I reached out, answered it.

A woman said, 'Why don't you let the dead bury the dead?'

'Who is this?'

'Leave the dead alone. Let the dead stay buried.'

'Who is this?'

A click. I turned on a light and looked at my watch. It was around one thirty. I'd been sleeping an hour, if that.

Who had called me? It was a voice I'd heard before but I couldn't place it. Lynn London? I didn't think so.

I got out of bed, flipped pages in my notebook, picked up the phone again. When the hotel operator came on I read off a number to him. He put the call through and I listened as it rang twice.

A woman answered it. Same woman who'd just told me to leave the dead alone. I'd heard her voice once before that, and remembered it now.

I had nothing to say to her that wouldn't wait a day or two. Without saying anything, I replaced the receiver and went back to bed.

ELEVEN

After breakfast the next day I called Charles London's office. He hadn't come in yet. I gave my name and said I'd call later.

I spent another dime calling Frank Fitzroy at the Eighteenth Precinct. 'Scudder,' I said. 'Where are they holding Pinell?'

'They had him downtown. Then I think they shunted him out to Rikers Island. Why?'

'I'd like to see him. What are my chances?'

'Not good.'

'You could go out there,' I suggested. 'I could just be a fellow officer along for the ride.'

'I don't know, Matt.'

'You'd get something for your time.'

'That's not it. Believe me. Thing is, this fucker fell in our laps and I'd hate to see him walk on a technicality. We ring in an unauthorized visitor and his lawyer gets wind of it and gets a wild hair up his ass and it could screw up the whole case. You follow me?'

'It doesn't seem very likely.'

'Maybe not, but it's a chance I'm in no rush to take. What do you want from him, anyway?'

'I don't know.'

'Maybe I could ask him a question or two for you. Assuming I could get to see him, which I'm not sure I could. His lawyer may have cut off the flow. But if you've got a specific question –'

I was in the phone booth in my hotel lobby and someone was knocking on the door. I told Frank to hang on for a second and opened the door a crack. It was Vinnie, the desk man, to tell me I had a call. I asked who it was and he said it was a woman and she hadn't given her name. I wondered if it was the same one who'd called last night.

I told him to switch it to the house phone and I'd take it in a minute. I uncovered the mouthpiece of the phone I was holding and told Frank I couldn't think of anything in particular that I wanted to ask Louis Pinell, but that I'd keep his offer in mind. He asked if I was getting anyplace with my investigation.

'I don't know,' I said. 'It's hard to tell. I'm putting in the hours.'

'Giving what's-his-name his money's worth. London.'

'I suppose so. I have a feeling most of it is wasted motion.'

'It's always that way, isn't it? There's days when I figure I must waste ninety percent of my time. But you have to do that to come up with the ten percent that's not a waste.'

'That's a point.'

'Even if you could see Pinell, that'd be part of the wasted ninety percent. Don't you think?'

'Probably.'

I finished up with him, went over to the desk and picked up the house phone. It was Anita.

She said, 'Matt? I just wanted to tell you that the check came.'

'That's good. I'm sorry it's not more.'

'It came at a good time.'

I sent money for her and the boys when I had it to send. She never called just to say it had arrived.

I asked how the boys were.

'They're fine,' she said. 'Of course they're in school now.'

'Of course.'

'I guess it's been a while since you've seen them.'

I felt a little red pinprick of anger. Had she called just to tell me that? Just to push a little guilt button? 'I'm on a case,' I said. 'Soon as it's finished, whenever that is, maybe they can come in and we'll catch a game at the Garden. Or a boxing match.'

'They'd like that.'

'So would I.' I thought of Jan, relieved that her kids were on the other side of the country, relieved she didn't have to visit them anymore, and guilty over her relief. 'I'd like that very much,' I said.

'Matt, the reason I called –'

'Yes?'

'Oh, God,' she said. She sounded sad and tired. 'It's Bandy,' she said.

'Bandy?'

'The dog. You remember Bandy.'

'Of course. What about him?'

'Oh, it's sad,' she said. 'The vet said he ought to be put to sleep. He said there's really nothing to be done for him at this point.'

'Oh,' I said. 'Well, I suppose if that's what has to be done –'

'I already had him put to sleep. On Friday.'

'Oh.'

'I guess I thought you would want to know.'

'Poor Bandy,' I said. 'He must have been twelve years old.'

'He was fourteen.'

'I didn't realize he was that old. That's a long life for a dog.'

'It's supposed to be the equivalent of ninety-eight for a human being.'

'What was the matter with him?'

'The vet said he just wore out. His kidneys were in bad shape. And he was almost blind. You knew that, didn't you?'

'No.'

'For the past year or two his eyesight was failing. It was so sad, Matt. The boys sort of lost interest in him. I think that was the saddest part. They loved him when they were younger but they grew up and he got old and they lost interest.' She started to cry. I stood there and held the phone to my ear and didn't say anything.

She said, 'I'm sorry, Matt.'

'Don't be silly.'

'I called you because I wanted to tell somebody and who else could I tell? Do you remember when we got him?'

'I remember.'

'I wanted to call him Bandit because of his facial markings, his mask. You said something about give-a-dog-a-bad-name, but we were already calling him Bandy. So we decided it was short for Bandersnatch.'

'From *Alice in Wonderland*.'

'The vet said he didn't feel anything. He just went to sleep. He took care of disposing of the body for me.'

'That's good.'

'He had a good life, don't you think? And he was a good dog. He was such a clown. He could always break me up.'

She talked for a few more minutes. The conversation just wore out, like the dog. She thanked me again for the check and I said again that I wished it could have been more. I told her to tell the boys I'd be seeing them as soon as I was finished with my current case. She said she'd be sure to tell them. I hung up the phone and went outside.

The sun was screened by clouds and there was a chill wind

blowing. Two doors down from the hotel is a bar called McGovern's. They open early.

I went in. The place was empty except for two old men, one behind the bar, one in front of it. The bartender's hand trembled slightly as he poured me a double shot of Early Times and backed it up with a glass of water.

I hoisted the glass, wondered at the wisdom of paying an early visit to London's office with bourbon on my breath, then decided it was a pardonable eccentricity in an unofficial private detective. I thought about poor old Bandy, but of course I wasn't really thinking about the dog. For me, and probably for Anita, he was one of the few threads that had still linked us. Rather like the marriage, he'd taken his sweet time dying.

I drank the drink and got out of there.

London's office was on the sixteenth floor of a twenty-eight-story building on Pine Street. I shared the elevator with two men in forest-green work clothing. One carried a clipboard, the other a tool kit. Neither spoke, nor did I.

I felt like a rat in a maze by the time I found London's office. His name was the first of four lettered on the frosted glass door. Inside, a receptionist with a slight British accent invited me to have a seat, then spoke quietly into a telephone. I looked at a copy of *Sports Illustrated* until a door opened and Charles London beckoned me into his private office.

It was a fair-sized room, comfortable without being luxurious. There was a view of the harbor from his window, only partially blocked by surrounding buildings. We stood on either side of his desk, and I sensed something in the air between us. For a moment I regretted that bourbon at McGovern's, then realized it had nothing to do with the screen that seemed to separate us.

'I wish you'd called,' he said. 'You'd have been able to save a trip down here.'

'I called and they told me you hadn't come in yet.'

'I got a message that you would call later.'

'I thought I'd save a call.'

He nodded. His outfit looked the same as he'd worn to Armstrong's, except that the tie was different. I'm sure the suit and shirt were different, too. He probably had six identical suits, and two drawers of white shirts.

He said, 'I'm going to have to ask you to drop the case, Mr Scudder.'

'Oh?'

'You seem unsurprised.'

'I picked up the vibration walking in here. Why?'

'My reasons aren't important.'

'They are to me.'

He shrugged. 'I made a mistake,' he said. 'I sent you on a fool's errand. It was a waste of money.'

'You already wasted the money. You might as well let me give you something for it. I can't give it back because I already spent it.'

'I wasn't expecting a refund.'

'And I didn't come here to ask for any additional money. So what are you saving by telling me to drop the case?'

The pale blue eyes blinked twice behind the rimless glasses. He asked me if I wouldn't sit down. I said I was comfortable standing. He remained standing himself.

He said, 'I behaved foolishly. Seeking vengeance, retribution. Troubling the waters. Either that man killed her or some other maniac did and there's probably no way we'll ever know for sure. I was wrong to set you to work raking up the past and disturbing the present.'

'Is that what I've been doing?'

'I beg your pardon?'

'Raking up the past and disturbing the present? Maybe that's a good definition of my role. When did you decide to call me off?'

'That's not important.'

'Ettinger got to you, didn't he? It must have been yesterday. Saturday's a busy day at the store, they sell a lot of tennis rackets. He probably called you last night, didn't he?' When he hesitated I said, 'Go ahead. Tell me it's not important.'

'It's not. More to the point, it's not your business, Mr Scudder.'

'I got a wake-up call around one thirty last night from the second Mrs Ettinger. Did she give you a call about the same time?'

'I don't know what you're talking about.'

'She's got a distinctive voice. I heard it the day before when I called Ettinger at home and she told me he was at the Hicksville store. She called last night to tell me to let the dead stay buried. That seems to be what you want, too.'

'Yes,' he said. 'That's what I want.'

I picked a paperweight from the top of his desk. An inch-long brass label identified it as a piece of petrified wood from the Arizona desert.

86

'I can understand what Karen Ettinger's afraid of. Her husband might turn out to be the killer, and that would really turn her world upside down. You'd think a woman in her position would want to know one way or the other. How comfortable could she be from here on in, living with a man she half-suspects of killing his first wife? But people are funny that way. They can push things out of their minds. Whatever happened was years ago and in Brooklyn. And the wench is dead, right? People move and their lives change, so there's nothing for her to worry about, is there?'

He didn't say anything. His paperweight had a piece of black felt on its bottom to keep it from scratching his desk. I replaced it, felt-side down.

I said, 'You wouldn't be worried about Ettinger's world, or his wife's world. What's it to you if they get hassled a little? Unless Ettinger had a way to put pressure on you, but I don't think that's it. I don't think you'd be all that easy to push around.'

'Mr Scudder –'

'It's something else, but what? Not money, not a physical threat. Oh, hell, I know what it is.'

He avoided my eyes.

'Her reputation. You're afraid of what I'll find in the grave with her. Ettinger must have told you she was having an affair. He told me she wasn't, but I don't think he's that deeply committed to the truth. As a matter of fact, it does look as though she was seeing a man. Maybe more than one man. That may go against the grain of your sense of propriety, but it doesn't weigh too much against the fact that she was murdered. She may have been killed by a lover. She may have been killed by her husband. There are all sorts of possibilities but you don't want to look at any of them because in the course of it the world might find out that your daughter wasn't a virgin.'

For a moment I thought he was going to lose his temper. Then something went out of his eyes. 'I'm afraid I'll have to ask you to leave now,' he said. 'I have some calls to make and I have an appointment scheduled in fifteen minutes.'

'I guess Mondays are busy in insurance. Like Saturdays in sporting goods.'

'I'm sorry that you're embittered. Perhaps later you'll appreciate my position, but –'

'Oh, I appreciate your position,' I said. 'Your daughter was killed for no reason by a madman and you adjusted to that reality. Then you had a new reality to adjust to, and that turned out to mean coming to grips with the possibility that someone had a reason to kill her, and that it might be a good reason.' I shook my head, impatient with myself for talking too much. 'I came here to pick up a picture of your daughter,' I said. 'I don't suppose you happened to bring it.'

'Why would you want it?'

'Didn't I tell you the other day?'

'But you're off the case now,' he said. He might have been explaining something to a slow child. 'I don't expect a refund, but I want you to discontinue your investigation.'

'You want to fire me.'

'If you'd prefer to put it that way.'

'But you never hired me in the first place. So how can you fire me?'

'Mr Scudder –'

'When you open up a can of worms you can't just decide to stuff the worms back in the can. There are a lot of things set in motion and I want to see where they lead. I'm not going to stop now.'

He had an odd look on his face, as though he was a little bit afraid of me. Maybe I'd raised my voice, or looked somehow menacing.

'Relax,' I told him. 'I won't be disturbing the dead. The dead are beyond disturbance. You had a right to ask me to drop the case and I've got the right to tell you to go to hell. I'm a private citizen pursuing an unofficial investigation. I could do it more efficiently if I had your help, but I can get along without it.'

'I wish you'd let it go.'

'And I wish you'd back me up. And wishes aren't horses, not for either of us. I'm sorry this isn't turning out the way you wanted it to. I tried to tell you that might be the case. I guess you didn't want to listen.'

On the way down, the elevator stopped at almost every floor. I went out to the street. It was still overcast, and colder than I remembered it. I walked a block and a half until I found a bar. I had a quick double bourbon and left. A few blocks further along I stopped at another bar and had another drink.

I found a subway, headed for the uptown platform, then changed my mind and waited for a train bound for Brooklyn. I got out at Jay Street and walked up one street and down another and wound up in Boerum Hill. I stopped at a Pentecostal church on Schermerhorn. The bulletin board was full of notices in

Spanish. I sat there for a few minutes, hoping things would sort themselves out in my mind, but it didn't work. I found my thoughts bouncing back and forth among dead things – a dead dog, a dead marriage, a dead woman in her kitchen, a dead trail.

A balding man wearing a sleeveless sweater over a maroon shirt asked me something in Spanish. I suppose he wanted to know if he could help me. I got up and left.

I walked around some more. A curious thing, I thought, was that I felt somehow more committed to the pursuit of Barbara Ettinger's killer than I had before her father fired me. It was still as hopeless a quest as it had ever been, doubly hopeless now that I wouldn't even have the cooperation of my client. And yet I seemed to believe what I had said to him about forces having been set in motion. The dead were indeed beyond disturbance, but I had set about disturbing the living and sensed that it would lead somewhere.

I thought of poor old Bandersnatch, always game to chase a stick or go for a walk. He'd bring one of his toys to you to signal his eagerness to play. If you just stood there he'd drop it at your feet, but if you tried to take it away from him he'd set his jaw and hang on grimly.

Maybe I'd learned it from him.

I went to the building on Wyckoff Street. I rang Donald Gilman and Rolfe Waggoner's bell. They weren't in. Neither was Judy Fairborn. I walked on past the building where Jan had lived with – what was his name? Edward. Eddie.

I stopped at a bar and had a drink. Just a straight shot of bourbon, not a double. Just a little something, maintenance drinking against the chill in the air.

I decided I was going to see Louis Pinell. For one thing, I'd ask him if he used a different icepick each time he killed. The autopsies hadn't indicated anything one way or the other. Perhaps forensic medicine isn't that highly developed yet.

I wondered where he got the icepicks. An icepick struck me as a damned old-fashioned instrument. What would you ever use it for outside of murder? People didn't have iceboxes any more, didn't have blocks of ice brought by the iceman. They filled trays with water to make ice cubes or had a gadget in their refrigerator that produced the cubes automatically.

The refrigerator in Syosset had had an automated ice maker.

Where did you get an icepick? How much did they cost? I was suddenly full of icepick questions. I walked around, found a five-

and-ten, asked a clerk in the housewares department where I'd find an icepick. She shunted me to the hardware department, where another clerk told me they didn't carry icepicks.

'I guess they're out of date,' I said.

She didn't bother to answer. I walked around some more, stopped at a storefront that sold hardware and kitchen things. The fellow behind the counter was wearing a camel-hair cardigan and chewing the stub of a cigar. I asked if he carried icepicks and he turned without a word and came back with one stapled to a piece of cardboard.

'Ninety-eight cents,' he said. 'Is one-oh-six with the tax.'

I didn't really want it. I had just wondered at price and availability. I paid for it anyway. Outside I stopped at a wire trash basket and discarded the brown paper bag and the piece of cardboard and examined my purchase. The blade was four or five inches long, the point sharp. The handle was a cylinder of dark wood. I held it alternately in one hand and then the other, dropped it back in my pocket.

I went back into the store. The man who'd sold it to me looked up from his magazine. 'I just bought that icepick from you,' I said.

'Something wrong with it?'

'It's fine. You sell many of them?'

'Some.'

'How many?'

'Don't keep track,' he said. 'Sell one now and then.'

'What do people buy them for?'

He gave me the guarded look you get when people begin to wonder about your identity. 'Whatever they want,' he said. 'I don't guess they pick their teeth with 'em, but anything else they want.'

'You been here long?'

'How's that?'

'You had this store a long time?'

'Long enough.'

I nodded, left. I didn't ask him who'd bought an icepick from him nine years ago. If I had, he wouldn't have been the only one doubting my sanity. But if someone had asked him that question right after Barbara Ettinger was killed, if someone had asked him and every other housewares and hardware dealer in that part of Brooklyn, and if they'd shown around the appropriate photographs and asked a few other appropriate questions, maybe they would have come up with Barbara's killer then and there.

No reason to do so. No reason to think it was anything but what it looked like, another score for the Icepick Prowler.

I walked around, my hand gripping the butt end of the icepick in my pocket. Handy little thing. You couldn't slash with it, you could only stab, but it would still do a pretty good job on someone.

Was it legal to carry it? The law classified it not as a deadly weapon but as a dangerous instrument. Deadly weapons are things like loaded guns, switch knives, gravity knives, daggers, billies, blackjacks and brass knuckles, articles with no function but murderous assault. An icepick had other uses, though the man who sold it hadn't managed to tell me any of them.

Still, that didn't mean you could carry it legally. A machete's a dangerous instrument in the eyes of the law, not a deadly weapon, but you're not allowed to carry one through the streets of New York.

I took the thing out of my pocket a couple of times and looked at it. Somewhere along the way I dropped it through a sewer grating.

Had the icepick used on Barbara Ettinger vanished the same way? It was possible. It was even possible that it had been dropped down that very sewer grating. All kinds of things were possible.

The wind was getting worse instead of better. I stopped for another drink.

I lost track of the time. At one point I looked at my watch and it was twenty-five minutes of four. I remembered that I was supposed to meet Lynn London at four o'clock. I didn't see how I could get there on time. Still, she was in Chelsea, it wouldn't take all that long –

Then I caught myself. What was I worrying about? Why break my neck to keep an appointment when she wouldn't be keeping it herself? Because her father would have talked to her, either early that morning or late the night before, and she'd know by now that there'd been a change in the London family policy. Matthew Scudder was no longer representing the best interests of the Londons. He was persisting in his folly for reasons of his own, and perhaps he had the right to do this, but he couldn't count on the cooperation of Charles London or his schoolmarm daughter.

'You say something?'

I looked up, met the warm brown eyes of the bartender. 'Just talking to myself,' I said.

'Nothin' wrong with that.'

I liked his attitude. 'Might as well give me another,' I said. 'And take something for yourself while you're at it.'

I called Jan twice from Brooklyn and her line was busy both times. When I got back to Manhattan I called her again from Armstrong's and got another busy signal. I finished a cup of coffee with a shot in it and tried her again and the line was still busy.

I had the operator check the line. She came back and told me the receiver was off the hook. There's a way they can make the phone ring even if you've taken it off the hook, and I thought about identifying myself as a policeman and getting her to do that, but decided to let it go.

I had no right to interrupt the woman. Maybe she was asleep. Maybe she had company.

Maybe there was a man there, or a woman. It was no business of mine.

Something settled in my stomach and glowed there like a hot coal. I had another cup of bourbon-flavored coffee to drown it.

The evening hurried on by. I didn't really pay it too much attention. My mind tended to drift.

I had things to think about.

At one point I found myself on the phone, dialing Lynn London's number. No answer. Well, she'd told me she had tickets for a concert. And I couldn't remember why I was calling her, anyway. I'd already decided there was no point. That was why I'd missed my appointment with her.

Not that she'd have shown up herself. Would have left me standing there, feeling stupid.

So I called Jan again. Still busy.

I thought about going over there. Wouldn't take too long by cab. But what was the point? When a woman takes her phone off the hook it's not because she's hoping you'll come knock on her door.

Hell with her.

Back at the bar, somebody was talking about the First Avenue Slasher. I gathered he was still at large. One of the surviving victims had described how the man had attempted to start a

92

conversation with him before showing his weapon and attacking.

I thought about the little article I'd read about muggers asking you the time or directions. Don't talk to strangers, I thought.

'That's the trouble with this place tonight,' I said. 'Too many strangers.'

A couple of people looked at me. From behind the bar, Billie asked me if I was all right.

'I'm fine,' I assured him. 'Just that it's too crowded tonight. No room to breathe.'

'Probably a good night to turn in early.'

'You said it.'

But I didn't feel like turning in, just like getting the hell out of there. I went around the corner to McGovern's and had a quick one. The place was dead so I didn't hang around. I hit Polly's Cage across the street and left when the jukebox started getting on my nerves.

The air outside was bracing. It struck me that I'd been drinking all day and that it added up to a hell of a lot of booze, but I seemed to be handling it fine. It wasn't affecting me at all. I was wide awake, clear-minded, clear-headed. It'd be hours before I'd be able to sleep.

I circled the block, stopped at a hole in the wall on Eighth Avenue, stopped again at Joey Farrell's. I felt restless and combative and got out of there when the bartender said something that irritated me. I don't remember what it was.

Then I was walking. I was on Ninth Avenue across the street from Armstrong's, walking south, and there was something hanging in the air that was putting me on my guard. Even as I was wondering at the feeling, a young man stepped out of a doorway ten yards ahead of me.

He had a cigarette in one hand. As I approached he moved purposefully into my path and asked me for a match.

That's how the bastards do it. One stops you and sizes you up. The other moves in behind you, and you get a forearm across the windpipe, a knife at your throat.

I don't smoke but I generally have a pack of matches in my pocket. I cupped my hands, scratched a match. He tucked the unlit cigarette between his lips and leaned forward, and I flipped the burning match in his face and went in under it, grabbing and shoving hard, sending him reeling into the brick well behind him.

I whirled myself, ready for his partner.

93

There was nobody behind me. Nothing but an empty street.

That made it simpler. I kept turning, and I was facing him when he came off the wall with his eyes wide and his mouth open. He was my height but lighter in build, late teens or early twenties, uncombed dark hair and a face white as paper in the light of the streetlamps.

I moved in quick and hit him in the middle. He swung at me and I sidestepped the punch and hit him again an inch or two above his belt buckle. That brought his hands down and I swung my right forearm in an arc and hit him in the mouth with my elbow. He drew back and clapped both hands to his mouth.

I said, 'Turn around and grab that wall! Come on, you fucker. Get your hands on the wall!'

He said I was crazy, that he hadn't done anything. The words came out muffled through the hands he was holding to his mouth.

But he turned around and grabbed the wall.

I moved in, hooked a foot in front of his, drew his foot back so that he couldn't come off the wall in a hurry.

'I didn't do nothing,' he said. 'What's the matter with you?'

I told him to put his head against the wall.

'All I did was ask you for a match.'

I told him to shut up. I frisked him and he stood still for it. A little blood trickled from the corner of his mouth. Nothing serious. He was wearing one of those leather jackets with a pile collar and two big pockets in front. Bomber jackets, I think they call them. The pocket on the left held a wad of Kleenex and a pack of Winston Lights. The other pocket held a knife. A flick of my wrist and the blade dropped into place.

A gravity knife. One of the seven deadly weapons.

'I just carry it,' he said.

'For what?'

'Protection.'

'From who? Little old ladies:'

I took a wallet off his hip. He had ID that indicated he was Anthony Sforczak and he lived in Woodside, Queens. I said, 'You're a long ways from home, Tony.'

'So?'

He had two tens and some singles in his wallet. In another pants pocket I found a thick roll of bills secured by a rubber band, and in the breast pocket of his shirt, under the leather jacket, I found one of those disposable butane lighters.

'It's out of fluid,' he said.

94

I flicked it. Flame leaped from it and I showed it to him. The heat rose and he jerked his head to the side. I released the thumbcatch and the flame died.

'It was out before. Wouldn't light.'

'So why keep it? Why not throw it away?'

'It's against the law to litter.'

'Turn around.'

He came off the wall slowly, eyes wary. A little line of blood trailed from the corner of his mouth down over his chin. His mouth was starting to puff up some where my elbow had caught him.

He wouldn't die of it.

I gave him the wallet and the cigarette lighter. I tucked the roll of bills in my own pocket.

'That's my money,' he said.

'You stole it.'

'Like hell I did! What are you gonna do, keep it?'

'What do you think?' I flicked the knife open and held it so that the light glinted off the face of the blade. 'You better not turn up in this part of the city again. Another thing you better not do is carry a blade when half the department's looking for the First Avenue Slasher.'

He stared at me. Something in his eyes said he wished I didn't have that knife in my hand. I met his gaze and closed the knife, dropped it on the ground behind me.

'Go ahead,' I said. 'Be my guest.'

I balanced on the balls of my feet, waiting for him. For a moment he might have been considering it, and I was hoping he'd make a move. I could feel the blood singing in my veins, pulsing in my temples.

He said, 'You're crazy, you know? What you are is crazy,' and he edged off ten or twenty yards, then half-ran to the corner.

I stood watching until he was out of sight.

The street was still empty. I found the gravity knife on the pavement and put it in my pocket. Across the street, Armstrong's door opened and a young man and woman emerged. They walked down the street holding hands.

I felt fine. I wasn't drunk. I'd had a day of maintenance drinking, nothing more. Look how I'd handled the punk. Nothing wrong with my instincts, nothing slow about my reflexes. The booze wasn't getting in the way. Just a matter of taking on fuel, of keeping a full tank. Nothing wrong with that.

TWELVE

I came suddenly awake. There was no warm-up period. It was as abrupt as turning on a transistor radio.

I was on my bed in my hotel room, lying on top of the covers with my head on the pillow. I had piled my clothes on the chair but slept in my underwear. There was a foul taste in my dry mouth and I had a killer headache.

I got up. I felt shaky and awful, and a sense of impending doom hung in the air, as though if I turned around quickly I could look Death in the eye.

I didn't want a drink but knew I needed one to take the edge off the way I felt. I couldn't find the bourbon bottle and then I finally found it in the wastebasket. Evidently I'd finished it before I went to bed. I wondered how much it had contained.

No matter. It was empty now.

I held out a hand, studied it. No visible tremors. I flexed the fingers. Not as steady as Gibraltar, maybe, but not a case of the shakes, either.

Shaky inside, though.

I couldn't remember returning to the hotel. I probed gingerly at my memory and couldn't get any further than the boy scuttling down the street and around the corner. Anthony Sforczak, that was his name.

See? Nothing wrong with my memory.

Except that it ran out at that point. Or perhaps a moment later, when the young couple came out of Armstrong's and walked up the street holding hands. Then it all went blank, coming into focus again with me coming to in my hotel room. What time was it, anyway?

My watch was still on my wrist. Quarter after nine. And it was light outside my window, so that means a.m. Not that I really had to look to be sure. I hadn't lost a day, just the length of time it took me to walk half a block home and get to bed.

96

Assuming I'd come straight home.

I stripped off my underwear and got into the shower. While I was under the spray I could hear my phone ringing. I let it ring. I spent a long time under the hot spray, then took a blast of cold for as long as I could stand it, which wasn't very long. I toweled dry and shaved. My hand wasn't as steady as it might have been but I took my time and didn't cut myself.

I didn't like what I saw in the mirror. A lot of red in the eyes. I thought of Havermeyer's description of Susan Potowski, her eyes swimming in blood. I didn't like my red eyes, or the mesh of broken blood vessels on my cheekbones and across the bridge of my nose.

I knew what put them there. Drink put them there. Nothing else. I could forget about what it might be doing to my liver because my liver was tucked away where I didn't have to look at it every morning.

And where nobody else could see it.

I got dressed, put on all clean clothes, stuffed everything else in my laundry bag. The shower helped and the shave helped and the clean clothes helped, but in spite of all three I could feel remorse settling over my shoulders like a cape. I didn't want to look at the previous night because I knew I wasn't going to like what I'd see there.

But what choice did I have?

I put the roll of bills in one pocket, the gravity knife in the other. I went downstairs and out, walking past the desk without breaking stride. I knew there'd be messages there but I figured they'd keep.

I decided not to stop at McGovern's but when I got there I turned in. Just one quick drink to still the invisible shaking. I drank it like the medicine it was.

Around the corner I sat in a rear pew at St Paul's. For what seemed like a long time I didn't even think. I just sat there.

Then the thoughts started. No way to stop them, really.

I'd been drunk the night before and hadn't known it. I'd probably been drunk fairly early in the day. There were patches in Brooklyn that I couldn't remember clearly, and I didn't seem to have any recollection of the subway ride back to Manhattan. For that matter, I couldn't be sure I'd ridden the subway. I might have taken a cab.

I remembered talking to myself in a Brooklyn bar. I must have been drunk then. I didn't tend to talk to myself when I was sober.

Not yet, anyway.

All right, I could live with all that. I drank too goddamn much, and when you do that with consistency there are going to be times when you get drunk without wanting to. This wasn't the first time and I didn't suspect it would be the last. It came with the territory.

But I'd been drunk when I was playing Hero Cop on Ninth Avenue, drunk with the booze for high-octane fuel. My street-smart instincts that warned me about a mugging were less a source of pride the morning after.

Maybe he just wanted a match.

My gorge rose at the thought and I tasted bile at the back of my throat. Maybe he was just another kid from Woodside having himself a night on the town. Maybe he'd been a mugger only in my mind, my drunken mind. Maybe I'd beaten him and robbed him for no good reason at all.

But he'd asked for a match when he had a working lighter.

So? That was an icebreaker as old as tobacco. Ask for a match, strike up a conversation. He could have been a male hustler. He would hardly have been the first gay man to put on a bomber jacket.

He was carrying a gravity knife.

So? Frisk the city and you could stock an arsenal. Half the city was carrying something to protect it from the other half. The knife was a deadly weapon and he was breaking a law carrying it, but it didn't prove anything.

He knew how to grab that wall. It wasn't his first frisk.

And that didn't prove anything either. There are neighbor-hoods where you can't grow up without getting stopped and tossed once a week by the cops.

And the money? The roll of bills?

He could have come by it honestly. Or he could have earned it in any of innumerable dishonest ways and still not have been a mugger.

And my vaunted cop instincts? Hell, the minute he came out of the doorway I'd known he was going to approach me.

Right. And I'd also known his partner was moving in behind me, knew it as if I'd had eyes in the back of my head. Except there was nobody there. So much for the infallibility of instinct.

I took out the gravity knife, opened it. Suppose I'd been carrying it the night before. More realistically, suppose I'd still

98

been carrying the icepick I'd bought in Boerum Hill. Would I have limited myself to a couple of body punches and a forearm smash to the face? Or would I have worked with the materials at hand?

I felt shaky, and it was more than the hangover.

I closed the knife and put it away. I took out the roll of bills, removed the rubber band, counted the cash. I made it a hundred and seventy dollars in five and tens.

If he was a mugger, why didn't he have the knife in his hand? How come it was in his jacket pocket with the flap buttoned down?

Or *was* the flap buttoned?

Didn't matter. I sorted the money and added it to my own. On my way out I lit a couple of candles, then slipped seventeen dollars into the poor box.

At the corner of Fifty-seventh I dropped the gravity knife into a sewer.

THIRTEEN

My cab driver was an Israeli immigrant and I don't think he'd ever heard of Rikers Island. I told him to follow the signs for LaGuardia Airport. When we got close I gave him directions. I got out at a luncheonette at the foot of the bridge that spans Bowery Bay and the channel of the East River that separates the island from the rest of Queens.

Lunch hour had come and gone and the place was mostly empty. A few men in work clothes were seated at the counter. About halfway down a man sat in a booth with a cup of coffee and looked up expectantly at my approach. I introduced myself and he said he was Marvin Hiller.

'My car's outside,' he said. 'Or did you want to grab a cup of coffee? The only thing is I'm a little bit rushed. I had a long morning in Queens Criminal Court and I'm supposed to be at my dentist's in forty-five minutes. If I'm late I'm late.'

I told him I didn't care about coffee. He paid his tab and we went outside and rode his car over the bridge. He was a pleasant and rather earnest man a few years younger than I and he looked like what he was, a lawyer with an office on Queens Boulevard in Elmhurst. One of his clients, one who'd be contributing very little toward the rent on that office, was Louis Pinell.

I'd gotten his name from Frank Fitzroy and managed to get his secretary to beep him and call me at the hotel. I'd expected a flat turndown on my request for clearance to see Pinell and got just the reverse. 'Just so it's kosher,' he had said, 'why don't you meet me out there and we'll drive over together. You'll probably get more out of him that way. He's a little more comfortable about talking with his lawyer present.'

Now he said, 'I don't know what you'll be able to get from him. I suppose you mostly want to satisfy yourself that he didn't kill the Ettinger woman.'

'I suppose.'

'I would think he's in the clear on that one. The evidence is pretty clear-cut. If it was just his word I'd say forget it, because who knows what they remember and what they make up when they're as crazy as he is?'

'He's really crazy?'

'Oh, he's a bedbug,' Hiller said. 'No question about it. You'll see for yourself. I'm his attorney, but between ourselves I see my job as a matter of making sure he never gets out without a leash. It's a good thing I drew this case.'

'Why's that?'

'Because anybody crazy enough to want to could get him off without a whole lot of trouble. I'm going to plead him, but if I made a fight the State's case wouldn't stand up. All they've got is his confession and you could knock that out a dozen different ways, including that he was cuckoo at the time he confessed. They've got no evidence, not after nine years. There's lawyers who think the advocate system means they should go to bat for a guy like Lou and put him back on the streets.'

'He'd do it again.'

'Of course he'd do it again. He had a fucking icepick in his pocket when they collared him. Again between ourselves, I think lawyers with that attitude ought to be in jail alongside their clients. But in the meantime here I am, playing God. What do you want to ask Lou?'

'There was another Brooklyn killing. I might ask him a few questions about that.'

'Sheepshead Bay. He copped to that one.'

'That's right. I don't know what else I'll ask him. I'm probably wasting my time. And yours.'

'Don't worry about it.'

Thirty or forty minutes later we were driving back to the mainland and I was apologizing again for wasting his time.

'You did me a favor,' he said. 'I'm going to have to make another dentist's appointment. You ever have periodontal surgery?'

'No.'

'You're a wise man. This guy's my wife's cousin and he's pretty good, but what they do is they carve your gums. They do a section of your mouth at a time. Last time I went I wound up taking codeine every four hours for a week. I walked around in this perpetual fog. I suppose it's worth it in the long run, but don't feel you took me away from something enjoyable.'

'If you say so.'

I told him he could drop me anywhere but he insisted on giving me a lift to the subway stop at Northern Boulevard. On the way we talked a little about Pinell. 'You can see why they picked him up on the street,' he said. 'That craziness is right there in his eyes. One look and you see it.'

'There are a lot of street crazies.'

'But he's dangerous-crazy and it shows. And yet I'm never nervous in his presence. Well, I'm not a woman and he hasn't got an icepick. That might have something to do with it.'

At the subway entrance I got out of the car and hesitated for a moment, and he leaned toward me, one arm over the back of the seat. We both seemed reluctant to take leave of each other. I liked him and sensed that he held me in similar regard.

'You're not licensed,' he said. 'Isn't that what you said?'

'That's right.'

'Couldn't you get a license?'

'I don't want one.'

'Well, maybe I could throw some work your way all the same, if the right sort of thing came along.'

'Why would you want to?'

'I don't know. I liked your manner with Lou. And I get the feeling with you that you think the truth is important.' He chuckled. 'Besides, I owe you. You spared me a half-hour in the dentist's chair.'

'Well, if I ever need a lawyer—'

'Right. You know who to call.'

I just missed a Manhattan-bound train. While I waited for the next one on the elevated platform I managed to find a phone in working order and tried Lynn London's number. I'd checked the hotel desk before I called Hiller, and there'd been a message from her the night before, probably wondering why I hadn't shown up. I wondered if she'd been the one who called during my shower. Whoever it was hadn't elected to leave a message. The desk man said the caller had been a woman, but I'd learned not to count too heavily on his powers of recollection.

Lynn's number didn't answer. No surprise. She was probably still in school, or on her way home. Had she mentioned any afternoon plans? I couldn't remember.

I retrieved my dime, started to put it and my notebook away. Was there anyone else I should call? I flipped pages in my notebook, struck by how many names and numbers and addresses I'd written down, considering how little I'd managed to accomplish.

Karen Ettinger? I could ask her what she was afraid of. Hiller had just told me he sensed that I thought the truth was important. Evidently she thought it was worth hiding.

It'd be a toll call, though. And I didn't have much change.

Charles London? Frank Fitzroy? An ex-cop on the Upper West Side? His ex-wife on the Lower East Side?

Mitzi Pomerance? Jan Keane?

Probably still had the phone off the hook.

I put the notebook away, and the dime. I could have used a drink. I'd had nothing since that one eye-opener at McGovern's. I'd eaten a late breakfast since then, had drunk several cups of coffee, but that was it.

I looked over the low wall at the rear of the platform. My eye fastened on red neon in a tavern window. I'd just missed a train. I could have a quick one and be back in plenty of time for the next one.

I sat down on a bench and waited for my train.

I changed trains twice and wound up at Columbus Circle. The sky was darkening by the time I hit the street, turning that particular cobalt blue that it gets over New York. There were no messages waiting for me at my hotel. I called Lynn London from the lobby.

This time I reached her. 'The elusive Mr Scudder,' she said. 'You stood me up.'

'I'm sorry.'

'I waited for you yesterday afternoon. Not for long, because I didn't have too much time available. I suppose something came up, but you didn't call, either.'

I remembered how I had considered keeping the appointment and how I'd decided against it. Alcohol had made the decision for me. I'd been in a warm bar and it was cold outside.

'I'd just spoken to your father,' I said. 'He asked me to drop the case. I figured he'd have been in touch with you to tell you not to cooperate with me.'

'So you just decided to write off the Londons, is that it?' There was a trace of amusement in her voice. 'I was here waiting, as I said. Then I went out and kept my date for the evening, and when I got home my father called. To tell me he'd ordered you off the case but that you intended to persist with it all the same.'

So I could have seen her. Alcohol had made the decision, and had made it badly.

'He told me not to offer you any encouragement. He said he'd made a mistake raking up the past to begin with.'

'But you called me. Or was that before you spoke to him?'

'Once before and once after. The first call was because I was angry with you for standing me up. The second call was because I was angry with my father.'

'Why?'

'Because I don't like being told what to do. I'm funny that way. He says you wanted a picture of Barbara. I gather he refused to give it to you. Do you still want one?'

Did I? I couldn't recall now what I'd planned to do with it. Maybe I'd make the rounds of hardware stores, showing it to everyone who sold icepicks.

'Yes,' I said. 'I still want one.'

'Well, I can supply that much. I don't know what else I can give you. But one thing I can't give you at the moment is time. I was on my way out the door when the phone range. I've got my coat on. I'm meeting a friend for dinner, and then I'm going to be busy this evening.'

'With group therapy.'

'How did you know that? Did I mention it the last time we talked? You have a good memory.'

'Sometimes.'

'Just let me think. Tomorrow night's also impossible. I'd say come over tonight after therapy but by then I generally feel as though I've been through the wringer. After school tomorrow there's a faculty meeting, and by the time that's over – look, could you come to the school?'

'Tomorrow?'

'I've got a free period from one to two. Do you know where I teach?'

'A private school in the Village, but I don't know which one.'

'It's the Devonhurst School. Sounds very preppy, doesn't it? Actually it's anything but. And it's in the East Village. Second Avenue between Tenth and Eleventh. The east side of the street closer to Eleventh than Tenth.'

'I'll find it.'

'I'll be in Room Forty-one. And Mr Scudder? I wouldn't want to be stood up a second time.'

I went around the corner to Armstrong's. I had a hamburger and a small salad, then some bourbon in coffee. They switch bartenders at eight, and when Billie came in a half-hour before his shift started I went over to him.

'I guess I was pretty bad last night,' I said.

'Oh, you were okay,' he said.

'It was a long day and night.'

'You were talking a little loud,' he said. 'Aside from that you were your usual self. And you knew to leave here and make it an early night.'

Except I hadn't made it an early night.

I went back to my table and had another bourbon and coffee. By the time I was finished with it, the last of my hangover was gone. I'd shaken off the headache fairly early on, but the feeling of being a step or two off the pace had persisted throughout the day.

Great system: the poison and the antidote come in the same bottle.

I went to the phone, dropped a dime. I almost dialed Anita's number and sat there wondering why. I didn't want to talk about a dead dog, and that was as close as we'd come to a meaningful conversation in years.

I dialed Jan's number. My notebook was in my pocket but I didn't have to get it out. The number was just right there at hand.

'It's Matthew,' I said. 'I wondered if you felt like company.'

'Oh.'

'Unless you're busy.'

'No, I'm not. As a matter of fact, I'm a little under the weather. I was just settling in for a quiet evening in front of the television set.'

'Well, if you'd rather be alone—'

'I didn't say that.' There was a pause. 'I wouldn't want to make it a late evening.'

'Neither would I.'

'You remember how to get here?'

'I remember.'

On the way there I felt like a kid on a date. I rang her bell according to the code and stood at the curb. She tossed me the key. I went inside and rode up in the big elevator.

She was wearing a skirt and sweater and had doeskin slippers on her feet. We stood looking at each other for a moment and then I handed her the paper bag I was carrying. She took out the two bottles, one of Teacher's Scotch, the other of the brand of Russian vodka she favored.

'The perfect hostess gift,' she said. 'I thought you were a bourbon drinker.'

'Well, it's a funny thing. I had a clear head the other morning, and it occurred to me that Scotch might be less likely to give me a hangover.'

She put the bottles down. 'I wasn't going to drink tonight,' she said.

'Well, it'll keep. Vodka doesn't go bad.'

'Not if you don't drink it. Let me fix you something. Straight, right?'

'Right.'

It was stilted at first. We'd been close to one another, we'd spent a night in bed together, but we were nevertheless stiff and awkward with each other. I started talking about the case, partly because I wanted to talk to someone about it, partly because it was what we had in common. I told her how my client had tried to take me off the case and how I was staying with it anyway. She didn't seem to find this unusual.

Then I talked about Pinell.

'He definitely didn't kill Barbara Ettinger,' I said, 'and he definitely did commit the icepick murder in Sheepshead Bay. I didn't really have much doubt about either of those points but I wanted to have my own impressions to work with. And I just plain wanted to see him. I wanted some sense of the man.'

'What was he like?'

'Ordinary. They're always ordinary, aren't they? Except I don't know that that's the right word for it. The thing about Pinell is that he looked insignificant.'

'I think I saw a picture of him in the paper.'

'You don't get the full effect from a photograph. Pinell's the kind of person you don't notice. You see guys like him delivering lunches, taking tickets in a movie theater. Slight build, furtive manner, and a face that just won't stay in your memory.'

' "The Banality of Evil." '

'What's that?'

She repeated the phrase. 'It's the title of an essay about Adolf Eichmann.'

'I don't know that Pinell's evil. He's crazy. Maybe evil's a form of insanity. Anyway, you don't need a psychiatrist's report to know he's crazy. It's right there in his eyes. Speaking of eyes, that's another thing I wanted to ask him.'

'What?'

'If he stabbed them all in both eyes. He said he did. He did that right away, before he went to work turning their bodies into pincushions.'

She shuddered. 'Why?'

'That was the other thing I wanted to ask him. Why the eyes? It turned out he had a perfectly logical reason. He did it to avoid detection.'

'I don't follow you.'

'He thought a dead person's eyes would retain the last image they perceived before death. If that were the case you could obtain a picture of the murderer by scanning the victim's retina. He was just guarding against this possibility by destroying their eyes.'

'Jesus.'

'The funny thing is that he's not the first person to have that theory. During the last century some criminologists believed the same thing Pinell hit on. They just figured it was a matter of time before the necessary technology existed for recovering the image from the retina. And who knows that it won't be possible someday? A doctor could give you all sorts of reasons why it'll never be physiologically possible, but look at all the things that would have seemed at least as farfetched a hundred years ago. Or even twenty years ago.'

'So Pinell's just a little ahead of his time, is that it?' She got up, carried my empty glass to the bar. She filled it and poured a glass of vodka for herself. 'I do believe that calls for a drink. "Here's looking at you, kid." That's as close as I can come to an imitation of Humphrey Bogart. I do better with clay.'

She sat down and said, 'I wasn't going to drink anything today. Well, what the hell.'

'I want to go fairly light myself.'

She nodded, her eyes aimed at the glass in her hand. 'I was glad when you called, Matthew. I didn't think you were going to.'

'I tried to get you last night. I kept getting a busy signal.'

'I had the phone off the hook.'

'I know.'

'You had them check it? I just wanted to keep the world away last night. When I'm in here with the door locked and the phone off the hook and the shades down, that's when I'm really safe. Do you know what I mean?'

'I think so.'

'See, I didn't wake up with a clear head Sunday morning. I got drunk Sunday night. And then I got drunk again last night.'

'Oh.'

'And then I got up this morning and took a pill to stop the shakes and decided I'd stay away from it for a day or two. Just to get off the roller-coaster, you know?'

'Sure.'

'And here I am with a glass in my hand. Isn't that a surprise?'

'You should have said something, Jan. I wouldn't have brought the vodka.'

'It's no big deal.'

'I wouldn't have brought the Scotch, either. I had too much to drink last night myself. We could be together tonight without drinking.'

'You really think so?'

'Of course.'

Her large gray eyes looked quite bottomless. She stared sadly at me for a long moment, then brightened. 'Well, it's too late to test that hypothesis right now, isn't it? Why don't we just make the best of what we have?'

We didn't do all that much drinking. She had enough vodka to catch up with me and then we both coasted. She played some records and we sat together on the couch and listened to them, not talking much. We started making love on the couch and then went into the bedroom to finish the job.

We were good together, better than we'd been Saturday night. Novelty is a spice, but when the chemistry is good between lovers, familiarity enhances their love-making. I got out of myself some, and felt a little of what she felt.

Afterward we went back to the couch and I started talking about the murder of Barbara Ettinger. 'She's buried so goddamn deep,' I said. 'It's not just the amount of time that's gone by. Nine years is a long time, but there are people who died nine years ago and you could walk through their lives and find everything pretty much as they left it. The same people in the houses next door and everybody leading the same kind of life.

'With Barbara, everybody's gone through a sea-change. You closed the day-care center and left your husband and moved here. Your husband took the kids and beat it to California. I was one of the first cops on the scene, and God knows my life turned upside down since then. There were three cops who investigated the case in Sheepshead Bay, or started to. Two of them are dead and one left the force and his wife and lives in a furnished room and stands guard in a department store.'

'And Doug Ettinger's remarried and selling sporting goods.'

I nodded. 'And Lynn London's been married and divorced, and half the neighbors on Wyckoff Street have moved somewhere or other. It's as though every wind on earth's been busy blowing sand on top of her grave. I know Americans lead mobile lives. I read somewhere that every year twenty percent of the country changes its place of residence. Even so, it's as though every wind on earth's been busy blowing sand on top of her grave. It's like digging for Troy.'

' "Deep with the first dead." '

'How's that?'

'I don't know if I remember it right. Just a second.' She crossed the room, searched the bookshelves, removed a slim volume and paged through it. 'It's Dylan Thomas,' she said, 'and it's in here somewhere. Where the hell is it? I'm sure it's in here. Here it is.'

She read:

'Deep with the first dead lies London's daughter,
Robed in the long friends,
The grains beyond age, the dark veins of her mother,
Secret by the unmourning water
Of the riding Thames.
After the first death, there is no other.'

'London's daughter,' I said.

'As in the city of London. But that must be what made me think of it. Deep with the first dead lies Charles London's daughter.'

'Read it again.'

She did.

'Except there's a door there somewhere if I could just find the handle to it. It wasn't some nut that killed her. It was someone with a reason, someone she knew. Someone who purposely made it look like Pinell's handiwork. And the killer's still around. He didn't die or drop out of sight. He's still around. I don't have any grounds to believe that but it's a feeling I can't shake.'

'You think it's Doug?'

'If I don't, I'm the only one who doesn't. Even his wife thinks he did it. She may not know that's what she thinks, but why else is she scared of what I'll find?'

'But you think it's somebody else?'

'I think an awful lot of lives changed radically after her death. Maybe her dying had something to do with those changes. With some of them, anyway.'

'Doug's obviously. Whether he killed her or not.'

'Maybe it affected other lives, too.'

'Like a stone in a pond? The ripple effect?'

'Maybe. I don't know just what happened or how. I told you, it's a matter of a hunch, a feeling. Nothing concrete that I can point at.'

'Your cop instincts, is that it?'

I laughed. She asked what was funny. I said, 'It's not so funny. I've had all day to wonder about the validity of my cop instincts.'

'How do you mean?'

And so I wound up telling her more than I'd planned. About everything from Anita's phone call to a kid with a gravity knife. Two nights ago I'd found out what a good listener she was, and she was no worse at it this time around.

When I was done she said, 'I don't know why you're down on yourself. You could have been killed.'

'If it was really a mugging attempt.'

'What were you supposed to do, wait until he stuck a knife into you? And why was he carrying a knife in the first place? I don't know what a gravity knife is, but it doesn't sound like something you carry around in case you need to cut a piece of string.'

'He could have been carrying it for protection.'

'And the roll of money? It sounds to me as though he's one of those closet cases who pick up gay men and rob them, and sometimes beat them up or kill them while they're at it to prove how straight they are. And you're worrying because you gave a kid like that a bloody lip?'

I shook my head. 'I'm worrying because my judgment wasn't sound.'

'Because you were drunk.'

'And didn't even know it.'

'Was your judgment off the night you shot the two holdup men? The night that Puerto Rican girl got killed?'

'You're a pretty sharp lady, aren't you?'

'A fucking genius.'

'That's the question, I guess. And the answer is no, it wasn't. I hadn't had much to drink and I wasn't feeling it. But—'

'But you got echoes just the same.'

'Right.'

'And didn't want to look straight at them, any more than Karen Ettinger wants to look straight at the fact that she thinks her husband might have murdered his first wife.'

'A very sharp lady.'

'They don't come any sharper. Feel better now?'

'Uh-huh.'

'Talking helps. But you kept it so far inside you didn't even know it was there.' She yawned. 'Being a sharp lady is tiring work.'

'I can believe it.'

'Want to go to bed?'

'Sure.'

But I didn't stay the night. I thought I might, but I was still awake when her breathing changed to indicate that she was sleeping. I lay first on one side and then on the other, and it was clear I wasn't ready to sleep. I got out of bed and padded quietly into the other room.

I dressed, then stood at the window and looked out at Lispenard Street. There was plenty of Scotch left but I didn't want to drink any of it.

I let myself out. A block away on Canal Street I managed to flag a cab. I got uptown in time to catch the last half-hour or so at Armstrong's, but I said the hell with it and went straight to my room.

I got to sleep eventually.

FOURTEEN

I had a night of dreams and shallow sleep. The dog, Bandy, turned up in one of the dreams. He wasn't really dead. His death had been faked as part of some elaborate scam. He told me all this, told me too that he'd always been able to talk but had been afraid to disclose this talent. 'If I'd only known,' I marveled, 'what conversations we could have had!'

I awoke refreshed and clearheaded and fiercely hungry. I had bacon and eggs and home fries at the Red Flame and read the *News*. They'd caught the First Avenue Slasher, or at the least had arrested someone they said was the Slasher. A photograph of the suspect bore a startling resemblance to the police artist's sketch that had run earlier. That doesn't happen too often.

I was on my second cup of coffee when Vinnie slid into the booth across from me. 'Woman in the lobby,' he said.

'For me?'

He nodded. 'Young, not bad-looking. Nice clothes, nice hair. Gave me a couple of bucks to point you out when you came in. I don't even know if you're comin' back, so I figured I'd take a chance, look here and there and see if I could find you. I got Eddie coverin' the desk for me. You comin' back to the hotel?'

'I hadn't planned to.'

'What you could do, see, you could look her over and gimme a sign to point you out or not point you out. I'd just as soon earn the couple of bucks, but I'm not gonna go and retire on it, you know what I mean? If you want to duck this dame –'

'You can point me out,' I said. 'Whoever she is.'

He went back to the desk. I finished my coffee and the paper and took my time returning to the hotel. When I walked in Vinnie nodded significantly toward the wing chair over by the cigarette machine, but he needn't have bothered. I'd have spotted her without help. She looked utterly out of place, a well-groomed, well-coiffed, color-coordinated suburban princess who'd found her way to the wrong part of Fifty-seventh Street. A few blocks east she might have been having an adventure, making the rounds of the art galleries, looking for a print that would go well with the mushroom-toned drapes in the family room.

I let Vinnie earn his money, strolled past her, stood waiting for the elevator. Its doors were just opening when she spoke my name.

I said, 'Hello, Mrs Ettinger.'

'How –'

'Saw your picture on your husband's desk. And I probably would have recognized your voice, although I've only heard it over the phone.' The blonde hair was a little longer than in the picture in Douglas Ettinger's photo cube, and the voice in person was less nasal, but there was no mistaking her. 'I heard your voice a couple of times. Once when I called you, once when you called me, and again when I called you back.'

'I thought that was you,' she said. 'It frightened me when the phone rang and you didn't say anything.'

'I just wanted to make sure I'd recognized the voice.'

'I called you since then. I called twice yesterday.'

'I didn't get any messages.'

'I didn't leave any. I don't know what I'd have said if I reached you. Is there someplace more private where we can talk?'

I took her out for coffee, not to the Red Flame but to another similar place down the block. On the way out Vinnie tipped me a wink and a sly smile. I wonder how much money she'd given him.

Less, I'm sure, than she was prepared to give me. We were no sooner settled with our coffee than she put her purse on the table and gave it a significant tap.

'I have an envelope in here,' she announced. 'There's five thousand dollars in it.'

'That's a lot of cash to be carrying in this town.'

'Maybe you'd like to carry it for me.' She studied my face, and when I failed to react she leaned forward, dropping her voice conspiratorially. 'The money's for you, Mr Scudder. Just do what Mr London already asked you to do. Drop the case.'

'What are you afraid of, Mrs Ettinger?'

'I just don't want you poking around in our lives.'

'What is it you think I might find there?' Her hand clutched her purse, seeking security in the presumptive power of five

thousand dollars. Her nail polish was the color of iron rust.
Gently I said, 'Do you think your husband killed his first wife?'

'No!'

'Then what have you got to be afraid of?'

'I don't know.'

'When did you meet your husband, Mrs Ettinger?'

She met my eyes, didn't answer.

'Before his wife was killed?' Her fingers kneaded her handbag.
'He went to college on Long Island. You're younger than he is,
but you could have known him then.'

'That was before he even knew her,' she said. 'Long before
they were married. Then we happened to run into each other
again after her death.'

'And you were afraid I'd find that out?'

'I –'

'You were seeing him before she died, weren't you?'

'You can't prove that.'

'Why would I have to prove it? Why would I even want to
prove it?'

She opened the purse. Her fingers clumsy with the clasp but
she got the bag open and took out a manila bank envelope. 'Five
thousand dollars,' she said.

'Put it away.'

'Isn't it enough? It's a lot of money. Isn't five thousand dollars
a lot of money for doing nothing?'

'It's too much. You didn't kill her, did you, Mrs Ettinger?'

'Me?' She had trouble getting a grip on the question. 'Me? Of
course not.'

'But you were glad when she died.'

'That's horrible,' she said. 'Don't say that.'

'You were having an affair with him. You wanted to marry
him, and then she was killed. How could you help being glad?'

Her eyes were pitched over my shoulder, gazing off into the
distance. Her voice was as remote as her gaze. She said, 'I didn't
know she was pregnant. He said . . . he said he hadn't known
that either. He told me they weren't sleeping together. Having
sex, I mean. Of course they slept together, they shared a bed, but
he said they weren't having sex. I believed him.'

The waitress was approaching to refill our coffee cups. I held
up a hand to ward off the interruption. Karen Ettinger said, 'He
said she was carrying another man's child. Because it couldn't
have been his baby.'

'Is that what you told Charles London?'

'I never spoke to Mr London.'

'Your husband did, though, didn't he? Is that what he told him? Is that what London was afraid would come out if I stayed on the case?'

Her voice was detached, remote. 'He said she was pregnant by another man. A black man. He said the baby would have been black.'

'That's what he told London.'

'Yes.'

'Had he ever told you that?'

'No. I think it was just something he made up to influence Mr London.' She looked at me, and her eyes showed me a little of the person hidden beneath the careful suburban exterior. 'Just like the rest of it was something he made up for my sake. It was probably his baby.'

'You don't think she was having an affair?'

'Maybe. Maybe she was. But she must have been sleeping with him, too. Or else she would have been careful not to get pregnant. Women aren't stupid.' She blinked her eyes several times. 'Except about some things. Men always tell their girlfriends that they've stopped sleeping with their wives. And it's always a lie.'

'Do you think that –'

She rolled right over my question. 'He's probably telling her that he's not sleeping with me anymore,' she said, her tone very matter-of-fact. 'And it's a lie.'

'Telling whom?'

'Whoever he's having an affair with.'

'Your husband is currently having an affair with someone?'

'Yes,' she said, and frowned. 'I didn't know that until just now. I knew it, but I didn't know that I knew it. I wish you had never taken this case. I wish Mr London had never heard of you in the first place.'

'Mrs Ettinger –'

She was standing now, her purse gripped in both hands, her face showing her pain. 'I had a good marriage,' she insisted. 'And what have I got now? Will you tell me that? What have I got now?'

FIFTEEN

I don't suppose she wanted an answer. I certainly didn't have one for her, and she didn't hang around to find out what else I might have to say. She walked stiffly out of the coffee shop. I stayed long enough to finish my own coffee, then left a tip and paid the check. Not only hadn't I taken her five thousand dollars, but I'd wound up buying her coffee.

It was a nice day out and I thought I'd kill a little time by walking part of the way to my appointment with Lynn London. As it turned out I walked all the way downtown and east, stopping once to sit on a park bench and another time for coffee and a roll. When I crossed Fourteenth Street I ducked into Dan Lynch's and had the first drink of the day. I'd thought earlier that I might switch to Scotch, which had once again spared me a hangover, but I'd ordered a shot of bourbon with a short beer for a chaser before I remembered my decision. I drank it down and enjoyed the warmth of it. The saloon had a rich beery smell and I enjoyed that, too, and would have liked to linger awhile. But I'd already stood up the schoolteacher once.

I found the school, walked in. No one questioned my entering it or stopped me in the corridors. I located Room *41* and stood in the doorway for a moment, studying the woman seated at the blond oak desk. She was reading a book and unaware of my presence. I knocked on the open door and she looked up at me.

'I'm Matthew Scudder,' I said.

'And I'm Lynn London. Come in. Close the door.'

She stood up and we shook hands. There was no place for me to sit, just child-sized desks. The children's art work and test papers, some marked with gold or silver stars, were tacked on bulletin boards. There was a problem in long division worked out in yellow chalk on the blackboard. I found myself checking the arithmetic.

'You wanted a picture,' Lynn London was saying. 'I'm afraid

I'm not much on family memorabilia. This was the best I could do. This was Barbara in college.'

I studied the photo, glanced from it to the woman standing beside me. She caught the eye movement. 'If you're looking for a resemblance,' she said, 'don't waste your time. She looked like our mother.'

Lynn favored her father. She had the same chilly blue eyes. Like him she wore glasses, but hers had heavy rims and rectangular lenses. Her brown hair was pulled back and coiled in a tight bun on the back of her head. There was a severity in her face, a sharpness to her features, and although I knew she was only thirty-three she looked several years older. There were lines at the corners of her eyes, deeper ones at the corners of her mouth.

I couldn't get much from Barbara's picture. I'd seen police photos of her after death, high-contrast black and white shot in the kitchen on Wyckoff Street, but I wanted something that would give me a sense of the person and Lynn's photograph didn't supply that, either. I may have been looking for more than a photograph could furnish.

She said, 'My father's afraid you'll drag Barbara's name through the mud. Will you?'

'I hadn't planned on it.'

'Douglas Ettinger told him something and he's afraid you'll tell it to the world. I wish I knew what it was.'

'He told your father that your sister was carrying a black man's child.'

'Holy Jesus. Is that true?'

'What do you think?'

'I think Doug's a worm. I've always thought that. Now I know why my father hates you.'

'Hates *me?*'

'Uh-huh. I wondered why. In fact I wanted to meet you mostly to find out what kind of man would inspire such a strong reaction in my father. You see, if it weren't for you he wouldn't have been given that piece of information about his sainted daughter. If he hadn't hired you, and if you hadn't talked to Doug – you did talk to Doug, I assume?'

'I met him. At the store in Hicksville.'

'If you hadn't, he wouldn't have told my father something my father emphatically did not want to be told. I think he'd prefer to believe that both of his daughters are virgins. Well, he may not care so much about me. I had the temerity to get divorced so that makes me beyond redemption. He'd be sick if I got into an interracial romance, because after all there's a limit, but I don't think he cares if I have affairs. I'm already damaged goods.' Her voice was flat, less bitter than the words she was speaking. 'But Barbara was a saint. If I got killed he wouldn't hire you in the first place, but if he did he wouldn't care what you found. With Barbara it's a different story altogether.'

'Was she a saint?'

'We weren't that close.' She looked away, picked up a pencil from the desk top. 'She was my big sister. I put her on a pedestal and wound up seeing her feet of clay, and I went through a period of holier-than-thou contempt for her. I might have outgrown that but then she was killed, so I had all that guilt over the way I'd felt about her.' She looked at me. 'This is one of the things I've been working on in the therapy.'

'Was she having an affair while she was married to Ettinger?'

'She wouldn't have told me if she had been. The one thing she did tell me was that he was playing around. She said he made passes at their friends and that he was screwing his welfare clients. I don't know if that was true or not. He never made a pass at me.'

She said that last as if it was one more item on a long list of resentments. I talked with her for another ten minutes and didn't learn anything beyond the fact that Barbara Ettinger's death had had an impact on her sister's life, and that wasn't news. I wondered how different Lynn had been nine years ago, and how different she might have turned out if Barbara had lived. Perhaps it was all there already, all locked in place, the bitterness, the emotional armor. I wondered – although I could probably have guessed – what Lynn's own marriage had been like. Would she have married the same man if Barbara had been alive? Would she have divorced him if she did?

I left there with a useless photograph and a head full of irrelevant – or unanswerable – questions. I left, too, glad to escape from the woman's cramped personality. Dan Lynch's bar was just a couple blocks uptown, and I turned toward it, remembering the dark wood, the warmth, the boozy, beery aroma.

They were all afraid I'd dig her up, I thought, and it was impossible because she was buried impossibly deep. The bit of poetry Jan had read came to mind and I tried to recall just how it went. *Deep with the first dead.* Was that right?

I decided I wanted the exact wording. More than that, I

wanted the whole poem. I had a vague recollection of a branch library somewhere around there on Second Avenue. I walked a block north, didn't find it, turned around and walked downtown. There was indeed a library, right where I'd remembered it, a squarish three-story building with a nicely ornamented marble facade. A sign in the door gave the hours, and they were closed on Wednesdays.

All of the branch libraries have cut back on their hours, added closed days. Part of the financial pinch. The city can't afford anything, and the administration goes around like an old miser closing off unused rooms in a sprawling cold house. The police force is ten thousand men below what it used to be. Everything drops but the rents and the crime rate.

I walked another block and hit St Marks Place and knew there'd be a bookstore around, and one that would most likely have a poetry section. The busiest commercial block of St Marks Place, and as trendy a block as the East Village possesses, runs between Second and Third Avenues. I turned right and walked toward Third, and two-thirds of the way down the block I found a bookstore. They had a paperback edition of the collected poems of Dylan Thomas. I had to go through it a couple of times before I spotted the poem I was looking for, but it was there and I read it all the way through. 'A refusal to Mourn the Death by Fire of a Child in London' was the title. There were parts I didn't think I understood, but I liked the sound of them anyway, the weight and shape of the words.

The poem was long enough to discourage me from trying to copy it into my notebook. Besides, maybe I'd want to look at some of the other poems. I paid for the book and slipped it into my pocket.

Funny how little things nudge you in one direction or another. I had tired myself with all the walking I'd done. I wanted to catch a subway home, but I also wanted a drink and I stood for a moment on the sidewalk in front of the bookstore, trying to decide what to do and where to go. While I was standing there, two patrolmen walked by in uniform. Both of them looked impossibly young, and one was so fresh-faced his uniform looked like a costume.

Across the street, a shop sign read 'Haberman's.' I don't know what they sold there.

I thought of Burton Havermeyer. I might have thought of him without having seen the cop or having my memory jostled by a name not unlike his. In any event I thought of him, and remembered that he had once lived on this street, that his wife still lived here. I couldn't remember the address, but it was still in my notebook. 212 St Marks Place, along with the telephone number.

There was still no reason to go look at the building she lived in. He wasn't even part of the case I was working on, because my meeting with Louis Pinell had satisfied me that the little psychopath had killed Susan Potowski and had not killed Barbara Ettinger. But Havermeyer's life had been changed, and in a way that interested me, a way not unlike that in which mine had been changed by another death.

St Marks Place starts at Third Avenue and the numbers get higher as you go eastward. The block between Second and First was more residential and less commercial. A couple of the row houses had ornate windows and letterboards near the entrance to indicate that they were churches. There was a Ukrainian church, a Polish Catholic church.

I walked to First Avenue, waited for the light, walked on across. I made my way down a quiet block, its houses less prepossessing and in poorer repair than on the preceding block. One of a group of parked cars I passed was a derelict, stripped of tires and hubcaps, the radio pulled out, the interior gutted. On the other side of the street three bearded and longhaired men in Hell's Angels colors were trying to get a motorcyle started.

The last number on the block was 132. The street deadended at the corner, where Avenue A formed the western boundary of Tompkins Square Park. I stood there looking at the house number, then at the park, first at one and then at the other.

From Avenue A east to the river are the blocks they call Alphabet City. The population runs to junkies and muggers and crazies. Nobody decent lives there on purpose, not if they can afford to live anywhere else.

I dragged out my notebook. The address was still the same, 212 St Marks Place.

I walked through Tompkins Square and across Avenue B. On my way through the park, drug dealers offered to sell me dope and pills and acid. Either I didn't look like a cop to them or they just didn't care.

On the other side of Avenue B, the numbers started at 300. And the street signs didn't call it St Marks Place. It was East Eighth Street there.

I went back through the park again. At 130 St Marks Place

120

there was a bar called Blanche's Tavern. I went in. The place was a broken-down bucket of blood that smelled of stale beer and stale urine and bodies that needed washing. Perhaps a dozen of the bodies were there, most of them at the bar, a couple at tables. The place went dead silent when I walked into it. I guess I didn't look as though I belonged there, and I hope to God I never do.

I used the phone book first. The precinct in Sheepshead Bay could have made a mistake, or Antonelli could have read the number to me wrong, or I could have copied it incorrectly. I found him listed, Burton Havermeyer on West 103rd, but I didn't find any Havermeyers listed on St Marks Place.

I was out of dimes. The bartender gave me change. His customers seemed more relaxed now that they realized I had no business with them.

I dropped a dime in the slot, dialed the number in my book. No answer.

I went out and walked a few doors to 112 St Marks Place. I checked the mail boxes in the vestibule, not really expecting to find the name Havermeyer, then went back outside. I wanted a drink but Blanche's wasn't where I wanted to have it.

Any port in a storm. I had a straight shot of bourbon at the bar, a stop-shelf brand. To my right, two men were discussing some mutual friends. 'I told her not to go home with him,' one of them was saying. 'I told her he was no good and he'd beat her up and rip her off, and she went anyhow, took him on home, and he beat her up and ripped her off. So where's she get off coming and crying to me?'

I tried the number again. On the fourth ring a boy answered it. I thought I'd misdialed, asked if I had the Havermeyer residence. He told me I did.

I asked if Mrs Havermeyer was there.

'She's next door,' he said. 'Is it important? Because I could get her.'

'Don't bother. I have to check the address for a delivery. What's the house number there?'

'Two twelve.'

'Two twelve what?'

He started to tell me the apartment number. I told him I needed to know the name of the street.

'Two twelve St Marks Place,' he said.

I had a moment of the sort I have now and then had in dreams, where the sleeping mind confronts an impossible inconsistency and breaks through to the realization that it is dreaming. Here I was talking to some fresh-voiced child who insisted he lived at an address that did not exist.

Or perhaps he and his mother lived in Tompkins Square Park, with the squirrels.

I said, 'What's that between?'

'Huh?'

'What are the cross streets? What block are you on?'

'Oh,' he said. 'Third and Fourth.'

'What?'

'We're between Third and Fourth Avenues.'

'That's impossible,' I said.

'Huh?'

I looked away from the phone, half-expecting to see something entirely different from the interior of Blanche's Tavern. A lunar landscape, perhaps. St Marks Place started at Third Avenue and ran east. There was no St Marks Place between Third and Fourth Avenues.

I said, 'Where?'

'Huh? Look, mister, I don't –'

'Wait a minute.'

'Maybe I should get my mother. I –'

'What borough?'

'Huh?'

'Are you in Manhattan? Brooklyn? The Bronx? Where are you, son?'

'Brooklyn.'

'Are you sure?'

'Yes, I'm sure.' He sounded close to tears. 'We live in Brooklyn. What do you want, anyway? What's the matter, are you crazy or something?'

'It's all right,' I said. 'You've been a big help. Thanks a lot.'

I hung up, feeling like an idiot. Street names repeated through the five boroughs. I'd had no grounds to assume she lived in Manhattan.

I thought back, replayed what I could of my earlier conversation with the woman. If anything, I might have known that she didn't live in Manhattan. 'He's in Manhattan,' she had said of her husband. She wouldn't have put it that way if she'd been in Manhattan herself.

But what about my conversation with Havermeyer? 'You're wife's still in the East Village,' I'd said, and he'd agreed with me.

Well, maybe he'd just wanted the conversation to end. It was easier to agree with me than to explain that there was another St Marks Place in Brooklyn.

Still ...

I left Blanche's and hurried west to the bookstore where I'd bought the book of poems. They had a Hagstrom pocket atlas of the five boroughs. I looked up St Marks Place in the back, turned to the appropriate map, found what I was looking for.

St Marks Place, in Brooklyn as in Manhattan, extends for only three blocks. To the east, across Flatbush Avenue, the same street continues at an angle as St Marks Avenue, stretching under that name clear to Brownsville.

To the west, St Marks Place stops at Third Avenue – just as it does at an altogether different Third Avenue in Manhattan. On the other side of Third, Brooklyn's St Marks Place has another name.

Wyckoff Street.

SIXTEEN

It must have been around three o'clock when I spoke with the boy. It was between six thirty and seven by the time I mounted the stoop of his building on West 103rd. I'd found things to do during the intervening hours.

I rang a couple of bells but not his, and someone buzzed me in. Whoever it was peered at me from a doorway on the third floor but didn't challenge my right to pass. I stood at Havermeyer's door and listened for a moment. The television was on, tuned to the local news.

I didn't really expect him to shoot through the door but he did wear a gun as a security guard, and although he probably left it in the store each night I couldn't be sure he didn't have another one at home. They teach you to stand at the side of a door when you knock on it, so I did. I heard his footsteps approach the door, then his voice asking who it was.

'Scudder,' I said.

He opened the door. He was in street clothes and probably left not only the gun but the entire uniform at the store each night. He had a can of beer in one hand. I asked if I could come in. His reaction time was slow but at length he nodded and made room for me. I entered and drew the door shut.

He said, 'Still on that case, huh? Something I can do for you?'

'Yes.'

'Well, I'll be glad to help if I can. Meantime, how about a beer?'

I shook my head. He looked at the can of beer he was holding, moved to set it down on a table, went over and turned off the television set. He held the pose for a moment and I studied his face in profile. He didn't need a shave this time. He turned slowly, expectantly, as if waiting for the blow to fall.

I said, 'I know you killed her, Burt.'

I watched his deep brown eyes. He was rehearsing his denial, running it through his mind, and then there was a moment when he decided not to bother. Something went out of him.

'When did you know?'

'A couple of hours ago.'

'When you left here Sunday I couldn't figure whether you knew or not. I thought maybe you were going cat-and-mouse with me. But I didn't get that feeling. I felt close to you, actually. I felt we were a couple of ex-cops, two guys who left the force for personal reasons. I thought maybe you were playing a part, setting a trap, but it didn't feel like it.'

'I wasn't.'

'How did you find out?'

'St Marks Place. You didn't live in the East Village after all. You lived in Brooklyn three blocks away from Barbara Ettinger.'

'Thousands of people lived that close to her.'

'You let me go on thinking you lived in the East Village. I don't know if I'd have had a second thought about it if I'd known from the beginning that you had lived in Brooklyn. Maybe I would have. But most likely I wouldn't. Brooklyn's a big place. I didn't know there was a St Marks Place in it so I certainly didn't know where it was in relation to Wyckoff Street. For all I knew, it could have been out in Sheepshead Bay near your precinct. But you lied about it.'

'Just to avoid getting into a long explanation. It doesn't prove anything.'

'It gave me a reason to take a look at you. And the first thing I took a look at was another lie you told me. You said you and your wife didn't have any kids. But I talked to your boy on the phone this afternoon, and I called back and asked him his father's name and how old he was. He must have wondered what I was doing asking him all those questions. He's twelve. He was three years old when Barbara Ettinger was killed.'

'So?'

'You used to take him to a place on Clinton Street. The Happy Hours Child Care Center.'

'You're guessing.'

'No.'

'They're out of business. They've been out of business for years.'

'They were still in business when you left Brooklyn. Did you keep tabs on the place?'

'My ex-wife must have mentioned it,' he said. Then he

shrugged. 'Maybe I walked past there once. When I was in Brooklyn visiting Danny.'

'The woman who ran the day-care center is living in New York. She'll remember you.'

'After nine years?'

'That's what she says. And she kept records, Burt. The ledgers with the names and addresses of students and their parents, along with the record of payments. She packed all that stuff in a carton when she closed the business and never bothered to go through it and throw out the things she didn't need to keep anymore. She opened the box today. She says she remembers you. You always brought the boy, she said. She never met your wife but she does remember you.'

'She must have a good memory.'

'You were usually in uniform. That's an easy thing to remember.'

He looked at me for a moment, then turned and walked over to the window and stood looking out of it. I don't suppose he was looking at anything in particular.

'Where'd you get the icepick, Burt?'

Without turning he said, 'I don't have to admit to anything. I don't have to answer any questions.'

'Of course you don't.'

'Even if you were a cop I wouldn't have to say anything. And you're not a cop. You've got no authority.'

'You're absolutely right.'

'So why should I answer your questions?'

'You've been sitting on it a long time, Burt.'

'So?'

'Doesn't it get to you a little? Keeping it inside all that time?'

'Oh, God,' he said. He went over to a chair, dropped into it. 'Bring me that beer,' he said. 'Could you do that for me?'

I gave it to him. He asked me if I was sure I didn't want one for myself. No thanks, I said. He drank some beer and I asked him where he got the icepick.

'Some store,' he said. 'I don't remember.'

'In the neighborhood?'

'I think in Sheepshead Bay. I'm not sure.'

'You knew Barbara Ettinger from the day-care center.'

'And from the neighborhood. I used to see her around the neighborhood before I started taking Danny to the center.'

'And you were having an affair with her?'

126

'Who told you that? No, I wasn't having an affair with her. I wasn't having an affair with anybody.'

'But you wanted to.'

'No.'

I waited but he seemed willing to leave it there. I said, 'Why did you kill her, Burt?'

He looked at me for a moment, then looked down, then looked at me again. 'You can't prove anything,' he said.

I shrugged.

'You can't. And I don't have to tell you anything.' A deep breath, a long sigh. 'Something happened when I saw the Potowski woman,' he said. 'Something happened.'

'What do you mean?'

'Something happened to *me*. Inside of me. Something came into my head and I couldn't get rid of it. I remember standing and hitting myself in the forehead but I couldn't get it out of my mind.'

'You wanted to kill Barbara Ettinger.'

'No. Don't help me out, okay? Let me find the words by myself.'

'I'm sorry.'

'I looked at the dead woman and it wasn't her I saw on the floor, it was my wife. Every time the picture came back to me, the murder scene, the woman on the floor, I saw my wife in the picture. And I couldn't get it out of my head to kill her that way.'

He took a little sip of beer. Over the top of the can he said, 'I used to think about killing her. Plenty of times I thought that it was the only way out. I couldn't stand being married. I was alone, my parents were dead, I never had any brothers or sisters, and I thought I needed somebody. Besides, I knew she needed me. But it was wrong. I hated being married. It was around my neck like a collar that's too small for you, it was choking me and I couldn't get out of it.'

'Why couldn't you just leave her?'

'How could I leave her? How could I do that to her? What kind of a man leaves a woman like that?'

'Men leave women every day.'

'You don't understand, do you?' Another sigh. 'Where was I? Yeah. I used to think about killing her. I would think about it, and I would think, sure, and the first thing they'd do is check you inside and out, and one way or another they'll hang it on you, because they always go to the husband first and ninety percent of the time that's who did it, and they'll break your story down and break you down and where does that leave you? But then I saw the Potowski woman and it was all there. I could kill her and make it look like the Icepick Prowler had one more on his string. I saw what we did with the Potowski killing. We just bucked it to Midtown North, we didn't hassle the husband or anything like that.'

'So you decided to kill her.'

'Right.'

'Your wife.'

'Right.'

'Then how does Barbara Ettinger come into this?'

'Oh, God,' he said.

I waited him out.

'I was afraid to kill her. My wife, I mean. I was afraid something would go wrong. I thought, suppose I start and I can't go through with it? I had the icepick and I would take it out and look at it and – I remember now, I bought it on Atlantic Avenue. I don't even know if the store's still there.'

'It doesn't matter.'

'I know. I had visions of, you know, starting to stab her and stopping, of not being able to finish the job, and the things that were going through my mind were driving me crazy. I guess I *was* crazy. Of course I was.'

He drank from the beer can. 'I killed her for practice,' he said.

'Barbara Ettinger.'

'Yes. I had to find out if I could do it. And I told myself it would be a precaution. One more icepick killing in Brooklyn, so that when my wife got murdered three blocks away it would be just one more in the string. And it would be the same. Maybe no matter how I did it they'd notice a difference between it and the real icepick killings, but they would never have a reason to suspect me of killing some stranger like the Ettinger woman, and then my wife would be killed the same way, and – but that was just what I was telling myself. I killed her because I was afraid to kill my wife and I had to kill someone.'

'You had to kill someone?'

'I *had* to.' He leaned forward, sat on the edge of his chair. 'I couldn't get it out of my mind. Do you know what it's like when you can't get something out of your mind?'

'Yes.'

'I couldn't think who to pick. And then one day I took Danny to the day-care center and she and I talked the way we always did, and the idea came to me. I thought of killing her and the thought fit.'

'What do you mean, "the thought fit"?'

'She belonged in the picture. I could see her, you know, on the kitchen floor. So I started watching her. When I wasn't working I would hang around the neighborhood and keep tabs on her.'

She had sensed that someone was following her, watching her. And she'd been afraid, ever since the Potowski murder, that someone was stalking her.

'And I decided it would be all right to kill her. She didn't have any children. Nobody was dependent upon her. And she was immoral. She flirted with me, she flirted with men at the day-care center. She had men to her apartment when her husband was out. I thought, if I screwed it up and they knew it wasn't the Icepick Prowler, there would be plenty of other suspects. They'd never get to me.'

I asked him about the day of the murder.

'My shift ended around noon that day. I went over to Clinton Street and sat in a coffee shop at the counter where I could keep an eye on the place. When she left early I followed her. I was across the street watching her building when a man went into it. I knew him, I'd seen him with her before.'

'Was he black?'

'Black? No. Why?'

'No reason.'

'I don't remember what he looked like. He was with her for a half-hour or so. Then he left. I waited a little while longer, and something told me, I don't know, I just knew this was the right time. I went up and knocked on her door.'

'And she let you in?'

'I showed her my shield. And I reminded her that she knew me from the day-care center, that I was Danny's father. She let me in.'

'And?'

'I don't want to talk about it.'

'Are you sure of that?'

I guess he thought it over. Then he said, 'We were in the kitchen. She was making me a cup of coffee, she had her back to me, and I put one hand over her mouth and jabbed the icepick into her chest. I wanted to get her heart right away, I didn't want her to suffer. I kept stabbing her in the heart and she collapsed in my arms and I let her fall to the floor.' He raised his liquid brown eyes to mine. 'I think she was dead right then,' he said. 'I think she died right away.'

'And you went on stabbing her.'

'When I thought about it before I did it, I always went crazy and stabbed over and over like a maniac. I had that picture in my mind. But I couldn't do it that way. I had to make myself stab her and I was sick, I thought I was going to throw up, and I had to keep on sticking that icepick into her body and –' He broke off, gasping for breath. His face was drawn and his pale complexion was ghostly.

'It's all right,' I said.

'Oh, God.'

'Take it easy, Burt.'

'God, God.'

'You only stabbed one of her eyes.'

'It was so *hard*,' he said. 'Her eyes were wide open. I knew she was dead, I knew she couldn't see anything, but those eyes were just staring at me. I had the hardest time making myself stab her in the eye. I did it once and then I just couldn't do it again. I tried but I just couldn't do it again.'

'And then?'

'I left. No one saw me leave. I just left the building and walked away. I put the icepick down a sewer. I thought, I did it, I killed her and I got away with it, but I didn't feel as though I got away with anything. I felt sick to my stomach. I thought about what I had done and I couldn't believe I'd really done it. When the story was on television and in the papers I couldn't believe it. I thought that someone else must have done it.'

'And you didn't kill your wife.'

He shook his head. 'I knew I could never do something like that again. You know something? I've thought about all of it, over and over, and I think I was out of my mind. In fact I'm sure of it. Something about seeing Mrs Potowski, those pools of blood in her eyes, those stab wounds all over her body, it did something to me. It made me crazy, and I went on being crazy until Barbara Ettinger was dead. Then I was all right again, but she was dead.

'All of a sudden certain things were clear. I couldn't stay married anymore, and for the first time I realized I didn't have to. I could leave my wife and Danny. I had thought that would be a horrible thing to do, but here I'd been planning on killing her, and now I'd actually killed somebody and I knew how much more horrible that was than anything else I could possibly do to her, like leaving.'

I led him through it again, went over a few points. He finished his beer but didn't get another. I wanted a drink, but I didn't want beer and I didn't want to drink with him. I didn't hate him. I don't know exactly what I felt for him. But I didn't want to drink with him.

He broke a silence to say, 'Nobody can prove any of this. It doesn't matter what I told you. There are no witnesses and there's no evidence.'

'People could have seen you in the neighborhood.'

'And still remember nine years later? And remember what day it was?'

He was right, of course. I couldn't imagine a District Attorney who'd even try for an indictment. There was nothing to make a case out of.

I said, 'Why don't you put a coat on, Burt.'

'What for?'

'We'll go down to the Eighteenth Precinct and talk to a cop named Fitzroy. You can tell him what you told me.'

'That'd be pretty stupid, wouldn't it?'

'Why?'

'All I have to do is keep on the way I've been. All I have to do is keep my mouth shut. Nobody can prove anything. They couldn't even try to prove anything.'

'That's probably true.'

'And you want me to confess.'

'That's right.'

His expression was childlike. 'Why?'

To tie off the ends, I thought. To make it neat. To show Frank Fitzroy that he was right when he said I just might solve the case.

What I said was, 'You'll feel better.'

'That's a laugh.'

'How do you feel now, Burt?'

'How do I feel?' He considered the question. Then, as if surprised by his answer, 'I feel okay.'

'Better than when I got here?'

'Yeah.'

'Better than you've felt since Sunday?'

'I suppose so.'

'You never told anybody, did you?'

'Of course not.'

'Not a single person in nine years. You probably didn't think about it much, but there were times when you couldn't help thinking about it, and you never told anybody.'

'So?'

'That's a long time to carry it.'

'God.'

'I don't know what they'll do with you, Burt. You may not do any time. Once I talked a murderer into killing himself, and he did it, and I wouldn't do that again. And another time I talked a murderer into confessing because I convinced him he would probably kill himself if he didn't confess first. I don't think you'd do that. I think you've lived with this for nine years and maybe you could go on living with it. But do you really want to? Wouldn't you rather let go of it?'

'God,' he said. He put his head in his hands. 'I'm all mixed up,' he said.

'You'll be all right.'

'They'll put my picture in the papers. It'll be on the news. What's that going to make it like for Danny?'

'You've got to worry about yourself first.'

'I'll lose my job,' he said. 'What'll happen to me?'

I didn't answer that one. I didn't have an answer.

'Okay,' he said suddenly.

'Ready to go?'

'I guess.'

On the way downtown he said, 'I think I knew Sunday. I knew you'd keep poking at it until you found out I did it. I had an urge to tell you right then.'

'I got lucky. A couple of coincidences put me on St Marks Place and I thought of you and had nothing better to do than see the house where you used to live. But the numbers stopped at One-three-two.'

'If it wasn't that concidence there would have been another one. It was all set from the minute you walked into my apartment. Maybe earlier than that. Maybe it was a sure thing from the minute I killed her. Some people get away with murder but I guess I'm not one of them.'

'Nobody gets away with it. Some people just don't get caught.'

'Isn't that the same thing?'

''You didn't get caught for nine years, Burt. What were you getting away with?'

'Oh,' he said. 'I get it.'

And just before we got to the One-Eight I said, 'There's something I don't understand. Why did you think it would be easier to kill your wife than to leave her? You said several times that it would be such a terrible thing to leave a woman like her, that it would be a contemptible act, but men and women leave each other all the time. You couldn't have been worried about what your parents would think because you didn't have any family left. What made it such a big deal?'

'Oh,' he said. 'You don't know.'

'Don't know what?'

'You haven't met her. You didn't go out there this afternoon, did you?'

'No.'

(*'I never see him ... I never see my former husband ... I don't see my husband and I don't see the check. Do you see? Do you?'*)

'The Potowski woman, with her eyes staring up through the blood. When I saw her like that it just hit me so hard I couldn't deal with it. But you wouldn't understand that because you don't know about her.'

(*'Perhaps he has a phone and perhaps it's in the book. You could look it up. I know you'll excuse me if I don't offer to look it up for you.'*)

The answer was floating out there. I could very nearly reach out and touch it. But my mind wouldn't fasten onto it.

He said, 'My wife is blind.'

SEVENTEEN

It turned out to be a long night, although the trip to Twentieth
Street was the least of it. I shared a cab down with Burton
Havermeyer. We must have talked about something en route
but I can't remember what. I paid for the cab, took Havermeyer
to the squad room and introduced him to Frank Fitzroy, and that
was pretty much the extent of my contribution. I, after all, was
not the arresting officer. I had no official connection with the
case and had performed no official function. I didn't have to be
around while a stenographer took down Havermeyer's statement, nor was I called upon to make a statement of my own.

Fitzroy slipped away long enough to walk me down to the
corner and buy me a drink at P. J. Reynolds.

I didn't much want to accept his invitation. I wanted a drink,
but I wasn't much more inclined to drink with him than with
Havermeyer. I felt closed off from everyone, locked up tight
within myself where dead women and blind women couldn't get
at me.

The drinks came and we drank them, and he said, 'Nice piece
of work, Matt.'

'I got lucky.'

'You don't get that kind of luck. You make it. Something got
you onto Havermeyer in the first place.'

'More luck. The other two cops from the Six-One were dead.
He was odd man in.'

'You could have talked to him on the phone. Something made
you go see him.'

'Lack of anything better to do.'

'And then you asked him enough questions so that he told a
couple of lies that could catch him up further down the line.'

'And I was in the right place at the right time, and the right
shop sign caught my eye when the right pair of cops walked in
front of me.'

'Oh, shit,' he said, and signaled the bartender. 'Put yourself down if you want.'

'I just don't think I did anything to earn a field promotion to Chief of Detectives. That's all.'

The bartender came around. Fitzroy pointed to our glasses and the bartender filled them up again. I let him pay for this round, as he had paid for the first one.

He said, 'You won't get any official recognition out of this, Matt. You know that, don't you?'

'I'd prefer it that way.'

'What we'll tell the press is the reopening of the case with the arrest of Pinell made him conscience-stricken, and he turned himself in. He talked it over with you, another ex-cop like himself, and decided to confess. How does that sound?'

'It sounds like the truth.'

'Just a few things left out is all. What I was saying, you won't get anything official out of it, but people around the department are gonna know better. You follow me?'

'So?'

'So you couldn't ask for a better passport back onto the force is what it sounds like to me. I was talking to Eddie Koehler over at the Sixth. You wouldn't have any trouble getting 'em to take you on again.'

'It's not what I want.'

'That's what he said you'd say. But are you sure it isn't? All right, you're a loner, you got a hard-on for the world, you hit this stuff –' he touched his glass '– a little harder than you maybe should. But you're a cop, Matt, and you didn't stop being one when you gave the badge back.'

I thought for a moment, not to consider his proposal but to weigh the words of my reply. I said, 'You're right, in a way. But in another way you're wrong, and I stopped being a cop *before* I handed in my shield.'

'All because of that kid that died.'

'Not just that.' I shrugged. 'People move and their lives change.'

'Well,' he said, and then he didn't say anything for a few minutes, and then we found something less unsettling to talk about. We discussed the impossibility of keeping three-card monte dealers off the street, given that the fine for the offense is seventy-five dollars and the profit somewhere between five hundred and a thousand dollars a day. 'And there's this one judge,' he said, 'who told a whole string of them he'd let 'em off

135

without a fine if they'd promise not to do it again. "Oh, Ah promises, yo' honah." To save seventy-five dollars, those assholes'd promise to grow hair on their tongues.'

We had a third round of drinks, and I let him pay for that round, too, and then he went back to the station house and I caught a cab home. I checked the desk for messages, and when there weren't any I went around the corner to Armstrong's, and that's where it got to be a long night.

But it wasn't a bad one. I drank my bourbon in coffee, sipping it, making it last and my mood didn't turn black or ugly. I talked to people intermittently but spent a lot of time replaying the day, listening to Havermeyer's explanation. Somewhere in the course of things I gave Jan a call to tell her how things had turned out. Her line was busy. Either she was talking to someone or she had the phone off the hook, and this time I didn't get the operator to find out which.

I had just the right amount to drink, for a change. Not so much that I blacked out and lost my memory. But enough to bring sleep without dreams.

By the time I got down to Pine Street the next day, Charles London knew what to expect. The morning papers had the story. The line they carried was pretty much what I'd expected from what Fitzroy had said. I was mentioned by name as the fellow ex-cop who'd heard Havermeyer's confession and escorted him in so he could give himself up for the murder of Barbara Ettinger.

Even so, he didn't look thrilled to see me.

'I owe you an apology,' he said. 'I managed to become convinced that your investigation would only have a damaging effect upon a variety of people. I thought –'

'I know what you thought.'

'It turned out that I was wrong. I'm still concerned about what might come out in a trial, but it doesn't look as though there will be a trial.'

'You don't have to worry about what comes out anyway,' I said. 'Your daughter wasn't carrying a black baby.' He looked as though he'd been slapped. 'She was carrying her husband's baby. She may very well have been having an affair, probably in retaliation for her husband's behavior, but there's no evidence that it had an interracial element. That was an invention of your former son-in-law's.'

'I see.' He took his little walk to the window and made sure

136

that the harbor was still out there. He turned to me and said, 'At least this has turned out well, Mr Scudder.'

'Oh?'

'Barbara's killer has been brought to justice. I no longer have to worry who might have killed her, or why. Yes, I think we can say it's turned out well.'

He could say it if he wanted. I wasn't sure that justice was what Burton Havermeyer had been brought to, or where his life would go from here. I wasn't sure where justice figured in the ordeal that was just beginning for Haverymeyer's son and his blind ex-wife. And if London didn't have to worry that Douglas Ettinger had killed his daughter, what he'd learned about Ettinger's character couldn't have been monumentally reassuring.

I thought, too, of the fault lines I'd already detected in Ettinger's second marriage. I wondered how long the blonde with the sunny suburban face would hold her space in his desktop cube. If they split, would he be able to go on working for his second father-in-law?

Finally, I thought how people could adjust to one reality after another if they put their minds to it. London had begun by believing that his daughter had been killed for no reason at all, and he'd adjusted to that. Then he came to believe that she had indeed been killed for a reason, and by someone who knew her well. And he'd set about adjusting to that. Now he knew that she'd been killed by a near-stranger for a reason that had nothing much to do with her. Her death had come in a dress rehearsal for murder, and in dying she'd preserved the life of the intended victim. You could see all that as part of some great design or you could see it as further proof that the world was mad, but either way it was a new reality to which he would surely adjust.

Before I left he gave me a check for a thousand dollars. A bonus, he said, and he assured me he wanted me to have it. I gave him no argument. When money comes with no strings on it, take it and put it in your pocket. I was still enough of a cop at heart to remember that much.

I tried Jan around lunchtime and there was no answer. I tried her again later in the afternoon and the line was busy three times running. It was around six when I finally reached her.

'You're hard to get hold of,' I said.

'I was out some. And then I was on the phone.'

'I was out some myself.' I told her a lot of what had happened since I'd left her loft the previous afternoon, armed with the knowledge that Havermeyer's boy Danny had attended the Happy Hours Child Care Center. I told her why Barbara Ettinger had been killed, and I told her that Havermeyer's wife was blind.

'Jesus,' she said.

We talked a little more, and I asked her what she was doing about dinner. 'My client gave me a thousand dollars that I didn't do a thing to earn,' I said, 'and I feel a need to spend some of it frivolously before I piss the rest of it away on necessities.'

'I'm afraid tonight's out,' she said. 'I was just making myself a salad.'

'Well, do you want to hit a couple of high spots after you finish your salad? Anyplace but Blanche's Tavern is fine with me.'

There was a pause. Then she said, 'The thing is, Matthew, I have something on tonight.'

'Oh.'

'And it's not another date. I'm going to a meeting.'

'A meeting?'

'An AA meeting.'

'I see.'

'I'm an alcoholic, Matthew. I've got to face the fact and I've got to deal with it.'

'I didn't have the impression that you drank that much.'

'It's not how much you drink. It's what it does to you. I have blackouts. I have personality changes. I tell myself I'm not going to drink and I do. I tell myself I'm going to have one drink and the next morning the bottle's empty. I'm an alcoholic.'

'You were in AA before.'

'That's right.'

'I thought it didn't work for you.'

'Oh, it was working fine. Until I drank. This time I want to give it a chance.'

I thought for a minute. 'Well, I think that's great,' I said.

'You do?'

'Yes, I do,' I said, and meant it. 'I think it's terrific. I know it works for a lot of people and there's no reason why you can't make it work. You're going to a meeting tonight?'

'That's right. I was at one this afternoon.'

'I thought they only had them at night.'

'They have them all the time, and all over the city.'

'How often do you have to go?'

'You don't have to do anything. They recommend ninety

meetings in the first ninety days, but you can go to more. I have plenty of time. I can go to a lot of them.'

'That's great.'

'After the meeting this afternoon I was on the phone with somebody I knew when I was in the program last time. And I'm going to a meeting tonight, and that'll get me through today, and I'll have one day of sobriety.'

'Uh-huh.'

'That's how it's done, you see. You take it one day at a time.'

'That's great.' I wiped my forehead. It gets warm in a phone booth with the door closed. 'When do those meetings end? Ten or ten thirty something like that?'

'Ten o'clock.'

'Well, suppose –'

'But people generally go out for coffee afterward.'

'Uh-huh. Well, suppose I came by around eleven? Or later, if you figure you'll want to spend more than an hour over coffee.'

'I don't think that's a very good idea, Matthew.'

'Oh.'

'I want to give this a fair shot. I don't want to start sabotaging myself before I even get started.'

I said, 'Jan? I wasn't planning to come over and drink with you.'

'I know that.'

'Or in front of you, as far as that goes. I won't drink when I'm with you. That's no problem.'

'Because you can stop anytime you want to.'

'I can certainly not drink when we're together.'

Another pause, and when she spoke I could hear the strain in her voice. 'God,' she said. 'Matthew, darling, it's not quite that simple.'

'Oh?'

'One of the things they tell us is that we're powerless over people, places and things.'

'I don't know what that means.'

'It means to avoid those elements that can increase our desire to drink.'

'And I'm one of those elements?'

'I'm afraid so.'

I cracked the phone booth door, let a little air in. I said, 'Well, what does that mean, exactly? That we never see each other again?'

'Oh, God.'

'Just tell me the rules so I'll understand.'

'Jesus, God. I can't think in terms of never again. I can't even think in terms of never having a drink again. I'm supposed to take it a day at a time, so let's do this in terms of today.'

'You don't want to see me today.'

'Of *course* I want to see you today! Oh, Jesus. Look, if you want to come over around eleven –'

'No,' I said.

'What?'

'I said no. You were right the first time and I shouldn't be doing a number on you. I'm like my client, that's all. I've just got to adjust to a new reality. I think you're doing the right thing.'

'Do you really?'

'Yes. And if I'm somebody you ought to stay away from, I think that's what you'd better do for the time being. And if we're supposed to get together later on, well, it'll happen.'

A pause. Then, 'Thank you, Matthew.'

For what? I got out of the booth and went back upstairs to my room. I put on a clean shirt and tie and treated myself to a good steak dinner at the Slate. It's a hangout for cops from John Jay College and Midtown North, but I was lucky enough not to see anyone that I knew. I had a big meal all by myself, with a martini in front and a brandy afterward.

I walked back to Ninth Avenue and passed St Paul's. The church itself was closed now. I descended a narrow flight of steps to the basement. Not the big room in front where they have Bingo a couple nights a week, but a smaller room on the side where they have the meetings.

When you live in a neighborhood you know where different things are. Whether you have any interest in them or not.

I stood in front of the door for a minute or two. I felt a little lightheaded, a little congested in the chest. I decided that was probably from the brandy. It's a powerful stimulant. I'm not used to it, don't drink it often.

I opened the door and looked in. A couple dozen people sitting in folding chairs. A table holding a big coffee urn and a few stacks of Styrofoam cups. Some slogans taped to the wall – *Easy Does It, Keep It Simple.* The fucking wisdom of the ages.

She was probably in a room like this downtown. Some church basement in SoHo, say.

Best of luck, lady.

I stepped back, let the door shut, walked up the stairs. I had visions of the door opening behind me, people chasing after me and dragging me back. Nothing like that happened.

The tight feeling was still there in my chest.

The brandy, I told myself. Probably be a good idea to stay away from it. Stick to what you're used to. Stick to bourbon.

I went on over to Armstrong's. A little bourbon would take the edge off the brandy rush. A little bourbon would take the edge off almost anything.

EIGHT MILLION WAYS
TO DIE

In memory of
BILLY DUGAN
CLIFF
BOSTON JOHN
BAMBI
MARK THE DWARF
and
RED-HAIRED MAGGIE

The death of a beautiful woman is,
unquestionably, the most poetical topic in
the world.

EDGAR ALLAN POE

ONE

I saw her entrance. It would have been hard to miss. She had blonde hair that was close to white, the sort that's called towhead when it belongs to a child. Hers was plaited in heavy braids that she'd wrapped around her head and secured with pins. She had a high smooth forehead and prominent cheekbones and a mouth that was just a little too wide. In her western-style boots she must have run to six feet, most of her length in her legs. She was wearing designer jeans the color of burgundy and a short fur jacket the color of champagne. It had been raining on and off all day, and she wasn't carrying an umbrella or wearing anything on her head. Beads of water glinted like diamonds on her plaited hair.

She stood for a moment in the doorway getting her bearings. It was around three-thirty on a Wednesday afternoon, which is about as slow as it gets at Armstrong's. The lunch crowd was long gone and it was too early for the after-work people. In another fifteen minutes a couple of schoolteachers would stop in for a quick one, and then some nurses from Roosevelt Hospital whose shift ended at four, but for the moment there were three or four people at the bar and one couple finishing a carafe of wine at a front table and that was it. Except for me, of course, at my usual table in the rear.

She made me right away, and I caught the blue of her eyes all the way across the room. But she stopped at the bar to make sure before making her way between the tables to where I was sitting.

She said, 'Mr Scudder? I'm Kim Dakkinen. I'm a friend of Elaine Mardell's.'

'She called me. Have a seat.'

'Thank you.'

She sat down opposite me, placed her handbag on the table between us, took out a pack of cigarettes and a disposable lighter, then paused with the cigarette unlit to ask if it was all right if she smoked. I assured her that it was.

Her voice wasn't what I'd expected. It was quite soft, and the only accent it held was Midwestern. After the boots and the fur and the severe facial planes and the exotic name, I'd been anticipating something more out of a masochist's fantasy: harsh and stern and European. She was younger, too, than I'd have guessed at first glance. No more than twenty-five.

She lit her cigarette and positioned the lighter on top of the cigarette pack. The waitress, Evelyn, had been working days for the past two weeks because she'd landed a small part in an off-Broadway showcase. She always looked on the verge of a yawn. She came to the table while Kim Dakkinen was playing with her lighter. Kim ordered a glass of white wine. Evelyn asked me if I wanted more coffee, and when I said yes Kim said, 'Oh, are you having coffee? I think I'd like that instead of wine. Would that be all right?'

When the coffee arrived she added cream and sugar, stirred, sipped, and told me she wasn't much of a drinker, especially early in the day. But she couldn't drink it black the way I did, she'd never been able to drink black coffee, she had to have it sweet and rich, almost like dessert, and she supposed she was just lucky but she'd never had a weight problem, she could eat anything and never gain an ounce, and wasn't that lucky?

I agreed that it was.

Had I known Elaine long? For years, I said. Well, she hadn't really known her that long herself, in fact she hadn't even been in New York too terribly long, and she didn't know her that well either, but she thought Elaine was awfully nice. Didn't I agree? I agreed. Elaine was very levelheaded, too, very sensible, and that was something, wasn't it? I agreed it was something.

I let her take her time. She had acres of small talk, she smiled and held your eyes with hers when she talked, and she could probably have walked off with the Miss Congeniality award in any beauty contest she didn't win outright, and if it took her awhile to get to the point that was fine with me. I had no place else to go and nothing better to do.

She said, 'You used to be a policeman.'

'A few years back.'

'And now you're a private detective.'

'Not exactly.' The eyes widened. They were a very vivid blue, an unusual shade, and I wondered if she were wearing contact

146

lenses. The soft lenses sometimes do curious things to eye color, altering some shades, intensifying others.

'I don't have a license,' I explained. 'When I decided I didn't want to carry a badge anymore I didn't figure I wanted to carry a license, either.' Or fill out forms or keep records or check in with the tax collector. 'Anything I do is very unofficial.'

'But it's what you do? It's how you make your living?'

'That's right.'

'What do you call it? What you do.'

You could call it hustling a buck, except that I don't hustle a whole lot. The work finds me. I turn down more than I handle, and the jobs I accept are ones I can't think of a way to turn down. Right now I was wondering what this woman wanted from me, and what excuse I'd find to say no.

'I don't know what to call it,' I told her. 'You could say that I do favors for friends.'

Her face lit up. She'd been doing a lot of smiling ever since she walked in the door but this was the first smile that got as far as her eyes. 'Well, hell, that's perfect,' she said. 'I could use a favor. As far as that goes, I could use a friend.'

'What's the problem?'

She bought some thinking time by lighting another cigarette, then lowered her eyes to watch her hands as she centered the lighter on top of the pack. Her nails were well manicured, long but not awkward, lacquered the color of tawny port. She wore a gold ring set with a large square-cut green stone on the third finger of her left hand. She said, 'You know what I do. Same as Elaine.'

'So I gathered.'

'I'm a hooker.'

I nodded. She straightened in her seat, squared her shoulders, adjusted the fur jacket, opened the clasp at her throat. I caught a trace of her perfume. I'd smelled that spicy scent before but couldn't recall the occasion. I picked up my cup, finished my coffee.

'I want out.'

'Of the life?'

She nodded. 'I've been doing this for four years. I came here four years ago in July. August, September, October, November. Four years and four months. I'm twenty-three years old. That's young, isn't it?'

'Yes.'

'It doesn't feel so young.' She adjusted the jacket again,

refastened the clasp. Light glinted off her ring. 'When I got off the bus four years ago I had a suitcase in one hand and a denim jacket over my arm. Now I've got this. It's ranch mink.'

'It's very becoming.'

'I'd trade it for the old denim jacket,' she said, 'if I could have the years back. No, I wouldn't. Because if I had them back I'd just do the same thing with them, wouldn't I? Oh to be nineteen again and know what I know now, but the only way that could be is if I started tricking at fifteen, and then I'd be dead by now. I'm just rambling. I'm sorry.'

'No need.'

'I want to get out of the life.'

'And do what? Go back to Minnesota?'

'Wisconsin. No, I won't be going back. There's nothing there for me. Just because I want out doesn't mean I have to go back.'

'Okay.'

'I can make lots of trouble for myself that way. I reduce things to two alternatives, so if A is no good that means I'm stuck with B. But that's not right. There's the whole rest of the alphabet.'

She could always teach philosophy. I said, 'Where do I come in, Kim?'

'Oh. Right.'

I waited.

'I have this pimp.'

'And he won't let you leave?'

'I haven't said anything to him. I think maybe he knows, but I haven't said anything and *he* hasn't said anything and –' Her whole upper body trembled for a moment, and small beads of perspiration glistened on her upper lip.

'You're afraid of him.'

'How'd you guess?'

'Has he threatened you?'

'Not really.'

'What does that mean?'

'He never threatened me. But I *feel* threatened.'

'Have other girls tried to leave?'

'I don't know. I don't know much about his other girls. He's very different from other pimps. At least from the ones I know about.'

They're all different. Just ask their girls. 'How?' I asked her.

'He's more refined. Subdued.'

Sure. 'What's his name?'

'Chance.'

'First name or last name?'

'It's all anybody ever calls him. I don't know if it's a first name or a last name. Maybe it's neither, maybe it's a nickname. People in the life, they'll have different names for different occasions.'

'Is Kim your real name?'

She nodded. 'But I had a street name. I had a pimp before Chance, his name was Duffy. Duffy Green, he called himself, but he was also Eugene Duffy and he had another name he used sometimes that I forget.' She smiled at a memory. 'I was so green when he turned me out. He didn't pick me up right off the bus but he might as well.'

'He a black man?'

'Duffy? Sure. So is Chance. Duffy put me on the street. The Lexington Avenue stroll, and sometimes when it was hot there we'd go across the river to Long Island City.' She closed her eyes for a moment. When she opened them she said, 'I just got this rush of memory, what it was like on the street. My street name was Bambi. In Long Island City we did the johns in their cars. They would drive in from all over Long Island. On Lexington we had a hotel we could use. I can't believe I used to do that, I used to live like that. God, I was *green*! I wasn't innocent. I knew what I came to New York for, but I was green all right.'

'How long were you on the street?'

'It must have been five, six months. I wasn't very good. I had the looks and I could, you know, perform, but I didn't have street smarts. And a couple of times I had anxiety attacks and I couldn't function. Duffy gave me stuff but all it ever did was make me sick.'

'Stuff?'

'You know. Drugs.'

'Right.'

'Then he put me in this house, and that was better, but he didn't like it because he had less control that way. There was this big apartment near Columbus Circle and I went to work there like you would go to an office. I was in the house, I don't know, maybe another six months. Just about that. And then I went with Chance.'

'How did that happen?'

'I was with Duffy. We were at this bar. Not a pimp bar, a jazz club, and Chance came and sat at our table. We all three sat and talked, and then they left me at the table and went off and talked some more, and Duffy came back alone and said I was to go with Chance. I thought he meant I should do him, you know, like a trick, and I was pissed because this was supposed to be our evening together and why should I be working. See, I didn't take Chance for a pimp. Then he explained that I was going to be Chance's girl from now on. I felt like a car he just sold.'

'Is that what he did? Did he sell you to Chance?'

'I don't know what he did. But I went with Chance and it was all right. It was better than with Duffy. He took me out of that house and put me on a phone and it's been, oh, three years now.'

'And you want me to get you off the hook.'

'Can you do it?'

'I don't know. Maybe you can do it yourself. Haven't you said anything to him? Hinted at it, talked about it, something like that?'

'I'm afraid.'

'Of what?'

'That he'd kill me or mark me or something. Or that he'd talk me out of it.' She leaned forward, put her port-tipped fingers on my wrist. The gesture was clearly calculated but nonetheless effective for it. I breathed in her spicy scent and felt her sexual impact. I wasn't aroused and didn't want her but I could not be unaware of her sexual strength. She said, 'Can't you help me, Matt?' And, immediately, 'Do you mind if I call you Matt?'

I had to laugh. 'No,' I said. 'I don't mind.'

'I make money but I don't get to keep it. And I don't really make more money than I did on the street. But I have a little money.'

'Oh?'

'I have a thousand dollars.'

I didn't say anything. She opened her purse, found a plain white envelope, got a finger under the flap and tore it open. She took a sheaf of bills from it and placed them on the table between us.

'You could see him for me,' she said.

I picked up the money, held it in my hand. I was being offered the opportunity to serve as intermediary between a blonde whore and a black pimp. It was not a role I'd ever hungered for.

I wanted to hand the money back. But I was nine or ten days out of Roosevelt Hospital and I owed money there, and on the first of the month my rent would be due, and I hadn't sent anything to Anita and the boys in longer than I cared to remember. I had money in my wallet and more money in the bank but it didn't add up to much, and Kim Dakkinen's money was as good as anybody else's and easier to come by, and what difference did it make what she'd done to earn it?

I counted the bills. They were used hundreds and there were ten of them. I left five on the table in front of me and handed the other five to her. Her eyes widened a little and I decided she had to be wearing contacts. Nobody had eyes that color.

I said, 'Five now and five later. If I get you off the hook.'

'Deal,' she said, and grinned suddenly. 'You could have had the whole thousand in front.'

'Maybe I'll work better with an incentive. You want some more coffee?'

'If you're having some. And I think I'd like something sweet. Do they have desserts here?'

'The pecan pie's good. So's the cheesecake.'

'I love pecan pie,' she said. 'I have a terrible sweet tooth but I never gain an ounce. Isn't that lucky?'

TWO

There was a problem. In order for me to talk to Chance I had to find him, and she couldn't tell me how to do it.

'I don't know where he lives,' she said. 'Nobody does.'

'Nobody?'

'None of his girls. That's the big guessing game if a couple of us should happen to be together and he's not in the room. Trying to guess where Chance lives. One night I remember this girl Sunny and I were together and we were just goofing, coming up with one outrageous idea after another. Like he lives in this tenement in Harlem with his crippled mother, or he has this mansion in Sugar Hill, or he has a ranch house in the suburbs and commutes. Or he keeps a couple of suitcases in his car and lives out of them, just sleeping a couple hours a night at one of our apartments.' She thought a moment. 'Except he never sleeps when he's with me. If we do go to bed he'll just lie there afterward for a little while and then he's up and dressed and out. He said once he can't sleep if there's another person in the room.'

'Suppose you have to get in touch with him?'

'There's a number to call. But it's an answering service. You can call the number any time, twenty-four hours a day, and there's always an operator that answers. He always checks in with his service. If we're out or something, he'll check in with them every thirty minutes, every hour.'

She gave me the number and I wrote it in my notebook. I asked here where he garaged his car. She didn't know. Did she remember the car's license number?

She shook her head. 'I never notice things like that. His car is a Cadillac.'

'There's a surprise. Where does he hang out?'

'I don't know. If I want to reach him I leave a message. I don't go out looking for him. You mean is there a regular bar he drinks in? There's lot of places he'll go sometimes, but nothing regular.'

'What kind of things does he do?'

'What do you mean?'

'Does he go to ball games? Does he gamble? What does he do with himself?'

She considered the question. 'He does different things,' she said.

'What do you mean?'

'Depending who he's with. I like to go to jazz clubs so if he's with me that's where we'll go. I'm the one he calls if he's looking for that kind of an evening. There's another girl, I don't even know her, but they go to concerts. You know, classical music. Carnegie Hall and stuff. Another girl, Sunny, digs sports, and he'll take her to ball games.'

'How many girls has he got?'

'I don't know. There's Sunny and Nan and the girl who likes classical music. Maybe there's one or two others. Maybe more. Chance is very private, you know? He keeps things to himself.'

'The only name you've got for him is Chance?'

'That's right.'

'You've been with him, what, three years? And you've got half a name and no address and the number of his answering service.'

She looked down at her hands.

'How does he pick up the money?'

'From me, you mean? Sometimes he'll come by for it.'

'Does he call first?'

'Not necessarily. Sometimes. Or he'll call and tell me to bring it to him. At a coffee shop or a bar or something, or to be on a certain corner and he'll pick me up.'

'You give him everything you make?'

A nod. 'He found me my apartment, he pays the rent, the phone, all the bills. We'll shop for my clothes and he'll pay. He likes picking out my clothes. I give him what I make and he gives me back some, you know, for walking-around money.'

'You don't hold anything out?'

'Sure I do. How do you think I got the thousand dollars? But it's funny, I don't hold out much.'

The place was filling up with office workers by the time she left. By then she'd had enough coffee and switched to white wine. She had one glass of the wine and left half of it. I stayed with black coffee. I had her address and phone in my notebook along with Chance's answering service, but I didn't have a whole lot more than that.

On the other hand, how much did I need? Sooner or later I would get hold of him, and when I did I would talk to him, and if it broke right I'd throw a bigger scare into him than he'd managed to throw into Kim. And if not, well, I still had five hundred dollars more than I had when I woke up that morning.

After she left I finished my coffee and cracked one of her hundreds to pay my tab. Armstrong's is on Ninth Avenue between Fifty-seventh and Fifty-eighth, and my hotel is around the corner on Fifty-seventh Street. I went to it, checked the desk for mail and messages, then called Chance's service from the pay phone in the lobby. A woman answered on the third ring, repeating the four final digits of the number and asking if she could help me.

'I want to speak to Mr Chance,' I said.

'I expect to speak with him soon,' she said. She sounded middle-aged, with a chain smoker's rasp to her voice. 'May I take a message for him?'

I gave her my name and my phone number at the hotel. She asked what my call was in reference to. I told her it was personal.

When I hung up the phone I felt shaky, maybe from all the coffee I'd been sipping all day. I wanted a drink. I thought about going across the street to Polly's Cage for a quick one, or hitting the liquor store two doors down from Polly's and picking up a pint of bourbon. I could envision the booze, Jim Beam or J. W. Dant, some no-nonsense brown whiskey in a flat pint bottle.

I thought, C'mon, it's raining out there, you don't want to go out in the rain. I left the phone booth and turned toward the elevator instead of the front door and went up to my room. I locked myself in and pulled the chair over to the window and watched the rain. The urge to drink went away after a few minutes. Then it came back and then it went away again. It came and went for the next hour, winking on and off like a neon sign. I stayed where I was and watched the rain.

Around seven I picked up the phone in my room and called Elaine Mardell. Her machine answered, and when the beep sounded I said, 'This is Matt. I saw your friend and I wanted to thank you for the referral. Maybe one of these days I can return the favor.' I hung up and waited another half hour. Chance didn't return my call.

I wasn't especially hungry but I made myself go downstairs for something to eat. It had quit raining. I went over to the Blue Jay and ordered a hamburger and fries. A guy two tables over was having a beer with his sandwich and I decided to order one when the waiter brought my burger, but by the time that happened I'd changed my mind. I ate most of the hamburger and about half of the fries and drank two cups of coffee, then ordered cherry pie for dessert and ate most of it.

It was almost eight-thirty when I left there. I stopped at my hotel – no messages – and then walked the rest of the way to Ninth Avenue. There used to be a Greek bar on the corner, Antares and Spiro's, but it's a fruit and vegetable market now. I turned uptown and walked past Armstrong's and across Fifty-eighth Street, and when the light changed I crossed the avenue and walked on up past the hospital to St Paul's. I walked around the side and down a narrow flight of stairs to the basement. A cardboard sign hung from the doorknob, but you'd have to be looking for it to see it.

AA, it said.

They were just getting started when I walked in. There were three tables set up in a U, with people seated on either sides of the tables and perhaps a dozen other chairs arranged at the back. Another table off to the side held refreshments. I got a Styrofoam cup and drew coffee from the urn, then took a chair at the rear. A couple of people nodded to me and I nodded back.

The speaker was a fellow about my age. He was wearing a herringbone tweed jacket over a plaid flannel shirt. He told the story of his life from his first drink in his early teens until he came into the program and got sober four years ago. He was married and divorced a few times, cracked up several cars, lost jobs, hit a few hospitals. Then he stopped drinking and started going to meetings and things got better. '*Things* didn't get better,' he said, correcting himself. '*I* got better.'

They say that a lot. They say a lot of things a lot and you get to hear the same phrases over and over. The stories are pretty interesting, though. People sit up there in front of God and everybody and tell you the goddamnedest things.

He spoke for half an hour. Then they took a ten-minute break and passed the basket for expenses. I put in a dollar, then helped myself to another cup of coffee and a couple of oatmeal cookies. A fellow in an old army jacket greeted me by name. I remembered his name was Jim and returned the greeting. He asked me how things were going and I told him they were going all right.

'You're here and you're sober,' he said. 'That's the important thing.'

'I suppose.'

'Any day I don't take a drink is a good day. You're staying sober a day at a time. The hardest thing in the world is for an alcoholic to not drink and you're doing it.'

Except I wasn't. I'd been out of the hospital for nine or ten days. I would stay sober for two or three days and then I would pick up a drink. Mostly it was a drink or two drinks or three drinks and it stayed under control, but Sunday night I'd been bad drunk, drinking bourbon at a Blarney Stone on Sixth Avenue where I didn't figure to run into anybody I knew. I couldn't remember leaving the bar and didn't know how I got home, and Monday morning I had the shakes and a dry mouth and felt like walking death.

I didn't tell him any of this.

After ten minutes they started the meeting again and went around the room. People would say their names and say they were alcoholics and thank the speaker for his qualification, which is what they call the life story that he told. Then they would go on to talk about how they'd identified with the speaker, or recall some memory from their drinking days, or speak about some difficulty they were dealing with in the course of trying to lead a sober life. A girl not much older than Kim Dakkinen talked about problems with her lover, and a gay man in his thirties described a hassle he'd had that day with a customer at his travel agency. It made a funny story and got a lot of laughs.

One woman said, 'Staying sober is the easiest thing in the world. All you have to do is don't drink, go to meetings, and be willing to change your whole fucking life.'

When it got to me I said, 'My name is Matt. I'll pass.'

The meeting ended at ten. I stopped at Armstrong's on my way home and took a seat at the bar. They tell you to stay out of bars if you're trying not to drink but I'm comfortable there and the coffee's good. If I'm going to drink I'll drink and it doesn't matter where I am.

By the time I left there the early edition of the *News* was on the street. I picked it up and went back to my room. There was still no message from Kim Dakkinen's pimp. I called his service again, which established that he had received my message. I left another message and said that it was important I hear from him as soon as possible.

I showered and put on a robe and read the paper. I read the national and international stories but I can never really focus on them. Things have to be on a smaller scale and happen closer to home before I can relate to them.

There was plenty to relate to. Two kids in the Bronx threw a young woman in front of the D train. She'd lain flat and, although six cars passed over her before the motorman got the train stopped, she'd escaped without injury.

Down on West Street, near the Hudson docks, a prostitute had been murdered. Stabbed, the story said.

A housing authority cop in Corona was still in critical condition. Two days ago I'd read how he'd been attacked by two men who hit him with lengths of pipe and stole his gun. He had a wife and four children under ten.

The telephone didn't ring. I didn't really expect it to. I couldn't think of any reason for Chance to return my call outside of curiosity, and perhaps he remembered what that had done to the cat. I could have identified myself as a cop – Mr Scudder was easier to ignore than Police Officer Scudder, or Detective Scudder – but I didn't like to run that kind of game if I didn't have to. I was willing to let people jump to conclusions but reluctant to give them a push.

So I'd have to find him. That was just as well. It would give me something to do. In the meantime the messages I left with his service would fix my name in his head.

The elusive Mr Chance. You'd think he'd have a mobile phone unit in his pimpmobile, along with the bar and the fur upholstery and the pink velvet sun visor. All those touches of class.

I read the sports pages and then went back to the hooker stabbing in the Village. The story was very sketchy. They didn't have a name or any description beyond identifying the victim as being about twenty-five years old.

I called the *News* to see if they had a name for the victim and was told they weren't giving out that information. Pending notification of kin, I suppose. I called the Sixth Precinct but Eddie Koehler wasn't on duty and I couldn't think of anyone else at the Sixth who might know me. I got out my notebook and decided it was too late to call her, that half the women in the city were hookers and there was no reason to suppose she'd been the one to get sliced up underneath the West Side Highway. I put the notebook away, and ten minutes later I dug it out again and dialed her number.

I said, 'It's Matt Scudder, Kim. I just wondered if you happened to speak to your friend since I saw you.'

'No, I haven't. Why?'

'I thought I might reach him through his service. I don't think he's going to get back to me, so tomorrow I'll have to go out and look for him. You haven't said anything to him about wanting out?'

'Not a word.'

'Good. If you see him before I do, just act as though nothing's changed. And if he calls and wants you to meet him somewhere, call me right away.'

'At the number you gave me?'

'Right. If you reach me I'll be able to keep the appointment in your place. If not, just go ahead and play it straight.'

I talked a little while longer, calming her down some after having alarmed her with the call in the first place. At least I knew she hadn't died on West Street. At least I could sleep easy.

Sure. I killed the light and got into bed and just lay there for a long time, and then I gave up and got up and read the paper again. The thought came to me that a couple of drinks would take the edge off and let me sleep. I couldn't banish the thought but I could make myself stay where I was, and when four o'clock came I told myself to forget it because the bars were closed now. There was an after-hours on Eleventh Avenue but I conveniently forgot about it.

I turned off the light and got in bed again and thought about the dead hooker and the housing cop and the woman who'd been run over by the subway train, and I wondered why anyone would think it a good idea to stay sober in this city, and I held onto that thought and fell asleep with it.

THREE

I got up around ten-thirty, surprisingly well rested after six hours of skimming the surface of sleep. I showered and shaved, had coffee and a roll for breakfast, and went over to St Paul's. Not to the basement this time but to the church proper, where I sat in a pew for ten minutes or so before lighting a couple of candles and slipping fifty dollars into the poor box. At the post office on Sixtieth Street I bought a two-hundred-dollar money order and an envelope with the stamp embossed. I mailed the money order to my ex-wife in Syosset. I tried to write a note to enclose but it came out apologetic. The money was too little and too late but she would know that without my having to tell her. I wrapped the money order in a blank sheet of paper and mailed it that way.

It was a gray day, on the cool side, with the threat of more rain. There was a raw wind blowing and it cut around corners like a scatback. In front of the Coliseum a man was chasing his hat and cursing, and I reached up reflexively and gave a tug to the brim of mine.

I walked most of the way to my bank before deciding I didn't have enough of Kim's advance left to necessitate formal financial transactions. I went to my hotel instead and paid half of the coming month's rent on account. By then I had only one of the hundreds intact and I cracked that into tens and twenties while I was at it.

Why hadn't I taken the full thousand in front? I remembered what I'd said about an incentive. Well, I had one.

My mail was routine – a couple of circulars, a letter from my congressman. Nothing I had to read.

No message from Chance. Not that I'd expected one.

I called his service and left another message just for the hell of it.

I got out of there and stayed out all afternoon. I took the

subway a couple of times but mostly walked. It kept threatening to rain but it kept not raining, and the wind got even more of an edge to it but never did get my hat. I hit two police precinct houses and a few coffee shops and half a dozen gin mills. I drank coffee in the coffee shops and Coca-Cola in the bars, and I talked to a few people and made a couple of notes. I called my hotel desk a few times. I wasn't expecting a call from Chance but I wanted to be in touch in case Kim called. But no one had called me. I tried Kim's number twice and both times her machine answered. Everybody's got one of those machines and someday all the machines will start dialing and talk to each other. I didn't leave any messages.

Toward the end of the afternoon I ducked into a Times Square theater. They had two Clint Eastwood movies paired, ones where he's a rogue cop who settles things by shooting the bad guys. The audience looked to be composed almost entirely of the sort of people he was shooting. They cheered wildly every time he blew somebody away.

I had pork fried rice and vegetables at a Cuban Chinese place on Eighth Avenue, checked my hotel desk again, stopped at Armstrong's and had a cup of coffee. I got into a conversation at the bar and thought I'd stay there awhile, but by eight-thirty I'd managed to get out the door and across the street and down the stairs to the meeting.

The speaker was a housewife who used to drink herself into a stupor while her husband was at his office and the kids were at school. She told how her kid would find her passed out on the kitchen floor and she convinced him it was a yoga exercise to help her back. Everybody laughed.

When it was my turn I said, 'My name is Matt. I'll just listen tonight.'

Kelvin Small's is on Lenox Avenue at 127th Street. It's a long narrow room with a bar running the length of it and a row of banquette tables opposite the bar. There's a small bandstand all the way at the back, and on it two dark-skinned blacks with close-cropped hair and horn-rimmed sunglasses and Brooks Brothers suits played quiet jazz, one on a small upright piano, the other using brushes on cymbals. They looked and sounded like half of the old Modern Jazz Quartet.

It was easy for me to hear them because the rest of the room went silent when I cleared the threshold. I was the only white man in the room and everybody stopped for a long look at me.

There were a couple of white women, seated with black men at the banquette tables, and there were two black women sharing a table, and there must have been two dozen men in every shade but mine.

I walked the length of the room and went into the men's room. A man almost tall enough for pro basketball was combing his straightened hair. The scent of his pomade vied with the sharp reek of marijuana. I washed my hands and rubbed them together under one of those hot-air dryers. The tall man was still working on his hair when I left.

Conversation died again when I emerged from the men's room. I walked toward the front again, walked slowly and let my shoulders roll. I couldn't be sure about the musicians, but aside from them I figured there wasn't a man in the room who hadn't taken at least one felony bust. Pimps, drug dealers, gamblers, policy men. Nature's noblemen.

A man on the fifth stool from the front caught my eye. It took a second to place him because when I knew him years ago he had straight hair, but now he was wearing it in a modified Afro. His suit was lime green and his shoes were the skin of some reptile, probably an endangered species.

I moved my head toward the door and walked on past him and out. I walked two doors south on Lenox and stood next to a streetlamp. Two or three minutes went by and he came on out, walking loose-limbed and easy. 'Hey, Matthew,' he said, and extended his hand for a slap. 'How's my man?'

I didn't slap his hand. He looked down at it, up at me, rolled his eyes, gave his head an exaggerated shake, clapped his hands together, dusted them against his trouser legs, then placed them on his slim hips. 'Been some time,' he said. 'They run out of your brand downtown? Or do you just come to Harlem to use the little boy's room?'

'You're looking prosperous, Royal.'

He preened a little. His name was Royal Waldron and I once knew a black cop with a bullet head who rang changes through Royal Flush to Flush Toilet and called him The Crapper. He said, 'Well, I buy and sell. You know.'

'I know.'

'Give the folks an honest deal and you will never miss a meal. That's a rhyme my mama taught me. How come you uptown, Matthew?'

'I'm looking for a guy.'

'Maybe you found him. You off the force these days?'

'For some years now.'

'And you lookin' to buy something? What do you want and what can you spend?'

'What are you selling?'

'Most anything.'

'Business still good with all these Colombians?'

'Shit,' he said, and one hand brushed the front of his pants. I suppose he had a gun in the waistband of the lime green pants. There were probably as many handguns as people in Kelvin Small's. 'Them Colombians be all right,' he said. 'You just don't ever want to cheat them is all. You didn't come up here to buy stuff.'

'No.'

'What you want, man?'

'I'm looking for a pimp.'

'Shit, you just walked past twenty of 'em. And six, seven hoes.'

'I'm looking for a pimp named Chance.'

'Chance.'

'You know him?'

'I might know who he is.'

I waited. A man in a long coat was walking along the block, stopping at each storefront. He might have been looking in the windows except that you couldn't; every shop had steel shutters that descended like garage doors at the close of business. The man stopped in front of each closed store and studied the shutters as if they held meaning for him.

'Window shopping,' Royal said.

A blue-and-white police car cruised by, slowed. The two uniformed officers within looked us over. Royal wished them a good evening. I didn't say anything and neither did they. When the car drove off he said, 'Chance don't come here much.'

'Where would I find him?'

'Hard to say. He'll turn up anyplace but it might be the last place you would look. He don't hang out.'

'So they tell me.'

'Where you been lookin'?'

I'd been to a coffee shop on Sixth Avenue and Forty-fifth Street, a piano bar in the Village, a pair of bars in the West Forties. Royal took all this in and nodded thoughtfully.

'He wouldn't be at Muffin-Burger,' he said, 'on account he don't run no girls on the street. That I *know* of. All the same, he might be there anyway, you dig? Just to *be* there. What I say, he'll turn up anywhere, but he don't hang out.'

'Where should I look for him, Royal?'

He named a couple of places. I'd been to one of them already and had forgotten to mention it. I made a note of the others. I said, 'What's he like, Royal?'

'Well, shit,' he said. 'He a pimp, man.'

'You don't like him.'

'He ain't to like or not like. My friends is business friends, Matthew, and Chance and I got no business with each other. We don't neither of us buy what the other be sellin'. He don't want to buy no stuff and I don't want to buy no pussy.' His teeth showed in a nasty little smile. 'When you the man with all the candy, you don't never have to pay for no pussy.'

One of the places Royal mentioned was in Harlem, on St Nicholas Avenue. I walked over to 125th Street. It was wide and busy and well lit, but I was starting to feel the not entirely irrational paranoia of a white man on a black street.

I turned north at St Nicholas and walked a couple of blocks to the Club Cameroon. It was a low-rent version of Kelvin Small's with a jukebox instead of live music. The men's room was filthy, and in the stall toilet someone was inhaling briskly. Snorting cocaine, I suppose.

I didn't recognize anyone at the bar. I stood there and drank a glass of club soda and looked at fifteen or twenty black faces reflected in the mirrored back bar. It struck me, not for the first time that evening, that I could be looking at Chance and not knowing it. The description I had for him would fit a third of the men present and stretch to cover half of those remaining. I hadn't been able to see a picture of him. My cop contacts didn't recognize the name, and if it was his last name he didn't have a yellow sheet in the files.

The men on either side had turned away from me. I caught sight of myself in the mirror, a pale man in a colorless suit and a gray topcoat. My suit could have stood pressing and my hat would have looked no worse if the wind had taken it, and here I stood, isolated between these two fashion plates with their wide shoulders and exaggerated lapels and fabric-covered buttons. The pimps used to line up at Phil Kronfeld's Broadway store for suits like that, but Kronfeld's was closed and I had no idea where they went these days. Maybe I should find out, maybe Chance had a charge account and I could trace him that way.

163

Except people in the life didn't have charges because they did everything with cash. They'd even buy cars with cash, bop into Potamkin's and count out hundred dollar bills and take home a Cadillac.

The man on my right crooked a finger at the bartender. 'Put it right in the same glass,' he said. 'Let it build up a taste.' The bartender filled his glass with a jigger of Hennessy and four or five ounces of cold milk. They used to call that combination a White Cadillac. Maybe they still do.

Maybe I should have tried Potamkin's.

Or maybe I should have stayed home. My presence was creating tension and I could feel it thickening the air in the little room. Sooner or later someone would come over and ask me what the fuck I thought I was doing there and it was going to be hard to come up with an answer.

I left before it could happen. A gypsy cab was waiting for the light to change. The door on my side was dented and one fender was crumpled, and I wasn't sure what that said about the driver's ability. I got in anyway.

Royal had mentioned another place on West Ninety-sixth and I let the cab drop me there. It was after two by this time and I was starting to tire. I went into yet another bar where yet another black man was playing piano. This particular piano sounded out of tune, but it might have been me. The crowd was a fairly even mix of black and white. There were a lot of interracial couples, but the white women who were paired with black men looked more like girlfriends than hookers. A few of the men were dressed flashily, but nobody sported the full pimp regalia I'd seen a mile and a half to the north. If the room carried an air of fast living and cash transactions, it was nevertheless subtler and more muted than the Harlem clubs, or the ones around Times Square.

I put a dime in the phone and called my hotel. No messages. The desk clerk that night was a mulatto with a cough-syrup habit that never seemed to keep him from functioning. He could still do the *Times* crossword puzzle with a fountain pen. I said, 'Jacob, do me a favor. Call this number and ask to speak to Chance.'

I gave him the number. He read it back and asked if that was Mr Chance. I said just Chance.

'And if he comes to the phone?'

'Just hang up.'

I went to the bar and almost ordered a beer but made it a Coke instead. A minute later the phone rang and a kid answered it. He looked like a college student. He called out, asking if there was anyone there named Chance. Nobody responded. I kept an eye on the bartender. If he recognized the name he didn't show it. I'm not even certain he was paying attention.

I could have played that little game at every bar I'd been to, and maybe it would have been worth the effort. But it had taken me three hours to think of it.

I was some detective. I was drinking all the Coca-Cola in Manhattan and I couldn't find a goddamned pimp. My teeth would rot before I got hold of the son of a bitch.

There was a jukebox, and one record ended and another began, something by Sinatra, and it triggered something, made some mental connection for me. I left my Coke on the bar and caught a cab going downtown on Columbus Avenue. I got off at the corner of Seventy-second Street and walked half a block west to Poogan's Pub. The clientele was a little less Superspade and a little more Young Godfather but I wasn't really looking for Chance anyway. I was looking for Danny Boy Bell.

He wasn't there. The bartender said, 'Danny Boy? He was in earlier. Try the Top Knot, that's just across Columbus. He's there when he's not here.'

And he was there, all right, on a bar stool all the way at the back. I hadn't seen him in years but he was no mean trick to recognize. He hadn't grown and he wasn't any darker.

Danny Boy's parents were both dark-skinned blacks. He had their features but not their color. He was an albino, as unpigmented as a white mouse. He was quite slender and very short. He claimed to be five two but I've always figured he was lying by an inch and a half or so.

He was wearing a three-piece banker's-stripe suit and the first white shirt I'd seen in a long time. His tie showed muted red and black stripes. His black shoes were highly polished. I don't think I've ever seen him without a suit and tie, or with scuffed shoes.

He said, 'Matt Scudder. By God, if you wait long enough everybody turns up.'

'How are you, Danny?'

'Older. It's been years. You're less than a mile away and when's the last time we saw each other? It has been, if you'll excuse the expression, a coon's age.'

'You haven't changed much.'

He studied me for a moment. 'Neither have you,' he said, but his voice lacked conviction. It was a surprisingly normal voice to issue from such an unusual person, of medium depth, unaccented. You expected him to sound like Johnny in the old Philip Morris commercials.

He said, 'You were just in the neighborhood? Or you came looking for me?'

'I tried Poogan's first. They told me you might be here.'

'I'm flattered. Purely a social visit, of course.'

'Not exactly.'

'Why don't we take a table? We can talk of old times and dead friends. And whatever mission brought you here.'

The bars Danny Boy favored kept a bottle of Russian vodka in the freezer. That was what he drank and he liked it ice-cold but without any ice cubes rattling around in his glass and diluting his drink. We settled in at a booth in the back and a speedy little waitress brought his drink of choice and Coke for me. Danny Boy lowered his eyes to my glass, than raised them to my face.

'I've been cutting back some,' I said.

'Makes good sense.'

'I guess.'

'Moderation,' he said. 'I tell you, Matt, those old Greeks knew it all. Moderation.'

He drank half his drink. He was good for perhaps eight like it in the course of a day. Call it a quart a day, all in a body that couldn't go more than a hundred pounds, and I'd never seen him show the effects. He never staggered, never slurred his words, just kept on keeping on.

So? What did that have to do with me?

I sipped my Coke.

We sat there and told each other stories. Danny Boy's business, if he had one, was information. Everything you told him got filed away in his mind, and by putting bits of data together and moving them around he brought in enough dollars to keep his shoes shined and his glass full. He would bring people together, taking a slice of their action for his troubles. His own hands stayed clean while he held a limited partnership in a lot of short-term enterprises, most of them faintly illicit. When I was on the force he'd been one of my best sources, an unpaid snitch who took his recompense in information.

He said, 'You remember Lou Rudenko? Louie the Hat, they call him.' I said I did. 'You hear about his mother?'

'What about her?'

'Nice old Ukrainian lady, still lived in the old neighborhood on East Ninth or Tenth, wherever it was. Been a widow for years. Must have been seventy, maybe closer to eighty. Lou's got to be what, fifty?'

'Maybe.'

'Doesn't matter. Point is this nice little old lady has a gentleman friend, a widower the same age as she is. He's over there a couple nights a week and she cooks Ukrainian food for him and maybe they go to a movie if they can find one that doesn't have people fucking all over the screen. Anyway, he comes over one afternoon, he's all excited, he found a television set on the street. Somebody put it out for the garbage. He says people are crazy, they throw perfectly good things away, and he's handy at fixing things and her own set's on the fritz and this one's a color set and twice the size of hers and maybe he can fix it for her.'

'And?'

'And he plugs it in and turns it on to see what happens, and what happens is it blows up. He loses an arm and an eye and Mrs Rudenko, she's right in front of it when it goes, she's killed instantly.'

'What was it, a bomb?'

'You got it. You saw the story in the paper?'

'I must have missed it.'

'Well, it was five, six months ago. What they worked out was somebody rigged the set with a bomb and had it delivered to somebody else. Maybe it was a mob thing and maybe it wasn't, because all the old man knew was what block he picked the set up on, and what does that tell you? Thing is, whoever received the set was suspicious enough to put it right out with the garbage, and it wound up killing Mrs Rudenko. I saw Lou and it was a funny thing because he didn't know who to get mad at. "It's this fucking city," he told me. "It's this goddamn fucking city." But what sense does that make? You live in the middle of Kansas and a tornado comes and picks your house up and spreads it over Nebraska. That's an act of God, right?'

'That's what they say.'

'In Kansas God uses tornadoes. In New York he uses gaffed television sets. Whoever you are, God or anybody else, you work with the materials at hand. You want another Coke?'

'Not right now.'

'What can I do for you?'

'I'm looking for a pimp.'

167

'Diogenes was looking for an honest man. You have more of a field to choose from.'

'I'm looking for a particular pimp.'

'They're all particular. Some of them are downright finicky. Has he got a name?'

'Chance.'

'Oh, sure,' Danny Boy said. 'I know Chance.'

'You know how I can get in touch with him?'

He frowned, picked up his empty glass, put it down. 'He doesn't hang out anywhere,' he said.

'That's what I keep hearing.'

'It's the truth. I think a man should have a home base. I'm always here or at Poogan's. You're at Jimmy Armstrong's, or at least you were the last I heard.'

'I still am.'

'See? I keep tabs on you even when I don't see you. Chance. Let me think. What's today, Thursday?'

'Right. Well, Friday morning.'

'Don't get technical. What do you want with him, if you don't mind the question?'

'I want to talk to him.'

'I don't know where he is now but I might know where he'll be eighteen or twenty hours from now. Let me make a call. If that girl shows up, order me another drink, will you? And whatever you're having.'

I managed to catch the waitress's eye and told her to bring Danny Boy another glass of vodka. She said, 'Right. And another Coke for you?'

I'd been getting little drink urges off and on ever since I sat down and now I got a strong one. My gorge rose at the thought of another Coke. I told her to make it ginger ale this time. Danny Boy was still on the phone when she brought the drinks. She put the ginger ale in front of me and the vodka on his side of the table. I sat there and tried not to look at it and my eyes couldn't find anywhere else to go. I wished he would get back to the table and drink the damn thing.

I breathed in and breathed out and sipped my ginger ale and kept my hands off his vodka and eventually he came back to the table. 'I was right,' he said. 'He'll be at the Garden tomorrow night.'

'Are the Knicks back? I thought they were still on the road.'

'Not the main arena. Matter of fact I think there's some rock concert. Chance'll be at the Felt Forum for the Friday night fights.'

'He always goes?'

'Not always, but there's a welterweight named Kid Bascomb at the top of the prelim card and Chance has an interest in the young man.'

'He owns a piece of him?'

'Could be, or maybe it's just an intellectual interest. What are you smiling at?'

'The idea of a pimp with an intellectual interest in a welterweight.'

'You never met Chance.'

'No.'

'He's not the usual run.'

'That's the impression I'm getting.'

'Point is, Kid Bascomb's definitely fighting, which doesn't mean Chance'll definitely be there, but I'd call it odds on. You want to talk to him, you can do it for the price of a ticket.'

'How will I know him?'

'You never met him? No, you just said you didn't. You wouldn't recognize him if you saw him?'

'Not in a fight crowd. Not when half the house is pimps and players.'

He thought about it. 'This conversation you're going to have with Chance,' he said. 'Is it going to upset him a lot?'

'I hope not.'

'What I'm getting at, is he likely to have a powerful resentment against whoever points him out?'

'I don't see why he should.'

'Then what it's going to cost you, Matt, is the price of not one but two tickets. Be grateful it's an off-night at the Forum and not a title bout at the Main Garden. Ringside shouldn't be more than ten or twelve dollars, say fifteen at the outside. Thirty dollars at the most for our tickets.'

'You're coming with me?'

'Why not? Thirty dollars for tickets and fifty for my time. I trust your budget can carry the weight?'

'It can if it has to.'

'I'm sorry I have to ask you for money. If it were a track meet I wouldn't charge you a cent. But I've never cared for boxing. If it's any consolation, I'd want at least a hundred dollars to attend a hockey game.'

'I guess that's something. You want to meet me there?'

'Out in front. At nine – that should give us plenty of lee-way. How does that sound?'

'Fine.'

'I'll see if I can't wear something distinctive,' he said, 'so that you'll have no trouble recognizing me.'

FOUR

He wasn't hard to recognize. His suit was a dove gray flannel and with it he wore a bright red vest over a black knit tie and another white dress shirt. He had sunglasses on, dark lenses in metal frames. Danny Boy contrived to sleep when the sun was out – neither his eyes nor his skin could take it – and wore dark glasses even at night unless he was in a dimly lit place like Poogan's or the Top Knot. Years ago he'd told me that he wished the world had a dimmer switch and you could just turn the whole thing down a notch or two. I remember thinking at the time that that was what whiskey did. It dimmed the lights and lowered the volume and rounded the corners.

I admired his outfit. He said, 'You like the vest? I haven't worn it in ages. I wanted to be visible.'

I already had our tickets. The ringside price was $15. I'd bought a pair of $4.50 seats that would have put us closer to God than to the ring. They got us through the gate, and I showed them to an usher down front and slipped a folded bill into his hand. He put us in a pair of seats in the third row.

'Now I might have to move you gentlemen,' he said, 'but probably not, and I guarantee you ringside.'

After he'd moved off Danny Boy said, 'There's always a way, isn't there? What did you give him?'

'Five dollars.'

'So the seats set you back fourteen dollars instead of thirty. What do you figure he makes in a night?'

'Not much on a night like this. When the Knicks or Rangers play he might make five times his salary in tips. Of course he might have to pay somebody off.'

'Everybody's got an angle,' he said.

'It looks that way.'

'I mean everybody. Even me.'

That was my cue. I gave him two twenties and a ten. He put

the money away, then took his first real look around the auditorium. 'Well, I don't see him,' he said, 'but he'll probably just show for the Bascomb fight. Let me take a little walk.'

'Sure.'

He left his seat and moved around the room. I did some looking around myself, not trying to spot Chance but getting a sense of the crowd. There were a lot of men who might have been in the Harlem bars the previous night, pimps and dealers and gamblers and other uptown racket types, most of them accompanied by women. There were some white mob types; they were wearing leisure suits and gold jewelry and they hadn't brought dates. In the less expensive seats the crowd was the sort of mixed bag that turns up for any sporting event, black and white and Hispanic, singles and couples and groups, eating hot dogs and drinking beer from paper cups and talking and joking and, occasionally, having a look at the action in the ring. Here and there I saw a face straight out of any OTB horse room, one of those knobby on-the-come Broadway faces that only gamblers get. But there weren't too many of those. Who bets prizefights anymore?

I turned around and looked at the ring. Two Hispanic kids, one light and one dark, were being very careful not to risk serious injury. They looked like lightweights to me, and the fair-skinned kid was rangy with a lot of reach. I started getting interested, and in the final round the darker of the two figured out how to get in under the other kid's jab. He was working the body pretty good when they rang the bell. He got the decision, and most of the booing came from one spot in the audience. The other boy's friends and family, I suppose.

Danny Boy had returned to his seat during the final round. A couple minutes after the decision, Kid Bascomb climbed over the ropes and did a little shadowboxing. Moments later his opponent entered the ring. Bascomb was very dark, very muscular, with sloping shoulders and a powerful chest. His body might have been oiled the way the light glinted on it. The boy he was fighting was an Italian kid from South Brooklyn named Vito Canelli. He was carrying some fat around the waist and he looked soft as bread dough, but I had seen him before and knew him for a smart fighter.

Danny Boy said, 'Here he comes. Center aisle.'

I turned and looked. The same usher who'd taken my five bucks was leading a man and woman to their seats. She was about five five, with shoulder-length auburn hair and skin like fine porcelain. He was six one or two, maybe 190 pounds. Broad shoulders, narrow waist, trim hips. His hair was natural, short rather than long, and his skin was a rich brown. He was wearing a camel's-hair blazer and brown flannel slacks. He looked like a professional athlete or a hot lawyer or an up-and-coming black businessman.

I said, 'You're sure?'

Danny Boy laughed. 'Not your usual pimp, is he? I'm sure. That's Chance. I hope your friend didn't put us in his seats.'

He hadn't. Chance and his girl were in the first row and a good deal closer to the center. They took their seats and he tipped the usher, acknowledged greetings from some of the other spectators, then approached Kid Bascomb's corner and said something to the fighter and his handlers. They huddled together for a moment. Then Chance returned to his seat.

'I think I'll leave now,' Danny Boy said. 'I don't really want to watch these two fools pummel each other. I hope you don't need me to introduce you?' I shook my head. 'Then I'll slip out before the mayhem commences. In the ring, that is. Will he have to know I fingered him, Matt?'

'He won't hear it from me.'

'Good. If I can be of further service –'

He made his way up the aisle. He probably wanted a drink and the bars in Madison Square Garden don't stock ice-cold Stolichnaya.

The announcer was introducing the fighters, calling out their ages and weights and hometowns. Bascomb was twenty-two and undefeated. Canelli didn't figure to change his status tonight.

There were two seats empty next to Chance. I thought about taking one but stayed where I was. The warning buzzer sounded, then the bell for round one. It was a slow, thoughtful round, with neither fighter anxious to commit himself. Bascomb jabbed nicely but Canelli managed to be out of range most of the time. Nobody landed anything solid.

The pair next to Chance were still empty at the round's end. I walked over there and sat next to him. He was looking very intently at the ring. He must have been aware of my presence but didn't indicate it if he was.

I said, 'Chance? My name is Scudder.'

He turned, looked at me. His eyes were brown flecked with gold. I thought of my client's eyes, that unreal blue. He'd been at her apartment last night while I was barhopping, dropped in unannounced to pick up some money. She'd told me about it

173

earlier, called me at the hotel around noon. 'I was afraid,' she'd said. 'I thought, suppose he asks about you, asks me some kind of questions. But it was cool.'

Now he said, 'Matthew Scudder. You left some messages with my service.'

'You didn't return my calls.'

'I don't know you. I don't call people I don't know. And you've been asking around town for me.' His voice was deep and resonant. It sounded trained, as if he'd gone to broadcasting school. 'I want to watch this fight,' he said.

'All I want is a few minutes conversation.'

'Not during the fight and not between rounds.' A frown came and went. 'I want to be able to concentrate. I bought that seat you're sitting in, you see, so I'd have some privacy.'

The warning buzzer sounded. Chance turned, focused his eyes on the ring. Kid Bascomb was standing and his seconds were hauling the stool out of the ring. 'Go back to your seat,' Chance said, 'and I'll talk to you after the fight ends.'

'It's a ten-rounder?'

'It won't go ten.'

It didn't. In the third or fourth round Kid Bascomb started getting to Canelli, punishing him with the jab, putting a couple of combinations together. Canelli was smart but the Kid was young and fast and strong, with a way of moving that reminded me a little of Sugar Ray. Robinson, not Leonard. In the fifth round he staggered Canelli with a short right hand to the heart and if I'd had a bet on the Italian I'd have written it off then and there.

Canelli looked strong by the end of the round but I'd seen the expression on his face when the blow landed, and I wasn't surprised a round later when Kid Bascomb dropped him with a looping left hook. He was up at three and took an eight-count, and then the Kid was all over him, hitting him with everything but the ring posts. Canelli went down again and got right up and the ref jumped between the two of them and looked in Canelli's eyes and stopped it.

There was some halfhearted booing from the diehards who never want a fight stopped, and one of Canelli's cornermen was insisting his fighter could have gone on, but Canelli himself seemed just as happy the show was over. Kid Bascomb did a little war dance and took his bows, then climbed nimbly over the ropes and left the ring.

On his way out he stopped to talk to Chance. The girl with the auburn hair sat forward and rested a hand on the fighter's glossy black arm. Chance and the Kid talked for a moment or two, and then the Kid headed for his dressing room.

I left my seat, walked over to Chance and the girl. They were standing by the time I got there. He said, 'We're not staying for the main bout. If you'd planned on watching it —'

The top of the card matched two middleweights, a Panamanian contender and a black boy from South Philadelphia with a reputation as a spoiler. It would probably be a good bout, but that wasn't what I'd come for. I told him I was ready to leave.

'Then why don't you come with us,' he suggested. 'I have a car nearby.' He headed up the aisle with the girl at his side. A few people said hello to him and some of them told him that the Kid had looked good in there. Chance didn't say much in reply. I tagged along, and when we got outside and hit the fresh air I realized for the first time how stale and smoky it had been inside the Garden.

On the street he said, 'Sonya, this is Matthew Scudder. Mr Scudder, Sonya Hendryx.'

'It's nice to meet you,' she said, but I didn't believe her. Her eyes told me she was withholding judgment until Chance cued her in one way or the other. I wondered if she was the Sunny that Kim had mentioned, the sports fan Chance took to ball games. I wondered, too, if I would have pegged her for a hooker if I'd met her in other circumstances. I couldn't see anything unmistakably whorish about her, and yet she didn't look at all out of place hanging on a pimp's arm.

We walked a block south and half a block east to a parking lot where Chance collected his car and tipped the attendant enough to get thanked with more than the usual degree of enthusiasm. The car surprised me, just as the clothes and manner had surprised me earlier. I was expecting a pimpmobile, complete with custom paint and interior and the usual wretched excess, and what showed up was a Seville, the small Cadillac, silver on the outside with a black leather interior. The girl got in back, Chance sat behind the wheel, and I sat in front next to him.

The ride was smooth, silent. The car's interior smelled of wood polish and leather. Chance said, 'There's a victory party for Kid Bascomb. I'll drop Sonya there now and join her after we've concluded our business. What did you think of the fight?'

'I thought it was hard to figure.'

'Oh?'

'It looked fixed but the knockout looked real.'

He glanced at me, and I saw interest in his gold-flecked eyes for the first time. 'What makes you say that?'

'Canelli had an opening twice in the fourth round and he didn't follow it up either time. He's too smart a fighter for that. But he was trying to get through the sixth and he couldn't. At least that's how it looked from my seat.'

'You ever box, Scudder?'

'Two fights at the Y when I was twelve or thirteen years old. Balloon gloves, protective headgear, two-minute rounds. I was too low and clumsy for it, I could never manage to land a punch.'

'You have an eye for the sport.'

'Well, I guess I've seen a lot of fights.'

He was silent for a moment. A cab cut us off and he braked smoothly, avoiding a collision. He didn't swear or hit the horn. He said, 'Canelli was set to go in the eighth. He was supposed to give the Kid his best fight until then, but not to get out in front or the knockout might not look right. That's why he held back in round four.'

'But the Kid didn't know it was set up.'

'Of course not. Most of his fights have been straight until tonight, but a fighter like Canelli could be dangerous to him, and why chance a bad mark on his record at this stage? He gains experience fighting Canelli and he gains confidence by beating him.' We were on Central Park West now, heading uptown. 'The knockout was real. Canelli would have gone in the tank in the eighth, but we hoped the Kid might get us home early, and you saw him do that. What do you think of him?'

'He's a comer.'

'I agree.'

'Sometimes he telegraphs the right. In the fourth round –'

'Yes,' he said. 'They've worked with him on that. The problem is that he generally manages to get away with it.'

'Well, he wouldn't have gotten by with it tonight. Not if Canelli had been looking to win.'

'Yes. Well, perhaps it's as well that he wasn't.'

We talked boxing until we got to 104th Street, where Chance turned the car around in a careful U-turn and pulled up next to a fire hydrant. He killed the motor but left the keys. 'I'll be right down,' he said, 'after I've seen Sonya upstairs.'

She hadn't said a word since she told me it was nice to meet me. He walked around the car and opened the door for her, and they strolled to the entrance of one of the two large apartment buildings that fronted on that block. I wrote the address in my notebook. In no more than five minutes he was back behind the wheel and we were heading downtown again.

Neither of us spoke for half a dozen blocks. Then he said, 'You wanted to talk to me. It doesn't have anything to do with Kid Bascomb, does it?'

'No.'

'I didn't really think so. What does it have to do with?'

'Kim Dakkinen.'

His eyes were on the road and I couldn't see any change in his expression. He said, 'Oh? What about her?'

'She wants out.'

'Out? Out of what?'

'The life,' I said. 'The relationship she has with you. She wants you to agree to ... break things off.'

We stopped for a light. He didn't say anything. The light changed and we went another block or two and he said, 'What's she to you?'

'A friend.'

'What does that mean? You're sleeping with her? You want to marry her? Friend's a big word, it covers a lot of ground.'

'This time it's a small word. She's a friend, she asked me to do her a favor.'

'By talking to me.'

'That's right.'

'Why couldn't she talk to me herself? I see her frequently, you know. She wouldn't have had to run around the city asking after me. Why, I saw her just last night.'

'I know.'

'Do you? Why didn't she say anything when she saw me?'

'She's afraid.'

'Afraid of me?'

'Afraid you might not want her to leave.'

'And so I might beat her? Disfigure her? Stub out cigarettes on her breasts?'

'Something like that.'

He fell silent again. The car's ride was hypnotically smooth. He said, 'She can go.'

'Just like that?'

'How else? I'm not a white slaver, you know.' His tone put an ironic stress on the term. 'My women stay with me out of their own will, such will as they possess. They're under no duress. You know Nietzsche? "Women are like dogs, the more you beat them the more they love you." But I don't beat them, Scudder. It never seems to be necessary. How does Kim come to have you for a friend?'

'We have an acquaintance in common.'

He glanced at me. 'You were a policeman. A detective, I believe. You left the force several years ago. You killed a child and resigned out of guilt.'

That was close enough for me to let it pass. A stray bullet of mine had killed a young girl named Estrellita Rivera, but I don't know that it was guilt over the incident that propelled me out of the police department. What it had done, really, was change the way the world looked to me, so that being a cop was no longer something I wanted to do. Neither was being a husband and a father and living on Long Island, and in due course I was out of work and out of the marriage and living on Fifty-seventh Street and putting in the hours at Armstrong's. The shooting unquestionably set those currents in motion, but I think I was pointed in those directions anyway and would have gotten there sooner or later.

'Now you're a sort of half-assed detective,' he went on. 'She hire you?'

'More or less.'

'What's that mean?' He didn't wait for clarification. 'Nothing against you, but she wasted her money. Or *my* money, according to how you look at it. If she wants to end our arrangement all she has to do is tell me so. She doesn't need anyone to do her talking for her. What's she plan to do? I hope she's not going back home.'

I didn't say anything.

'I suspect she'll stay in New York. But will she stay in the life? I'm afraid it's the only trade she knows. What else will she do? And where will she live? I provide their apartments, you know, and pay their rent and pick out their clothes. Well, I don't suppose anyone asked Ibsen where Nora would find an apartment. I believe this is where you live, if I'm not mistaken.'

I looked out the window. We were in front of my hotel. I hadn't been paying attention.

'I assume you'll be in touch with Kim,' he said. 'If you want, you can tell her you intimidated me and sent me slinking off into the night.'

'Why would I do that?'

'So she'll think she got her money's worth from you.'

'She got her money's worth,' I said, 'and I don't care whether she knows it or not. All I'll tell her is what you've told me.'

'Really? While you're at it, you can let her know that I'll be coming to see her. Just to satisfy myself that all of this is really her idea.'

'I'll mention it.'

'And tell her she has no reason to fear me.' He sighed. 'They think they're irreplaceable. If she had any notion how easily she can be replaced she'd most likely hang herself. The buses bring them, Scudder. Every hour of every day they stream into Port Authority ready to sell themselves. And every day a whole slew of others decide there must be a better way than waiting tables or punching a cash register. I could open an office, Scudder, and take applications, and there'd be a line halfway around the block.'

I opened the door. He said, 'I enjoyed this. Especially earlier. You have a good eye for boxing. Please tell that silly blonde whore that nobody's going to kill her.'

'I'll do that.'

'And if you need to talk to me, just call my service. I'll return your calls now that I know you.'

I got out, closed the door. He waited for an opening, made a U-turn, turned again at Eighth Avenue and headed uptown. The U-turn was illegal and he ran the light making his left turn on Eighth, but I don't suppose it worried him much. I couldn't recall the last time I'd seen a cop ticket anyone for a moving violation in the city of New York. Sometimes you'll see five cars go on through after a light turns red. Even the buses do it these days.

After he made his turn I took out my notebook, made an entry. Across the street, near Polly's Cage, a man and woman were having a loud argument. 'You call yourself a man?' she demanded. He slapped her. She cursed him and he slapped her again.

Maybe he'd beat her senseless. Maybe this was a game they played five nights out of seven. Try to break up that sort of thing and as likely as not they'll both turn on you. When I was a rookie cop, my first partner would do anything to avoid interfering in a domestic argument. Once, facing down a drunken husband, he'd been assaulted from behind by the wife. The husband had knocked out four of her teeth but she leaped to his defense, breaking a bottle over her savior's head. He wound up with fifteen stitches and a concussion, and he used to run his forefinger over the scar when he told me the story. You couldn't see the scar, his hair covered it, but his finger went right to the spot.

'I say let 'em kill each other,' he used to say. 'It don't matter if she phoned in the complaint herself, she'll still turn on you. Let 'em fucking kill each other.'

Across the street, the woman said something I didn't catch and the man hit her low with his closed fist. She cried out in what sounded like real pain. I put my notebook away and went into my hotel.

I called Kim from the lobby. Her machine answered and I had started to leave a message when she picked up the receiver and interrupted me. 'I leave the machine on sometimes when I'm home,' she explained, 'so I can see who it is before I answer. I haven't heard from Chance since I spoke to you earlier.'

'I just left him a few minutes ago.'

'You saw him?'

'We rode around in his car.'

'What did you think?'

'I think he's a good driver.'

'I meant –'

'I know what you meant. He didn't seem terribly upset to hear that you want to leave him. He assured me that you've got nothing to fear from him. According to him, you didn't need me as your champion. All you had to do was tell him.'

'Yes, well, he'd say that.'

'You don't think it's true?'

'Maybe it is.'

'He said he wants to hear it from you, and I gather he also wants to make some arrangements about your leaving the apartment. I don't know if you're afraid to be alone with him or not.'

'I don't know either.'

'You can keep the door locked and talk to him through it.'

'He has keys.'

'Don't you have a chain lock?'

'Yes.'

'You can use that.'

'I suppose.'

'Shall I come over?'

'No, you don't have to do that. Oh, I suppose you want the rest of the money, don't you?'

'Not until you've talked to him and everything's settled. But I'll come over there if you want somebody on your side when he turns up.'

'Is he coming tonight?'

'I don't know when he's coming. Maybe he'll handle the whole thing over the phone.'

'He might not come until tomorrow.'

'Well, I could hole up on the couch if you wanted.'

'Do you think it's necessary?'

'Well, it is if you think it is, Kim. If you're uncomfortable –'

'Do you think I have anything to be afraid of?'

I thought for a moment, replayed the scene with Chance, assessed my own reactions after the fact. 'No,' I said. 'I don't think so. But I don't really know the man.'

'Neither do I.'

'If you're nervous –'

'No, it's silly. Anyway it's late. I'm watching a movie on cable, but when it ends I'm going to sleep. I'll put the chain lock on. That's a good idea.'

'You've got my number.'

'Yes.'

'Call me if anything happens, or if you just want to call me. All right?'

'Sure.'

'Just to put your mind at rest, I think you spent some money you didn't have to spend, but it was money you held out so maybe it doesn't matter.'

'Absolutely.'

'The point is I think you're off the hook. He's not going to hurt you.'

'I think you're right. I'll probably call you tomorrow. And Matt? Thanks.'

'Get some sleep,' I said.

I went upstairs and tried to take my own advice but I was wired. I gave up and got dressed and went around the corner to Armstrong's. I would have had something to eat but the kitchen was closed. Trina told me she could get me a piece of pie if I wanted. I didn't want a piece of pie.

I wanted two ounces of bourbon, neat, and another two ounces in my coffee, and I couldn't think of a single goddamned reason not to have it. It wouldn't get me drunk. It wouldn't put

181

me back in the hospital. That had been the result of a bout of uncontrolled round-the-clock drinking, and I'd learned my lesson. I couldn't drink that way anymore, not safely, and I didn't intend to. But there was a fairly substantial difference between a nightcap and going out on a toot, wasn't there?

They tell you not to drink for ninety days. You're supposed to go to ninety meetings in ninety days and stay away from the first drink one day at a time, and after ninety days you can decide what you want to do next.

I'd had my last drink Sunday night. I'd been to four meetings since then, and if I went to bed without a drink I'd have five days.

So?

I had one cup of coffee, and on the way back to the hotel I stopped at the Greek deli and picked up a cheese danish and a half pint of milk. I ate the pastry and drank a little of the milk in my room.

I turned out the light, got into bed. Now I had five days. So?

FIVE

I read the paper while I ate breakfast. The housing cop in Corona was still in critical condition but his doctors now said they expected him to live. They said there might be some paralysis, which in turn might be permanent. It was too early to tell.

In Grand Central Station, someone had mugged a shopping-bag lady and had stolen two of her three bags. And, in the Gravesend section of Brooklyn, a father and son with arrest records for pornography and what the paper described as links to organized crime bolted from a car and sought sanctuary in the first house they could run to. Their pursuers opened up on them with pistols and a shotgun. The father was wounded, the son was shot dead, and the young wife and mother who'd just recently moved into the house was hanging something in a hall closet when enough of the shotgun blast came through the door to take most of her head off.

They have noon meetings six days a week at the YMCA on Sixty-third Street. The speaker said, 'Just let me tell you how I got here. I woke up one morning and I said to myself, "Hey, it's a beautiful day and I never felt better in my life. My health's tiptop, my marriage is in great shape, my career's going beautifully, and my state of mind has never been better. I think I'll go join AA."'

The room rocked with laughter. After his talk they didn't go around the room. You raised your hand and the speaker called on you. One young fellow said shyly that he'd just reached ninety days. He got a lot of applause. I thought about raising my hand and tried to figure out what I might say. All I could think to talk about was the woman in Gravesend, or perhaps Lou Rudenko's mother, slain by a salvaged television set. But what did either of those deaths have to do with me? I was still looking for something to say when time ran out and we all stood up and

183

said the Lord's Prayer. It was just as well. I probably wouldn't have gotten around to raising my hand anyway.

After the meeting I walked for awhile in Central Park. The sun was out for a change and it was the first good day all week. I took a good long walk and watched the kids and the runners and the cyclists and the roller skaters and tried to reconcile all that wholesome innocent energy with the dark face of the city that showed itself every morning in the newspaper.

The two worlds overlap. Some of these riders would be robbed of their bicycles. Some of these strolling lovers would return home to burglarized apartments. Some of these laughing kids would pull holdups, and shoot or stab, and some would be held up or shot or stabbed, and a person could give himself a headache trying to make sense out of it.

On my way out of the park at Columbus Circle a bum with a baseball jacket and one milky eye hustled me for a dime toward a pint of wine. A few yards to the left of us, two colleagues of his shared a bottle of Night Train and watched our transaction with interest. I was going to tell him to piss off, then surprised myself by giving him a buck. Maybe I was reluctant to shame him in front of his friends. He started to thank me more effusively than I could stomach, and then I guess he saw something in my face that stopped him cold. He backed off and I crossed the street and headed home.

There was no mail, just a message to call Kim. The clerk's supposed to note the time of the call on the slip but this place isn't the Waldorf. I asked if he remembered the time of the call and he didn't.

I called her and she said, 'Oh, I was hoping you'd call. Why don't you come over and pick up the money I owe you?'

'You heard from Chance?'

'He was here about an hour ago. Everything worked out perfectly. Can you come over?'

I told her to give me an hour. I went upstairs and showered and shaved. I got dressed, then decided I didn't like what I was wearing and changed. I was fussing with the knot of my tie when I realized what I was doing. I was dressing for a date.

I had to laugh at myself.

I put on my hat and coat and got out of there. She lived in Murray Hill, Thirty-eighth between Third and Lex. I walked over to Fifth, took a bus, then walked the rest of the way east.

Her building was a prewar apartment house, brickfronted, fourteen stories, with a tile floor and potted palms in the lobby. I gave my name to the doorman and he called upstairs on the intercom and established that I was welcome before pointing me to the elevator. There was something deliberately neutral about his manner, and I decided that he knew Kim's profession and assumed I was a john and was being very careful not to smirk.

I got off at the twelfth floor and walked to her door. It opened as I approached it. She stood framed in the doorway, all blonde braids and blue eyes and cheekbones, and for a moment I could picture her carved on the prow of a Viking ship. 'Oh, Matt,' she said, and reached to embrace me. She was just about my height and she gave me a good hard hug and I felt the pressure of firm breasts and thighs and recognized the sharp tang of her scent. 'Matt,' she said, drawing me inside, closing the door. 'God, I'm so grateful to Elaine for suggesting I get in touch with you. You know what you are? You're my hero.'

'All I did was talk to the man.'

'Whatever you did, it worked. That's all I care about. Sit down, relax a moment. Can I get you anything to drink?'

'No thanks.'

'Some coffee?'

'Well, if it's no trouble.'

'Sit down. It's instant, if that's all right. I'm too lazy to make real coffee.'

I told her instant was fine. I sat down on the couch and waited while she made the coffee. The room was a comfortable one, attractively if sparsely furnished. A recording of solo jazz piano played softly on the stereo. An all-black cat peered cautiously around the corner at me, then disappeared from view.

The coffee table held a few current magazines – *People, TV Guide, Cosmopolitan, Natural History*. A framed poster on the wall over the stereo advertised the Hopper show held a couple years back at the Whitney. A pair of African masks decorated another wall. A Scandinavian area rug, its abstract pattern a whirl of blue and green, covered the central portion of the limed oak floor.

When she returned with the coffee I admired the room. She said she wished she could keep the apartment. 'But in a way,' she said, 'it's good I can't, you know? I mean, to go on living here, and then there'd be people showing up. You know. Men.'

'Sure.'

'Plus the fact that none of this is me. I mean, the only thing in this room that I picked out is the poster. I went to that show and I wanted to take some of it home with me. The way that man painted loneliness. People together but not together, looking off in different directions. It got to me, it really did.'

'Where will you live?'

'Someplace nice,' she said confidently. She perched on the couch beside me, one long leg folded up beneath her, her coffee cup balanced on the other knee. She was wearing the same wine-colored jeans she'd worn at Armstrong's, along with a lemon yellow sweater. She didn't seem to be wearing anything under the sweater. Her feet were bare, the toe nails the same tawny port as her fingernails. She'd been wearing bedroom slippers but kicked them off before sitting down.

I took in the blue of her eyes, the green of her square-cut ring, then found my eyes drawn to the rug. It looked as though someone had taken each of those colors and beaten them with a wire whisk.

She blew on her coffee, sipped it, leaned far forward and set the cup on the coffee table. Her cigarettes were on the table and she lit one. She said, 'I don't know what you said to Chance but you really made an impression on him.'

'I don't see how.'

'He called this morning and said he would be coming over, and when he got here I had the door on the chain lock, and somehow I just knew I didn't have anything to fear from him. You know how sometimes you just know something?'

I knew, all right. The Boston Strangler never had to break a door down. All his victims opened the door and let him in.

She pursed her lips, blew out a column of smoke. 'He was very nice. He said he hadn't realized I was unhappy and that he had no intention of trying to hold me against my will. He seemed hurt that I could have thought that of him. You know something? He had me just about feeling guilty. And he had me feeling I was making a big mistake, that I was throwing something away and I'd be sorry I couldn't ever get it back. He said, "You know, I never take a girl back," and I thought, God, I'm burning my bridges. Can you imagine?'

'I think so.'

'Because he's such a con artist. Like I'm walking away from a great job and forfeiting my stake in the corporate pension plan. I mean, come *on!*'

'When do you have to be out of the apartment?'

'He said by the end of the month. I'll probably be gone before then. Packing's no big deal. None of the furniture's mine. Just clothes and records, and the Hopper poster, but do you want to know something? I think that can stay right here. I don't think I need the memories.'

I drank some of my coffee. It was weaker than I preferred it. The record ended and was followed by a piano trio. She told me again how I had impressed Chance. 'He wanted to know how I happened to call you,' she said. 'I was vague, I said you were a friend of a friend. He said I didn't need to hire you, that all I'd had to do was talk to him.'

'That's probably true.'

'Maybe. But I don't think so. I think I would have started talking to him, assuming I could work up the nerve, and we'd get into this conversation and gradually I would turn around and the whole subject would be shunted off to the side. And I'd leave it shunted off to the side, you know, because without ever coming out and saying it he'd manage to give me the impression that leaving him wasn't something I was going to be allowed to do. He might not say, "Look, bitch, you stay where you're at or I'll ruin your face." He might not say it, but that's what I'd hear.'

'Did you hear it today?'

'No. That's the point. I didn't.' Her hand fastened on my arm just above the wrist. 'Oh, before I forget,' she said, and my arm took some of her weight as she got up from the couch. Then she was across the room rummaging in her purse, and then she was back on the couch handing me five hundred-dollar bills, presumably the ones I'd returned to her three days earlier.

She said, 'It seems like there ought to be a bonus.'

'You paid me well enough.'

'But you did such a good job.'

She had one arm draped over the back of the sofa and she was leaning toward me. I looked at her blonde braids coiled around her head and thought of a woman I know, a sculptor with a loft in Tribeca. She did a head of Medusa with snakes for hair and Kim had the same broad brow and high cheekbones as Jan Keane's piece of sculpture.

The expression was different, though. Jan's Medusa had looked profoundly disappointed. Kim's face was harder to read.

I said, 'Are those contacts?'

'What? Oh, my eyes? That's their natural color. It's kind of weird, isn't it?'

'It's unusual.'

Now I could read her face. It was anticipation that I saw there.

187

'Beautiful eyes,' I said.

The wide mouth softened into the beginning of a smile. I moved a little toward her and she came at once into my arms, fresh and warm and eager. I kissed her mouth, her throat, her lidded eyes.

Her bedroom was large and flooded with sunlight. The floor was thickly carpeted. The king-size platform bed was unmade, and the black kitten napped on a chintz-covered boudoir chair. Kim drew the curtains, glanced shyly at me, then began to undress.

Ours was a curious passage. Her body was splendid, the stuff of fantasy, and she gave herself with evident abandon. I was surprised by the intensity of my own desire, and yet it was almost wholly physical. My mind remained oddly detached from her body and from my own. I might have been viewing our performance from a distance.

The resolution provided relief and release and precious little pleasure. I drew away from her and felt as though I was in the midst of an infinite wasteland of sand and dry brush. There was a moment of astonishing sadness. Pain throbbed at the back of my throat and I felt myself close to tears.

Then the feeling passed. I don't know what brought it on or what took it away.

She said, 'Well now,' and smiled, and rolled on her side to face me and put a hand on my arm. 'That was nice, Matt,' she said.

I got dressed, turned down the offer of another cup of coffee. She took my hand at the doorway, thanked me again, and said she'd let me know her address and phone once she got relocated. I told her to feel free to call anytime for any reason. We didn't kiss.

In the elevator I remembered something she'd said. '*It seems like there ought to be a bonus.*' Well, that was as good a word for it as any.

I walked all the way back to the hotel. I stopped a few times along the way, once for coffee and a sandwich, once in a church on Madison Avenue where I was going to put fifty dollars into the poor box until I realized I couldn't. Kim had paid me in hundreds and I didn't have enough in smaller bills.

I don't know why I tithe, or how I got in the habit in the first place. It was one of the things I began doing after I left Anita and the boys and moved into Manhattan. I don't know what the churches do with the money and I'm sure their need for it is no greater than my own, and of late I've tried to break myself of the habit. But whenever some money comes in I find there's a restlessness that comes with it that I cannot shed until I've handed over 10 percent of the sum to one church or another. I suppose it's superstition. I suppose I think that, having started this, I have to keep it up or something terrible will happen.

God knows it doesn't make any sense. Terrible things happen anyway, and will go on happening whether I give all or none of my income to churches.

This particular tithe would have to wait. I sat for a few minutes anyway, grateful for the peace the empty church provided. I let my mind wander for awhile. After I'd been there a few minutes an elderly man seated himself on the other side of the aisle. He closed his eyes and looked to be in deep concentration.

I wondered if he was praying. I wondered what prayer was like, and what people got out of it. Sometimes, in one church or another, it occurs to me to say a prayer, but I wouldn't know how to go about it.

If there'd been candles to light I would have lit one, but the church was Episcopalian and there weren't.

I went to the meeting that night at St Paul's but couldn't keep my mind on the qualification. I kept drifting off. During the discussion the kid from the noon meeting told how he'd reached his ninety days, and once again he got a round of applause. The speaker said, 'You know what comes after your ninetieth day? Your ninety-first day.'

I said, 'My name is Matt. I'll pass.'

I made it an early night. I fell asleep easily but kept waking up out of dreams. They withdrew from the edge of thought as I tried to catch hold of them.

I got up finally, went out for breakfast, bought a paper and brought it back to the room. There's a Sunday noon meeting within walking distance. I'd never been to it but I had seen it listed in the meeting book. By the time I thought of going, it was already half over. I stayed in my room and finished the paper.

Drinking used to fill up the hours. I used to be able to sit in Armstrong's for hours, drinking coffee with bourbon in it, not getting loaded, just sipping one cup after another while the hours went by. You try and do the same thing without the booze and it doesn't work. It just doesn't work.

Around three I thought of Kim. I reached for the phone to call

189

her and had to stop myself. We'd gone to bed because that was the sort of gift she knew how to bestow and one I didn't know how to reject, but that didn't make us lovers. It didn't make us anything to one another, and whatever business we'd had with each other was finished.

I remembered her hair and Jan Keane's Medusa and thought of calling Jan. And what would the conversation be like?

I could tell her I was halfway through my seventh sober day. I hadn't had any contact with her since she started going to meetings herself. They'd told her to stay away from people, places and things associated with drink, and I was in that category as far as she was concerned. I wasn't drinking today and I could tell her that, but so what? It didn't mean she would want to see me. For that matter, it didn't mean I would want to see her.

We'd had a couple evenings when we had a good time drinking together. Maybe we could have the same kind of enjoyment sober. But maybe it would be like sitting in Armstrong's for five hours with no bourbon in the coffee.

I got as far as looking up her number but never made the call.

The speaker at St Paul's told a really low-bottom story. He'd been a heroin addict for several years, kicked that, then drank his way down to the Bowery. He looked as though he'd seen hell and remembered what it looked like.

During the break, Jim cornered me by the coffee urn and asked me how it was going. I told him it was going okay. He asked how long I'd been sober now.

'Today's my seventh day,' I said.

'Jesus, that's great,' he said. 'That's really great, Matt.'

During the discussion I thought maybe I'd speak up when it was my turn. I didn't know that I'd say I was an alcoholic because I didn't know that I was, but I could say something about it being my seventh day, or just that I was glad to be there, or something. But when it got to me I said what I always say.

After the meeting Jim came up to me while I was carrying my folded chair to where they stack them. He said, 'You know, a bunch of us generally stop over to the Cobb's Corner for coffee after the meeting. Just to hang out and shoot the breeze. Why don't you come along?'

'Gee, I'd like to,' I said, 'but I can't tonight.'

'Some other night, then.'

'Sure,' I said. 'Sounds good, Jim.'

I could have gone. I didn't have anything else to do. Instead I went to Armstrong's and ate a hamburger and a piece of cheesecake and drank a cup of coffee. I could have had the identical meal at Cobb's Corner.

Well, I always like Armstrong's on a Sunday night. You get a light crowd then, just the regulars. After I was done with my meal I carried my coffee cup over to the bar and chatted for awhile with a CBS technician named Manny and a musician named Gordon. I didn't even feel like drinking.

I went home and went to bed. I got up in the morning with a sense of dread and wrote it off as the residue of an unremembered dream. I showered and shaved and it was still there. I got dressed, went downstairs, dropped a bag of dirty clothes at the laundry and left a suit and a pair of pants at the dry cleaners. I ate breakfast and read the *Daily News*. One of their columnists had interviewed the husband of the woman who'd caught the shotgun blast in Gravesend. They'd just moved into that house, it was their dream house, their chance for a decent life in a decent neighborhood. And then these two gangsters, running for their lives, had picked that particular house to run to. 'It was as if the finger of God had pointed to Clair Ryzcek,' the columnist wrote.

In the 'Metro Briefs' section, I learned that two Bowery derelicts had fought over a shirt one of them had found in a trash can in the Astor Place BMT subway station. One had stabbed the other dead with an eight-inch folding knife. The dead man was fifty-two, his killer thirty-three. I wondered if the item would have made the paper if it hadn't taken place below-ground. When they kill each other in Bowery flophouses, it's not news.

I kept thumbing through the paper as if I expected to find something, and the vague feeling of foreboding persisted. I felt faintly hungover and I had to remind myself I'd had nothing to drink the night before. This was my eighth sober day.

I went to the bank, put some of my five-hundred-dollar fee in my account, changed the rest into tens and twenties. I went to St Paul's to get rid of fifty bucks but there was a mass going on. I went to the Sixty-third Street Y instead and listened to the most boring qualification I'd heard yet. I think the speaker mentioned every drink he'd had from the age of eleven on. He droned on in a monotone for forty solid minutes.

I sat in the park afterward, bought a hotdog from a vendor, ate it. I got back to the hotel around three, took a nap, went out again around four-thirty. I picked up a *Post* and took it around the corner to Armstrong's. I must have looked at the headline when I bought the paper but somehow it didn't register. I sat down and ordered coffee and looked at the front page and there it was.

CALL GIRL SLASHED TO RIBBONS, it said.

I knew the odds and I also knew that the odds didn't matter. I sat for a moment with my eyes closed and the paper clenched in my fists, trying to alter the story by sheer force of will. Color, the very blue of her northern eyes, flashed behind my closed eyelids. My chest was tight and I could feel that pulse of pain again at the back of my throat.

I turned the goddamned page and there it was on page three just the way I knew it would be. She was dead. The bastard had killed her.

SIX

Kim Dakkinen had died in a room on the seventeenth floor of the Galaxy Downtowner, one of the new high-rise hotels on Sixth Avenue in the Fifties. The room had been rented to a Mr Charles Owen Jones of Fort Wayne, Indiana, who had paid cash in advance for a one-night stay upon checking in at 9:15 p.m. Sunday, after having phoned ahead for a room half an hour earlier. Since a preliminary check revealed no one of Mr Jones's name in Fort Wayne, and since the street address he'd entered on the registration card did not seem to exist, he was presumed to have given a false name.

Mr Jones had made no calls from his room, nor had he billed any charges to his hotel account. After an indeterminable number of hours he had left, and he'd done so without bothering to drop off his key at the desk. Indeed, he'd hung the DO NOT DISTURB sign on the door of his room, and the housekeeping staff had scrupulously honored it until shortly after the 11:00 a.m. checkout time Monday morning. At that time one of the maids put through a call to the room. When the phone went unanswered she knocked on the door; when that brought no response she opened it with her passkey.

She walked in on what the *Post* reporter called 'a scene of indescribable horror.' A nude woman lay on the carpet at the foot of the unmade bed. Bed and carpet were soaked with her blood. The woman had died of multiple wounds, having been stabbed and slashed innumerable times with what a deputy medical examiner guessed might have been a bayonet or machete. Her killer had hacked her face into 'an unrecognizable mess,' but a photograph retrieved by an enterprising reporter from Miss Dakkinen's 'luxurious Murray Hill apartment' showed what he'd had to work with. Kim's blonde hair was quite different in the photograph, flowing down over her shoulders with one single braid wrapped around the crown like a tiara. She was clear-eyed and radiant in the photo, and looked like a grown-up Heidi.

Identification had been made on the basis of the woman's purse, found at the scene. A sum of cash in the purse had enabled police investigators to rule out money as a motive in the slaying.

No kidding.

I put down the paper. I noticed without much surprise that my hands were shaking. I was even shakier on the inside. I caught Evelyn's eye, and when she came over I asked her to bring me a double shot of bourbon.

She said, 'Are you sure, Matt?'

'Why not?'

'Well, you haven't been drinking. Are you sure you want to start?'

I thought, What's it to you, kid? I took a breath and let it out and said, 'Maybe you're right.'

'How about some more coffee?'

'Sure.'

I went back to the story. A preliminary examination fixed the time of death some time around midnight. I tried to think what I'd been doing when he killed her. I'd come to Armstrong's after the meeting, but what time had it been when I'd left? I made it a fairly early night, but even so it had probably been close to midnight by the time I packed it in. Of course the time of death was approximate, so I might have been already asleep when he started to chop her life away.

I sat there and I kept drinking coffee and I read the story over and over and over.

From Armstrong's I went to St Paul's. I sat in a rear pew and tried to think. Images kept bouncing back and forth, flashes of my two meetings with Kim intercut with my conversation with Chance.

I put fifty futile dollars in the poor box. I lit a candle and stared at it as if I expected to see something dancing in its flame.

I went back and sat down again. I was still sitting there when a soft-spoken young priest came over and told me apologetically that they would be closing for the night. I nodded, got to my feet.

'You seem disturbed,' he offered. 'Could I help you in any way?'

'I don't think so.'

'I've seen you come in here from time to time. Sometimes it helps to talk to someone.'

Does it? I said, 'I'm not even Catholic, Father.'

'That's not a requirement. If there's something troubling you –'

'Just some hard news, Father. The unexpected death of a friend.'

'That's always difficult.'

I was afraid he'd hand me something about God's mysterious plan, but he seemed to be waiting for me to say more. I managed to get out of there and stood for a moment on the sidewalk, wondering where to go next.

It was around six-thirty. The meeting wasn't for another two hours. You could get there an hour early and sit around and have coffee and talk to people, but I never did. I had two hours to kill and I didn't know how.

They tell you not to let yourself get too hungry. I hadn't had anything to eat since that hotdog in the park. I thought of food and my stomach turned at the notion.

I walked back to my hotel. It seemed as though every place I passed was a bar or a liquor store. I went up to my room and stayed there.

I got to the meeting a couple of minutes early. Half a dozen people said hello to me by name. I got some coffee and sat down.

The speaker told an abbreviated drinking story and spent most of the time telling of all the things that had happened to him since he got sober four years ago. His marriage had broken up, his youngest son had been killed by a hit-and-run driver, he'd gone through a period of extended unemployment and several bad bouts of clinical depression.

'But I didn't drink,' he said. 'When I first came here you people told me there's nothing so bad that a drink won't make it worse. You told me the way to work this program is not drink even if my ass falls off. I'll tell you, sometimes I think I stay sober on sheer fucking stubbornness. That's okay. I figure whatever works is fine with me.'

I wanted to leave at the break. Instead I got a cup of coffee and took a couple of Fig Newtons. I could hear Kim telling me that she had an awful sweet tooth. *'But I never gain an ounce. Aren't I lucky?'*

I ate the cookies. It was like chewing straw but I chewed them and washed them down.

During the discussion one woman got into a long riff about

her relationship. She was a pain in the ass, she said the same thing every night. I tuned out.

I thought, My name is Matt and I'm an alcoholic. A woman I know got killed last night. She hired me to keep her from getting killed and I wound up assuring her that she was safe and she believed me. And her killer conned me and I believed him, and she's dead now, and there's nothing I can do about it. And it eats at me and I don't know what to do about that, and there's a bar on every corner and a liquor store on every block, and drinking won't bring her back to life but neither will staying sober, and why the hell do I have to go through this? Why?

I thought, My name is Matt and I'm an alcoholic and we sit around in these goddamned rooms and say the same damned things all the time and meanwhile out there all the animals are killing each other. We say Don't drink and go to meetings and we say The important thing is you're sober and we say Easy does it and we say One day at a time and while we natter on like brainwashed zombies the world is coming to an end.

I thought, My name is Matt and I'm an alcoholic and I need help.

When they got to me I said, 'My name is Matt. Thanks for your qualification. I enjoyed it. I think I'll just listen tonight.'

I left right after the prayer. I didn't go to Cobb's Corner and I didn't go to Armstrong's, either. Instead I walked to my hotel and past it and halfway around the block to Joey Farrell's on Fifty-eighth Street.

They didn't have much of a crowd. There was a Tony Bennett record on the jukebox. The bartender was nobody I knew.

I looked at the back bar. The first bourbon that caught my eye was Early Times. I ordered a straight shot with water back. The bartender poured it and set it on the bar in front of me.

I picked it up and looked at it. I wonder what I expected to see.

I drank it down.

SEVEN

It was no big deal. I didn't even feel the drink at first, and then what I experienced was a vague headache and the suggestion of nausea.

Well, my system wasn't used to it. I'd been away from it for a week. When was the last time I'd gone a full week without a drink?

I couldn't remember. Maybe fifteen years, I thought. Maybe twenty, maybe more.

I stood there, a forearm on the bar, one foot on the bottom rung of the bar stool beside me, and I tried to determine just what it was that I felt. I decided that something didn't hurt quite so much as it had a few minutes ago. On the other hand, I felt a curious sense of loss. But of what?

'Another?'

I started to nod, then caught myself and shook my head. 'Not right now,' I said. 'You want to let me have some dimes? I have to make a couple of calls.'

He changed a dollar for me and pointed me toward the pay phone. I closed myself into the booth and took out my notebook and pen and started making calls. I spent a few dimes learning who was in charge of the Dakkinen case and a couple more reaching him, but finally I was plugged into the squad room at Midtown North. I asked to speak to Detective Durkin and a voice said, 'Just a minute,' and 'Joe? For you,' and after a pause another voice said, 'This is Joe Durkin.'

I said, 'Durkin, my name is Scudder. I'd like to know if you've made an arrest in the Dakkinen murder.'

'I didn't get that name,' he said.

'It's Matthew Scudder, and I'm not trying to get information out of you, I'm trying to give it. If you haven't arrested the pimp yet I may be able to give you a lead.'

After a pause he said, 'We haven't made any arrests.'

'She had a pimp.'

'We know that.'

'Do you have his name?'

'Look, Mr Scudder –'

'Her pimp's name is Chance. That may be a first or last name or it may be an alias. There's no yellow sheet on him, not under that name.'

'How would you know about a yellow sheet?'

'I'm an ex-cop. Look, Durkin, I've got a lot of information and all I want to do is give it to you. Suppose I just talk for a few minutes and then you can ask anything you want.'

'All right.'

I told him what I knew about Chance. I gave him a full physical description, added a description of his car and supplied the license number. I said he had a minimum of four girls on his string and that one of them was a Ms Sonya Hendryx, possibly known as Sunny, and I described her. 'Friday night he dropped Hendryx at 444 Central Park West. It's possible she lives there but more likely that she was going to attend a victory party for a prizefighter named Kid Bascomb. Chance has some sort of interest in Bascomb and it's probable that someone in that building was throwing a party for him.'

He started to interrupt but I kept going. I said, 'Friday night Chance learned that the Dakkinen girl wanted to end their relationship. Saturday afternoon he visited her on East Thirty-eighth Street and told her he had no objection. He told her to vacate the apartment by the end of the month. It was his apartment, he rented it and installed her in it.'

'Just a minute,' Durkin said, and I heard papers rustle. 'The tenant of record is a Mr David Goldman. That's also the name Dakkinen's phone's listed in.'

'Have you been able to trace David Goldman?'

'Not yet.'

'My guess is you won't, or else Goldman'll turn out to be a lawyer or accountant Chance uses to front for him. I'll tell you this much, Chance doesn't look like any David Goldman I ever met.'

'You said he was black.'

'That's right.'

'You met him.'

'That's right. Now he doesn't have a particular hangout, but there are several places he frequents.' I ran down the list. 'I wasn't able to learn where he lives. I gather he keeps that a secret.'

'No problem,' Durkin said. 'We'll use the reverse directory. You gave us his phone number, remember? We'll look it up and get the address that way.'

'I think the number's his answering service.'

'Well, they'll have a number for him.'

'Maybe.'

'You sound doubtful.'

'I think he likes to keep himself hard to find,' I said.

'How'd you happen to find him? What's your connection to all of this, Scudder?'

I felt like hanging up. I'd given them what I had and I didn't feel like answering questions. But I was a lot easier to find than Chance, and if I hung up on Durkin he could have me picked up in no time.

I said, 'I met him Friday night. Miss Dakkinen asked me to intercede for her.'

'Intercede how?'

'By telling him she wanted to get off the hook. She was scared to tell him herself.'

'So you told him for her.'

'That's right.'

'What, are you a pimp yourself, Scudder? She go from his stable to yours?'

My grip tightened on the receiver. I said, 'No, that's not my line, Durkin. Why? Is your mother looking for a new connection?'

'What in –'

'Just watch your fucking mouth, that's all. I'm handing you things on a plate and I never had to call you at all.'

He didn't say anything.

I said, 'Kim Dakkinen was a friend of a friend. If you want to know about me there used to be a cop named Guzik who knew me. Is he still at Midtown North?'

'You're a friend of Guzik's?'

'We never liked each other much but he can tell you I'm straight. I told Chance she wanted out and he said it was fine with him. He saw her the next day and told her the same thing. Then last night somebody killed her. You still have the time of death figured as midnight?'

'Yeah, but that's approximate. It was twelve hours later that they found her. And the condition of the corpse, you know, the ME probably wanted to move on to something else.'

'Bad.'

'The one I feel sorry for is that poor little chambermaid. She's from Ecuador, I think she's an illegal, barely speaks a word of English, and she had to walk in on that.' He snorted. 'You want to look at the body, give us a positive make? You'll see something'll stick in your memory.'

'Don't you have an identification?'

'Oh, yeah,' he said. 'We got fingerprints. She was arrested once a few years back in Long Island City. Loitering with intent, fifteen days suspended. No arrests since then.'

'She worked in a house after that,' I said. 'And then Chance put her in the apartment on Thirty-eighth Street.'

'A real New York odyssey. What else have you got, Scudder? And how do I get hold of you if I need you?'

I didn't have anything else. I gave him my address and phone. We said a few more polite things to each other and I hung up and the phone rang. I owed forty-five cents for going over the three minutes my dime had bought me. I broke another dollar at the bar, put the money in the slot, and returned to the bar to order another drink. Early Times, straight up, water back.

This one tasted better. And after it hit bottom I felt something loosen up inside me.

At the meetings they tell you it's the first drink that gets you drunk. You have one and it triggers an irresistible compulsion and without meaning it you have another and another and you wind up drunk again. Well, maybe I wasn't an alcoholic because that wasn't what was happening. I'd had two drinks and I felt a whole lot better than I did before I'd had them and I certainly didn't feel any need to drink anymore.

I gave myself a chance, though. I stood there for a few minutes and thought about having a third drink.

No. No, I really didn't want it. I was fine the way I was.

I left a buck on the bar, scooped the rest of my change, and headed for home. I walked past Armstrong's and didn't feel like stopping in. I certainly didn't have the urge to stop for a drink.

The early *News* would be out by now. Did I want to walk down to the corner for it?

No, the hell with it.

I stopped at the desk. No messages. Jacob was on duty, riding a gentle codeine buzz, filling in the squares of a crossword puzzle.

I said, 'Say, Jacob, I want to thank you for what you did the other night. Making that phone call.'

'Oh, well,' he said.

'No, that was terrific,' I said. 'I really appreciate it.'

I went upstairs and got ready for bed. I was tired and felt out of breath. For a moment, just before sleep came, I experienced again that odd sensation of having lost something. But what could I have lost?

I thought, Seven days. You had seven sober days and most of an eighth, and you lost them. They're gone.

EIGHT

I bought the *News* the next morning. A new atrocity had already driven Kim Dakkinen off the front page. Up in Washington Heights a young surgeon, a resident at Columbia Presbyterian, had been shot dead in a robbery attempt on Riverside Drive. He hadn't resisted his assailant, who had shot him for no apparent reason. The victim's widow was expecting their first child in early February.

The call-girl slashing was on an inside page. I didn't learn anything I hadn't heard the previous night from Durkin.

I walked around a lot. At noon I dropped over to the Y but got restless and left during the qualification. I had a pastrami sandwich at a Broadway deli and drank a bottle of Prior Dark with it. I had another beer around dinnertime. At eight-thirty I went over to St Paul's, walked once around the block and returned to my hotel without entering the basement meeting room. I made myself stay in my room. I felt like a drink, but I'd had two beers and I decided that two drinks a day would be my ration. As long as I didn't exceed that quota I didn't see how I could get in trouble. It didn't matter whether I had them first thing in the morning or last thing at night, in my room or at a bar, alone or in company.

The following day, Wednesday, I slept late and ate a late breakfast at Armstrong's. I walked to the main library and spent a couple hours there, then sat in Bryant Park until the drug dealers got on my nerves. They've so completely taken over the parks that they assume only a potential customer would bother coming there, so you can't read a paper without being constantly offered uppers and downers and pot and acid and God knows what else.

I went to the eight-thirty meeting that night. Mildred, one of the regulars, got a round of applause when she announced that it was her anniversary, eleven years since her last drink. She said she didn't have any secret, she just did it a day at a time.

I thought that if I went to bed sober I'd have one day. I decided, what the hell, I'd do that. After the meeting I went over to Polly's Cage instead and had my two drinks. I got into a discussion with a guy and he wanted to buy me a third drink, but I told the bartender to make it Coke instead. I was quietly pleased with myself, knowing my limit and sticking to it.

Thursday I had a beer with dinner, went to the meeting and left on the break. I stopped in at Armstrong's but something kept me from ordering a drink there and I didn't stay long. I was restless, I walked in and out of Farrell's and Polly's without ordering a drink in either place. The liquor store down the block from Polly's was still open. I bought a fifth of J. W. Dant and took it back to my room.

I took a shower first and got ready for bed. Then I broke the seal on the bottle, poured about two ounces of bourbon in a water glass, drank it down and went to sleep.

Friday I had another two ounces first thing when I got out of bed. I really felt the drink and it was a good feeling. I went all day without having another. Then around bedtime I had one more and fell asleep.

Saturday I awoke clearheaded with no desire for a morning drink. I couldn't get over how well I was controlling my drinking. I almost felt like going to a meeting and sharing my secret with them, but I could imagine the reaction I'd get. Knowing looks, knowing laughter. Holier-than-thou sobriety. Besides, just because I could control my drinking didn't mean I was justified in recommending it to other people.

I had two drinks before bed. I barely felt them, but Sunday morning I woke up a little rocky and poured myself a generous eye-opener to start the day. It did the job. I read the paper, then checked the meeting book and found an afternoon meeting in the Village. I went down there on the subway. The crowd was almost entirely gay. I left at the break.

I went back to the hotel and took a nap. After dinner I finished reading the paper and decided to have my second drink. I poured two or three ounces of bourbon into my glass and drank it off. I sat down and read some more but I couldn't concentrate very well on what I was reading. I thought of having another drink but I reminded myself I'd already had two that day.

Then I realized something. I'd had my morning drink more than twelve hours ago. More time had elapsed since then than had separated it from my last drink the night before. So that drink had long since left my system, and shouldn't properly be counted as part of *today's* drinks.

Which meant I was entitled to another drink before I went to bed.

I was pleased with having figured that out, and decided to reward myself for my insight by making the drink a respectable one. I filled the water glass to within a half inch of the top and took my time drinking it, sitting in my chair with it like a model in one of those Man of Distinction ads. I had the sense to realize that it was the number of drinks that was significant, not their size, and then it struck me that I'd cheated myself. My first drink, if you could call it that, had been a short measure. In a sense, I owed myself about four ounces of bourbon.

I poured what I judged to be four ounces and drained the glass.

I was pleased to note that the drinks hadn't had any discernible effect on me. I certainly wasn't drunk. As a matter of fact, I felt better than I'd felt in a long time. Too good, in fact, to sit around the room. I'd go out, find a congenial spot, have a Coke or a cup of coffee. Not a drink, because in the first place I didn't want any more and, just as important, I'd already had my two drinks for the day.

I had a Coke at Polly's. On Ninth Avenue I had a glass of ginger ale at a gay bar called Kid Gloves. Some of the other drinkers looked faintly familiar, and I wondered if any of them had been at the meeting that afternoon in the Village.

A block further downtown I realized something. I'd been controlling my drinking for days now, and before that I'd been off the sauce entirely for over a week, and that proved something. Hell, if I could limit myself to two drinks a day, that was fairly strong evidence that I didn't *need* to limit myself to two drinks a day. I'd had my problems with alcohol in the past, I couldn't very well deny it, but evidently I had outgrown that stage in my life.

So, although I certainly didn't *need* another drink, I could just as certainly have one if I wanted one. And I did want one, as a matter of fact, so why not have it?

I went into the saloon and ordered a double bourbon with water back. I remember the bartender had a shiny bald head, and I remember him pouring the drink, and I remember picking it up.

That's the last thing I remember.

NINE

I woke up suddenly, consciousness coming on abruptly and at top volume. I was in a hospital bed.

That was the first shock. The second came a little later when I found out it was Wednesday. I couldn't remember anything after I picked up that third drink Sunday night.

I'd had occasional blackouts for years. Sometimes I'd lose the last half hour of the night. Sometimes I'd lose a few hours.

I'd never lost two whole days before.

They didn't want to let me go. I'd been admitted late the previous night and they wanted to keep me in detox for a full five days.

An intern said, 'The booze isn't even out of your system yet. You'll walk around the corner and pick up a drink five minutes after you get out of here.'

'No I won't.'

'You just went through detox here a couple of weeks ago. It's on your chart. We cleaned you up and how long did you last?'

I didn't say anything.

'You know how you got here last night? You had a convulsion, a full-scale grand mal seizure. Ever have one of those before?'

'No.'

'Well, you'll have them again. If you keep on drinking you can pretty much count on it. Not every time, but sooner or later. And sooner or later you'll die of it. If you don't die of something else first.'

'Stop it.'

He grabbed me by the shoulder. 'No, I won't stop it,' he said. 'Why the hell should I stop it? I can't be polite and considerate of your feelings and expect to cut through all your bullshit at the same time. Look at me. *Listen* to me. You're an alcoholic. If you drink you'll die.'

I didn't say anything.

He had it all figured out. I would spend ten days in detox. Then I'd go to Smithers for twenty-eight days of alcoholic rehabilitation. He let up on that part when he found out I didn't have medical insurance or the couple of thousand dollars rehab would cost, but he was still holding out for a five-day stay in the detox ward.

'I don't have to stay,' I said. 'I'm not going to drink.'

'Everybody says that.'

'In my case it's true and you can't keep me here if I don't agree to stay. You have to let me sign out.'

'If you do you'll be signing out AMA. Against Medical Advice.'

'Then that's what I'll do.'

He looked angry for a moment. Then he shrugged. 'Suit yourself,' he said cheerfully. 'Next time maybe you'll listen to advice.'

'There won't be a next time.'

'Oh, there'll be a next time, all right,' he said. 'Unless you fall on your face closer to some other hospital. Or die before you get here.'

The clothes they brought me were a mess, dirty from rolling in the street, the shirt and jacket stained with blood. I'd been bleeding from a scalp wound when they brought me in and they'd stitched it up for me. I had evidently sustained the wound during the seizure, unless I'd acquired it earlier in my adventures.

I had enough cash on me for the hospital bill. A minor miracle, that.

It had rained during the morning and the streets were still wet. I stood on the sidewalk and felt the confidence drain out of me. There was a bar right across the street. I had money in my pocket for a drink and I knew it would make me feel better.

I went back to my hotel instead. I had to get up the nerve to approach the desk and collect my mail and messages, as if I'd done something shameful and owed some profound apology to the desk clerk. The worst of it was not knowing what I might have done during the time I was in blackout.

Nothing showed in the clerk's expression. Maybe I'd spent

most of the lost time in my room, drinking in isolation. Maybe I'd never returned to the hotel since I left it Sunday night.

I went upstairs and ruled out the latter hypothesis. I'd evidently returned sometime either Monday or Tuesday, because I'd finished the bottle of J. W. Dant and there was a half-full quart of Jim Beam on the bureau beside the empty Dant bottle. The dealer's label indicated it was from a store on Eighth Avenue.

I thought, Well, here's the first test. Either you drink or you don't.

I poured the bourbon down the sink, rinsed out both bottles and put them in the trash.

The mail was all junk. I got rid of it and looked at my messages. Anita had called Monday morning. Someone named Jim Faber had called Tuesday night and left a number. And Chance had called once last night and once this morning.

I took a long hot shower and a careful shave and put on clean clothes. I threw out the shirt and socks and underwear I'd worn home from the hospital and put the suit aside. Maybe the dry cleaner would be able to do something with it. I picked up my messages and went through them again.

My ex-wife Anita. Chance, the pimp who'd killed Kim Dakkinen. And somebody named Faber. I didn't know anybody named Faber, unless he was some drunk who'd become a long-lost buddy during my drunken wanderings.

I discarded the slip with his number and weighed a trip downstairs against the hassle of placing a call through the hotel operator. If I hadn't poured out the bourbon I might have had a drink just about then. Instead I went downstairs and called Anita from the lobby booth.

It was a curious conversation. We were carefully polite, as we often are, and after we'd circled one another like first-round prizefighters she asked me why I'd called. 'I'm just returning your call,' I said. 'I'm sorry it took me awhile.'

'Returning my call?'

'There's a message that you called Monday.'

There was a pause. Then she said, 'Matt, we spoke Monday night. You called me back. Don't you remember?'

I felt a chill, as if someone had just scraped a piece of chalk on a blackboard. 'Of course I remember,' I said. 'But how did this slip get back in my box? I thought you'd called a second time.'

'No.'

'I must have dropped the message slip and then some helpful

207

idiot returned it to my box, and it got handed to me just now and I thought it was another call.'

'That's what must have happened.'

'Sure,' I said. 'Anita, I'd had a couple drinks when I spoke to you the other night. My memory's a little vague. You want to remind me what we talked about in case there's anything I forgot?'

We had talked about orthodontia for Mickey. I'd told her to get another opinion. I remembered that part of the conversation, I assured her. Was there anything else? I had said I was hoping to send more money soon, a more substantial contribution than I'd made lately, and paying for the kid's braces shouldn't be any problem. I told her I remembered that part, too, and she said that was about all, except that of course I'd talked to the children. Oh, sure, I told her. I remembered my conversation with the boys. And that was all? Well, then, my memory wasn't so bad after all, was it?

I was shaking when I hung up the phone. I sat there and tried to summon up a memory of the conversation she had just described and it was hopeless. Everything was a blank from the moment just before the third drink Sunday night to the time I'd come out of it in the hospital. Everything, all of it, gone.

I tore up the message slip, tore it in half again, put the scraps in my pocket. I looked at the other message. The number Chance had left was his service number. I called Midtown North instead. Durkin wasn't in but they gave me his home number.

He sounded groggy when he answered. 'Gimme a second, lemme light a cigarette,' he said. When he came back on the line he sounded all right. 'I was watching teevee,' he said, 'and I went and fell asleep in front of the set. What's on your mind, Scudder?'

'That pimp's been trying to reach me. Chance.'

'Trying to reach you how?'

'By phone. He left a number for me to call. His answering service. So he's probably in town, and if you want me to set him up –'

'We're not looking for him.'

For an awful moment I thought I must have spoken to Durkin during my blackout, that one of us had called the other and I didn't remember it. But he went on talking and I realized that hadn't happened.

'We had him over at the station house and we sweated him,' he explained. 'We put out a pickup order but he wound up coming in on his own accord. He had a slick lawyer with him and he was pretty slick himself.'

'You let him go?'

'We didn't have one damn thing to hold him on. He had an alibi for the whole stretch from several hours before the estimated time of death to six or eight hours after. The alibi looks solid and we haven't got anything to stack up against it. The clerk who checked Charles Jones into the Galaxy can't come up with a description. I mean he can't say for sure if the man he signed in was black or white. He sort of thinks he was white. How'd you like to hand that to the DA?'

'He could have had someone else rent the room. Those big hotels, they don't keep any track of who goes in and out.'

'You're right. He could have had someone rent the room. He also could have had someone kill her.'

'Is that what you figure he did?'

'I don't get paid to figure. I know we haven't got a case against the son of a bitch.'

I thought for a moment. 'Why would he call me?'

'How would I know?'

'Does he know I steered you to him?'

'He didn't hear it from me.'

'Then what does he want with me?'

'Why don't you ask him yourself?'

It was warm in the booth. I cracked the door, let a little air in. 'Maybe I'll do that.'

'Sure. Scudder? Don't meet him in a dark alley, huh? Because if he's got some kind of a hard-on for you, you want to watch your back.'

'Right.'

'And if he does nail you, leave a dying message, will you? That's what they always do on television.'

'I'll see what I can do.'

'Make it clever,' he said. 'but not *too* clever, you know? Keep it simple enough so I can figure it out.'

I dropped a dime and called his service. The woman with the smoker's rasp to her voice said, 'Eight-oh-nine-two. May I help you?'

I said, 'My name's Scudder. Chance called me and I'm returning his call.'

She said she expected to be speaking to him soon and asked

for my number. I gave it to her and went upstairs and stretched out on the bed.

A little less than an hour later the phone rang. 'It's Chance,' he said. 'I want to thank you for returning my call.'

'I just got the message an hour or so ago. Both of the messages.'

'I'd like to speak with you,' he said. 'Face to face, that is.'

'All right.'

'I'm downstairs, I'm in your lobby. I thought we could get a drink or a cup of coffee in the neighborhood. Could you come down?'

'All right.'

TEN

He said, 'You still think I killed her, don't you?'

'What does it matter what I think?'

'It matters to me.'

I borrowed Durkin's line. 'Nobody pays me to think.'

We were in the back booth of a coffee shop a few doors from Eighth Avenue. My coffee was black. His was just a shade lighter than his skin tone. I'd ordered a toasted English muffin, figuring that I probably ought to eat something, but I hadn't been able to bring myself to touch it.

He said, 'I didn't do it.'

'All right.'

'I have what you might call an alibi in depth. A whole roomful of people can account for my time that night. I wasn't anywhere near that hotel.'

'That's handy.'

'What's that supposed to mean?'

'Whatever you want it to mean.'

'You're saying I could have hired it done.'

I shrugged. I felt edgy, sitting across the table from him, but more than that I felt tired. I wasn't afraid of him.

'Maybe I could have. But I didn't.'

'If you say so.'

'God *damn*,' he said, and drank some of his coffee. 'She anything more to you than you let on that night?'

'No.'

'Just a friend of a friend?'

'That's right.'

He looked at me, and his gaze was like a too-bright light shining in my eyes. 'You went to bed with her,' he said. Before I could respond he said, 'Sure, that's what you did. How else would she say thank you? The woman only spoke one language.

I hope that wasn't the only compensation you got, Scudder. I hope she didn't pay the whole fee in whore's coin.'

'My fees are my business,' I said. 'Anything that happened between us is my business.'

He nodded. 'I'm just getting a fix on where you're coming from, that's all.'

'I'm not coming from anyplace and I'm not going anywhere. I did a piece of work and I was paid in full. The client's dead and I didn't have anything to do with that and it doesn't have anything to do with me. You say you had nothing to do with her death. Maybe that's true and maybe it isn't. I don't know and I don't have to know and I don't honestly give a damn. That's between you and the police. I'm not the police.'

'You used to be.'

'But I'm not anymore. I'm not the police and I'm not the dead girl's brother and I'm not some avenging angel with a flaming sword. You think it matters to me who killed Kim Dakkinen? You think I give a damn?'

'Yes.'

I looked at him.

He said, 'Yes, I think it matters to you. I think you care who killed her. That's why I'm here.' He smiled gently. 'See,' he said, 'what I want is to hire you, Mr Matthew Scudder. I want you to find out who killed her.'

I took a while before I believed he was serious. Then I did what I could to talk him out of it. If there was any kind of trail leading to Kim's killer, I told him, the police had the best chance of finding and following it. They had the authority and the manpower and the talent and the connections and the skills. I had none of the above.

'You're forgetting something,' he said.

'Oh?'

'They won't be looking. Far as they're concerned, they already *know* who killed her. They got no evidence so they can't do anything with it, but that's their excuse not to kill themselves trying. They'll say, "Well, we know Chance killed her but we can't prove it so let's work on something else." God knows they got plenty other things to work on. And if they did work on it, all they'd be looking for is some way to hang it onto me. They wouldn't even look to see if there's somebody else on earth with a reason for wanting her dead.'

'Like who?'

'That's what you would be looking to find out.'

'Why?'

'For money,' he said, and smiled again. 'I wasn't asking you to work for free. I have a lot of money coming in, all of it cash. I can pay a good fee.'

'That's not what I meant. Why would you want me on the case? Why would you want the killer found, assuming I had any chance of finding him? It's not to get you off the hook because you're not on the hook. The cops haven't got a case against you and they're not likely to come up with one. What's it to you if the case stays on the books as unsolved?'

His gaze was calm, steady. 'Maybe I'm concerned about my reputation,' he suggested.

'How? It looks to me as though your reputation gets a boost. If the word on the street is that you killed her and got away with it, the next girl who wants to quit your string is going to have something else to think about. Even if you didn't have anything to do with her murder, I can see where you'd be just as happy to take the credit for it.'

He flicked his index finger a couple times against his empty coffee cup. He said, 'Somebody killed a woman of mine. Nobody should be able to do that and get away with it.'

'She wasn't yours when she got killed.'

'Who knew that? You knew it and she knew it and I knew it. My other girls, did they know? Did the people in the bars and on the street know? Do they know now? Far as the world knows, one of my girls got killed and the killer's getting away with it.'

'And that hurts your reputation?'

'I don't see it helping it any. There's other things. My girls are afraid. Kim got killed and the guy who did it is still out there. Suppose he repeats?'

'Kills another prostitute?'

'Kills another of mine,' he said levelly. 'Scudder, that killer's a loaded gun and I don't know who he's pointed at. Maybe killing Kim's a way for somebody to get at me. Maybe another girl of mine is next on his list. I know one thing. My business is hurting already. I told my girls not to take any hotel tricks, that's for starters, and not to take any new johns if there's anything funny about them. That's like telling them to leave the phone off the hook.'

The waiter drifted over with a pot of coffee and refilled our cups. I still hadn't touched my English muffin and the melted butter was starting to congeal. I got him to take it away. Chance added milk to his coffee. I remembered sitting with Kim while she drank hers heavily diluted with cream and sugar.

I said, 'Why me, Chance?'

'I told you. The cops aren't going to kill themselves. The only way somebody's going to give this his best shot is if he's earning my money for it.'

'There's other people who work private. You could hire a whole firm, get 'em working around the clock.'

'I never did like team sports. Rather see somebody go one on one. 'Sides, you got an inside track. You knew the woman.'

'I don't know how much of an edge that gives me.'

'And I know you.'

'Because you met me once?'

'And liked your style. That counts some.'

'Does it? The only thing you know about me is I know how to look at a boxing match. That's not a whole lot.'

'It's something. But I know more than that. I know how you handle yourself. And I've asked around, you know. A lot of folks know you and most of 'em said good things about you.'

I was silent for a minute or two. Then I said, 'It could have been a psycho that killed her. That's what he made it look like so maybe that's what it was.'

'Friday I learn she wants out of my string of girls. Saturday I tell her it's cool. Sunday some crazy man flies in from Indiana and chops her up, just by coincidence. You figure?'

'Coincidences happen all the time,' I said, 'but no, I don't think it was coincidence.' God, I felt tired. I said, 'I don't much want the case.'

'Why not?'

I thought, Because I don't want to have to do anything. I want to sit in a dark corner and turn the world off. I want a drink, damn it.

'You could use the money,' he said.

That was true enough. I hadn't gotten all that much mileage out of my last fee. And my son Mickey needed braces on his teeth, and after that there'd be something else.

I said, 'I've got to think it over.'

'All right.'

'I can't concentrate right now. I need a little time to sort out my thoughts.'

'How much time?'

Months, I thought. 'A couple of hours. I'll call you sometime tonight. Is there a number where I can reach you or do I just call the service?'

'Pick a time,' he said. 'I'll meet you in front of your hotel.'

'You don't have to do that.'

'It's too easy to say no over the phone. I figure the odds are better face to face. Besides, if the answer's yes we'll want to talk some. And you'll want some money from me.'

I shrugged.

'Pick a time.'

'Ten?'

'In front of your hotel.'

'All right,' I said. 'If I had to answer now, it'd be no.'

'Then it's good you got until ten.'

He paid for the coffee. I didn't put up a fight.

I went back to the hotel and up to the room. I tried to think straight and couldn't. I couldn't seem to sit still, either. I kept moving from the bed to the chair and back again, wondering why I hadn't given him a final no right away. Now I had the aggravation of getting through the hours until ten o'clock and then finding the resolve to turn down what he was offering.

Without thinking too much about what I was doing I put on my hat and coat and went around the corner to Armstrong's. I walked in the door not knowing what I was going to order. I went up to the bar and Billie started shaking his head when he saw me coming. He said, 'I can't serve you, Matt. I'm sorry as hell.'

I felt the color mounting in my face. I was embarrassed and I was angry. I said, 'What are you talking about? Do I look drunk to you?'

'No.'

'Then how the hell did I get to be eighty-six around here?'

His eyes avoided mine. 'I don't make the rules,' he said. 'I'm not saying you're not welcome here. Coffee or a Coke or a meal, hell, you're a valued longtime customer. But I'm not allowed to sell you booze.'

'Who says?'

'The boss says. When you were in here the other night –'

Oh, God. I said, 'I'm sorry about that Billie. I'll tell you the truth, I had a couple of bad nights. I didn't even know I came in here.'

'Don't worry about it.'

Christ, I wanted to hide behind something. 'Was I very bad, Billie? Did I make trouble?'

'Aw, shit,' he said. 'You were drunk, you know? It happens, right? I used to have this Irish landlady, I came in bagged one night and apologized the next day, and she would say, 'Jaysus, son, it could happen to a bishop.' You didn't make any trouble, Matt.'

'Then –'

'Look,' he said, and leaned forward. 'I'll just repeat what I was told. He told me, he said, if the guy wants to drink himself to death I can't stop him, and if he wants to come in here he's welcome, but I'm not selling him the booze. This isn't me talking, Matt. I'm just saying what was said.'

'I understand.'

'If it was up to me –'

'I didn't come in for a drink anyway,' I said. 'I came in for coffee.'

'In that case –'

'In that case the hell with it,' I said. 'In that case I think what I want is a drink and it shouldn't be all that hard to find somebody willing to sell it to me.'

'Matt, don't take it that way.'

'Don't tell me how to take it,' I said. 'Don't give me that shit.'

There was something clean and satisfying about the rage I felt. I stalked out of there, my anger burning with a pure flame, and stood on the sidewalk trying to decide where to go for a drink.

Then someone was calling my name.

I turned. A fellow in an army jacket was smiling gently at me. I couldn't place him at first. He said it was good to see me and asked how I was doing, and then of course I knew who it was.

I said, 'Oh, hi, Jim. I'm okay, I guess.'

'Going to the meeting? I'll walk with you.'

'Oh,' I said. 'Gee, I don't think I'm going to be able to make it tonight. I have to see a guy.'

He just smiled. Something clicked, and I asked him if his last name was Faber.

'That's right,' he said.

'You called me at the hotel.'

'Just wanted to say hello. Nothing important.'

'I didn't recognize the name. Otherwise I would have called you back.'

'Sure. You sure you don't want to tag along to the meeting, Matt?'

'I wish I could. Oh, Jesus.'

He waited.

'I've been having a little trouble, Jim.'

'That's not so unusual, you know.'

I couldn't look at him. I said, 'I started drinking again. I went, I don't know, seven or eight days. Then I started again, and I was doing okay, you know, controlling it, and then one night I got into trouble.'

'You got in trouble when you picked up the first one.'

'I don't know. Maybe.'

'That's why I called,' he said gently. 'I figured maybe you could use a little help.'

'You knew?'

'Well, you were in pretty rocky shape at the meeting Monday night.'

'I was at the meeting?'

'You don't remember, do you? I had a feeling you were in a blackout.'

'Oh my God.'

'What's the matter?'

'I went there drunk? I showed up drunk at an AA meeting?'

He laughed. 'You make it sound like a mortal sin. You think you're the first person who ever did that?'

I wanted to die. 'But it's terrible,' I said.

'What's so terrible?'

'I can never go back. I can never walk into that room.'

'You're ashamed of yourself, aren't you?'

'Of course.'

He nodded. 'I was always ashamed of my blackouts. I didn't want to know about them and I was always afraid of what I might have done. Just for the record, you weren't so bad. You didn't make trouble. You didn't talk out of turn. You spilled a cup of coffee –'

'Oh, God.'

'It's not as if you spilled it *on* anybody. You were just drunk, that's all. In case you were wondering, you didn't look to be having a very good time. Matter of fact, you looked pretty miserable.'

I found the courage to say, 'I wound up in the hospital.'

'And you're out already?'

'I signed myself out this afternoon. I had a convulsion, that's how I got there.'

'That'll do it.'

We walked a little ways in silence. I said, 'I wouldn't be able to stay for the whole meeting. I have to meet a guy at ten o'clock.'

'You could stay for most of the meeting.'

'I guess so.'

It seemed to me as though everybody was staring at me. Some people said hello to me and I found myself reading implications into their greetings. Others didn't say anything and I decided they were avoiding me because my drunkenness had offended them. I was so maddeningly self-conscious I wanted to jump out of my own skin.

I couldn't stay in my seat during the qualification. I kept going back to the coffee urn. I was sure my constant visits to the urn were drawing disapproval but I seemed irresistibly drawn to it.

My mind kept going off on tangents of its own. The speaker was a Brooklyn fireman and he had a very lively story but I couldn't keep my mind on it. He told how everyone in his firehouse had been a heavy drinker and how anyone who didn't drink that way got transferred out. 'The captain was an alcoholic and he wanted to surround himself with other alcoholics,' he explained. 'He used to say, "Give me enough drunken firemen and I'll put out any fire there is." And he was right. Man, we would do anything, we would go in anywhere, take any crazy goddamned chances. Because we were too drunk to know better.'

It was such a goddamned puzzle. I'd been controlling my drinking and it had worked fine. Except when it didn't.

On the break I put a buck in the basket and went to the urn for still another cup of coffee. This time I managed to make myself eat an oatmeal cookie. I was back in my seat when the discussion started.

I kept losing the thread but it didn't seem to matter. I listened as well as I could and I stayed there as long as I could. At a quarter of ten I got up and slipped out the door as unobtrusively as possible. I had the feeling every eye in the place was on me and I wanted to assure them all that I wasn't going for a drink, that I had to meet somebody, that it was a business matter.

It struck me later that I could have stayed for the end. St Paul's was only five minutes from my hotel. Chance would have waited.

Maybe I wanted an excuse to leave before it was my turn to talk.

*

I was in the lobby at ten o'clock. I saw his car pull up and I went out the door and crossed the sidewalk to the curb. I opened the door, got in, swung it shut.

He looked at me.

'That job still open?'

He nodded. 'If you want it.'

'I want it.'

He nodded again, put the car in gear, and pulled away from the curb.

ELEVEN

The circular drive in Central Park is almost exactly six miles around. We were on our fourth counterclockwise lap, the Cadillac cruising effortlessly. Chance did most of the talking. I had my notebook out, and now and then I wrote something in it.

At first he talked about Kim. Her parents were Finnish immigrants who had settled on a farm in western Wisconsin. The nearest city of any size was Eau Claire. Kim had been named Kiraa and grew up milking cows and weeding the vegetable garden. When she was nine years old her older brother began abusing her sexually, coming into her room every night, doing things to her, making her do things to him.

'Except one time she told the story and it was her uncle on her mother's side, and another time it was her father, so maybe it never happened at all outside of her mind. Or maybe it did and she changed it to keep it from being so real.'

During her junior year in high school she had an affair with a middle-aged realtor. He told her he was going to leave his wife for her. She packed a suitcase and they drove to Chicago, where they stayed for three days at the Palmer House, ordering all their meals from room service. The realtor got maudlin drunk the second day and kept telling her he was ruining her life. He was in better spirits the third day, but the following morning she awoke to find him gone. A note explained that he had returned to his wife, that the room was paid for four more days, and that he would never forget Kim. Along with the note he left six hundred dollars in a hotel envelope.

She stayed out the week, had a look at Chicago, and slept with several men. Two of them gave her money without being asked. She'd intended to ask the others but couldn't bring herself to do so. She thought about going back to the farm. Then, on her final night at the Palmer House, she picked up a fellow hotel guest, a Nigerian delegate to some sort of trade conference.

'That burned her bridges,' Chance said. 'Sleeping with a black man meant she couldn't go back to the farm. First thing the next morning she went and caught a bus for New York.'

She'd been all wrong for the life until he took her away from Duffy and put her in her own apartment. She had the looks and the bearing for the carriage trade, and that was good because she hadn't had the hustle to make it on the street.

'She was lazy,' he said, and thought for a moment. 'Whores are lazy.'

He'd had six women working for him. Now, with Kim dead, he had five. He talked about them for a few moments in general terms, then got down to cases, supplying names and addresses and phone numbers and personal data. I made a lot of notes. We finished our fourth circuit of the park and he pulled off to the right, exited at West Seventy-second Street, drove two blocks and pulled over to the curb.

'Be a minute,' he said.

I stayed where I was while he made a call from a booth on the corner. He'd left the motor idling. I looked at my notes and tried to see a pattern in the wisps and fragments I'd been given.

Chance returned to the car, checked the mirror, swung us around in a deft if illegal U-turn. 'Just checking with my service,' he said. 'Just keeping in touch.'

'You ought to have a phone in the car.'

'Too complicated.'

He drove downtown and east, pulling up next to a fire hydrant in front of a white brick apartment house on Seventeenth between Second and Third. 'Collection time,' he told me. Once again he left the motor idling, but this time fifteen minutes elapsed before he reappeared, striding jauntily past the liveried doorman, sliding nimbly behind the wheel.

'That's Donna's place,' he said. 'I told you about Donna.'

'The poet.'

'She's all excited. She got two poems accepted by this magazine in San Francisco. She'll get six free copies of the issue the poems appear in. That's as much pay as she'll get, just copies of the magazine.'

A light turned red in front of us. He braked for it, looked left and right, then coasted through the light.

'Couple times,' he said, 'she's had poems in magazines that pay you for them. Once she got twenty-five dollars. That's the best she ever did.'

'It sounds like a hard way to make a living.'

'A poet can't make any money. Whores are lazy but this one's not lazy when it comes to her poems. She'll sit for six or eight hours to get the words right, and she's always got a dozen batches of poems in the mail. They come back from one place and she sends 'em out someplace else. She spends more on postage than they'll ever pay her for the poems.' He fell silent for a moment, then laughed softly. 'You know how much money I just took off of Donna? Eight hundred dollars, and that's just for the past two days. Of course there's days when her phone won't ring once.'

'But it averages out pretty well.'

'Pays better than poems.' He looked at me. 'Want to go for a ride?'

'Isn't that what we've been doing?'

'We been going around in circles,' he said. 'Now I'm gonna take you to a whole nother world.'

We drove down Second Avenue, through the Lower East Side, and over the Williamsburg Bridge into Brooklyn. Coming off the bridge we took enough turns to throw off my sense of direction, and the street signs didn't help much. I didn't recognize the names. But I watched the neighborhood change from Jewish to Italian to Polish and had a fair idea of where we were.

On a dark, silent street of two-family frame houses, Chance slowed in front of a three-story brick structure with a garage door in the middle. He used a remote-control unit to raise the door, then closed it after we had driven in. I followed him up a flight of stairs and into a spacious high-ceilinged room.

He asked if I knew where we were. I guessed Greenpoint. 'Very good,' he said. 'I guess you know Brooklyn.'

'I don't know this part of it very well. The meat market signs advertising kielbasa were a tip-off.'

'I guess. Know whose house we're in? Ever hear of a Dr Casimir Levandowski?'

'No.'

'No reason why you should have. He's an old fellow. Retired, confined to a wheelchair. Eccentric, too. Keeps himself to himself. This place used to be a firehouse.'

'I thought it must have been something like that.'

'Two architects bought it some years ago and converted it. They pretty much gutted the interior and started from scratch. They must have had a few dollars to play with because they didn't cut many corners. Look at the floors. Look at the window

222

moldings.' He pointed out details, commented on them. 'Then they got tired of the place or each other, I don't know what, and they sold out to old Dr Levandowski.'

'And he lives here?'

'He don't exist,' he said. His speech patterns kept shifting, from ghetto to university and back again. 'The neighbors never see the old doc. They just see his faithful black servant and all they see him do is drive in and drive out. This is my house, Matthew. Can I give you the ten-cent tour?'

It was quite a place. There was a gym on the top floor, fully equipped with weights and exercise machines and furnished with sauna and Jacuzzi. His bedroom was on the same floor, and the bed, covered with a fur spread, was centered beneath a skylight. A library on the second floor contained one whole wall of books and an eight-foot pool table.

There were African masks all over the place, and occasional groups of free-standing African sculpture. Chance pointed out a piece from time to time, naming the tribe that had produced it. I mentioned having seen African masks at Kim's apartment.

'Poro Society masks,' he said. 'From the Dan tribe. I keep one or two African things in all my girls' apartments. Not the most valuable things, of course, but not junk, either. I don't own any junk.'

He took a rather crudely fashioned mask from the wall and presented it for my inspection. The eye openings were square, the features all geometrically precise, the overall effect powerful in its primitiveness. 'This is Dogon,' he said. 'Take hold of it. You can't appreciate sculpture with your eyes alone. The hands have to participate. Go ahead, handle it.'

I took the mask from him. Its weight was greater than I anticipated. The wood that composed it must have been very dense.

He lifted a telephone from a low teakwood table and dialed a number. He said, 'Hey, darlin'. Any messages?' He listened for a moment, then put the phone down. 'Peace and quiet,' he said. 'Shall I make some coffee?'

'Not if it's any trouble.'

He assured me it wasn't. While the coffee brewed he told me about his African sculpture, how the craftsmen who produced it did not think of their work as art. 'Everything they make has a specific function,' he explained. 'It's to guard your house or keep off spirits or to use in a particular tribal rite. If a mask doesn't have the power in it anymore they'll throw it away and somebody'll carve a new one. The old one's trash, you burn it up or toss it away cause it's no good.'

He laughed. 'Then the Europeans came and discovered African art. Some of those French painters got their inspiration from tribal masks. Now you've got a situation where there are carvers in Africa spending all their time making masks and statues for export to Europe and America. They follow the old forms because that's what their customers want, but it's a funny thing. Their work's no good. It doesn't have any feeling in it. It's not real. You look at it and you take it in your hand, and you do the same with the real thing, and you can tell the difference right away. If you have any feeling at all for the stuff. Funny, isn't it?'

'It's interesting.'

'If I had any of the junk around I'd show you, but I don't own any. I bought some when I was starting out. You have to make mistakes to develop a feel for it. But I got rid of that stuff, burned it in the fireplace there.' He smiled. 'The very first piece I bought, I still have it. It's hanging in the bedroom. A Dan mask. Poro Society. I didn't know shit about African art but I saw it in an antique shop and I responded to the mask's artistic integrity.' He stopped, shook his head. 'Hell I did. What happened was I looked at that piece of smooth black wood and I was looking in a mirror. I saw myself, I saw my father, I was looking back through the damned ages. You know what I'm talking about?'

'I'm not sure.'

'Hell. Maybe I don't know either.' He gave his head a shake. 'What do you figure one of those old carvers'd make of this? He'd say, "Shit, what's this crazy nigger want with all these old masks? Why'd he go and hang 'em all over the damn wall?" That coffee's ready. You take yours black, right?'

He said, 'How's a detective go about detecting, anyway? Where do you start?'

'By going around and talking to people. Unless Kim got killed coincidentally by a maniac, her death grew out of her life.' I tapped my notebook. 'There's a lot you don't know about her life.'

'I guess.'

'I'll talk to people and see what they can tell me. Maybe it'll fit together and point somewhere. Maybe not.'

'My girls'll know it's cool to talk to you.'

'That'll help.'

'Not that they necessarily know anything, but if they do.'

'Sometimes people know things without knowing they know them.'

'And sometimes they tell without knowing they told.'

'That's true, too.'

He stood up, put his hands on his hips. 'You know,' he said, 'I didn't figure to bring you here. I didn't figure you needed to know about this house. And I brought you without you even asking.'

'It's quite a house.'

'Thank you.'

'Was Kim impressed with it?'

'She never saw it. None of 'em ever did. There's an old German woman comes here once a week to clean. Makes the whole place shine. She's the only woman's ever been inside of this house. Since I owned it, anyway, and the architects who used to live here didn't have much use for women. Here's the last of the coffee.'

It was awfully good coffee. I'd had too much of it already but it was too good to pass up. When I complimented it earlier he'd told me it was a mixture of Jamaica Blue Mountain and a dark roast Colombian bean. He'd offered me a pound of it, and I'd told him it wouldn't be much use to me in a hotel room.

I sipped the coffee while he made yet another call to his service. When he hung up I said, 'You want to give me the number here? Or is that one secret you want to keep?'

He laughed. 'I'm not here that much. It's easier if you just call the service.'

'All right.'

'And this number wouldn't do you much. I don't know it myself. I'd have to look at an old phone bill to make sure I got it right. And if you dialed it, nothing would happen.'

'Why's that?'

'Because the bells won't ring. The phones are to make calls out. When I set this place up I got telephone service and I put in extensions so I'd never be far from a phone, but I never gave the number to anybody. Not even my service, not anybody.'

'And?'

'And I was here one night, I think I was playing pool, and the damn phone rang. I like to jumped. It was somebody wanted to know did I want a subscription to the *New York Times*. Then two days later I got another call and it was a wrong number, and I realized the only calls I was ever going to get were wrong numbers and somebody selling something, and I took a screwdriver and went around and opened up each of the phones, and there's this little clapper that rings the bell when a current passes through a particular wire, and I just took the little clapper off each of the phones. I dialed the number once from another phone, and you think it rings because there's no telling the clapper's gone, but there's no bell going off in this house.'

'Clever.'

'No doorbell, either. There's a thing you ring by the door outside, but it's not connected to anything. That door's never been opened since I moved in, and you can't see in the windows, and there's burglar alarms on everything. Not that you get much burglary in Greenpoint, a nice settled Polish neighborhood like this, but old Dr Levandowski, he likes his security and he likes his privacy.'

'I guess he does.'

'I'm not here much, Matthew, but when that garage door closes behind me it keeps the whole world out. Nothing touches me here. Nothing.'

'I'm surprised you brought me here.'

'So am I.'

We saved the money for last. He asked how much I wanted. I told him I wanted twenty-five hundred dollars.

He asked what that bought.

'I don't know,' I said. 'I don't charge by the hour and I don't keep track of my expenses. If I wind up laying out a lot of money or if the thing goes on too long, I might wind up asking you for more money. But I'm not going to send you a bill and I'm not going to sue you if you don't pay.'

'You keep it all very informal.'

'That's right.'

'I like that. Cash on the line and no receipts. I don't mind paying a price. The women bring in a lot of money, but there's a lot that has to go out, too. Rent. Operating costs. Payoffs. You got a whore installed in a building, you pay off the building. You can't give the doorman twenty dollars for Christmas and let it go at that, same as any other tenant. It's more like twenty a month and a hundred for Christmas, and it's the same for all the building employees. It adds up.'

'It must.'

'But there's a lot left. And I don't blow it on coke or waste it gambling. You said what? Twenty-five hundred? I paid more than twice that for the Dogon mask I gave you to hold. I paid $6,200, plus the auction galleries charge buyers a 10 percent commission these days. Comes to what? $6,820. And then there's sales tax.'

I didn't say anything. He said, 'Shit, I don't know what I'm proving. That I'm nigger-rich, I guess. Wait here a minute.' He came back with a sheaf of hundreds and counted out twenty-five of them. Used bills, out of sequence. I wondered how much cash he kept around the house, how much he habitually carried on his person. Years ago I'd known a loan shark who made it a rule never to walk out his door with less than ten thousand dollars in his pocket. He didn't keep it a secret, and everybody who knew him knew about the roll he carried.

Nobody ever tried to take it off him, either.

He drove me home. We took a different route back, over the Pulaski Bridge into Queens and through the tunnel to Manhattan. Neither of us talked much, and somewhere along the way I must have dozed off because he had to put a hand on my shoulder to waken me.

I blinked, straightened up in my seat. We were at the curb in front of my hotel.

'Door-to-door delivery service,' he said.

I got out and stood on the curb. He waited for a couple of cabs to pass, then made his U-turn. I watched until the Cadillac was out of sight.

Thoughts struggled in my brain like exhausted swimmers. I was far too tired to think. I went up to bed.

TWELVE

'**I** didn't know her all that well. I met her a year or so ago at the beauty parlor and we had a cup of coffee together, and reading between the lines of her conversation I figured out she wasn't the Avon lady. We exchanged numbers and we would talk now and then over the phone, but we never got close. Then whenever it was, a couple weeks ago, she called and wanted to get together. I was surprised. We'd been out of touch for months.'

We were in Elaine Mardell's apartment on Fifty-first between First and Second. White shag carpet on the floor, bold abstract oils on the walls, something inoffensive on the stereo. I had a cup of coffee. Elaine was drinking a diet soda.

'What did she want?'

'She told me she was leaving her pimp. She wanted to make the break without getting hurt. Which is where you came in, remember?'

I nodded. 'Why'd she come to you?'

'I don't know. I had the feeling she didn't have too many friends. It wasn't the sort of thing she could talk over with one of Chance's other girls, and she probably wouldn't have wanted to discuss it with someone who was out of the life altogether. And she was young, you know, compared to me. She may have seen me as a sort of wise old aunt.'

'That's you, all right.'

'Isn't it just? What was she, about twenty-five?'

'She said twenty-three. I think it said twenty-four in the papers.'

'Jesus, that's young.'

'I know.'

'More coffee, Matt?'

'I'm fine.'

'You know why I think she picked me to have that little

conversation with? I think it's because I don't have a pimp.' She settled herself in her seat, uncrossed and recrossed her legs. I remembered other times in this apartment, one of us on the couch, the other on the Eames chair, the same sort of unobtrusive music softening the room's hard edges.

I said, 'You never had one, did you?'

'No.'

'Do most girls?'

'The ones she knew did. I think you pretty much have to on the street. Somebody's got to defend your right to a particular corner and bail you out when you get arrested. When you work out of an apartment like this, well, that's different. But even so, most of the hookers I know have boyfriends.'

'Is that the same thing as a pimp?'

'Oh, no. A boyfriend isn't running a batch of girls. He just happens to be your boyfriend. And you don't turn your money over to him. But you buy him a lot of things, just because you want to, and you help out with cash when he hits a rough spot in life, or if there's some business opportunity he wants to take advantage of, or because he needs a little loan and, gee, it's not like you were *giving* him the money. That's what a boyfriend is.'

'Sort of a one-woman pimp.'

'Sort of, except every girl swears her boyfriend's different, her relationship's different, and what never changes is who earns the money and who spends it.'

'And you never had a pimp, did you? Or a boyfriend?'

'Never. I had my palm read once and the woman who did it was impressed. "You have a double head line, dear," she told me. "Your head rules your heart."' She came over, showed me her hand. 'It's this line right here. See?'

'Looks good to me.'

'Damn straight.' She went back for her glass of soda, then came and sat on the couch beside me. She said, 'When I learned what happened to Kim, the first thing I did was call you. But you weren't in.'

'I never got the message.'

'I didn't leave one. I hung up and called a travel agent I know. A couple hours later I was on a plane for Barbados.'

'Were you afraid you were on somebody's list?'

'Hardly that. I just figured Chance killed her. I didn't think he'd start knocking off all her friends and relations. No, I just knew it was time for a break. A week at a beachfront hotel. A little sun in the afternoon, a little roulette at night, and enough steel-drum music and limbo dancing to hold me for a long time.'

'Sounds good.'

'Second night out I met a fellow at the poolside cocktail party. He was staying at the next hotel over. Very nice fellow, tax lawyer, got divorced a year and a half ago and then went through a tough little affair with someone too young for him, and he's over that now, and who does he meet but me.'

'And?'

'And we had a nice little romance for the rest of the week. Long walks on the beach. Snorkeling, tennis. Romantic dinners. Drinks on my terrace. I had a terrace looking out at the sea.'

'Here you've got one looking at the East River.'

'It's not the same. We had a great time, Matt. Good sex, too. I thought I'd have my work cut out for me, you know, acting shy. But I didn't have to act. I *was* shy, and then I got over my shyness.'

'You didn't tell him –'

'Are you kidding? Of course not. I told him I work for art galleries. I restore paintings. I'm a free-lance art restoration expert. He thought that was really fascinating and he had a lot of questions. It would have been easier if I'd had the sense to pick something a little more humdrum, but, see, I *wanted* to be fascinating.'

'Sure.'

She had her hands in her lap and she was looking at them. Her face was unlined but her years were beginning to show themselves on the back of her hands. I wondered how old she was. Thirty-six? Thirty-eight?

'Matt, he wanted to see me in the city. We weren't telling each other it was love, nothing like that, but there was this sense that we might have something that might go somewhere, and he wanted to follow it up and see where it led. He lives in Merrick. You know where that is?'

'Sure, out on the Island. It's not that far from where I used to live.'

'Is it nice out there?'

'Parts of it are very nice.'

'I gave him a phony number. He knows my name but the phone here is unlisted. I haven't heard from him and I don't expect to. I wanted a week in the sun and a nice little romance, and that's what I had, but once in a while I think I could call him and make up something about the wrong number. I could lie my way out of that one.'

'Probably.'

'But for what? I could even lie my way into being his wife or girlfriend or something. And I could give up this apartment and drop my john book in the incinerator. But for what?' She looked at me. 'I've got a good life. I save my money. I always saved my money.'

'And invested it,' I remembered. 'Real estate, isn't it? Apartment houses in Queens?'

'Not just Queens. I could retire now if I had to and I'd get by all right. But why would I want to retire and what do I need with a boyfriend?'

'Why did Kim Dakkinen want to retire?'

'Is that what she wanted?'

'I don't know. Why did she want to leave Chance?'

She thought it over, shook her head. 'I never asked.'

'Neither did I.'

'I've never been able to understand why a girl would have a pimp in the first place, so I don't need an explanation when somebody tells me she wants to get rid of one.'

'Was she in love with anybody?'

'Kim? Could be. She didn't mention it if she was.'

'Was she planning to leave the city?'

'I didn't get that impression. But she wouldn't tell me if she was, would she?'

'Hell,' I said. I put my empty cup on the end table. 'She was involved someway with someone. I just wish I knew who.'

'Why?'

'Because that's the only way I'm going to find out who killed her.'

'You think that's how it works?'

'That's usually how it works.'

'Suppose I got killed tomorrow. What would you do?'

'I guess I'd send flowers.'

'Seriously.'

'Seriously? I'd check tax lawyers from Merrick.'

'There's probably a few of them, don't you think?'

'Could be. I don't suppose there's too many who spent a week in Barbados this month. You said he stayed at the next hotel down the beach from you? I don't think he'd be hard to find, or that I'd have much trouble tying him to you.'

'Would you actually do all that?'

231

'Why not?'

'No one would be paying you.'

I laughed. 'Well, you and I, we go back a ways, Elaine.'

And we did. When I was on the force we'd had an arrangement. I helped her out when she needed the kind of hand a cop could provide, whether with the law or with an unruly john. She, in turn, had been available to me when I wanted her. What, I wondered suddenly, had that made me? Neither pimp nor boyfriend, but what?

'Matt? Why did Chance hire you?'

'To find out who killed her.'

'Why?'

I thought of the reasons he'd given. 'I don't know,' I said.

'Why'd you take the job?'

'I can use the money, Elaine.'

'You don't care that much about money.'

'Sure I do. It's time I started providing for my old age. I've got an eye on these apartment houses in Queens.'

'Very funny.'

'I'll bet you're some landlady. I'll bet they love it when you come around to collect the rent.'

'There's a management firm that takes care of all that. I never see my tenants.'

'I wish you hadn't told me that. You just ruined a great fantasy.'

'I'll bet.'

I said, 'Kim took me to bed after I finished the job for her. I went over there and she paid me and then afterward we went to bed.'

'And?'

'It was like a tip, almost. A friendly way of saying thank you.'

'Beats ten dollars at Christmas time.'

'But would she do that? If she was involved with somebody, I mean. Would she just go to bed with me for the hell of it?'

'Matt, you're forgetting something.'

She looked, for just a moment, like somebody's wise old aunt. I asked what I was forgetting.

'Matt, she was a hooker.'

'Were you a hooker in Barbados?'

'I don't know,' she said. 'Maybe I was and maybe I wasn't. But I can tell you this much. I was damn glad when the mating dance was over and we were in bed together because for a change I knew what I was doing. And going to bed with guys is what I do.'

I thought a moment. Then I said, 'When I called earlier you said to give you an hour. Not to come over right away.'

'So?'

'Because you had a john booked?'

'Well, it wasn't the meter reader.'

'Did you need the money?'

'Did I need the money? What kind of question is that? I *took* the money.'

'But you would have made the rent without it.'

'And I wouldn't have missed any meals, or had to wear the panty hose with the runs in it. What's this all about?'

'So you saw the guy today because that's what you do.'

'I suppose.'

'Well, you're the one who asked why I took the job.'

'It's what you do,' she said.

'Something like that.'

She thought of something and laughed. She said, 'When Heinrich Heine was dying – the German poet?'

'Yeah?'

'When he was dying he said, 'God will pardon me. It's His profession.'

'That's not bad.'

'It's probably even better in German. I shtup and you detect and God pardons.' She lowered her eyes. 'I just hope He does,' she said. 'When it's my turn in the barrel, I hope He's not down in Barbados for the weekend.'

THIRTEEN

When I left Elaine's the sky was growing dark and the streets were thick with rush-hour traffic. It was raining again, a nagging drizzle that slowed the commuters to a crawl. I looked at the swollen river of cars and wondered if one of them held Elaine's tax lawyer. I thought about him and tried to guess how he might have reacted when the number she gave him turned out to be a fake.

He could find her if he wanted to. He knew her name. The phone company wouldn't give out her unlisted number, but he wouldn't have to be too well connected to find somebody who could pry it out of them for him. Failing that, he could trace her without too much trouble through her hotel. They could tell him her travel agent and somewhere along the line he could pick up her address. I'd been a cop, I automatically thought of this sort of thing, but couldn't anybody make this sort of connection? It didn't seem terribly complicated to me.

Perhaps he'd been hurt when her number proved phony. Perhaps knowing she didn't want to see him would keep him from wanting to see her. But wouldn't his first thought be that the mistake might have been an accident? Then he'd try Information, and might guess that the unobtainable number differed from what she'd given him by no more than a transposed couple of digits. So why wouldn't he pursue it?

Maybe he never called her in the first place, never even learned that the number was phony. Maybe he'd discarded her number in the airplane washroom on the way home to his wife and kids.

Maybe he had a few guilt-ridden moments now and then, thinking of the art restorer waiting by her telephone for his call. Maybe he would find himself regretting his haste. No need, after all, to have thrown her number away. He might have been able to fit in a date with her from time to time. No reason she had to

234

learn about the wife and kids. The hell, she'd probably be grateful for someone to take her away from her paint tubes and turpentine.

Halfway home I stopped at a deli and had soup and a sandwich and coffee. There was a bizarre story in the *Post*. Two neighbors in Queens had been arguing for months because of a dog that barked in its owner's absence. The previous night, the owner was walking the dog when the animal relieved itself on a tree in front of the neighbor's house. The neighbor happened to be watching and shot at the dog from an upstairs window with a bow and arrow. The dog's owner ran back into his house and came out with a Walther P-38, a World War II souvenir. The neighbor also ran outside with his bow and arrow, and the dog's owner shot him dead. The neighbor was eighty-one, the dog's owner was sixty-two, and the two men had lived side by side in Little Neck for over twenty years. The dog's age wasn't given, but there was a picture of him in the paper, straining against a leash in the hands of a uniformed police officer.

Midtown North was a few blocks from my hotel. It was still raining in the same halfhearted fashion when I went over there a little after nine that night. I stopped at the front desk and a young fellow with a moustache and blow-dry hair pointed me to the staircase. I went up a flight and found the detective squad room. There were four plainclothes cops sitting at desks, a couple more down at the far end watching something on television. Three young black males in a holding pen paid some attention when I entered, then lost interest when they saw I wasn't their lawyer.

I approached the nearest desk. A balding cop looked up from the report he was typing. I told him I had an appointment with Detective Durkin.

A cop at another desk looked up and caught my eye. 'You must be Scudder,' he said. 'I'm Joe Durkin.'

His handshake was overly firm, almost a test of masculinity. He waved me into a chair and took his own seat, stubbed out a cigarette in an overflowing ashtray, lit a fresh one, leaned back and looked at me. His eyes were that pale shade of gray that doesn't show you a thing.

He said, 'Still raining out there?'

'Off and on.'

'Miserable weather. You want some coffee?'

'No thanks.'

'What can I do for you?'

I told him I'd like to see whatever he could show me on the Kim Dakkinen killing.

'Why?'

'I told somebody I'd look into it.'

'You told somebody you'd look into it? You mean you got a client?'

'You could say that.'

'Who?'

'I can't tell you that.'

A muscle worked along the side of his jaw. He was around thirty-five and a few pounds overweight, enough to make him look a little older than his years. He hadn't lost any hair yet and it was all dark brown, almost black. He wore it combed flat down on his head. He should have borrowed a blow dryer from the guy downstairs.

He said, 'You can't hold that out. You don't have a license and it wouldn't be privileged information even if you did.'

'I didn't know we were in court.'

'We're not. But you come in here asking a favor –'

I shrugged. 'I can't tell you my client's name. He has an interest in seeing her killer caught. That's all.'

'And he thinks that'll happen faster if he hires you.'

'Evidently.'

'You think so too?'

'What I think is I got a living to make.'

'Jesus,' he said. 'Who doesn't?'

I'd said the right thing. I wasn't a threat now. I was just a guy going through the motions and trying to turn a dollar. He sighed, slapped the top of his desk, got up and crossed the room to a bank of filing cabinets. He was a chunkily built, bandy-legged man with his sleeves rolled up and his collar open, and he walked with the rolling gait of a sailor. He brought back a manila accordion file, dropped into his chair, found a photograph in the files and pitched it onto the desk.

'Here,' he said. 'Feast your eyes.'

It was a five-by-seven black and white glossy of Kim, but if I hadn't known that I don't see how I could have recognized her. I looked at the picture, fought off a wave of nausea, and made myself go on looking at it.

'Really did a job on her,' I said.

'He got her sixty-six times with what the doc thinks was

probably a machete or something like it. How'd you like the job of counting? I don't know how they do that work. I swear it's a worse job than the one I got.'

'All that blood.'

'Be grateful you're seeing it in black and white. It was worse in color.'

'I can imagine.'

'He hit arteries. You do that, you get spurting, you get blood all over the room. I never saw so much blood.'

'He must have gotten blood all over himself.'

'No way to avoid it.'

'Then how did he get out of there without anybody noticing?'

'It was cold that night. Say he had a coat, he'd put that on over whatever else he was wearing.' He drew on his cigarette. 'Or maybe he wasn't wearing any clothes when he did the number on her. The hell, she was in her birthday suit, maybe he didn't want to feel overdressed. Then all he'd have to do afterward was take a shower. There was a nice beautiful bathroom there and he had all the time in the world so why not use it?'

'Were the towels used?'

He looked at me. The gray eyes were still unreadable, but I sensed a little more respect in his manner. 'I don't remember any soiled towels,' he said.

'I don't suppose they're something you'd notice, not with a scene like that in the same room.'

'They ought to be inventoried, though.' He thumbed through the file. 'You know what they do, they take pictures of everything, and everything that might turn out to be evidence gets bagged and labeled and inventoried. Then it goes down to the warehouse, and when it's time to prepare a case nobody can find it.' He closed the file for a moment, leaned forward. 'You want to hear something? Two, three weeks ago I get a call from my sister. She and her husband live over in Brooklyn. The Midwood section. You familiar with the area?'

'I used to be.'

'Well, it was probably nicer when you knew it. It's not so bad. I mean, the whole city's a cesspool, so it's not so bad in comparison. Why she called, they came home and found out there'd been a burglary. Somebody broke in, took a portable teevee, a typewriter, some jewelry. She called me to find out how to report it, who to call and everything. First thing I asked her is has she got insurance. No, she says, they didn't figure it was worth it. I told her to forget it. Don't report it, I told her. You'd just be wasting your time.

'So she says how are they gonna catch the guys if she doesn't report it? So I explain how nobody's got the time to investigate a burglary anymore. You fill out a report and it goes in a file, but you don't run around looking to see who did it. Catching a burglar in the act is one thing, but investigating, hell, it's low priority, nobody's got time for it. She says okay, she can understand that, but suppose they happen to recover the goods? If she never reported the theft in the first place, how will the stuff get returned to her? And then I had to tell her just how fucked up the whole system is. We got warehouses full of stolen goods we recovered, and we got files full of reports people filled out, stuff lost to burglars, and we can't get the shit back to the rightful owners. I went on and on, I won't bore you with it, but I don't think she really wound up believing me. Because you don't want to believe it's that bad.'

He found a sheet in the file, frowned at it. He read, 'One bath towel, white. One hand towel, white. Two wash cloths, white. Doesn't say used or unused.' He drew out a sheaf of glossies and went rapidly through them. I looked over his shoulder at interior shots of the room where Kim Dakkinen had died. She was in some but not all of the pictures; the photographer had documented the murder scene by shooting virtually every inch of the hotel room.

A shot of the bathroom showed a towel rack with unused linen on it.

'No dirty towels,' he said.

'He took them along.'

'Huh?'

'He had to wash up. Even if he just threw a topcoat over his bloody clothes. And there aren't enough towels there. There ought to be at least two of everything. A double room in a class hotel, they give you more than one bath towel and one hand towel.'

'Why would he take 'em along?'

'Maybe to wrap the machete in.'

'He had to have a case for it in the first place, some kind of a bag to get it into the hotel. Why couldn't he take it out the same way?'

I agreed that he could have.

'And why wrap it in the dirty towels? Say you took a shower and dried yourself off and you wanted to wrap a machete before you put it in your suitcase. There's clean towels there. Wouldn't you wrap it in a clean one instead of sticking a wet towel in your bag?'

'You're right.'

'It's a waste of time worrying about it,' he said, tapping the photo against the top of his desk. 'But I shoulda noticed the missing towels. That's something I should have thought of.'

We went through the file together. The medical report held few surprises. Death was attributed to massive hemorrhaging from multiple wounds resulting in excessive loss of blood. I guess you could call it that.

I read through witness interrogation reports, made my way through all the other forms and scraps of paper that wind up in a homicide victim's file. I had trouble paying attention. My head was developing a dull ache and my mind was spinning its wheels. Somewhere along the way Durkin let me go through the rest of the file on my own. He lit a fresh cigarette and went back to what he'd been typing earlier.

When I'd had as much as I could handle I closed the file and gave it back to him. He returned it to the cabinet, detouring on the way back to make a stop at the coffee machine.

'I got 'em both with cream and sugar,' he said, setting mine before me. 'Maybe that's not how you like it.'

'It's fine,' I said.

'Now you know what we know,' he said. I told him I appreciated it. He said, 'Listen, you saved us some time and aggravation with the tip about the pimp. We owed you one. If you can turn a buck for yourself, why not?'

'Where do you go from here?'

He shrugged. 'We proceed in normal fashion with our investigation. We run down leads and assemble evidence until such time as we have something to present to the district attorney's office.'

'That sounds like a recording.'

'Does it?'

'What happens next, Joe?'

'Aw, Jesus,' he said. 'The coffee's terrible, isn't it?'

'It's okay.'

'I used to think it was the cups. Then one day I brought my own cup, you know, so I was drinking it out of china instead of Styrofoam. Not fancy china, just, you know, an ordinary china cup like they give you in a coffee shop. You know what I mean.'

'Sure.'

'It tasted just as bad out of a real cup. And the second day after I brought the cup I was writing out an arrest report on some scumbag and I knocked the fucking cup off the desk and broke it. You got someplace you gotta be?'

'No.'

'Then let's go downstairs,' he said. 'Let's go around the corner.'

FOURTEEN

He took me around the corner and a block and a half south on Tenth Avenue to a tavern that belonged at the end of somebody's qualification. I didn't catch the name and I'm not sure if it had one. They could have called it Last Stop Before Detox. Two old men in thrift-shop suits sat together at the bar, drinking in silence. A Hispanic in his forties stood at the far end of the bar, sipping an eight-ounce glass of red wine and reading the paper. The bartender, a rawboned man in a tee shirt and jeans, was watching something on a small black and white television set. He had the volume turned way down.

Durkin and I took a table and I went to the bar to get our drinks, a double vodka for him, ginger ale for myself. I carried them back to our table. His eyes registered my ginger ale without comment.

It could have been a medium-strength scotch and soda. The color was about right.

He drank some of his vodka and said, 'Aw, Jesus, that helps. It really helps.'

I didn't say anything.

'What you were asking before. Where do we go from here. Can't you answer that yourself?'

'Probably.'

'I told my own sister to buy a new teevee and a new typewriter and hang some more locks on the door. But don't bother calling the cops. Where do we go with Dakkinen? We don't go anywhere.'

'That's what I figured.'

'We know who killed her.'

'Chance?' He nodded. 'I thought his alibi looked pretty good.'

'Oh, it's gilt-edged. It's bottled in bond. So what? He still could have done it. The people he says he was with are people who would lie for him.'

'You think they were lying?'

'No, but I wouldn't swear they weren't. Anyway, he could have hired it. We already talked about that.'

'Right.'

'If he did it he's clear. We're not going to be able to put a dent in that alibi. If he hired it we're not gonna find out who he hired. Unless we get lucky. That happens sometimes, you know. Things fall in your lap. One guy says something in a gin joint and somebody with a grudge passes it on, and all of a sudden we know something we didn't know before. But even if that happens, we'll be a long way from putting a case together. Meanwhile, we don't figure to kill ourselves over it.'

What he was saying was no surprise but there was something deadening about the words. I picked up my ginger ale and looked at it.

He said, 'Half the job is knowing the odds. Working the cases where you got a chance, letting the others flap in the breeze. You know the murder rate in this town?'

'I know it keeps going higher.'

'Tell me about it. It's up every year. All crimes are up every year, except we're starting to get a statistical drop in some of the less serious ones because people aren't bothering to report them. Like my sister's burglary. You got mugged coming home and all that happened was he took your money? Well, shit, why make a federal case out of it, right? Be grateful you're alive. Go home and say a prayer of thanks.'

'With Kim Dakkinen –'

'Screw Kim Dakkinen,' he said. 'Some dumb little bitch comes fifteen hundred miles to peddle her ass and give the money to a nigger pimp, who cares if somebody chopped her up? I mean why didn't she stay in fucking Minnesota?'

'Wisconsin.'

'I meant Wisconsin. Most of 'em come from Minnesota.'

'I know.'

'The murder rate used to be around a thousand a year. Three a day in the five boroughs. That always seemed high.'

'High enough.'

'It's just about double that now.' He leaned forward. 'But that's *nothing*, Matt. Most homicides are husband-wife things, or two friends drinking together and one of 'em shoots the other and doesn't even remember it the next day. That rate never changes. It's the same as it always was. What's changed are stranger murders, where the killer and the victim don't know each other. That's the rate that shows you how dangerous it is to live somewhere. If you just take the stranger murders, if you throw out the other cases and put the stranger murders on a graph, the line goes up like a rocket.'

'There was a guy in Queens yesterday with a bow and arrow,' I said, 'and the guy next door shot him with a .38.'

'I read about that. Something about a dog shitting on the wrong lawn?'

'Something like that.'

'Well, that wouldn't be on the chart. That's two guys who knew each other.'

'Right.'

'But it's all part of the same thing. People keep killing each other. They don't even stop and think, they just go ahead and do it. You been off the force what, a couple years now? I'll tell you this much. It's a lot worse than you remember.'

'I believe you.'

'I mean it. It's a jungle out there and all the animals are armed. Everybody's got a gun. You realize the number of people out there walking around with a piece? Your honest citizen, he's gotta have a gun now for his own protection, so he gets one and somewhere down the line he shoots himself or his wife or the guy next door.'

'The guy with the bow and arrow.'

'Whatever. But who's gonna tell him not to have a gun?' He slapped his abdomen, where his service revolver was tucked under his belt. 'I gotta carry this,' he said. 'It's regulations. But I'll tell you, I wouldn't walk around out there without it. I'd feel naked.'

'I used to think that. You get used to it.'

'You don't carry anything?'

'Nothing.'

'And it doesn't bother you?'

I went to the bar and got fresh drinks, more vodka for him, more ginger ale for me. When I brought them back to the table Durkin drank the whole thing in one long swallow and sighed like a tire going flat. He cupped his hands and lit a cigarette, inhaled deeply, blew out the smoke as if in a hurry to be rid of it.

'This fucking city,' he said.

It was hopeless, he said, and he went on to tell me just how hopeless it was. He rang changes on the whole criminal justice system, from the cops to the courts to the jails, explaining how none of it worked and all of it was getting worse every day. You

243

couldn't arrest a guy and then you couldn't convict him and finally you couldn't keep the son of a bitch in jail.

'The prisons are overcrowded,' he said, 'so the judges don't want to hand out long sentences and the parole boards release people early. And the DA's let the guys cop to a reduced charge, they plea bargain good cases down to nothing, because the court calendars are so jammed up and the courts are so careful to protect the rights of the accused that you just about need a photo of the guy committing the crime in order to get a conviction, and then you might get a reversal because you were violating his civil rights by taking his photograph without prior permission. And in the meantime there's no cops. The department's got ten thousand men below what it had twelve years ago. Ten thousand fewer cops on the street!'

'I know.'

'Twice as many crooks and a third less cops and you wonder why it's not safe to walk down the street. You know what it is? The city's broke. There's no money for cops, no money to keep the subways running, no money for anything. The whole country's leaking money, it's all winding up in Saudi fucking Arabia. All those assholes are trading in their camels for Cadillacs while this country goes down the fucking tubes.' He stood up. 'My turn to buy.'

'No, I'll get them. I'm on expenses.'

'Right, you got a client.' He sat down. I came back with another round and he said, 'What are you drinking there?'

'Just ginger ale.'

'Yeah, I thought that's what it looked like. Whyntcha have a real drink?'

'I'm sort of cutting back on it these days.'

'Oh yeah?' The gray eyes focused on me as he registered this information. He picked up his glass and drank about half of it, set it down on the worn wooden table with a thunk. 'You got the right idea,' he said, and I thought he meant the ginger ale, but he had shifted gears by then. 'Quitting the job. Getting out. You know what I want? All I want is six more years.'

'Then you got your twenty?'

'Then I got my twenty,' he said, 'and then I got my pension, and then I'm fucking well gone. Out of this job and out of this shithole of a city. Florida, Texas, New Mexico, someplace warm and dry and clean. Forget Florida, I heard things about Florida, all the fucking Cubans, they got crime like you get here. Plus they got all the dope coming in there. Those crazy Colombians. You know about the Colombians?'

I thought of Royal Waldron. 'A fellow I know says they're all right,' I said. 'He said you just don't want to cheat 'em.'

'You bet your ass you don't want to cheat 'em. You read about those two girls over in Long Island City? Must have been six, eight months ago. Sisters, one's twelve and one's fourteen, and they found 'em in the back room of this out-of-business gas station, hands tied behind their backs, each of 'em shot twice in the head with a small-caliber weapon, I think a .22, but who gives a shit?' He drank the rest of his drink. 'Well, it didn't figure. No sex angle, nothing. It's an execution, but who executes a couple of teenage sisters?

'Well, it clears itself up, because a week later somebody breaks into the house where they lived and shoots their mother. We found her in the kitchen with dinner still cooking on the stove. See, the family's Colombian, and the father's in the cocaine business, which is the chief industry down there outside of smuggling emeralds –'

'I thought they grew a lot of coffee.'

'That's probably a front. Where was I? The point is, the father turns up dead a month later in whatever's the capital of Colombia. He crossed somebody and he ran for it, and they wound up getting him in Colombia, but first they killed his kids and his wife. See, the Colombians, they play by a different set of rules. You fuck with them and they don't just kill you. They wipe out your whole family. Kids, any age, it don't matter. You got a dog and a cat and some tropical fish, they're dead too.'

'Jesus.'

'The Mafia was always considerate about family. They'd even make sure to arrange a hit so your family wouldn't be there to see it happen. Now we got criminals that kill the whole family. Nice?'

'Jesus.'

He put his palms on the table for leverage, hoisted himself to his feet. 'I'm getting this round,' he announced. 'I don't need some pimp payin' for my drinks.'

Back at the table he said, 'He's your client, right? Chance?' When I failed to respond he said, 'Well, shit, you met with him last night. He wanted to see you, and now you got a client that you won't say his name. Two and two's gotta be four, doesn't it?'

245

'I can't tell you how to add it.'

'Let's just say I'm right and he's your client. For the sake of argument. You won't be givin' nothin' away.'

'All right.'

He leaned forward. 'He killed her,' he said. 'So why would he hire you to investigate it?'

'Maybe he didn't kill her.'

'Oh, sure he did.' He dismissed the possibility of Chance's innocence with a wave of his hand. 'She says she's quitting him and he says okay and the next day she's dead. Come on, Matt. What's that if it's not cut and dried?'

'Then we get back to your question. Why'd he hire me?'

'Maybe to take the heat off.'

'How?'

'Maybe he'll figure we'll figure he must be innocent or he wouldn't have hired you.'

'But that's not what you figured at all.'

'No.'

'You think he'd really think that?'

'How do I know what some coked-up spade pimp is gonna think?'

'You figure he's a cokehead?'

'He's got to spend it on something, doesn't he? It's not gonna go for country-club dues and a box at the charity ball. Lemme ask *you* something.'

'Go ahead.'

'You think there's a chance in the world he didn't kill her? Or set her up and hire it done?'

'I think there's a chance.'

'Why?'

'For one thing, he hired me. And it wasn't to take the heat off because what heat are we talking about? You already said there wasn't going to be any heat. You're planning to clear the case and work on something else.'

'He wouldn't necessarily know that.'

I let that pass. 'Take it from another angle,' I suggested. 'Let's say I never called you.'

'Called me when?'

'The first call I made. Let's say you didn't know she was breaking with her pimp.'

'If we didn't get it from you we'd of gotten it somewhere else.'

'Where? Kim was dead and Chance wouldn't volunteer the information. I'm not sure anybody else in the world knew.'

Except for Elaine, but I wasn't going to bring her into it. 'I don't think you'd have gotten it. Not right off the bat, anyway.'

'So?'

'So how would you have figured the killing then?'

He didn't answer right away. He looked down at his near-empty glass, and a couple of vertical frown lines creased his forehead. He said, 'I see what you mean.'

'How would you have pegged it?'

'The way we did before you called. A psycho. You know we're not supposed to call 'em that anymore? There was a departmental directive went out about a year ago. From now on we don't call 'em psychos. From now on it's EDPs.'

'What's an EDP?'

'Emotionally Disturbed Person. That's what some asshole on Centre Street's got nothing better to worry about. The whole city's up to its ass in more nuts than a fruitcake and our first priority is how we refer to them. We don't want to hurt their feelings. No, I'd figure a psycho, some new version of Jack the Ripper. Calls up a hooker, invites her over, chops her up.'

'And if it was a psycho?'

'You know what happens then. You hope you get lucky with a piece of physical evidence. In this case fingerprints were hopeless, it's a transient hotel room, there's a million latents and no place to start with them. Be nice if there was a big bloody fingerprint and you knew it belonged to the killer, but we didn't have that kind of luck.'

'Even if you did –'

'Even if we did, a single print wouldn't lead anywhere. Not until we had a suspect. You can't get a make from Washington on a single print. They keep saying you're gonna be able to eventually, but –'

'They've been saying that for years.'

'It'll never happen. Or it will, but I'll have my six years by then and I'll be in Arizona. Barring physical evidence that leads somewhere, I guess we'd be waiting for the nut to do it again. You get another couple of cases with the same MO and sooner or later he fucks up and you got him, and then you match him to some latents in the room at the Galaxy and you wind up with a case.' He drained his glass. 'Then he plea bargains his way to manslaughter and he's out in three years tops and he does it again, but I don't want to get started on that again. I honest to Christ don't want to get started on that again.'

I bought our next round. Any compunctions he had about having a pimp's money pay for his booze seemed to have been dissolved by the same alcohol that had given rise to them. He was visibly drunk now, but only if you knew where to look. The eyes had a glaze on them, and there was a matching glaze on his whole manner. He was holding up his end of a typical alcoholic conversation, wherein two drunks take polite turns talking aloud to their own selves.

I wouldn't have noticed this if I'd been matching him drink for drink. But I was sober, and as the booze got to him I felt the gulf widening between us.

I tried to keep the conversation on the subject of Kim Dakkinen but it wouldn't stay there. He wanted to talk about everything that was wrong with New York.

'You know what it is,' he said, leaning forward, lowering his voice, as if we weren't the only two customers in the bar by now, just us and the bartender. 'I'll tell you what it is. It's niggers.'

I didn't say anything.

'And spics. The blacks and the Hispanics.'

I said something about black and Puerto Rican cops. He rode right over it. 'Listen, don't tell me,' he said. 'I got a guy I been partnered with a lot, Larry Haynes his name is, maybe you know him –' I didn't '– and he's as good as they come. I'd trust the man with my life. Shit, I *have* trusted him with my life. He's black as coal and I never met a better man in or out of the department. But that's got nothing to do with what I'm talking about.' He wiped his mouth with the back of his hand. 'Look,' he said, 'you ever ride the subway?'

'When I have to.'

'Well, shit, nobody rides it by choice. It's the whole city in a nutshell, the equipment breaks down all the time, the cars are filthy with spray paint and they stink of piss and the transit cops can't make a dent in the crime down there, but what I'm talking about, shit, *I* get on a subway and I look around and you know where I am? I'm in a fucking foreign country.'

'What do you mean?'

'I mean everybody's black or Spanish. Or oriental, we got all these new Chinese immigrants coming in, plus there's the Koreans. Now the Koreans are perfect citizens, they open up all these great vegetable markets all over the city, they work twenty hours a day and send their kids to college, but it's all part of something.'

'Part of what?'

'Oh, shit, it sounds ignorant and bigoted but I can't help it. This used to be a white city and now there's days when I feel like I'm the only white man left in it.'

The silence stretched. Then he said, 'They smoke on the subway now. You ever notice?'

'I've noticed.'

'Never used to happen. A guy might murder both his parents with a fire axe but he wouldn't dare light up a cigarette on the subway. Now you got middle-class people lighting their cigarettes, puffing away. Just in the last few months. You know how it started?'

'How?'

'Remember about a year ago? A guy was smoking on the PATH train and a PATH cop asked him to put it out, and the guy drew a gun and shot the cop dead? Remember?'

'I remember.'

'That's what started it. You read about that and whoever you are, a cop or a private citizen, you're not in a rush to tell the guy across the aisle to put out his fucking cigarette. So a few people light up and nobody does anything about it, and more people do it, and who's gonna give a shit about smoking in the subway when it's a waste of time to report a major crime like burglary? Stop enforcing a law and people stop respecting it.' He frowned. 'But think about that PATH cop. You like that for a way to die? Ask a guy to put out a cigarette and bang, you're dead.'

I found myself telling him about Rudenko's mother, dead of a bomb blast because her friend had brought home the wrong television set. And so we traded horror stories. He told of a social worker, lured onto a tenement roof, raped repeatedly and thrown off the building to her death. I recalled something I'd read about a fourteen-year-old shot by another boy the same age, both of them strangers to each other, the killer insisted that his victim had laughed at him. Durkin told me about some child-abuse cases that had ended in death, and about a man who had smothered his girlfriend's infant daughter because he was sick of paying for a baby-sitter everytime the two of them went to the movies. I mentioned the woman in Gravesend, dead of a shotgun blast while she hung clothes in her closet. There was an air of *Can You Top This?* to our dialogue.

He said, 'The mayor thinks he's got the answer. The death penalty. Bring back the big black chair.'

'Think it'll happen?'

'No question the public wants it. And there's one way it works and you can't tell me it doesn't. You fry one of these bastards and at least you know he's not gonna do it again. The hell, I'd vote for it. Bring back the chair and televise the fucking executions, run commercials, make a few dollars and hire a few more cops. You want to know something?'

'What?'

'We *got* the death penalty. Not for murderers. For ordinary citizens. Everybody out there runs a better chance of getting killed than a killer does of getting the chair. We get the death penalty five, six, seven times a day.'

He had raised his voice and the bartender was auditing our conversation now. We'd lured him away from his program.

Durkin said, 'I like the one about the exploding television set. I don't know how I missed that one. You think you heard 'em all but there's always something new, isn't there?'

'I guess.'

'There are eight million stories in the naked city,' he intoned. 'You remember that program? Used to be on television some years back.'

'I remember.'

'They had that line at the end of every show. "There are eight million stories in the naked city. This has been one of them."'

'I remember it.'

'Eight million stories,' he said. 'You know what you got in this city, this fucked-up toilet of a naked fucking city? You know what you got? You got eight million ways to die.'

I got him out of there. Outside in the cool night air he fell silent. We circled a couple of blocks, wound up down the street from the station house. His car was a Mercury a few years old. It had been beaten up a little around the corners. The license plate had a prefix which would indicate to other cops that this was a vehicle used for police business and not to be ticketed. Some of the more knowledgeable crooks could also recognize it as a cop's car.

I asked if he was okay to drive. He didn't much care for the question. He said, 'What are you, a cop?' and then the absurdity of the remark struck him and he started to laugh. He clung to the car's open door for support, helpless with laughter, and swung back and forth on the car door. 'What are you, a cop?' he said, giggling. 'What are you, a cop?'

That mood passed like a fast cut in a film. In an instant he was

250

serious and apparently sober, eyes narrowed, jaw thrust forward like a bulldog's. 'Listen,' he said, voice low and hard. 'Don't be so goddamn superior, you understand?'

I didn't know what he was talking about.

'You sanctimonious bastard. You're no better than I am, you son of a bitch.'

He pulled out and drove off. He seemed to be driving all right for as far as I was able to track him. I hoped he didn't have too far to go.

FIFTEEN

I walked straight back to my hotel. The liquor stores were closed but the bars were still open. I passed them without much effort, resisted too the call of street whores on Fifty-seventh Street on either side of the Holiday Inn. I gave Jacob a nod, confirmed that I'd had no calls, and went upstairs.

Sanctimonious bastard. No better than I am. He'd been ugly drunk, with that defensive belligerence of the drinker who had exposed too much of himself. His words didn't mean anything. He'd have addressed them to any companion, or to the night itself.

Still, they echoed in my head.

I got into bed but couldn't sleep, got up and put the light on and sat on the edge of the bed with my notebook. I looked over some of the notes I made, then jotted down a point or two from our conversation in the bar on Tenth Avenue. I made a few further notes to myself, playing with ideas like a kitten with a yarn ball. I put the notebook down when the process reached a point of diminishing returns, with the same thoughts turning over and over upon themselves. I picked up a paperback I'd bought earlier but couldn't get into it. I kept reading the same paragraph without getting the sense of it.

For the first time in hours I really wanted a drink. I was anxious and edgy and wanted to change it. There was a deli with a cooler full of beer just three doors from the hotel, and when had beer ever led me into a blackout?

I stayed where I was.

Chance hadn't asked my reason for working for him. Durkin had accepted money as a valid motive. Elaine was willing to believe I was doing it because it was what I did, even as she turned tricks and God pardoned sinners. And it was all true, I could indeed use the money and detecting was what I did insofar as I did anything, it was as much of a profession as I had.

But I had another motive, and perhaps it was a deeper one. Searching for Kim's killer was something I could do instead of drinking.

For awhile, anyway.

When I woke up the sun was shining. By the time I showered and shaved and hit the street it was gone, tucked away behind a bank of clouds. It came and went all day, as if whoever was in charge didn't want to commit himself.

I ate a light breakfast, made some phone calls, then walked over to the Galaxy Downtowner. The clerk who'd checked in Charles Jones wasn't on duty. I'd read his interrogation report in the file and didn't really expect I could get more out of him than the cops could.

An assistant manager let me look at Jones's registration card. He'd printed 'Charles Owen Jones' on the line marked 'Name,' and on the 'Signature' line he'd printed 'C. O. JONES' in block capitals. I pointed this out to the assistant manager, who told me the discrepancy was common. 'People will put their full name on one line and a shorter version on the other,' he said. 'Either way is legal.'

'But this isn't a signature.'

'Why not?'

'He printed it.'

He shrugged. 'Some people print everything,' he said. 'The fellow made a telephone reservation and paid cash in advance. I wouldn't expect my people to question a signature under such circumstances.'

That wasn't my point. What had struck me was that Jones had managed to avoid leaving a specimen of his handwriting, and I found that interesting. I looked at the name where he'd printed it in full. The first three letters of *Charles*, I found myself thinking, were also the first three letters of *Chance*. And what, pray tell, did that signify? And why look for ways to hang my own client?

I asked if there'd been any previous visits by our Mr Jones in the past few months. 'Nothing in the past *year*,' he assured me. 'We carry previous registrations alphabetically in our computer and one of the detectives had that information checked. If that's all –'

'How many other guests signed their names in block caps?'

'I've no idea.'

'Suppose you let me look through the registration cards for the past two, three months.'

'To look for what?'

'People who print like this guy.'

'Oh, I really don't think so,' he said. 'Do you realize how many cards are involved? This is a 635-room hotel. Mr –'

'Scudder.'

'Mr Scudder. That's over eighteen thousand cards a month.'

'Only if all your guests leave after one night.'

'The average stay is three nights. Even so, that's over six thousand registration cards a month, twelve thousand cards in two months. Do you realize how long it would take to look at twelve thousand cards?'

'A person could probably do a couple thousand an hour,' I said, 'since all he'd be doing is scanning the signature to see if it's in script or in block caps. We're just talking about a couple of hours. I could do it or you could have some of your people do it.'

He shook his head. 'I couldn't authorize that,' he said. 'I really couldn't. You're a private citizen, not a policeman, and while I did want to cooperate there's a limit to my authority here. If the police should make an official request –'

'I realize I'm asking a favor.'

'If it were the sort of favor I could grant –'

'It's an imposition,' I went on, 'and I'd certainly expect to pay for the time involved, the time and inconvenience.'

It would have worked at a smaller hotel, but here I was wasting my time. I don't think he even realized I was offering him a bribe. He said again that he'd be glad to go along if the police made the request for me, and this time I let it lie. I asked instead if I could borrow the Jones registration card long enough to have a photocopy made.

'Oh, we have a machine right here,' he said, grateful to be able to help. 'Just wait one moment.'

He came back with a copy. I thanked him and he asked if there was anything else, his tone suggesting he was confident there wouldn't be. I said I'd like a look at the room she died in.

'But the police have quite finished there,' he said. 'The room's in a transitional state now. The carpet had to be replaced, you see, and the walls painted.'

'I'd still like to see it.'

'There's really nothing to see. I think there are workmen in there today. The painters are gone, I believe, but I think the carpet installers –'

'I won't get in their way.'

He gave me a key and let me go up myself. I found the room and congratulated myself on my ability as a detective. The door was locked. The carpet installers looked to be on their lunch break. The old carpet had been removed, and new carpet covered about a third of the floor, with more of it rolled up awaiting installation.

I spent a few minutes there. As the man had assured me, there was really nothing to see. The room was as empty of traces of Kim as it was of furniture. The walls were bright with fresh paint and the bathroom fairly sparkled. I walked around like some psychic practitioner, trying to pick up vibrations through the tips of my fingers. If there were any vibrations present, they eluded me.

The window faced downtown, the view chopped up by the facades of other tall buildings. Through a gap between two of them I could catch a glimpse of the World Trade Center all the way downtown.

Had she had time to look out the window? Had Mr Jones looked out the window, before or afterward?

I took the subway downtown. The train was one of the new ones, its interior a pleasing pattern of yellow and orange and tan. The inscribers of graffiti had already scarred it badly, scrawling their indecipherable messages over every available space.

I didn't notice anyone smoking.

I got off at West Fourth and walked south and west to Morton Street, where Fran Schecter had a small apartment on the top floor of a four-story brownstone. I rang her bell, announced myself over the intercom, and was buzzed through the vestibule door.

The stairwell was full of smells – baking smells on the first floor, cat odor halfway up, and the unmistakable scent of marijuana at the top. I thought that you could draw a building's profile from the aromas in its stairwell.

Fran was waiting for me in her doorway. Short curly hair, light brown in color, framed a round baby face. She had a button nose, a pouty mouth, and cheeks a chipmunk would have been proud of.

She said, 'Hi, I'm Fran. And you're Matt. Can I call you Matt?' I assured her that she could, and her hand settled on my arm as she steered me inside.

The marijuana reek was much stronger inside. The apartment

255

was a studio. One fairly large room with a pullman kitchen on one wall. The furniture consisted of a canvas sling chair, a pillow sofa, some plastic milk crates assembled as shelves for books and clothes, and a large waterbed covered with a fake-fur spread. A framed poster on one wall over the waterbed showed a room interior, with a railway locomotive emerging from the fireplace.

I turned down a drink, accepted a can of diet soda. I sat with it on the pillow sofa, which turned out to be more comfortable than it looked. She took the sling chair, which must have been more comfortable than it looked.

'Chance said you're investigating what happened to Kim,' she said. 'He said to tell you whatever you want to know.'

There was a breathless little-girl quality to her voice and I couldn't tell how much of it was deliberate. I asked her what she knew about Kim.

'Not much. I met her a few times. Sometimes Chance'll take two girls at once out to dinner or a show. I guess I met everyone at one time or another. I just met Donna once, she's on her own trip, it's like she's lost in space. Have you met Donna?' I shook my head. 'I like Sunny. I don't know if we're friends exactly, but she's the only one I'd call up to talk to. I'll call her once, twice a week, or she'll call me, you know, and we'll talk.'

'But you never called Kim?'

'Oh, no. I never had her number, even.' She thought for a moment. 'She had beautiful eyes. I can close my eyes and picture the color of them.'

Her own eyes were large, somewhere between brown and green. Her eyelashes were unusually long, and it struck me that they were probably false. She was a short girl of the body type they call a pony in Las Vegas chorus lines. She was wearing faded Levi's with the cuffs turned up and a hot pink sweater that was stretched tight over her full breasts.

She hadn't known that Kim had planned to leave Chance, and she found the information interesting. 'Well, I can understand that,' she said after some thought. 'He didn't really care for her, you know, and you don't want to stay forever with a man who doesn't care for you.'

'What makes you say he didn't care for her?'

'You pick these things up. I suppose he was glad to have her around, like she didn't make trouble and she brought in the bread, but he didn't have a feeling for her.'

'Does he have a feeling for the others?'

'He has a feeling for me,' she said.

'And anybody else?'

'He likes Sunny. Everybody likes Sunny, she's fun to be with. I don't know if he *cares* for her. Or Donna, I'm sure he doesn't care for Donna, but I don't think she cares for him either. I think that's strictly business on both sides. Donna, I don't think Donna cares for anybody. I don't think she knows there are people in the world.'

'How about Ruby?'

'Have you met her?' I hadn't. 'Well, she's like, you know, exotic. So he'd like that. And Mary Lou's very intelligent and they go to concerts and shit, like Lincoln Center, classical music, but that doesn't mean he has a feeling for her.'

She started to giggle. I asked her what was so funny. 'Oh, I just flashed that I'm the typical dumb hooker, thinks she's the only one the pimp loves. But you know what it is? I'm the only one he can relax with. He can come up here and take his shoes off and let his mind roll out. Do you know what a karmic tie is?'

'No.'

'Well, it has something to do with reincarnation. I don't know if you believe in that.'

'I never thought about it much.'

'Well, I don't know if I believe in it either, but sometimes I think Chance and I knew each other in another life. Not necessarily as lovers or man and wife or anything like that. Like we could have been brother and sister, or maybe he was my father or I was his mother. Or we could even have both been the same sex because that can change from one lifetime to another. I mean we could have been sisters or something Anything, really.'

The telephone cut into her speculations. She crossed the room to answer it, standing with her back to me, one hand propped against her hip. I couldn't hear her conversation. She talked for a moment or two, then covered the mouthpiece and turned to me.

'Matt,' she said, 'I don't want to hassle you, but do you have any idea how long we're gonna be?'

'Not long.'

'Like could I tell somebody it would be cool to come over in an hour?'

'No problem.'

She turned again, finished the conversation quietly, hung up. 'That was one of my regulars,' she said. 'He's a real nice guy. I told him an hour.'

She sat down again. I asked her if she'd had the apartment

before she hooked up with Chance. She said she'd been with Chance for two years and eight months and no, before that she shared a bigger place in Chelsea with three other girls. Chance had had this apartment all ready for her. All she'd had to do was move into it.

'I just moved my furniture in,' she said. 'Except the waterbed. That was already here. I had a single bed that I got rid of. And I bought the Magritte poster, and the masks were here.' I hadn't noticed the masks and had to turn in my seat to see them, a grouping of three solemn ebony carvings on the wall behind me. 'He knows about them,' she said. 'What tribe made them and everything. He knows things like that.'

I said that the apartment was an unlikely one for the use being made of it. She frowned, puzzled.

'Most girls in the game live in doorman buildings,' I said. 'With elevators and all.'

'Oh, right. I didn't know what you meant. Yes, that's true.' She grinned brightly. 'This is something different,' she said. 'The johns who come here, they don't think they're johns.'

'How do you mean?'

'They think they're friends of mine,' she explained. 'They think I'm this spacey Village chick, which I am, and that they're my friends, which they are. I mean, they come here to get laid, let's face it, but they could get laid quicker and easier in a massage parlor, no muss no fuss no bother, dig? But they can come up here and take off their shoes and smoke a joint, and it's a sort of a raunchy Village pad, I mean you have to climb three flights of stairs and then you roll around in a waterbed. I mean, I'm not a hooker. I'm a girlfriend. I don't get paid. They give me money because I got rent to pay and, you know, I'm a poor little Village chick who wants to make it as an actress and she's never going to. Which I'm not, and I don't care much, but I still take dancing lessons a couple mornings a week and I have an acting class with Ed Kovens every Thursday night, and I was in a showcase last May for three weekends in Tribeca. We did Ibsen, *When We Dead Awake*, and do you believe that three of my johns came?'

She chatted about the play, then began telling me how her clients brought her presents in addition to the money they gave her. 'I never have to buy any booze. In fact I have it to give away because I don't drink myself. And I haven't bought any grass in ages. You know who gets the best grass? Wall Street guys. They'll buy an ounce and we'll smoke a little and they'll leave me the ounce.' She batted her long lashes at me. 'I kind of like to smoke,' she said.

'I guessed that.'

'Why? Do I seem stoned?'

'The smell.'

'Oh, right. I don't smell it because I'm here, but when I go out and then I come back in, whew! It's like a friend of mine has four cats and she swears they don't smell, but the smell could knock you down. It's just that she's used to it.' She shifted in her seat. 'Do you ever smoke, Matt?'

'No.'

'You don't drink and you don't smoke, that's terrific. Can I get you another diet soda?'

'No thanks.'

'Are you sure? Look, would it bother you if I smoked a quick joint? Just to unwind a little.'

'Go ahead.'

'Because I've got this fellow coming over and it'll help me be in the mood.'

I told her it was fine with me. She fetched a plastic baggie of marijuana from a shelf over the stove and hand-rolled a cigarette with evident expertise. 'He'll probably want to smoke,' she said, and manufactured two more cigarettes. She lit one, put everything else away, and returned to the sling chair. She smoked the joint all the way down, chattering about her life between drags, finally stubbing the tiny roach and setting it aside for later. Her manner didn't change visibly for having smoked the thing. Perhaps she'd been smoking throughout the day and had been stoned when I arrived. Perhaps she just didn't show the effects of the drug, as some drinkers don't show their drinks.

I asked if Chance smoked when he came to see her and she laughed at the idea. 'He never drinks, never smokes. Same as you. Hey, is that where you know him from? Do you both hang out in a nonbar together? Or maybe you both have the same undealer.'

I managed to get the conversation back to Kim. If Chance didn't care for Kim, did Fran think she might have been seeing someone else?

'He didn't care for her,' she said. 'You know something? I'm the only one he loves.'

I could taste the grass in her speech now. Her voice was the same, but her mind made different connections, switching along paths of smoke.

'Do you think Kim had a boyfriend?'

'I have boyfriends. Kim had tricks. All of the others have tricks.'

'If Kim had someone special –'

'Sure, I can dig it. Somebody who wasn't a john, and that's why she wanted to split with Chance. That what you mean?'

'It's possible.'

'And then he killed her.'

'Chance?'

'Are you crazy? Chance never cared enough about her to kill her. You know how long it'd take to replace her? Shit.'

'You mean the boyfriend killed her.'

'Sure.'

'Why?'

''Cause he's on the spot. She leaves Chance, there she is, all ready for happily ever after, and what does he want with that? I mean he's got a wife, he's got a job, he's got a family, he's got a house in Scarsdale –'

'How do you know all this?'

She sighed. 'I'm just speedballing, baby. I'm just throwing chalk at the blackboard. Can you dig it? He's a married guy, he digs Kim, it's kicky being in love with a hooker and having her in love with you, and that way you get it for free, but you don't want anybody turning your life around. She says, Hey, I'm free now, time to ditch your wife and we'll run into the sunset, and the sunset's something he watches from the terrace at the country club and he wants to keep it that way. Next thing you know, zip, she's dead and he's back in Larchmont.'

'It was Scarsdale a minute ago.'

'Whatever.'

'Who would he be, Fran?'

'The boyfriend? I don't know. Anybody.'

'A john?'

'You don't fall in love with a john.'

'Where would she meet a guy? And what kind of guy would she meet?'

She struggled with the notion, shrugged and gave up. The conversation never got any further than that. I used her phone, talked for a moment, then wrote my name and number on a pad next to the phone.

'In case you think of anything,' I said.

'I'll call you if I do. You going? You sure you don't want another soda?'

'No thanks.'

'Well,' she said. She came over to me, stifled a lazy yawn with the back of her hand, looked up at me through the long lashes. 'Hey, I'm really glad you could come over,' she said. 'Anytime you feel like company, you know, give me a call, okay? Just to hang out and talk.'

'Sure.'

'I'd like that,' she said softly, coming up onto her toes, planting an astonishing kiss on my cheek. 'I'd really like that, Matt,' she said.

Halfway down the stairs I started laughing. How automatically she'd slipped into her whore's manner, warm and earnest at parting, and how good she was at it. No wonder those stockbrokers didn't mind climbing all those stairs. No wonder they turned out to watch her try to be an actress. The hell, she *was* an actress, and not a bad one, either.

Two blocks away I could still feel the imprint of her kiss on my cheek.

SIXTEEN

Donna Campion's apartment was on the tenth floor of the white brick building on East Seventeenth Street. The living room window faced west, and the sun was making one of its intermittent appearances when I got there. Sunlight flooded the room. There were plants everywhere, all of them vividly green and thriving, plants on the floor and the windowsills, plants hanging in the window, plants on ledges and tables throughout the room. The sunlight streamed through the curtain of plants and cast intricate patterns on the dark parquet flooring.

I sat in a wicker armchair and sipped a cup of black coffee. Donna was perched sideways on a backed oak bench about four feet wide. It had been a church pew, she'd told me, and it was English oak, Jacobite or possibly Elizabethan, dark with the passing years and worn smooth by three or four centuries of pious bottoms. Some vicar in rural Devon had decided to redecorate and in due course she'd bought the little pew at a University Place auction gallery.

She had the face to go with it, a long face that tapered from a high broad forehead to a pointed chin. Her skin was very pale, as if the only sunlight she ever got was what passed through the screen of plants. She was wearing a crisp white blouse with a Peter Pan collar and a short pleated skirt of gray flannel over a pair of black tights. Her slippers were doeskin, with pointed toes.

A long narrow nose, a small thin-lipped mouth. Dark brown hair, shoulder length, combed straight back from a well-defined widow's peak. Circles under her eyes, tobacco stains on two fingers of her right hand. No nail polish, no jewelry, no visible makeup. No prettiness, certainly, but a medieval quality that came quite close to beauty.

She didn't look like any whore I'd ever met. She did look like a poet, though, or what I thought a poet ought to look like.

She said, 'Chance said to give you my complete cooperation. He said you're trying to find out who killed the Dairy Queen.'

'The Dairy Queen?'

'She looked like a beauty queen, and then I learned she was from Wisconsin, and I thought of all that robust milk-fed innocence. She was a sort of regal milkmaid.' She smiled softly. 'That's my imagination talking. I didn't really know her.'

'Did you ever meet her boyfriend?'

'I didn't know she had one.'

Nor had she known that Kim had been planning to leave Chance, and she seemed to find the information interesting. 'I wonder,' she said. 'Was she an emigrant or an immigrant?'

'What do you mean?'

'Was she going from or to? It's a matter of emphasis. When I first came to New York I was coming *to*. I'd also just made a break with my family and the town I grew up in, but that was secondary. Later on, when I split with my husband, I was running from. The act of leaving was more important than the destination.'

'You were married?'

'For three years. Well, together for three years. Lived together for one year, married for two.'

'How long ago was that?'

'Four years?' She worked it out. 'Five years this coming spring. Although I'm still married, technically. I never bothered to get a divorce. Do you think I should?'

'I don't know.'

'I probably ought to. Just to tie off a loose end.'

'How long have you been with Chance?'

'Going on three years. Why?'

'You don't seem the type.'

'Is there a type? I don't suppose I'm much like Kim. Neither regal nor a milkmaid.' She laughed. 'I don't know which is which, but we're like the colonel's lady and Judy O'Grady.'

'Sisters under the skin?'

She looked surprised that I'd recognized the quotation. She said, 'After I left my husband I was living on the Lower East Side. Do you know Norfolk Street? Between Stanton and Rivington?'

'Not specifically.'

'I knew it very specifically. I lived there and I had these little jobs in the neighborhood. I worked in a Laundromat, I waited tables. I clerked in shops. I would quit the jobs or the jobs would quit me and there was never enough money and I hated where I was living and I was starting to hate my life. I was going to call my husband and ask him to take me back just so he would take care of me. I kept thinking about it. One time I dialed his number but the line was busy.'

And so she'd drifted almost accidentally into selling herself. There was a store owner down the block who kept coming on to her. One day without preplanning it she heard herself say, 'Look, if you really want to ball me, would you give me twenty dollars?' He'd been flustered, blurting that he hadn't known she was a hooker. 'I'm not,' she told him, 'but I need the money. And I'm supposed to be a pretty good fuck.'

She started turning a few tricks a week. She moved from Norfolk Street to a better block in the same neighborhood, then moved again to Ninth Street just east of Tompkins Square. She didn't have to work now but there were other hassles to contend with. She was beaten up once, robbed several times. Again she found herself thinking of calling her ex-husband.

Then she met a girl in the neighborhood who worked in a midtown massage parlor. Donna tried out there and liked the security of it. There was a man in front to deal with anyone who tried to cause trouble, and the work itself was mechanical, almost clinical in its detachment. Virtually all her tricks were manual or oral. Her own flesh was uninvaded, and there was no illusion of intimacy beyond the pure fact of physical intimacy.

At first she welcomed this. She saw herself as a sexual technician, a kind of physiotherapist. Then it turned on her.

'The place had Mafia vibes,' she said, 'and you could smell death in the drapes and carpets. And it got like a job, I worked regular hours, I took the subway back and forth. It sucked – I love that word – it sucked the poetry right out of me.'

And so she'd quit and resumed free-lancing, and somewhere along the way Chance found her and everything fell into place. He'd installed her in this apartment, the first decent place she ever had in New York, and he got her phone number circulating and took all the hassles away. Her bills got paid, her apartment got cleaned, everything got done for her, and all she had to do was work on her poems and mail them off to magazines and be nice and charming whenever the telephone rang.

'Chance takes all the money you earn,' I said. 'Doesn't that bother you?'

'Should it?'

'I don't know.'

'It's not real money anyway,' she said. 'Fast money doesn't last. If it did, all the drug dealers would own the stock exchange. But that kind of money goes out the way it comes in.' She swung her legs around, sat facing forward on the church pew. 'Anyway,' she said, 'I have everything I want. All I ever wanted was to be left alone. I wanted a decent place to live and time to do my work. I'm talking about my poetry.'

'I realize that.'

'You know what most poets go through? They teach, or they work a straight job, or they play the poetry game, giving readings and lectures and writing out proposals for foundation grants and getting to know the right people and kissing the right behinds. I never wanted to do all that shit. I just wanted to make poems.'

'What did Kim want to do?'

'God knows.'

'I think she was involved with somebody. I think that's what got her killed.'

'Then I'm safe,' she said. 'I'm involved with no one. Of course you could argue that I'm involved with mankind. Would that put me in grave danger, do you suppose?'

I didn't know what she meant. With her eyes closed she said, '"Any man's death diminishes me, because I am involved in Mankind," John Donne. Do you know how she was involved, or with whom?'

'No.'

'Does her death diminish me, do you suppose? I wonder if I was involved with her. I didn't know her, not really, and yet I wrote a poem about her.'

'Could I see it?'

'I suppose so, but I don't see how it could tell you anything. I wrote a poem about the Big Dipper but if you want to know anything real about it you'd have to go to an astronomer, not to me. Poems are never about what they're about, you know. They're all about the poet.'

'I'd still like to see it.'

This seemed to please her. She went to her desk, a modern version of the old rolltop, and found what she was looking for almost immediately. The poem was hand-lettered on white bond paper with an italic-nibbed pen.

'I type them up for submission,' she said, 'but I like to see how they look on the page this way. I taught myself to do calligraphy. I learned from a book. It's easier than it looks.'

I read:

265

Bathe her in milk, let the white stream run
Pure in its bovine baptism,
Heal the least schism
Under the soonest sun. Take her
Hand, tell her it doesn't matter,
Milk's not to cry over. Scatter
Seed from a silver gun. Break her
Bones in a mortar, shatter
Wine bottles at her feet, let green glass
Sparkle upon her hand. Let it be done.
Let the milk run.
Let it flow down, down to the ancient grass.

I asked if I could copy it into my notebook. Her laugh was light, merry. 'Why? Does it tell who killed her?'

'I don't know what it tells me. Maybe if I keep it I'll figure out what it tells me.'

'If you figure out what it means,' she said, 'I hope you'll tell *me*. That's an exaggeration. I sort of know what I'm getting at. But don't bother copying it. You can have that copy.'

'Don't be silly. That's your copy.'

She shook her head. 'It's not finished. It needs more work. I want to get her eyes into it. If you met Kim you must have noticed her eyes.'

'Yes.'

'I originally wanted to contrast the blue eyes with the green glass, that's how that image got there in the first place, but the eyes disappeared when I wrote it. I think they were in an earlier draft but somewhere along the line they dropped out.' She smiled. 'They were gone in a wink. I've got the silver and the green and the white and I left the eyes out.' She stood with her hand on my shoulder, looking down at the poem. 'It's what, twelve lines? I think it should be fourteen anyway. Sonnet length, even if the lines are irregular. I don't know about *schism*, either. Maybe an off-rhyme would be better. Spasm, chasm, something.'

She went on, talking more to herself than to me, discussing possible revisions in the poem. 'By all means keep that,' she concluded. 'It's a long way from final form. It's funny. I haven't even looked at it since she was killed.'

'You wrote it before she was killed?'

'Completely. And I don't think I ever thought of it as finished, even though I copied it in pen and ink. I'll do that with drafts. I can get a better idea of what does and doesn't work that way. I'd have kept on working on this one if she hadn't been killed.'

'What stopped you? The shock?'

'Was I shocked? I suppose I must have been. "This could happen to me." Except of course I don't believe that. It's like lung cancer, it happens to other people. "Any man's death diminishes me." Did Kim's death diminish me? I don't think so. I don't think I'm as involved in mankind as John Donne was. Or as he said he was.'

'Then why did you put the poem aside?'

'I didn't put it aside. I left it aside. That's nitpicking, isn't it?' She considered this. 'Her death changed how I saw her. I wanted to work on the poem, but I didn't want to get her death into it. I had enough colors. I didn't need blood in there, too.'

SEVENTEEN

I had taken a cab from Morton Street to Donna's place on East Seventeenth. Now I took another to Kim's building on Thirty-seventh. As I paid the driver I realized I hadn't made it to the bank. Tomorrow was Saturday, so I'd have Chance's money on my hands all weekend. Unless some mugger got lucky.

I lightened the load some by slipping five bucks to the doorman for a key to Kim's apartment, along with some story about acting as the tenant's representative. For five dollars he was eager to believe me. I went up to the elevator and let myself in.

The police had been through the place earlier. I didn't know what they were looking for and couldn't say what they found. The sheet in the file Durkin showed me hadn't said much, but nobody writes down everything that comes to his attention.

I couldn't know what the officers on the scene might have noticed. For that matter, I couldn't be sure what might have stuck to their fingers. There are cops who'll rob the dead, doing so as a matter of course, and they are not necessarily men who are especially dishonest in other matters.

Cops see too much of death and squalor, and in order to go on dealing with it they often have the need to dehumanize the dead. I remember the first time I helped remove a corpse from a room in an SRO hotel. The deceased had died vomiting blood and had lain there for several days before his death was discovered. A veteran patrolman and I wrestled the corpse into a body bag and on the way downstairs my companion made sure the bag hit every single step. He'd have been more careful with a sack of potatoes.

I can still recall the way the hotel's other residents looked at us. And I can remember how my partner went through the dead man's belongings, scooping up the little cash he had to his name, counting it deliberately and dividing it with me.

I hadn't wanted to take it. 'Put it in your pocket,' he told me. 'What do you think happens to it otherwise? Somebody else takes it. Or it goes to the state. What's the state of New York gonna do with forty-four dollars? Put it in your pocket, then buy yourself some perfumed soap and try to get this poor fucker's stink off your hands.'

I put it in my pocket. Later on, I was the one who bounced bagged corpses down the stairs, the one who counted and divided their leavings.

Someday, I suppose, it'll come full circle, and I'll be the one in the bag.

I spent over an hour there. I went through drawers and closets without really knowing what I was looking for. I didn't find very much. If she'd had a little black book full of telephone numbers, the call girl's legendary stock in trade, someone else had found it before I did. Not that I had any reason to assume she'd had such a book. Elaine kept one, but Fran and Donna had both told me they didn't.

I didn't find any drugs or drug paraphernalia, which proved little in and of itself. A cop might appropriate drugs just as he'd take money from the dead. Or Chance might have picked up any contraband that he found lying around. He'd said that he visited the apartment once after her death. I noticed, though, that he'd left the African masks. They glared at me from their spot on the wall, guarding the premises on behalf of whatever eager young whore Chance would install in Kim's place.

The Hopper poster was still in place over the stereo. Would that stay behind for the next tenant, too?

Her spoor was all over the place. I breathed it when I went through the clothes in her dresser drawers and in her closet. Her bed was unmade. I lifted the mattress, looked under it. No doubt others had done so before me. I didn't find anything and I let the mattress fall back into place, and her spicy scent rose from the rumpled bedclothing and filled my nostrils.

In the living room, I opened a closet and found her fur jacket, other coats and jackets, and a shelf full of wine and liquor bottles. A fifth of Wild Turkey caught my eye, and I swear I could taste that rich overproof bourbon, could feel the bite of it in my throat, the hot rush flowing down to my stomach, the warmth spreading clear to my toes and fingers. I closed the door, crossed the room and sat down on the couch. I hadn't wanted a drink, hadn't so much as thought of a drink in hours, and the unexpected glimpse of a bottle of booze had caught me unawares.

I went back to the bedroom. She had a jewelry box on the top of her dressing table and I went through it. A lot of earrings, a couple of necklaces, a string of unconvincing pearls. Several bangle bracelets, including an attractive one made of ivory and trimmed in what looked to be gold. A gaudy class ring from LaFollette High in Eau Claire, Wisconsin. The ring was gold, stamped 14K on the inside, heavy enough by the feel of it to be worth something.

Who would get all of this? There had been some cash in her bag at the Galaxy Downtowner, four hundred bucks and change according to the note in her file, and that would probably wind up going to her parents in Wisconsin. But would they fly in and claim her coats and sweaters? Would they take possession of the fur jacket, the high school ring, the ivory bracelet?

I stayed long enough to make a few notes and managed to get out of there without again opening the front closet. I rode the elevator to the lobby, waved at the doorman and nodded at an entering tenant, an elderly woman with a small short-haired dog on a rhinestone-studded leash. The dog yipped at me, and I wondered for the first time what had become of Kim's little black kitten. I'd seen no traces of the animal, no litter pan in the bathroom. Someone must have taken it.

I caught a cab at the corner. I was paying it off in front of my hotel when I found Kim's key with my pocket change. I hadn't remembered to return it to the doorman, and he hadn't thought to ask me for it.

There was a message for me. Joe Durkin had called and left his number at the precinct. I called and was told he was out but was expected back. I left my name and number.

I went up to my room, feeling winded and tired. I lay down but I couldn't get any rest that way, couldn't turn off the tapes in my head. I went downstairs again, had a cheese sandwich and french fries and coffee. Over a second cup of coffee I took Donna Campion's poem out of my pocket. Something about it was trying to get through to me but I couldn't figure out what. I read it again. I didn't know what the poem meant, assuming that it was intended to have any literal meaning. But it seemed to me that some element of it was winking at me, trying to get my attention, and I was just too brain damaged to catch on.

I went over to St Paul's. The speaker told a horrible story in a

270

chatty matter-of-fact fashion. Both his parents had died of alcoholism, his father of acute pancreatitis, his mother of suicide committed while drunk. Two brothers and a sister had died of the disease. A third brother was in a state hospital with a wet brain.

'After I was sober a few months,' he said, 'I started hearing how alcohol kills brain cells, and I got worried about how much brain damage I might have. So I went to my sponsor and told him what was on my mind. "Well," he said, "maybe you've had some brain damage. It's possible. But let me ask you this. Are you able to remember where the meetings are from one day to the next? Can you find your way to them without any trouble?" "Yeah," I told him, "I can manage that all right." "Well then," he said, "you got all the brain cells you need for the time being."'

I left on the break.

There was another message from Durkin at the hotel desk. I called right back and he was out again. I left my name and number and went upstairs. I was having another look at Donna's poem when the phone rang.

It was Durkin. He said, 'Hey, Matt. I just wanted to say I hope I didn't give you the wrong impression last night.'

'About what?'

'Oh, things in general,' he said. 'Once in a while the whole business gets to me, you know what I mean? I have the need to break out, drink too much, run off at the mouth. I don't make a habit of it but once in a while I have to do it.'

'Sure.'

'Most of the time I love the job, but there's things that get to you, things you try not to look at, and every now and then I have to get all that shit out of my system. I hope I didn't get out of line there toward the end.'

I assured him that he'd done nothing wrong. I wondered how clearly he recalled the previous evening. He'd been drunk enough to be in a blackout, but not everybody has blackouts. Maybe he was just a little vague, and uncertain how I'd taken his outbursts.

I thought of what Billie's landlady had told him. 'Forget it,' I said. 'It could happen to a bishop.'

'Hey, I got to remember that one. It could happen to a bishop. And probably does.'

'Probably.'

'You getting anywhere with your investigation? Coming up with anything?'

'It's hard to tell.'

'I know what you mean. If there's anything I can do for you –'

'Matter of fact, there is.'

'Oh?'

'I went over to the Galaxy Downtowner,' I said. 'Talked to an assistant manager. He showed me the registration card Mr Jones signed.'

'The famous Mr Jones.'

'There was no signature on it. The name was hand-printed.'

'Figures.'

'I asked if I could go through the cards for the past few months and see if there were any other hand-printed signatures, and how they compared to Jones's printing. He couldn't authorize it.'

'You should have slipped him a few bucks.'

'I tried. He didn't even know what I was getting at. But you could have him pull the printed cards. He wouldn't do it for me because I've got no official standing, but he'd hop to it if a cop made the request.'

He didn't say anything for a moment. Then he asked if I thought it was going to lead anywhere.

'It might,' I said.

'You think whoever did it stayed at the hotel before? Under some other name?'

'It's possible.'

'But not his own name, or he would have signed it in script instead of being cute. So what we'd wind up with, assuming we got very lucky and there was a card to be found and we actually came up with it, what we'd have is another alias for the same son of a bitch, and we wouldn't be any closer'n we are now to knowing who he is.'

'There's another thing you could do, while you were at it.'

'What's that?'

'Have other hotels in the area check their registrations for, oh, the past six months or a year.'

'Check 'em for what? Printed registrations. Come on, Matt. You know the man-hours you're talking about?'

'Not printed registrations. Have them check for guests named Jones. I'm talking about hotels like the Galaxy Downtowner, modern hotels in that price range. Most of them'll be like the Galaxy and have their registrations on computer. They can pull their Jones registrations in five or ten minutes, but not unless someone with a tin shield asks 'em to.'

'And then what have you got?'

'You pull the appropriate cards, look for a guest named Jones, probably with the first initial *C* or the initials *CO*, and you compare printing and see if you find him anywhere. If you come up with anything you see where it leads. I don't have to tell you what to do with a lead.'

He was silent again. 'I don't know,' he said at length. 'It sounds pretty thin.'

'Maybe it is.'

'I'll tell you what I think it is. I think it's a waste of time.'

'It's not a waste of all that much time. And it's not that thin. Joe, you'd do it if the case wasn't already closed in your mind.'

'I don't know about that.'

'Of course you would. You think it's a hired killer or a lunatic. If it's a hired killer you want to close it out and if it's a lunatic you want to wait until he does it again.'

'I wouldn't go that far.'

'You went that far last night.'

'Last night was last night, for Christ's sake. I already explained about last night.'

'It wasn't a hired killer,' I said. 'And it wasn't a lunatic just picking her out of the blue.'

'You sound like you're sure of it.'

'Reasonably sure.'

'Why?'

'No hired hitman goes crazy that way. What did he hit her, sixty times with a machete?'

'I think it was sixty-six.'

'Sixty-six, then.'

'And it wasn't necessarily a machete. Something *like* a machete.'

'He had her strip. Then he butchered her like that, he got so much blood on the walls that they had to paint the room. When did you ever hear of a professional hit like that?'

'Who knows what kind of animal a pimp hires? Maybe he tells the guy to make it ugly, do a real job on her, make an example out of her. Who knows what goes through his mind?'

'And then he hires me to look into it.'

'I admit it sounds weird, Matt, but –'

'It can't be a crazy, either. It was somebody who *went* crazy, but it's not a psycho getting his kicks.'

'How do you know that?'

'He's too careful. Printing his name when he signed in. Carrying the dirty towels away with him. This is a guy who took the trouble to avoid leaving a shred of physical evidence.'

'I thought he used the towels to wrap the machete.'

'Why would he do that? After he washed the machete he'd put it back in the case the way he brought it. Or, if he wanted to wrap it in towels, he'd use clean towels. He wouldn't carry away the towels he washed up with unless he wanted to keep them from being found. But towels can hold things – a hair, a bloodstain – and he knew he might be a suspect because he knew something linked him to Kim.'

'We don't know for sure the towels were dirty, Matt. We don't know he took a shower.'

'He chopped her up and put blood all over the walls. You think he got out of there without washing up?'

'I guess not.'

'Would you take wet towels home for a souvenir? He had a reason.'

'Okay.' A pause. 'A psycho might not want to leave evidence. You're saying he's someone who knew her, who had a reason to kill her. You can't be sure of that.'

'Why did he have her come to the hotel?'

'Because that's where he was waiting. Him and his little machete.'

'Why didn't he take his little machete to her place on Thirty-seventh Street?'

'Instead of having her make house calls?'

'Right. I spent the day talking to hookers. They aren't nuts about outcalls because of the travel time. They'll do them, but they usually invite the caller to come to their place instead, tell him how much more comfortable it is. She probably would have done that but he wasn't having any.'

'Well, he already paid for the room. Wanted to get his money's worth.'

'Why wouldn't he just as soon go to her place?'

He thought about it. 'She had a doorman,' he said. 'Maybe he didn't want to walk past the doorman.'

'Instead he had to walk through a whole hotel lobby and sign a registration card and speak to a desk clerk. Maybe he didn't want to pass that doorman because the doorman had seen him before. Otherwise a doorman's a lot less of a challenge than an entire hotel.'

'That's pretty iffy, Matt.'

'I can't help it. Somebody did a whole batch of things that don't make sense unless he knew the girl and had a personal reason for wanting her dead. He may be emotionally disturbed. Perfectly levelheaded people don't generally go batshit with a machete. But he's more than a psycho picking women at random.'

'How do you figure it? A boyfriend?'

'Something like that.'

'She splits with the pimp, tells the boyfriend she's free, and he panics?'

'I was thinking along those lines, yes.'

'And goes crazy with a machete? How does that mesh with your profile of a guy who decides he'd rather stay home with his wife?'

'I don't know.'

'Do you know for sure she had a boyfriend?'

'No,' I admitted.

'These registration cards. Charles O. Jones and all his aliases, if he ever had any. You think they're gonna lead anywhere?'

'They could.'

'That's not what I asked you, Matt.'

'Then the answer's no. I don't think they're going to lead to anything.'

'But you still think it's worth doing.'

'I'd have gone through the cards myself at the Galaxy Downtowner,' I reminded him. 'On my own time, if the guy would have let me.'

'I suppose we could run the cards.'

'Thanks, Joe.'

'I suppose we can run the other check, too. First-class commercial hotels in the area, their Jones registrations for the past six months or whatever. That what you wanted?'

'That's right.'

'The autopsy showed semen in her throat and esophagus. You happen to notice that?'

'I saw it in the file last night.'

'First he had her blow him, then he chopped her up with his boy scout hatchet. And you figure it was a boyfriend.'

'The semen could have been from an earlier contact. She was a hooker, she had a lot of contacts.'

'I suppose,' he said. 'You know, they can type semen now. It's not like a fingerprint, more like a blood type. Makes useful circumstantial evidence. But you're right, with her lifestyle it doesn't rule a guy out if the semen type's not a match.'

'And it doesn't rule him in if it does.'

'No, but it'd fucking well give him a headache. I wish she'd scratched him, got some skin under her nails. That always helps.'

'You can't have everything.'

'For sure. If she blew him, you'd think she could have wound up with a hair or two between her teeth. Whole trouble is she's too ladylike.'

'That's the trouble, all right.'

'And my trouble is I'm starting to believe there's a case here, with a killer at the end of a rainbow. I got a desk full of shit I haven't got time for and you've got me pulling my chain with this one.'

'Think how good you'll look if it breaks.'

'I get the glory, huh?'

'Somebody might as well.'

I had three more hookers to call, Sunny and Ruby and Mary Lou. Their numbers were in my notebook. But I'd talked to enough whores for one day. I called Chance's service, left word for him to call me. It was Friday night. Maybe he was at the Garden, watching a couple of boys hit each other. Or did he just go when Kid Bascomb was fighting?

I took out Donna Campion's poem and read it. In my mind's eye all the poem's colors were overlaid with blood, bright arterial blood that faded from scarlet to rust. I reminded myself that Kim had been alive when the poem was written. Why, then, did I sense a note of doom in Donna's lines? Had she picked up on something? Or was I seeing things that weren't really there?

She'd left out the gold of Kim's hair. Unless the sun was supposed to cover that base. I saw those gold braids wrapped around her head and thought of Jan Keane's Medusa. Without giving it too much thought I picked up the phone and placed a call. I hadn't dialed the number in a long time but memory supplied it, pushing it at me as a magician forces a card on one.

It rang four times. I was going to hang up when I heard her voice, low pitched, out of breath.

I said, 'Jan, it's Matt Scudder.'

'Matt! I was just thinking of you not an hour ago. Give me a minute, I just walked in the door, let me get my coat off … There. How've you been? It's so good to hear from you.'

'I've been all right. And you?'

'Oh, things are going well. A day at a time.'

The little catchphrases. 'Still going to those meetings?'

'Uh-huh. I just came from one, as a matter of fact. How are you doing?'

'Not so bad.'

'That's good.'

What was it, Friday? Wednesday, Thursday, Friday. 'I've got three days,' I said.

'Matt, that's wonderful!'

What was so wonderful about it? 'I suppose,' I said.

'Have you been going to meetings?'

'Sort of. I'm not sure I'm ready for all that.'

We talked a little. She said maybe we'd run into each other at a meeting one of these days. I allowed that it was possible. She'd been sober almost six months, she'd qualified a couple of times already. I said it would be interesting sometime to hear her story. She said, 'Hear it? God, you're *in* it.'

She was just getting back to sculpture. She'd put it all on hold when she got sober, and it was hard to make the clay do what she wanted it to do. But she was working at it, trying to keep it all in perspective, putting her sobriety first and letting the rest of her life fall into shape at its own pace.

And what about me? Well, I said, I had a case, I was looking into a matter for an acquaintance. I didn't go into detail and she didn't press. The conversation slowed, and there were a few pauses in it, and I said, 'Well, I just thought I'd call and say hello.'

'I'm glad you did, Matthew.'

'Maybe we'll run into each other one of these days.'

'I'd like that.'

I hung up and remembered drinking in her loft on Lispenard Street, warming and mellowing as the booze worked its magic in our veins. What a fine sweet evening that had been.

At meetings you'll hear people say, 'My worst day sober is better than my best day drunk.' And everybody nods like a plastic dog on a Puerto Rican's dashboard. I thought about that night with Jan and looked around my little cell of a room and tried to figure out why this night was better than the other had been.

I looked at my watch. The liquor stores were closed. The bars, though, would be open for hours yet.

I stayed where I was. Outside, a squad car went by with its

siren open. The sound died down, the minutes slipped by, and my phone rang.

It was Chance. 'You been working,' he said with approval. 'I've been getting reports. The girls cooperate okay?'

'They've been fine.'

'You getting anywhere?'

'It's hard to tell. You pick up a piece here and a piece there and you never know if they're going to fit together. What did you take from Kim's apartment?'

'Just some money. Why?'

'How much?'

'Couple hundred. She kept cash in the top dresser drawer. It was no secret hiding place, just where she kept it. I looked around some to see if she had any holdout money stashed anywhere, but I couldn't find any. Didn't turn up any bankbooks, safe-deposit keys. Did you?'

'No.'

'Or any money? S'pose it's finders keepers if you did, but I'm just asking.'

'No money. That's all you took?'

'And a picture a nightclub photographer took of her and me. Couldn't see any rightful reason to leave that for the police. Why?'

'I just wondered. You went there before the police picked you up?'

'They didn't pick me up. I walked in voluntarily. And yes, I went there first, and it was before they got there, far as that goes. Or the couple hundred would have been gone.'

Maybe, maybe not. I said, 'Did you take the cat?'

'The cat?'

'She had a little black kitten.'

'Right, she did. I never thought about the kitten. No, I didn't take it. I would have put out food for it if I thought. Why? Is it gone?'

I said it was, and its litter box too. I asked if the kitten had been around when he went to the apartment but he didn't know. He hadn't noticed a kitten, but then he hadn't been looking for one.

'And I was moving quickly, you know. I was in and out in five minutes. Kitten could have brushed against my ankles and I might not have paid it any mind. What's it matter? Kitten didn't kill her.'

'No.'

'You don't think she took the kitten to the hotel, do you?'

'Why would she do that?'

'*I* don't know, man. I don't know why we're *talking* about the kitten.'

'Somebody must have taken it. Somebody besides you must have gone to her apartment after she died and took the kitten out of there.'

'You sure the kitten wasn't there today? Animals get scared when a stranger comes around. They hide.'

'The kitten wasn't there.'

'Could have walked out when the cops came. Doors open, kitten runs out, goodbye kitty.'

'I never heard of a cat taking its litter pan along.'

'Maybe some neighbor took it. Heard it meowing, like they do, and didn't want it to go hungry.'

'Some neighbor with a key?'

'Some people exchange keys with a neighbor. In case they get locked out. Or the neighbor could have got the key from the doorman.'

'That's probably what happened.'

'Must be.'

'I'll check with the neighbors tomorrow.'

He whistled softly. 'You chase down everything, don't you? Little thing like a kitten, you're at it like a dog at a bone.'

'That's the way it's done. Goyakod.'

'How's that?'

'Goyakod,' I said, and spelled it out. 'It stands for Get Off Your Ass and Knock On Doors.'

'Oh, I like that. Say it again?'

I said it again.

'"Get off your ass and knock on doors." I like that.'

EIGHTEEN

Saturday was a good day for knocking on doors. It usually is because more people are at home than during the week. This Saturday the weather didn't invite them out. A fine rain was falling out of a dark sky and there was a stiff wind blowing, whipping the rain around.

Wind sometimes behaves curiously in New York. The tall buildings seem to break it up and put a spin on it, like english on a billiard ball, so that it takes odd bounces and blows in different directions on different blocks. That morning and afternoon it seemed to be always in my face. I would turn a corner and it would turn with me, always coming at me, always driving the spray of rain at me. There were moments when I found it invigorating, others when I hunched my shoulders and lowered my head and cursed the wind and the rain and myself for being out in them.

My first stop was Kim's building, where I nodded and walked past the doorman, key in hand. I hadn't seen him before and I doubt that I was any more familiar to him than he was to me, but he didn't challenge my right to be there. I rode upstairs and let myself into Kim's apartment.

Maybe I was making sure the cat was still missing. I had no other reason to go in. The apartment was as I had left it, as far as I could tell, and I couldn't find a kitten or a litter pan anywhere. While I thought of it I checked the kitchen. There were no cans or boxes of cat food in the cupboards, no bag of kitty litter, no nonspill bowl for a cat to eat out of. I couldn't detect any cat odor in the apartment, and I was beginning to wonder if my memory of the animal might have been a false one. Then, in the refrigerator, I found a half-full can of Puss 'n Boots topped with a plastic lid.

How about that, I thought. The great detective found a clue.

Not long after that the great detective found a cat. I walked up and down the hallway and knocked on doors. Not everyone was home, rainy Saturday or no, and the first three people who were had no idea that Kim had ever owned a cat, let alone any information on its present whereabouts.

The fourth door that opened to my knock belonged to an Alice Simkins, a small woman in her fifties whose conversation was guarded until I mentioned Kim's cat.

'Oh, Panther,' she said. 'You've come for Panther. You know, I was afraid someone would. Come in, won't you?'

She led me to an upholstered chair, brought me a cup of coffee, and apologized for the excess of furniture in the room. She was a widow, she told me, and had moved to this small apartment from a suburban house, and while she'd rid herself of a great many things she'd made the mistake of keeping too much furniture.

'It's like an obstacle course in here,' she said, 'and it's not as if I just moved in yesterday. I've been here almost two years. But because there's no real urgency I seem to find it all too easy to put it off and put it off.'

She had heard about Kim's death from someone in the building. The following morning she was at her desk at the office when she thought of Kim's cat. Who would feed it? Who would take care of it?

'I made myself wait until lunch hour,' she said, 'because I decided I just wasn't crazy enough to run out of the office lest a kitten go an extra hour without food. I fed the kitten and cleaned out the litter pan and freshened its water, and I checked on it that evening when I came home from the office, and it was evident that no one had been in to care for it. I thought about the poor little thing that night, and the next morning when I went to feed it I decided it might as well live with me for the time being.' She smiled. 'It seems to have adjusted. Do you suppose it misses her?'

'I don't know.'

'I don't suppose it'll miss me, either, but I'll miss it. I never kept a cat before. We had dogs years ago. I don't think I'd want to keep a dog, not in the city, but a cat doesn't seem to be any trouble. Panther was declawed so there's no problem of furniture scratching, although I almost wish he'd scratched some of this furniture, it might move me to get rid of it.' She laughed softly. 'I'm afraid I took all his food from her apartment. I can get all of that together for you. And Panther's hiding somewhere, but I'm sure I can find him.'

I assured her I hadn't come for the cat, that she could keep the animal if she wanted. She was surprised, and obviously relieved. But if I hadn't come for the cat, what was I there for? I gave her an abbreviated explanation of my role. While she was digesting that I asked her how she'd gained access to Kim's apartment.

'Oh, I had a key. I'd given her a key to my apartment some months ago. I was going out of town and wanted her to water my plants, and shortly after I came back she gave me her key. I can't remember why. Did she want me to feed Panther? I really can't remember. Do you suppose I can change his name?'

'I beg your pardon?'

'It's just that I don't much care for the cat's name, but I don't know if it's proper to change it. I don't believe he recognizes it. What he recognizes is the whirr of the electric can opener, announcing that dinner is served.' She smiled. 'T. S. Eliot wrote that every cat has a secret name, known only to the cat himself. So I don't suppose it really matters what name *I* call him.'

I turned the conversation to Kim, asked how close a friend she'd been.

'I don't know if we were friends,' she said. 'We were neighbors. We were good neighbors, I kept a key to her apartment, but I'm not sure we were friends.'

'You knew she was a prostitute?'

'I suppose I knew. At first I thought she was a model. She had the looks for it.'

'Yes.'

'But somewhere in the course of things I gathered what her actual profession was. She never mentioned it. I think it may have been her failure to discuss her work that made me guess what it was. And then there was that black man who visited her frequently. Somehow I found myself assuming he was her pimp.'

'Did she have a boyfriend, Mrs Simkins?'

'Besides the black man?' She thought about it, and while she did so a black streak darted across the rug, leaped onto a couch, leaped again and was gone. 'You see?' the woman said. 'He's not at all like a panther. I don't know what he is like, but he's nothing like a panther. You asked if she had a boyfriend.'

'Yes.'

'I just wonder. She must have had some sort of secret plan because she hinted at it the last time we talked – that she'd be moving away, that her life was going to take a turn for the better. I'm afraid I wrote it off as a pipe dream.'

282

'Why?'

'Because I assumed she meant she and her pimp were going to run off into the sunset and live happily ever after, only she wouldn't say as much to me because she'd never come out and told me that she *had* a pimp, that she was a prostitute. I understand pimps will assure a girl that their other girls are unimportant, that as soon as enough money's saved they'll go off and buy a sheep station in Australia or something equally realistic.'

I thought of Fran Schecter on Morton Street, convinced she and Chance were bound by karmic ties, with innumerable lifetimes ahead of them.

'She was planning on leaving her pimp,' I said.

'For another man?'

'That's what I'm trying to find out.'

She'd never seen Kim with anyone in particular, never paid much attention to the men who visited Kim's apartment. Such visitors were few at night, anyway, she explained, and she herself was at work during the day.

'I thought she'd bought the fur herself,' she said. 'She was so proud of it, as if someone had bought it for her, but I thought she wanted to conceal her shame at having had to buy it for herself. I'll bet she did have a boyfriend. She showed it off with that air, as if it had been a gift from a man, but she didn't come out and say so.'

'Because the relationship was a secret.'

'Yes. She was proud of the fur, proud of the jewelry. You said she was leaving her pimp. Is that why she was killed?'

'I don't know.'

'I try not to think about her having been killed, or how or why it happened. Did you ever read a book called *Watership Down?*' I hadn't. 'There's one colony of rabbits in the book; a sort of semidomesticated colony. The food's in good supply there because human beings leave food for the rabbits. It's sort of rabbit heaven, except that the men who do this do so in order to set snares and provide themselves with a rabbit dinner from time to time. And the surviving rabbits, they never refer to the snare, they never mention any of their fellows who've been killed that way. They have an unspoken agreement to pretend that the snare does not exist, and that their dead companions never existed.' She'd been looking to one side as she spoke. Now her eyes found mine. 'Do you know, I think New Yorkers are like those rabbits. We live here for whatever it is that the city provides – the culture, the job opportunities, whatever it is. And we look the other way when the city kills off our friends and neighbors. Oh, we read about it and we talk about it for a day or two days but then we blink it all away. Because otherwise we'd have to do something about it, and we can't. Or we'd have to move, and we don't want to move. We're like those rabbits, aren't we?'

I left my number, told her to call if she thought of anything. She said she would. I took the elevator to the lobby, but when it got there I stayed in the car and rode it back to twelve again. Just because I'd located the black kitten didn't mean I'd be wasting my time knocking on a few more doors.

Except that's what I did. I talked to half a dozen people and didn't learn a thing, other than that they and Kim did a good job of keeping to themselves. One man had even managed to miss out on the knowledge that a neighbor of his had been murdered. The others knew that much, but not a great deal more.

When I'd run out of doors to knock on I found myself approaching Kim's door, key in hand. Why? Because of the fifth of Wild Turkey in the front closet?

I put her key in my pocket and got out of there.

The meeting book led me to a noon meeting just a few blocks from Kim's. The speaker was just finishing her qualification when I walked in. At first glance I thought she was Jan, but when I took another look I saw there was no real resemblance. I got a cup of coffee and took a seat at the back.

The room was crowded, thick with smoke. The discussion seemed to center itself on the spiritual side of the program, and I wasn't too clear on what that was, nor did anything I hear clarify it for me.

One guy said something good, though, a big fellow with a voice like a load of gravel. 'I came in here to save my ass,' he said, 'and then I found out it was attached to my soul.'

If Saturday was a good day for knocking on doors, it was equally good for visiting hookers. While a Saturday-afternoon trick may not be unheard of, it's the exception.

I ate some lunch, then rode uptown on the Lexington IRT. The car was uncrowded, and directly opposite me a black kid in a pea jacket and heavy-soled boots was smoking a cigarette. I remembered my conversation with Durkin and wanted to tell the kid to put out the cigarette.

Jesus, I thought, mind your own business. Leave it alone.

I got off at Sixty-eighth Street and walked a block north and two blocks east. Ruby Lee and Mary Lou Barcker lived in apartment buildings diagonally opposite one another. Ruby's was on the southwest corner and I went there first because I came to it first. The doorman announced me over the intercom and I shared the elevator with a florist's delivery boy. He had his arms full of roses and the car was heavy with their scent.

Ruby opened the door to my knock, smiled coolly, led me inside. The apartment was sparsely if tastefully furnished. The furniture was contemporary and neutral, but there were other items to give the place an oriental cast – a Chinese rug, a group of Japanese prints in black lacquered frames, a bamboo screen. They weren't enough to render the apartment exotic, but Ruby managed that all by herself.

She was tall, though not so tall as Kim, and her figure was lithe and willowy. She showed it off in a black sheath dress with a skirt slit to show a flash of thigh when she walked. She put me in a chair and offered me a drink, and I heard myself ask for tea. She smiled and came back with tea for both of us. It was Lipton's, I noted. God knows what I expected.

Her father was half French and half Senegalese, her mother Chinese. She'd been born in Hong Kong, lived for a time in Macao, then came to America via Paris and London. She didn't tell me her age and I didn't ask, nor could I have possibly guessed it. She might have been twenty or forty-five or almost anything in between.

She had met Kim once. She didn't really know anything about her, didn't know much about any of the girls. She herself had been with Chance for a time and found their arrangement comfortable.

She didn't know if Kim had had a boyfriend. Why, she wondered, would a woman want two men in her life? Then she would have to give money to both of them.

I suggested that Kim might have had a different sort of relationship with her boyfriend, that he might have given her gifts. She seemed to find the idea baffling. Did I mean a customer? I said that was possible. But a customer was not a boyfriend, she said. A customer was just another man in a long line of men. How could one feel anything for a customer?

*

285

Across the street, Mary Lou Barcker poured me a Coke and set out a plate of cheese and crackers. 'So you met the Dragon Lady,' she said. 'Striking, isn't she?'

'That's putting it mildly.'

'Three races blended into one absolutely stunning woman. Then the shock comes. You open the door and nobody's home. Come here a minute.'

I joined her at the window, looked where she was pointing.

'That's her window,' she said. 'You can see her apartment from mine. You'd think we'd be great friends, wouldn't you? Dropping in at odd hours to borrow a cup of sugar or complain about premenstrual tension. Figures, doesn't it?'

'And it hasn't worked out that way?'

'She's always polite. But she's just not there. The woman doesn't relate. I've known a lot of johns who've gone over there. I've steered some business her way, as far as that goes. A guy'll say he's had fantasies about oriental girls, for example. Or I might just tell a guy that I know a girl he might like. You know something? It's the safest thing in the world. They're grateful because she *is* beautiful, she *is* exotic, and I gather she knows her way around a mattress, but they almost never go back. They go once and they're glad they went, but they don't go back. They'll pass her number on to their buddies instead of ringing it again themselves. I'm sure she keeps busy but I'll bet she doesn't know what a steady trick is, I'll bet she's never had one.'

She was a slender woman, dark haired, a little taller than average, with precise features and small even teeth. She had her hair pulled back and done in a chignon, I think they call it, and she was wearing aviator glasses, the lenses tinted a pale amber. The hair and the glasses combined to give her a rather severe look, an effect of which she was by no means unaware. 'When I take off the glasses and let my hair down,' she said at one point, 'I look a whole lot softer, a good deal less threatening. Of course some johns want a woman to look threatening.'

Of Kim she said, 'I didn't know her well. I don't know any of them really well. What a crew they are! Sunny's the goodtime party girl, she thinks she's made a huge leap in status by becoming a prostitute. Ruby's a sort of autistic adult, untouched by human minds. I'm sure she's socking away the dollars, and one of these days she'll go back to Macao or Port Said and open up an opium den. Chance probably knows she's holding out and has the good sense to let her.'

She put a slice of cheese on a biscuit, handed it to me, took some for herself, sipped her red wine. 'Fran's a charming kook out of *Wonderful Town*. I call her the Village Idiot. She's raised self-deception to the level of an art form. She must have to smoke a ton of grass to support the structure of illusion she's created. More Coke?'

'No thanks.'

'You sure you wouldn't rather have a glass of wine? Or something stronger?'

I shook my head. A radio played unobtrusively in the background, tuned to one of the classical music stations. Mary Lou took off her glasses, breathed on them, wiped them with a napkin.

'And Donna,' she said. 'Whoredom's answer to Edna St Vincent Millay. I think the poetry does for her what the grass does for Fran. She's a good poet, you know.'

I had Donna's poem with me and showed it to Mary Lou. Vertical frown lines appeared in her forehead as she scanned the lines.

'It's not finished,' I said. 'She still has work to do on it.'

'I don't know how poets know when they're finished. Or painters. How do they know when to stop? It baffles me. This is supposed to be about Kim?'

'Yes.'

'I don't know what it means, but there's something, she's onto something here.' She thought for a moment, her head cocked like a bird's. She said, 'I guess I thought of Kim as the archetypical whore. A spectacular ice blonde from the northern Midwest, the kind that was just plain born to walk through life on a black pimp's arm. I'll tell you something. I wasn't surprised when she was murdered.'

'Why not?'

'I'm not entirely sure. I was shocked but not surprised. I guess I expected her to come to a bad end. An abrupt end. Not necessarily as a murder victim, but as some sort of victim of the life. Suicide, for instance. Or one of those unholy combinations of pills and liquor. Not that she drank much, or took drugs as far as I know. I suppose I expected suicide, but murder would do as well, wouldn't it? To get her out of the life. Because I couldn't see her going on with it forever. Once that corn-fed innocence left her she wouldn't be able to handle it. And I couldn't see her finding her way out, either.'

'She *was* getting out. She told Chance she wanted out.'

'Do you know that for a fact?'

'Yes.'

'And what did he do?'

'He told her it was her decision to make.'

'Just like that?'

'Evidently.'

'And then she got killed. Is there a connection?'

'I think there has to be. I think she had a boyfriend and I think the boyfriend's the connection. I think he's why she wanted to get away from Chance and I think he's also the reason she was killed.'

'But you don't know who he was.'

'No.'

'Does anybody have a clue?'

'Not so far.'

'Well, I'm not going to be able to change that. I can't remember the last time I saw her, but I don't remember her eyes being agleam with true love. It would fit though. A man got her into this. She'd probably need another man to get her out.'

And then she was telling me how she'd gotten into it. I hadn't thought to ask but I got to hear it anyway.

Someone had pointed Chance out to her at an opening in SoHo, one of the West Broadway galleries. He was with Donna, and whoever pointed him out told Mary Lou he was a pimp. Fortified by an extra glass or two of the cheap wine they were pouring, she approached him, introduced herself, told him she'd like to write a story about him.

She wasn't exactly a writer. At the time she'd been living in the West Nineties with a man who did something incomprehensible in Wall Street. The man was divorced and still half in love with his ex-wife, and his bratty kids came over every weekend, and it wasn't working out. Mary Lou did free-lance copy editing and had a part-time proofreading job, and she'd published a couple of articles in a feminist monthly newspaper.

Chance met with her, took her out to dinner, and turned the interview inside out. She realized over cocktails that she wanted to go to bed with him, and that the urge stemmed more from curiosity than sexual desire. Before dinner was over he was suggesting that she forget about some surface article and write something real, a genuine inside view of a prostitute's life. She was obviously fascinated, he told her. Why not use that fascination, why not go with it, why not buy the whole package for a couple of months and see where she went with it?

She made a joke out of the suggestion. He took her home after dinner, didn't make a pass, and managed to remain oblivious to her sexual invitation. For the next week she couldn't get his proposal out of her mind. Everything about her own life seemed unsatisfactory. Her relationship was exhausted, and she sometimes felt she only stayed with her lover out of reluctance to hunt an apartment of her own. Her career was dead-ended and unsatisfying, and the money she earned wasn't enough to live on.

'And the book,' she said, 'the book was suddenly everything. De Maupassant obtained human flesh from a morgue and ate it so that he could describe its taste accurately. Couldn't I spend a month as a call girl in order to write the best book ever written on the subject?'

Once she accepted Chance's offer, everything was taken care of. Chance moved her out of her place on West Ninety-fourth and installed her where she was now. He took her out, showed her off, took her to bed. In bed he told her precisely what to do, and she found this curiously exhilarating. Other men in her experience had always been reticent that way, expecting you to read their minds. Even johns, she said, had trouble telling you what they wanted.

For the first few months she still thought she was doing research for a book. She took notes every time a john left, writing down her impressions. She kept a diary. She detached herself from what she was doing and from who she was, using her journalistic objectivity as Donna used poetry and as Fran used marijuana.

When it dawned on her that whoring was an end in itself she went through an emotional crisis. She had never considered suicide before, but for a week she hovered on its brink. Then she worked it out. The fact that she was whoring didn't mean she had to label herself a whore. This was something she was doing for a while. The book, just an excuse to get into the life, might someday turn out to be something she really wanted to do. It didn't really matter. Her individual days were pleasant enough, and the only thing that was unsettling was when she pictured herself living this way forever. But that wouldn't happen. When the time was right, she would drift out of the life as effortlessly as she had drifted in.

'So that's how I keep my particular cool, Matt. I'm not a hooker. I'm just "into hooking." You know, there are worse ways to spend a couple of years.'

'I'm sure there are.'

'Plenty of time, plenty of creature comforts. I read a lot, I get to movies and museums and Chance likes to take me to concerts. You know the bit about the blind men and the elephant? One grabs the tail and thinks the elephant is like a snake, another touches the side of the elephant and thinks it's like a wall?'

'So?'

'I think Chance is the elephant and his girls are the blind men. We each see a different person.'

'And you all have some African sculpture on the premises.'

Hers was a statue about thirty inches high, a little man holding a bundle of sticks in one hand. His face and hands were rendered in blue and red beadwork, while all the rest of him was covered with small seashells.

'My household god,' she said. 'That's a Batum ancestor figure from Cameroun. Those are cowry shells. Primitive societies all over the world use the cowry shell as a medium of exchange, it's the Swiss franc of the tribal world. You see how it's shaped?'

I went and had a look.

'Like the female genitalia,' she said. 'So men automatically use it to buy and sell. Can I get you some more of that cheese?'

'No thanks.'

'Another Coke?'

'No.'

'Well,' she said, 'if there's anything you'd like, just let me know what it is.'

NINETEEN

Just as I was leaving her building, a cab pulled up in front to discharge a passenger. I got in and gave the address of my hotel.

The windshield wiper on the driver's side didn't work. The driver was white; the picture on the posted license showed a black man. A sign cautioned, NO SMOKING/DRIVER ALLERGIC. The cab's interior reeked of marijuana.

'Can't see a fucking thing,' the driver said.

I sat back and enjoyed the ride.

I called Chance from the lobby, went up to my room. About fifteen minutes later he got back to me. 'Goyakod,' he said. 'I'll tell you, I like that word. Knock on many doors today?'

'A few.'

'And?'

'She had a boyfriend. He bought her presents and she showed them off.'

'To who? To my girls?'

'No, and that's what makes me sure it was something she wanted to keep secret. It was one of her neighbors who mentioned the gifts.'

'Neighbor turn out to have the kitten?'

'That's right.'

'Goyakod. Damn if it don't work. You start with a missing cat and you wind up with a clue. What presents?'

'A fur and some jewelry.'

'Fur,' he said. 'You mean that rabbit coat?'

'She said it was ranch mink.'

'Dyed rabbit,' he said. 'I bought her that coat, took her shopping and paid cash for it. Last winter, that was. The neighbor said it was mink, shit, I'd like to sell the neighbor a couple of minks just like it. Give her a good price on 'em.'

'Kim said it was mink.'

'Said it to the neighbor?'

'Said it to me.' I closed my eyes, pictured her at my table in Armstrong's. 'Said she came to town in a denim jacket and now she was wearing ranch mink and she'd trade it for the denim jacket if she could have the years back.'

His laughter rang through the phone wire. 'Dyed rabbit,' he said with certainty. 'Worth more than the rag she got off the bus with, maybe, but no king's ransom. And no boyfriend bought it for her 'cause *I* bought it for her.'

'Well –'

'Unless I was the boyfriend she was talking about.'

'I suppose that's possible.'

'You said jewelry. All she had was costume, man. You see the jewelry in her jewelry box? Wasn't nothing valuable there.'

'I know.'

'Fake pearls, a school ring. The one nice thing she had was somethin' else I got her. Maybe you saw it. The bracelet?'

'Was it ivory, something like that?'

'Elephant tusk ivory, *old* ivory, and the fittings are gold. The hinge and the clasp. Not a lot of gold, but gold's gold, you know?'

'You bought it for her?'

'Got it for a hundred dollar bill. Cost you three hundred in a shop, maybe a little more, if you were to find one that nice.'

'It was stolen?'

'Let's just say I didn't get no bill of sale. Fellow who sold it to me, he never said it was stolen. All he said was he'd take a hundred dollars for it. I should have picked that up when I got the photograph. See, I bought it 'cause I liked it, and then I gave it to her because I wasn't about to wear it, see, and I thought it'd look good on her wrist. Which it did. You still think she had a boyfriend?'

'I think so.'

'You don't sound so sure no more. Or maybe you just sound tired. You tired?'

'Yes.'

'Knockin' on too many doors. Wha'd this boyfriend of hers do besides buy her all these presents that don't exist?'

'He was going to take care of her.'

'Well, shit,' he said. 'That's what *I* did, man. What else did I do for that girl but take care of her?'

*

292

I stretched out on the bed and fell asleep with my clothes on. I'd knocked on too many doors and talked to too many people. I was supposed to see Sunny Hendryx, I'd called and told her I would be coming over, but I took a nap instead. I dreamed of blood and a woman screaming, and I woke up bathed in sweat and with a metallic taste in the back of my mouth.

I showered and changed my clothes. I checked Sunny's number in my notebook, dialed it from the lobby. No answer.

I was relieved. I looked at my watch, headed over to St Paul's.

The speaker was a soft-spoken fellow with receding light brown hair and a boyish face. At first I thought he might be a clergyman.

He turned out to be a murderer. He was homosexual, and one night in a blackout he had stabbed his lover thirty or forty times with a kitchen knife. He had, he said quietly, faint memories of the incident, because he'd kept going in and out of blackout, coming to with the knife in his hand, being struck by the horror of it, and then slipping back into the darkness. He'd served seven years at Attica and had been sober three years now on the outside.

It was disturbing, listening to him. I couldn't decide how I felt about him. I didn't know whether to be glad or sorry that he was alive, that he was out of prison.

On the break I got to talking with Jim. Maybe I was reacting to the qualification, maybe I was carrying Kim's death around with me, but I started talking about all the violence, all the crime, all the killings. 'It gets to me,' I said. 'I pick up the paper and I read some damn thing or other and it gets to me.'

'You know that vaudeville routine? "Doctor, it hurts when I do this." "So don't do this!"'

'So?'

'So maybe you should stop picking up the paper.' I gave him a look. 'I'm serious,' he said. 'Those stories bother me, too. So do the stories about the world situation. If the news was good they wouldn't put it in the paper. But one day it struck me, or maybe I got the idea from somebody else, but it came to me that there was no law saying I had to read that crap.'

'Just ignore it.'

'Why not?'

'That's the ostrich approach, isn't it? What I don't look at can't hurt me?'

'Maybe, but I see it a little differently. I figure I don't have to make myself crazy with things I can't do anything about anyway.'

'I can't see myself overlooking that sort of thing.'

'Why not?'

I thought of Donna. 'Maybe I'm involved with mankind.'

'Me too,' he said. 'I come here, I listen, I talk. I stay sober. That's how I'm involved in mankind.'

I got some more coffee and a couple of cookies. During the discussion people kept telling the speaker how much they appreciated his honesty.

I thought, Jesus, I never did anything like that. And my eyes went to the wall. They hang these slogans on the wall, gems of wisdom like Keep It Simple and Easy Does It, and the sign my eyes went to as if magnetized read There But For The Grace Of God.

I thought, no, screw that. I don't turn murderous in blackouts. Don't tell me about the grace of God.

When it was my turn I passed.

TWENTY

Danny Boy held his glass of Russian vodka aloft so that he could look at the light shine through it. 'Purity. Clarity. Precision,' he said, rolling the words, pronouncing them with elaborate care. 'The best vodka is a razor, Matthew. A sharp scalpel in the hand of a skilled surgeon. It leaves no ragged edges.'

He tipped back the glass and swallowed an ounce or so of purity and clarity. We were at Poogan's and he was wearing a navy suit with a red stripe that barely showed in the bar's half-light. I was drinking club soda with lime. At another stop along the way a freckled-faced waitress had informed me that my drink was called a Lime Rickey. I had a feeling I'd never ask for it by that name.

Danny Boy said, 'Just to recapitulate. Her name was Kim Dakkinen. She was a big blonde, early twenties, lived in Murray Hill, got killed two weeks ago in the Galaxy Downtowner.'

'Not quite two weeks ago.'

'Right. She was one of Chance's girls. And she had a boyfriend, and that's what you want. The boyfriend.'

'That's right.'

'And you're paying for whoever can give you the skinny on this. How much?'

I shrugged. 'A couple of dollars.'

'Like a bill? Like a half a K? How many dollars?'

I shrugged again. 'I don't know, Danny. It depends on the information and where it comes from and where it goes. I haven't got a million dollars to play with but I'm not strapped either.'

'You said she was one of Chance's girls.'

'Right.'

'You were looking for Chance a little over two weeks ago,

Matthew. And then you took me to the boxing matches just so I could point him out to you.'

'That's right.'

'And a couple of days after that, your big blonde had her picture in the papers. You were looking for her pimp, and now she's dead, and here you are looking for her boyfriend.'

'So?'

He drank the rest of his vodka. 'Chance know what you're doing?'

'He knows.'

'You talk to him about it?'

'I've talked to him.'

'Interesting.' He raised his empty glass to the light, squinted through it. Checking it, no doubt, for purity and clarity and precision. He said, 'Who's your client?'

'That's confidential.'

'Funny how people looking for information are never looking to furnish it. No problem. I can ask around, put the word out in certain quarters. That's what you want?'

'That's what I want.'

'Do you know anything about this boyfriend?'

'Like what?'

'Like is he old or young, wise or straight, married or single? Does he walk to school or take his lunch?'

'He may have given her presents.'

'That narrows the field.'

'I know.'

'Well,' he said, 'all we can do is try.'

It was certainly all *I* could do. I'd gone back to the hotel after the meeting and found a message waiting for me. *Call Sunny*, it said, and included the number which I'd called earlier. I rang her from the booth in the lobby and got no answer. Didn't she have a machine? Didn't they all have machines nowadays?

I went to my room but I couldn't stay in it. I wasn't tired, the nap had taken the edge off my tiredness, and all the coffee I'd drunk at the meeting had me restless and edgy. I went through my notebook and reread Donna's poem and it struck me that I was very likely looking for an answer someone else already knew.

That's very often the case in police work. The easiest way to find out something is to ask someone who knows. The hard part is figuring out who that person is, the one with the answer.

Who might Kim have confided in? Not the girls I'd talked to so far. Not her neighbor on Thirty-seventh Street. Who, then?

Sunny? Maybe. But Sunny wasn't answering her phone. I tried her again, placing the call through the hotel switchboard.

No answer. Just as well. I didn't much feel like spending the next hour drinking ginger ale with yet another hooker.

What had they done, Kim and her faceless friend? If they'd spent all their time behind closed doors, rolling together on a mattress and swearing eternal love, never saying a word to anyone else, then I might be up against it. But maybe they'd gone out, maybe he'd shown her off in some circle or other. Maybe he talked to somebody who talked to somebody else, maybe –

I wouldn't learn the answers in my hotel room. The hell, it wasn't such a bad night. The rain had quit sometime during the meeting and the wind had died down some. Time to get off my ass, time to take a few taxis and spend a little money. I didn't seem to be putting it in the bank or stuffing it into poor boxes or shipping it home to Syosset. Might as well spread it around.

And so I'd been doing that. Poogan's Pub was perhaps the ninth place I'd hit and Danny Boy Bell perhaps the fifteenth person I'd talked to. Some of the places were ones I'd visited while looking for Chance, but others were not. I tried saloons in the Village, gin joints in Murray Hill and Turtle Bay, singles bars on First Avenue. I kept doing this after I left Poogan's, spending frequent small sums on cabs and drink orders, having the same conversation over and over again.

No one knew anything. You live in hope when you run that sort of fool's errand. There's always the chance that you'll deliver your spiel and the person you're talking to will turn and point and say, 'That's him, that's her boyfriend, that big guy in the corner over there.'

It almost never happens that way. What does happen, if you're lucky, is that the word gets around. There may be eight million people in the goddamned city but it's amazing how they all talk to each other. If I did this right, it wouldn't be long before a fair share of those eight million knew that a dead whore had a boyfriend and a guy named Scudder was looking for him.

Two cabbies in a row refused to go to Harlem. There's a law that says they have to. If an orderly fare requests a destination anywhere in the five boroughs of New York City, the driver has to take him there. I didn't bother citing the relevant statute. It was easier to walk a block and catch a subway.

The station was a local stop, the platform deserted. The attendant sat in the bulletproof token booth, locked in. I wondered if she felt secure in there. New York taxis have thick plexiglas partitions to protect the drivers, but the cabbies I'd hailed weren't willing to go uptown, partition or no.

Not long ago an attendant had had a heart attack in one of those token booths. The CPR team couldn't get into the locked booth to revive him and so the poor bastard had died in there. Still, I suppose they protect more people than they kill.

Of course they hadn't protected the two women at the Broad Channel stop on the A train. A couple of kids had a grudge against an attendant who'd reported them for turnstile jumping, so they'd filled a fire extinguisher with gasoline, pumped it into the booth, and lit a match. The whole booth exploded, inciner-ated both women. One more way to die.

That had been in the paper a year ago. Of course there was no law saying I had to read the papers.

I bought tokens. When my train came I rode it uptown. I worked Kelvin Small's and a few other places on Lenox Avenue. I ran into Royal Waldron at a rib joint, had the same conversation with him I'd been having with everybody else. I drank a cup of coffee on 125th Street, walked the rest of the way to St Nicholas, had a glass of ginger ale at the bar of Club Cameroon.

The statue in Mary Lou's apartment was from Cameroun. An ancestor statue, encrusted with cowry shells.

I found no one at the bar I knew well enough to talk to. I looked at my watch. It was getting late. On Saturday night the bars in New York close an hour early, at three instead of four. I've never understood why. Perhaps so that the heavy hitters can sober up in time for church.

I motioned to the bartender, asked about after-hours joints. He just looked at me, his face impassive. I found myself laying my rap on him, telling him I was looking for information about Kim's boyfriend. I knew I wasn't going to get an answer from him, knew I wouldn't get the time of day from him, but I was getting the message across all the same. He'd hear me and so would the men on either side of me, and they'd all talk to people, and that was how it worked.

"Fraid I can't help you,' he said. 'Whatever you lookin' for, you lookin' awful far uptown for it.'

*

I suppose the boy followed me out of the bar. I didn't notice, and I should have. You have to pay attention to that sort of thing.

I was walking along the street, my mind jumping all over the place, from Kim's mysterious boyfriend to the speaker who'd stabbed his lover. By the time I sensed movement alongside of me there was no time left to react. I was just starting to turn when his hand fastened on my shoulder and propelled me into the mouth of the alley.

He came right in after me. He was an inch or so shorter than me but his bushy Afro made up those two inches and more. He was eighteen or twenty or twenty-two, with a drooping moustache and a burn scar on one cheek. He was wearing a flight jacket with zippered pockets and a pair of tight black jeans, and he had a little gun in his hand and it was pointed right at me.

He said, 'Motherfucker, fucking motherfucker. Gimme your money, you motherfucker. Gimme it, gimme all of it, gimme it or you dead, you motherfucker.'

I thought, Why didn't I get to the bank? Why didn't I leave some of it at my hotel? I thought, Jesus, Mickey could forget getting his teeth straightened, St Paul's could forget about their ten percent.

And I could forget about tomorrow.

'Motherfucking honky bastard, dirty motherfucker –'

Because he was going to kill me. I reached in my pocket for my wallet and I looked at his eyes and at his finger on the trigger and I knew it. He was working himself up, he was primed, and whatever money I had wasn't going to be enough for him. He'd be scoring big, better than two grand, but I'd be dead whatever money I had.

We were in an alley about five feet wide, just a gap between two brick tenements. Light from a streetlamp spilled into the alley, illuminating the passage for another ten or fifteen yards beyond where we stood. There was rain-soaked litter on the ground, scraps of paper, beer cans, broken bottles.

Fine place to die. Fine *way* to die, not even a very original one. Shot dead by a mugger, crime in the streets, a terse paragraph on a back page.

I drew the wallet out of my pocket. I said, 'You can have it, everything I've got, you're welcome to it,' knowing it wasn't enough, knowing he'd resolved to shoot me for five dollars or five thousand. I extended the wallet, hand shaking, and I dropped it.

'I'm sorry,' I said, 'very sorry, I'll get it,' and bent to retrieve it, hoping he'd bend forward also, figuring he had to. I bent at the knees and I gathered my feet under me and I thought *Now!* and I straightened up hard and fast, slapping at the gun as I drove my head full force into his chin.

The gun went off, deafening in that enclosed space. I thought I must have been hit but I didn't feel anything. I grabbed and butted him again, then shoved hard and he stumbled back against the wall behind him, eyes glazed, the gun held loose in his hand. I kicked his wrist and the gun went flying.

He came off the wall, his eyes full of murder. I feinted with a left and hit him with my right in the pit of the stomach. He made a retching sound and doubled up, and I grabbed that son of a bitch, one hand gripping the nylon flight jacket, the other tangled up in his mop of hair, and I ran him right into the wall, three quick steps that ended with his face smacking into the bricks. Three, four times I drew him back by the hair and smashed his face into the wall. When I let go of him he dropped like a marionette with the strings cut, sprawling on the floor of the alley.

My heart was pounding as if I'd run at top speed up ten flights of stairs. I couldn't catch my breath. I leaned against the brick wall, panting for breath, waiting for the cops to come.

Nobody came. There had been a noisy scuffle, hell, there had been a gunshot, but nobody came and nobody was going to come. I looked down at the young man who would have killed me if he could. He lay with his mouth open, showing teeth broken off at the gumline. His nose was smashed flat against his face and blood flowed from it in a stream.

I checked, made sure I wasn't shot. Sometimes, I understand, you can take a bullet and not feel it at the time. Shock and adrenalin anesthetize the pain. But he'd missed me. I examined the wall behind where I was standing, found a fresh indentation in the brick where the bullet had dug out a chip before ricocheting. I figured out where I'd been standing and calculated that he hadn't missed me by much.

Now what?

I found my wallet, put it back in my pocket. I rooted around until I located the gun, a .32-caliber revolver with a spent cartridge in one of its chambers and live rounds in the other five. Had he killed anyone else with it? He'd seemed nervous, so maybe I'd been scheduled to be his first. Then again, maybe some people always get nervous before they pull the trigger, just as some actors always feel anxious before they step on stage.

I knelt down and frisked him. He had a switch knife in one pocket, another knife tucked into his sock. No wallet, no ID, but he had a thick roll of bills on his hip. I slipped off the rubber band and gave the roll a fast count. He had over three hundred dollars, the bastard. He hadn't been looking to make the rent money or score a bag of dope.

And what the hell was I going to do with him?

Call the cops? And hand them what? No evidence, no witnesses, and the guy on the ground was the one who'd sustained the damages. There was nothing good enough for a courtroom, not even anything to hold him on. They'd rush him to the hospital, fix him up, even give him his money back. No way to prove it was stolen. No way to prove it wasn't rightfully his.

They wouldn't give him the gun back. But they couldn't hang a weapons charge on him, either, because I couldn't prove he'd been carrying it.

I put his roll of bills in my own pocket, took out the gun that I'd placed there earlier. I turned the gun over and over in my hand, trying to recall the last time I'd handled one. It had been a while.

He lay there, his breath bubbling through the blood in his nose and throat, and I crouched at his side. After a moment or two I stuck the gun into his ruined mouth and let my finger curl around the trigger.

Why not?

Something stopped me, and it wasn't fear of punishment, not in this world or the next. I'm not sure what it was, but after what seemed like a long time I sighed and withdrew the gun from his mouth. There were traces of blood on the barrel, glowing like brass in the soft light of the alley. I wiped the gun on his jacket front, put it back in my pocket.

I thought, Damn you, goddamn you, what am I going to do with you?

I couldn't kill him and I couldn't hand him to the cops. What could I do? Leave him there?

What else?

I stood up. A wave of dizziness came over me and I stumbled, reached out, caught onto the wall for support. After a moment the dizziness passed and I was all right.

I took a deep breath, let it out. I bent down again and grabbed him by the feet, dragged him some yards back into the alley to a ledge about a foot high, the top frame of a barred basement window. I stretched him out across the alley on his back with his feet up on the ledge and his head wedged against the opposite wall.

I stamped full force on one of his knees, but that didn't do it. I had to jump into the air and come down with both feet. His left leg snapped like a matchstick on my first attempt, but it took me four times to break the right one. He remained unconscious throughout, moaning a bit, then crying out when the right leg broke.

I stumbled, fell, landed on one knee, got up again. Another wave of dizziness hit me, this one accompanied by nausea, and I clung to the wall and gave myself up to dry heaves. The dizziness passed, and the nausea, but I still couldn't catch my breath and I was shaking like a leaf. I held my hand out in front of me and watched my fingers tremble. I'd never seen anything like that before. I'd faked the shaking when I took out my wallet and dropped it, but this shaking was perfectly real, and I couldn't control it by force of will. My hands had a will of their own and they wanted to shake.

The shakes were even worse on the inside.

I turned, took a last look at him. I turned again and made my way over the littered pavement to the street. I was still shaking and it wasn't getting any better.

Well, there was a way to stop the shakes, the ones on the outside and the inner ones as well. There was a specific remedy for that specific disease.

Red neon winked at me from the other side of the street. BAR, it said.

TWENTY-ONE

didn't cross the street. The kid with the smashed face and broken legs was not the only mugger in the neighborhood, and it struck me that I wouldn't want to meet another one with drink in me.

No, I had to get to my home ground. I was only going to have one drink, maybe two, but I couldn't guarantee that was all I would have, nor could I say with assurance what one or two drinks would do to me.

The safe thing would be to get back to my neighborhood, have one or at the most two shots in a bar, then take a couple of beers back to my room.

Except that there was no safe way to drink. Not for me, not anymore. Hadn't I proved that? How many times did I have to go on proving it?

So what was I supposed to do? Shake until I fell apart? I wasn't going to be able to sleep without a drink. I wasn't going to be able to sit still without a drink, for Christ's sake.

Well, fuck it. I had to have one. It was medicinal. Any doctor who looked at me would prescribe it.

Any doctor? How about that intern at Roosevelt. I could feel his hand on my shoulder, right where the mugger had grabbed me to shove me into the alley. *'Look at me. Listen to me. You're an alcoholic. If you drink you'll die.'*

I'd die anyway, in one of eight million ways. But if I had the choice, at least I could die closer to home.

I walked over to the curb. A gypsy cab, the only kind that cruises Harlem, slowed as it approached. The driver, a middle-aged Hispanic woman wearing a brimmed cap over kinky red hair, decided I looked all right. I got in the back seat, closed the door, told her to take me to Fifty-eighth and Ninth.

On the way there my mind was all over the place. My hands were still trembling, though not so violently as before, but the internal shakes were as bad as ever. The ride seemed to take forever, and then before I knew it the woman was asking me which corner I wanted. I told her to pull up in front of Armstrong's. When the light changed she nosed the cab across the intersection and stopped where I'd told her. When I made no move she turned around to see what was wrong.

I'd just remembered that I couldn't get a drink at Armstrong's. Of course they might have forgotten by now that Jimmy had eighty-sixed me, but maybe they hadn't, and I felt myself burning with resentment already at the thought of walking in there and being refused service. No, fuck them, I wouldn't walk through their goddamned door.

Where, then? Polly's would be closed, they never ran all the way to closing hour. Farrell's?

That was where I'd had the first drink after Kim's death. I'd had eight sober days before I picked up that drink. I remembered that drink. Early Times, it was.

Funny how I always remember what brand I was drinking. It's all the same crap, but that's the sort of detail that sticks in your mind.

I'd heard someone make that very observation at a meeting a while back.

What did I have now? Four days? I could go up to my room and just make myself stay there and when I woke up I'd be starting my fifth day.

Except that I'd never fall asleep. I wouldn't even stay in the room. I'd try, but I couldn't stay anywhere, not the way I felt right now, not with only my own whirling mind to keep me company. If I didn't drink now I'd drink an hour from now.

'Mister? You okay?'

I blinked at the woman, then dug my wallet out of my pocket and found a twenty. 'I want to make a phone call,' I said. 'From the booth right there on the corner. You take this and wait for me. All right?'

Maybe she'd drive off with the twenty. I didn't really care. I walked to the corner, dropped a dime, stood there listening to the dial tone.

It was too late to call. What time was it? After two, much too late for a social call.

Hell, I could go to my room. All I had to do was stay put for an hour and I'd be in the clear. At three the bars would close.

So? There was a deli that would sell me beer, legally or not. There was an after-hours on Fifty-first, way west between

304

Eleventh and Twelfth. Unless it had closed by now; I hadn't been there in a long time.

There was a bottle of Wild Turkey in Kim Dakkinen's front closet. And I had her key in my pocket.

That scared me. The booze was right there, accessible to me at any hour, and if I went there I'd never stop after one or two drinks. I'd finish the bottle, and when I did there were a lot of other bottles to keep it company.

I made my call.

She'd been sleeping. I heard that in her voice when she answered the phone.

I said, 'It's Matt. I'm sorry to call you so late.'

'That's all right. What time is it? God, it's after two.'

'I'm sorry.'

'It's all right. Are you okay, Matthew?'

'No.'

'Have you been drinking?'

'No.'

'Then you're okay.'

'I'm falling apart,' I said. 'I called you because it was the only way I could think of to keep from drinking.'

'You did the right thing.'

'Can I come over?'

There was a pause. Never mind, I thought. Forget it. One quick drink at Farrell's before they closed, then back to the hotel. Never should have called her in the first place.

'Matthew, I don't know if it's a good idea. Just take it an hour at a time, a minute at a time if you have to, and call me as much as you want. I don't mind if you wake me, but –'

I said, 'I almost got killed half an hour ago. I beat a kid up and broke his legs for him. I'm shaking like I never shook before in my life. The only thing that's going to make me feel right is a drink and I'm afraid to take one and scared I'll do it anyway. I thought being with someone and talking with someone might get me through it but it probably wouldn't anyway, and I'm sorry, I shouldn't have called. I'm not your responsibility. I'm sorry.'

'Wait!'

'I'm here.'

'There's a clubhouse on St Marks Place where they have meetings all night long on the weekends. It's in the book, I can look it up for you.'

'Sure.'

'You won't go, will you?'

'I can't talk up at meetings. Forget it, Jan. I'll be all right.'

'Where are you?'

'Fifty-eighth and Ninth.'

'How long will it take you to get here?'

I glanced over at Armstrong's. My gypsy cab was still parked there. 'I've got a cab waiting,' I said.

'You remember how to get here?'

'I remember.'

The cab dropped me in front of Jan's six-story loft building on Lispenard. The meter had eaten up most of the original twenty dollars. I gave her another twenty to go with it. It was too much but I was feeling grateful, and could afford to be generous.

I rang Jan's bell, two long and three short, and went out in front so that she could toss the key down to me. I rode the industrial elevator to the fifth floor and stepped out into her loft.

'That was quick,' she said. 'You really did have a cab waiting.'

She'd had time to dress. She was wearing old Lee jeans and a flannel shirt with a red-and-black checkerboard pattern. She's an attractive woman, medium height, well fleshed, built more for comfort than for speed. A heart-shaped face, her hair dark brown salted with gray and hanging to her shoulders. Large well-spaced gray eyes. No makeup.

She said, 'I made coffee. You don't take anything in it, do you?'

'Just bourbon.'

'We're fresh out. Go sit down, I'll get the coffee.'

When she came back with it I was standing by her Medusa, tracing a hair-snake with my fingertip. 'Her hair reminded me of your girl here,' I said. 'She had blonde braids but she wrapped them around her head in a way that made me think of your Medusa.'

'Who?'

'A woman who got killed. I don't know where to start.'

'Anywhere,' she said.

*

I talked for a long time and I skipped all over the place, from the beginning to that night's events and back and forth again. She got up now and then to get us more coffee, and when she came back I'd start in where I left off. Or I'd start somewhere else. It didn't seem to matter.

306

I said, 'I didn't know what the hell to do with him. After I'd knocked him out, after I'd searched him. I couldn't have him arrested and I couldn't stand the thought of letting him go. I was going to shoot him but I couldn't do it. I don't know why. If I'd just smacked his head against the wall a couple more times it might have killed him, and I'll tell you, I'd have been glad of it. But I couldn't shoot him while he was lying there unconscious.'

'Of course not.'

'But I couldn't leave him there, I didn't want him walking the streets. He'd just get another gun and do it again. So I broke his legs. Eventually the bones'll knit and he'll be able to resume his career, but in the meantime he's off the streets.' I shrugged. 'It doesn't make any sense. But I couldn't think of anything else to do.'

'The important thing is you didn't drink.'

'Is that the important thing?'

'I think so.'

'I almost drank. If I'd been in my own neighborhood, or if I hadn't reached you. God knows I wanted to drink. I *still* want to drink.'

'But you're not going to.'

'No.'

'Do you have a sponsor, Matthew?'

'No.'

'You should. It's a big help.'

'How?'

'Well, a sponsor's someone you can call anytime, someone you can tell anything to.'

'You have one?'

She nodded. 'I called her after I spoke to you.'

'Why?'

'Because I was nervous. Because it calms me down to talk to her. Because I wanted to see what she would say.'

'What did she say?'

'That I shouldn't have told you to come over.' She laughed. 'Fortunately, you were already on your way.'

'What else did she say?'

The big gray eyes avoided mine. 'That I shouldn't sleep with you.'

'Why'd she say that?'

'Because it's not a good idea to have relationships during the first year. And because it's a terrible idea to get involved with anybody who's newly sober.'

'Christ,' I said. 'I came over because I was jumping out of my skin, not because I was horny.'

'I know that.'

'Do you do everything your sponsor says?'

'I try to.'

'Who is this woman that she's the voice of God on earth?'

'Just a woman. She's my age, actually she's a year and a half younger. But she's been sober almost six years.'

'Long time.'

'It seems like a long time to me.' She picked up her cup, saw it was empty, put it down again. 'Isn't there someone you could ask to be your sponsor?'

'Is that how it works? You have to ask somebody?'

'That's right.'

'Suppose I asked you?'

She shook her head. 'In the first place, you should get a male sponsor. In the second place, I haven't been sober long enough. In the third place we're friends.'

'A sponsor shouldn't be a friend?'

'Not that kind of friend. An AA friend. In the fourth place, it ought to be somebody in your home group so you have frequent contact.'

I thought unwillingly of Jim. 'There's a guy I talk to sometimes.'

'It's important to pick someone you can talk to.'

'I don't know if I can talk to him. I suppose I could.'

'Do you respect his sobriety?'

'I don't know what that means.'

'Well, do you –'

'This evening I told him I got upset by the stories in the newspapers. All the crime in the streets, the things people keep doing to each other. It gets to me, Jan.'

'I know it does.'

'He told me to quit reading the papers. Why are you laughing?'

'It's just such a program thing to say.'

'People talk the damnedest crap. "I lost my job and my mother's dying of cancer and I'm going to have to have my nose amputated but I didn't drink today so that makes me a winner."'

'They really sound like that, don't they?'

'Sometimes. What's so funny?'

'"I'm going to have my nose amputated." A *nose* amputated?'

'Don't laugh,' I said. 'It's a serious problem.'

A little later she was telling me about a member of her home group whose son had been killed by a hit-and-run driver. The man had gone to a meeting and talked about it, drawing strength from the group, and evidently it had been an inspirational experience all around. He'd stayed sober, and his sobriety had enabled him to deal with the situation and bolster the other members of his family while fully experiencing his own grief.

I wondered what was so wonderful about being able to experience your grief. Then I found myself speculating what would have happened some years ago if I'd stayed sober after an errant bullet of mine ricocheted and fatally wounded a six-year-old girl named Estrellita Rivera. I'd dealt with the resultant feelings by pouring bourbon on them. It had certainly seemed like a good idea at the time.

Maybe it hadn't been. Maybe there were no shortcuts, no detours. Maybe you had to go through things.

I said, 'You don't worry about getting hit by a car in New York. But it happens here, the same as anywhere else. Did they ever catch the driver?'

'No.'

'He was probably drunk. They usually are.'

'Maybe he was in a blackout. Maybe he came to the next day and never knew what he'd done.'

'Jesus,' I said, and thought of that night's speaker, the man who stabbed his lover. 'Eight million stories in the Emerald City. And eight million ways to die.'

'The naked city.'

'Isn't that what I said?'

'You said the Emerald City.'

'I did? Where did I get that from?'

'*The Wizard of Oz*. Remember? Dorothy and Toto in Kansas? Judy Garland going over the rainbow?'

'Of course I remember.'

'"Follow the Yellow Brick Road." It led to the Emerald City, where the wonderful wizard lived.'

'I remember. The Scarecrow, the Tin Man, the Cowardly Lion, I remember the whole thing. But where'd I get emeralds from?'

'You're an alcoholic,' she suggested. 'You're missing a couple of brain cells, that's all.'

I nodded. 'Must be it,' I said.

The sky was turning light when we went to sleep. I slept on the couch wrapped up in a couple of spare blankets. At first I thought I wouldn't be able to sleep, but the tiredness came over me like a towering wave. I gave up and let it take me wherever it wanted.

I can't say where it took me because I slept like a dead man. If I dreamed at all I never knew about it. I awoke to the smells of coffee perking and bacon frying, showered, shaved with a disposable razor she'd laid out for me, then got dressed and joined her at a pine plank table in the kitchen. I drank orange juice and coffee and ate scrambled eggs and bacon and whole-wheat muffins with peach preserves, and I couldn't remember when my appetite had been so keen.

There was a group that met Sunday afternoons a few blocks to the east of us, she informed me. She made it one of her regular meetings. Did I feel like joining her?

'I ought to do some work,' I said.

'On a Sunday?'

'What's the difference?'

'Are you really going to be able to accomplish anything on a Sunday afternoon?'

I hadn't really accomplished anything since I'd started. Was there anything I could do today?

I got out my notebook, dialed Sunny's number. No answer. I called my hotel. Nothing from Sunny, nothing from Danny Boy Bell or anyone else I'd seen last night. Well, Danny Boy would still be sleeping at this hour, and so might most of the others.

There was a message to call Chance. I started dialing his number, then stopped myself. If Jan was going to a meeting, I didn't want to sit around her loft waiting for him to call back. Her sponsor might not approve.

The meeting was on the second floor of a synagogue on Forsythe Street. You couldn't smoke there. It was an unusual experience being in an AA meeting that wasn't thick with cigarette smoke.

There were about fifty people there and she seemed to know most of them. She introduced me to several people, all of whose names I promptly forgot. I felt self-conscious, uncomfortable with the attention I was getting. My appearance didn't help, either. While I hadn't slept in my clothes, they looked as though I had, showing the effects of last night's fight in the alley.

And I was feeling the fight's effects, too. It wasn't until we left her loft that I realized how much I ached. My head was sore where I'd butted him and I had a bruise on one forearm and one shoulder was black and blue and ached. Other muscles hurt when I moved. I hadn't felt anything after the incident but all those aches and pains turn up the next day.

I got some coffee and cookies and sat through the meeting. It was all right. The speaker qualified very briefly, leaving the rest of the meeting for discussion. You had to raise your hand to get called on.

Fifteen minutes from the end, Jan raised her hand and said how grateful she was to be sober and how much of a role her sponsor played in her sobriety, how helpful the woman was when she had something bothering her or didn't know what to do. She didn't get more specific than that. I had a feeling she was sending me a message and I wasn't too crazy about that.

I didn't raise my hand.

Afterward she was going out with some people for coffee and asked me if I'd like to come along. I didn't want any more coffee and I didn't want company, either. I made an excuse.

Outside, before we went separate ways, she asked me how I felt. I said I felt all right.

'Do you still feel like drinking?'

'No,' I said.

'I'm glad you called last night.'

'So am I.'

'Call anytime, Matthew. Even in the middle of the night if you have to.'

'Let's hope I don't have to.'

'But if you do, call. All right?'

'Sure.'

'Matthew? Promise me one thing?'

'What?'

'Don't have a drink without calling me first.'

'I'm not going to drink today.'

'I know. But if you ever decide to, if you're going to, call me first. Promise?'

'Okay.'

On the subway heading uptown I thought about the conversation and felt foolish for having made the promise. Well, it had made her happy. What was the harm in it if it made her happy?

There was another message from Chance. I called from the lobby, told his service I was back at my hotel. I bought a paper and took it upstairs with me to kill the time it took him to call back.

The lead story was a honey. A family in Queens – father,

311

mother, two kids under five – had gone for a ride in their shiny new Mercedes. Someone pulled up next to them and emptied both barrels of a shotgun into the car, killing all four of them. A police search of their apartment in Jamaica Estates had revealed a large amount of cash and a quantity of uncut cocaine. Police theorized the massacre was drug related.

No kidding.

There was nothing about the kid I'd left in the alley. Well, there wouldn't be. The Sunday papers were already on the street when he and I encountered one another. Not that he'd be much likelier to make tomorrow's paper, or the next day's. If I'd killed him he might have earned a paragraph somewhere, but what was the news of a black youth with a pair of broken legs?

I was pondering that point when someone knocked on my door.

Funny. The maids have Sunday off, and the few visitors I get call from downstairs. I got my coat off the chair, took the .32 from the pocket. I hadn't gotten rid of it yet, or of the two knives I'd taken from my broken-legged friend. I carried the gun over to the door and asked who it was.

'Chance.'

I dropped the gun in a pocket, opened the door. 'Most people call,' I said.

'The fellow down there was reading. I didn't want to disturb him.'

'That was considerate.'

'That's my trademark.' His eyes were taking me in, appraising me. They left me to scan my room. 'Nice place,' he said.

The words were ironic but the tone of voice was not. I closed the door, pointed to a chair. He remained standing. 'It seems to suit me,' I said.

'I can see that. Spartan, uncluttered.'

He was wearing a navy blazer and gray flannel slacks. No topcoat. Well, it was a little warmer today and he had a car to get around in.

He walked over to my window, looked out of it. 'Tried you last night,' he said.

'I know.'

'You didn't call back.'

'I didn't get the message until a little while ago and I wasn't where I could be reached.'

'Didn't sleep here last night?'

'No.'

312

He nodded. He had turned to face me and his expression was guarded and hard to read. I hadn't seen that look on his face before.

He said, 'You speak to all my girls?'

'All but Sunny.'

'Yeah. You didn't see her yet, huh?'

'No. I tried her a few times last night and again around noon today. I didn't get any answer.'

'You didn't.'

'No. I had a message from her last night, but when I called back she wasn't there.'

'She called you last night.'

'That's right.'

'What time?'

I tried to remember. 'I left the hotel around eight and got back a little after ten. The message was waiting for me. I don't know what time it came in. They're supposed to put the time on the message slip but they don't always bother. Anyway, I probably threw away the slip.'

'No reason to hang onto it.'

'No. What difference does it make when she called?'

He looked at me for a long moment. I saw the gold flecks in the deep brown eyes. He said, 'Shit, I don't know what to do. I'm not used to that. Most of the time I at least *think* I know what to do.'

I didn't say anything.

'You're my man, like you're working for me. But I don't know as I'm sure what that means.'

'I don't know what you're getting at, Chance.'

'Shit,' he said. 'Question is, how much can I trust you? What I keep coming back to is whether I can or not. I *do* trust you. I mean, I took you to my *house*, man. I never took anybody else to my house. Why'd I do that?'

'I don't know.'

'I mean, was I showing off? Was I saying something along the lines of, Look at the class this here nigger has got? Or was I inviting you inside for a look at my soul? Either way, shit, I got to believe I trust you. But am I right to do it?'

'I can't decide that for you.'

'No,' he said, 'you can't.' He pinched his chin between thumb and forefinger. 'I called her last night. Sunny. Couple of times, same as you, didn't get no answer. Well, okay, that's cool. No machine, but that's cool, too, 'cause sometimes she'll forget to put it on. Then I called again, one-thirty, two o'clock maybe, and again no answer, so what I did, I drove over there. Naturally I got a key. It's my apartment. Why shouldn't I have a key?'

By now I knew where this was going. But I let him tell it himself.

'Well, she was there,' he said. 'She's still there. See, what she is, she's dead.'

TWENTY-TWO

She was dead, all right. She lay on her back, nude, one arm flung back over her head and her face turned to that side, the other arm bent at the elbow with the hand resting on her rib cage just below her breast. She was on the floor a few feet from her unmade bed, her auburn hair spread out above and behind her head, and alongside her lipsticked mouth an ellipse of vomit floated on the ivory carpet like scum on a pond. Between her well-muscled white thighs, the carpet was dark with urine.

There were bruises on her face and forehead, another on her shoulder. I touched her wrist automatically, groping for a pulse, but her flesh was far too cold to have any life left in it.

Her eye was open, rolled up into her head. I wanted to coax the eyelid shut with a fingertip. I left it alone.

I said, 'You move her?'

'No way. I didn't touch a thing.'

'Don't lie to me. You tossed Kim's apartment after she was dead. You must have looked around.'

'I opened a couple of drawers. I didn't take anything.'

'What were you looking for?'

'I don't know, man. Just anything I ought to know about. I found some money, couple hundred dollars. I left it there. I found a bankbook. I left it, too.'

'What did she have in the bank?'

'Under a thousand. No big deal. What I found, she had a ton of pills. That's how she did this here.'

He pointed to a mirrored vanity across the room from the corpse. There, among innumerable jars and bottles of makeup and scent, were two empty plastic vials containing prescription labels. The patient's name on both was S. Hendryx, although the prescriptions had been written by different physicians and filled at different pharmacies, both nearby. One prescription had been for Valium, the other for Seconal.

315

'I always looked in her medicine chest,' he was saying. 'Just automatically, you know? And all she ever had was this antihistamine stuff for her hay fever. Then I open this drawer last night and it's a regular drugstore in there. All prescription stuff.'

'What kind of stuff?'

'I didn't read every label. Didn't want to leave any prints where they shouldn't be. From what I saw, it's mostly downs. A lot of tranks. Valium, Librium, Elavil. Sleeping pills like the Seconal here. A couple things of ups, like whatchacallit, Ritalin. But mostly downs.' He shook his head. 'There's things I never heard of. You'd need a doctor to tell you what everything was.'

'You didn't know she took pills?'

'Had no idea. Come here, look at this.' He opened a dresser drawer carefully so as not to leave prints. 'Look,' he said, pointing. At one side of the drawer, beside a stack of folded sweaters, stood perhaps two dozen pill bottles.

'That's somebody who's into this shit pretty heavy,' he said. 'Somebody who's scared to run out. And I didn't know about it. That gets to me, Matt. You read that note?'

The note was on the vanity, anchored with a bottle of Norell cologne. I nudged the bottle aside with the back of my hand and carried the note over to the window. She'd written it in brown ink on beige notepaper and I wanted to read it in decent light.

I read:

Kim, you were lucky. You found someone to do it for you, I have to do it myself.

If I had the guts I would use the window. I could change my mind halfway down and laugh the rest of the way. But I haven't got the guts and the razor blade didn't work.

I hope I took enough this time.
It's no use. The good times are all used up. Chance, I'm sorry. You showed me good times but they're gone. The crowds went home in the eighth inning. All the cheering stopped. Nobody's even keeping score anymore.

There's no way off the merry-go-round. She grabbed the brass ring and it turned her finger green.

Nobody's going to buy me emeralds. Nobody's going to give me babies. Nobody's going to save my life.

I'm sick of smiling. I'm tired of trying to catch up and catch on. All the good times are gone.

I looked out the window across the Hudson at the Jersey skyline. Sunny had lived and died on the thirty-second floor of a high-rise apartment complex called Lincoln View Gardens, though I hadn't seen any trace of garden beyond the potted palms in the lobby.

'That's Lincoln Center down there,' Chance said.

I nodded.

'I should have put Mary Lou here. She likes concerts, she could just walk over. Thing is, she used to live on the West Side. So I wanted to move her to the East Side. You want to do that, you know. Make a big change in their lives right away.'

I didn't much care about the philosophy of pimping. I said, 'She do this before?'

'Kill herself?'

'Try to. She wrote "I hope I took enough this time." Was there a time she didn't take enough?'

'Not since I've known her. And that's a couple years.'

'What does she mean when she says the razor blade didn't work?'

'I don't know.'

I went to her, examined the wrist of the arm stretched out above her head. There was a clearly perceptible horizontal scar. I found an identical scar on her other wrist. I stood up, read the note again.

'What happens now, man?'

I got out my notebook and copied what she'd written word for word. I used a Kleenex to remove what prints I'd left on it, then put it back where I'd found it and anchored it again with the cologne bottle.

I said, 'Tell me again what you did last night.'

'Just what I already told you. I called her and I got a feeling, I don't know why, and I came here.'

'What time?'

'After two. I didn't notice the exact time.'

'You came right upstairs?'

'That's right.'

'The doorman see you?'

'We sort of nodded at each other. He knows me, thinks I live here.'

'Will he remember you?'

317

'Man, I don't know what he remembers and what he forgets.'

'He just work weekends or was he on Friday as well?'

'I don't know. What's the difference?'

'If he's been on every night he might remember he saw you but not remember when. If he just works Saturdays –'

'I get you.'

In the small kitchen a bottle of Georgi vodka stood on the sink board with an inch's depth of liquor left in it. Beside it was an empty cardboard quart of orange juice. A glass in the sink held a residue of what looked like a mixture of the two, and there'd been a faint trace of orange in the reek of her vomit. You didn't need to be much of a detective to put those pieces together. Pills, washed down with a batch of strong screwdrivers, their sedative effect boosted by the alcohol.

I hope I took enough this time.

I had to fight the impulse to pour the last of the vodka down the drain.

'How long were you here, Chance?'

'I don't know. Didn't pay attention to the time.'

'Talk to the doorman on the way out?'

He shook his head. 'I went down to the basement and out through the garage.'

'So he wouldn't have seen you.'

'Nobody saw me.'

'And while you were here –'

'Like I said. I looked in the drawers and closets. I didn't touch many things and I didn't move anything.'

'You read the note?'

'Yeah. But I didn't pick it up to do it.'

'Make any phone calls?'

'My service, to check in. And I called you. But you weren't there.'

No, I hadn't been there. I'd been breaking a boy's legs in an alley three miles to the north.

I said, 'No long-distance calls.'

'Just those two calls, man. That ain't a long distance. You can just about throw a rock from here to your hotel.'

And I could have walked over last night, after my meeting, when her number failed to answer. Would she still have been alive by then? I imagined her, lying on the bed, waiting for the pills and vodka to do their work, letting the phone ring and ring and ring. Would she have ignored the doorbell the same way?

Maybe. Or maybe she'd have been unconscious by then. But I

might have sensed that something was wrong, might have summoned the super or kicked the door in, might have gotten to her in time –

Oh, sure. And I could have saved Cleopatra from the fucking asp, too, if I hadn't been born too late.

I said, 'You had a key to this place?'

'I have keys to all their places.'

'So you just let yourself in.'

He shook his head. 'She had the chain lock on. That's when I knew something was wrong. I used the key and the door opened two, three inches and stopped on account of the chain, and I knew there was trouble. I busted the chain and came on in and just knew I was gonna find something I didn't want to see.'

'You could have gone right out. Left the chain on, gone home.'

'I thought of that.' He looked full at me and I was seeing his face less armored than I'd seen it before. 'You know something? When that chain was on, the thought came to me right away that she killed herself. First thing I thought of, *only* thing I thought of. Reason I broke that chain, I figured maybe she was still alive, maybe I could save her. But it was too late.'

I went to the door, examined the chain lock. The chain itself had not broken; rather, the assembly had ripped loose from its moorings on the doorjamb and hung from the door itself. I hadn't noticed it when we let ourselves into the apartment.

'You broke this when you came in?'

'Like I said.'

'The chain could have been unfastened when you let yourself in. Then you could have locked it and broken it from inside.'

'Why would I do that?'

'To make it look as though the apartment was locked from the inside when you got here.'

'Well, it was. I didn't have to. I don't get where you're comin' from, man.'

'I'm just making sure she was locked in when you got here.'

'Didn't I say she was?'

'And you checked the apartment? There wasn't anybody else here?'

'Not unless they was hiding in the toaster.'

It was a pretty clear suicide. The only thing problematic was his earlier visit. He'd sat on the knowledge of her death for over twelve hours without reporting it.

I thought for a moment. We were north of Sixtieth Street, so that put us in the Twentieth Precinct and out of Durkin's bailiwick. They'd close it as a suicide unless the medical evidence didn't match, in which case his earlier visit would come to light later on.

I said, 'There's a few ways we could do it. We could say that you couldn't reach her all night and you got worried. You talked to me this afternoon and we came over here together. You had a key. You opened the door and we found her and called it in.'

'All right.'

'But the chain lock gets in the way. If you weren't here before, how did it get broken? If somebody else broke it, who was he and what was he doing here?'

'What if we say we broke it getting in?'

I shook my head. 'That doesn't work. Suppose they come up with solid evidence that you were here last night. Then I'm caught swearing to a lie. I could lie for you to the extent of treating something you told me as confidential, but I'm not going to get nailed to a lie that cuts across the grain of the facts. No, I have to say the chain lock was broken when we got here.'

'So it's been broken for weeks.'

'Except the break's fresh. You can see where the screws came out of the wood. The one thing you don't want to do is get caught in that kind of a lie, where your story and the evidence wind up pointing in different directions. I'll tell you what I think you have to do.'

'What's that?'

'Tell the truth. You came here, you kicked the door in, she was dead and you split. You drove around, tried to sort things out in your mind. And you wanted to reach me before you did anything, and I was hard to reach. Then you called me and we came here and called it in.'

'That's the best way?'

'It looks like it to me.'

'All because of that chain thing?'

'That's the most obvious loose end. But even without the chain lock you're better off telling the truth. Look, Chance, you didn't kill her. She killed herself.'

'So?'

'If you didn't kill her, the best thing you can do is tell the truth. If you're guilty, the best thing to do is say nothing, not a word. Call a lawyer and keep your mouth shut. But anytime you're innocent, just tell the truth. It's easier, it's simpler, and it saves trying to remember what you said before. Because I'll tell you one thing. Crooks lie all the time and cops know it and they hate it. And once they get hold of a lie they pull on it until something comes loose. You're looking to lie to save yourself a hassle, and it might work, it's an obvious suicide, you might get by with it, but if it doesn't work you're going to get ten times the hassle you're trying to avoid.'

He thought about it, then sighed. 'They're gonna ask why I didn't call right away.'

'Why didn't you?'

''Cause I didn't know what to do, man. I didn't know whether to shit or go blind.'

'Tell them that.'

'Yeah, I guess.'

'What did you do after you got out of here?'

'Last night? Like you said, I drove around some. Drove around the park a few times. Drove over the George Washington Bridge, up the Palisades Parkway. Like a Sunday drive, only a little early.' He shook his head at the memory. 'Came back, drove over to see Mary Lou. Let myself in, didn't have to bust no chain lock. She was sleepin'. I got in bed with her, woke her up, stayed with her a little. Then I went on home.'

'To your house?'

'To my house. I'm not gonna tell 'em about my house.'

'No need to. You got a little sleep at Mary Lou's.'

'I never sleep when someone else is around. I can't. But they don't have to know that.'

'No.'

'I was at my house for awhile. Then I came on into town, lookin' for you.'

'What did you do at your house?'

'Slept some. A couple hours. I don't need a whole lot of sleep, but I got what I needed.'

'Uh-huh.'

'And I was just there, you know?' He walked over to the wall, took a staring mask from the nail where it hung. He started telling me about it, the tribe, their geographical location, the purpose of the mask. I didn't pay much attention. 'Now I got fingerprints on it,' he said. 'Well, that's okay. You can tell 'em while we were waiting for them I took the mask off the wall and told you it's history. I might as well tell the truth. Wouldn't want to get caught in some nasty old little white lie.' He smiled at the last phrase. 'Little black lie,' he said. 'Whyn't you make that call?'

TWENTY-THREE

It wasn't half the hassle it might have been. I didn't know either of the cops who came out from the Twentieth, but it couldn't have gone much smoother if I had. We answered questions on the scene and went back to the station house on West Eighty-second to give our statements. The on-scene medical evidence all seemed to be consistent with what we'd reported. The cops were quick to point out that Chance should have called in as soon as he found the dead girl, but they didn't really jump on him for taking his time. Walking in on an unexpected corpse is a shock, even if you're a pimp and she's a whore, and this, after all, was New York, the city of the uninvolved, and what was remarkable was not that he'd called it in late but that he'd called it in at all.

I was at ease by the time we got to the station house. I'd only been anxious early on when it occurred to me that it might occur to them to frisk us. My coat was a small-time arsenal, still holding the gun and the two knives I'd taken from the kid in the alley. The knives were both illegal weapons. The gun was that and possibly more; God only knew what kind of a provenance it had. But we'd done nothing to rate a frisk, and, happily, we didn't get one.

'Whores'll kill themselves,' Joe Durkin said. 'It's something they do, and this one had a history. You saw the wrist scars? Those were a few years old, according to the report. What you might not know is she tried the pill route a little less than a year ago. A girlfriend took her over to St Clare's to get her stomach pumped.'

'There was something in the note. She hoped she had enough this time, something like that.'

'Well, she got her wish.'

We were at the Slate, a Tenth Avenue steak house that draws

a lot of cops from John Jay College and Midtown North. I'd been back at my hotel, changing my clothes, finding places to stow the weapons and some of the money I'd been carrying, when he called to suggest I buy him a dinner. 'I thought I'd hit you up for a meal now,' he said, 'before all your client's girls are dead and your expense account gets trimmed.'

He had the mixed grill and drank a couple of Carlsbergs with it. I ordered the chopped sirloin and drank black coffee with my meal. We talked a little about Sunny's suicide but it didn't carry us very far. He said, 'If it wasn't for the other one, the blonde, you wouldn't even think to look at it twice. All the medical evidence fits in with suicide. The bruises, that's easy. She was groggy, she didn't know what she was doing, she fell and bumped into things. Same reason she was on the floor instead of the bed. There was nothing special about the bruises. Her prints were where they belonged – the bottle, the glass, the pill bottles. The note matches other samples of her handwriting. If we buy your guy's story, she was even in a locked room when he found her. Locked from inside, the chain on. You figure that for the truth?'

'His whole story sounded true to me.'

'So she killed herself. It even fits with the Dakkinen death two weeks ago. They were friends and she was depressed by what happened to her friend. You see any way it was anything but suicide?'

I shook my head. 'It's the hardest kind of suicide to stage. What do you do, stuff the pills down her throat with a funnel? Make her take them at gunpoint?'

'You can dissolve the contents, let her take them without knowing it. But they found traces of the Seconal capsules in the stomach contents. So forget that. It's suicide.'

I tried to remember the annual suicide rate in the city. I couldn't even come up with an educated guess, and Durkin was no help. I wondered what the rate was, and if it was on the rise like everything else.

Over coffee he said, 'I had a couple of clerks go through the registration cards at the Galaxy Downtowner since the first of the year. Pulling the block-printed ones. Nothing ties into the Jones registration.'

'And the other hotels?'

'Nothing that fits. A batch of people called Jones, it's a common enough name, but they're all signatures and credit cards and they look bona fide. Waste of time.'

'Sorry.'

'Why? Ninety percent of what I do is a waste of time. You were right, it was worth checking. If this had been a big case, front-page stuff, top brass putting pressure on, you can believe I'd have thought of it myself and we'd be checking every hotel in the five boroughs. How about you?'

'What about me?'

'You getting anywhere with Dakkinen?'

I had to think. 'No,' I said, finally.

'It's aggravating. I went over the file again and you know what got stuck in my throat? That desk clerk.'

'The one I talked to?'

'That was a manager, assistant manager, something like that. No, the one who checked the killer in. Now here's a guy comes in, prints his name instead of writing it, and pays cash. Those are two unusual things for a person to do, right? I mean, who pays cash in front for a hotel nowadays? I don't mean in a hot-pillow joint, I mean a decent hotel where you're going to spend sixty or eighty dollars for a room. Everything's plastic nowadays, credit cards, that's the whole business. But this guy paid cash and the desk clerk doesn't remember shit about him.'

'Did you check him out?'

He nodded. 'I went and talked to him last night. Well, he's this South American kid, up from one of those countries. He was in a fog when I talked to him. He was probably in a fog when the killer checked in. He probably lives his life in a fog. I don't know where his fog comes from, whether he smokes it or snorts it or what he does, but I think he probably comes by it honestly. You know the percentage of this city that's stoned all the time?'

'I know what you mean.'

'You see 'em at lunch hour. Office workers, midtown, Wall Street, I don't care what neighborhood you're talking about. They buy the fucking joints in the street and spend their lunch hour smoking 'em in the park. How does anybody get any work done?'

'I don't know.'

'And there's all these pillheads. Like this woman who killed herself. Taking all those pills all the time, and she wasn't even breaking the law. Drugs.' He sighed, shook his head, smoothed his dark hair. 'Well, what I'm gonna have is a brandy,' he said, 'if you think your client can afford it.'

*

I got over to St Paul's in time for the last ten minutes of the meeting. I had coffee and a cookie and barely listened to what was being said. I didn't even have to say my name, and I ducked out during the prayer.

I went back to the hotel. There were no messages. I'd had a couple of calls, the desk man told me, but nobody'd left a name. I went upstairs and tried to sort out how I felt about Sunny's suicide, but all I seemed to feel so far was numb. It was tempting to beat myself up with the thought that I might have learned something if I hadn't saved her interrogation for last, might even have said or done something to forestall her suicide, but I couldn't get much mileage out of that one. I'd talked to her on the phone. She could have said something and she hadn't. And suicide, after all, was something she'd tried at least twice in the past, and very likely a time or two of which there'd been no record.

Try something long enough, sooner or later you get it right.

In the morning I had a light breakfast and went over to the bank, where I deposited some cash and bought a money order. I went to the post office and mailed it to Anita. I hadn't given a whole lot of thought to my son's orthodontia and now I could forget it altogether.

I walked on to St Paul's and lit a candle for Sonya Hendryx. I sat in a pew, giving myself a few minutes to remember Sunny. There wasn't much to remember. We'd barely met. I couldn't even recall very clearly what she looked like because her image in death pushed my dim memory of the living Sunny to the side.

It occurred to me that I owed the church money. Ten percent of Chance's fee came to $250, and they were further entitled to a tithe of the three hundred bucks and change I'd taken off the kid who'd tried mugging me. I didn't have an exact count but $350 struck me as a fair estimate, so I could give them $285 and call it even.

But I'd put most of my money in the bank. I had a few hundred dollars in my wallet but if I gave the church $285 I'd be strapped for walk-around money. I weighed the nuisance of another trip to the bank, and then the fundamental insanity of my little game struck me like a kidney punch.

What was I doing anyway? Why did I figure I owed anybody money? And who did I owe it to? Not the church, I didn't belong to any church. I gave my tithes to whatever house of worship came along at the right time.

To whom, then, was I in debt? To God?

Where was the sense in that? And what was the nature of this debt? How did I owe it? Was I repaying borrowed funds? Or had I invented some sort of bribe scheme, some celestial protection racket?

I'd never had trouble rationalizing it before. It was just a custom, a minor eccentricity. I didn't file a tax return so I paid a tithe instead.

I'd never really let myself ask myself why.

I wasn't sure I liked the answer. I remembered, too, a thought that had crossed my mind momentarily in that alley off St Nicholas Avenue – that I was going to get killed by this boy because I hadn't paid my tithe. Not that I'd really believed it, not that I thought the world worked that way, but how remarkable that I'd had such a thought at all.

After awhile I took out my wallet, counted out the $285. I sat there with the money in my hand. Then I put it all back in my wallet, all but a dollar.

At least I could pay for the candle.

That afternoon I walked all the way to Kim's building. The weather wasn't bad and I didn't have anything better to do. I walked past the doorman and let myself into her apartment.

The first thing I did was pour the bottle of Wild Turkey down the sink.

I don't know how much sense that made. There was plenty of other booze there and I didn't feel like doing my Carrie Nation imitation. But the Wild Turkey had taken on the status of a symbol. I pictured the bottle every time I thought of going to that apartment, and the picture was accompanied more often than not by a vivid memory of the taste and smell. When the last of it went down the sink I was able to relax.

Then I went back to the front closet and checked out the fur coat hanging there. A label sewn to the lining identified the garment as consisting of dyed lapin. I used the Yellow Pages, called a furrier at random and learned that *lapin* was the French word for 'rabbit.' 'You could find it in a dictionary,' I was told. 'A regular American dictionary. It's an English word now, it came into the language from the fur business. Plain old rabbit.'

Just as Chance had said.

On the way home something triggered the thought of having a beer. I don't even recall what the stimulus was, but the response was a picture of myself with a shoulder pressed against a bar and one foot up on the brass rail, bell-shaped glass in hand, sawdust on the floor, my nostrils full of the smell of a musty old tavern.

It wasn't a strong drink urge and I never considered acting on it, but it put me in mind of what I'd promised Jan. Since I wasn't going to have a drink I felt no compulsion to call her but decided to anyway. I spent a dime and dialed her number from a booth around the corner from the main public library.

Our conversation had traffic noises for competition, and so we kept it brief and light. I didn't get around to telling her about Sunny's suicide. I didn't mention the bottle of Wild Turkey, either.

I read the *Post* while I ate dinner. Sunny's suicide had had a couple of paragraphs in the *News* that morning, which is as much as it merited, but the *Post* would hype anything that might sell papers, and their hook was that Sunny had the same pimp as Kim, who'd been chopped to pieces in a hotel just two weeks ago. Nobody had been able to turn up a picture of Sunny so they ran the shot of Kim again.

The story, though, couldn't fulfill the promise of the head-lines. All they had was a suicide and some airy speculation that Sunny had killed herself because of what she knew about Kim's murder.

I couldn't find anything about the boy whose legs I'd broken. But there was the usual complement of crime and deaths scattered throughout the paper. I thought about what Jim Faber had said about giving up newspapers. It didn't seem like I'd be giving up all that much.

After dinner I picked up my mail at the desk. The mail was the usual junk, along with a phone message to call Chance. I called his service and he rang back to ask how things were going. I said that they weren't, really. He asked if I was going to keep at it.

'For a while,' I said. 'Just to see if it goes anywhere.'

The cops, he said, had not been hassling him. He'd spent his day arranging funeral services for Sunny. Unlike Kim, whose body had been shipped back to Wisconsin, Sunny didn't have parents or kin to claim her. There was a question about when Sunny's body would be released from the morgue, so he'd made arrangements to have a memorial service at Walter B. Cooke's on West Seventy-second Street. That would take place Thursday, he told me, at two in the afternoon.

'I should have done the same for Kim,' he said, 'but I never thought of it. It's mostly for the girls. They're in a state, you know.'

'I can imagine.'

'They're all thinking the same thing. That business about death comes in threes. They're all worrying about who's next.'

I went to my meeting that night. It struck me during the qualification that a week ago I'd been in a blackout, wandering around doing God knows what.

'My name's Matt,' I said when my turn came. 'I'll just listen tonight. Thanks.'

When the meeting broke up a guy followed me up the stairs to street level, then fell into step with me. He was about thirty, wearing a plaid lumber jacket and a peaked cap. I couldn't recall seeing him before.

He said, 'Your name is Matt, right?' I allowed that it was. 'You like that story tonight?'

'It was interesting,' I said.

'You wanna hear an interesting story? I heard a story about a man uptown with a broken face and two broken legs. That's some story, man.'

I felt a chill. The gun was in my dresser drawer, all rolled up in a pair of socks. The knives were in the same drawer.

He said, 'You got some pair of balls, man. You got *cojones*, you know what I mean?' He cupped his groin with one hand like a baseball player adjusting his jock. 'All the same,' he said, 'you don' wanna look for trouble.'

'What are you talking about?'

He spread his hands. 'What do I know? I'm Western Union, man. I bring the message, tha's all I do. Some chick gets herself iced in a hotel, man, is one thing, but who her friends are is another. Is not important, you know?'

'Who's the message from?'

He just looked at me.

'How'd you know to find me at the meeting?'

'Followed you in, followed you out.' He chuckled. 'That *maricón* with the broken legs, that was too much, man. That was too much.'

TWENTY-FOUR

Tuesday was largely devoted to a game of Follow the Fur.

It started in that state that lies somewhere between dreaming and full consciousness. I'd awakened from a dream and dozed off again, and I found myself running a mental videotape of my meeting with Kim at Armstrong's. I began with a false memory, seeing her as she must have been when she arrived on the bus from Chicago, a cheap suitcase in one hand, a denim jacket tight on her shoulders. Then she was sitting at my table, her hand at her throat, light glinting off her ring while she toyed with the clasp at the throat of her fur jacket. She was telling me that it was ranch mink but she'd trade it for the denim jacket she'd come to town in.

The whole sequence played itself off and my mind moved on to something else. I was back in that alley in Harlem, except now my assailant had help. Royal Waldron and the messenger from the night before were flanking him on either side. The conscious part of my mind tried to get them the hell out of there, perhaps to even the odds a little, and then a realization screamed at me and I tossed my legs over the side of my bed and sat up, the dream images all scurrying off into the corners of the mind where they live.

It was a different jacket.

I showered and shaved and got out of there. I cabbed first to Kim's building to check her closet yet again. The lapin coat, the dyed rabbit Chance had bought her, was not the garment I had seen in Armstrong's. It was longer, it was fuller, it didn't fasten with a clasp at the throat. It was not what she'd been wearing, not what she'd described as ranch mink and offered to trade for her old denim jacket.

Nor was the jacket I remembered to be found anywhere else in the apartment.

I took another cab to Midtown North. Durkin wasn't on duty.

I got another cop to call him at home and finally got unofficial access to the file, and yes, the inventory of impounded articles found in the room at the Galaxy Downtowner included a fur jacket. I checked the photos in the file and couldn't find the jacket in any of them.

A subway took me downtown to One Police Plaza, where I talked to some more people and waited while my request went through some channels and around others. I got to one office just after the guy I was supposed to see left for lunch. I had my meeting book with me, and it turned out there was a meeting less than a block away at St Andrew's Church, so I killed an hour there. Afterward I got a sandwich at a deli and ate it standing up.

I went back to One Police Plaza and finally got to examine the fur jacket Kim had had with her when she died. I couldn't have sworn it was the one I'd seen in Armstrong's but it seemed to match my memory. I ran my hand over the rich fur and tried to replay the tape that had run in my mind that morning. It all seemed to go together. This fur was the right length, the right color, and there was a clasp at the throat that her port-tipped fingers might have toyed with.

The label sewn to the lining told me it was genuine ranch mink and that a furrier named Arvin Tannenbaum had made it.

The Tannenbaum firm was on the third floor of a loft building on West Twenty-ninth, right in the heart of the fur district. It would have simplified things if I could have taken Kim's fur along, but NYPD cooperation, official or otherwise, only went so far. I described the jacket, which didn't help much, and I described Kim. A check of their sales records revealed the purchase of a mink jacket six weeks previously by Kim Dakkinen, and the sales slip led us to the right salesman and he remembered the sale.

The salesman was round faced and balding, with watery blue eyes behind thick lenses. He said, 'Tall girl, very pretty girl. You know, I read that name in the newspaper and it rang a bell but I couldn't think why. Terrible thing, such a pretty girl.'

She'd been with a gentleman, he recalled, and it was the gentleman who had paid for the coat. Paid cash for it, he remembered. And no, that wasn't so unusual, not in the fur business. They only did a small volume of retail sales and a lot of it was people in the garment trade or people who knew somebody in the trade, although of course anyone could walk in off the street and buy any garment in the place. But mostly it was cash because the customer didn't usually want to wait for his check to clear, and besides a fur was often a luxury gift for a luxury friend, so to speak, and the customer was happier if no record of the transaction existed. Thus payment in cash, thus the sales slip not in the buyer's name but in Miss Dakkinen's.

The sale had come to just under twenty-five hundred dollars with the tax. A lot of cash to carry, but not unheard of. I'd been carrying almost that myself not too long ago.

Could he describe the gentleman? The salesman sighed. It was much easier, he explained, to describe the lady. He could picture her now, those gold braids wrapped around her head, the piercing blue of her eyes. She'd tried on several jackets, she looked quite elegant in fur, but the man –

Thirty-eight, forty years old, he supposed. Tall rather than short, as he remembered, but not tall as the girl had been tall.

'I'm sorry,' he said. 'I have a sense of him but I can't picture him. If he'd been wearing a fur I could tell you more than you'd want to know about it, but as it was –'

'What was he wearing?'

'A suit, I think, but I don't remember it. He was the type of man who'd wear a suit. I can't recall what he was wearing, though.'

'Would you recognize him if you saw him again?'

'I might pass him on the street and not think twice.'

'Suppose he was pointed out to you.'

'Then I would probably recognize him, yes. You mean like a lineup? Yes, I suppose so.'

I told him he probably remembered more than he thought he did. I asked him the man's profession.

'I don't even know his name. How would I know what he did for a living?'

'Your impression,' I said. 'Was he an auto mechanic? A stockbroker? A rodeo performer?'

'Oh,' he said, and thought it over. 'Maybe an accountant,' he said.

'An accountant?'

'Something like that. A tax lawyer, an accountant. This is a game, I'm just guessing, you understand that –'

'I understand. What nationality?'

'American. What do you mean?'

'English, Irish, Italian –'

'Oh,' he said. 'I see, more of the game. I would say Jewish, I would say Italian, I would say dark, Mediterranean. Because she was so blonde, you know? A contrast. I don't know that he was dark, but there was a contrast. Could be Greek, could be Spanish.'

'Did he go to college?'

'He didn't show me a diploma.'

'No, but he must have talked, to you or to her. Did he sound like college or did he sound like the streets?'

'He didn't sound like the streets. He was a gentleman, an educated man.'

'Married?'

'Not to her.'

'To anybody?'

'Aren't they always? You're not married, you don't have to buy mink for your girlfriend. He probably bought another one for his wife, to keep her happy.'

'Was he wearing a wedding ring?'

'I don't remember a ring.' He touched his own gold band. 'Maybe yes, maybe no. I don't recall a ring.'

He didn't recall much, and the impressions I'd pried out of him were suspect. They might have been valid, might as easily have grown out of an unconscious desire to supply me with the answers he thought I wanted. I could have kept going – *All right, you don't remember his shoes, but what kind of shoes would a guy like him wear? Chukka boots? Penny loafers? Cordovans? Adidas? What!* But I'd reached and passed a point of diminishing returns. I thanked him and got out of there.

There was a coffee shop on the building's first floor, just a long counter with stools and a takeout window. I sat over coffee and tried to assess what I had.

She had a boyfriend. No question. Somebody bought her that jacket, counted out hundred dollar bills, kept his own name out of the transaction.

Did the boyfriend have a machete? There was a question I hadn't asked the fur salesman. *'All right, use your imagination. Picture this guy in a hotel room with the blonde. Let's say he wants to chop her. What does he use? An axe? A cavalry saber? A machete? Just give me your impression.'*

Sure. He was an accountant, right? He'd probably use a pen. A Pilot Razor Point, deadly as a sword in the hands of a samurai. Zip zip, take that, you bitch.

The coffee wasn't very good. I ordered a second cup anyway. I interlaced my fingers and looked down at my hands. That was

332

the trouble, my fingers meshed well enough but nothing else did. What kind of accountant type went batshit with a machete? Granted, anyone could explode that way, but this had been a curiously planned explosion, the hotel room rented under a false name, the murder performed with no traces left of the murderer's identity.

Did that sound like the same man who bought the fur?

I sipped my coffee and decided it didn't. Nor did the picture I got of the boyfriend jibe with the message I'd been given after last night's meeting. The fellow in the lumber jacket had been muscle, pure and simple, even if he hadn't been called upon to do anything more with that muscle than flex it. Would a mild-mannered accountant command that sort of muscle?

Not likely.

Were the boyfriend and Charles Owen Jones one and the same? And why such an elaborate alias, middle name and all? People who used a surname like Smith or Jones for an alias usually picked Joe or John to go with it. Charles Owen Jones?

Maybe his name was Charles Owens. Maybe he'd started to write that, then changed his mind in the nick of time and dropped the last letter of Owens, converting it to a middle name. Did that make sense?

I decided that it didn't.

The goddamned room clerk. It struck me that he hadn't been interrogated properly. Durkin had said he was in a fog, and evidently he was South American, possibly somewhat at a loss in English. But he'd have had to be reasonably fluent to get hired by a decent hotel for a position that put him in contact with the public. No, the problem was that nobody pushed him. If he'd been questioned the way I questioned the fur salesman, say, he'd have let go of something. Witnesses always remember more than they think they remember.

The room clerk who checked in Charles Owen Jones was named Octavio Calderón, and he'd worked last on Saturday when he was on the desk from four to midnight. Sunday afternoon he'd called in sick. There had been another call yesterday and a third call an hour or so before I got to the hotel and braced the assistant manager. Calderón was still sick. He'd be out another day, maybe longer.

I asked what was the matter with him. The assistant manager sighed and shook his head. 'I don't know,' he said. 'It's hard to get a straight answer out of these people. When they want to turn evasive their grasp of the English language weakens considerably. They slip off into the convenient little world of *No comprendo.*'

'You mean you hire room clerks who can't speak English?'

'No, no. Calderón's fluent. Someone else called in for him.' He shook his head again. 'He's a very diffident young man, 'Tavio is. I suspect he reasoned that if he had a friend make the call, I couldn't intimidate him over the phone. The implication, of course, is that he's not hale and hearty enough to get from his bed to the phone. I gather he lives in some sort of rooming house with the telephone in the hallway. Someone with a much heavier Latin accent than 'Tavio made the call.'

'Did he call yesterday?'

'Someone called for him.'

'The same person who called today?'

'I'm sure I don't know. One Hispanic voice over the phone is rather like another. It was a male voice both times. I think it was the same voice, but I couldn't swear to it. What difference does it make?'

None that I could think of. How about Sunday? Had Calderón done his own telephoning then?

'I wasn't here Sunday.'

'You have a phone number for him?'

'It rings in the hall. I doubt that he'll come to the phone.'

'I'd like the number anyway.'

He gave it to me, along with an address on Barnett Avenue in Queens. I'd never heard of Barnett Avenue and I asked the assistant manager if he knew what part of Queens Calderón lived in.

'I don't know anything about Queens,' he said. 'You're not going out there, are you?' He made it sound as though I'd need a passport, and supplies of food and water. 'Because I'm sure 'Tavio will be back on the job in a day or two.'

'What makes you so sure?'

'It's a good job,' he said. 'He'll lose it if he's not back soon. And he must know that.'

'How's his absenteeism record?'

'Excellent. And I'm sure his sickness is legitimate enough. Probably one of those viruses that runs its course in three days. There's a lot of that going around.'

I called Octavio Calderón's number from a pay phone right there in the Galaxy lobby. It rang for a long time, nine or ten rings, before a woman answered it in Spanish. I asked for Octavio Calderón.

'*No está aquí,*' she told me.

I tried to form questions in Spanish. *Es enfermo?* Is he sick? I couldn't tell if I was making myself understood. Her replies were delivered in a Spanish that was very different in inflection from the Puerto Rican idiom I was used to hearing around New York, and when she tried to accommodate me in English her accent was heavy and her vocabulary inadequate. *No está aquí,* she kept saying, and it was the one thing she said that I understood with no difficulty. *No está aquí.* He is not here.

I went back to my hotel. I had a pocket atlas for the five boroughs in my room and I looked up Barnett Avenue in the Queens index, turned to the appropriate page and hunted until I found it. It was in Woodside. I studied the map and wondered what a Hispanic rooming house was doing in an Irish neighborhood.

Barnett Avenue extended only ten or twelve blocks, running east from Forty-third Street and ending at Woodside Avenue. I had my choice of trains. I could take either the E or F on the Independent line or the IRT Flushing Line.

Assuming I wanted to go there at all.

I called again from my room. Once again the phone rang for a long time. This time a man answered it. I said, 'Octavio Calderón, *por favor.*'

'*Momento,*' he said. Then there was a thumping sound, as if he let the receiver hang from its cord and it was knocking against the wall. Then there was no sound at all except that of a radio in the background tuned to a Latin broadcast. I was thinking about hanging up by the time he came back on the line.

'*No está aquí,*' he said, and rang off before I could say anything in any language.

I looked in the pocket atlas again and tried to think of a way to avoid a trip to Woodside. It was rush hour already. If I went now I'd have to stand up all the way out there. And what was I going to accomplish? I'd have a long ride jammed into a subway car like a sardine in a can so that someone could tell me *No está aquí* face to face. What was the point? Either he was taking a drug-assisted vacation or he was really sick, and either way I didn't stand much chance of getting anything out of him. If I actually managed to run him down, I'd be rewarded with *No lo se* instead of *No está aquí*. I don't know, he's not here, I don't know, he's not here –

Shit.

Joe Durkin had done a follow-up interrogation of Calderón on Saturday night, around the time that I was passing the word to every snitch and hanger-on I could find. That same night I took a gun away from a mugger and Sunny Hendryx washed down a load of pills with vodka and orange juice.

The very next day, Calderón called in sick. And the day after that a man in a lumber jacket followed me in and out of an AA meeting and warned me off Kim Dakkinen's trail.

The phone rang. It was Chance. There'd been a message that he'd called, but evidently he'd decided not to wait for me to get back to him.

'Just checking,' he said. 'You getting anywhere?'

'I must be. Last night I got a warning.'

'What kind of a warning?'

'A guy told me not to go looking for trouble.'

'You sure it was about Kim?'

'I'm sure.'

'You know the guy?'

'No.'

'What are you fixing to do?'

I laughed. 'I'm going to go looking for trouble,' I said. 'In Woodside.'

'Woodside?'

'That's in Queens.'

'I know where Woodside is, man. What's happening in Woodside?'

I decided I didn't want to get into it. 'Probably nothing,' I said, 'and I wish I could save myself the trip, but I can't. Kim had a boyfriend.'

'In Woodside?'

'No, Woodside's something else. But it's definite she had a boyfriend. He bought her a mink jacket.'

He sighed. 'I *told* you about that. Dyed rabbit.'

'I know about the dyed rabbit. It's in her closet.'

'So?'

'She also had a short jacket, ranch mink. She was wearing it the first time I met her. She was also wearing it when she went to the Galaxy Downtowner and got killed. It's in a lockbox at One Police Plaza.'

'What's it doin' there?'

'It's evidence.'

'Of what?'

'Nobody knows. I got to it and I traced it and I talked to the man who sold it to her. She's the buyer of record, her name's on the sales slip, but there was a man with her and he counted out the money and paid for it.'

'How much?'

'Twenty-five hundred.'

He thought it over. 'Maybe she held out,' he said. 'Be easy to do, couple hundred a week, you know they hold out from time to time. I wouldn'ta missed it.'

'The man paid out the money, Chance.'

'Maybe she gave it to him to pay with. Like a woman'll slip a man money for a restaurant check, so it don't look bad.'

'How come you don't want it to be that she had a boyfriend?'

'Shit,' he said. 'I don't care about that. I want it to be whatever way it was. I just can't believe it, that's all.'

I let it go.

'Could be a trick instead of a boyfriend. Sometimes a john wants to pretend like he's a special friend, he don't have to pay, so he wants to give presents instead of cash. Maybe he was just a john and she was like hustling him for the fur.'

'Maybe.'

'You think he was a boyfriend?'

'That's what I think, yes.'

'And he killed her?'

'I don't know who killed her.'

'And whoever killed her wants you to drop the whole thing.'

'I don't know,' I said. 'Maybe the killing had nothing to do with the boyfriend. Maybe it was a psycho, the way the cops want to figure it, and maybe the boyfriend just doesn't want to get roped into any investigation.'

'He wasn't in it and he wants to stay out of it. That what you mean?'

'Something like that.'

'I don't know, man. Maybe you should let it go.'

'Drop the investigation?'

'Maybe you should. A warning, shit, you don't want to get killed over it.'

'No,' I said. 'I don't.'

'What are you gonna do, then?'

'Right now I'm going to catch a train to Queens.'

'To Woodside.'

'Right.'

'I could bring the car around. Drive you out there.'

'I don't mind the subway.'

'Be faster in the car. I could wear my little chauffeur's cap. You could sit in the back.'

'Some other time.'

'Suit yourself,' he said. 'Call me after, huh?'

'Sure.'

I wound up taking the Flushing line to a stop at Roosevelt Avenue and Fifty-second Street. The train came up out of the ground after it left Manhattan. I almost missed my stop because it was hard to tell where I was. The station signs on the elevated platforms were so disfigured with graffiti that their messages were indecipherable.

A flight of steel steps led me back down to street level. I checked my pocket atlas, got my bearings, and set out for Barnett Avenue. I hadn't walked far before I managed to figure out what a Hispanic rooming house was doing in Woodside. The neighborhood wasn't Irish anymore. There were still a few places with names like the Emerald Tavern and the Shamrock scattered in the shadow of the El, but most of the signs were Spanish and most of the markets were *bodegas* now. Posters in the window of the Tara Travel Agency offered charter flights to Bogotá and Caracas.

Octavio Calderón's rooming house was a dark two-story frame house with a front porch. There were five or six plastic lawn chairs lined up on the porch, and an upended orange crate holding magazines and newspapers. The chairs were unoccupied, which wasn't surprising. It was a little chilly for porch sitting.

I rang the doorbell. Nothing happened. I heard conversation within, and several radios playing. I rang the bell again, and a middle-aged woman, short and very stout, came to the door and opened it. '*Sí?*' she said, expectant.

'Octavio Calderón,' I said.

'*No está aquí.*'

She may have been the woman I spoke to the first time I called. It was hard to tell and I didn't care a whole lot. I stood there talking through the screen door, trying to make myself understood in a mixture of Spanish and English. After awhile she went away and came back with a tall hollow-cheeked man with a severely trimmed moustache. He spoke English, and I told him that I wanted to see Calderón's room.

But Calderón wasn't there, he told me.

'*No me importa*,' I said. I wanted to see his room anyway. But there was nothing to see, he replied, mystified. Calderón was not there. What was I to gain by seeing a room?

They weren't refusing to cooperate. They weren't even particularly reluctant to cooperate. They just couldn't see the point. When it became clear that the only way to get rid of me, or at least the easiest way, was to show me to Calderón's room, that was what they did. I followed the woman down a hallway and past a kitchen to a staircase. We climbed the stairs, walked the length of another hallway. She opened a door without knocking on it, stood aside and gestured for me to enter.

There was a piece of linoleum on the floor, an old iron bedstead with the mattress stripped of linen, a chest of drawers in blonde maple, and a little writing table with a folding chair in front of it. A wing chair slipcovered in a floral print stood on the opposite side of the room near the window. There was a table lamp with a patterned paper shade on the chest of drawers, an overhead light fixture with two bare bulbs in the center of the ceiling.

And that's all there was.

'*Entiende usted ahora? No está acquí.*'

I went through the room mechanically, automatically. It could hardly have been emptier. The small closet held nothing but a couple of wire hangers. The drawers in the blonde chest and the single drawer in the writing table were utterly empty. Their corners had been wiped clean.

With the hollow-cheeked man as interpreter, I managed to question the woman. She wasn't a mine of information in any language. She didn't know when Calderón had left. Sunday or Monday, she believed. Monday she had come into his room to clean it and discovered he had removed all his possessions, leaving nothing behind. Understandably enough, she took this to mean that he was relinquishing the room. Like all of her tenants, he had paid by the week. He'd had a couple of days left before his rent was due, but evidently he had had someplace else to go, and no, it was not remarkable that he had left without telling her. Tenants did that with some frequency, even when they were not behind in their rent. She and her daughter had given the room a good cleaning, and now it was ready to be rented to someone else. It would not be vacant long. Her rooms never stood vacant long.

Had Calderón been a good tenant. *Sí*, an excellent tenant, but she had never had trouble with her tenants. She rented only to Colombians and Panamanians and Ecuadorians and never had trouble with any of them. Sometimes they had to move suddenly because of the Immigration Service. Perhaps that was why Calderón had left so abruptly. But that was not her business. Her business was cleaning his room and renting it to someone else.

Calderón wouldn't have had trouble with Immigration, I knew. He wasn't an illegal or he wouldn't have been working at the Galaxy Downtowner. A big hotel wouldn't employ an alien without a green card.

He'd had some other reason for leaving in a hurry.

I spent about an hour interviewing other tenants. The picture of Calderón that emerged didn't help a bit. He was a quiet young man who kept to himself. His hours at work were such that he was likely to be out when the other tenants were at home. He did not, to anyone's knowledge, have a girlfriend. In the eight months that he'd lived on Barnett Avenue, he had not had a visitor of either sex, nor had he had frequent phone calls. He'd lived elsewhere in New York before moving to Barnett Avenue, but no one knew his previous address or even if it had been in Queens.

Had he used drugs? Everyone I spoke to seemed quite shocked by the suggestion. I gathered that the fat little landlady ran a tight ship. Her tenants were all regularly employed and they led respectable lives. If Calderón smoked marijuana, one of them assured me, he certainly hadn't done so in his room. Or the landlady would have detected the smell and he would have been asked to leave.

'Maybe he is homesick,' a dark-eyed young man suggested. 'Maybe he is fly back to Cartagena.'

'Is that where he came from?'

'He is Colombian. I think he say Cartagena.'

So that was what I learned in an hour, that Octavio Calderón had come from Cartagena. And nobody was too certain of that either.

TWENTY-FIVE

I called Durkin from a Dunkin' Donuts on Woodside Avenue. There was no booth, just a pay phone mounted on the wall. A few feet from me a couple of kids were playing one of those electronic games. Somebody else was listening to disco music on a satchel-sized portable radio. I cupped the telephone mouthpiece with my hand and told Durkin what I'd found out.

'I can put out a pickup order on him. Octavio Calderón, male Hispanic, early twenties. What is he, about five seven?'

'I never met him.'

'That's right, you didn't. I can check the hotel for a description. You sure he's gone, Scudder? I talked to him just a couple of days ago.'

'Saturday night.'

'I think that's right. Yeah, before the Hendryx suicide. Right.'

'That's still a suicide?'

'Any reason why it shouldn't be?'

'None that I know of. You talked to Calderón Saturday night and that's the last anybody's seen of him.'

'I have that effect on a lot of people.'

'Something spooked him. You think it was you?'

He said something but I couldn't hear it over the din. I asked him to repeat it.

'I said he didn't seem to be paying that much attention. I thought he was stoned.'

'The neighbors describe him as a pretty straight young man.'

'Yeah, a nice quiet boy. The kind that goes batshit and wipes out his family. Where are you calling from, it's noisy as hell there?'

'A donut shop on Woodside Avenue.'

'Couldn't you find a nice quiet bowling alley? What's your guess on Calderón? You figure he's dead?'

'He packed everything before he left his room. And some-body's been calling in sick for him. That sounds like a lot of trouble to go through if you're going to kill somebody.'

'The calling in sounds like a way to give him a head start. Let him get a few extra miles before they start the blood-hounds.'

'That's what I was thinking.'

'Maybe he went home,' Durkin said. 'They go home all the time, you know. It's a new world these days. My grandparents came over here, they never saw Ireland again outside of the annual calendar from Treaty Stone Wines & Liquors. These fucking people are on a plane to the islands once a month and they come back carrying two chickens and another fucking relative. Of course, my grandparents worked, maybe that's the difference. They didn't have welfare giving 'em a trip around the world.'

'Calderón worked.'

'Well, good for him, the little prick. Maybe what I'll check is the flights out of Kennedy the past three days. Where's he from?'

'Somebody said Cartagena.'

'What's that, a city? Or is it one of those islands?'

'I think it's a city. And it's in either Panama or Colombia or Ecuador or she wouldn't have rented him a room. I think it's Colombia.'

'The gem of the ocean. The calling in fits if he went home. He had somebody phone for him so the job'd be there when he gets back. He can't call up every afternoon from Cartagena.'

'Why'd he clear out of the room?'

'Maybe he didn't like it there. Maybe the exterminator came and knocked off all his pet cockroaches. Maybe he owed rent and he was skipping.'

'She said no. He was paid up through the week.'

He was silent a moment. Then, reluctantly, he said, 'Some-body spooked him and he ran.'

'It looks that way, doesn't it?'

'I'm afraid it does. I don't think he left the city, either. I think he moved a subway stop away, picked himself a new name, and checked into another furnished room. There's something like half a million illegals in the five boroughs. He doesn't have to be Houdini to hide where we're not gonna find him.'

'You could get lucky.'

'Always a chance. I'll check the morgue first, and then the airlines. We'll stand the best chance if he's dead or out of the country.' He laughed, and I asked what was so funny. 'If he's dead or out of the country,' he said, 'he's not gonna be a whole lot of good to us, is he?'

The train back to Manhattan was one of the worst, its interior vandalized beyond recognition. I sat in a corner and tried to fight off a wave of despair. My life was an ice floe that had broken up at sea, with the different chunks floating off in different directions. Nothing was ever going to come together, in this case or out of it. Everything was senseless, pointless, and hopeless.

Nobody's going to buy me emeralds. Nobody's going to give me babies. Nobody's going to save my life.

All the good times are gone.

Eight million ways to die, and among them there's a wide variety suitable for the do-it-yourselfer. For all that was wrong with the subways, they still did the job when you threw yourself in front of them. And the city has no end of bridges and high windows, and stores stay open twenty-four hours a day selling razor blades and clothesline and pills.

I had a .32 in my dresser drawer, and my hotel room window was far enough from the pavement to make death a certainty. But I've never tried that sort of thing, and I've somehow always known I never will. I'm either too scared or too stubborn, or perhaps my particular despair is never as unequivocal as I think it is. Something seems to keep me going.

Of course all bets were off if I drank. I'd heard a man at a meeting who told of coming out of a blackout on the Brooklyn Bridge. He was over the railing and he had one foot in space when he came to. He retrieved the foot, climbed back over the railing, and got the hell out of there.

Suppose he'd come to a second later, with both feet in the air.

If I drank I'd feel better.

I couldn't get the thought out of my head. The worst of it was that I knew it was true. I felt horrible, and if I had a drink the feeling would go away. I'd regret it in the long run, I'd feel as bad and worse again in the long run, but so what? In the long run we're all dead.

I remembered something I'd heard at a meeting. Mary, one of the regulars at St Paul's, had said it. She was a birdlike woman with a tiny voice, always well dressed and well groomed and soft-spoken. I'd heard her qualify once, and evidently she'd been the next thing to a shopping-bag lady before she hit bottom.

343

One night, speaking from the floor, she'd said. 'You know, it was a revelation to me to learn that I don't have to be comfortable. Nowhere is it written that I *must* be comfortable. I always thought if I felt nervous or anxious or unhappy I had to do something about it. But I learned that's not true. Bad feelings won't kill me. Alcohol will kill me, but my feelings won't.'

The train plunged into the tunnel. As it dropped below ground level all the lights went out for a moment. Then they came back on again. I could hear Mary, pronouncing each word very precisely. I could see her, her fine-boned hands resting one on top of the other in her lap as she spoke.

Funny what comes to mind.

When I emerged from the subway station at Columbus Circle I still wanted a drink. I walked past a couple of bars and went to my meeting.

The speaker was a big beefy Irishman from Bay Ridge. He looked like a cop, and it turned out he'd been one, retiring after twenty years and currently supplementing his city pension as a security guard. Alcohol never interfered with his job or his marriage, but after a certain number of years it began to get to him physically. His capacity decreased, his hangovers worsened, and a doctor told him his liver was enlarged.

'He told me the booze was threatening my life,' he said. 'Well, I wasn't some derelict, I wasn't some degenerate drunk, I wasn't some guy who had to drink to get rid of the blues. I was just your normal happy-go-lucky guy who liked a shot an' a beer after work and a six-pack in front of the television set. So if it's gonna kill me, the hell with it, right? I walked out of that doctor's office and resolved to stop drinking. And eight years later that's just what I did.'

A drunk kept interrupting the qualification. He was a well-dressed man and he didn't seem to want to make trouble. He just seemed incapable of listening quietly, and after his fifth or sixth outburst a couple of members escorted him out and the meeting went on.

I thought how I'd come to the meeting myself in blackout. God, had I been like that?

I couldn't keep my mind on what I was hearing. I thought about Octavio Calderón and I thought about Sunny Hendryx and I thought how little I'd accomplished. I'd been just a little bit out of synch from the very beginning. I could have seen Sunny before she killed herself. She might have done it anyway,

344

I wasn't going to carry the weight for her self-destruction, but I could have learned something from her first.

And I could have talked to Calderón before he did his disappearing act. I'd asked for him on my first visit to the hotel, then forgot about him when he proved temporarily unavailable. Maybe I couldn't have gotten anything out of him, but at least I might have sensed that he was holding something back. But it didn't occur to me to pursue him until he'd already checked out and headed for the woods.

My timing was terrible. I was always a date late and a dollar short, and it struck me that it wasn't just this one case. It was the story of my life.

Poor me, poor me, pour me a drink.

During the discussion, a woman named Grace got a round of applause when she said it was her second anniversary. I clapped for her, and when the applause died down I counted up and realized today was my seventh day. If I went to bed sober, I'd have seven days.

How far did I get before my last drink? Eight days?

Maybe I could break that record. Or maybe I couldn't, maybe I'd drink tomorrow.

Not tonight, though. I was all right for tonight. I didn't feel any better than I'd felt before the meeting. My opinion of myself was certainly no higher. All the numbers on the scorecard were the same, but earlier they'd added up to a drink and now they didn't.

I didn't know why that was. But I knew I was safe.

TWENTY-SIX

There was a message at the desk to call Danny Boy Bell. I dialed the number on the slip and the man who answered said, 'Poogan's Pub.' I asked for Danny Boy and waited until he came on the line.

He said, 'Matt, I think you should come up and let me buy you a ginger ale. That's what I think you should do.'

'Now?'

'What better time?'

I was almost out of the door when I turned, went upstairs, and got the .32 out of my dresser. I didn't really think Danny Boy would set me up but I didn't want to bet my life that he wouldn't. Either way, you never knew who might be drinking in Poogan's.

I'd received a warning last night and I'd spent the intervening hours disregarding it. And the clerk who gave me Danny Boy's message had volunteered that I'd had a couple of other calls from people who'd declined to leave their names. They might have been friends of the chap in the lumber jacket, calling to offer a word to the wise.

I dropped the gun into a pocket, went out and hailed a cab.

Danny Boy insisted on buying the drinks, vodka for himself, ginger ale for me. He looked as natty as ever, and he'd been to the barber since I last saw him. His cap of tight white curls was closer to his scalp, and his manicured nails showed a coating of clear polish.

He said, 'I've got two things for you. A message and an opinion.'

'Oh?'

'The message first. It's a warning.'

'I thought it might be.'

'You should forget about the Dakkinen girl.'

'Or what?'

'Or what? Or else, I suppose. Or you get what she got, something like that. You want a specific warning so you can decide whether it's worth it or not?'

'Who's the warning come from, Danny?'

'I don't know.'

'What spoke to you? A burning bush?'

He drank off some of his vodka. 'Somebody talked to somebody who talked to somebody who talked to me.'

'That's pretty roundabout.'

'Isn't it? I could give you the person who talked to me, but I won't, because I don't do that. And even if I did it wouldn't do you any good, because you probably couldn't find him, and if you did he still wouldn't talk to you, and meanwhile somebody's probably going to whack you out. You want another ginger ale?'

'I've still got most of this one.'

'So you do. I *don't* know who the warning's from, Matt, but from the messenger they used I'd guess it's some very heavy types. And what's interesting is I get absolutely nowhere trying to find anybody who saw Dakkinen on the town with anybody but our friend Chance. Now if she's going with somebody with all this firepower, you'd think he'd show her around, wouldn't you? Why not?'

I nodded. For that matter, why would she need me to ease her out of Chance's string?

'Anyway,' he was saying, 'that's the message. You want the opinion?'

'Sure.'

'The opinion is I think you should heed the message. Either I'm getting old in a hurry or this town's gotten nastier in the past couple of years. People seem to pull the trigger a lot quicker than they used to. They used to need more of a reason to kill. You know what I mean?'

'Yes.'

'Now they'll do it unless they've got a reason not to. They'll sooner kill than not. It's an automatic response. I'll tell you, it scares me.'

'It scares everybody.'

'You had a little scene uptown a few nights back, didn't you? Or was somebody making up stories?'

'What did you hear?'

'Just that a brother jumped you in the alley and wound up with multiple fractures.'

'News travels.'

'It does for a fact. Of course there's more dangerous things in this city than a young punk on angel dust.'

'Is that what he was on?'

'Aren't they all? I don't know. I stick to basics, myself.' He underscored the line with a sip of his vodka. 'About Dakkinen,' he said. 'I could pass a message back up the line.'

'What kind of message?'

'That you're letting it lay.'

'That might not be true, Danny Boy.'

'Matt –'

'You remember Jack Benny?'

'Do I remember Jack Benny? Of course I remember Jack Benny.'

'Remember that bit with the stickup man? The guy says, "Your money or your life," and there's a long pause, a really long pause, and Benny says, "I'm thinking it over."'

'That's the answer? You're thinking it over?'

'That's the answer.'

Outside on Seventy-second Street I stood in the shadows in the doorway of a stationery store, waiting to see if anyone would follow me out of Poogan's. I stood there for a full five minutes and thought about what Danny Boy had said. A couple of people left Poogan's while I was standing there but they didn't look like anything I had to worry about.

I went to the curb to hail a cab, then decided I might as well walk half a block to Columbus and get one going in the right direction. By the time I got to the corner I decided it was a nice night and I was in no hurry, and an easy stroll fifteen blocks down Columbus Avenue would probably do me good, make sleep come that much easier. I crossed the street and headed downtown and before I'd covered a block I noticed that my hand was in my coat pocket and I was holding onto the little gun.

Funny. No one had followed me. What the hell was I afraid of?

Just something in the air.

I kept walking, displaying all the street smarts I hadn't shown Saturday night. I stayed at the edge of the sidewalk near the curb, keeping my distance from buildings and doorways. I looked left and right, and now and then I turned to see if anyone was moving up behind me. And I went on clutching the gun, my finger resting lightly alongside the trigger.

I crossed Broadway, walked on past Lincoln Center and O'Neal's. I was on the dark block between Sixtieth and Sixty-first, across the street from Fordham, when I heard the car behind me and spun around. It was slanting across the wide avenue toward me and had cut off a cab. Maybe it was his brakes I heard, maybe that's what made me turn.

I threw myself down on the pavement, rolled away from the street toward the buildings, came up with the .32 in my hand. The car was even with me now, its wheels straightened out. I'd thought it was going to vault the curb but it wasn't. And the windows were open and someone was leaning out the rear window, looking my way, and he had something in his hand –

I had the gun pointed at him. I was prone, elbows braced in front of me, holding the gun in both hands. I had my finger on the trigger.

The man leaning out the window threw something, tossed it underhand. I thought, *Jesus, a bomb,* and I aimed at him and felt the trigger beneath my finger, felt it tremble like some little live thing, and I froze, I froze, I couldn't pull the fucking trigger.

Time froze, too, like a stop-frame sequence in a film. Eight or ten yards from me a bottle struck the brick wall of a building and smashed. There was no explosion beyond the shattering of the glass. It was just an empty bottle.

And the car was just a car. I watched now as it went on careening south on Ninth Avenue, six kids in it, six drunken kids, and they might well kill somebody, they were drunk enough to do it, but when they did it would be an accident. They weren't professional killers, hitmen dispatched to murder me. They were just a bunch of kids who'd had more to drink than they could handle. Maybe they'd cripple someone, maybe they'd total their car, maybe they'd make it home without bending a fender.

I got up slowly, looked at the gun in my hand. Thank God I hadn't fired it. I could have shot them, I could have killed them.

God knows I'd wanted to. I'd *tried* to, thinking logically enough that they were trying to kill me.

But I'd been unable to do it. And if it *had* been pros, if the object I'd seen had been not a whiskey bottle but the gun or bomb I'd thought it was, I'd have been no more able to pull the trigger. They'd have killed me and I'd have died with an unfired revolver in my hands.

Jesus.

I dropped the useless gun in my pocket. I held out my hand, surprised that it wasn't shaking. I didn't even feel particularly shaky inside, and I was damned if I could figure out why not.

I went over to examine the broken bottle, if only to make sure it was just that and not a Molotov cocktail that had providentially failed to ignite. But there was no puddle, no reek of gasoline. There was a slight whiskey smell, unless I imagined it, and a label attached to one chunk of glass indicated that the bottle had contained J & B Scotch. Other fragments of green glass sparkled like jewels in the light of the streetlamp.

I bent over and picked up a little cube of glass. I placed it in the palm of my hand and stared at it like a gypsy at a crystal. I thought of Donna's poem and Sunny's note and my own slip of the tongue.

I started walking. It was all I could do to keep from running.

TWENTY-SEVEN

'**J**esus, I need a shave,' Durkin said. He'd just dropped what was left of his cigarette into what was left of his coffee, and he was running one hand over his cheek, feeling the stubble. 'I need a shave, I need a shower, I need a drink. Not necessarily in that order. I put out an APB on your little Colombian friend. Octavio Ignacio Calderón y La Barra. Name's longer'n he is. I checked the morgue. They haven't got him down there in a drawer. Not yet, anyway.'

He opened his top desk drawer, withdrew a metal shaving mirror and a cordless electric shaver. He leaned the mirror against his empty coffee cup, positioned his face in front of it and began shaving. Over the whirr of the shaver he said, 'I don't see anything in her file about a ring.'

'Mind if I look?'

'Be my guest.'

I studied the inventory sheet, knowing the ring wouldn't be on it. Then I went over the photographs of the death scene. I tried to look only at her hands. I looked at every picture, and in none of them could I spot anything that suggested she was wearing a ring.

I said as much to Durkin. He switched off the shaver, reached for the photographs, went through them carefully and deliberately. 'It's hard to see her hands in some of these,' he complained. 'All right, there's definitely no ring on that hand. What's that, the left hand? No ring on the left hand. Now in this shot, okay, definitely no ring on that hand. Wait a minute. Shit, that's the left hand again. It's not clear in this one. Okay, here we go. That's definitely her right hand and there's no ring on it.' He gathered the photos together like cards to be shuffled and dealt. 'No ring,' he said. 'What's that prove?'

'She had a ring when I saw her. Both times I saw her.'

'And?'

351

'And it disappeared. It's not at her apartment. There's a ring in her jewelry box, a high school class ring, but that's not what I remember seeing on her hand.'

'Maybe your memory's false.'

I shook my head. 'The class ring doesn't even have a stone. I went over there before I came here, just to check my memory. It's one of those klutzy school rings with too much lettering on it. It's not what she was wearing. She wouldn't have worn it, not with this mink and the wine-colored nails.'

I wasn't the only one who'd said so. After my little epiphany with the bit of broken glass, I'd gone straight to Kim's apartment, then used her phone to call Donna Campion. 'It's Matt Scudder,' I said. 'I know it's late, but I wanted to ask you about a line in your poem.'

She'd said, 'What line? What poem?'

'Your poem about Kim. You gave me a copy.'

'Oh, yes. Just give me a moment, will you? I'm not completely awake.'

'I'm sorry to call so late, but –'

'That's all right. What was the line?'

'Shatter/Wine bottles at her feet, let green glass/Sparkle upon her hand.'

'*Sparkle*'s wrong.'

'I've got the poem right here, it says –'

'Oh, I know that's what I wrote,' she said, 'but it's wrong. I'll have to change it. I *think*. What about the line?'

'Where did you get the green glass from?'

'From the shattered wine bottles.'

'Why green glass on her hand? What's it a reference to?'

'Oh,' she said. 'Oh, I see what you mean. Her ring.'

'She had a ring with a green stone, didn't she?'

'That's right.'

'How long did she have it?'

'I don't know.' She thought it over. 'The first time I saw it was just before I wrote the poem.'

'You're sure of that?'

'At least that's the first time I noticed it. It gave me a handle on the poem, as a matter of fact. The contrast of the blue of her eyes and the green of the ring, but then I lost the blue when I got working on the poem.'

She'd told me something along those lines when she first showed me the poem. I hadn't known then what she was talking about.

She wasn't sure when that might have been. How long had she been working on one or another version of the poem? Since a month before Kim's murder? Two months?

'I don't know,' she said. 'I have trouble placing events in time. I don't tend to keep track.'

'But it was a ring with a green stone.'

'Oh, yes. I can picture it now.'

'Do you know where she got it? Who gave it to her?'

'I don't know anything about it,' she said. 'Maybe –'

'Yes?'

'Maybe she shattered a wine bottle.'

To Durkin I said, 'A friend of Kim's wrote a poem and mentioned the ring. And there's Sunny Hendryx's suicide note.' I got out my notebook, flipped it open. I read, '"There's no way off the merry-go-round. She grabbed the brass ring and it turned her finger green. Nobody's going to buy me emeralds."'

He took the book from me. 'She meaning Dakkinen, I suppose,' he said. 'There's more here. "Nobody's going to give me babies. Nobody's going to save my life." Dakkinen wasn't pregnant and neither was Hendryx, so what's this shit about babies? And neither one of them had her life saved.' He closed the book with a snap, handed it across the desk to me. 'I don't know where you can go with this,' he said. 'It doesn't look to me like something you can take to the bank. Who knows when Hendryx wrote this? Maybe after the booze and the pills started working, and who can say where she was coming from?'

Behind us, two men in plainclothes were putting a young white kid in the holding cage. A desk away, a sullen black woman was answering questions. I picked up the top photo on the stack and looked at Kim Dakkinen's butchered body. Durkin switched on the razor and finished shaving.

'What I don't understand,' he said, 'is what you think you got. You think she had a boyfriend and the boyfriend gave her the ring. Okay. You also figured she had a boyfriend and he gave her the fur jacket, and you traced that and it looks as though you were right, but the jacket won't lead to the boyfriend because he kept his name out of it. If you can't trace him with a jacket that we've got, how can you trace him with a ring that all we know about it is it's missing? You see what I mean?'

'I see what you mean.'

'That Sherlock Holmes thing, the dog that didn't bark, well what you got is a ring that isn't there, and what does it prove?'

353

'It's gone.'

'Right.'

'Where'd it go?'

'Same place a bathtub ring goes. Down the fucking drain. How do I know where it went?'

'It disappeared.'

'So? Either it walked away or someone took it.'

'Who?'

'How do I know who?'

'Let's say she wore it to the hotel where she was killed.'

'You can't know that.'

'Let's just say so, all right?'

'Okay, run with it.'

'Who took it? Some cop yank it off her finger?'

'No,' he said. 'Nobody'd do that. There's people who'll take cash if it's loose, we both know that, but a ring off a murder victim's finger?' He shook his head. 'Besides, nobody was alone with her. It's something nobody'd do with somebody else watching.'

'How about the maid? The one who discovered the body?'

'Jesus, no way. I questioned the poor woman. She took one look at the body and started screaming and she'd still be screaming now if she had the breath left. You couldn'ta got her close enough to Dakkinen to touch her with a mop handle.'

'Who took the ring?'

'Assuming she wore it there –'

'Right.'

'So the killer took it.'

'Why?'

'Maybe he's queer for jewelry. Maybe green's his favorite color.'

'Keep going.'

'Maybe it's valuable. You got a guy who goes around killing people, his morals aren't the best. He might not draw the line at stealing.'

'He left a few hundred dollars in her purse, Joe.'

'Maybe he didn't have time to go through her bag.'

'He had time to take a shower, for Christ's sake. He had time to go through her bag. In fact, we don't know that he didn't go through her bag. We just know he didn't take the money.'

'So?'

'But he took the ring. He had time to take hold of her bloody hand and tug it off her finger.'

'Maybe it came off easy. Maybe it wasn't a snug fit.'

'Why'd he take it?'

'He wanted it for his sister.'

'Got any better reasons?'

'No,' he said. 'No, goddamn it, I don't have any better reasons. What are you getting at? He took it because it could be traced to him?'

'Why not?'

'Then why didn't he take the fur? We fucking *know* a boyfriend bought her the fur. Maybe he didn't use his name, but how can he be sure of what he let slip and what the salesman remembers? He took towels, for Christ's sake, so he wouldn't leave a fucking pubic hair behind, but he left the fur. And now you say he took the ring. Where did this ring come from besides left field? Why have I got to hear about this ring tonight when I never heard of it once in the past two and a half weeks?'

I didn't say anything. He picked up his cigarettes, offered me one. I shook my head. He took one for himself and lit it. He took a drag, blew out a column of smoke, then ran a hand over his head, smoothing down the dark hair that already lay flat upon his scalp.

He said, 'Could be there was some engraving. People do that with rings, engraving on the inside. To Kim from Freddie, some shit like that. You think that's it?'

'I don't know.'

'You got a theory?'

I remembered what Danny Boy Bell had said. If the boyfriend commanded such muscle, was so well connected, how come he hadn't shown her off? And if it was someone else with the muscle and the connections and the insufficient words to the wise, how did that someone else fit in with the boyfriend? Who was this accountant type who paid for her mink, and why wasn't I getting a smell of him from anywhere else?

And why did the killer take the ring?

I reached into my pocket. My fingers touched the gun, felt its cool metal, slipped beneath it to find the little cube of broken green glass that had started all of this. I took it from my pocket and looked at it, and Durkin asked me what it was.

'Green glass,' I said.

'Like the ring.'

I nodded. He took the piece of glass from me, held it to the light, dropped it back in my palm. 'We don't know she wore the ring to the hotel,' he reminded me. 'We just said so for the sake of argument.'

'I know.'

'Maybe she left it at the apartment. Maybe someone took it from there.'

'Who?'

'The boyfriend. Let's say he didn't kill her, let's say it was an EDP like I said from the beginning –'

'You really use that expression?'

'You get so you use the expressions they want you to use, you know how it works. Let's say the psycho killed her and the boyfriend's worried he'll be tied into it. So he goes to the apartment, he's got a key, and he takes the ring. Maybe he bought her other presents and he took them, too. He would've taken the fur, too, but it was in the hotel. Why isn't that theory just as good as the killer yanking the ring off her finger?'

Because it wasn't a psycho, I thought. Because a psycho killer wouldn't be sending men in lumber jackets to warn me off, wouldn't be passing messages to me through Danny Boy Bell. Because a psycho wouldn't have worried about handwriting or fingerprints or towels.

Unless he was some sort of Jack the Ripper type, a psycho who planned and took precautions. But that wasn't it, that couldn't be it, and the ring had to be significant. I dropped the piece of glass back into my pocket. It meant something, it had to mean something.

Durkin's phone rang. He picked it up, said 'Joe Durkin' and 'Yeah, right, right.' He listened, grunting acknowledgment from time to time, darting a pointed look in my direction, making notes on a memo pad.

I went over to the coffee machine and got us both coffee. I couldn't remember what he took in his coffee, then remembered how bad the coffee was out of that machine and added cream and sugar to both cups.

He was still on the phone when I got back to the desk. He took the coffee, nodded his thanks, sipped it, lit a fresh cigarette to go with it. I drank some of my own coffee and made my way through Kim's file, hoping something I saw might bridge a gap for me. I thought of my conversation with Donna. What was wrong with the word *sparkle*? Hadn't the ring sparkled on Kim's finger? I remembered how it had looked with the light striking it. Or was I just fabricating the memory to reinforce my own theory? And did I even have a theory? I had a missing ring and no hard evidence that the ring had even existed. A poem, a suicide note, and my own remark about eight million stories in the Emerald City. Had the ring triggered that subconsciously? Or was I just identifying with the crew on the Yellow Brick Road, wishing I had a brain and a heart and a dose of courage?

Durkin said, 'Yeah, it's a pisser, all right. Don't go 'way, okay? I'll be right out.'

He hung up, looked at me. His expression was a curious one, self-satisfaction mixed with something that might have been pity.

He said, 'The Powhattan Motel, you know where Queens Boulevard cuts the Long Island Expressway? It's just past the intersection. I don't know just where, Elmhurst or Rego Park. Right about where they run into each other.'

'So?'

'One of those adult motels, waterbeds in some of the rooms, X-rated movies on the teevee. They get cheaters, the hot-sheet trade, take a room for two hours. They'll turn a room five, six times a night if they get the volume, and a lot of it's cash, they can skim it. Very profitable, motels like that.'

'What's the point?'

'Guy drove up, rented a room a couple of hours ago. Well, that business, you make up the room soon as the customer leaves it. Manager noticed the car was gone, went to the room. Do Not Disturb sign hanging on the door. He knocks, no answer, he knocks again, still no answer. He opens the door and guess what he finds?'

I waited.

'Cop named Lennie Garfein responded to the call, first thing that struck him was the similarity to what we had at the Galaxy Downtowner. That was him on the phone. We won't know until we get the medical evidence, direction of thrust, nature of wounds, all that, but it sure as hell sounds identical. Killer even took a shower, took the towels with him when he left.'

'Was it –'

'Was it what?'

It wasn't Donna. I'd just spoken to her. Fran, Ruby, Mary Lou –

'Was it one of Chance's women?'

'Hell,' he said, 'how do I know who Chance's women are? You think all I do is keep tabs on pimps?'

'Who was it?'

'Not one of anybody's women,' he said. He crushed out his

cigarette, started to help himself to a fresh one, changed his mind and pushed it back into the pack. 'Not a woman,' he said.

'Not –'

'Not who?'

'Not Calderón. Octavio Calderón, the room clerk.'

He let out a bark of laughter. 'Jesus, what a mind you got,' he said. 'You really want things to make sense. No, not a woman, and not your boy Calderón either. This was a transsexual hooker off the Long Island City stroll. Preoperative, from what Garfein said. Means the tits are there, the silicone implants, but she's still got her male genitals. You hear me? *Her* male genitals. Jesus, what a world. Of course maybe she got the operation tonight. Maybe that was surgery there, with a machete.'

I couldn't react. I sat there, numb. Durkin got to his feet, put a hand on my shoulder. 'I got a car downstairs. I'm gonna run out there, take a look at what they got. You want to tag along?'

TWENTY-EIGHT

he body was still there, sprawled full-length on the king-size bed. It had bled white, leaving the skin with the translucence of old china. Only the genitalia, hacked almost beyond recognition, identified the victim as male. The face was that of a woman. So was the smooth and hairless skin, the slender but full-breasted body.

'She'd fool you,' Garfein said. 'See, she had the preliminary surgery. The breast implants, the Adam's apple, the cheekbones. And of course the hormone shots all along. That keeps down the beard and the body hair, makes the skin nice and feminine. Look at the wound in the left breast there. You can see the silicone sac. See?'

Blood all over, and the smell of fresh death in the air. Not the stale reek of a late-found corpse, not the stench of decomposition, but the horrible odor of a slaughterhouse, the raw throat-catching smell of fresh blood. I felt not so much nauseated as overpowered, oppressed by the warmth and density of the air.

'What was lucky is I recognized her,' Garfein was saying. 'That way I knew right off she was a pross and that made the connection in my mind with that case of yours, Joe. Was the one you caught as bloody as this?'

'Same thing,' Durkin said.

I said, 'You recognized her?'

'Oh, right away. I did a hitch not that long ago with the Pussy Posse over in Long Island City. They still got a stroll there, they've had street prostitution in that same location for forty or fifty years, but now you're getting a lot of middle-class people moving in there, converting lofts for residential use, buying up the old brownstones and converting them back from rooming houses to nice homes. They sign the lease in the daytime and then they move in and they look at what's around them and they aren't happy, and the pressure comes down to clean up the street.' He pointed at the figure on the bed. 'I must have arrested her, oh, say three times.'

'You know her name?'

'Which name do you want? They've all got more than one. Her street name was Cookie. That was the name that came to me when I saw her. Then I called in to the station house at Fiftieth and Vernon and had somebody pull her file. She was calling herself Sara but back when she made her bar mitzvah the name they wrote down was Mark Blaustein.'

'She had a bar mitzvah?'

'Who knows? I wasn't invited. But she's a nice Jewish girl from Floral Park is the point I'm making. A nice Jewish girl who used to be a nice Jewish boy.'

'Sara Blaustein?'

'Sara Bluestone a/k/a Sara Blue. A/k/a Cookie. Notice the hands and feet? They're on the large side for a girl. That's one way you can tell a transsexual. Of course it's not foolproof, you get girls with big hands and boys with small ones. She'd fool you, wouldn't she?'

I nodded.

'She would have had the rest of the surgery soon. Probably already had herself scheduled for the operation. Law says they have to live as a woman for a year before Medicaid'll pick up the tab. Of course they all got Medicaid, they all got welfare. They'll turn ten or twenty tricks a night, all quickie blow jobs in the john's cars for ten or twenty bucks a pop, they'll bring in a couple of hundred dollars a night seven nights a week, all of it tax free, and they got Medicaid and welfare and the ones with kids get ADC and half the pimps are on SSI.'

He and Durkin batted that ball around a little. Meanwhile the technical people were busy around us, measuring things, taking photographs, dusting for prints. We got out of their way and stood together in the motel parking lot.

Durkin said, 'You know what we got, don't you? We got us Jack the fucking Ripper.'

'I know it,' Garfein said.

'You get anything with the other guests? She musta made some noise.'

'You kidding? Cheaters? "I didn't see nothin', I didn't hear nothin', I gotta go now." Even if she did some screaming, in a job like this everybody'd figure it was a new way to have fun. Assuming they weren't too busy having their own fun to notice.'

'First he checks into a decent midtown hotel and phones up a fancy call girl. Then he picks up a TV streetwalker and drags her to a cheater's motel. You figure the cock and balls came as a shock to him?'

Garfein shrugged. 'Maybe. You know, half your street prostitutes are guys in drag. Some sections it's more than half.'

'The West Side docks it's a lot more than half.'

'I've heard that,' Garfein said. 'You talk to the johns, some of 'em'll admit they prefer if it's a guy. They say a guy gives better head. Of course there's nothing queer about them, see, because they're just receiving it.'

'Well, go figure a john,' Durkin said.

'Whether he knew or not, I don't think it put him off much. He went and did his number all the same.'

'Figure he had sex with her?'

'Hard to tell unless there's traces on the sheets. He doesn't figure as her first trick of the evening.'

'He took a shower?'

Garfein shrugged, showed his hands palms up. 'Don't know,' he said. 'The manager says there's towels missing. When they make up the room they put out two bath towels and two hand towels, and both of the bath towels are missing.'

'He took towels from the Galaxy.'

'Then he probably took 'em here, but who knows in a dump like this? I mean who knows if they always remember to make up the room right. Same with the shower. I don't figure they gave it a scrub after the last party left.'

'Maybe you'll find something.'

'Maybe.'

'Fingerprints, something. You see any skin under her nails?'

'No. But that's not to say the lab boys won't.' A muscle worked in his jaw. 'I'll say one thing. Thank God I'm not a medical examiner or a technician. It's bad enough being a cop.'

'Amen to that,' Durkin said.

I said, 'If he picked her up on the street, somebody might have seen her get into the car.'

'A couple of guys are out there now trying to take statements. We might get something. If anybody saw anything, and if they remember, and if they feel like talking.'

'Lots of ifs,' Durkin said.

'The manager here must have seen him,' I said. 'What does he remember?'

'Not a whole lot. Let's go talk to him some more.'

*

361

The manager had a night worker's sallow complexion and a pair of red-rimmed eyes. There was alcohol on his breath but he didn't have a drinker's way about him, and I guessed he'd tried to fortify himself with liquor after discovering the body. It only made him vague and ineffectual. 'This is a decent place,' he insisted, and the statement was so palpably absurd no one responded to it. I suppose he meant murder wasn't a daily occurrence.

He never saw Cookie. The man who had presumably killed her had come in alone, filled out the card, paid cash. This was not unusual. It was common practice for the woman to wait in the car while the man checked in. The car had not stopped directly in front of the office, so he hadn't seen it while the man was checking in. In fact he hadn't really seen the car at all.

'You saw it was missing,' Garfein reminded him. 'That's how you knew the room was empty.'

'Except it wasn't. I opened the door and –'

'You thought it was empty because the car was gone. How'd you know it was gone if you never saw it?'

'The parking space was empty. There's a space in front of each unit, the spaces are numbered same as the units. I looked out, that space was empty, that meant his car was gone.'

'They always park in the proper spaces?'

'They're supposed to.'

'Lots of things people are supposed to do. Pay their taxes, don't spit on the sidewalk, cross only at corners. A guy's in a hurry to dip his wick, what does he care about a number on a parking space? You got a look at the car.'

'I –'

'You looked once, maybe twice, and the car was parked in the space. Then you looked later and it wasn't and that's when you decided they were gone. Isn't that what happened?'

'I guess so.'

'Describe the car.'

'I didn't really look at it. I looked to see that it was there, that's all.'

'What color was it?'

'Dark.'

'Terrific. Two door? Four door?'

'I didn't notice.'

'New? Old? What make?'

'It was a late-model car,' he said. 'American. Not a foreign car.

As far as the make, when I was a kid they all looked different. Now every car's the same.'

'He's right,' Durkin said.

'Except American Motors,' he said. 'A Gremlin, a Pacer, those you can tell. The rest all look the same.'

'And this wasn't a Gremlin or a Pacer.'

'No.'

'Was it a sedan? A hatchback?'

'I'll tell you the truth,' the man said. 'All I noticed is it was a car. It says on the card, the make and model, the plate number.'

'You're talking about the registration card?'

'Yeah. They have to fill all that in.'

The card was on the desk, a sheet of clear acetate over it to preserve prints until the lab boys had their shot at it. *Name: Martin Albert Ricone. Address:* 211 Gilford Way. City: Fort Smith, Arkansas. Make of Auto: Chevrolet. Year: 1980. *Model: Sedan. Color: Black. License No.: LJK-914. Signature: M. A. RICONE.*

'Looks like the same hand,' I told Durkin. 'But who can tell with printing?'

'The experts can say. Same as they can tell you if he had the same light touch with the machete. Guy likes forts, you notice? Fort Wayne, Indiana and Fort Smith, Arkansas.'

'A subtle pattern begins to emerge,' Garfein said.

'Ricone,' Durkin said. 'Must be Italian.'

'M. A. Ricone sounds like the guy who invented the radio.'

'That's Marconi,' Durkin said.

'Well, that's close. This guy's Macaroni. Stuck a feather in his hat and called it Macaroni.'

'Stuck a feather up his ass,' Durkin said.

'Maybe he stuck it up Cookie's ass and maybe it wasn't a feather. Martin Albert Ricone, that's a fancy alias. What did he use last time?'

'Charles Owen Jones,' I said.

'Oh, he likes middle names. He's a cute fucker, isn't he?'

'Very cute,' Durkin said.

'The cute ones, the really cute ones, usually everything means something. Like *Jones* is slang, it means a habit. You know, like a heroin jones. Like a junkie says he's got a hundred-dollar jones, that's what his habit costs him per day.'

'I'm really glad you explained that for me,' Durkin said.

'Just trying to be helpful.'

''Cause I only got fourteen years in, I never had any contact yet with smack addicts.'

'So be a smart fuck,' Garfein said.

'The license plate go anywhere?'

'It's gonna go the same place as the name and address. I got a call in to Arkansas Motor Vehicles but it's a waste of time. A place like this, even the legitimate guests make up the plate number. They don't park in front of the window when they sign in so our guy here can't check. Not that he would anyway, would you?'

'There's no law says I have to check,' the man said.

'They use false names, too. Funny our boy used Jones at the Galaxy and Ricone here. They must get a lot of Joneses here, along with the usual run of Smiths and Browns. You get a lot of Smiths?'

'There's no law says I'm supposed to check ID,' the man said.

'Or wedding rings, huh?'

'Or wedding rings or marriage licenses or anything. Consenting adults, the hell, it's none of my business.'

'Maybe Ricone means something in Italian,' Garfein suggested.

'Now you're thinking,' Durkin said. He asked the manager if he had an Italian dictionary. The man stared at him, baffled. 'And they call this place a motel,' he said, shaking his head. 'There's probably no Gideon Bibles, either.'

'Most of the rooms have them.'

'Jesus, really? Right next to the television with the X-rated movies, right? Conveniently located near the waterbed.'

'Only two of the units have waterbeds,' the poor bastard said. 'There's an extra charge for a waterbed.'

'Good thing our Mr Ricone's a cheap prick,' Garfein said. 'Cookie'da wound up underwater.'

'Tell me about this guy,' Durkin said. 'Describe him again.'

'I told you –'

'You're gonna get to tell this again and again. How tall was he?'

'Tall.'

'My height? Shorter? Taller?'

'I –'

'What was he wearing? He have a hat on? He wearing a tie?'

'It's hard to remember.'

'He walks in the door, asks you for a room. Now he's filling

364

out the card. Pays you in cash. What do you get for a room like that, incidentally?'

'Twenty-eight dollars.'

'That's not such a bad deal. I suppose the porn movies are extra.'

'It's coin-operated.'

'Handy. Twenty-eight's fair, and it's a good deal for you if you can flip the room a few times a night. How'd he pay you?'

'I told you. Cash.'

'I mean what kind of bills? What'd he give you, a pair of fifteens?'

'A pair of –'

'He give you a twenty and a ten?'

'I think it was two twenties.'

'And you gave him twelve bucks back? Wait, there must have been tax, right?'

'It's twenty-nine forty with the tax.'

'And he gave you forty bucks and you gave him the change.' Something registered. 'He gave me two twenties and forty cents in change,' the man said. 'And I gave him a ten and a one.'

'See? You remember the transaction.'

'Yeah, I do. Sort of.'

'Now tell me what he looked like. He white?'

'Yeah, sure. White.'

'Heavy? Thin?'

'Thin but not too thin. On the thin side.'

'Beard?'

'No.'

'Moustache?'

'Maybe. I don't know.'

'There was something about him, though, something that stuck in your memory.'

'What?'

'That's what we're trying to get, John. That what they call you? John?'

'Mostly it's Jack.'

'Okay, Jack. You're doin' fine now. What about his hair?'

'I didn't pay attention to his hair.'

'Sure you did. He bent over to sign in and you saw the top of his head, remember?'

'I don't –'

'Full head of hair?'

'I don't –'

'They'll sit him down with one of our artists,' Durkin said, 'and he'll come up with something. And when this fucking psycho ripper steps on his cock one of these days, when we catch him in the act or on his way out the door, he'll look as much like the police artist's sketch as I look like Sara fucking Blaustein. She looked like a woman, didn't she?'

'Mostly she looked dead.'

'I know. Meat in a butcher's window.' We were in his car, driving over the bumpy surface of the Queensboro Bridge. The sky was starting to lighten up already. I was beyond tiredness by now, with the ragged edges of my emotions perilously close to the surface. I could feel my own vulnerability; the smallest thing could nudge me to tears or laughter.

'You gotta wonder what it would be like,' he said.

'What?'

'Picking up somebody who looked like that. On the street or in a bar, whatever. Then you get her someplace and she takes her clothes off and surprise. I mean, how do you react?'

'I don't know.'

''Course if she already had the operation, you could go with her and never know. Her hands didn't look so big to me. There's women with big hands and men with little hands, far as that goes.'

'Uh-huh.'

'She had a couple rings on, speaking of her hands. You happen to notice?'

'I noticed.'

'One on each hand, she had.'

'So?'

'So he didn't take 'em.'

'Why would he take her rings?'

'You were saying he took Dakkinen's.'

I didn't say anything.

Gently he said, 'Matt, you don't still think Dakkinen got killed for a reason?'

I felt rage swelling up within me, bulging like an aneurysm in a blood vessel. I sat there trying to will it away.

'And don't tell me about the towels. He's a ripper, he's a cute fucking psycho who makes plans and plays by his own private rules. He's not the first case like that to come along.'

'I got warned off the case, Joe. I got very professionally warned off the case.'

'So? She got killed by a psycho and there could still be something about her life that some friends of hers don't want to come out in the open. Maybe she had a boyfriend and he's a married guy, just like you figured, and even if what she died of was scarlet fucking fever he wouldn't want you poking around in the ashes.'

I gave myself the Miranda warning. *You have the right to remain silent*, I told myself, and exercised the right.

'Unless you figure Dakkinen and Blaustein are tied together. Long-lost sisters, say. Excuse me, brother and sister. Or maybe they were brothers, maybe Dakkinen had her operation a few years ago. Tall for a girl, wasn't she?'

'Maybe Cookie was a smokescreen,' I said.

'How's that?'

I went on talking in spite of myself. 'Maybe he killed her to take the heat off,' I said. 'Make it look like a train of random murders. To hide his motive for killing Dakkinen.'

'To take the heat off. What heat, for Christ's sake?'

'I don't know.'

'There's been no fucking heat. There will be now. Nothing turns the fucking press on like a series of random killings. The readers eat it up, they pour it on their corn flakes. Anything gives 'em a chance to run a sidebar on the original Jack the Ripper, those editors go crazy for it. You talk about heat, there'll be enough heat now to scorch his ass for him.'

'I suppose.'

'You know what you are, Scudder? You're stubborn.'

'Maybe.'

'Your problem is you work private and you only carry one case at a time. I got so much shit on my desk it's a pleasure when I get to let go of something, but with you it's just the opposite. You want to hang onto it as long as you can.'

'Is that what it is?'

'I don't know. It sounds like it.' He took one hand off the wheel, tapped me on the forearm. 'I don't mean to bust balls,' he said. 'I see something like that, somebody chopped up like that, I try to clamp a lid on it and it comes out in other directions. You did a lot of good work.'

'Did I?'

'No question. There were things we missed. It might give us a little jump on the psycho, some of the stuff you came up with. Who knows?'

Not I. All I knew was how tired I was.

He fell silent as we drove across town. In front of my hotel he braked to a stop and said, 'What Garfein said there. Maybe Ricone means something in Italian.'

'It won't be hard to check.'

'Oh, of course not. Everything should be that easy to run down. No, we'll check, and you know what we'll find? It'll turn out it means Jones.'

I went upstairs and got out of my clothes and into bed. Ten minutes later I got up again. I felt unclean and my scalp itched. I stood under a too-hot shower and scrubbed myself raw. I got out of the shower, told myself it didn't make any sense to shave before going to bed, then lathered up and shaved anyway. When I was done I put a robe on and sat down on the edge of my bed, then moved to the chair.

They tell you not to let yourself get too hungry, too angry, too lonely or too tired. Any of the four can put you off balance and turn you in the direction of a drink. It seemed to me that I'd touched all four bases. I'd boxed that particular compass in the course of the day and night. Oddly enough, I didn't feel the urge for a drink.

I got the gun from my coat pocket, I started to return it to the dresser drawer, then changed my mind and sat in the chair again, turning the gun in my hands.

When was the last time I'd fired a gun?

I didn't really have to think very hard. It had been that night in Washington Heights when I chased two holdup men into the street, shot them down and killed that little girl in the process. In the time I remained on the force after that incident, I never had occasion to draw my service revolver, let alone discharge it. And I certainly hadn't fired a gun since I left the force.

And tonight I'd been unable to do it. Because something clued me that the car I was aiming at held drunken kids instead of assassins? Because some subtle intuitive perception made me wait until I was certain what I was shooting at?

No. I couldn't make myself believe that.

I had frozen. If instead of a kid with a whiskey bottle I'd seen a thug with a tommy gun, I wouldn't have been any more capable of squeezing the trigger. My finger'd been paralyzed.

I broke the gun, shook the bullets out of the cylinder, closed it up again. I pointed the empty weapon at the wastebasket across the room and squeezed the trigger a couple of times. The *click* the hammer made as it fell upon an empty chamber was surprisingly loud and sharp in my little room.

I aimed at the mirror over the dresser. *Click!*

Proved nothing. It was empty, I knew it was empty. I could take the thing to a pistol range, load it and fire at targets, and that wouldn't prove anything either.

It bothered me that I'd been unable to fire the gun. And yet I was grateful it had happened that way, because otherwise I'd have emptied the gun into that car of kids, probably killed a few of them, and what would that have done to my peace of mind? Tired as I was, I went a few hard rounds with that particular conundrum. I was glad I hadn't shot anyone and frightened of the implications of not shooting, and my mind went around and around, chasing its tail.

I took off the robe, got into bed, and couldn't even begin to loosen up. I got dressed again in street clothes, used the back end of a nail file as a screwdriver, and took the revolver apart for cleaning. I put its parts in one pocket, and in another I stowed the four live cartridges along with the two knives I'd taken from the mugger.

It was morning and the sky was bright. I walked over to Ninth Avenue and up to Fifty-eighth Street, where I dropped both knives into a sewer grating. I crossed the street and walked to another grating and stood near it with my hands in my pockets, one holding the four cartridges, the other touching the pieces of the disassembled revolver.

Why carry a gun you're not going to shoot? Why own a gun you can't carry?

I stopped in a deli on the way back to the hotel. The customer ahead of me bought two six-packs of Old English 800 Malt Liquor. I picked out four candy bars and paid for them, ate one as I walked and the other three in my room. Then I took the revolver's parts from my pocket and put them back together again. I loaded four of the six chambers and put the gun in the dresser drawer.

I got into bed, told myself I'd stay there whether I could sleep or not, and smiled at the thought as I felt myself drifting off.

TWENTY-NINE

The telephone woke me. I fought my way out of sleep like an underwater swimmer coming up for air. I sat up, blinking and trying to catch my breath. The phone was still ringing and I couldn't figure out what was making that damned sound. Then I caught on and answered it.

It was Chance. 'Just saw the paper,' he said. 'What do you figure? That the same guy as got Kim?'

'Give me a minute,' I said.

'You asleep?'

'I'm awake now.'

'Then you don't know what I'm talkin' about. There was another killing, this time in Queens, some sex-change street-walker cut to ribbons.'

'I know.'

'How do you know if you been sleeping?'

'I was out there last night.'

'Out there in Queens?'

He sounded impressed. 'Out there on Queens Boulevard,' I told him. 'With a couple of cops. It was the same killer.'

'You sure of that?'

'They didn't have the scientific evidence sorted out when I was there. But yes, I'm sure of it.'

He thought about it. 'Then Kim was just unlucky,' he said. 'Just in the wrong place at the wrong time.'

'Maybe.'

'Just maybe?'

I got my watch from the nightstand. It was almost noon. 'There are elements that don't fit,' I said. 'At least it seems that way to me. A cop last night told me my problem is I'm too stubborn. I've only got the one case and I don't want to let go of it.'

'So?'

'He could be right, but there are still some things that don't fit. What happened to Kim's ring?'

'What ring?'

'She had a ring with a green stone.'

'Ring,' he said, and thought about it. 'Was it Kim had that ring? I guess it was.'

'What happened to it?'

'Wasn't it in her jewelry box?'

'That was her class ring. From high school back home.'

'Yeah, right. I recall the ring you mean. Big green stone. Was a birthstone ring, something like that.'

'Where'd she get it?'

'Out of a Crackerjack box, most likely. Think she said she bought it for herself. It was just a piece of junk, man. Chunk of green glass is all.'

Shatter wine bottles at her feet.

'It wasn't an emerald?'

'You shuckin', man? You know what emeralds cost?'

'No.'

'More'n diamonds. Why's the ring important?'

'Maybe it's not.'

'What do you do next?'

'I don't know,' I said. 'If Kim got killed by a psycho striking at random, I don't know what I can do that the cops can't do better. But there's somebody who wants me off the case, and there's a hotel clerk who got scared into leaving town, and there's a missing ring.'

'That maybe doesn't mean anything.'

'Maybe.'

'Wasn't there something in Sunny's note about a ring turning somebody's finger green? Maybe it was a cheap ring, turned Kim's finger green, and she got rid of it.'

'I don't think that's what Sunny meant.'

'What did she mean, then?'

'I don't know that either.' I took a breath. 'I'd like to connect Cookie Blue and Kim Dakkinen,' I said. 'That's what I'd like to do. If I can manage that I can probably find the man who killed them both.'

'Maybe. You be at Sunny's service tomorrow?'

'I'll be there.'

'Then I'll see you. Maybe we can talk a little afterward.'

'Fine.'

'Yeah,' he said. 'Kim and Cookie. What could they have in common?'

'Didn't Kim work the streets for a while? Didn't she take a bust on that Long Island City stroll?'

'Years ago.'

'She had a pimp named Duffy, didn't she? Did Cookie have a pimp?'

'Could be. Some of the TVs do. Most of 'em don't, from what I know. Maybe I could ask around.'

'Maybe you could.'

'I haven't seen Duffy in months. I think I heard he was dead. But I'll ask around. Hard to figure, though, that a girl like Kim had anything in common with a little Jewish queen from the Island.'

A Jewish queen and a Dairy Queen, I thought, and thought of Donna.

'Maybe they were sisters,' I suggested.

'Sisters?'

'Under the skin.'

I wanted breakfast, but when I hit the street I bought a paper before I did anything else, and I could see right away that it wasn't going to make a good accompaniment for my bacon and eggs. *Hotel Ripper Claims Second Victim*, the top teaser headline announced. And then, in big block caps, SEX-CHANGE HOOKER BUTCHERED IN QUEENS.

I folded it, tucked it under my arm. I don't know what I thought I was going to do first, read the paper or eat, but my feet decided for me and picked neither of those choices. I walked two blocks before I realized I was heading for the Y on West Sixty-third, and that I was going to get there just in time for the twelve-thirty meeting.

What the hell, I thought. Their coffee was as good as anybody else's.

I got out of there an hour later and had breakfast in a Greek joint around the corner on Broadway. I read the paper while I ate. It didn't seem to bother me now.

There wasn't much in the story I didn't already know. The victim was described as having lived in the East Village; I'd somehow assumed she lived across the river in Queens. Garfein had mentioned Floral Park, just across the line in Nassau County, and evidently that was where she'd grown up. Her

372

parents, according to the *Post*, had both died several years earlier in an air crash. Mark/Sara/Cookie's sole surviving relative was a brother, Adrian Blaustein, a wholesale jeweler residing in Forest Hills with offices on West Forty-seventh Street. He was out of the country and had not yet been notified of his brother's death.

His brother's death? Or his sister's? How did a relative relate to someone who'd changed sex? How did a respectable business-man regard a brother-turned-sister who turned quick tricks in strangers' parked cars? What would Cookie Blue's death mean to Adrian Blaustein?

What did it mean to me?

Any man's death diminishes me, because I am involved in mankind. Any man's death, any woman's death, any death in between. But did it diminish me? And was I truly involved?

I could still feel the trigger of the .32 trembling beneath my finger.

I ordered another cup of coffee and turned to a story about a young soldier home on furlough, playing pickup basketball at a sandlot game in the Bronx. A gun had apparently fallen out of some bystander's pocket, discharging on impact, and the bullet had struck this young serviceman and killed him instantly. I read the story through a second time and sat there shaking my head at it.

One more way to die. Jesus, there really were eight million of them, weren't there?

At twenty to nine that evening I slipped into the basement of a church on Prince Street in SoHo. I got myself a cup of coffee, and while I looked for a seat I scanned the room for Jan. She was near the front on the right-hand side. I sat further back near the coffee.

The speaker was a woman in her thirties who drank for ten years and spent the last three of them on the Bowery, panhan-dling and wiping windshields to get money for wine. 'Even on the Bowery,' she said, 'there are some people who know how to take care of themselves. Some of the men down there always carry a razor and a bar of soap. I gravitated straight to the other kind, the ones who don't shave and don't wash and don't change their clothes. A little voice in my head said, "Rita, you're right where you belong."'

During the break I ran into Jan on her way to the coffee urn. She seemed pleased to see me. 'I was in the neighborhood,' I

373

explained, 'and it got to be meeting time. It occurred to me I might see you here.'

'Oh, this is one of my regular meetings,' she said. 'We'll go for coffee after, okay?'

'Sure.'

A dozen of us wound up around a couple of tables in a coffee shop on West Broadway. I didn't take a very active part in the conversation, or pay too much attention to it. Eventually the waiter distributed separate checks. Jan paid hers and I paid mine and the two of us headed downtown toward her place.

I said, 'I didn't just happen to be in the neighborhood.'

'There's a big surprise.'

'I wanted to talk to you. I don't know if you read today's paper –'

'About the killing in Queens? Yes, I did.'

'I was out there. I'm all wound up and I feel the need to talk about it.'

We went up to her loft and she made a pot of coffee. I sat with a cup of coffee in front of me and by the time I stopped talking and took a sip it was cold. I brought her up to date, told her about Kim's fur jacket, about the drunken kids and the broken wine bottle, about the trip to Queens and what we'd found there. And I told her, too, how I'd spent this afternoon, riding the subway across the river and walking around Long Island City, returning to knock on doors in Cookie Blue's East Village tenement, then crossed the island to work the gay bars on Christopher Street and up and down West Street.

By then it had been late enough to get in touch with Joe Durkin and learn what the lab had come up with.

'It was the same killer,' I told Jan. 'And he used the same weapon. He's tall, right handed, and pretty powerful, and he keeps a sharp edge on his machete, or whatever the hell he uses.'

Phone checks with Arkansas yielded nothing. The Fort Smith street address was a phony, predictably enough, and the auto license plate belonged to an orange Volkswagen owned by a nursery school teacher in Fayetteville.

'And she only drove it on Sundays,' Jan said.

'Something like that. He made up the whole Arkansas business the same as he made up Fort Wayne, Indiana. But the license plate was real, or almost real. Somebody thought to check the hot-car sheet, and there was a navy blue Impala stolen off the street in Jackson Heights just a couple hours before Cookie was killed. The plate number's the same as he used checking in except for a pair of digits reversed, and of course it's a New York plate instead of Arkansas.

'The car fits the motel clerk's description, such as it was. It also fits what they got from some other hookers who were on the stroll when Cookie was picked up. They say there was a car like that cruising around for a while before the dude in it made up his mind and picked up Cookie.

'The car hasn't turned up yet, but that doesn't mean he's still driving it. It can take a long time before an abandoned stolen car turns up. Sometimes the thieves leave 'em in a No Parking zone and the police tow truck hauls them to the pound. That's not supposed to happen, somebody's supposed to check towed cars against the hot sheet, but it doesn't always go the way it's supposed to. It doesn't matter. It'll turn out the killer dumped the car twenty minutes after he finished with Cookie, and that he wiped it clean of prints.'

'Matt, can't you let go of it?'

'Of the whole business?'

She nodded. 'It's police procedure from here on in, isn't it? Sifting evidence, running down all the details.'

'I suppose so.'

'And it's not as though they're likely to put this on the shelf and forget about it, the way you thought they might when it was just Kim who was dead. The papers wouldn't let them shelve it even if they wanted to.'

'That's true.'

'So is there a reason why you have to push yourself on this? You already gave your client his money's worth.'

'Did I?'

'Didn't you? I think you worked harder for the money than he did.'

'I guess you're right.'

'So why stay with it? What can you do that the whole police force can't.'

I wrestled with that one. After a moment I said, 'There's got to be a connection.'

'What kind of connection?'

'Between Kim and Cookie. Because, damnit, otherwise they don't make sense. A psycho killer always has a pattern for what he's doing, even if it only exists in his own mind. Kim and Cookie didn't look alike and didn't have similar lives. For Christ's sake, they weren't even the same sex to start with. Kim worked off a phone in her own apartment and had a pimp.

Cookie was a transsexual streetwalker doing the johns in their cars. She was an outlaw. Chance is doing some double-checking to see if she had a pimp nobody knew about, but it doesn't look likely.'

I drank some cold coffee. 'And he *picked* Cookie,' I went on. 'He took his time, he drove up and down those streets, he made sure he got her and not somebody else. Where's the connection? It's not a matter of type. She was a completely different physical type from Kim.'

'Something in her personal life?'

'Maybe. Her personal life's hard to trace. She lived in the East Village and tricked in Long Island City. I couldn't find anybody in the West Side gay bars who knew her. She didn't have a pimp and she didn't have a lover. Her neighbors on East Fifth Street never knew she was a prostitute, and only a few of them suspected she wasn't a woman. Her only family's her brother and he doesn't even know she's dead.'

I talked some more. *Ricone* wasn't an Italian word, and if it was a name it was an uncommon one. I'd checked telephone directories for Manhattan and Queens without finding a single Ricone listed.

When I ran dry she got more coffee for both of us and we sat for a few minutes without speaking. Then I said, 'Thanks.'

'For the coffee?'

'For listening. I feel better now. I had to talk my way through it.'

'Talking always helps.'

'I suppose so.'

'You don't talk at meetings, do you?'

'Jesus, I couldn't talk about this stuff.'

'Not specifically, maybe, but you could talk about what you're going through and the way it makes you feel. That might help more than you think, Matt.'

'I don't think I could do it. Hell, I can't even say I'm an alcoholic. "My name is Matt and I pass." I could phone it in.'

'Maybe that'll change.'

'Maybe.'

'How long have you been sober, Matt?'

I had to think. 'Eight days.'

'Gee, that's terrific. What's so funny?'

'Something I've noticed. One person asks another how long he's been sober, and whatever the answer is, the reply is, "Gee, that's terrific, that's wonderful." If I said eight days or eight

376

years the reaction'd be the same. "Gee, isn't that great, isn't that terrific."'

'Well, it is.'

'I guess.'

'What's terrific is that you're sober. Eight years is terrific and so is eight days.'

'Uh-huh.'

'What's the matter?'

'Nothing. Sunny's funeral is tomorrow afternoon.'

'Are you going?'

'I said I would.'

'Are you worried about that?'

'Worried?'

'Nervous, anxious.'

'I don't know about that. I'm not looking forward to it.' I looked into her large gray eyes, then looked away. 'Eight days is as long as I've gone,' I said casually. 'I had eight days last time, and then I drank.'

'That doesn't mean you have to drink tomorrow.'

'Oh, shit, I know that. I'm not going to drink tomorrow.'

'Take someone with you.'

'What do you mean?'

'To the funeral. Ask someone from the program to go along with you.'

'I couldn't ask anyone to do that.'

'Of course you could.'

'Who? There's nobody I know well enough to ask.'

'How well do you have to know somebody to sit next to them at a funeral?'

'Well?'

'Well what?'

'Would you go with me? Never mind, I don't want to put you on the spot.'

'I'll go.'

'Really?'

'Why not? Of course I might look pretty dowdy. Next to all those flashy hookers.'

'Oh, I don't think so.'

'No?'

'No, I don't think so at all.'

I tipped up her chin and tasted her mouth with mine. I touched her hair. Dark hair, lightly salted with gray. Gray to match her eyes.

She said, 'I was afraid this would happen. And then I was afraid it wouldn't.'

'And now?'

'Now I'm just afraid.'

'Do you want me to leave?'

'Do I want you to leave? No, I don't want you to leave. I want you to kiss me again.'

I kissed her. She put her arms around me and drew me close and I felt the warmth of her body through our clothing.

'Ah, darling,' she said.

Afterward, lying in her bed and listening to my own heartbeat, I had a moment of utter loneliness and desolation. I felt as though I had taken the cover off a bottomless well. I reached over and laid a hand on her flank, and the physical contact cut the thread of my mood.

'Hello,' I said.

'Hello.'

'What are you thinking?'

She laughed. 'Nothing very romantic. I was trying to guess what my sponsor's going to say.'

'Do you have to tell her?'

'I don't have to do anything, but I will tell her. "Oh, by the way, I hopped into bed with a guy who's eight days sober."'

'That's a mortal sin, huh?'

'Let's just say it's a no-no.'

'What'll she give you? Six Our Fathers?'

She laughed again. She had a good laugh, full and hearty. I'd always liked it.

'She'll say, "Well, at least you didn't drink. That's the important thing." And she'll say, "I hope you enjoyed it."'

'Did you?'

'Enjoy it?'

'Yeah.'

'Hell, no. I was faking orgasm.'

'Both times, huh?'

'You betcha.' She drew close to me, put her hand on my chest. 'You'll stay over, won't you?'

'What would your sponsor say?'

'Probably that I might as well hang for a sheep as a lamb. Oh, shit, I almost forgot.'

'Where are you going?'

'Gotta make a phone call.'

'You're actually calling your sponsor?'

She shook her head. She'd put a robe on and now she was paging through a small address book. She dialed a number and said, 'Hi, this is Jan. You weren't sleeping, were you? Look, this is out of left field, but does the word *Ricone* mean anything to you?' She spelled it. 'I thought it might be a dirty word or something. Uh-huh.' Then she listened for a moment and said, 'No, nothing like that. I'm doing crossword puzzles in Sicilian, that's all. On nights when I can't sleep. Listen, you can only spend so much time reading the Big Book.'

She finished the conversation, hung up and said, 'Well, it was a thought. I figured if it was a dialect or an obscenity it might not be in the dictionary.'

'What obscenity did you think it might be? And when did the thought happen to cross your mind?'

'None of your business, wiseass.'

'You're blushing.'

'I know, I can feel it. That'll teach me to try to help a friend solve a murder.'

'No good deed goes unpunished.'

'That's what they say. Martin Albert Ricone and Charles Otis Jones? Are those the names he used?'

'Owen. Charles Owen Jones.'

'And you think it means something.'

'It has to mean something. Even if he's a lunatic, anything that elaborate would have to mean something.'

'Like Fort Wayne and Fort Smith?'

'Like that, maybe, but I think the names he used are more significant than that. Ricone's such an unusual name.'

'Maybe he started by writing *Rico*.'

'I thought of that. There are plenty of Ricos in the phone book. Or maybe he's from Puerto Rico.'

'Why not? Everybody else is. Maybe he's a Cagney fan.'

'Cagney?'

'In the death scene. "Mother of mercy, is this the end of Rico?" Remember?'

'I thought that was Edward G. Robinson.'

'Maybe it was. I was always drunk when I watched the "Late Show" and all those Warner Brothers gangsters tend to merge in my mind. It was one of those ballsy guys. "Mother of mercy, is this the —"'

'Some pair of balls,' I said.

'Huh?'

'Jesus Christ.'

'What's the matter?'

'He's a comedian. A fucking comedian.'

'What are you talking about?'

'The killer. C. O. Jones and M. A. Ricone. I thought they were names.'

'They're not?'

'*Cojones. Maricón.*'

'That's Spanish.'

'Right.'

'*Cojones* means "balls," doesn't it?'

'And *maricón* means "faggot." I don't think there's an e on the end of it, though.'

'Maybe it's especially nasty with an E on the end.'

'Or maybe he's just a lousy speller.'

'Well, hell,' she said. 'Nobody's perfect.'

THIRTY

Around mid-morning I went home to shower and shave and put on my best suit. I caught a noon meeting, ate a Sabrett hotdog on the street, and met Jan as arranged at the papaya stand at Seventy-second and Broadway. She was wearing a knit dress, dove gray with touches of black. I'd never seen her in anything that dressy.

We went around the corner to Cooke's, where a professionally sympathetic young man in black determined which set of bereaved we belonged to and ushered us through a hallway to Suite Three, where a card in a slot on the open door said HENDRYX. Inside, there were perhaps six rows of four chairs each on either side of a center aisle. In the front, to the left of the lectern on a raised platform, an open casket stood amid a glut of floral sprays. I'd sent flowers that morning but I needn't have bothered. Sunny had enough of them to see a Prohibition era mobster on his way to the Promised Land.

Chance had the aisle seat in the front row on the right. Donna Campion was seated beside him, with Fran Schecter and Mary Lou Barcker filling out the row. Chance was wearing a black suit, a white shirt, and a narrow black silk tie. The women were all wearing black, and I wondered if he'd taken them shopping the previous afternoon.

He turned at our entrance, got to his feet. Jan and I walked over there and I managed the introductions. We stood awkwardly for a moment, and then Chance said, 'You'll want to view the body,' and gave a nod toward the casket.

Did anyone ever want to view a body? I walked over there and Jan walked beside me. Sunny was laid out in a brightly colored dress on a casket lining of cream-colored satin. Her hands, clasped upon her breast, held a single red rose. Her face might have been carved from a block of wax, and yet she certainly looked no worse than when I'd seen her last.

Chance was standing beside me. He said, 'Talk to you a moment?'

'Sure.'

Jan gave my hand a quick squeeze and slipped away. Chance and I stood side by side, looking down at Sunny.

I said, 'I thought the body was still at the morgue.'

'They called yesterday, said they were ready to release it. The people here worked late getting her ready. Did a pretty good job.'

'Uh-huh.'

'Doesn't look much like her. Didn't look like her when we found her, either, did it?'

'No.'

'They'll cremate the body after. Simpler that way. The girls look right, don't they? The way they're dressed and all?'

'They look fine.'

'Dignified,' he said. After a pause he said, 'Ruby didn't come.'

'I noticed.'

'She doesn't believe in funerals. Different cultures, different customs, you know? And she always kept to herself, hardly knew Sunny.'

I didn't say anything.

'After this is over,' he said, 'I be taking the girls to their homes, you know. Then we ought to talk.'

'All right.'

'You know Parke Bernet? The auction gallery, the main place on Madison Avenue. There's a sale tomorrow and I wanted to look at a couple of lots I might bid on. You want to meet me there?'

'What time?'

'I don't know. This here won't be long. Be out of here by three. Say four-fifteen, four-thirty?'

'Fine.'

'Say, Matt?' I turned. ''Preciate your coming.'

There were perhaps ten more mourners in attendance by the time the service got underway. A party of four blacks sat in the middle on the left-hand side, and among them I thought I recognized Kid Bascomb, the fighter I'd watched the one time I met Sunny. Two elderly women sat together in the rear, and another elderly man sat by himself near the front. There are lonely people who drop in on the funerals of strangers as a way of passing the time, and I suspected these three were of their number.

Just as the service started, Joe Durkin and another plain-clothes detective slipped into a pair of seats in the last row.

The minister looked like a kid. I don't know how thoroughly he'd been briefed, but he talked about the special tragedy of a life cut short in its prime, and about God's mysterious ways, and about the survivors being the true victims of such apparently senseless tragedy. He read passages from Emerson, Teilhard de Chardin, Martin Buber, and the Book of Ecclesiastes. Then he suggested that any of Sunny's friends who wished to might come forward and say a few words.

Donna Campion read two short poems which I assumed she'd written herself. I learned later that they were by Sylvia Plath and Anne Sexton, two poets who had themselves committed suicide. Fran Schecter followed her and said, 'Sunny, I don't know if you can hear me but I want to tell you this anyway,' and went on to say how she'd valued the dead girl's friendship and cheerfulness and zest for living. She started off light and bubbly herself and wound up breaking down in tears, and the minister had to help her off stage. Mary Lou Barcker spoke just two or three sentences, and those in a low monotone, saying that she wished she'd known Sunny better and hoped she was at peace now.

Nobody else came forward. I had a brief fantasy of Joe Durkin mounting the platform and telling the crowd how the NYPD was going to get it together and win this one for the Gipper, but he stayed right where he was. The minister said a few more words – I wasn't paying attention – and then one of the attendants played a recording, Judy Collins singing 'Amazing Grace.'

Outside, Jan and I walked for a couple of blocks without saying anything. Then I said, 'Thanks for coming.'

'Thanks for asking me. God, that sounds foolish. Like a conversation after the Junior Prom. "Thanks for asking me. I had a lovely time."' She took a handkerchief from her purse, dabbed at her eyes, blew her nose. 'I'm glad you didn't go to that alone,' she said.

'So am I.'

'And I'm glad I went. It was so sad and so beautiful. Who was that man who spoke to you on the way out?'

'That was Durkin.'

'Oh, was it? What was he doing there?'

'Hoping to get lucky, I suppose. You never know who'll show up at a funeral.'

'Not many people showed up at this one.'

'Just a handful.'

'I'm glad we were there.'

'Uh-huh.'

I bought her a cup of coffee, then put her in a cab. She insisted she could take the subway but I got her into a cab and made her take ten bucks for the fare.

A lobby attendant at Parke Bernet directed me to the second-floor gallery where Friday's African and Oceanic art was on display. I found Chance in front of a set of glassed-in shelves housing a collection of eighteen or twenty small gold figurines. Some represented animals while others depicted human beings and various household articles. One I recall showed a man sitting on his haunches and milking a goat. The largest would fit easily in a child's hand, and many of them had a droll quality about them.

'Ashanti gold weights,' Chance explained. 'From the land the British called the Gold Coast. It's Ghana now. You see plated reproductions in the shops. Fakes. These are the real thing.'

'Are you planning to buy them?'

He shook his head. 'They don't speak to me. I try to buy things that do. I'll show you something.'

We crossed the room. A bronze head of a woman stood mounted on a four-foot pedestal. Her nose was broad and flattened, her cheekbones pronounced. Her throat was so thickly ringed by bronze necklaces that the overall appearance of the head was conical.

'A bronze sculpture of the lost Kingdom of Benin,' he announced. 'The head of a queen. You can tell her rank by the number of necklaces she's wearing. Does she speak to you, Matt? She does to me.'

I read strength in the bronze features, cold strength and a merciless will.

'Know what she says? She says, "Nigger, why you be lookin' at me dat way? You know you ain't got de money to take me home."' He laughed. 'The presale estimate is forty to sixty thousand dollars.'

'You won't be bidding?'

'I don't know what I'll be doing. There are a few pieces I wouldn't mind owning. But sometimes I come to auctions the way some people go to the track even when they don't feel like betting. Just to sit in the sun and watch the horses run. I like the way an auction room feels. I like to hear the hammer drop. You seen enough? Let's go.'

His car was parked at a garage on Seventy-eighth Street. We rode over the Fifty-ninth Street Bridge and through Long Island City. Here and there street prostitutes stood along the curb singly or in pairs.

'Not many out last night,' he said. 'I guess they feel safer in daylight.'

'You were here last night?'

'Just driving around. He picked up Cookie around here, then drove out Queens Boulevard. Or did he take the expressway? I don't guess it matters.'

'No.'

We took Queens Boulevard. 'Want to thank you for coming to the funeral,' he said.

'I wanted to come.'

'Fine-looking woman with you.'

'Thank you.'

'Jan, you say her name was?'

'That's right.'

'You go with her or –'

'We're friends.'

'Uh-huh.' He braked for a light. 'Ruby didn't come.'

'I know.'

'What I told you was a bunch of shit. I didn't want to contradict what I told the others. Ruby split, she packed up and went.'

'When did this happen?'

'Sometime yesterday, I guess. Last night I had a message on my service. I was running around all yesterday, trying to get this funeral organized. I thought it went okay, didn't you?'

'It was a nice service.'

'That's what I thought. Anyway, there's a message to call Ruby and a 415 area code. That's San Francisco. I thought, huh? And I called, and she said she had decided to move on. I thought it was some kind of a joke, you know? Then I went over there and checked her apartment, and all her things were gone. Her clothes. She left the furniture. That makes three empty apartments I got, man. Big housing shortage, nobody can find a place to live, and I'm sitting on three empty apartments. Something, huh?'

'You sure it was her you spoke to?'

'Positive.'

'And she was in San Francisco?'

'Had to be. Or Berkeley or Oakland or some such place. I dialed the number, area code and all. She had to be out there to have that kind of number, didn't she?'

'Did she say why she left?'

'Said it was time to move on. Doing her inscrutable oriental number.'

'You think she was afraid of getting killed?'

'Powhattan Motel,' he said, pointing. 'That's the place, isn't it?'

'That's the place.'

'And you were out here to find the body.'

'It had already been found. But I was out here before they moved it.'

'Must have been some sight.'

'It wasn't pretty.'

'That Cookie worked alone. No pimp.'

'That's what the police said.'

'Well, she coulda had a pimp that they didn't know about. But I talked to some people. She worked alone, and if she ever knew Duffy Green, nobody ever heard tell of it.' He turned right at the corner. 'We'll head back to my house, okay?'

'All right.'

'I'll make us some coffee. You liked that coffee I fixed last time, didn't you?'

'It was good.'

'Well, I'll fix us some more.'

His block in Greenpoint was almost as quiet by day as it had been by night. The garage door ascended at the touch of a button. He lowered it with a second touch of the button and we got out of the car and walked on into the house. 'I want to work out some,' he said. 'Do a little lifting. You like to work out with weights?'

'I haven't in years.'

'Want to go through the motions?'

'I think I'll pass.'

My name is Matt and I pass.

'Be a minute,' he said.

He went into a room, came out wearing a pair of scarlet gym shorts and carrying a hooded terry-cloth robe. We went to the room he'd fitted out as a gym, and for fifteen or twenty minutes he worked out with loose weights and on the Universal machine. His skin became glossy with perspiration as he worked and his heavy muscles rippled beneath it.

'Now I want ten minutes in the sauna,' he said. 'You didn't earn the sauna by pumping the iron, but we could grant a special dispensation in your case.'

'No thanks.'

'Want to wait downstairs then? Be more comfortable.'

I waited while he took a sauna and shower. I studied some of his African sculpture, thumbed through a couple of magazines. He emerged in due course wearing light blue jeans and a navy pullover and rope sandals. He asked if I was ready for coffee. I told him I'd been ready for half an hour.

'Won't be long,' he said. He started it brewing, then came back and perched on a leather hassock. He said, 'You want to know something? I make a lousy pimp.'

'I thought you were a class act. Restraint, dignity, all of that.'

'I had six girls and I got three. And Mary Lou'll be leaving soon.'

'You think so?'

'I know it. She's a tourist, man. You ever hear how I turned her out?'

'She told me.'

'First tricks she did, she got to tell herself she was a reporter, a journalist, this was all research. Then she decided she was really into it. Now she's finding out a couple of things.'

'Like what?'

'Like you can get killed, or kill yourself. Like when you die there's twelve people at your funeral. Not much of a turnout for Sunny, was there?'

'It was on the small side.'

'You could say that. You know something? I could have filled that fucking room three times over.'

'Probably.'

'Not just probably. Definitely.' He stood up, clasped his hands behind his back, paced the floor. 'I thought about that. I could have taken their biggest suite and filled it. Uptown people, pimps and whores, and the ringside crowd. Could have mentioned it to people in her building. Might be she had some neighbors who would have wanted to come. But see, I didn't want too many people.'

'I see.'

'It was really for the girls. The four of them. I didn't know they'd be down to three when I organized the thing. Then I thought, shit, it might be pretty grim, just me and the four girls. So I told a couple of other people. It was nice of Kid Bascomb to come, wasn't it?'

'Yes.'

'I'll get that coffee.'

He came back with two cups. I took a sip, nodded my approval.

'You'll take a couple pounds home with you.'

'I told you last time. It's no good to me in a hotel room.'

'So you give it to your lady friend. Let her make you a cup of the best.'

'Thanks.'

'You just drink coffee, right? You don't drink booze?'

'Not these days.'

'But you used to.'

And probably will again, I thought. But not today.

'Same as me,' he said. 'I don't drink, don't smoke dope, don't do any of that shit. Used to.'

'Why'd you stop?'

'Didn't go with the image.'

'Which image? The pimp image?'

'The connoisseur,' he said. 'The art collector.'

'How'd you learn so much about African art?'

'Self-taught,' he said. 'I read everything I could find, went around to the dealers and talked to them. And I had a feel for it.' He smiled at something. 'Long time ago I went to college.'

'Where was that?'

'Hofstra. I grew up in Hempstead. Born in Bedford-Stuyvesant, but my folks bought a house when I was two, three years old. I don't even remember Bed-Stuy.' He had returned to the hassock and he was leaning back, his hands clasped around his knees for balance. 'Middle-class house, lawn to mow and leaves to rake and a driveway to shovel. I can slip in and out of the ghetto talk, but it's mostly a shuck. We weren't rich but we lived decent. And there was enough money to send me to Hofstra.'

'What did you study.'

'Majored in art history. And didn't learn shit about African art there, incidentally. Just that dudes like Braque and Picasso got a lot of inspiration from African masks, same as the Impressionists got turned on by Japanese prints. But I never took a look at an African carving until I got back from Nam.'

'When were you over there?'

'After my third year of college. My father died, see. I could have finished all the same but, I don't know, I was crazy enough to drop out of school and enlist.' His head was back and his eyes were closed. 'Did a ton of drugs over there. We had everything. Reefer, hash, acid. What I liked, I liked heroin. They did it different there. You used to get it in cigarettes, used to smoke it.'

'I never heard of that.'

'Well, it's wasteful,' he said. 'But it was so cheap over there. They grew the opium in those countries and it was cheap. You get a real muzzy high that way, smoking skag in a cigarette. I was stoned that way when I got the news that my mother died. Her pressure was always high, you know, and she had a stroke and died. I wasn't nodding or anything but I was high from a skag joint and I got the news and I didn't feel anything, you know? And when it wore off and I was straight again I still didn't feel anything. First time I felt it was this afternoon, sitting there listening to some hired preacher reading Ralph Waldo Emerson over a dead whore.' He straightened up and looked at me. 'I sat there and wanted to cry for my mama,' he said, 'but I didn't. I don't guess I'll ever cry for her.'

He broke the mood by getting us both more coffee. When he came back he said, 'I don't know why I pick you to tell things to. Like with a shrink, I suppose. You took my money and now you have to listen.'

'All part of the service. How did you decide to be a pimp?'

'How did a nice boy like me get into a business like this?' He chuckled, then stopped and thought for a moment. 'I had this friend,' he said. 'A white boy from Oak Park, Illinois. That's outside of Chicago.'

'I've heard of it.'

'I had this act for him, that I was from the ghetto, that I'd done it all, you know? Then he got killed. It was stupid, we weren't near the line, he got drunk and a jeep ran over him. But he was dead and I wasn't telling those stories anymore, and my mama was dead and I knew when I got home I wasn't going back to college.'

He walked over to the window. 'And I had this girl over there,' he said, his back to me. 'Little bit of a thing, and I'd go over to her place and smoke skag and lay around. I'd give her money, and, you know, I found out she was taking my money and giving it to her boyfriend, and here I was having fantasies of marrying this woman, bringing her back Stateside. I wouldn't have done it, but I was thinking about it, and then I found out she wasn't but a whore. I don't know why I ever thought she was anything else, but a man'll do that, you know.'

'I thought about killing her, but shit, I didn't want to do that. I wasn't even that angry. What I did, I stopped smoking, I stopped drinking, I stopped all kinds of getting high.'

'Just like that?'

'Just like that. And I asked myself, Okay, what do you want to be? And the picture filled in, you know, a few lines here and a few lines there. I was a good little soldier for the rest of my hitch. Then I came back and went into business.'

'You just taught yourself?'

'Shit, I *invented* myself. Gave myself the name Chance. I started out in life with a first name and a middle name and a last name, and wasn't any of them Chance. I gave myself a name and created a style and the rest just fell into place. Pimping's easy to learn. The whole thing is power. You just act like you already got it and the women come and give it to you. That's all it really is.'

'Don't you have to have a purple hat?'

'It's probably easiest if you look and dress the part. But if you go and play against the stereotype they think you're something special.'

'Were you?'

'I was always fair with them. Never knocked them around, never threatened them. Kim wanted to quit me and what did I do? Told her to go ahead and God bless.'

'The pimp with the heart of gold.'

'You think you're joking. But I cared for them. And I had a heavenly dream for a life, man. I really did.'

'You still do.'

He shook his head. 'No,' he said. 'It's slipping away. Whole thing's slipping away and I can't hold onto it.'

THIRTY-ONE

We left the converted firehouse with me in the back seat and Chance wearing a chauffeur's cap. A few blocks away he pulled over and returned the cap to the glove compartment while I joined him in front. The commuter traffic had pretty much thinned out by then and we made the trip into Manhattan quickly and in relative silence. We were a little aloof with each other, as if we'd already shared more than either of us had anticipated.

No messages at the desk. I went upstairs, changed my clothes, paused on the way out the door and got the .32 from my dresser drawer. Was there any point in carrying a gun I seemed unable to fire? I couldn't see any, but I put it in my pocket anyway.

I went downstairs and bought a paper, and without thinking too much about it I walked around the corner and took a table in Armstrong's. My usual corner table. Trina came over, said it had been a long time, and took my order for a cheeseburger and a small salad and coffee.

After she headed for the kitchen I got a sudden flash of a martini, straight up and bone dry and ice cold in a stemmed glass. I could see it, I could smell the odor of juniper and the tang of a lemon twist. I could feel the bite as it hit bottom.

Jesus, I thought.

The urge for a drink passed as suddenly as it had come on me. I decided it was a reflex, a reaction to the atmosphere of Armstrong's. I'd done so much drinking here for so long, I'd been eighty-sixed here after my last bender, and I hadn't crossed the threshold since. It was only natural that I'd think of a drink. It didn't mean I had to have one.

I ate my meal, drank a second cup of coffee afterward. I read my newspaper, paid my check, left a tip. Then it was time to go over to St Paul's.

The qualification was an alcoholic version of the American Dream. The speaker was a poor boy from Worcester, Mass. who worked his way through college, rose to a vice-presidency at one of the television networks, then lost it all drinking. He went all the way down, wound up in Los Angeles drinking Sterno in Pershing Square, then found AA and got it all back.

It would have been inspiring if I could have kept my mind on it. But my attention kept straying. I thought about Sunny's funeral, I thought about what Chance had told me, and I found my thoughts wandering all over the whole case, trying to make sense out of it.

Damnit, it was all there. I just wasn't looking at it right.

I left during the discussion, before it was my turn to speak. I didn't even feel like saying my name tonight. I walked back to my hotel, fighting the urge to stop in at Armstrong's for a minute or two.

I called Durkin. He was out. I hung up without leaving a message and called Jan.

No answer. Well, she was probably still at her meeting. And she'd go out for coffee afterward, probably wouldn't get home until after eleven.

I could have stayed at my own meeting until it ended, then gone to coffee with some of the others. I could join them now, as far as that went. The Cobb's Corner where they hung out wasn't all that far away.

I thought about it. And decided I didn't really want to go there.

I picked up a book but couldn't make sense out of it. I tossed it down, got undressed, went into the bathroom and ran the shower. But I didn't need a shower, for Christ's sake, I just had a shower that morning, and the most strenuous activity I'd had all day was watching Chance working out with weights. What the hell did I need with a shower?

I turned the water off and got dressed again.

Jesus, I felt like a caged lion. I picked up the phone. I might have called Chance but you couldn't just call the son of a bitch, you had to call his service and wait for him to call back, and I didn't feel like doing that. I called Jan, who was still out, and I called Durkin. He wasn't there either, and once again I decided against leaving a message.

Maybe he was at that place on Tenth Avenue, unwinding with a couple of belts. I thought about going over there and looking for him, and it struck me that it wasn't Durkin I'd be looking for, that all I wanted was an excuse to walk through the door of that bucket of blood and put my foot upon the brass rail.

Did they even have a brass rail? I closed my eyes and tried to picture the place, and in an instant I was recalling everything about it, the smells of spilled booze and stale beer and urine, that dank tavern smell that welcomes you home.

I thought, You've got nine days and you went to two meetings today, a noon meeting and an evening meeting, and you've never been closer to a drink. What the hell's the matter with you?

If I went to Durkin's boozer I'd drink. If I went to Farrell's or Polly's or Armstrong's I would drink. If I stayed in my room I'd go crazy, and when I went crazy enough I'd get away from those four walls and what would I do? I'd go out, to one bar or another, and I'd drink.

I made myself stay there. I'd gotten through the eighth day and there was no reason why I couldn't get through the ninth. I sat there and every now and then I looked at my watch and sometimes a whole minute went by between looks. Finally it got to be eleven o'clock and I went downstairs and hailed a taxi.

There's a midnight meeting seven nights a week at the Moravian Church on the corner of Thirtieth and Lexington. The doors open about an hour before meeting time. I got there and took a seat, and when the coffee was ready I got myself a cup.

I didn't pay attention to the qualification or the discussion. I just sat there and let myself feel safe. There were a lot of newly sober people in the room, a lot of people who were having a hard time. Why else would they be there at that hour?

There were some people who hadn't stopped drinking yet, too. They had to put one of them out, but the others didn't make any trouble. Just a roomful of people getting through one more hour.

When the hour was up I helped fold the chairs and empty the ashtrays. Another chair folder introduced himself as Kevin and asked me how long I'd been sober. I told him it was my ninth day.

'That's great,' he said. 'Keep coming back.'

They always say that.

I went outside and signaled a passing cab, but when he cut over and started to brake I changed my mind and waved him off. He gunned his engine as he drove away.

I didn't want to go back to the room.

So instead I walked seven blocks north to Kim's building,

393

bluffed my way past her doorman, let myself into her apartment. I knew there was a closetful of booze there but it didn't bother me. I didn't even feel the need to pour it down the sink, as I'd done with the bottle of Wild Turkey earlier.

In her bedroom, I went through her jewelry. I wasn't really looking for the green ring. I picked up the ivory bracelet, unfastened the clasp, tried it for size on my own wrist. It was too small. I got some paper towels from the kitchen and wrapped the bracelet carefully, put it in my pocket.

Maybe Jan would like it. I'd pictured it on her wrist a few times – at her loft, during the funeral service.

If she didn't like it she didn't have to wear it.

I went over, picked up the phone. The service hadn't been disconnected yet. I supposed it would be sooner or later, just as sooner or later the apartment would be cleaned and Kim's things removed from it. But for now it was still as if she'd just stepped out for a moment.

I hung up the phone without calling anyone. Somewhere around three o'clock I got undressed and went to sleep in her bed. I didn't change the linen, and it seemed to me that her scent, still faintly discernible, constituted a presence in the room.

If so, it didn't keep me awake. I went right off to sleep.

I woke up bathed in perspiration, convinced that I'd solved the case in a dream and then forgot the solution. I showered and dressed and got out of there.

There were several messages at my hotel, all of them from Mary Lou Barcker. She'd called just after I left the night before and a couple of times that morning.

When I called her she said, 'I've been trying to reach you. I would have called you at your girlfriend's but I couldn't remember her last name.'

'Her number's unlisted.' And I wasn't there, I thought, but left it unsaid.

'I'm trying to reach Chance,' she went on. 'I thought you might have talked to him.'

'Not since around seven last night. Why?'

'I can't get hold of him. The only way I know is to call his service –'

'That's the only way I know.'

'Oh. I thought you might have a special number.'

'Only the service.'

394

'I've called there. He always returns his calls. I've left, God, I don't know how many messages and he hasn't called me back.'

'Has that ever happened before?'

'Not for this length of time. I started trying him late yesterday afternoon. What time is it, eleven o'clock? That's over seventeen hours. He wouldn't go that long without checking with his service.'

I thought back to our conversation at his house. Had he checked with his service in all the time we were together? I didn't think he had.

Other times we'd been together he called in every half hour or so.

'And it's not just me,' she was saying. 'He hasn't called Fran, either. I checked with her and she called him and he never returned her calls.'

'What about Donna?'

'She's here with me. Neither of us wanted to be alone. And Ruby, I don't know where Ruby is. Her number doesn't answer.'

'She's in San Francisco.'

'She's where?'

I gave her a brief explanation, then listened as she relayed the information to Donna. 'Donna's quoting Yeats,' she told me. 'Things fall apart, the center cannot hold.' Even I can recognize that. Apt, though. Things are falling apart all over the place.'

'I'm going to try to get hold of Chance.'

'Call me when you do?'

'I will.'

'Meanwhile Donna's staying here and we're not booking any tricks or answering the door. I already told the doorman not to let anybody come up.'

'Good.'

'I invited Fran to come over here but she said she didn't want to. She sounded very stoned. I'm going to call her again and instead of inviting her to come over I'm going to *tell* her to come over.'

'Good idea.'

'Donna says the three little pigs will all be hiding in the brick house. Waiting for the wolf to come down the chimney. I wish she'd stick to Yeats.'

I couldn't get anywhere with his answering service. They were happy to take my message but wouldn't disclose whether Chance had called in recently. 'I expect to hear from him shortly,' a woman told me, 'and I will see that he receives your message.'

I called Brooklyn information and got the number for the house in Greenpoint. I dialed it and let it ring for a dozen times. I'd remembered what he'd told me about removing the clappers from the bells of his telephones, but I thought it was worth a check.

I called Parke Bernet. The sale of African and Oceanic art and artifacts was scheduled for two o'clock.

I had a shower and a shave, had a roll and a cup of coffee and read the paper. The *Post* managed to keep the Motel Ripper on the front page, but it took some stretching to do it. A man in the Bedford Park section of the Bronx had stabbed his wife three times with a kitchen knife, then called the police to tell them what he'd done. This normally would have rated two paragraphs on the back page at the most, but the *Post* put it on the front page and topped it with a teaser headline that wondered, DID THE MOTEL RIPPER INSPIRE HIM?

I went to a meeting at twelve-thirty and got to Parke Bernet a few minutes after two. The auction was being held in a different room from the one where the sale lots had been displayed. You had to have a sale catalog to get a seat, and the catalogs cost five dollars. I explained I was just looking for someone and scanned the room. Chance wasn't there.

The attendant didn't want me to hang around unless I bought a catalog, and it was easier to do that than argue with him. I gave him the five dollars and wound up registering and getting a bidder's number while I was at it. I didn't want to register, I didn't want a bidder's number, I didn't want the goddamned catalog.

I sat there for almost two hours while one lot after another went under the hammer. By two-thirty I was fairly certain he wasn't going to show but I stayed in my seat because I couldn't think of anything better to do. I paid minimal attention to the auction and looked around every couple of minutes for Chance. At twenty to four the Benin bronze was offered for bids and sold for $65,000, which was just a little higher than the estimate. It was the star of the sale and quite a few bidders left once it had been sold. I hung on a few minutes longer, knowing he wasn't coming, just trying to grapple with the same thing I'd been grappling with for days.

It seemed to me that I already had all the pieces. It was just a question of fitting them together.

Kim. Kim's ring and Kim's mink jacket. *Cojones. Maricón.*
The towels. The warning. Calderón. Cookie Blue.

I got up and left. I was crossing the lobby when a table full of
catalogs of past sales caught my eye. I picked up a catalog of a
jewelry auction held that spring and leafed through it. It didn't
tell me anything. I put it back and asked the lobby attendant if
the gallery had a resident expert on gems and jewelry. 'You want
Mr Hillquist,' he said, and told me what room to go to and
pointed me in the right direction.

Mr Hillquist sat at an uncluttered desk as if he'd been waiting
all day for me to consult him. I gave him my name and told him
I wanted some vague approximation of the value of an emerald.
He asked if he could see the stone, and I explained that I didn't
have it with me.

'You would have to bring it in,' he explained. 'The value of a
gem depends upon so many variables. Size, cut, color, brilliance –'

I put my hand in my pocket, touched the .32, felt around for
the bit of green glass. 'It's about this size,' I said, and he fitted a
jeweler's loupe into one eye and took the piece of glass from me.
He looked at it, went absolutely rigid for an instant, then fixed
his other eye warily upon me.

'This is not an emerald,' he said carefully. He might have been
talking to a small child, or to a lunatic.

'I know that. It's a piece of glass.'

'Yes.'

'It's the approximate size of the stone I'm talking about. I'm a
detective, I'm trying to get some idea of the value of a ring that
has disappeared since I saw it, I –'

'Oh,' he said, and sighed. 'For a moment I thought –'

'I know what you thought.'

He took the loupe from his eye, set it on the desk in front of
him. 'When you sit here,' he said, 'you are at the absolute mercy
of the public. You wouldn't believe the people who come here,
the things they show me, the questions they ask.'

'I can imagine.'

'No, you can't.' He picked up the bit of green glass and shook
his head at it. 'I still can't tell you the value. Size is only one of
several considerations. There's also color, there's clarity, there's
brilliance. Do you even know that the stone is an emerald? Did
you test it for hardness?'

'No.'

'So it could even be colored glass. Like the, uh, treasure you've
given me here.'

397

'For all I know it is glass. But I want to know what it could be worth if it did happen to be an emerald.'

'I think I see what you mean.' He frowned at the piece of glass. 'You have to understand that my every inclination is to avoid naming any sort of a figure. You see, even assuming the stone is a genuine emerald, its range in value could be considerable. It could be extremely valuable or very nearly worthless. It could be seriously flawed, for example. Or it could simply be a very low grade stone. There are mail order firms that actually offer emeralds by the carat for some ridiculous sum, forty or fifty dollars the carat, and what they're selling is no bargain, either. Yet they are genuine emeralds, however worthless they may be as gemstones.'

'I see.'

'Even a gem-quality emerald could vary enormously in value. You could buy a stone this size –' he weighed the chunk of glass in his hand '– for a couple thousand dollars. And that would be a good stone, not industrial-grade corundum from western North Carolina. On the other hand, a stone of the highest quality, the best color, perfect brilliance, unflawed, not even Peruvian but the very best Colombian emerald, might bring forty or fifty or sixty thousand dollars. And even that's approximate and imprecise.'

He had more to say but I wasn't paying attention. He hadn't really told me anything, hadn't added a fresh piece to the puzzle, but he'd given the box a good shake. Now I could see where everything went.

I took the cube of green glass with me when I left.

THIRTY-TWO

Around ten-thirty that night I walked in and out of Poogan's Pub on West Seventy-second Street. A light rain had begun falling an hour or so earlier. Most of the people on the street were carrying umbrellas. I wasn't, but I had a hat, and I paused on the sidewalk to straighten it and adjust its brim.

Across the street I saw a Mercury sedan with its motor riding.

I turned to my left and walked to the Top Knot. I spotted Danny Boy at a table in back but went to the bar anyway and asked for him. I must have spoken loudly because people looked at me. The bartender motioned toward the rear and I went back there and joined him.

He already had company. He was sharing his table with a slender fox-faced girl whose hair was as white as his own, but in her case nature couldn't take the credit. Her eyebrows were severely plucked and her forehead had a shine to it. Danny Boy introduced her as Bryna. 'Rhymes with angina,' he said, 'among other things.' She smiled, showing sharp little canine teeth.

I pulled a chair out and sat down heavily. I said, 'Danny Boy, you can pass the word. I know all about Kim Dakkinen's boyfriend. I know who killed her and I know why she was killed.'

'Matt, are you all right?'

'I'm fine,' I said. 'You know why I had so much trouble getting a line on Kim's boyfriend? Because he wasn't an action guy, that's why. Didn't go to clubs, didn't gamble, didn't hang out. Wasn't connected.'

'You been drinking, Matt?'

'What are you, the Spanish Inquisition? What do you care if I've been drinking or not?'

'I just wondered. You're talking loud, that's all.'

'Well, I'm trying to tell you about Kim,' I said. 'About her boyfriend. See, he was in the jewelry business. He didn't get rich, he didn't starve. He made a living.'

'Bryna,' he said, 'suppose you powder your nose for a few minutes.'

'Oh, let her stay,' I told him. 'Her nose doesn't look shiny to me.'

'Matt —'

'What I'm telling you's no secret, Danny Boy.'

'Suit yourself.'

'This jeweler,' I went on. 'The way it looks, he started seeing Kim as a john. But something happened. One way or another, he fell for her.'

'These things happen.'

'They do indeed. Anyway, he fell in love. Meanwhile, some people got in touch with him. They had some precious stones that never went through Customs and that they had no bill of sale for. Emeralds. Colombian emeralds. Real quality stuff.'

'Matt, would you please tell my why in the hell you're telling me all this?'

'It makes an interesting story.'

'You're not just telling me, you're telling the whole room. Do you know what you're doing?'

I looked at him.

'Okay,' he said, after a moment. 'Bryna, pay attention, darling. The crazy man wants to talk about emeralds.'

'Kim's boyfriend was going to be the middleman, handling the sale of the emeralds for the men who'd brought them into the country. He did this sort of thing before, made a few dollars for himself. But now he was in love with an expensive lady and he had a reason to want some real money. So he tried a cross.'

'How?'

'I don't know. Maybe he switched some stones. Maybe he held out. Maybe he decided to grab the whole bundle and run with it. He must have told Kim something because on the strength of it she told Chance she wanted out. She wasn't going to be turning tricks anymore. If I were going to guess, I'd say he did a switch and went out of the country to unload the good stuff. Kim got herself free of Chance while he was gone, and when he got back it was going to be Happily Ever After time. But he never came back.'

'If he never came back, who killed her?'

'The people he crossed. They decoyed her to that room at the Galaxy Downtowner. She probably thought she was going to be meeting him there. She wasn't hooking any more, she wouldn't have gone to a hotel room to meet a john. In fact she'd never been much on hotel tricks. But suppose she gets a call from somebody who says he's a friend and the boyfriend's afraid to come to her place because he thinks he's being followed, so would she please meet him at the hotel?'

'And she went.'

'Sure she went. She got all dressed up, she wore the presents he gave her, the mink jacket and the emerald ring. The jacket wasn't worth a fortune because the guy wasn't rich, he didn't have money to burn, but he could give her a terrific emerald because the emeralds didn't cost him anything. He was in the business, he could take one of those smuggled stones and have it set in a ring for her.'

'So she went over and got killed.'

'Right.'

Danny Boy drank some vodka. 'Why? You figure they killed her to get the ring back?'

'No. They killed her to kill her.'

'Why?'

'Because they were Colombians,' I said, 'and that's how they do it. When they have a reason to hit somebody they go for the whole family.'

'Jesus.'

'Maybe they figure it's a deterrent,' I said. 'I could see where it might be. The cases make the papers pretty regularly, especially in Miami. A whole family gets waxed because somebody burned somebody else in a coke deal. Colombia's a rich little country. They've got the best coffee, the best marijuana, the best cocaine.'

'And the best emeralds?'

'That's right. Kim's jeweler wasn't a married guy. I figured he was, that's why he was so hard to get a line on, but he never married. Maybe he never fell in love until he fell in love with Kim, and maybe that's why he was ready to kick his life over. Anyway, he was a bachelor. No wife, no kids, no living parents. You want to rub out his family, what do you do? You kill his girlfriend.'

Bryna's face was as white as her hair now. She didn't like stories where they killed the girlfriend.

'The killing was pretty professional,' I went on, 'in that the killer was careful about evidence. He covered his tracks pretty well. But something made him do a butcher job instead of a couple of quick bullets from a silenced handgun. Maybe he had a thing about prostitutes, or maybe it was women in general. One way or another, he went and did a number on Kim.

'Then he cleaned up, packed the dirty towels along with the machete, and got out of there. He left the fur jacket and he left the money in the purse but he took her ring.'

'Because it was worth so much money?'

'Possibly. There's no hard evidence on the ring, and for all I know it was cut glass and she bought it for herself. But it might have been an emerald, and even if it wasn't the killer might have thought it was. It's one thing to leave a few hundred dollars on a dead body to show you don't rob the dead. It's something else to leave an emerald that might be worth fifty thousand dollars, especially if it's your emerald in the first place.'

'I follow you.'

'The room clerk at the Galaxy Downtowner was a Colombian, a young kid named Octavio Calderón. Maybe that was a coincidence. There are a lot of Colombians in town these days. Maybe the killer picked the Galaxy because he knew somebody who worked there. It doesn't matter. Calderón probably recognized the killer, or at least knew enough about him to keep his mouth shut. When a cop came back to have another talk with him, Calderón disappeared. Either the killer's friends told him to disappear or Calderón decided he'd be safer somewhere else. Back home in Cartagena, say, or another rooming house in another part of Queens.'

Or maybe he got killed, I thought. That was possible, too. But I didn't think so. When these people killed, they liked to leave the corpses in plain sight.

'There was another whore that got killed.'

'Sunny Hendryx,' I said. 'That was a suicide. Maybe Kim's death triggered that, so maybe the man who killed Kim has some moral responsibility for Sunny's death. But she killed herself.'

'I'm talking about the street hustler. The TV.'

'Cookie Blue.'

'That's the one. Why did she get killed? To throw you off the track? Except you weren't on the track to begin with.'

'No.'

'Then why? You think the first killing turned the killer nuts? Triggered something in him that made him want to do it again?'

'I think that's part of it,' I said. 'Nobody would do a second butcher job like that unless he enjoyed the first one. I don't know if he had sex with either of his victims, but the kick he got out of the killings had to be sexual.'

'So he just picked up Cookie for the hell of it?'

Bryna blanched again. It was bad enough hearing about someone who got killed for being the wrong person's girlfriend. It was even worse hearing about a girl getting killed at random.

'No,' I said, 'Cookie was killed for a specific reason. The killer went looking for her and passed up a batch of other street-walkers until he found her. Cookie was family.'

'Family? Whose family?'

'The boyfriend's.'

'He had two sweeties, this jeweler? A call girl and a transvestite hustler?'

'Cookie wasn't his sweetie. Cookie was his brother.'

'Cookie –'

'Cookie Blue started life as Mark Blaustein. Mark had an older brother named Adrian who went into the jewelry business. Adrian Blaustein had a girlfriend named Kim and some business associates from Colombia.'

'So Cookie and Kim were connected.'

'They had to be connected. I'm sure they never met each other. I don't think Mark and Adrian had any contact in recent years. That may explain why it took the killer so long to find Cookie. But I knew there had to be some kind of link. I told someone earlier that they were sisters under the skin. That wasn't far off. They were almost sisters-in-law.'

He thought about this, then told Bryna to give us a few moments alone. This time I didn't interfere. She left the table and Danny Boy motioned to the waitress. He ordered vodka for himself and asked me what I wanted.

'Nothing right now,' I said.

When she brought back the vodka he took a careful little sip and set the glass down. 'You've been to the cops,' he said.

'No cops.'

'Why not?'

'Just didn't get around to it yet.'

'You had to come here instead.'

'That's right.'

'I can keep my mouth shut, Matt, but Bryna the Vagina wouldn't know how. She thinks unexpressed thoughts build up inside your head and explode your skull, and she's not taking any chances. Anyway, you were talking loud enough for half the room to pick up on what you were saying.'

403

'I know that.'

'I figured you did. What do you want?'

'I want the killer to know what I know.'

'That shouldn't take long.'

'I want you to pass it on, Danny Boy. I'm leaving here, I'm walking back to my neighborhood. I'll probably spend a couple of hours in Armstrong's. Then I'll walk around the corner to my room.'

'You're gonna get killed, Matt.'

'This fucker only kills girls,' I said.

'Cookie was only half a girl. Maybe he's working his way up to men.'

'Maybe.'

'You want him to make a move on you.'

'Looks that way, doesn't it?'

'Looks to me as though you're crazy, Matt. I tried to head you off the minute you came over here. Tried to cool you down some.'

'I know.'

'It's probably too late now. Whether I pass it on or not.'

'It was too late before then. I was uptown before I came down here. You know a man named Royal Waldron?'

'Sure, I know Royal.'

'He and I talked some. Royal's been known to do a little business with some fellows from Colombia.'

'He would,' Danny Boy said. 'The business he's in.'

'So they probably already know. But you could pass it on anyway, just for insurance.'

'Insurance,' he said. 'What's the opposite of life insurance?'

'I don't know.'

'Death insurance. They may be waiting outside for you right now, Matt.'

'It's possible.'

'Why don't you go pick up the phone and call the cops? They could send a car and you go somewhere and make a statement. Let the bastards earn their money.'

'I want the killer,' I said. 'I want him one-on-one.'

'You're not Latin. Where'd you get this *macho* hangup?'

'Just pass the word, Danny Boy.'

'Sit down a minute.' He leaned forward, dropped his voice. 'You don't want to walk out of here without a piece. Just sit here a minute and I'll get you something.'

'I don't need a gun.'

404

'No, of course not. Who needs one? You can take his machete away from him and make him eat it. Then break both his legs and leave him in an alley.'

'Something like that.'

'Will you let me get you a gun?' His eyes searched mine. 'You've already got one,' he said. 'On you, right now. Haven't you?'

'I don't need a gun,' I said.

And I didn't. On the way out of the Top Knot I put my hand in my pocket and felt the butt and barrel of the little .32. Who needed it? A little gun like that doesn't have a whole lot of stopping power anyway.

Especially when you can't make yourself squeeze the trigger.

I went outside. It was still raining but no harder than before. I tugged the brim of my hat and took a good look around.

The Mercury sedan was parked on the other side of the street. I recognized it by its crimped fenders. While I was standing there the driver started the engine.

I walked over to Columbus Avenue. While I waited for the light to change I saw that the Mercury had come around in a U-turn and was approaching. The light changed and I walked across the street.

I had the gun in my hand and my hand in my pocket. My index finger was on the trigger. I remembered how the trigger had trembled beneath my finger not too long ago.

I'd been on this same street then.

I walked on downtown. A couple of times I looked over my shoulder. The Mercury stayed a little less than a block behind me all the way.

I never relaxed, but I was especially tense when I got to the block where I'd drawn the gun once before. I couldn't help looking back, expecting to see a car careening toward me. I spun around involuntarily once at the sound of brakes screeching, then realized the sound was a good two blocks away.

Nerves.

I passed the spot where I'd dropped to the pavement and rolled. I checked the place where the bottle had broken. There was still some broken glass there, though I couldn't be sure it was the same broken glass. A lot of bottles get broken every day.

I kept walking all the way to Armstrong's. When I got there I went in and ordered a piece of pecan pie and a cup of coffee. I kept my right hand in my pocket while my eyes scanned the room, checking everybody out. After I was done with the pie I put my hand back in my pocket and drank my coffee left-handed.

After awhile I ordered more coffee.

The telephone rang. Trina answered it, walked over to the bar. There was a heavyset fellow there with dark blond hair. She said something to him and he went to the phone. He talked for a few minutes, looked around the room, came over to my table. Both of his hands were where I could see them.

He said, 'Scudder? My name's George Lightner, I don't think we met.' He pulled a chair out and sat in it. 'That was Joe just now,' he said. 'There's no activity out there, nothing at all. They're laying doggo in the Mercury plus he's got two sharp-shooters in second-floor windows across the street.'

'Good.'

'I'm in here, and there's the two fellows at the front table. I figured you made us when you walked in.'

'I made them,' I said. 'I figured you were either a cop or the killer.'

'Jesus, what a thought. This is a nice place. You more or less hang out here, huh?'

'Not as much as I used to.'

'It's pleasant here. I'd like to come back sometime when I can drink something instead of coffee. They're selling a lot of coffee tonight, what with you and me and the two guys down front.'

'It's pretty good coffee.'

'Yeah, it's not bad. Better than the shit in the station house.' He lit a cigarette with a Zippo lighter. 'Joe said there's no activity elsewhere either. There's two men staked out down-town with your girlfriend. There's a couple others with the three hookers on the East Side.' He grinned. 'That's the detail I shoulda drawn. Can't win 'em all, huh?'

'I guess not.'

'How long you want to stay here? Joe's guess is that the guy's either set up by now or he's not gonna move tonight. We can cover you every step from here back to the hotel. Of course we can't insure against the possibility of a sniper firing from a rooftop or a high window. We did a rooftop check earlier but there's no guarantee.'

'I don't think he'll do it from a distance.'

'Then we're in pretty good shape. And you're wearing the bulletproof vest.'

'Yes.'

406

'That's a help. Of course it's mesh, it doesn't always stop a blade, but nobody's about to let him get that close to you. We figure if he's out there he'll make a move between here and the doorway of your hotel.'

'That's what I figure, too.'

'When do you want to run the gauntlet?'

'A few minutes,' I said. 'I might as well finish this coffee.'

'Listen,' he said, rising, 'what the hell. Enjoy it.'

He returned to his spot at the bar. I finished my coffee, got up, went to the lavatory. There I checked my .32 and made sure I had a round under the hammer and three more rounds to back it up. I could have asked Durkin for a couple more cartridges to fill the empty chambers. For that matter, he'd have given me a larger gun with more of a punch to it. But he didn't even know I was carrying the .32 and I hadn't wanted to tell him. The way things were set up, I wasn't going to have to shoot anybody. The killer was supposed to walk right into our arms.

Except it wasn't going to happen that way.

I paid the check, left a tip. It wasn't going to work. I could feel it. The son of a bitch wasn't out there.

I walked out the door. The rain had let up some. I looked at the Mercury and glanced at the buildings across the street, wondering where the police sharpshooters were planted. It didn't matter. They weren't going to have any work to do tonight. Our quarry wasn't taking the bait.

I walked down to Fifty-seventh Street, staying close to the curb just in case he'd managed to find a spot in a dark doorway. I walked slowly and hoped I was right and he wouldn't try to do it from a distance, because a bulletproof vest doesn't always stop a bullet and it doesn't do anything to protect you from a head shot.

But it didn't matter. He wasn't there. Damnit, I knew he wasn't there.

Still, I breathed easier when I walked into my hotel. I may have been disappointed but I was also relieved.

There were three plainclothesmen in the lobby. They identified themselves right away. I stood around with them for a few minutes, and then Durkin came in alone. He went into a huddle with one of them, then came over to me.

'We struck out,' he said.

'Looks that way.'

'Shit,' he said. 'We didn't leave many loopholes. Maybe he smelled something but I don't see how. Or maybe he flew home to fucking Bogotá yesterday and we're setting a trap for somebody who's on another continent.'

'It's possible.'

'You can go get some sleep, anyway. If you're not too wired to unwind. Have a couple of drinks, knock yourself out for eight hours.'

'Good idea.'

'The guys have had the lobby staked out all night. There've been no visitors, no check-ins. I'm gonna keep a guard down here all night.'

'You think it's necessary?'

'I think it can't hurt.'

'Whatever you say.'

'We gave it our best shot, Matt. It's worth it if we can smoke the fucker out because God knows how we could get anyplace combing the city for emerald smugglers. Sometimes you get lucky and sometimes you don't.'

'I know.'

'We'll catch the cocksucker sooner or later. You know that.'

'Sure.'

'Well,' he said, and shifted his weight awkwardly. 'Well, listen. Get some sleep, huh?'

'Sure.'

I rode up on the elevator. He wasn't in South America, I thought. I knew damned well he wasn't in South America. He was here in New York and he was going to kill again because he liked it.

Maybe he'd done it before. Maybe Kim was the first time he found out it felt good to him. But he'd liked it enough to do it again the same way, and the next time he wouldn't need an excuse. Just a victim and a hotel room and his trusty machete.

Have a couple of drinks, Durkin had suggested.

I didn't even feel like a drink.

Ten days, I thought. Just go to bed sober and you've got ten days.

I took the gun out of my pocket and put it on the dresser. I was still carrying the ivory bracelet in another pocket and I took it out and set it down next to the gun, still wrapped in paper towels from Kim's kitchen. I got out of my slacks and jacket, hung them in the closet, and took off my shirt. The bulletproof vest was a tricky thing to get out of and a cumbersome thing to wear, and most of the cops I knew hated wearing them. On the other hand, nobody likes getting shot.

I took the thing off and draped it over the dresser next to the gun and bracelet. Bulletproof vests aren't just bulky, they're also warm, and I'd perspired inside this one and my undershirt had dark circles under the arms. I took off the undershirt and my shorts and my socks, and something clicked, some little alarm went off, and I was turning toward the bathroom door when it flew open.

He sailed through it, a big man, olive skinned, wild-eyed. He was as naked as I was and there was a machete in his hand with a gleaming foot-long blade.

I threw the mesh at him. He swung the machete and knocked it aside. I grabbed the gun off the dresser and dove out of his way. The blade arced down, missing me, and his arm rose again and I shot him four times in the chest.

THIRTY-THREE

The LL train starts at Eighth Avenue, crosses Manhattan along Fourteenth Street, and winds up way the hell out in Canarsie. Its first stop across the river in Brooklyn is at Bedford Avenue and North Seventh Street. I left it there and walked around until I found his house. It took me a while and I took a couple of wrong turns, but it was a good day for walking, the sun out, the sky clear, and a little warmth in the air for a change.

There was a heavy windowless door to the right of the garage. I poked the doorbell but got no response, and I couldn't hear the bell sounding within. Hadn't he said something about disconnecting the bell? I jabbed it again, heard nothing.

There was a brass knocker mounted on the door and I used it. Nothing happened. I cupped my hands and shouted, 'Chance, open up! It's Scudder.' Then I pounded on the door some more, with the knocker and with my hands.

The door looked and felt awfully solid. I gave it a tentative nudge with my shoulder and decided it was unlikely I could kick it in. I could break a window and get in that way, but in Greenpoint some neighbor would call the cops, or pick up a gun and come over himself.

I banged on the door some more. A motor worked, and a winch began lifting the electrically-operated garage door.

'This way,' he said. 'Before you knock my damn door down.'

I went in through the garage and he pushed a button to lower the door again. 'My front door doesn't open,' he said. 'Didn't I show you that before? It's all sealed shut with bars and shit.'

'That's great if you have a fire.'

'Then I go out a window. But when'd you ever hear of the firehouse burning down?'

He was dressed as I'd last seen him, in light blue denim pants and a navy blue pullover. 'You forgot your coffee,' he said. 'Or I

410

forgot to give it to you. Day before yesterday, remember? You were gonna take a couple pounds home with you.'

'You're right, I forgot.'

'For your girlfriend. Fine-looking woman. I got some coffee made. You'll have a cup, won't you?'

'Thanks.'

I went into the kitchen with him. I said, 'You're a hard man to get hold of.'

'Well, I sort of stopped checking with my service.'

'I know. Have you heard a newscast lately? Or read a paper?'

'Not lately. You drink it black, right?'

'Right. It's all over, Chance.' He looked at me. 'We got the guy.'

'The guy. The killer.'

'That's right. I thought I'd come out and tell you about it.'

'Well,' he said. 'I guess I'd like to hear it.'

I went through the whole thing in a fair amount of detail. I was used to it by now. It was the middle of the afternoon and I'd been telling the story to one person or another ever since I'd put four bullets into Pedro Antonio Marquez a little after two in the morning.

'So you killed him,' Chance said. 'How do you feel about that?'

'It's too early to tell.'

I knew how Durkin felt about it. He couldn't have been happier. 'When they're dead,' he had said, 'you know they're not going to be back on the street in three years, doing it again. And this one was a fucking animal. He had that taste of blood and he liked it.'

'It's the same guy?' Chance wanted to know. 'There's no question?'

'No question. They got confirmation from the manager of the Powhattan Motel. They also matched a couple of latent prints, one from the Powhattan and one from the Galaxy, so that ties him to both killings. And the machete's the weapon used in both killings. They even found minute traces of blood where the hilt meets the handle, and the type matches either Kim or Cookie, I forget which one.'

'How'd he get into your hotel?'

'He walked right through the lobby and rode up in the elevator.'

'I thought they had the place staked out.'

'They did. He walked right past them, picked up his key at the desk and went to his room.'

'How could he do that?'

'Easiest thing in the world,' I said. 'He checked in the day before, just in case. He was setting things up. When he got the word that I was looking for him, he went back to my hotel, went up to his room, then went to my room and let himself in. The locks in my hotel aren't much of a challenge. He took off his clothes and sharpened his machete and waited for me to come home.'

'And it almost worked.'

'It should have worked. He could have waited behind the door and killed me before I knew what was happening. Or he could have stayed in the bathroom a few more minutes and given me time to get into bed. But he got too much of a kick out of killing and that's what screwed him up. He wanted us both naked when he took me out, so he waited in the bathroom, and he couldn't wait for me to get into bed because he was too keyed up, too excited. Of course if I hadn't had the gun handy he'd have killed me anyway.'

'He couldn't have been all alone.'

'He was alone as far as the killings were concerned. He probably had partners in the emerald operation. The cops may get somewhere looking for them and they may not. Even if they do, there's no real way to make a case against anybody.'

He nodded. 'What happened to the brother? Kim's boyfriend, the one who started everything.'

'He hasn't turned up. He's probably dead. Or he's still running, and he'll live until his Colombian friends catch up with him.'

'Will they do that?'

'Probably. They're supposed to be relentless.'

'And that room clerk? What's his name, Calderón?'

'That's right. Well, if he's holed up somewhere in Queens, he can read about it in the paper and ask for his old job back.'

He started to say something, then changed his mind and took both our cups back to the kitchen to refill them. He came back with them and gave me mine.

'You were up late,' he said.

'All night.'

'You been to sleep at all?'

'Not yet.'

'Myself, I doze off in a chair now and then. But when I get in bed I can't sleep, I can't even lie there. I go work out and take a sauna and a shower and drink some more coffee and sit around some more. Over and over.'

'You stopped calling your service.'

'I stopped calling my service. I stopped leaving the house. I guess I been eating. I take something from the refrigerator and eat it without paying attention. Kim's dead and Sunny's dead and this Cookie's dead, and maybe the brother's dead, the boyfriend, and what's-his-name is dead. The one you shot, I disremember his name.'

'Marquez.'

'Marquez is dead, and Calderón disappeared, and Ruby's in San Francisco. And the question is where's Chance, and the answer is I don't know. Where I think I am is out of business.'

'The girls are all right.'

'So you said.'

'Mary Lou isn't going to be turning tricks anymore. She's glad she did it, she learned a lot from it, but she's ready for a new stage in her life.'

'Yeah, well, I called that one. Didn't I tell you after the funeral?'

I nodded. 'And Donna thinks she can get a foundation grant, and she can earn money through readings and workshops. She says she's reached a point where selling herself is starting to undermine her poetry.'

'She's pretty talented, Donna. Be good if she could make it on her poetry. You say she's getting a grant?'

'She thinks she's got a shot at it.'

He grinned. 'Aren't you gonna tell me the rest of it? Little Fran just got a Hollywood contract and she's gonna be the next Goldie Hawn.'

'Maybe tomorrow,' I said. 'For now she just wants to live in the Village and stay stoned and entertain nice men from Wall Street.'

'So I still got Fran.'

'That's right.'

He'd been pacing the floor. Now he dropped onto the hassock again. 'Be a cinch to get five, six more of them,' he said. 'You don't know how easy it is. Easiest thing in the world.'

'You told me that once before.'

'It's the truth, man. So many women just waiting to be told what to do with their damn lives. I could walk out of here and have me a full string in no more than a week's time.' He shook his head ruefully. 'Except for one thing.'

'What's that?'

'I don't think I can do that anymore.' He stood up again. 'Damn, I been a good pimp! And I liked it. I tailored a life for myself and it fit me like my own skin. And you know what I went and did?'

'What?'

'I outgrew it.'

'It happens.'

'Some spic goes crazy with a blade and I'm out of business. You know something? It would have happened anyway, wouldn't it?'

'Sooner or later.' Just as I'd have left the police force even if a bullet of mine hadn't killed Estrellita Rivera. 'Lives change,' I said. 'It doesn't seem to do much good to fight it.'

'What am I gonna do?'

'Whatever you want.'

'Like what?'

'You could go back to school.'

He laughed. 'And study art history? Shit, I don't want to do that. Sit in classrooms again? It was bullshit then, I went into the fuckin' army to get away from it. You know what I thought about the other night?'

'What?'

'I was gonna build a fire. Pile all the masks in the middle of the floor, spill a little gas on 'em, put a match to 'em. Go out like one of those Vikings and take all my treasures with me. I can't say I thought about it for long. What I could do, I could sell all this shit. The house, the art, the car. I guess the money'd last me a time.'

'Probably.'

'But then what'd I do?'

'Suppose you set up as a dealer?'

'Are you crazy, man? Me deal drugs? I can't even pimp no more, and pimping's cleaner'n dealing.'

'Not drugs.'

'What, then?'

'The African stuff. You seem to own a lot of it and I gather the quality's high.'

'I don't own any garbage.'

'So you told me. Could you use that as your stock to get you

414

started? And do you know enough about the field to go into the business?'

He frowned, thinking. 'I was thinking about this earlier,' he said.

'And?'

'There's a lot I don't know. But there's a lot I do know, plus I got a feel for it and that's something you can't get in a classroom or out of a book. But shit, you need more'n that to be a dealer. You need a whole manner, a personality to go with it.'

'You invented Chance, didn't you?'

'So? Oh, I dig. I could invent some nigger art dealer same way I invented myself as a pimp.'

'Couldn't you?'

''Course I could.' He thought once more. 'It might work,' he said. 'I'll have to study it.'

'You got time.'

'Plenty of time.' He looked intently at me, the gold flecks glinting in his brown eyes. 'I don't know what made me hire you,' he said. 'I swear to God I don't. If I wanted to look good or what, the superpimp avenging his dead whore. If I knew where it was going to lead –'

'It probably saved a few lives,' I said. 'If that's any consolation.'

'Didn't save Kim or Sunny or Cookie.'

'Kim was already dead. And Sunny killed herself and that was her choice, and Cookie was going to be killed as soon as Marquez tracked her down. But he'd have gone on killing if I hadn't stopped him. The cops would have landed on him sooner or later but there'd have been more dead women by then. He never would have stopped. It was too much of a turn-on for him. When he came out of the bathroom with the machete, he had an erection.'

'You serious?'

'Absolutely.'

'He came at you with a hard-on?'

'Well, I was more afraid of the machete.'

'Well, yeah,' he said. 'I could see where you would be.'

He wanted to give me a bonus. I told him it wasn't necessary, that I'd been adequately paid for my time, but he insisted, and when people insist on giving me money I don't generally argue. I told him I'd taken the ivory bracelet from Kim's apartment. He laughed and said he'd forgotten all about it, that I was welcome to it and he hoped my lady would like it. It would be part of my bonus, he said, along with the cash and two pounds of his specially-blended coffee.

'And if you like the coffee,' he said, 'I can tell you where to get more of it.'

He drove me back into the city. I'd have taken the subway but he insisted he had to go to Manhattan anyway to talk to Mary Lou and Donna and Fran and get things smoothed out. 'Might as well enjoy the Seville while I can,' he said. 'Might wind up selling it to raise cash for operating expenses. Might sell the house, too.' He shook his head. 'I swear it suits me, though. Living here.'

'Get the business started with a government loan.'

'You jiving?'

'You're a minority group member. There's agencies just waiting to lend you money.'

'What a notion,' he said.

In front of my hotel he said, 'That Colombian asshole, I still can't remember his name.'

'Pedro Marquez.'

'That's him. When he registered at your hotel, is that the name he used?'

'No, it was on his ID.'

'That's what I thought. Like he was C. O. Jones and M. A. Ricone, and I wondered what dirty word he used for you.'

'He was Mr Starudo,' I said. 'Thomas Edward Starudo.'

'T. E. Starudo? *Testarudo?* That a curse in Spanish?'

'Not a curse. But it's a word.'

'What's it mean?'

'Stubborn,' I said. 'Stubborn or pig-headed.'

'Well,' he said, laughing. 'Well, hell, you can't blame him for that one, can you?'

THIRTY-FOUR

In my room I put the two pounds of coffee on the dresser, then went and made sure nobody was in the bathroom. I felt silly, like an old maid looking under the bed, but I figured it would be a while before I got over it. And I wasn't carrying a gun any more. The .32 had been impounded, of course, and the official story was that Durkin had issued it to me for my protection. He hadn't even asked how I'd really come by it. I don't suppose he cared.

I sat in my chair and looked at the place on the floor where Marquez had fallen. Some of his bloodstains remained in the rug, along with traces of the chalk marks they place around dead bodies.

I wondered if I'd be able to sleep in the room. I could always get them to change it, but I'd been here a few years now and I'd grown accustomed to it. Chance had said it suited me, and I suppose it did.

How did I feel about having killed him?

I thought it over and decided I felt fine. I didn't really know anything about the son of a bitch. To understand all is to forgive all, they say, and maybe if I knew his whole story I'd understand where the blood lust came from. But I didn't have to forgive him. That was God's job not mine.

And I'd been able to squeeze the trigger. And there'd been no ricochets, no bad bounces, no bullets that went wide. Four shots, all in the chest. Good detective work, good decoy work, and good shooting at the end.

Not bad.

I went downstairs and around the corner. I walked to Armstrong's, glanced in the window, but went on walking to Fifty-eighth and around the corner and halfway down the block. I went into Joey Farrell's and stood at the bar.

Not much of a crowd. Music on the jukebox, some baritone crooner backed up with a lot of strings.

'Double Early Times,' I said. 'With water back.'

I stood there, not really thinking of anything, while the bearded barman poured the drink and drew the chaser and set them both before me. I had placed a ten dollar bill on the counter. He cracked it, brought my change.

I looked at the drink. Light danced in the rich amber fluid. I reached for it, and a soft inner voice murmured *Welcome home.*

I withdrew my hand. I left the drink on the bar and took a dime from my pile of change. I went to the phone and dropped the dime and dialed Jan's number.

No answer.

Fine, I thought. I'd kept my promise. Of course I might have misdialed, or the phone company might have fucked up. Such things have been known to happen.

I put the dime back in the slot and dialed again. I let it ring a dozen times.

No answer.

Fair enough. I got my dime back and returned to the bar. My change was as I'd left it, and so were the two glasses in front of me, the bourbon and the water.

I thought, *Why?*

The case was finished, solved, wrapped up. The killer would never kill anyone again. I had done a whole lot of things right and felt very good about my role in the proceedings. I wasn't nervous, I wasn't anxious, I wasn't depressed. I was fine, for Christ's sake.

And there was a double shot of bourbon on the bar in front of me. I hadn't wanted a drink, I hadn't even thought of a drink, and here I was with a drink in front of me and I was going to swallow it.

Why? What the hell was the matter with me?

If I drank the fucking drink I would end up dead or in the hospital. It might take a day or a week or a month but that was how it would play. I knew that. And I didn't want to be dead and I didn't want to go to the hospital, but here I was in a gin joint with a drink in front of me.

Because –

Because what?

Because –

I left the drink on the bar. I left my change on the bar. I got out of there.

At half past eight I walked down the flight of basement stairs and into the meeting room at St Paul's. I got a cup of coffee and some cookies and took a seat.

I thought, You almost drank. You're eleven days sober and you went into a bar you had no reason to be in and ordered a drink for no reason at all. You almost picked up the drink, you were that close to it, you almost blew eleven days after the way you sweated to get them. What the hell is the matter with you?

The chairman read the preamble and introduced the speaker. I sat there and tried to listen to his story and I couldn't. My mind kept returning to the flat reality of that glass of bourbon. I hadn't wanted it, I hadn't even thought about it, and yet I'd been drawn to it like iron filings to a magnet.

I thought, My name is Matt and I think I'm going crazy.

The speaker finished what he was saying. I joined in the applause. I went to the bathroom during the break, less out of need than to avoid having to talk to anybody. I came back to the room and got yet another cup of coffee that I neither needed nor wanted. I thought about leaving the coffee and going back to my hotel. The hell, I'd been up two days and a night without a break. Some sleep would do me more good than a meeting I couldn't pay attention to in the first place.

I kept my coffee cup and took it to my seat and sat down.

I sat there during the discussion. The words people spoke rolled over me like waves. I just sat there, unable to hear a thing.

Then it was my turn.

'My name is Matt,' I said, and paused, and started over. 'My name is Matt,' I said, 'and I'm an alcoholic.'

And the goddamnedest thing happened. I started to cry.

WHEN THE SACRED GINMILL CLOSES

And so we've had another night
Of poetry and poses
And each man knows he'll be alone
When the sacred ginmill closes

DAVE VAN RONK

ONE

The windows at Morrissey's were painted black. The blast was loud enough and close enough to rattle them. It chopped off conversation in midsyllable, froze a waiter in midstride, making of him a statue with a tray of drinks on his shoulder and one foot in the air. The great round noise died out like dust settling, and for a long moment afterward the room remained hushed, as if with respect.

Someone said, 'Jesus Christ,' and a lot of people let out the breath they'd been holding. At our table, Bobby Ruslander reached for a cigarette and said, 'Sounded like a bomb.'

Skip Devoe said, 'Cherry bomb.'

'Is that all?'

'It's enough,' Skip said. 'Cherry bomb's major ordnance. Same charge had a metal casing instead of a paper wrapper, you'd have a weapon instead of a toy. You light one of those little mothers and forget to let go of it, you're gonna have to learn to do a lot of basic things left-handed.'

'Sounded like more than a firecracker,' Bobby insisted. 'Like dynamite or a grenade or something. Sounded like fucking World War Three, if you want to know.'

'Get the actor,' Skip said affectionately. 'Don't you love this guy? Fighting it out in the trenches, storming the windswept hills, slogging through the mud. Bobby Ruslander, battle-scarred veteran of a thousand campaigns.'

'You mean *bottle*-scarred,' somebody said.

'Fucking actor,' Skip said, reaching to rumple Bobby's hair. '"Hark I hear the cannon's roar." You know that joke?'

'I told *you* the joke.'

'"Hark I hear the cannon's roar." When'd you ever hear a shot fired in anger? Last time they had a war,' he said, 'Bobby brought a note from his shrink. "Dear Uncle Sam, Please excuse Bobby's absence, bullets make him crazy."'

'My old man's idea,' Bobby said.

'But you tried to talk him out of it. "Gimmie a gun," you said. "I wanna serve my country."'

Bobby laughed. He had one arm around his girl and picked up his drink with his free hand. He said, 'All I said was it sounded like dynamite to me.'

Skip shook his head. 'Dynamite's different. They're all different, different kinds of a bang. Dynamite's like one loud note, and a flatter sound than a cherry bomb. They all make a different sound. Grenade's completely different, it's like a chord.'

'The lost chord,' somebody said, and somebody else said, 'Listen to this, it's poetry.'

'I was going to call my joint Horseshoes & Hand Grenades,' Skip said. 'You know what they say, coming close don't count outside of horseshoes and hand grenades.'

'It's a good name,' Billie Keegan said.

'My partner hated it,' Skip said. 'Fucking Kasabian, he said it didn't sound like a saloon, sounded like some kind of candy-ass boutique, some store in SoHo sells toys for private-school kids. I don't know, though. Horseshoes & Hand Grenades, I still like the sound of it.'

'Horseshit and Hand Jobs,' somebody said.

'Maybe Kasabian was right, if that's what everybody woulda wound up calling it.' To Bobby he said, 'You want to talk about the different sounds they make, you should hear a mortar. Someday get Kasabian to tell you about the mortar. It's a hell of a story.'

'I'll do that.'

'Horseshoes & Hand Grenades,' Skip said. 'That's what we shoulda called the joint.'

Instead he and his partner had called their place Miss Kitty's. Most people assumed a reference to 'Gunsmoke,' but their inspiration had been a whorehouse in Saigon. I did most of my own drinking at Jimmy Armstrong's, on Ninth Avenue between Fifty-seventh and Fifty-eighth. Miss Kitty's was on Ninth just below Fifty-sixth, and it was a little larger and more boisterous than I liked. I stayed away from it on the weekends, but late on a weekday night when the crowd thinned down and the noise level dropped, it wasn't a bad place to be.

I'd been in there earlier that night. I had gone first to Armstrong's, and around two-thirty there were only four of us left – Billie Keegan behind the bar and I in front of it and a couple of nurses who were pretty far gone on Black Russians. Billie locked up and the nurses staggered off into the night and the two of us went down to Miss Kitty's, and a little before four Skip closed up, too, and a handful of us went on down to Morrissey's.

Morrissey's wouldn't close until nine or ten in the morning. The legal closing hour for bars in the city of New York is 4:00 a.m., an hour earlier on Saturday nights, but Morrissey's was an illegal establishment and was thus not bound by regulations of that sort. It was one flight up from street level in one of a block of four-story brick houses on Fifty-first Street between Eleventh and Twelfth Avenues. About a third of the houses on the block were abandoned, their windows boarded up or broken, some of their entrances closed off with concrete block.

The Morrissey brothers owned their building. It couldn't have cost them much. They lived in the upper two stories, let out the ground floor to an Irish amateur theater group, and sold beer and whiskey after hours on the second floor. They had removed all of the interior walls on the second floor to create a large open space. They'd stripped one wall to the brick, scraped and sanded and urethaned the wide pine floors, installed some soft lighting and decorated the walls with some framed Aer Lingus posters and a copy of Pearse's 1916 proclamation of the Irish Republic ('Irishmen and Irishwomen, in the name of God and of the dead generations ...'). There was a small service bar along one wall, and there were twenty or thirty square tables with butcher-block tops.

We sat at two tables pushed together. Skip Devoe was there, and Billie Keegan, the night bartender at Armstrong's. And Bobby Ruslander, and Bobby's girl for the evening, a sleepy-eyed redhead named Helen. And a fellow named Eddie Grillo who tended bar at an Italian restaurant in the West Forties, and another fellow named Vince who was a sound technician or something like that at CBS Television.

I was drinking bourbon, and it must have been either Jack Daniel's or Early Times, as those were the only brands the Morrisseys stocked. They also carried three or four scotches, Canadian Club, and one brand each of gin and vodka. Two beers, Bud and Heineken. A Cognac and a couple of odd cordials. Kahlúa, I suppose, because a lot of people were drinking Black Russians that year. Three brands of Irish whiskey, Bushmill's and Jameson and one called Power's, which nobody ever seemed to order but to which the Morrissey brothers were partial. You'd have thought they'd carry Irish beer, Guinness at least, but Tim Pat Morrissey had told me once that he didn't fancy the bottled Guinness, that it was awful stuff, that he only liked the draft stout and only on the other side of the Atlantic.

They were big men, the Morrisseys, with broad high foreheads and full rust-colored beards. They wore black trousers and highly polished black brogans and white shirts with the sleeves rolled to the elbow, and they wore white butcher's aprons that covered them to their knees. The waiter, a slim, clean-shaven youth, wore the same outfit, but on him it looked like a costume. I think he may have been a cousin. I think he'd have had to have been some sort of blood kin to work there.

They were open seven days a week, from around 2:00 a.m. to nine or ten. They charged three dollars for a drink, which was higher than the bars but reasonable compared to most after-hour joints, and they poured a good drink. Beer was two dollars. They would mix most of the common drinks, but it was no place to order a pousse-café.

I don't think the police ever gave the Morrisseys a hard time. While there was no neon sign out front, the place wasn't the best-kept secret in the neighborhood. The cops knew it was there, and that particular evening I noticed a couple of patrolmen from Midtown North and a detective I'd known years back in Brooklyn. There were two black men in the room and I recognized both of them; one I'd seen at ringside at a lot of fights, while his companion was a state senator. I'm sure the Morrissey brothers paid money to stay open, but they had some strong connections beyond the money they paid, ties to the local political clubhouse.

They didn't water the booze and they poured a good drink. Wasn't that as much of a character reference as any man needed?

Outside, another cherry bomb exploded. It was farther off, a block or two away, and it didn't slam the door shut on any conversations. At our table, the CBS guy complained that they were rushing the season. He said, 'The Fourth isn't until Friday, right? Today's what, the first?'

'It's been the second for the past two hours.'

'So that's still two days. What's the hurry?'

'They get these fucking fireworks and they get the itch,' Bobby Ruslander said. 'You know who's the worst? The fucking chinks. For a while there I was seein' this girl, she lived down near Chinatown. You'd get Roman candles in the middle of the night, you'd get cherry bombs, anything. Not just July, any time of the year. Comes to firecrackers, they're all little kids down there.'

'My partner wanted to call the joint Little Saigon,' Skip said. 'I told him, John, for Christ's sake, people're gonna think it's a Chinese restaurant, you're gonna get family groups from Rego Park ordering moo goo gai pan and two from Column B. He said what the hell's Chinese about Saigon? I told him, I said, John, you know that and I know that, but when it comes to the people from Rego Park, John, to them a slope is a slope and it all adds up to moo goo gai pan.'

Billie said, 'What about the people in Park Slope?'

'What about the people in Park Slope?' Skip frowned, thinking it over. 'The people in Park Slope,' he said. '*Fuck* the people in Park Slope.'

Bobby Ruslander's girl Helen said, very seriously, that she had an aunt in Park Slope. Skip looked at her. I picked up my glass. It was empty, and I looked around for the beardless waiter or one of the brothers.

So I was looking at the door when it flew open. The brother who kept the door downstairs stumbled through it and careened into a table. Drinks spilled and a chair tipped over.

Two men burst into the room behind him. One was about five-nine, the other a couple inches shorter. Both were thin. Both wore blue jeans and tennis sneakers. The taller one had on a baseball jacket, the shorter one a royal-blue nylon windbreaker. Both had billed baseball caps on their heads and blood-red kerchiefs knotted around their faces, forming triangular wedges that hid their mouths and cheeks.

Each had a gun in his hand. One had a snub-nosed revolver, the other a long-barreled automatic. The one with the automatic raised it and fired two shots into the stamped-tin ceiling. It didn't sound like a cherry bomb or a hand grenade, either.

They got in and out in a hurry. One went behind the bar and emerged with the Garcia y Vega cigar box where Tim Pat kept the night's receipts. There was a glass jar on top of the bar with a hand-lettered sign soliciting contributions for the families of IRA men imprisoned in the North of Ireland, and he scooped the bills out of it, leaving the silver.

While he was doing this, the taller man held a gun on the Morrisseys and had them turn out their pockets. He took the cash from their wallets and a roll of bills from Tim Pat. The shorter man set down the cigar box for a moment and went to the back of the room, removing a framed Aer Lingus poster of the Cliffs of Moher from the wall to expose a locked cupboard. He shot the lock off and withdrew a metal strongbox, tucked it unopened under his arm, went back to pick up the cigar box again, and ducked out the door and raced down the stairs.

His partner continued to hold the Morrisseys at gunpoint until he'd left the building. He had the gun centered at Tim Pat's chest, and for a moment I thought he was going to shoot. His gun was the long-barreled automatic, he'd been the one who put two bullets in the tin ceiling, and if he shot Tim Pat, he seemed unlikely to miss.

There was nothing I could do about it.

Then the moment passed. The gunman breathed out through his mouth, the red kerchief billowing with his breath. He backed to the door and out, fled down the stairs.

No one moved.

Then Tim Pat held a brief whispered conference with one of his brothers, the one who'd been keeping the door downstairs. After a moment the brother nodded and walked to the gaping cupboard at the back of the room. He closed it and hung the Cliffs of Moher poster where it had been.

Tim Pat spoke to his other brother, then cleared his throat. 'Gentlemen,' he said, and smoothed his beard with his big right hand. 'Gentlemen, if I may take a moment to explain the performance ye just witnessed. Two good friends of ours came in to ask for the loan of a couple of dollars, which we lent them with pleasure. None of us recognized them or took note of their appearance, and I'm sure no one in this room would know them should we by God's grace meet up with them again.' His fingertips dabbed at his broad forehead, moved again to groom his beard. 'Gentlemen,' he said, 'ye'd honor me and my brothers by havin' the next drink with us.'

And the Morrisseys bought a round for the house. Bourbon for me. Jameson for Billie Keegan, scotch for Skip, brandy for Bobby, and a scotch sour for his date. A beer for the guy from CBS, a brandy for Eddie the bartender. Drinks all around – for the cops, for the black politicians, for a roomful of waiters and bartenders and night people. Nobody got up and left, not with the house buying a round, not with a couple of guys out there with masks and guns.

The clean-shaven cousin and two of the brothers served the drinks. Tim Pat stood at the side with his arms folded on his white apron and his face expressionless. After everyone had been served, one of his brothers whispered something to Tim Pat and showed him the glass jar, empty except for a handful of coins. Tim Pat's face darkened.

'Gentlemen,' he said, and the room quieted down. 'Gentlemen, in the moment of confusion there was money taken as was contributed to Norad, money for the relief of the misfortunate wives and children of political prisoners in the North. Our loss is our own, myself and my brothers, and we'll speak no more of it, but them in the North with no money for food ...' He stopped for breath, continued in a lower voice. 'We'll let the jar pass amongst ye,' he said, 'and if some of ye should care to contribute, the blessings of God on ye.'

I probably stayed another half-hour, not much more than that. I drank the drink Tim Pat bought and one more besides, and that was enough. Billie and Skip left when I did. Bobby and his girl were going to stick around for a while, Vince had already left, and Eddie had joined another table and was trying to make points with a tall girl who waitressed at O'Neal's.

The sky was light, the streets empty still, silent with early dawn. Skip said, 'Well, Norad made a couple of bucks, anyway. There couldn't have been a whole lot Frank and Jesse took out of the jar, and the crowd coughed up a fair amount to fill it up again.'

'Frank and Jesse?'

'Well, those red hankies, for Christ's sake. You know, Frank and Jesse James. But that was ones and fives they took out of the jar, and it was all tens and twenties got put back into it, so the poor wives and wee childer in the North came out all right.'

Billie said, 'What do you figure the Morrisseys lost?'

'Jesus, I don't know. That strongbox could have been full of insurance policies and pictures of their sainted mither, but that would be a surprise all around, wouldn't it? I bet they walked with enough to send a lot of guns to the bold lads in Derry and Belfast.'

'You think the robbers were IRA?'

'The hell,' he said. He threw his cigarette into the gutter. 'I think the Morrisseys are. I think that's where their money goes. I figure—'

'Hey, guys! Wait up, huh?'

We turned. A man named Tommy Tillary was hailing us from the stoop of the Morrisseys' house. He was a heavyset fellow, full in the cheeks and jowls, big in the chest, big in the belly, too. He was wearing a summer-weight burgundy blazer and a pair of white pants. He was wearing a tie, too. He almost always wore a tie.

The woman with him was short and slender, with light brown hair that showed red highlights. She was wearing tight faded jeans and a pink button-down shirt with the sleeves rolled up. She looked very tired, and a little drunk.

He said, 'You guys know Carolyn? Course you do.' We all said hello to her. He said, 'I got a car parked around the corner, plenty of room for everybody. Drop you guys off.'

'It's a nice morning,' Billie said. 'I think I'd as soon walk, Tommy.'

'Oh, yeah?'

Skip and I said the same. 'Walk off some of the booze,' Skip said. 'Wind down, get ready for bed.'

'You sure? No trouble to run you home.' We were sure. 'Well, you mind walking as far as the car with us? That little demonstration back there, makes a person nervous.'

'Sure thing, Tom.'

'Nice morning, huh? Be a hot one today but it's beautiful right now. I swear I thought he was gonna shoot whatsisname, Tim Pat. You see the look on his face at the end there?'

'There was a moment,' Billie said, 'it could have gone either way.'

'I was thinking, there's gonna be shooting, back and forth, I'm looking to see which table to dive under. Fucking little tables, there's not a lot of cover, you know?'

'Not too much.'

'And I'm a big target, right? What are you smoking, Skip, Camels? Lemme try one of those if you don't mind. I smoke these filters and this time of night they got no taste left to them. Thanks. Was I imagining things or was there a couple of cops in the room?'

'There were a few, anyway.'

'They got to carry their guns on or off duty, isn't that right?'

He'd asked the question of me, and I agreed that there was a regulation to that effect.

'You'd think one of 'em would have tried something.'

'You mean draw down on the holdup men?'

'Something.'

'It's a good way to get people killed,' I said. 'Throwing lead around a crowded room like that.'

'I guess there'd be a danger of ricochets.'

430

'Why'd you say that?'

He looked at me, surprised by the snap in my tone. 'Why, the brick walls, I guess,' he said. 'Even shooting into the tin ceiling the way he did, a bullet could glance off, do some damage. Couldn't it?'

'I guess,' I said. A cab cruised by, its off-duty light lit, a passenger sharing the front seat with the driver. I said. 'On or off duty, a cop wouldn't start anything in a situation like that unless someone else had already started shooting. There were a couple of bulls in the room tonight who probably had their hands on their guns toward the end there. If that fellow'd shot Tim Pat, he'd probably have been dodging bullets on the way out the door. *If* anybody had a clear shot at him.'

'And if they were sober enough to see straight,' Skip put in.

'Makes sense,' Tommy said. 'Matt, didn't you break up a bar holdup a couple of years ago? Somebody was saying something about it.'

'That was a little different,' I said. 'They'd already shot the bartender dead before I made a move. And I didn't spray bullets around inside, I went out into the street after them.' And I thought about that, and missed the next few sentences of the conversation. When I came back into focus Tommy was saying he'd expected to be held up.

'Lot of people in that room tonight,' he said. 'Night workers, people closed up their places and carrying cash on 'em. You'd think they would have passed the hat, wouldn't you?'

'I guess they were in a hurry.'

'I only got a few hundred on me, but I'd rather keep it than give it to a guy with a hanky on his face. You feel relieved not to get robbed, you're real generous when they pass the jug for whatchacallit, Norad? I gave twenty bucks to the widows and orphans, didn't think twice.'

'It's all staged,' Billie Keegan suggested. 'The guys with the handkerchiefs are friends of the family, they put on this little act every couple of weeks to boost the Norad take.'

'Jesus,' Tommy said, laughing at the idea. 'Be something, wouldn't it? There's my car, the Riv. Big boat'll carry everybody easy, you want to change your mind and let me run you on home.'

We all stayed with our decision to walk. His car was a maroon Buick Riviera with a white leather interior. He let Carolyn in, then walked around the car and unlocked his door, making a face at her failure to lean across the seat and unlock the door for him.

After they drove off, Billie said, 'They were at Armstrong's until one, one-thirty. I didn't expect to see 'em again tonight. I hope he's not driving back to Brooklyn tonight.'

'Is that where they live?'

'Where *he* lives,' he told Skip. 'She's here in the neighborhood. He's a married guy. Doesn't he wear a ring?'

'I never noticed.'

'Caro-lyn from the Caro-line,' Billie said. 'That's how he introduces her. She was sure shitfaced tonight, wasn't she? When he left earlier I thought for sure he was takin' her home – and come to think of it I guess he was. She was wearin' a dress earlier tonight, wasn't she, Matt?'

'I don't remember.'

'I could swear she was. Office clothes, anyway, not jeans and a Brooks shirt like she had on now. Took her home, gave her a bounce, then they got thirsty and by that time the stores were closed, so off we go to the neighborhood after-hours, T. P. Morrissey, Prop. What do you think, Matt? Have I got the makings of a detective?'

'You're doing fine.'

'He put on the same clothes but she changed. Now the question is will he go home to the wife or sleep over at Carolyn's and show up at the office tomorrow in the same outfit. The only problem is, who gives a shit?'

'I was just going to ask that,' Skip said.

'Yeah. One thing *he* asked, I'll ask it myself. Why didn't they stick up the customers tonight? There must have been a lot of guys carryin' a few hundred each and a couple with more than that.'

'Not worth it.'

'That's a few grand we're talking about.'

'I know,' Skip said. 'It's also another twenty minutes if you're gonna do it right, and that's in a room full of drunks with God knows how many of them carrying guns. I bet there were fifteen guns in that room.'

'Are you serious?'

'I'm not only serious, I bet I'm guessing low. For openers you got three or four cops. You got Eddie Grillo, right at our table.'

'Eddie carries a piece?'

'Eddie runs around with some pretty heavy guys, not even talking about who owns the joint where he works. There was a

432

guy named Chuck, I don't really know him, works at Polly's Cage—'

'I know who you mean. He walks around with a gun on him?'

'Either that or he walks around with a permanent hardon and he's built funny. Believe me, there's a whole lot of guys walk around packing iron. You tell a whole roomful to reach for their wallets, some of them'll reach for their guns instead. Meanwhile they're in and out in what, five minutes tops? I don't think it was five minutes from the door flying open and the bullets in the ceiling until they're out the door and Tim Pat's standing there with his arms crossed and a scowl on his face.'

'That's a point.'

'And whatever they'd of got from people's wallets, that's small change.'

'You figure the box was that heavy? What do you figure it held?'

Skip shrugged. 'Twenty grand.'

'Seriously?'

'Twenty grand, fifty grand, pick a number.'

'IRA money, you were saying earlier.'

'Well, what else do you figure they spend it on, Bill? I don't know what they take in but they do a nice business seven days a week and where's the overhead? They probably got the building for back taxes, and they live in half of it, so they got no rent to pay and no real payroll to come up with. I'm sure they don't report any income or pay any taxes, unless they pretend that playhouse on the ground floor shows a profit and pay a token tax on that. They have to be dragging ten or twenty grand a week out of that place and what do you think they spend it on?'

'They have to pay off to stay open,' I put in.

'Payoffs and political contributions, of course, but not ten or twenty K a week's worth. And they don't drive big cars, and they never go out and spend a dollar in somebody else's joint. I don't see Tim Pat buying emeralds for some sweet young thing, or his brothers putting grams of coke up their Irish noses.'

'Up your Irish nose,' Billie Keegan said.

'I liked Tim Pat's little speech, and then buying a round. Far as I know, that's the first time the Morrisseys ever set 'em up for the house.'

'Fucking Irish,' Billie said.

'Jesus, Keegan, you're drunk again.'

'Praise be to God, you're right.'

433

'What do you think, Matt? Did Tim Pat recognize Frank and Jesse?'

I thought about it. 'I don't know. What he was saying added up to "Keep out of this and we'll settle it ourselves." Maybe it was political.'

'Fucking-A right,' Billie said. 'The Reform Democrats were behind it.'

'Maybe Protestants,' Skip said.

'Funny,' Billie said. 'They didn't look Protestant.'

'Or some other IRA faction. There's different factions, aren't there?'

'Of course you rarely see Protestants with handkerchiefs over their faces,' Billie said. 'They usually tuck them in the breast pocks, the breast pockets—'

'Jesus, Keegan.'

'Fucking Protestants,' Billie said.

'Fucking Billie Keegan,' Skip said. 'Matt, we better walk this asshole home.'

'Fucking guns,' Billie said, back on that track suddenly. 'Go out for a nightcap and you're surrounded by fucking guns. You carry a gun, Matt?'

'Not me, Billie.'

'Really?' He put a hand on my shoulder for support. 'But you're a cop.'

'Used to be.'

'Private cop now. Even the rent-a-cop, security guard in a bookstore, guy tells you to check your briefcase on the way in, he's got a gun.'

'They're generally just for show.'

'You mean I won't get shot if I walk off with the Modern Library edition of *The Scarlet Letter?* You should of told me before I went and paid for it. You really don't carry a gun?'

'Another illusion shattered,' Skip said.

'What about your buddy the actor?' Billie demanded of him. 'Is little Bobby a gunslinger?'

'Who, Ruslander?'

'He'd shoot you in the back,' Billie said.

'If Ruslander carried a gun,' Skip said, 'it'd be a stage prop. It'd shoot blanks.'

'Shoot you in the back,' Billie insisted. 'Like whatsisname, Bobby the Kid.'

'You mean Billy the Kid.'

'Who are you to tell me what I mean? Does he?'

434

'Does he what?'

'Pack a piece, for Christ's sake. Isn't that what we've been talking about?'

'Jesus, Keegan, don't ask *me* what we've been talking about.'

'You mean you weren't paying attention either? *Jeezus.*'

Billie Keegan lived in a high-rise on Fifty-sixth near Eighth. He straightened up as we approached his building and appeared sober enough when he greeted the doorman. 'Matt, Skip,' he said. 'See you guys.'

'Keegan's all right,' Skip told me.

'He's a good man.'

'Not as drunk as he pretended, either. He was just riding it, enjoying himself.'

'Sure.'

'We keep a gun behind the bar at Miss Kitty's, you know. We got held up, the place I used to work before John and I opened up together. I was behind the stick in this place on Second Avenue in the Eighties, guy walked in, white guy, stuck a gun in my face and got the money from the register. Held up the customers, too. Only have five, six people in the joint at the time, but he took wallets off of them. I think he took their watches too, if I remember it right. Class operation.'

'Sounds it.'

'All the time I was being a hero in Nam, fucking Special Forces, I never had to stand and look at the wrong end of a gun. I didn't feel anything while it was going on, but later I felt angry, you know what I mean? I was in a rage. Went out, bought a gun, ever since then it's been with me when I been working. At that joint, and now in Miss Kitty's. I still think we should have called it Horseshoes & Hand Grenades.'

'You got a permit for it?'

'The gun?' He shook his head. 'It's not registered. You work saloons, you don't have too much trouble knowing where to go to buy a gun. I spent two days asking around and on the third day I was a hundred dollars poorer. We got robbed once since we opened the place. John was working, he left the gun right where it was and handed over whatever was in the till. He didn't rob the customers. John figured he was a junkie, said he didn't even think of the gun until the guy was out the door. Maybe, or maybe he thought of it and decided against it. I probably would have done the same thing, or maybe not. You don't really know until it happens, do you?'

435

'No.'

'You really haven't had a piece since you quit the cops? They say after a guy gets in the habit he feels naked without it.'

'Not me. I felt like I laid down a burden.'

'Oh, lawdie, I'se gwine lay my burden down. Like you lightened up some, huh?'

'Something like that.'

'Yeah. He didn't mean anything, incidentally. Talking about ricochets.'

'Huh? Oh, Tommy.'

'Tough Tommy Tillary. Something of an asshole, but not a bad guy. Tough Tommy, it's like calling a big guy Tiny. I'm sure he didn't mean anything.'

'I'm sure you're right.'

'Tough Tommy. There's something else they call him.'

'Telephone Tommy.'

'Or Tommy Telephone, right. He sells shit over the phone. I didn't think grown men did that. I thought it was for house-wives and they wind up making thirty-five cents an hour.'

'I gather it can be lucrative.'

'Evidently. You saw the car. We all saw the car. We didn't get to see her open the door for him, but we got to see the car. Matt, you want to come up and have one more before we call it a day? I got scotch and bourbon, I probably got some food in the fridge.'

'I think I'll just get on home, Skip. But thanks.'

'I don't blame you.' He drew on his cigarette. He lived at the Parc Vendome, across the street and a few doors west of my hotel. He threw his cigarette away and we shook hands, and five or six shots sounded a block or so from us.

'Jesus,' he said. 'Was that gunfire or half a dozen little firecrackers? Could you say for sure?'

'No.'

'Neither could I. Probably firecrackers, considering what day it is. Or the Morrisseys caught up with Frank and Jesse, or I don't know what. This is the second, right? July second?'

'I guess so.'

'Gonna be some summer,' he said.

TWO

Ll of this happened a long time ago.

It was the summer of '75, and in a larger context it seems in memory to have been a season in which nothing very important happened. Nixon's resignation had been a year earlier, and the coming year would bring the convention and the campaigns, the Olympics, the Bicentennial.

Meanwhile Ford was in the White House, his presence oddly comforting if not terribly convincing. A fellow named Abe Beame was in Gracie Mansion, although I never had the feeling he really believed he was mayor of New York, any more than Gerry Ford believed he was president of the United States of America.

Somewhere along the way Ford declined to help the city through a financial crisis, and the *News* headline read, '*Ford to City: Drop Dead!*'

I remember the headline but I don't recall whether it ran before, during or after that summer. I read that headline. I rarely missed the *News*, picking up an early edition on my way back to my hotel at night or scanning a later one over breakfast. I read the *Times* now and then as well, if there was a story I was following, and more often than not I'd pick up a *Post* during the afternoon. I never paid much attention to the international news or the political stuff, or anything much aside from sports and local crime, but I was at least peripherally aware of what was going on in the world, and it's funny how utterly it's all vanished.

What do I remember? Well, three months after the stickup at Morrissey's, Cincinnati would take a seven-game Series from the Red Sox. I remember that, and Fisk's home run in game six, and Pete Rose playing throughout as if all of human destiny rode on every pitch. Neither of the New York teams made the playoffs, but beyond that I couldn't tell you how they did, and I know I went to half a dozen games. I took my boys to Shea a couple of times, and I went a few times with friends. The Stadium was being renovated that year and both the Mets and Yanks were at Shea. Billie Keegan and I watched the Yankees play somebody, I remember, and they stopped the game because some idiots were throwing garbage onto the field.

Was Reggie Jackson with the Yankees that year? He was still in Oakland playing for Charlie Finley in '73, I remember the Series, the Mets losing badly. But when did Steinbrenner buy him for the Yankees?

What else? Boxing?

Did Ali fight that summer? I watched the second Norton fight on closed circuit, the one where Ali left the ring with a broken jaw and an unearned decision, but that was at least a year earlier, wasn't it? And then I'd seen Ali up close, ringside at the Garden. Earnie Shavers had fought Jimmy Ellis knocking him out early in the first round. For God's sake, I remember the punch that took Ellis out, remember the look on his wife's face two rows away from me, but when was that?

Not in '75, I'm sure of that. I must have gone to the fights that summer. I wonder who I watched.

Does it matter? I don't suppose it does. If it did I could go to the library and check the *Times Index*, or just hunt up a *World Almanac* for the year. But I already remember everything I really need to remember.

Skip Devoe and Tommy Tillary. Theirs are the faces I see when I think of the summer of '75. Between them, they were the season.

Were they friends of mine?

They were, but with a qualification. They were saloon friends. I rarely saw them – or anyone else, in those days – other than in a room where strangers gathered to drink liquor. I was still drinking then, of course, and I was at a point where the booze did (or seemed to do) more for me than it did to me.

A couple of years previously, my world had narrowed as if with a will of its own until it encompassed only a few square blocks south and west of Columbus Circle. I had left my marriage after a dozen years and two children, moving from Syosset, which is on Long Island, to my hotel, which was on West Fifty-seventh Street between Eighth and Ninth Avenues. I had at about the same time left the New York Police Department, where I'd put in about as many years with about as much to show for it. I supported myself, and sent checks irregularly to

Syosset, by doing things for people. I was not a private detective – private detectives are licensed and fill out reports and file tax returns. So I did favors for people, and they gave me money, and my rent always got paid and there was always money for booze, and intermittently I was able to put a check in the mail for Anita and the boys.

My world, as I said, had shrunk geographically, and within that area it confined itself largely to the room where I slept and the bars where I spent most of my waking hours. There was Morrissey's, but not all that often. I was off to bed more often than not by one or two, sometimes hung on until the bars closed, and only rarely went to an after-hours and made a full night of it.

There was Miss Kitty's, Skip Devoe's place. On the same block as my hotel, there was Polly's Cage, with its red-flocked bordello wallpaper and its crowd of after-work drinkers who thinned out by ten or ten-thirty; and McGovern's, a drab narrow room with unshielded overhead lights and customers who never said a word. I stopped in sometimes for a quick drink on a hard morning, and the bartender's hand shook when he poured it, as often as not.

On the same block there were two French restaurants, one next to the other. One of them, Mont-St-Michel, was always three-quarters empty. I took women there for dinner a few times over the years, and stopped in alone once in a while for a drink at the bar. The establishment next door had a good reputation and did a better business, but I don't think I ever set foot inside it.

There was a place over on Tenth Avenue called the Slate; they got a lot of cops from Midtown North and John Jay College, and I went there when I was in the mood for that kind of crowd. The steaks were good there, and the surroundings comfortable. There was a Martin's Bar on Broadway and Sixtieth with low-priced drinks and good corned beef and ham on the steam table; they had a big color set over the bar, and it wasn't a bad place to watch a ball game.

There was O'Neal's Baloon across from Lincoln Center – an old law still on the books that year prohibited calling a place a saloon, and they didn't know that when they ordered the sign, so they changed the first letter and said the hell with it. I'd stop in once in a while during the afternoon, but it was too trendy and upbeat at night. There was Antares and Spiro's, a Greek place at the corner of Ninth and Fifty-seventh. Not really my

439

kind of place, a lot of guys with bushy moustaches drinking ouzo, but I passed it every night on the way home and sometimes I'd stop in for a quick one.

There was the all-night newsstand at the corner of Fifty-seventh and Eighth. I generally bought the paper there, unless I bought it from the shopping-bag lady who hawked them on the sidewalk in front of the 400 Deli. She bought them for a quarter each from the newsstand – I think they were all a quarter that year, or maybe the *News* was twenty cents – and she sold them for the same price, which is a tough way to make a living. Sometimes I'd give her a buck and tell her to keep the change. Her name was Mary Alice Redfield, but I never knew that until a couple of years later, when someone stabbed her to death.

There was a coffee shop called the Red Flame and there was the 400 Deli. There were a couple of okay pizza stands, and there was a place that sold cheese steaks that nobody ever went to twice.

There was a spaghetti joint called Ralph's and a couple of Chinese restaurants. There was a Thai place that Skip Devoe was crazy about. There was Joey Farrell's on Fifty-eighth Street – they'd just opened the past winter. There was, hell, there were a lot of joints.

Mostly there was Armstrong's.

Christ, I lived there. I had my room to sleep in and I had other bars and restaurants to go to, but for a few years there, Jimmy Armstrong's was home to me. People who were looking for me knew to check for me there, and sometimes they called Armstrong's before they called the hotel. The place opened up around eleven, with a Filipino kid named Dennis behind the stick days. Billie Keegan took over around seven and closed at two or three or four, depending on the crowd and how he was feeling. (That was the weekday routine. There were different day and night bartenders on weekends, and the turnover among them was high.)

Waitresses came and went. They got acting jobs or broke up with their boyfriends or got new boyfriends or moved to Los Angeles or went home to Sioux Falls or had a fight with the Dominican kid in the kitchen or got fired for stealing or quit or got pregnant. Jimmy himself wasn't around much that summer. I think that was the year he was looking to buy land in North Carolina.

What can I say about the place? A long bar on the right hand side as you came in, tables on the left. Blue-checkered cloths on them. Dark wood-paneled walls. Pictures on the walls, and framed advertisements from old magazines. A deer's head was mounted incongruously on the back wall; my favourite table was right under the thing, so I didn't have to look at it.

The crowd was a mixed bag. Doctors and nurses from Roosevelt Hospital across the street. Professors and students from Fordham. People from the television studios – CBS was a block away, and ABC a short walk. And people who lived nearby, or kept shops in the neighborhood. A couple of classical musicians. A writer. Two Lebanese brothers who had just opened a shoe store.

Not many kids. When I first moved into the neighborhood Armstrong's had a jukebox with a nice selection of jazz and country blues, but Jimmy took it out early on and replaced it with a stereo system and classical music on tape. That kept the younger crowd out, to the delight of the waitresses who hated the kids for staying late, ordering little, and tipping hardly at all. It also kept the noise level down and made the room more suitable for long-haul maintenance drinking.

Which was what I was there for. I wanted to keep an edge on but I didn't want to get drunk, except once in a while. I mostly mixed my bourbon with coffee, moving to straight booze toward the end of an evening. I could read a paper there, and have a hamburger or a full meal, and as much or as little conversation as I was in the mood for. I wasn't always there all day and night, but it was a rare day that I didn't get in the door at least once, and some days I got there a few minutes after Dennis opened up and was still there when Billie was ready to close. Everybody's got to be someplace.

Saloon friends.

I got to know Tommy Tillary in Armstrong's. He was a regular, apt to turn up three or four nights out of seven. I don't recall the first time I was aware of him, but it was hard to be in a room with him and not notice him. He was a big fellow and his voice tended to carry. He wasn't raucous, but after a few drinks his voice filled a room.

He ate a lot of beef and drank a lot of Chivas Regal, and they both showed in his face. He must have been close to forty-five. He was getting jowly, and his cheeks were blooming with a tracery of broken capillaries.

I never knew why they called him Tough Tommy. Perhaps Skip was right, perhaps the name's intent was ironic. They called him Tommy Telephone because of his job. He worked in telephone sales, peddling investments over the phone from a bucket shop in the Wall Street area. I understand people change jobs a lot in that line of work. The ability to coax investment dollars out of strangers over a telephone line is a rather special talent, and its possessors can get work readily, moving from one employer to another at will.

That summer, Tommy was working for an outfit called Tannahill & Company, selling limited partnerships in real estate syndications. There were tax advantages, I gather, and the prospect of capital gains. I picked this up inferentially, because Tommy never pitched anything, to me or anyone else at the bar. I was there one time when an obstetrics resident from Roosevelt tried to ask him about his offerings. Tommy brushed him off with a joke.

'No, I'm serious,' the doctor insisted. 'I'm finally making a buck, I ought to start thinking about things like that.'

Tommy shrugged. 'You got a card?' The doctor didn't. 'Then write your phone on this and a good time to call you. You want a pitch, I'll call you and give you the full treatment. But I got to warn you, I'm irresistible over the phone.'

A couple of weeks later they ran into each other and the resident complained that Tommy hadn't called him.

'Jesus, I been meaning to,' Tommy said. 'First thing, I'll make a note of it now.'

He was acceptable company. He told dialect jokes and he told them reasonably well, and I laughed at my share of them. I suppose some of them were offensive, but they weren't often mean-spirited. If I was in a mood to reminisce about my days on the force, he was a good enough listener, and if the story I told was a funny one his laugh was as loud as anybody's.

He was, on balance, a little too loud and a little too cheery. He talked a little too much and he could get on your nerves. As I said, he'd turn up at Armstrong's three or four nights a week, and about half the time she was with him. Carolyn Cheatham, Carolyn from the Caro-line, with a soft you-all accent that, like certain culinary herbs, became stronger when you steeped it in alcohol. Sometimes she came in on his arm. Other times he'd get there first and she'd join him. She lived in the neighborhood and she and Tommy worked in the same office, and I figured – if I bothered to think about it – that the office romance had served to introduce Tommy to Armstrong's.

He followed sports. He bet with a bookie – mostly ball games,

442

sometimes horses – and he let you know when he won. He was a little too friendly, a little too indiscriminately friendly, and sometimes there was a chill in his eyes that belied the friendship in his voice. He had cold little eyes, and there was a softening around his mouth, a weakness there, but none of that got into his voice.

You could see how he'd be good over the phone.

Skip Devoe's first name was Arthur, but Bobby Ruslander was the only person I ever heard call him that. Bobby could get away with it. They'd been friends since fourth grade, they grew up on the same block in Jackson Heights. Skip had been christened Arthur Jr, and he'd acquired the nickname early on. 'Because he used to skip school all the time,' Bobby said, but Skip had another explanation.

'I had this uncle was in the navy and never got over it,' he told me once. 'My mother's brother. Bought me sailor suits, toy boats. I had this whole fleet and he called me Skipper, and pretty soon so did everybody else. Coulda been worse. There was a guy in our class everybody called Worm. Don't ask me why. Imagine if they still call him that. He's in bed with his wife: 'Oh, Wormy, put it in deeper.''

He was around thirty-four, thirty-five, about my height but lean and muscular. The veins showed on his forearms and the backs of his hands. There was no spare flesh on his face, and the skin followed the curve of the bone, giving him deeply sculpted cheeks. He had a hawk nose and piercing blue eyes that showed a little green under the right lighting. All of this combined with assurance and an easy manner to make him quite attractive to women, and he rarely had trouble finding a girl to go home with when he wanted one. But he was living alone and not keeping steady company with anyone, and seemed to prefer the regular company of other men. He had either lived with or been married to someone and it had ended a few years ago, and he seemed disinclined to get involved with anyone else.

Tommy Tillary got called Tough Tommy, and had a certain tough-guy quality to his manner. Skip Devoe actually *was* tough, but you had to sense it underneath the surface. It wasn't on display.

He'd been in the service, not the navy you'd have thought his uncle would have preconditioned him for but the army's Special Forces, the Green Berets. He enlisted fresh out of high school and got sent to Southeast Asia during the Kennedy years. He got

443

out sometime in the late Sixties, tried college and dropped out, then broke in behind the stick at an Upper East Side singles' bar. After a couple of years he and John Kasabian pooled their savings, signed a long lease on an out-of-business hardware store, spent what they had to remodel it, and opened up Miss Kitty's.

I saw him occasionally at his own place, but more often at Armstrong's, where he'd drop in frequently when he wasn't working. He was pleasant company, easy to be with, and not much rattled him.

There was something about him, though, and I think what it may have been was an air of cool competence. You sensed that he'd be able to handle just about anything that came along, and without working up a sweat. He came across as a man who could do things, one too who could make quick decisions in midaction. Maybe he acquired that quality wearing a green hat in Vietnam, or maybe I endowed him with it because I knew he'd been over there.

I'd met that quality most often in criminals. I have known several heavy heist men who had it, guys who took off banks and armored cars. And there was a long-haul driver for a moving company who was like that. I got to know him after he'd come back from the Coast ahead of schedule, found his wife in bed with a lover, and killed them both with his hands.

THREE

There was nothing in the papers about the robbery at Morrissey's, but for the next few days you heard a lot of talk about it around the neighborhood. The rumored loss Tim Pat and his brothers had sustained kept escalating. The numbers I heard ranged from ten thousand to a hundred thousand. Since only the Morrisseys and the gunmen would know, and neither were terribly likely to talk, one number seemed as good as the next.

'I think they got around fifty,' Billie Keegan told me the night of the Fourth. 'That's the number keeps coming up. Of course everybody and his brother was there and saw it.'

'What do you mean?'

'I mean so far there's been at least three guys assured me they were there when it happened, and I *was* there and can swear for a fact that they weren't. And they can supply bits of color that somehow slipped by me. Did you know that one of the gunmen slapped a woman around?'

'Really.'

'So I'm told. Oh, and one of the Morrissey brothers was shot, but it was only a flesh wound. I thought it was exciting enough the way it went down, but I guess it's a lot more dramatic when you're not there. Well, ten years after the 1916 Rising they say it was hard to find a man in Dublin who hadn't been part of it. That glorious Monday morning, when thirty brave men marched into the post office and ten thousand heroes marched out. What do you think, Matt? Fifty grand sound about right to you?'

Tommy Tillary had been there, and I figured he'd dine out on it. Maybe he did. I didn't see him for a couple of days, and when I did he never even mentioned the robbery. He'd discovered the secret of betting baseball, he told everybody around. You just bet against the Mets and the Yankees and they'd always come through for you.

Early the next week, Skip came by Armstrong's in midafternoon and found me at my table in the back. He'd picked up a dark beer at the bar and brought it with him. He sat down across from me and said he'd been at Morrissey's the night before.

'I haven't been there since I was there with you,' I told him.

'Well, last night was my first time since then. They got the ceiling fixed. Tim Pat was asking for you.'

'Me?'

'Uh-huh.' He lit a cigarette. 'He'd appreciate it if you could drop by.'

'What for?'

'He didn't say. You're a detective, aren't you? Maybe he wants you to find something. What do you figure he might have lost?'

'I don't want to get in the middle of that.'

'Don't tell me.'

'Some Irish war, just what I need to cut myself in on.'

He shrugged. 'You don't have to go. He said to ask you to drop by any time after eight in the evening.'

'I guess they sleep until then.'

'If they sleep at all.'

He drank some beer, wiped his upper lip with the back of his hand. I said, 'You were there last night? What was it like?'

'What it's always like. I told you they patched the ceiling, did a good job of it as far as I could tell. Tim Pat and his brothers were their usual charming selves. I just said I'd pass the word to you next time I ran into you. You can go or not go.'

'I don't think I will,' I said.

But the next night around ten, ten-thirty, I figured what the hell and went over there. On the ground floor, the theater troupe was rehearsing Brendan Behan's *The Quare Fellow*. It was scheduled to open Thursday night. I rang the upstairs bell and waited until one of the brothers came downstairs and cracked the door. He told me they were closed, that they didn't open until two. I told him my name was Matthew Scudder and Tim Pat had said he wanted to see me.

'Oh, sure, an' I didn't now ye in that light,' he said. 'Come inside and I'll tell himself you're here.'

I waited in the big room on the second floor. I was studying the ceiling, looking for patched bullet holes, when Tim Pat came in and switched on some more lights. He was wearing his usual garb, but without the butcher's apron.

You're good to come,' he said. 'Ye'll have a drink with me? And your drink is bourbon, is it not?'

He poured drinks and we sat down at a table. It may have been the one his brother fell into when he came stumbling through the door. Tim Pat held his glass to the light, tipped it back and drained it.

He said, 'Ye were here the night of the incident.'

'Yes.'

'One of those fine young lads left a hat behind, but misfortunately his mother never got around to sewing a name tape in it, so it's impossible to return it to him.'

'I see.'

'If I only knew who he was and where to find him, I could see that he got what was rightfully his.'

I'll bet you could, I thought.

'Ye were a policeman.'

'Not anymore.'

'Ye might hear something. People talk, don't they, and a man who keeps his eyes and ears open might do himself a bit of good.'

I didn't say anything.

He groomed his beard with his fingertips. 'My brothers and I,' he said, his eyes fixed on a point over my shoulder, 'would be greatly pleased to pay ten thousand dollars for the names and whereabouts of the two lads who visited us the other night.'

'Just to return a hat.'

'Why, we've a sense of obligation,' he said. 'Wasn't it your George Washington who walked miles through the snow to return a penny to a customer?'

'I think it was Abraham Lincoln.'

'Of course it was. George Washington was the other, the cherry tree. 'Father, I cannot tell a lie.' This nation's heroes are great ones for honesty.'

'They used to be.'

'And then himself, tellin' us all he's not a crook. Jaysus.' He shook his big head. 'Well, then,' he said. 'Do ye think ye'll be able to help us out?'

'I don't see what help I could be.'

'Ye were here and saw them.'

'They were wearing masks and they had caps on their heads.

447

In fact I could swear they both had their caps on when they left. You don't suppose you found somebody else's hat, do you?'

'Perhaps the lad dropped it on the stairs. If you hear anything, Matt, ye'll let us know?'

'Why not?'

'Are ye of Irish stock yourself, Matt?'

'No.'

'I'd have thought maybe one of your forebears was from Kerry. The Kerryman is famous for answering a question with a question.'

'I don't know who they were, Tim Pat.'

'If you learn anything ...'

'If I learn anything.'

'Ye've no quarrel with the price? It's a fair price?'

'No quarrel,' I said. 'It's a very fair price.'

It was a good price, the fairness of it notwithstanding. I said as much to Skip the next time I saw him.

'He didn't want to hire me,' I said. 'He wanted to post a reward. Ten K to the man who tells him who they are and where he can lay his hands on them.'

'Would you do it?'

'What, go hunting for them? I told you the other day I wouldn't take the job for a fee. I'm certainly not going to go nosing around on the come.'

He shook his head. 'Suppose you found out without trying. You walked around the corner on the way to buy a paper and there they were.'

'How would I recognize them?'

'How often do you see two guys wearing red kerchiefs for masks? No, seriously, say you recognized them. Or you got hold of the information, the word got out and some contact of yours from the old days put a flea in your ear. You used to have stool pigeons, didn't you?'

'Snitches,' I said. 'Every cop had them, you couldn't get anywhere without them. Still, I –'

'Forget *how* you find out,' he said. 'Just suppose it happened. Would you?'

'Would I –'

'Sell 'em out. Collect the ten grand.'

'I don't know anything about them.'

'Fine, let's say you don't know whether they're assholes or altar boys. What's the difference? Either way it's blood money, right? The Morrisseys find those kids, they gotta be dead as Kelsey's nuts, right?'

'I don't suppose Tim Pat wants to send them an invitation to a christening.'

'Or ask 'em to join the Holy Name Society. Could you do it?'

I shook my head. 'I can't answer that,' I said. 'It would depend on who they were and how bad I needed the money.'

'I don't think you'd do it.'

'I don't think I would either.'

'I sure as shit wouldn't,' he said. He tapped the ashes from his cigarette. 'There's enough people who would.'

'There's people who would kill for less than that.'

'I was thinking that myself.'

'There were a few cops in the room that night,' I said. 'You want to bet they'll know about the reward?'

'No bet.'

'Say a cop finds out who the holdup men were. He can't make a collar. There's no crime, right? Nothing ever got reported, no witnesses, nothing. But he can turn the two bums over to Tim Pat and walk with half a year's pay.'

'Knowing he's aided and abetted murder.'

'I'm not saying everybody would do it. But you tell yourself the guys are scum, they've probably killed people themselves, they're a cinch to kill someone sooner or later, and it's not like you know for certain the Morrisseys are going to kill them. Maybe they'll just break a few bones, just scare 'em a little. Try to get their money back, something like that. You can tell yourself that.'

'And believe it?'

'Most people believe what they want to believe.'

'Yeah,' he said. 'Can't argue with that.'

You decide something in your mind and then your body goes and decides something else. I wasn't going to have anything to do with Tim Pat's problem, and then I kept finding myself sniffing around it like a dog at a lamppost. The same night I assured Skip I wasn't playing, I wound up on Seventy-second Street at a place called Poogan's Pub, sitting at a rear table and buying iced Stolichnaya for a tiny albino Negro named Danny Boy Bell. Danny Boy was always interesting company, but he was also a prime snitch, an information broker who knew everyone and heard everything.

Of course he'd heard about the robbery at Morrissey's. He'd

heard a wide range of figures quoted for the take, and for his own part guessed that the right number was somewhere between fifty and a hundred thousand dollars.

'Whoever took it,' he said, 'they're not spending it in the bars. My sense of it is that it's an Irish thing, Matthew. Irish Irish, not the local Harps. You know, it went down right in the middle of Westy country, but I can't see the Westies taking off Tim Pat like that.'

The Westies are a loosely organized mob of toughs and killers, most of them Irish, and they've been operating in Hell's Kitchen since the turn of the century. Maybe longer, maybe since the Potato Famine.

'I don't know,' I said. 'With that kind of money involved –'

'If those two were Westies, if they were anybody from the neighborhood, it wouldn't be a secret for more than eight hours. Everybody on Tenth Avenue'd know it.'

'You're right.'

'Some kind of Irish thing, that's my best guess. You were there, you'd know this. The masks were red?'

'Red handkerchiefs.'

'A shame. If they were green or orange they'd be making some sort of political statement. I understand the brothers are offering a generous reward. Is that what brings you here, Matthew?'

'Oh, no,' I said. 'Definitely not.'

'Not doing a bit of exploratory work on speculation?'

'Absolutely not,' I said.

Friday afternoon I was drinking in Armstrong's and fell into conversation with a couple of nurses at the next table. They had tickets for an off-off-Broadway show that night. Dolores couldn't go, and Fran really wanted to but she wasn't sure she felt like going by herself, and besides they had the extra ticket.

And of course the show turned out to be *The Quare Fellow*. It didn't relate in any way to the incident at Morrissey's, it was just coincidentally being performed downstairs of the after-hours joint, and it hadn't been my idea in the first place, but what was I doing there? I sat on a flimsy wooden folding chair and watched Behan's play about imprisoned criminals in Dublin and wondered what the hell I was doing in the audience.

Afterward Fran and I wound up at Miss Kitty's with a group that included two of the members of the cast. One of them, a slim red-haired girl with enormous green eyes, was Fran's friend

Mary Margaret, and the reason why Fran had been so anxious to go. That was Fran's reason, but what was mine?

There was talk at the table of the robbery. I didn't raise the subject or contribute much to the discussion, but I couldn't stay out of it altogether because Fran told the group I was a former police detective and asked for my professional opinion of the affair. My reply was as noncommittal as I could make it, and I avoided mentioning that I'd been an eyewitness to the holdup.

Skip was there, so busy behind the bar with the Fridaynight crowd that I didn't bother to do more than wave hello at him. The place was mobbed and noisy, as it always was on weekends, but that was where everyone else had wanted to go, and I'd gone along.

Fran lived on Sixty-eighth between Columbus and Amsterdam. I walked her home, and at her door she said, 'Matt, you were a sweetheart to keep me company. The play was okay, wasn't it?'

'It was fine.'

'I thought Mary Margaret was good, anyway. Matt, would you mind awfully if I don't ask you to come up? I'm beat and I've got an early day tomorrow.'

'That's okay,' I said. 'Now that you mention it, so do I.'

'Being a detective?'

I shook my head. 'Being a father.'

The next morning Anita put the kids on the Long Island Rail Road and I picked them up at the station in Corona and took them to Shea and watched the Mets lose to the Astros. The boys would be going to camp for four weeks in August and they were excited about that. We ate hot dogs and peanuts and popcorn. They had Cokes, I had a couple of beers. There was some sort of special promotion that day, and the boys got free caps or pennants, I forget which.

Afterward I took them back to the city on the subway and to a movie at Loew's 83rd. We had pizza on Broadway after the film let out and took a cab back to my hotel, where I'd rented a twin-bedded room for them a floor below mine. They went to bed and I went up to my own room. After an hour I checked their room. They were sleeping soundly. I locked their door again and went around the corner to Armstrong's. I didn't stay long, maybe an hour. Then I went back to my hotel, checked the boys again, and went upstairs and to bed.

In the morning we went out for a big breakfast, pancakes and bacon and sausages. I took them up to the Museum of the American Indian in Washington Heights. There are a couple dozen museums in the city of New York, and when you leave your wife you get to discover them all.

It felt strange being in Washington Heights. It was in that neighborhood a few years earlier that I'd been having a few off-duty drinks when a couple of punks held up the bar and shot the bartender dead on their way out.

I went out into the street after them. There are a lot of hills in Washington Heights. They ran down one of them and I had to shoot downhill. I brought them both down, but one shot went wide and ricocheted, and it killed a small child named Estrellita Rivera.

Those things happen. There was a departmental hearing, there always is when you kill someone, and I was found to have acted properly and with justification.

Shortly thereafter I put in my papers and left the police department.

I can't say that one event caused the other. I can only say that the one led to the other. I had been the unwitting instrument of a child's death, and after that something was different for me. The life I had been living without complaint no longer seemed to suit me. I suppose it had ceased to suit me before then. I suppose the child's death precipitated a life change that was long overdue. But I can't say that for certain, either. Just that one thing led to another.

We took a train to Penn Station. I told the boys how good it had been to spend some time with them, and they told me what a good time they'd had. I put them on a train, made a phone call and told their mother what train they'd be on. She assured me she'd meet it, then mentioned hesitantly that it would be good if I sent money soon. Soon, I assured her.

I hung up and thought of the ten thousand dollars Tim Pat was offering. And shook my head, amused at the thought.

But that night I got restless and wound up down in the Village, stopping in a string of bars for one drink each. I took the A train to West Fourth Street and started at McBell's and worked my way west. Jimmy Day's, the 55, the Lion's Head, George Hertz's, the Corner Bistro. I told myself I was just having a couple of drinks, unwinding after the pressure of a weekend with my sons, settling myself down after awakening old memories with a visit to Washington Heights.

But I knew better. I was starting some half-assed purposeless investigation, trying to turn up a lead to the pair who'd hit Morrissey's.

I wound up in a gay bar called Sinthia's. Kenny, who owned the place, was minding the store, serving drinks to men in Levi's and ribbed tank tops. Kenny was slender, willowy, with dyed blond hair and a face that had been tucked and lifted enough to look no more than twenty-eight, which was about half as many years as Kenny had been on the planet.

'Matthew!' he called out. 'You can all relax now, girls. Law and order has come to Grove Street.'

Of course he didn't know anything about the robbery at Morrissey's. He didn't know Morrissey's to begin with; no gay man had to leave the Village to find a place where he could get a drink after closing. But the holdup men could have been gay as easily as not, and if they weren't spending their take elsewhere they might be spending it in the joints around Christopher Street, and anyhow that was the way you worked it, you nosed around, you worked all your sources, you put the word out and waited to see if anything came back to you.

But why was I doing this? Why was I wasting my time?

I don't know what would have happened – whether I would have kept at it or let go of it, whether I would have gotten someplace or ultimately turned away from a cold trail. I didn't seem to be getting anywhere, but that's often the way it is, and you go through the motions with no indication of progress until you get lucky and something breaks. Maybe something like that would have happened. Maybe not.

Instead, some other things happened to take my mind off Tim Pat Morrissey and his quest for vengeance.

For openers, somebody killed Tommy Tillary's wife.

453

FOUR

Tuesday night I took Fran to dinner at the Thai restaurant Skip Devoe liked so much. Afterward I walked her home, with a stop for after-dinner drinks at Joey Farrell's. In front of her building she pleaded an early day again, and I left her there and walked back to Armstrong's with a stop or two en route. I was in a sour mood, and a stomachful of unfamiliar food didn't help any. I probably hit the bourbon a little harder than usual, rolling out of there around one or two. I took the long way home, picked up the *Daily News*, and sat on the edge of my bed in my underwear taking a quick look at a couple of stories.

On one of the inside pages I read about a Brooklyn woman who'd been killed in the course of a burglary. I was tired and I'd had a lot to drink and the name didn't register.

But I woke up the next morning with something buzzing in my mind, half dream and half memory. I sat up and reached for the paper and found the story.

Margaret Tillary, forty-seven, had been stabbed to death in the upstairs bedroom of her home on Colonial Road, in the Bay Ridge section of Brooklyn, evidently having awakened in the course of a burglary. Her husband, securities salesman Thomas J. Tillary, had become concerned when his wife failed to answer the telephone Tuesday afternoon. He called a relative living nearby who entered the house, finding the premises ransacked and the woman dead.

'This is a good neighborhood,' a neighbor was quoted as saying. 'Things like this don't happen here.' But a police source cited a marked increase in area burglaries in recent months, and another neighbor referred obliquely to the presence of a 'bad element' in the neighborhood.

It's not a common name. There's a Tillary Street in Brooklyn, not far from the entrance to the Brooklyn Bridge, but I've no idea what war hero or ward heeler they named it after, or if he's a relative of Tommy's. There are several Tillerys in the Manhattan phone directory, spelled with an *e*. Thomas Tillary, securities salesman, Brooklyn – it seemed as though it had to be Telephone Tommy.

I took a shower and shaved and went out for breakfast. I thought about what I'd read and tried to figure out how I felt about it. It didn't seem real to me. I didn't know him well and I hadn't known her at all, had never known her name, had known only that she existed somewhere in Brooklyn.

I looked at my left hand, the ring finger. No ring, no mark. I had worn a wedding ring for years, and I had taken it off when I moved from Syosset to Manhattan. For months there had been a mark where the ring had been, and then one day I noticed that the mark was gone.

Tommy wore a ring. A yellow gold band, maybe three-eighths of an inch wide. And he wore a pinkie ring on his right hand, a high-school class ring, I think it must have been. I remembered it, sitting there over coffee in the Red Flame. A class ring with a blue stone on his right pinkie, a yellow gold band on his left ring finger.

I couldn't tell how I felt.

That afternoon I went to St. Paul's and lit a candle for Margaret Tillary. I had discovered churches in my retirement, and while I did not pray or attend services, I dropped in now and then and sat in the darkened silence. Sometimes I lit candles for people who had recently died, or for those longer dead who were on my mind. I don't know why I thought this was something I ought to do, nor do I know why I felt compelled to tuck a tenth of any income I received into the poor box of whatever church I next visited.

I sat in a rear pew and thought a bit about sudden death. When I left the church a light rain was falling. I crossed Ninth Avenue and ducked into Armstrong's. Dennis was behind the bar. I ordered bourbon neat, drank it straight down, and motioned for another and said I'd have a cup of coffee with it.

While I poured the bourbon into the coffee, he asked if I'd heard about Tillary. I said I'd read the story in the *News*.

'There's a piece in this afternoon's *Post*, too. Pretty much the same story. It happened the night before last is how they figure it. He evidently didn't make it home and he went straight to the office in the morning, and then after he called a few times to apologize and couldn't get through, he got worried.'

455

'It said that in the paper?'

'Just about. That would have been the night before last. He didn't come in while I was here. Did you see him?'

I tried to remember. 'I think so. The night before last yeah, I think he was here with Carolyn.'

'The Dixie Belle.'

'That's the one.'

'Wonder how she feels about now.' He used thumb and forefinger to smooth the points of his wispy moustache. 'Probably guilty for having her wish come true.'

'You think she wanted the wife dead?'

'I don't know. Isn't that a girl's fantasy when she's running around with a married guy? Look, I'm not married. What do I know about these things?'

The story faded out of the papers during the next couple of days. There was a death notice in Thursday's *News*. Margaret Wayland Tillary, beloved wife of Thomas, mother of the late James Alan Tillary, aunt of Mrs Richard Paulsen. There would be a wake that evening, a funeral service the following afternoon at Walter B. Cooke's, Fourth and Bay Ridge Avenues, in Brooklyn.

That night Billie Keegan said, 'I haven't seen Tillary since it happened. I'm not sure we're gonna see him again.' He poured himself a glass of JJ&S, the twelve-year-old Jameson that nobody else ever ordered. 'I bet we don't see him with her again.'

'The girlfriend?'

He nodded. 'What's got to be on both their minds is he was with her when his wife was getting knifed to death in Brooklyn. And if he'd only been home where he was supposed to be, di dah di dah di dah. You're fooling around and you want a quick bounce and a couple of laughs, the last thing you need is something to remind you how you got your wife killed by fooling around.'

I thought about it, nodded. 'The wake was tonight,' I said.

'Yeah? You go?' I shook my head. 'I don't know anybody that went.'

I left before closing. I had a drink at Polly's and another at Miss Kitty's. Skip was tense and remote. I sat at the bar and tried to ignore the man standing next to me without being actively hostile. He wanted to tell me how all the city's problems were the fault of the former mayor. I didn't necessarily disagree but I didn't want to hear about it.

456

I finished my drink and headed for the door. Halfway there Skip called my name. I turned and he motioned to me.

I walked back to the bar. He said, 'This is the wrong time for it, but I'd like to talk to you soon.

'Ask your advice, maybe throw a little work your way. You be around Jimmy's tomorrow afternoon?'

'Probably,' I said. 'If I don't go to the funeral.'

'Who died?'

'Tillary's wife.'

'Oh, the funeral's tomorrow? Are you thinking about going? I didn't know you were that close to the guy.'

'I'm not.'

'Then why would you want to go? Forget it, not my business. I'll look for you at Armstrong's around two, two-thirty. If you're not there I'll catch you some other time.'

I was there when he came in the next day around two-thirty. I had just finished lunch and was sitting over a cup of coffee when Skip came in and scanned the room from the doorway. He saw me and came on over and sat down.

'You didn't go,' he said. 'Well, it's no day for a funeral. I was just over at the gym, I felt silly sitting in the sauna after. The whole city's a sauna. What have you got there, some of that famous Kentucky coffee of yours?'

'Just plain coffee.'

'That'll never do.' He turned, beckoned the waitress. 'Let me have a Prior Dark,' he told her, 'and bring my father here something to put in his coffee.'

She brought a shot for me and a beer for him. He poured it slowly against the side of the glass, examined the half-inch head, took a sip, put the glass down.

He said, 'I might have a problem.'

I didn't say anything.

'This is confidential, okay?'

'Sure.'

'You know much about the bar business?'

'Just from the consumer's point of view.'

'I like that. You know it's all cash.'

'Of course.'

'A lot of places take plastic. We don't. Strictly cash. Oh, if we know you we'll take your check, or if you run a tab, whatever. But it's basically a cash business. I'd say ninety-five percent of

457

our gross is cash. As a matter of fact it's probably higher than that.'

'And?'

He took out a cigarette, tapped the end against his thumbnail. 'I hate talking about all this,' he said.

'Then don't.'

He lit the cigarette. 'Everybody skims,' he said. 'A certain percentage of the take comes right off the top before it gets recorded. It doesn't get listed in the books, it doesn't get deposited, it doesn't exist. The dollar you don't declare is worth two dollars that you do, because you don't pay tax on it. You follow me?'

'It's not all that hard to follow, Skip.'

'Everybody does it, Matt. The candy store, the newsie, everybody who takes in cash. Christ's sake, it's the American way – the president'd cheat on his taxes if he could get by with it.'

'The last one did.'

'Don't remind me. That asshole'd give tax fraud a bad name.' He sucked hard on the cigarette. 'We opened up, couple years ago, John kept the books. I yell at people, do the hiring and firing, he does the buying and keeps the books. Works out about right.'

'And?'

'Get to the point, right? Fuck it. From the beginning we keep two sets of books, one for us and one for Uncle.' His face darkened and he shook his head. 'Never made sense to me. I figured keep one phony set and that's that, but he says you need honest books so you'll know how you're doing. That make sense to you? You count your money and you know how you're doing, you don't need two sets of books to tell you, but he's the guy with the business head, he knows these things, so I say fine, do it.'

He picked up his glass, drank some beer. 'They're gone,' he said.

'The books.'

'John comes in Saturday mornings, does the week's bookkeeping. Everything was fine this past Saturday. Day before yesterday he has to check something, looks for the books, no books.'

'Both sets gone?'

'Only the dark set, the honest set.' He drank some beer, wiped his mouth with the back of his hand. 'He spent a day taking

Valium and going nuts by himself, then told me yesterday. And I been going nuts ever since.'

'How bad is it, Skip?'

'Aw, shit,' he said. 'It's pretty bad. We could go away for it.'

'Really?'

He nodded. 'It's all our records since we opened, and we been making money from the first week. I don't know why, it's just another joint, but we been pulling 'em in. And we've been stealing with both hands. They come up with the books, we're fucking *nailed*, you know? You can't call it a mistake, it's all down there in black and white, one set of figures, and there's another completely different set on each year's tax return. You can't even make up a story, all you can do is ask 'em where they want you, Atlanta or Leavenworth.'

We sat silent for a few moments. I drank some of my coffee. He lit another cigarette and blew smoke at the ceiling. Music played on the tape deck, something contra-puntal with woodwinds.

I said, 'What would you want me to do?'

'Find out who took 'em. Get 'em back.'

'Maybe John got rattled, misplaced them. He could have –'

He was shaking his head. 'I turned the office upside down yesterday afternoon. They're fuckin' gone.'

'They just disappeared? No signs of forced entry? Where did you keep 'em, under lock and key?'

'They're supposed to be locked up. Sometimes he would forget, leave 'em out, stick 'em in a desk drawer. You get careless, you know what I mean? You never have an incident, you take the whole thing for granted, and if you're rushed, you don't take the trouble to put things away where they belong. He tells me he locked up Saturday but in the next breath he admits maybe he didn't, it's a routine thing, he does the same thing every Saturday, so how do you remember one Saturday from the next? What's the difference? The stuff is capital-G Gone.'

'So somebody took it.'

'Right.'

'If they go the IRS with it –'

'Then we're dead. That's all. They can plant us next to whatsisname's wife, Tillary's. You miss the funeral, don't worry about it. I'll understand.'

'Was anything else missing, Skip?'

'Didn't seem to be.'

459

'So it was a very specific theft. Somebody walked in, took the books, and left.'

'Bingo.'

I worked it out in my mind. 'If it was somebody with a grudge against you, somebody you fired, say –'

'Yeah, I thought of that.'

'If they go to the Feds, you'll know about it when a couple of guys in suits come around and show you their ID. They'll take all your records, slap a lien on your bank accounts, and whatever else they do.'

'Keep talking, Matt. You're really making my day.'

'If it's not somebody who's got a hardon for you, then it's somebody looking to turn a dollar.'

'By selling the books.'

'Uh-huh.'

'To us.'

'You're the ideal customers.'

'I thought of that. So did Kasabian. Sit tight, he tells me. Sit tight, and whoever took 'em'll get in touch, and we worry about it then. Just sit tight in the meantime. Tight's no problem, it's the sitting that's getting to me. Can you get bail for cheating on taxes?'

'Of course.'

'Then I suppose I can get it and run out on it. Leave the country. Live the rest of my life in Nepal selling hash to hippies.'

'All that's still a long ways off.'

'I suppose.' He looked thoughtfully at his cigarette, drowned it in the dregs of his beer. 'I hate it when they do that,' he said thoughtfully. 'Send back glasses with butts floating in them. Disgusting.' He looked at me, his eyes probing mine. 'Anything you can do for me on this? I mean for hire.'

'I don't see what. Not at this point.'

'So in the meantime I just wait. That's always the hard part for me, always has been. I ran track in high school, the quarter-mile. I was lighter then. I smoked heavy, I smoked since I was thirteen, but you can do anything at that age and it doesn't touch you. Nothing touches kids, that's why they all think they're gonna live forever.' He drew another cigarette halfway out of the pack, put it back again. 'I loved the races, but waiting for the event to start, I hated that. Some guys would puke. I never puked but I used to feel like it. I would pee and then I'd think I had to pee again five minutes later.' He shook his head at the memory. 'And the same thing overseas, waiting to go into combat. I never minded combat, and there was a lot about it to mind. Things that bother me now, remembering them, but while they were going on it was a different story.'

'I can understand that.'

'Waiting, though, that was murder.' He pushed his chair back. 'What do I owe you, Matt?'

'For what? I didn't do anything.'

'For the advice.'

I waved the thought away. 'You can buy me that drink,' I said, 'and that'll be fine.'

'Done,' he said. He stood up. 'I may need a hand from you somewhere down the line.'

'Sure,' I said.

He stopped to talk to Dennis on the way out. I nursed my coffee. By the time I was done with it a woman two tables away had paid her check and left her newspaper behind. I read it, and had another cup of coffee with it, and a shot of bourbon to sweeten the coffee.

The afternoon crowd was starting to fill the room when I called the waitress over. I palmed her a buck and told her to put the check on my tab.

'No check,' she said. 'The gentleman paid it.'

She was new, she didn't know Skip by name. 'He wasn't supposed to do that,' I said. 'Anyway, I had a drink after he left. Put it on my tab, all right?'

'Talk to Dennis,' she said.

She went to take somebody's order before I could reply. I went to the bar and crooked a finger for Dennis. 'She tells me there's no check for my table,' I said.

'She speaks the truth.' He smiled. He often smiled, as if much of what he saw amused him. 'Devoe paid the check.'

'He wasn't supposed to do that. Anyway, I had a drink after he left and told her to put it on my tab, and she said to see you. Is this something new? Don't I have a tab?'

His smile broadened. 'Anytime you want one, but as a matter of fact you don't have one now. Mr Devoe covered it. Wiped the slate clean.'

'What did it come to?'

'Eighty dollars and change. I could probably come up with the exact figure if it mattered. Does it?'

'No.'

'He gave me a hundred dollars to cover your tab, the check

461

today, a tip for Lyddie and something to ease my own weariness of the soul. I suppose one could maintain that your most recent drink was not covered, but my inscrutable sense of the rightness of things is that it was.' Another wide smile. 'So you owe us nothing,' he said.

I didn't argue. If there was one thing I learned in the NYPD, it was to take what people gave me.

FIVE

I went back to my hotel, checked for mail and messages. There were none of either. The desk clerk, a loose-limbed black man from Antigua, said that he didn't mind the heat but he missed the ocean breezes.

I went upstairs and took a shower. My room was hot. There was an air-conditioner, but something was wrong with its cooling element. It moved the warm air around and gave it a chemical flavor but didn't do much about the heat or the humidity. I could shut it off and open the window from the top, but the air outside was no better. I stretched out and must have dozed off for an hour or so, and when I woke up I needed another shower.

I took it and then called Fran. Her roommate answered. I gave my name and waited what seemed like a long time for Fran to come to the phone.

I suggested dinner, and maybe a movie afterward if we felt up to it. 'Oh, I'm afraid I can't tonight, Matt,' she said. 'I have other plans. Maybe some other time?'

I hung up regretting that I'd called. I checked the mirror, decided I didn't really need a shave after all, got dressed and got out of there.

It was hot on the street, but it would cool down in a couple of hours. Meanwhile, there were bars all over the place, and their air-conditioners all worked better than mine.

Curiously, I didn't hit it all that hard. I was in a surly mood, gruff and ill-tempered, and that usually led me to take my drinks fast. But I was restless, and as a result I moved around a lot. There were even a few bars that I walked into and out of without ordering anything.

At one point I almost got into a fight. In a joint on Tenth Avenue a rawboned drunk with a couple of teeth missing

463

bumped into me and spilled part of his drink on me, then took exception to the way I accepted his apology. It was all over nothing – he was looking for a fight and I was very nearly ready to oblige him. Then one of his friends grabbed his arms from behind and another stepped between us, and I came to my senses and got out of there.

I walked east on Fifty-seventh. A couple of black hookers were working the pavement in front of the Holiday Inn. I noticed them more than I usually did. One, with a face like an ebony mask, challenged me with her eyes. I felt a rush of anger, and I didn't know who or what I was angry at.

I walked over to Ninth, up half a block to Armstrong's. I wasn't surprised to see Fran there. It was almost as if I had expected her to be there, seated at a table along the north wall. She had her back to me and hadn't noticed me come in.

Hers was a table for two, and her partner was no one I recognized. He had blond hair and eyebrows and an open young face, and he was wearing a slate-blue short-sleeved shirt with epaulets. I think they call it a safari shirt. He was smoking a pipe and drinking a beer. Her drink was something red in an oversize stemmed glass.

Probably a tequila sunrise. That was a big year for tequila sunrises.

I turned to the bar, and there was Carolyn. The tables were crowded but the bar was half empty, lightly attended for that hour on a Friday night. At her right, toward the door, a couple of beer drinkers stood talking baseball. To her left, there were three vacant stools in a row.

I took the middle one and ordered bourbon, a double with water back. Billie served it, saying something about the weather. I took a sip of my drink and shot a quick glance at Carolyn.

She didn't appear to be waiting for Tommy or for anyone else, nor did she look as though she'd just breezed in a few minutes ago. She was wearing yellow pedal pushers and a sleeveless lime-green blouse. Her light brown hair was combed to frame her little fox face. She was drinking something dark from a lowball glass.

At least it wasn't a tequila sunrise.

I drank some bourbon, glanced in spite of myself at Fran and was irritated with my own irritation. I'd had two dates with her, there was no great mutual attraction, no chemical magic, just two nights of leaving her at her door. And tonight I'd called her,

464

late, and she'd said she had other plans, and here she was, drinking a tequila sunrise with her other plan.

Where did I get off being mad about that?

I thought, I'll bet she doesn't tell him she's got an early day tomorrow. I bet the White Hunter there doesn't have to say goodnight downstairs.

To my right, a voice with a Piedmont softness to it said, 'I forget your name.'

I looked up.

'I believe we were introduced,' she said, 'but I don't recall your name.'

'It's Matthew Scudder,' I said, 'and you're right, Tommy introduced us. You're Carolyn.'

'Carolyn Cheatham. Have you seen him?'

'Tommy? Not since it happened.'

'Neither have I. Were you-all at the funeral?'

'No. I thought about going but I didn't get there.'

'Why would you go? You never met her, did you?'

'No.'

'Neither did I.' She laughed. There wasn't much mirth in it. 'Big surprise, I never met his wife. I would have gone this afternoon. But I didn't.' She took her lower lip between her teeth. 'Matt. Whyn't you buy me a drink? Or I'll buy you one, but come sit next to me so's I don't have to shout. Please?'

She was drinking Amaretto, a sweet almond-flavored liqueur that she took on the rocks. It tastes like dessert but it's almost as strong as whiskey.

'He told me not to come,' she said. 'To the funeral. It was someplace in Brooklyn, that's a whole foreign nation to me, Brooklyn, but a lot of people went from the office. I wouldn't have had to *know* how to get there, I could have had a ride, I could have been part of the office crowd, come to pay my respects along with everybody else. But he said not to, he said it wouldn't look right.'

Her bare arms were lightly dusted with golden hair. She was wearing perfume, a floral scent with an undertaste of musk.

'He said it wouldn't look right,' she said. 'He said it was a matter of respect for the dead.' She picked up her glass and stared into it.

She said, 'Respect. What's the man care about respect? What's he so much as know about respect, for the dead or for the living? I would just have been part of the office crowd. We both work there at Tannahill, far as anyone knows we're just friends. Lord's sake, all we ever were is friends.'

'Whatever you say.'

'Well, *shit*,' she said, drawling it, giving the word an extra syllable or two. 'Ah *don't* mean to say Ah wasn't fucking him. Ah surely don't mean that. But all it ever was was laughs and good times. He was married and went home to mama most every night' – she drank some Amaretto – 'and that was jes fine, believe me, because who in her right mind'd want Tommy Tillary around by the dawn's early light? Christ in the foothills, Matthew, did I spill this or drink it?'

We agreed that she was drinking them a little too fast. Sweet drinks, we assured each other, had a way of sneaking up on a person. It was this fancy New York Amaretto shit, she maintained. It wasn't like the bourbon she'd grown up on. You knew where you stood with bourbon.

I reminded her that I was a bourbon drinker myself, and it pleased her to learn this. Alliances have been forged on more tenuous bonds than that, and she sealed ours with a sip from my glass. I offered it to her, and she put her little hand on mine to steady the glass, sipping daintily at the liquor.

'Bourbon is low-down,' she said. 'You know what I mean?'

'Here I thought it was a gentleman's drink.'

'It's for a gentleman likes to get down in the dirt. Scotch is vests and ties and prep school. Bourbon is an old boy ready to let the animal out, ready to let the nasty show. Bourbon is sitting up on a hot night and not minding if you sweat.'

Nobody was sweating. We were in her apartment, sitting on her couch in a sunken living room set about a foot below the level of the kitchen and foyer. Her building was an Art Deco apartment house on Fifty-seventh just a few doors west of Ninth. A bottle of Maker's Mark from the store around the corner stood on top of her glass-and-wrought-iron coffee table. Her air-conditioner was on, quieter than mine and more effective. We were drinking out of rocks glasses but we weren't bothering with ice.

'You were a cop,' she said. 'Didn't he tell me that?'

'He could have.'

'And now you're a detective?'

'In a way.'

'Just so you're not a robber. Be something if I got myself stabbed by a burglar tonight, wouldn't it? He's with me and she

466

gets killed, and then he's with her and *I* get killed. Except I don't guess he's with her right about now, is he. She's in the ground by now.'

Her apartment was small but comfortable. The furniture had clean lines, the op art prints on the brick wall were framed simply in aluminum frames. From her window you could see the green copper roof of the Parc Vendome on the far corner.

'If a burglar came in here,' she said, 'I'd stand a better chance than she did.'

'Because you've got me to protect you?'

'Mmmm,' she said. 'Mah hero.'

We kissed then. I tipped up her chin and kissed her, and we moved into an easy clinch. I breathed in her perfume, felt her softness. We clung together for a moment or two, then withdrew and reached as if in synchronization for our drinks.

'Even if I was alone,' she said, picking up the conversation as readily as she'd picked up the drink. 'I could protect myself.'

'You're a karate black belt.'

'I'm a beaded belt, honey, to match my purse. No, I could protect myself with this here, just give me a minute and I'll show you.'

A pair of modern matte-black step tables flanked the sofa. She leaned across me to grope for something in the drawer of the one on my side. She was sprawled facedown across my lap. An inch of golden skin showed between the tops of the yellow pedal pushers and the bottom of her green blouse. I put my hand on her behind.

'Now quit that, Matthew! I'll forget what I'm looking for.'

'That's all right.'

'No it's not. Here. See?'

She sat up, a gun in her hand. It was the same matte-black finish as the table. It was a revolver, and looked to be a .32. A small gun, all black, with a one-inch barrel.

'Maybe you should put that away,' I said.

'I know how to behave around guns,' she said. 'I grew up in a house full of guns. Rifles, shotguns, handguns. My pa and both my brothers hunted. Quail, pheasants. Some ducks. I know about guns.'

'Is that one loaded?'

'Wouldn't be much good if it wasn't, would it? Can't point at a burglar and say *bang*. He loaded it 'fore he gave it to me.'

'Tommy gave it to you?'

'Uh-huh.' She held the gun at arm's length, sighted across the room at an imaginary burglar. 'Bang,' she said. 'He didn't leave me any shells, just the loaded gun. So if I was to shoot a burglar I'd have to ask him for more bullets the next day.'

'Why'd he give it to you?'

'Not to go duck hunting.' She laughed. 'For protection,' she said. 'I said how I got nervous sometimes, a girl living alone in this city, and one time he brought me this here. He said he bought it for her, to have it for protection, but she wouldn't have any part of it, wouldn't even take it in her hand.' She broke off and giggled.

'What's so funny?'

'Oh, that's what they all say. 'My wife won't even take it in her hand.' I got a dirty mind, Matthew.'

'Nothing wrong with that.'

'I told you bourbon was low-down. Brings out the beast in a person. You could kiss me.'

'You could put the gun away.'

'You got something against kissing a woman with a gun in her hand?' She rolled to her left, put the gun in the drawer and closed it. 'I keep it in the bedside table,' she explained, 'so it'll be handy if I need it in a hurry. This here makes up into a bed.'

'I don't believe you.'

'You don't huh? Want me to prove it to you?'

'Maybe you'd better.'

And so we did what grownups do when they find themselves alone together. The sofa opened up into an adequate bed and we lay upon it with the lights out and the room lit by a couple of candles in straw-wrapped wine bottles. Music played on an FM station. She had a sweet body, an eager mouth, perfect skin. She made a lot of enthusiastic noises and more than a few skillful moves, and afterward she cried some.

Then we talked and had a little more of the bourbon, and before long she dropped off to sleep. I covered her with the top sheet and a cotton blanket. I could have slept myself, but instead I put on my clothes and sent myself home. Because who in her right mind'd want Matt Scudder around by the dawn's early light?

On my way home I stopped at the little Syrian deli and had the clerk loosen the caps on two bottles of Molson Ale. I went up to my room and sat with my feet up on the windowsill and drank from one of the bottles.

I thought about Tillary. Where was he now? In the house where she died? Staying with friends or relatives?

I thought of him in the bars or Carolyn's bed while a burglar was killing his wife, and I wondered what he thought about that. Or if he thought about it.

And my own thoughts turned suddenly to Anita, out there in Syosset with the boys. I had a moment of fear for her, seeing her menaced, drawing back in terror from some unseen danger. I recognized the fear as irrational, and I was able after a moment to know it for what it was, something I'd brought home with me, something that clung to me now along with Carolyn Cheatham's scent. I was carrying around Tommy Tillary's guilt by proxy.

Well, the hell with that. I didn't need his guilt. I had plenty of my own.

SIX

The weekend was quiet. I talked to my sons, but they didn't come in. Saturday afternoon I earned a hundred dollars by accompanying one of the partners in the antique shop down the block from Armstrong's. We cabbed together to East Seventy-fourth Street, where we collected clothing and other possessions from his ex-lover's apartment. The lover was thirty or forty pounds overweight, bitter and bitchy.

'I don't believe this, Gerald,' he said. 'Did you actually bring a bodyguard or is this my summer replacement? Either way I don't know whether to be flattered or insulted.'

'Oh, I'm sure you'll work it out,' Gerald told him.

In the cab back to the West Side Gerald said, 'I really loved that cunt, Matthew, and I will be goddamned if I can figure out why. Thank you for this, Matthew. I could have hired a schlepper for five dollars an hour, but your presence was all the difference in the world. Did you see how ready he was to remember that the Handel lamp was his? The fucking *hell* it was his. When I met him he didn't know from Handel, not the lamps or the composer, either. All he knew was to *hondle*. You know that word, *hondle?* It means to haggle over a price, like if I were to try to pay you fifty dollars now instead of the hundred we agreed on. I'm just joking, dear. I have no problem with paying you the hundred, I think you were worth every penny of it.'

Sunday night Bobby Ruslander found me in Armstrong's. Skip was looking for me, he said. He was at Miss Kitty's, and if I got a minute why didn't I drop over? I had time then, and Bobby walked over there with me.

It was a little cooler; the worst of the heat wave had broken Saturday, and there had been some rain to cool the streets down a little. A fire truck raced past us as we waited for the light to change. When the siren died down, Bobby said, 'Crazy business.'

'Oh?'

'He'll tell you about it.'

As we crossed the street he said, 'I never see him like this, you know what I mean? He's always supercool, Arthur is.'

'Nobody else calls him Arthur.'

'Nobody ever did. Back when we're kids, nobody calls him Arthur. It was like going against type, you know? Everybody calls him Skip, I'm his best friend, *I* call him by his formal name.'

When we got there Skip tossed Bobby a bar towel and asked him to take over for him. 'He's a lousy bartender,' he announced, 'but he doesn't steal much.'

'That's what you think,' Bobby said.

We went in back and Skip closed the door. There were a couple of old desks, two swivel chairs and a straight-backed chair, a coatrack, a file cabinet, and a big old Mosler safe that was taller than I was. 'That's where the books shoulda been,' he said, pointing at the safe. 'Except we're too smart for that, me and John. There's an audit, that's the first place they're gonna look, right? So all that's in there is a thousand in cash and some papers and shit, the lease on this place, the partnership agreement, his divorce papers, shit like that. Terrific. We saved that crap and let somebody walk off with the store.'

He lit a cigarette. 'Safe was here when we took the place,' he said. 'Left over from when the joint was a hardware store, and it cost more to move than it was worth, so we inherited it. Massive fucker, isn't it? You could put a body in there if you had one around. That way nobody'd steal it. He called, the fucker who stole the books.'

'Oh?'

He nodded. 'It's a ransom pitch. "I got something of yours and you can have it back."'

'He name a price?'

'No. Said he'll be in touch.'

'You recognize the voice?'

'Uh-uh. Sounded phony.'

'How do you mean?'

'Like it wasn't his real voice I was hearing. Anyway, I didn't recognize it.' He clasped his hands, extended his arms to crack his knuckles. 'I'm supposed to sit around until I hear from him.'

'When did you get the call?'

471

'Couple hours ago. I was working, he called me here. Good start to the evening, I'll tell you.'

'At least he's coming to you instead of sending the stuff straight to the IRS.'

'Yeah, I thought of that. This way we get the chance to do something. If he went and dropped a dime on us, all we could do is bend over and take it.'

'Did you talk to your partner?'

'Not yet. I called his house, he wasn't in.'

'So you sit tight.'

'Yeah. That's a switch. What the hell have I been doing, hanging loose?' There was a water tumbler on his desk, a third full with a brownish liquid. He took a last drag on his cigarette and dropped it into the glass. 'Disgusting,' he said. 'I never want to see you do that, Matt. You don't smoke, do you?'

'Once in a great while.'

'Yeah? You have one now and then and don't get hooked? I know a guy takes heroin that way. You know him, too, for that matter. But these little fuckers' – he tapped the pack – 'I think they're more addictive than smack. You want one now?'

'No thanks.'

He stood up. 'The only things I don't get addicted to,' he said, 'are the ones I didn't like that much in the first place. Hey, thanks for coming by. There's nothing to do but wait, but I figured I wanted to keep you in the picture, let you know what's going on.'

'That's fine,' I said, 'but I want you to know you don't owe me anything for it.'

'What do you mean?'

'I mean don't go paying my bar tab for this.'

'Are you sore?'

'No.'

'It was just something I felt like doing.'

'I appreciate it, but it wasn't necessary.'

'Yeah, I guess.' He shrugged. 'When you're skimming you get to be very free with cash. You spend it on things that don't show. The hell with it. I can stand you a drink, though, can't I? In my own joint?'

'That you can do.'

'C'mon then,' he said, 'before fucking Ruslander gives the whole store away.'

Every time I went into Armstrong's I wondered if I'd run into

Carolyn, and each time I was more relieved than disappointed when I didn't. I could have called her, but I sensed that it was perfectly appropriate not to. Friday night had been just what each of us had evidently wanted, and it looked as though it had been complete in itself for both of us, and I was glad of that. As a fringe benefit, I was over whatever had had me bugged about Fran, and it was beginning to look as though it had been nothing much more complicated than old-fashioned horniness. I suppose a half-hour with one of the streetwalkers would have served me as well, if less pleasurably.

I didn't run into Tommy, either, and that, too, was a relief, and in no sense disappointing.

Then Monday morning I picked up the *News* and read that they'd pulled in a pair of young Hispanics from Sunset Park for the Tillary burglary and homicide. The paper ran the usual photo – two skinny youths, their hair unruly, one of them trying to hide his face from the camera, the other smirking defiantly, and each of them handcuffed to a broad-shouldered grimfaced Irishman in a suit. There was a caption to tell you which ones were the good guys, but you didn't really need it.

I was in Armstrong's that afternoon when the phone rang. Dennis put down the glass he was wiping and answered it. 'He was here a minute ago,' he said. 'I'll see if he stepped out.' He covered the mouthpiece with his hand and looked quizzically at me. 'Are you still here?' he asked. 'Or did you slip away while my attention was somehow diverted?'

'Who wants to know?'

'Tommy Tillary.'

You never know what a woman will decide to tell a man, or how a man will react to it. I didn't much want to find out, but I was better off learning over the phone than face-to-face. I nodded and Dennis passed the phone across the bar.

I said, 'Matt Scudder, Tommy. I was sorry to hear about your wife.'

'Thanks, Matt. Jesus, it feels like it happened a year ago. It was what, a little over a week?'

'At least they got the bastards.'

There was a pause. Then he said, 'Jesus. You haven't seen a paper, huh?'

'Sure I did. Two Spanish kids, had their pictures.'

'I guess you read this morning's *News*.'

'I generally do. Why?'

473

'But not this afternoon's *Post*.'

'No. Why, what happened? They turn out to be clean?'

'Clean,' he said, and snorted. Then he said, 'I figured you'd know. The cops came by early this morning, before I saw the story in the *News*, so I didn't even know about the arrest. Shit. Be easier if you already knew this.'

'I'm not following you, Tommy.'

'The two Latin lovers. Clean? Shit, the men's room in the Times Square subway station, that's how clean they are. The cops hit their place and found stuff from my house everywhere they looked. Jewelry they had descriptions of, a stereo that I gave them the serial number, everything. Monogrammed shit. I mean that's how clean they were, for Christ's sake.'

'So?'

'So they admitted the burglary but not the murder.'

'Crooks do that all the time, Tommy.'

'Lemme finish, huh? They admitted the burglary, but according to them it wasn't really a burglary. I was giving them all that stuff.'

'And they just came to pick it up in the middle of the night.'

'Yeah, right. No, their story was they were supposed to make it look like a burglary so I could collect from my insurance. I could claim a loss on top of what they were actually taking, and that way everybody's to the good.'

'What did the actual loss amount to?'

'Shit, *I* don't know. There were twice as many things turned up at their place as I ever listed when I made out a report. There's things I missed a few days after I filled out the report and other stuff I didn't know was gone until the cops found them. And they took things weren't covered. There was a fur of Peg's, we were gonna get a floater on it and we never did. And some of her jewelry, same story. I got a standard homeowner's policy, it didn't cover anywheres near everything they took. They got a set of sterling, it came down to us from her aunt, I swear I forgot we owned the stuff. And *it* wasn't covered, either.'

'It hardly sounds like an insurance setup.'

'No, of course not. How the hell could it be? Anyway, the important thing is according to them the house was empty when they hit it. Peg wasn't home.'

'And?'

'And I set them up is their story. They hit the place, they carted everything away, and then I came home with Peg and

474

stabbed her six, eight times, whatever it was, and left her there so it looked like it happened during a burglary.'

'How could the burglars testify that you stabbed your wife?'

'They couldn't. All they said was they didn't and she wasn't home when they were there and I had it arranged with them to do the burglary. The cops pieced the rest of it together.'

'What did they do, arrest you?'

'No. They came over to the hotel where I'm staying, it was early, I was just out of the shower. Now this was the first I knew that the spics were arrested, let alone that they were trying to do a job on me. They just wanted to talk, the cops, and at first I talked to them, and then I started to get the drift of what they were trying to put on me. So I said I wasn't saying anything more without my lawyer present, and I called him, and he left half his breakfast on the table and came over in a hurry, and he wouldn't let me say a word.'

'And they didn't take you in or book you?'

'No.'

'But they didn't entirely buy your story either?'

'No way. I didn't really tell 'em a story because Kaplan wouldn't let me say anything. They didn't drag me in because they don't have a case yet, but according to Kaplan they're going to be building one if they can. They told me not to leave town. You believe it? My wife's dead, the *Post* headline says "Quiz Husband in Burglary Murder," and what the hell do they think I'm gonna do? Am I going fishing for fucking trout in Montana? "Don't leave town." You see this shit on television, you think nobody in real life talks like that. Maybe television's where they get it from.'

I waited for him to tell me what he wanted from me. I didn't have long to wait.

'Why I called,' he said, 'is Kaplan thinks we ought to hire a detective. He figures maybe these guys talked around the neighborhood, maybe they bragged to their friends, maybe there's a way to prove they did the killing. He says the cops won't concentrate on that end if they're too busy trying to nail the lid shut on me.'

I explained that I didn't have any official standing, that I had no license and filed no reports.

'That's okay,' he insisted. 'I told Kaplan what I want is somebody I can trust, somebody'll do a job for me. I don't think they're gonna have any kind of a case at all, Matt, because I can account for my time and I couldn'ta been where I woulda hadda

475

be to do what they said I did. But the longer this shit drags on the worse it is for me. I want it cleared up, I want it in the papers that these Spanish assholes did it all and I had nothing to do with anything. I want that for me and for the people I do business with and for my relatives and Peg's relatives and all the wonderful people who voted for me. You remember the old "Amateur Hour"? "I want to thank mom and dad and Aunt Edith and my piano teacher Mrs Pelton and all the wonderful people who voted for me." Listen, you'll meet me and Kaplan in his office, hear what the man has to say, do me a hell of a big favor, and pick up a couple of bucks for yourself. What do you say, Matt?'

He wanted somebody he could trust. Had Carolyn from the Caroline told him how trustworthy I was?

What did I say? I said yes.

SEVEN

I took a train one stop into Brooklyn and met Tommy Tillary in Drew Kaplan's office on Court Street a few blocks from Brooklyn's Borough Hall. There was a Lebanese restaurant next door. At the corner a grocery store specializing in Middle Eastern imports stood next to an antique shop overflowing with stripped oak furniture and brass lamps and bedsteads. In front of Kaplan's building, a legless black man reposed on a platform with wheels. An open cigar box on one side of him held a couple of singles and a lot of coins. He was wearing horn-rimmed sunglasses, and a hand-lettered sign on the pavement in front of him said, 'Don't Be Fooled by the Sunglasses. Not Blind Just No Legs.'

Kaplan's office ran to wood paneling and leather chairs and oak file cabinets that might have come from the place on the corner. His name and the names of two partners were painted on the frosted glass of the hall door in old-fashioned gold and black lettering. Framed diplomas on the wall of his personal office showed he'd earned his BA at Adelphi, his LLB at Brooklyn Law. A lucite cube on top of a Victorian oak desk held photographs of his wife and young children. A bronzed railway spike served as a desktop paperweight. On the wall alongside the desk, a pendulum clock ticked away the afternoon.

Kaplan himself looked conservatively up-to-date in a tropical-weight gray pinstripe suit and a yellow pin-dot tie. He looked to be in his early thirties, which would fit the dates on the diplomas. He was shorter than I and of course much shorter than Tommy, trimly built, clean-shaven, with dark hair and eyes and a slightly lopsided smile. His handshake was medium-firm, his gaze direct but measuring, calculating.

Tommy wore his burgundy blazer over gray flannel trousers and white loafers. Strain showed at the corners of his blue eyes and around his mouth. His complexion was off, too, as if anxiety had caused the blood to draw inward, leaving the skin sallow.

'All we want you to do,' Drew Kaplan said, 'is find a key in one of their pants pockets, Herrera's or Cruz's, and trace it to a locker in Penn Station, and in the locker there's a foot-long knife with both their prints and her blood on it.'

'Is that what it's going to take?'

He smiled. 'Let's just say it wouldn't hurt. No, actually we're not in such bad shape. What they've got is some shaky testimony from a pair of Latins who've been in and out of trouble since they got weaned onto Tropicana. And they've got what looks to them like a good motive on Tommy's part.'

'Which is?'

I was looking at Tommy when I asked. His eyes slipped away from mine. Kaplan said, 'A marital triangle, a case of the shorts, and a strong money motive. Margaret Tillary came into some money this past spring upon the death of an aunt. The estate's not through probate yet but the value's somewhere in excess of half a million dollars.'

'Be less than that when they get done hackin' away at it,' Tommy said. 'A whole lot less.'

'Plus there's insurance. Tommy and his wife had a pair of straight-life policies, each naming the other as beneficiary, both with double-indemnity clauses and a face amount of' – he consulted a slip on his desk – 'a hundred and fifty thousand dollars, which doubled for accidental death is three hundred thousand. At this point we've got what begins to look like seven, eight hundred thousand motives for murder.'

'My lawyer talkin',' Tommy said.

'Same time, Tommy here's hurting a little for cash. He's having a bad year gambling, he's into the bookies and maybe they're starting to press him a little.'

'Not so it amounts to anything,' Tommy put in.

'I'm telling it the way the cops would tell it, all right? He owes some money around town, he's a couple of payments behind with the Buick. Meanwhile he's putting away this girl at the office, bouncing around the bars with her, sometimes not making it home altogether –'

'Hardly ever, Drew. I'd almost always make it home, an' if I couldn't grab a few hours in the sack I'd at least shower and change and have breakfast with Peg.'

'What was breakfast? Dexamyl?'

'Sometimes. I had an office to go to, a job to do.'

Kaplan sat on a corner of his desk, crossed his legs at the ankle. 'That'll do for motive,' he said. 'What they don't bother to notice is a couple of things. One, he loved his wife, and how many husbands cheat? What is it they say? Ninety percent admit they cheat and ten percent lie about it? Two, he's got debts but he's not in a crunch. He's a guy makes good money over the year but he runs hot and cold, and for years he's been fat one month and strapped the next.'

'You get used to it,' Tommy said.

'Plus the numbers sound like a fortune, but they're not unusual figures. A half-million is substantial, but as Tommy said it won't net out to that much after taxes, and part of it consists of title to the house he's been occupying for years. A hundred fifty thousand dollars' insurance on a breadwinner isn't high by any means, and having the same coverage on the wife isn't uncommon, a lot of insurance agents try to write policies that way. They make it sound logically balanced, so you overlook the fact that you don't really need that kind of coverage on someone you don't depend upon for income.' He spread his hands. 'Anyway, the policies were taken out over ten years ago. This isn't something he went and set up last week.'

He stood up, talked over to the window. Tommy had picked up the railway spike from the desk and was playing with it, slapping it against the palm of his hand, consciously or unconsciously matching the rhythm of the clock's pendulum.

Kaplan said, 'One of the killers, Angel Herrera, except I suppose he pronounces it Ahn-hell, did some odd jobs at the Tillary house last March or April. Spring cleaning, he hauled stuff out of the basement and attic, did a little donkey work for hourly wages. According to Herrera, that's how Tommy knew to contact him to fake the burglary. According to common sense, that's how Herrera and his buddy Cruz knew the house and what was in it and how to gain access.'

'How'd they do that?'

'Broke a small pane in the side door, reached in and unlocked it. Their story is Tommy left it open for them and must have broken the glass after. It's also their story that they left the place relatively neat.'

'Looked like a cyclone hit it,' Tommy said. 'I had to go there. Made me sick to look at it.'

'Their story is Tommy did that the same time he was murdering his wife. Except none of this works out if you take a good look at it. The times are all wrong. They went in around midnight, and the medical examiner places the time of death at between ten p.m. and four a.m. Now Tommy here never made it home from the office that evening. He worked past five, he met his friend for dinner, and he was with her in a variety of public places over the course of the evening.' He looked over at his client. 'We're lucky he's not much on discretion. His alibi'd be a whole lot thinner if he'd spent every minute in her apartment with the blinds drawn.'

'I was discreet as far as Peg was concerned,' Tommy said. 'In Brooklyn I was a family man. What I did in the city never hurt her.'

'After midnight his time's harder to account for,' Kaplan went on. 'The only substantiation for some of those hours is the girlfriend, because for a while they *were* in her apartment with the blinds drawn.'

You didn't have to draw the blinds, I thought. Nobody could see in.

'Plus there was some time she couldn't account for.'

'She fell asleep and I couldn't,' Tommy said, 'so I got dressed and went out for a couple of pops. But I wasn't gone that long, and she woke up when I got back. I had a helicopter, maybe I coulda got to Bay Ridge'n' back in that amount of time. Never do it in a Buick.'

'The thing is,' Kaplan said, 'even supposing there was time, or discounting the girlfriend's alibi altogether and only accepting the times substantiated by unbiased witnesses, how could he possibly have done it? Say he sneaks home sometime after the Spanish kids have paid their visit and before four a.m., which was the latest the murder could have taken place. Where was she all this time? According to Cruz and Herrera, there was nobody home. Well, where did he find her to kill her? What did he do, haul her around in the trunk all night?'

'Let's say he killed her before they got there,' I suggested.

'And I'm lookin' to *hire* this guy,' Tommy said. 'I got an instinct, you know what I mean?'

'Doesn't work,' Kaplan said. 'In the first place the times simply won't fit. He's alibied solid from before eight until past midnight, out in public with the girl. The ME says she was definitely alive at ten, that's the absolute earliest she could have been killed. Plus even forgetting the times it doesn't work. How could they go in, rob the whole house, and not see a dead woman in the bedroom? They were in that room, they were in possession of stolen articles from that room, I think they even

480

found prints in there. Well, the police found the corpse of Margaret Tillary in that room, too, and it's the sort of thing they probably would have noticed.'

'Maybe the body was covered up.' I thought of Skip's big Mosler safe. 'Locked in a closet they didn't look in.'

He shook his head. 'The cause of death was stabbing. There was a lot of blood and it was all over the place. The bed was soaked, the bedroom carpet.' We both avoided looking at Tommy. 'So she wasn't killed elsewhere,' he concluded. 'She was killed right there, and if it wasn't Herrera did it it was Cruz, and either way it wasn't Tommy.'

I looked for a hole in it and couldn't find one. 'Then I don't see what you need me for,' I said. 'The case against Tommy sounds pretty thin.'

'So thin there isn't any case.'

'Then –'

'The thing is,' he said, 'you get near a courtroom with something like this and even if you win you still lose. Because for the rest of your life all everybody remembers about you is you once stood trial for murdering your wife. Never mind that you won an acquittal. Everybody just figures some Jew lawyer bought a judge or conned a jury.'

'So I'll get a guinea lawyer,' Tommy said, 'and they'll think he threatened the judge and beat up the jury.'

'Besides,' Kaplan said, 'you never know which way a jury's going to jump. Remember, Tommy's alibi is he was with another woman at the time of the burglary. The woman's a colleague, they could choose to regard it as completely above-board, but did you see the piece in the *Post*? What juries'll go and do, they decide they don't believe the alibi because it's your girlfriend lying for you, and at the same time they label you a scumbag for getting your carrot scraped while your wife's getting killed.'

'You keep it up,' Tommy said, 'I'll find my own self guilty, the way you make it sound.'

'Plus he's hard to get a sympathetic jury for. He's a big handsome guy, a sharp dresser, and you'd love him in a gin joint but how much do you love him in a courtroom? He's a telephone securities salesman, perfectly respectable thing to be, calls you up, advises you how to invest your money. Fine. That means every clown who ever lost a hundred dollars on a stock tip or bought magazine subscriptions over the phone is going to

481

walk into the courtroom with a hardon for him. I'm telling you, I want to stay the hell *out* of court. I'll *win* in court, I know that, or worse comes to worst I'll win on appeal, but who needs it? This is a case that shouldn't be in the first place, and what I'd love is to clear it up before they even go so far as presenting a bill to the grand jury.'

'So from me you want –'

'Whatever you can find out, Matt. Whatever discredits Cruz and Herrera. I don't know what's there to find. I'd love it if you could find blood, their clothes with stains on it, anything like that. The point is that I don't know what's there to be found, and you were a cop and now you're working private, and you can get down in the streets and the bars and nose around. You familiar with Brooklyn?'

'Parts of it. I worked over here, off and on.'

'So you can find your way around.'

'Well enough. But wouldn't you be better off with a Spanish-speaker? I know enough to buy a beer in a bodega, but I'm a long way from fluent.'

'Tommy says he wants somebody he can trust, and he was very adamant about calling you in. I think he's right. A personal relationship's worth more than a dime's worth of *"Me llamo Matteo y como está usted?"'*

'That's the truth,' Tommy Tillary said. 'Matt, I know I can count on you, and that's worth a lot.'

I wanted to tell him all he could count on were his fingers, but why was I trying to talk myself out of a fee? His money was as good as anybody else's. I wasn't sure I liked him, but I was just as happy not to like the men I worked for. It bothered me less that way if I felt I was giving them less than full value.

And I didn't see how I could give him much. The case against him sounded loose enough to fall apart without my help. I wondered if Kaplan just wanted to create some activity to justify a high fee of his own, in the event that the whole thing blew itself out in a week's time. That was possible, and that wasn't my problem, either.

I said I would be glad to help. I said I hoped I would be able to come up with something useful.

Tommy said he was sure I could.

Drew Kaplan said, 'Now you'll want a retainer. I suppose that'll be an advance against a per diem fee plus expenses, or do you bill at hourly rates? Why are you shaking your head?'

'I'm unlicensed,' I said. 'I have no official standing.'

'That's no problem. We can carry you on the books as a consultant.'

'I don't want to be on the books at all,' I said. 'I don't keep track of my time or expenses. I pay my own expenses out of my own pocket. I get paid in cash.'

'How do you set your fees?'

'I think up a number. If I think I should have more coming when I'm finished, I say so. If you disagree, you don't have to pay me. I'm not going to take anybody to court.'

'It seems a haphazard way to do business,' Kaplan said.

'It's not a business. I do favors for friends.'

'And take money for them.'

'Is there anything wrong with taking money for a favor?'

'I don't suppose there is.' He looked thoughtful. 'How much would you expect for this favor?'

'I don't know what's involved,' I said. 'Suppose you let me have fifteen hundred dollars today. If things drag on and I feel entitled to more, I'll let you know.'

'Fifteen hundred. And of course Tommy doesn't know exactly what he's getting for that.'

'No,' I said. 'Neither do I.'

Kaplan narrowed his eyes. 'That seems high for a retainer,' he said. 'I'd have thought a third of that would be ample for starters.'

I thought of my antique dealer friend. Did I know what it was to *hondle*? Kaplan evidently did.

'It's not that much,' I said. 'It's one percent of the insurance money, and that's part of the reason for hiring an investigator, isn't it? The company won't pay off until Tommy's in the clear.'

Kaplan looked slightly startled. 'That's true,' he admitted, 'but I don't know that it's the reason for hiring you. The company will pay up sooner or later. I don't think your fee is necessarily high, it just seemed a disproportionately large sum to lay out in advance, and –'

'Don't argue price,' Tommy cut in. 'The fee sounds fine to me, Matt. The only thing is, being a little short right now, and coming up with fifteen C in cash –'

'Maybe your lawyer will front it to you,' I suggested.

Kaplan thought that was irregular. I went into the outer office while they talked it over. The receptionist was reading a copy of *Fate* magazine. A pair of hand-tinted etchings in antiqued frames showed scenes of nineteenth-century downtown Brooklyn. I was looking at them when Kaplan's door opened and he beckoned me back inside.

'Tommy's going to be able to borrow on the basis of his expectations from the insurance monies and his wife's estate,' he said. 'Meanwhile I can let you have the fifteen hundred. I hope you have no objection to signing a receipt?'

'None at all,' I said. I counted the bills, twelve hundreds and six fifties, all circulated bills out of sequence. Everybody seems to have some cash around, even lawyers.

He wrote out a receipt and I signed it. He apologized for what he called a little awkwardness around the subject of my fee. 'Lawyers are schooled to be very conventional human beings,' he said. 'I sometimes have a slow reaction time when it comes to adjusting to irregular procedure. I hope I wasn't offensive.'

'Not at all.'

'I'm glad of that. Now I won't be expecting written reports or a precise account of your movements, but you'll report to me as you go along and let me know what turns up? And please tell me too much rather than too little. It's hard to know what will prove useful.'

'I know that myself.'

'I'm sure you do.' He walked me to the door. 'And incidentally,' he said, 'your fee is only one-half of one percent of the insurance money. I think I mentioned that the policy had a double-indemnity clause, and murder is considered accidental.'

'I know,' I said. 'I've always wondered why.'

EIGHT

The Sixty-eighth Precinct is stationed on Sixty-fifth Street between Third and Fourth Avenues, straddling the approximate boundary of Bay Ridge and Sunset Park. On the south side of the street a housing project loomed; across from it, the station house looked like something from Picasso's cubist period, all blocky with cantilevered cubes and recessed areas. The structure reminded me of the building that houses the Two-three in East Harlem, and I learned later that the same architect designed them both.

The building was six years old then, according to the plaque in the entranceway that mentioned the architect, the police commissioner, the mayor, and a couple of other worthies making a bid for municipal immortality. I stood there and read the whole plaque as if it had a special message for me. Then I went up to the desk and said I was there to see Detective Calvin Neumann. The officer on duty made a phone call, then pointed me to the squad room.

The building's interior was clean and spacious and well lit. It had been open enough years, though, to begin to feel like what it was.

The squad room contained a bank of gray metal file cabinets, a row of green metal lockers, and twin rows of five-foot steel desks set back to back. A television set was on in one corner with nobody watching it. Half of the eight or ten desks were occupied. At the water cooler, a man in a suit talked with a man in his shirt sleeves. In the holding pen, a drunk sang something tuneless in Spanish.

I recognized one of the seated detectives but couldn't recall his name. He didn't look up. Across the room, another man looked familiar. I went up to a man I didn't know and he pointed out Neumann, two desks down on the opposite side.

He was filling in a form, and I stood while he finished what he was typing. He looked up then and said, 'Scudder?' and pointed to a chair. He swiveled around to face me and waved a hand at the typewriter.

'They don't tell you,' he said, 'the hours you're gonna spend typing crud. Nobody out there realizes how much of this job is clerical.'

'That's the part it's hard to get nostalgic about.'

'I don't think I'd miss it myself.' He yawned elaborately. 'Eddie Koehler gave you high marks,' he said. 'I gave him a call like you suggested. He said you're okay.'

'You know Eddie?'

He shook his head. 'But I know what a lieutenant is,' he said. 'I haven't got a whole lot to give you, but you're welcome to it. You may not get the same cooperation from Brooklyn Homicide.'

'Why's that?'

'They drew the case to start with. It got called in originally to the One-oh-four, which was actually wrong, it should have been ours, but that happens a lot. Then Brooklyn Homicide responded along with the One-oh-four, and they took the case away from the precinct guys.'

'When did you come into it?'

'When a favorite snitch of mine came up with a lot of talk coming out of the bars and bakeries on Third under the expressway. A nice mink coat at a real good price, but you got to keep this quiet because there's a lot of heat. Well, July's a funny time to sell fur coats in Sunset Park. A guy buys a coat for his señora, he wants her to be able to wear it that night. So my guy comes to me with the impression that Miguelito Cruz has a houseful of stuff he's looking to sell and it just might be he hasn't got sales slips for many of the items. With the mink and a couple other items he mentioned, I remembered the Tillary job on Colonial Road, and it was enough to get a judge to issue a search warrant.'

He ran a hand through his hair. It was medium brown, lighter where the sun had bleached it, and it was on the shaggy side. Cops were starting to wear their hair a little longer around about then, and the younger ones were beginning to show up in beards and moustaches. Neumann, though, was clean-shaven, his features regular except for a nose that had been broken and imperfectly reset.

'The stuff was in Cruz's house,' he said. 'He lives over on Fifty-first, the other side of the Gowanus Expressway. I have the address somewhere if you want it. Those are some pretty blighted blocks over by the Bush Terminal Warehouse, if you know where that is. A lot of empty lots and boarded-up buildings and others nobody bothered boarding up, or somebody opened them up again and there's junkies camped out there. Where Cruz lived wasn't so bad. You'll see it if you go over there.'

'He live alone?'

He shook his head. 'With his *abuela*. His grandmother. Little old lady, doesn't speak English, she probably ought to be in a home. Maybe they'll take her in at the Marien-Heim, it's right in the neighborhood. Old lady comes here from Puerto Rico, before she can learn English she winds up in a home with a German name. That's New York, right?'

'You found Tillary's possessions in the Cruz apartment?'

'Oh, yeah. No question. I mean the serial numbers matched on the record player. He tried to deny it. What else is new, right? 'Oh, I buy dis stuff on de street, it was some guy I met in a bar. I doan know hees name.' We told him, sure, Miguelito, but meanwhile a woman got cut bad in the house this stuff came out of, so it sure looks like you're gonna go away for murder one. The next minute he's copping to the burglary but insisting there was no dead woman when he was there.'

'He must have known a woman got killed there.'

'Of course, no matter who killed her. It was in the papers, right? One minute he says he didn't see the story, the next minute he didn't happen to recognize the address, you know how their stories keep changing.'

'Where does Herrera come in?'

'They're cousins or something. Herrera lives in a furnished room on Forty-eighth between Fifth and Sixth just a couple of blocks from the park. Lived there, anyway. Right now they're both living at the Brooklyn House of Detention and they'll be living there until they move upstate.'

'They both have sheets?'

'Be a surprise if they didn't, wouldn't it?' He grinned. 'They're your typical fuckups. A few juvenile arrests for gang stuff. They both beat a burglary charge a year and a half ago, a judge ruled there wasn't probable cause to justify a frisk.' He shook his head. 'The fucking rules you have to play by. Anyway, they beat that one, and another time they got collared for burglary and plea-bargained it to criminal trespass and got suspended sentences for it. And another time, another burglary case, the evidence disappeared.'

'It disappeared?'

'It got lost or misfiled or something, I don't know. It's a miracle anybody ever goes to jail in this city. You really need a death wish to wind up in prison.'

'So they did a fair amount of burglary.'

'It looks like. In-and-out stuff, nickel-and-dime crap. Kick the door in, grab a radio, run into the street and sell it on the street for five or ten dollars. Cruz was worse than Herrera. Herrera worked from time to time, pushing a hand truck in the garment center or delivering lunches, minimum-wage stuff. I don't think Miguelito ever held a job.'

'But neither of them ever killed anybody before.'

'Cruz did.'

'Oh?'

He nodded. 'In a tavern fight, him and another asshole fighting over some woman.'

'The papers didn't have that.'

'It never got to court. There were no charges pressed. There were a dozen witnesses reporting that the dead guy went after Cruz first with a broken bottle.'

'What weapon did Cruz use?'

'A knife. He said it wasn't his, and there were witnesses prepared to swear they'd seen somebody toss him the knife. And of course they hadn't happened to notice who it was did the tossing. We didn't have enough to make a case of weapon possession, let alone homicide.'

'But Cruz normally carried a knife?'

'You'd be more likely to catch him leaving the house without underwear.'

That was early afternoon, the day after I'd taken fifteen hundred dollars from Drew Kaplan. That morning I'd bought a money order and mailed it to Syosset. I paid my August rent in advance, settled a bar tab or two, and rode the BMT to Sunset Park.

It's in Brooklyn, of course, on the borough's western edge, above Bay Ridge and south and west of Green-Wood Cemetery. These days there's a fair amount of brownstoning going on in Sunset Park, with young urban professionals fleeing the Manhattan rents and renovating the old row houses, gentrifying the neighborhood. Back then the upwardly mobile young had not yet discovered the place, and the population was a mixture of

Latins and Scandinavians. Most of the former were Puerto Ricans, most of the latter Norwegians, and the balance was gradually shifting from Europe to the islands, from light to dark, but this was a process that had been going on for ages and there was nothing hurried about it.

I'd walked around some before my visit to the Six-eight, keeping mostly within a block or so of Fourth Avenue, the main commercial thoroughfare, and orienting myself intermittently by looking around for Saint Michael's Church. Few of the buildings stood more than three stories, and the egg-shaped church dome, set atop a two-hundred-foot tower, was visible a long ways off.

I walked north on Third Avenue now, on the right-hand side of the street, in the shade of the expressway overhead. As I neared Cruz's street I stopped in a couple of bars, more to immerse myself in the neighborhood than to ask any questions. I had a short shot of bourbon in one place, stuck to beer otherwise.

The block where Miguelito Cruz had lived with his grand-mother was as Neumann described it. There were several vast vacant lots, one of them staked out in cyclone fencing, the others open and rubble-strewn. In one, small children played in the burned-out shell of a Volkswagen beetle. Four three-story buildings with scalloped brick fronts stood in a row on the north side of the block, closer to Second Avenue than to Third. The buildings abutting the group on either side had been torn down, and the newly exposed brick side walls looked raw except for the graffiti spray-painted on their lower portions.

Cruz had lived in the building closest to Second Avenue, closest too to the river. The vestibule was a lot of cracked and missing tiles and peeling paint. Six mailboxes were set into one wall, their locks broken and repaired and broken again. There were no bells to ring, nor was there a lock on the front door. I opened it and walked up two flights of stairs. The stairwell held cooking smells, rodent smells, a faint ammoniac reek of urine. All old buildings housing poor people smell like that. Rats die in the walls, kids and drunks piss. Cruz's building was no worse than thousands.

The grandmother lived on the top floor, in a perfectly neat railroad flat filled with holy pictures and little candle-illumi-nated shrines. If she spoke any English, she didn't let me know it.

No one answered my knock at the apartment across the hall.

I worked my way through the building. On the second floor, the apartment directly below the Cruz apartment was occupied by a very dark-skinned Hispanic woman with what looked like five children under six years old. A television set and a radio were playing in the front room, another radio in the kitchen. The children were in constant motion and at least two of them were crying or yelling at all times. The woman was cooperative enough, but she didn't have much English and it was impossible to concentrate on anything in there.

Across the hall, no one responded to my knock. I could hear a television set playing and went on knocking. Finally the door opened. An enormously fat man in his underwear opened the door and walked back inside without a word, evidently assuming I would follow. He led me through several rooms littered with old newspapers and empty Pabst Blue Ribbon cans to the front room, where he sat in a sprung armchair watching a game show. The color on his set was curiously distorted, giving the panelists faces that were red one moment and green the next.

He was white, with lank hair that had been blond once but was mostly gray now. It was hard to estimate his age because of the weight he was carrying, but he was probably somewhere between forty and sixty. He hadn't shaved in several days and may not have bathed or changed his bed linen in months. He stank, and his apartment stank, and I stayed there anyway and asked him questions. He had three beers left from a six-pack when I went in there, and he drank them one after another and padded barefoot through the apartment to return with a fresh six-pack from the refrigerator.

His name was Illing, he said, Paul Illing, and he had heard about Cruz, it was on television, and he thought it was terrible but he wasn't surprised, hell no. He'd lived here all his life, he told me, and this had been a nice neighborhood once, decent people, respected theirselves and respected their neighbors. But now you had the wrong element, and what could you expect?

'They live like animals,' he told me. 'You wouldn't believe it.'

Angel Herrera's rooming house was a four-story red brick building, its ground floor given over to a coin laundry. Two men in their late twenties lounged on the stoop, drinking their beer from cans held in brown paper bags. I asked for Herrera's room. They decided I was a cop; the assumption showed in their faces, and the set of their shoulders. One of them told me to try the fourth floor.

There was a reek of marijuana smoke floating on top of the other smells in the hallway. A tiny woman, dark and bright-eyed, stood at the third-floor landing. She was wearing an apron and holding a folded copy of *El Diario*, one of the Spanish-language newspapers. I asked for Herrera's room.

'Twenty-two,' she said, and pointed upstairs. 'But he's not in. 'Her eyes fixed on mine. 'You know where he is?'

'Yes.'

'Then you know he is not here. His door is lock.'

'Do you have the key?'

She looked at me sharply. 'You a cop?'

'I used to be.'

Her laugh was loud, unexpected. 'Wha'd you get, laid off? They got no work for cops, all the crooks in jail? You want to go in Angel's room, come on, I let you in.'

A cheap padlock secured the door of Room 22. She tried three keys before finding the right one, then opened the door and entered the room ahead of me. A cord hung from the bare-bulb ceiling fixture over the narrow iron bedstead. She pulled it, then raised a window shade to illuminate the room a little more.

I looked out the window, walked around the room, examined the contents of the closet and the small bureau. There were several photographs in drugstore frames on top of the bureau, and half a dozen unframed snapshots. Two different women, several children. In one snapshot, a man and woman in bathing suits squinted into the sun, the surf behind them. I showed the photograph to the woman and she identified the man as Herrera. I had seen his photo in the paper, along with Cruz and the two arresting officers, but he looked completely different in the snapshot.

The woman, I learned, was Herrera's girlfriend. The woman who appeared in some of the other photos with the children was Herrera's wife in Puerto Rico. He was a good boy, Herrera was, the woman assured me. He was polite, he kept his room neat, he didn't drink too much or play his radio loud late at night. And he loved his babies, he sent money home to Puerto Rico when he had it to send.

Fourth Avenue had churches on the average of one to a block – Norse Methodist, German Lutheran, Spanish Seventh-Day Adventists, and one called the Salem Tabernacle. They were all closed, and by the time I got to it, so was Saint Michael's. I was ecumenical enough in my tithing, but the Catholics got most of my money simply because they kept longer hours, but by the time I left Herrera's rooming house and stopped for a quick one at the bar on the corner, Saint Michael's was locked up as tight as its Protestant fellows.

Two blocks away, between a bodega and an OTB parlor, a gaunt Christ writhed on the cross in the window of a storefront *iglesia*. There were a couple of backless benches inside in front of a small altar, and on one of them two shapeless women in black huddled silent and motionless.

I slipped inside and sat on one of the benches myself for a few moments. I had my hundred-fifty-dollar tithe ready and I'd have been as happy giving it to this hole in the wall as to some more imposing and long-established firm, but I couldn't think of an inconspicuous way to manage it. There was no poor box in evidence, no receptacle designed to accommodate donations. I didn't want to call attention to myself by finding someone in charge and handing him the money, nor did I feel comfortable just leaving it on the bench, say, where anybody could pick it up and walk off with it.

I walked out of there no poorer than I'd walked in.

I spent the evening in Sunset Park.

I don't know if it was work, or if I even thought I was doing Tommy Tillary any good. I walked the streets and worked the bars, but I wasn't looking for anyone and I didn't ask a lot of questions.

On Sixtieth Street east of Fourth Avenue I found a dark beery tavern called the Fjord. There were nautical decorations on the walls but they looked to have accumulated haphazardly over the years – a length of fishnet, a life preserver, and, curiously, a Minnesota Vikings football pennant. A black-and-white TV sat at one end of the bar, its volume turned down low. Old men sat with their shots and beers, not talking much, letting the night pass.

When I left there I flagged a gypsy cab and got the driver to take me to Colonial Road in Bay Ridge. I wanted to see the house where Tommy Tillary had lived, the house where his wife had died. But I wasn't sure of the address. That stretch of Colonial Road was mostly brick apartment houses and I was pretty sure that Tommy's place was a private house. There were a few such houses tucked in between the apartment buildings but I didn't have the number written down and wasn't sure of the cross streets. I told the cabdriver I was looking for the house where the woman was stabbed to death and he didn't know what the hell I was talking about, and seemed generally wary of me, as though I might do something unpredictable at any moment.

I suppose I was a little drunk. I sobered up on the way back to Manhattan. He wasn't that enthusiastic about taking me, but he set a price of ten dollars and I agreed to it and leaned back in my seat. He took the expressway, and en route I saw the tower of Saint Michael's and told the driver that it wasn't right, that churches should be open twenty-four hours a day. He didn't say anything, and I closed my eyes and when I opened them the cab was pulling up in front of my hotel.

There were a couple of messages for me at the desk. Tommy Tillary had called twice and wanted me to call him. Skip Devoe had called once.

It was too late to call Tommy, probably too late for Skip. Late enough, anyway, to call it a night.

NINE

I rode out to Brooklyn again the next day. I stayed on the train past the Sunset Park stations and got off at Bay Ridge Avenue. The subway entrance was right across the street from the funeral parlor Margaret Tillary had been buried from. Burial had been in Green-Wood Cemetery, two miles to the north. I turned and looked up Fourth Avenue, as if following the route of the funeral cortege with my eyes. Then I walked west on Bay Ridge Avenue toward the water.

At Third Avenue I looked to my left and saw the Verrazano Bridge off in the distance, spanning the Narrows between Brooklyn and Staten Island. I walked on, through a better neighborhood than the one I'd spent the previous day in, and at Colonial Road I turned right and walked until I found the Tillary house. I'd looked up the address before leaving my hotel and now found it easily. It may have been one of the houses I'd stared at the night before. The cab ride had since faded some from memory. It was indistinct, as if seen through a veil.

The house was a huge brick-and-frame affair three stories tall, just across the street from the southeast corner of Owl's Head Park. Four-story apartment buildings of red brick flanked the house. It had a broad porch, an aluminum awning, a steeply pitched roof. I mounted the steps to the porch and rang the doorbell. A four-note chime sounded within.

No one answered. I tried the door and it was locked. The lock didn't look terribly challenging, but I had no reason to force it.

A driveway ran past the house on its left-hand side. It led past a side door, also locked, to a padlocked garage. The burglars had broken a pane of glass in the side door, and it had been since replaced with a rectangle of cardboard cut from a corrugated carton and secured with metallic tape.

I crossed the street and sat in the park for a while. Then I moved to where I could observe the Tillary house from the other

494

side of the street. I was trying to visualize the burglary. Cruz and Herrera had had a car, and I wondered where they'd parked it. In the driveway, out of sight and close to the door they'd entered through? Or on the street, making a getaway a simpler matter? The garage could have been open then; maybe they stowed the car in it, so no one would see it in the driveway and wonder about it.

I had a lunch of beans and rice and hot sausage. I got to Saint Michael's by midafternoon. It was open this time, and I sat for a while in a pew off to the side, then lit a couple of candles. My $150 finally made it to the poor box.

I did what you do. Mostly, I walked around and knocked on doors and asked questions. I went back to both their residences, Herrera's and Cruz's. I talked to neighbors of Cruz's who hadn't been around the previous day, and I talked to some of the other tenants in Herrera's rooming house. I walked over to the Six-eight looking for Cal Neumann. He wasn't there, but I talked to a couple of cops in the station house and went out for coffee with one of them.

I made a couple of phone calls, but most of my activity was walking around and talking to people face-to-face, writing down bits and pieces in my notebook, going through the motions and trying not to question the point of my actions. I was amassing a certain amount of data but I had no idea whether or not it added up to anything. I didn't know what exactly I was looking for, or if there was anything there *to* look for. I suppose I was trying to perform enough action and produce enough information to justify, to myself and to Tommy and his lawyer, the fee I had already collected and largely dispersed.

By early evening I'd had enough. I took the train home. There was a message at the desk for me from Tommy Tillary, with his office number. I put it in my pocket and walked around the corner, and Billie Keegan told me Skip was looking for me.

'Everybody's looking for me,' I said.

'It's nice to be wanted,' Billie said. 'I had an uncle was wanted in four states. You had a phone message, too. Where'd I put it?' He handed me a slip. Tommy Tillary again, but a different phone number this time. 'Something to drink, Matt? Or did you just drop by to check your mail and messages?'

I'd been taking it easy in Brooklyn, mostly sticking with cups of coffee in bakeries and bodegas, drinking a little beer in the bars. I let Billie pour me a double bourbon and it went down easy.

495

'Looked for you today,' Billie said. 'Couple of us went out to the track. Thought you might want to come along.'

'I had work to do,' I said. 'Anyway, I'm not much for horses.'

'It's fun,' he said, 'if you don't take it serious.'

The number Tommy Tillary left turned out to be a hotel switchboard in Murray Hill. He came on the line and asked if I could drop by the Hotel. 'You know where it is? Thirty-seventh and Lex?'

'I ought to be able to find it.'

'They got a bar downstairs, nice quiet little place. It's full of these Jap businessmen in Brooks Brothers suits. Every once in a while they put down their scotches long enough to take snapshots of each other. Then they smile and order more drinks. You'll love it.'

I caught a cab and went over there, and he hadn't been exaggerating much. The cocktail lounge, plush and dimly lit, had a largely Japanese clientele that evening. Tommy was by himself at the bar, and when I walked in he pumped my hand and introduced me to the bartender.

We took our drinks to a table. 'Crazy place,' he said. 'Look at that, will you? You thought I was kidding about the cameras, didn't you? I wonder what they do with all the pictures. You'd need a whole room in your house just to keep them, the way they click 'em off.'

'There's no film in the cameras.'

'Be a kick, wouldn't it?' He laughed. 'No film in the cameras. Shit, they're probably not real Japs, either. Where I mostly been going, there's the Blueprint a block away on Park, and there's another place, a pub-type place, Dirty Dick's or something like that. But I'm staying here and I wanted you to be able to reach me. Is this okay for now or should we go somewhere else?'

'This is fine.'

'You sure? I never had a detective work for me before, I want to make sure I keep him happy.' He grinned, then let his face turn serious. 'I was just wondering,' he said, 'if you were, you know, making any progress. Getting any-place.'

I told him some of what I'd run into. He got very excited when he heard about the barroom stabbing.

'That's great,' he said. 'That ought to wrap it up for our little brown brothers, shouldn't it?'

'How do you figure that?'

'He's a knife artist,' he said, 'and he already killed somebody once and got away with it. Jesus, this is great stuff, Matt. I knew it was the right move to get you in on this. Have you talked to Kaplan yet?'

'No.'

'That's what you want to do. This is the kind of stuff he can use.'

I wondered at that. For openers, it struck me that Drew Kaplan should have been able to inform himself of Miguelito Cruz's no-bill for homicide without hiring a detective. Nor did it seem to me that the information would weigh heavily in a courtroom, or that you could even introduce it in court, for that matter. Anyway, Kaplan had said he was looking for something that would keep him and his client out of court in the first place, and I couldn't see how I'd uncovered anything that qualified.

'You want to fill Drew in on everything you come up with,' Tommy assured me. 'Some little bit you hand him, might not look like anything to you, and it might fit with something he already has and it's just what he needs, you know what I mean? Even if it looks like nothing all by itself.'

'I can see how that would work.'

'Sure. Call him once a day, give him whatever you got. I know you don't file reports, but you don't mind checking in regular by phone, do you?'

'No, of course not.'

'Great,' he said. 'That's great, Matt. Let me get us a couple more of these.' He went to the bar, came back with fresh drinks. 'So you been out in my part of the world, huh? Like it out there?'

'I like your neighborhood better than Cruz and Herrera's.'

'Shit, I hope so. What, were you out by the house? My house?'

I nodded. 'To get a sense of it. You have a key, Tommy?'

'A key? You mean a house key? Sure, I'd have to have a key to my own house, wouldn't I? Why? You want a key to the place, Matt?'

'If you don't mind.'

'Jesus, everybody's been through there, cops, insurance, not to mention the spics.' He took a ring of keys from his pocket, removed one and held it out to me. 'This is for the front door,' he said. 'You want the side door key too? That's how they went in, there's cardboard taped up where they broke a pane to let themselves in.'

'I noticed it this afternoon.'

'So what do you need with the key? Just pull off the cardboard and let yourself in. While you're at it, see if there's anything left worth stealing and carry it outta there in a pillowcase.'

'Is that how they did it?'

'Who knows how they did it? That's how they do it on television, isn't it? Jesus, look at that, will ya? They take each other's pictures, they trade cameras and take 'em all over again. There's a lot of 'em stay at this hotel, that's why they come in here.' He looked down at his hands, clasped loosely on the table in front of him. His pinkie ring had turned to one side and he reached to straighten it. 'The hotel's not bad,' he said, 'but I can't stay here forever. You pay day rates, it adds up.'

'Will you be moving back to Bay Ridge?'

He shook his head. 'What do I need with a place like that? It was too big for the two of us and I'd rattle around there by myself. Forgetting about the feelings connected with it.'

'How did you come to have such a large house for two people, Tommy?'

'Well, it wasn't for two.' He looked off, remembering. 'It was Peg's aunt's house. What happened, she put up the money to buy the place. She had some insurance money left after she buried her husband some years ago, and we needed a place to live because we had the baby coming. You knew we had a kid that died?'

'I think there was something in the paper.'

'In the death notice, yeah, I put it in. We had a boy, Jimmy. He wasn't right, he had congenital heart damage and some mental retardation. He died, it was just before his sixth birthday.'

'That's hard, Tommy.'

'It was harder for her. I think it woulda been worse than it was except he didn't live at home after the first few months. The medical problems, you couldn't really cope in a private home, you know what I mean? Plus the doctor took me aside and said, look, Mr Tillary, the more your wife gets attached to the kid, the rougher it's gonna be on her when the inevitable happens. Because they knew he wasn't gonna live more than a couple of years.'

Without saying anything he got up and brought back fresh drinks. 'So it was the three of us,' he went on, 'me and Peg and the aunt, and she had her room and her own bath an' all on the third floor, an' it was still a big house for three people, but the two women, you know, they kept each other company. And then when the old woman died, well, we talked about moving, but Peg was used to the house and used to the neighborhood.'

He took a breath and let his shoulders drop. 'What do I need, big house, drive back and forth or fight the subway, whole thing's a pain in the ass. Soon as all this clears up I'll sell the place, find myself a little apartment in the city.'

'What part of town?'

'You know, I don't even know. Around Gramercy Park is kind of nice. Or maybe the Upper East Side. Maybe buy a co-op in a decent building. I don't need a whole lot of space.' He snorted. 'I could move in with whatsername. You know. Carolyn.'

'Oh?'

'You know we work at the same place. I see her there every day. "I gave at the office."' He sighed. 'I been sort of stayin' away from the neighborhood until all of this is cleared up.'

'Sure.'

And then we got on the subject of churches, and I don't remember how. Something to the effect that bars kept better hours than churches, that churches closed early. 'Well, they got to,' he said, 'on account of the crime problem. Matt, when we were kids, who ever heard of somebody stealing from a church?'

'I suppose it happened.'

'I suppose it did but when did you ever hear of it? Nowadays you got a different class of people, they don't respect anything. Of course there's that church in Bensonhurst, I guess they keep whatever hours they want to.'

'What do you mean?'

'I think it's Bensonhurst. Big church, I forget the name of it. Saint Something or other.'

'That narrows it down.'

'Don't you remember? Couple of years ago two black kids stole something off the altar. Gold candlesticks, whatever the hell it was. And it turns out Dominic Tutto's mother goes to mass there every morning. The capo, runs half of Brooklyn?'

'Oh, right.'

'And the word went out, and a week later the candlesticks are back on the altar. Or whatever the hell they were. I think it was candlesticks.'

'Whatever.'

'And the punks who took 'em,' he said, 'disappeared. And the story I heard, well, you don't know if it was anything more than a story. I wasn't there, and I forget who I heard it from, but *he* wasn't there either, you know?'

'What did you hear?'

'I heard they hauled the two niggers to Tutto's basement,' he said, 'and hung 'em on meat hooks.' A flashbulb winked two tables away from us. 'And skinned 'em alive,' he said. 'But who knows? You hear all these stories, you don't know what to believe.'

'You should've been with us this afternoon,' Skip told me. 'Me and Keegan and Ruslander, we took my car and drove out to the Big A.' He drawled in imitation of W. C. Fields: 'Participated in the sport of kings, made our contribution to the improvement of the breed, yes indeed.'

'I was doing some work.'

'I'd have been better off working. Fucking Keegan, he's got a pocket full of miniatures, he's knocking 'em off one a race, he's got his pockets full of these little bottles. And he's betting horses on the basis of their names. There's this plater, Jill the Queen, hasn't won anything since Victoria was the queen, and Keegan remembers this girl named Jill he had this mad passion for in the sixth grade. So of course he bets the horse.'

'And the horse wins.'

'Of *course* the horse wins. The horse wins at something like twelve-to-one, and Keegan's got a ten-dollar win ticket on her, and he's saying he made a mistake. What mistake? "Her name was Rita," he says. "It was her sister's name was Jill. I remembered it wrong."'

'That's Billie.'

'Well, the whole afternoon was like that,' Skip said. 'He bets his old girlfriends and their sisters and he drinks half a quart of whiskey out of these little bottles, and Ruslander and I both lose I don't know, a hundred, hundred and fifty, and fucking Billie Keegan wins six hundred dollars by betting on girls' names.'

'How did you and Ruslander pick horses?'

'Well, you know the actor. He hunches his shoulders and talks out of the side of his mouth like a tout, and he talks to a couple of horsey-looking guys and comes back with a tip. The guys he talks to are probably other actors.'

'And you both followed his tips?'

'Are you crazy? I bet scientific.'

'You read the form?'

'I can't make sense out of it. I watch which ones have the odds drop when the smart money comes in, and also I go down and watch 'em walk around, and I notice which one takes a good crap.'

'Scientific.'

'Absolutely. Who wants to invest serious money in some fucking constipated horse? Some steed wracked with irregularity? My horses' – he lowered his eyes, mockshy – 'are M/O-kay.'

'And Keegan's crazy.'

'You got it. The man trivializes a scientific pursuit.' He leaned forward, ground out his cigarette. 'Ah, Jesus, I love this life,' he said. 'I swear to God I was born for it. I spend half my life running my own saloon and the other half in other people's saloons, with a sunny afternoon away from it now and then to get close to nature and commune with God's handiwork.' His eyes locked on mine. 'I love it,' he said levelly. 'That's why I'm gonna pay those cock-suckers.'

'You heard from them?'

'Before we left for the track. They presented their nonnegotiable demands.'

'How much?'

'Enough to make my bets seem somehow beside the point. Who cares if you win or lose a hundred dollars? And I don't bet heavy, it's not fun once it gets into serious money. *They* want serious money.'

'And you're going to pay it?'

He picked up his drink. 'We're meeting with some people tomorrow. The lawyer, the accountants. That's if Kasabian stops throwing up.'

'And then?'

'And then I suppose we try to negotiate the nonnegotiable, and then we fucking pay. What else are the lawyers and accountants going to tell us? Raise an army? Fight a guerrilla war? That's not the kind of answer you get from lawyers and accountants.' He took another cigarette from the pack, tapped it, held it up, looked at it, tapped it again, then lit it. 'I'm a machine that smokes and drinks,' he said through a cloud of smoke, 'and I'll tell you, I don't know why I fucking bother with any of it.'

'A minute ago you loved this life.'

'Was I the one who said that? You know the story about the guy bought a Volkswagen and his friend asks him how does he like it? "Well, it's like eating pussy,' the guy says. 'I'm crazy about it, but I don't take a whole lot of pride in it."'

TEN

I called Drew Kaplan the next morning before I went out to Brooklyn. His secretary said he was in a meeting, and could he call me back? I said I'd call him back, and I did forty minutes later when I got off the subway in Sunset Park. By then he'd gone for lunch. I told her I'd call back later.

That afternoon I managed to meet a woman who was friendly with Angel Herrera's girlfriend. She had strong Indio features and a face badly pitted by acne. She said it was a pity for Herrera that he had to go to jail, but it was probably good for her friend, because Herrera would never marry her or even live with her because he considered himself still married in Puerto Rico. 'An' his wife divorce him, but he doan accept it,' she said. 'So my fren, she wanna get pregnant, but he doan get her pregnant and he woan marry her. What's she want with him, you know? Better for her if he goes away for a while. Better for everybody.'

I called Kaplan again from a street corner phone booth and reached him this time. I got out my notebook and gave him what I had. None of it added up to anything as far as I could see, except for Cruz's prior arrest for manslaughter, which was something he should have known about, as he was quick enough to point out himself. 'That's not something an investigator should have to come up with,' he said. 'They should have put that on the table. True, you can't introduce it in court, but there's ways to use it. You may have earned your fee with that little bit of information. Not that I want to discourage you from digging for more.'

But when I'd hung up the phone I didn't really feel like digging for more. I went over to the Fjord and had a couple of drinks, but then a lanky kid with a lot of yellow hair and a blond Zapata moustache came in and tried to hustle me into a game on the shuffle-bowling machine. I wasn't interested and neither was anyone else, so he went and played the thing by himself, feigning noisy drunkenness, I suppose in an attempt to look like easy pickings. The noise drove me out of there, and I wound up walking all the way to Tommy's house on Colonial Road.

His key unlocked the front door. I walked in, half expecting the scene that had greeted the discoverer of Margaret Tillary's body, but of course things had been cleaned up and put right long ago, after the lab crew and the photographer had done their work and gone.

I walked through the rooms on the ground floor, found the side entrance that led to a vestibule off the kitchen, walked back through the kitchen and the dining room, trying to imagine myself into Cruz and Herrera's shoes as they moved through the rooms of the empty house.

Except it wouldn't have been empty. Margaret Tillary had been upstairs in her bedroom. Doing what? Sleeping? Watching television?

I climbed the stairs. A couple of the boards creaked underfoot. Had they done so the night of the burglary? Had Peg Tillary heard, and had she reacted? Maybe she thought it was Tommy's step, got out of bed to greet him. Maybe she knew it was someone else. Footsteps are recognizable to some people, and a stranger's footfall is unfamiliar, enough so sometimes to intrude on sleep.

She'd been killed in the bedroom. Up the stairs, open the door, find a woman cowering in there and stab her? Or maybe she'd come out of the bedroom door, expecting Tommy, or not expecting him but not thinking straight, confronting the burglar, people did that all the time, not thinking, outraged at the invasion of their home, acting as if their righteous indignation would serve them as armor.

Then she'd have seen the knife in his hand, and she'd have gone back inside the room, tried to shut the door, maybe, and he'd come in after her, and maybe she was screaming and he had to get to her to shut her up, and –

I kept seeing Anita backing away from a knife, kept turning the scene into our bedroom in Syosset.

Silly.

I walked over to one of the dressers, opened drawers, closed them. Her dresser, long and low. His was a highboy in the same French Provincial styling, part of a suite with the bed and a nightstand and a mirrored dressing table. I opened and closed drawers in his dresser. He'd left a lot of clothes behind, but he probably owned a lot of clothes.

I opened the closet door. She could have hidden in the closet, though not comfortably. It was full, the shelf loaded with a couple dozen shoe boxes, the rack packed with clothes on hangers. He must have taken a couple of suits and jackets with him, but the clothes he'd left behind were more than I owned.

There were bottles of perfume on the dressing table. I lifted the stopper of one and held it to my nose. The scent was lily-of-the-valley.

I was in the room for a long time. There are people who are psychically sensitive, they pick up things at a murder scene. Maybe everyone does, maybe the sensitive ones are simply better at figuring out what it is that they're attuned to. I had no illusions about my ability to glean vibrations from the room or the clothing or the furniture. Smell is the sense most directly hooked into the memory, but all her perfume did was remind me that an aunt of mine had smelled of that same floral scent.

I don't know what I thought I was doing there.

There was a television set in the bedroom. I turned it on, turned it off. She might have been watching it, she might not even have heard the burglar until he opened the door. But wouldn't he have heard the set? Why would he come into a room if he knew someone was there, when he could just slip away undetected?

Of course he could have had rape in mind. There hadn't been any rape, none detected in the autopsy, although that hardly proved the absence of intent. He might have achieved sexual release from the murder, might have been turned off by the violence, might have ...

Tommy had slept in this room, had lived with the woman who smelled of lilies-of-the-valley. I knew him from the bars, I knew him with a girl on his arm and a drink in his hand and his laugh echoing off paneled walls. I didn't know him in a room like this, in a house like this.

I went in and out of other rooms on the second floor. In what I suppose was the upstairs sitting room, photos in silver frames were grouped on top of a mahogany radio-phonograph console. There was a formal wedding picture, Tommy in a tuxedo, the bride in white with her bouquet all pink and white. Tommy was lean in the photo, and impossibly young. He was sporting a crew cut, which looked outlandish in 1975, especially in counterpoint to the formal clothes.

Margaret Tillary – she might still have been Margaret Wayland when the photo was taken – had been a tall woman, with strong features even then. I looked at her and tried to imagine her with years added. She'd probably put on a few pounds over the years. Most people did.

Most of the other photos showed people I didn't recognize. Relatives, I suppose. I didn't notice any of the son Tommy'd told me about.

One door led to a linen closet, another to a bathroom. A third opened on a flight of stairs leading to the third floor. There was a bedroom up there, its window affording a good view of the park. I drew up an armchair, its seat and back worked in needlepoint, and watched the traffic on Colonial Road and a baseball game in the park.

I imagined the aunt sitting as I was sitting, watching the world through her window. If I'd heard her name I didn't remember it, and when I thought of her the image that came to mind was some sort of generic aunt, some combination of the various unidentifiable female faces in the photographs downstairs mixed, I suppose, with elements of some aunts of my own. She was gone now, this unnamed composite aunt, and her niece was gone, and before long the house would be sold and other people living in it.

And it would be a piece of work, too, removing the traces of the Tillary occupancy. The aunt's bedroom and bathroom took up the front third of the top floor; the rest was a large open space given over to storage, with trunks and cardboard cartons fitted in under the pitched roof along with pieces of furniture that had been removed from service. Some were covered with cloths. Others were not. Everything was lightly coated with dust, and you could smell the dust in the air.

I went back to the aunt's bedroom. Her clothes were still in the dresser and closet, her toilet articles in the bathroom medicine chest. Easy enough to leave everything, if they didn't need the room.

I wondered what Herrera had hauled away. That was how he'd first come to the house, carting off jetsam after the aunt's death.

I sat in the chair again. I smelled the dust of the storage room, and the scent of the old woman's clothes, but I still held the lily-of-the-valley perfume in my nostrils and it overscored all of the other aromas. It cloyed now, and I wished I could stop smelling it. It seemed to me that I was smelling the memory of the scent more than the scent itself.

505

In the park across the street, two boys were playing a game of keep-away, with a third boy running vainly back and forth between them, trying to get the striped ball they tossed back and forth. I leaned forward, propping my elbows on the radiator to watch them. I tired of the game before they did. I left the chair facing the window and walked through the open area and down both flights of stairs.

I was in the living room, wondering what Tommy had around the house to drink and where he kept it, when someone cleared his throat a couple of yards behind me.

I froze.

ELEVEN

'Yeah,' a voice said. 'I sort of figured it was you. Whyntcha sit down, Matt. You look white as a ghost. You look like you seen one.'

I knew but couldn't place the voice. I turned, my breath still stuck in my chest, and I knew the man. He was sitting in an overstuffed armchair, deep in the room's long shadows. He was wearing a short-sleeved shirt open at the throat. His suit jacket was draped over the chair's arm, and the end of his tie peeped out of a pocket.

'Jack Diebold,' I said.

'The same,' he said. 'How you doin', Matt? I got to tell you you'd make the world's worst cat burglar. You were clompin' around up there like the horse cavalry.'

'You scared the shit out of me, Jack.'

He laughed softly. 'Well, what was I gonna do, Matt? A neighbor called in, lights on in the house, blah blah blah, and since I was handy and it was my case I took the squeal myself and came on over. I figured it was probably you. Guy from the Six-eight called me the other day, mentioned you were doin' something for this Tillary asshole.'

'Neumann called you? You're at Brooklyn Homicide now?'

'Oh, a while now. I made Detective First, shit, it's been almost two years.'

'Congratulations.'

'Thanks. Anyway, I came over, but I don't know it's you and I don't want to charge the stairs and I thought, shit, we'll let Mohammad come to the mountain for a change. I didn't mean to scare you.'

'The hell you didn't.'

'Well, you walked right past me, for God's sake, and you looked so funny goin' about it. What were you lookin' for just now?'

'Just now? I was trying to guess where he keeps his liquor.'

'Well, don't let me stop you. Find a couple of glasses too, while you're at it.'

A pair of cut-glass decanters stood on a sideboard in the dining room. Little silver nameplates around their necks identified them as Scotch and Rye. You needed a key to remove them from their silver caddy. The sideboard itself held linen in its center drawers, glassware on the right-hand side, bottles of whiskey and cordials on the left. I found a fifth of Wild Turkey and a couple of glasses, showed the bottle to Diebold. He nodded and I poured drinks for both of us.

He was a big man a couple of years my senior. He'd lost some hair since I'd seen him last, and he was heavy, but then he'd always been heavy. He looked at his glass for a moment, raised it to me, took a sip.

'Good stuff,' he said.

'Not bad.'

'What were you doin' up there, Matt? Lookin' for clues?' He stretched the last word.

I shook my head. 'Just getting the feel of it.'

'You're working for Tillary.'

I nodded. 'He gave me the key.'

'Shit, I don't care if you came down the chimney like Santy Claus. What's he want you to do for him?'

'Clear him.'

'Clear him? The cocksucker's already clear enough to see through. No way we're gonna tag him for it.'

'But you think he did it.'

He gave me a sour look. 'I don't think he did it,' he said, 'if doin' it means stickin' a knife in her. I'd love thinkin' he did but he's alibied better than a fuckin' Mafia don. He was out in public with this broad, a million people saw him, he's got charge-card receipts from a restaurant, for Christ's sake.' He drank the rest of his whiskey. 'I think he set her up.'

'Hired them to kill her?'

'Something like that.'

'They're not hired killers by trade, are they?'

'Shit, of course they're not. Cruz and Herrera, button men for the Sunset Park syndicate. Rubouts a specialty.'

'But you think he hired them.'

He came over and took the bottle from me, poured his glass half full. 'He set them up,' he said.

'How?'

He shook his head, impatient with the question. 'I wish I was the first person to question them,' he said. 'The guys from the Six-eight went over with a burglary warrant, they didn't know when they went in where the stuff was from. So they already talked to the PRs before I got a crack at 'em.'

'And?'

'First time out, they denied everything. 'I bought the stuff on the street.' You know how it goes.'

'Of course.'

'Then they didn't know anything about a woman who got killed. Now that was horseshit. They ran that story and then they changed it, or it died a natural death, because of course they knew, it was in the papers and on the television. Then the story was that there was no woman around when they did the job, and on top of that they were never upstairs of the first floor. Well, that's nice, but their fucking fingerprints were on the bedroom mirror and the dresser top and a couple of other places.'

'You had prints putting them in the bedroom? I didn't know that.'

'Maybe I shouldn't tell you. Except I can't see how it makes a difference. Yeah, we found prints.'

'Whose? Herrera's or Cruz's?'

'Why?'

'Because I was figuring Cruz for the one who knifed her.'

'Why him?'

'His record. And he carried a knife.'

'A flick knife. He didn't use it on the woman.'

'Oh?'

'She was killed with something had a blade six inches long and two or two-and-a-half inches wide. Whatever. A kitchen knife, it sounds like.'

'You didn't recover it, though.'

'No. She had a whole mess of knives in the kitchen, a couple of different sets. You keep house for twenty years, you accumulate knives. Tillary couldn't tell if one was missing. The lab took the ones we found, couldn't find blood on any of them.'

'So you think –'

'That one of 'em picked up a knife in the kitchen and went upstairs with it and killed her and then threw it down a sewer somewhere, or in the river, or who knows where.'

'Picked up a knife in the kitchen.'

'Or brought it along. Cruz carried a flick knife as a regular thing, but maybe he didn't want to use his own knife to kill the woman.'

'Figuring he came here planning to do it.'

'How else can you figure it?'

'I figure it was a burglary and they didn't know she was here.'

'Yeah, well, you want to figure it that way because you're trying to clear the prick. He goes upstairs and takes a knife along with him. Why the knife?'

'In case someone's up there.'

'Then why go upstairs?'

'He's looking for money. A lot of people keep cash in the bedroom. He opens the door, she's there, she panics, he panics –'

'And he kills her.'

'Why not?'

'Shit, it sounds as good as anything else, Matt.' He put his glass on the coffee table. 'One more session with 'em,' he said, 'and they woulda spilled.'

'They talked a lot as it was.'

'I know. You know what's the most important thing to teach a new recruit? How to read 'em Miranda-Escobedo in such a way that they don't attach any significance to it. 'You have the right to remain silent. Now I want you to tell me what really went down.' One more time and they woulda seen that the way to cop out on Tillary was to say he hired them to kill her.'

'That means admitting they did it.'

'I know, but they were admitting a little more each time. I don't know. I think I could've got more out of them. But once they got legal counsel on the spot, shit, that's the end of our cozy little conversations.'

'Why do you like Tillary for it? Just because he was playing around?'

'Everybody plays around.'

'That's what I mean.'

'The ones who kill their wives are the ones who aren't playing around and want to be. Or the ones who're in love with something sweet and young and want to marry it and keep it around forever. He's not in love with anybody but himself. Or doctors. Doctors are always killing their wives.'

'Then –'

'We got tons of motive, Matt. He owed money that he didn't have. And she was gettin' ready to dump him.'

'The girlfriend?'

'The wife.'

510

'I never heard that.'

'Who would you hear it from, him? She talked to a neighbor woman, she talked to a lawyer. The aunt dyin' made the difference. She came into the property, for one thing, and she didn't have the old woman around for company. Oh, we got lots of motive, my friend. If motive was enough to hang a man we could go shoppin' for a rope.'

Jack Diebold said, 'He's a friend of yours, huh? That's why you're involved?'

We had left the Tillary house somewhere in the early evening. I remember the sky was still light, but it was July and it stayed light well into the evening hours. I turned off the lights and put the bottle of Wild Turkey away. There wasn't much left in it. Diebold joked that I should wipe my prints off the bottle, and off the glasses we had used.

He was driving his own car, a Ford Fairlane that was showing a lot of rust. He chose the place, a plush steak-and-seafood restaurant near the approach to the Verrazano Bridge. They knew him there, and I sensed that there wouldn't be a check. Most cops have a certain number of restaurants where they can eat a certain number of free meals. This bothers some people, and I have never really understood why.

We ate well – shrimp cocktails, strip sirloins, hot pumpernickel rolls, stuffed baked potatoes. 'When we were growin' up,' Diebold said, 'a man who ate like this was treating himself right. You never heard a goddamned word about cholesterol. Now it's all you hear.'

'I know.'

'I had a partner, I don't know if you ever knew him. Gerry O'Bannon. You know him?'

'I don't think so.'

'Well, he got on this health kick. What started it was he quit smoking. I never smoked so I never had to quit, but he quit and then it was one thing after another. He lost a lot of weight, he changed his diet, he started jogging. He looked terrible, he looked all drawn, you know how guys get? But he was happy, he was really pleased with himself. Wouldn't go drinking, just order one beer and make it last, or he'd have one and then switch to club soda. The French stuff. Perrier?'

'Uh-huh.'

'Very popular all of a sudden, it's plain soda water and it costs more than beer. Figure it out and explain it to me sometime. He shot himself.'

'O'Bannon?'

'Yeah. I don't mean it's connected, losing the weight and drinking club soda and killing himself. The life you lead and the things you see, I'll tell you, a cop goes and eats his gun, I never figure it requires an explanation. You know what I mean?'

'I know what you mean.'

He looked at me. 'Yeah,' he said. 'Course you do.' And then the conversation took a turn in another direction, and a little while later, with a slab of hot apple pie topped with cheddar in front of Diebold and coffee poured for both of us, he returned to the subject of Tommy Tillary, identifying him as my friend.

'Sort of a friend,' I said. 'I know him around the bars.'

'Right, she lives up in your neighborhood, doesn't she? The girlfriend, I forget her name.'

'Carolyn Cheatham.'

'I wish she was all the alibi he had. But even if he got away from her for a few hours, what was the wife doing during the burglary? Waiting for Tommy to come home and kill her? I mean, take it to extremes, say she hides under the bed while they rifle the bedroom and get their prints on everything. They leave, she calls the cops, right?'

'He couldn't have killed her.'

'I know, and it drives me crazy. How come you like him?'

'He's not a bad guy. And I'm getting paid for this, Jack. I'm doing him a favor, but it's one I'm getting paid for. And it's a waste of my time and his money anyway, because you haven't got a case against him.'

'No.'

'You don't, do you?'

'Not even close.' He ate some pie, drank some coffee. 'I'm glad you're getting paid. Not just because I like to see a guy turn a buck. I'd hate to see you bust your balls for him for free.'

'I'm not busting anything.'

'You know what I mean.'

'Am I missing something, Jack?'

'Huh?'

'What did he do, steal baseballs from the Police Athletic League? How come you've got the red ass for him?'

He thought it over. His jaws worked. He frowned.

'Well, I'll tell you,' he said at length. 'He's a phony.'

'He sells stock and shit over the phone. Of course he's a phony.'

'More than that. I don't know how to explain it so it makes sense, but shit, you were a cop. You know how you get feelings.'

'Of course.'

'Well, I get a feeling with that guy. There's something about him that's wrong, something about her death.'

'I'll tell you what it is,' I said. 'He's glad she's dead and he's pretending he isn't. It gets him out of a jam and he's glad, but he's acting like a sanctimonious son of a bitch and that's what you're responding to.'

'Maybe that's part of it.'

'I think it's the whole thing. You're sensing that he's acting guilty. Well, he is. He feels guilty. He's glad she's dead, but at the same time he lived with the woman for I forget how many years, he had a life with her, part of him was busy being a husband while the other part was running around on her –'

'Yeah, yeah, I follow you.'

'So?'

'It's more than that.'

'Why does it have to be more? Look, maybe he did set up Cruz and whatsisname –'

'Hernandez.'

'No, not Hernandez. What the hell's his name?'

'Angel. Angel eyes.'

'Herrera. Maybe he set them up to go in, rob the place. Maybe he even had it in the back of his mind she might get in the way.'

'Keep going.'

'Except it's too iffy, isn't it? I think he just feels guilty for wishing she'd get killed, or being glad of it after the fact, and you're picking up on the guilt and that's why you like him for the murder.'

'No.'

'You sure?'

'I'm not sure that I'm sure of anything. You know, I'm glad you're gettin' paid. I hope you're costin' him a ton.'

'Not all that much.'

'Well, soak him all you can. Because at least it's costin' him money, even if that's all it's costin' him, and it's money he doesn't have to pay. Because we can't touch him. Even if those two changed their story, admitted the killing and said he put 'em up to it, that's not enough to put him away. And they're *not* gonna change their story, and who would ever hire them to commit murder anyway, and they wouldn't take a contract like that. I *know* they wouldn't. Cruz is a mean little bastard but Herrera's just a stupid guy, and – aw, shit.'

'What?'

'It just kills me to see him get away with it.'

'But he didn't do it, Jack.'

'He's gettin' away with *something*,' he said, 'and I hate to see it happen. You know what I hope? I hope he runs a red light sometime, in that fucking boat of his. What's it, a Buick he's got?'

'I think so.'

'I hope he runs a light and I tag him for it, that's what I hope.'

'Is that what Brooklyn Homicide does these days? A lot of traffic detail?'

'I just hope it happens,' he said. 'That's all.'

TWELVE

Diebold insisted on driving me home. When I offered to take the subway he told me not to be ridiculous, that it was midnight already and I was in no condition for public transportation.

'You'll pass out,' he said, 'and some bum'll steal the shoes off your feet.'

He was probably right. As it was I nodded off during the ride back to Manhattan, coming awake when he pulled up at the corner of Fifty-seventh and Ninth. I thanked him for the ride, asked him if he had time for a drink before he went back.

'Hey, enough's enough,' he said. 'I can't go all night like I used to.'

'You know, I think I'll call it a night myself,' I said.

But I didn't. I watched him pull away, started walking to my hotel, then turned and went around the corner to Armstrong's. The place was mostly empty. I went in, and Billie gave me a wave.

I went up to the bar. And she was there at the end of the bar, all alone, staring down into the glass on the bar in front of her. Carolyn Cheatham. I hadn't seen her since the night I'd gone home with her.

While I was trying to decide whether or not to say anything, she looked up and her eyes met mine. Her face was frozen with stubborn old pain. It took her a blink or two to recognize me, and when she did a muscle worked in her cheek and tears started to form in the corners of her eyes. She used the back of her hand to wipe them away. She'd been crying earlier; there was a tissue crumpled on the bar, black with mascara.

'My bourbon-drinking friend,' she said. 'Billie,' she said, 'this man is a gentleman. Will you please bring my gentleman friend a drink of good bourbon?'

Billie looked at me. I nodded. He brought a couple of ounces of bourbon and a mug of black coffee.

'I called you my gentleman friend,' Carolyn Cheatham said, 'but that has an unintentional connotation.' She pronounced her words with a drunk's deliberate care. 'You are a gentleman *and* a friend, but not a gentleman friend. My gentleman friend, on the other hand, is neither.'

I drank some of the bourbon, poured some of it into the coffee.

'Billie,' she said, 'do you know how you can tell that Mr Scudder is a gentleman?'

'He always removes his lady in the presence of a hat.'

'He is a bourbon drinker,' she said.

'That makes him a gentleman, huh, Carolyn?'

'It makes him a far cry removed from a hypocritical scotch-drinking son of a bitch.'

She didn't speak in a loud voice, but there was enough edge to her words to shut down conversations across the room. There were only three or four tables occupied, and the people sitting at them all picked the same instant to stop talking. For a moment the taped music was startlingly audible. It was one of the few pieces I could identify, one of the Brandenburg concertos. They played it so often there that even I was now able to tell what it was.

Then Billie said, 'Suppose a man drinks Irish whiskey, Carolyn. What does that make him?'

'An Irishman,' she said.

'Makes sense.'

'I'm drinking bourbon,' she said, and shoved her glass forward a significant inch. 'God damn it, I'm a *lady*.'

He looked at her, then looked at me. I nodded, and he shrugged and poured for her.

'On me,' I said.

'Thank you,' she said. 'Thank you, Matthew.' And her eyes started to water, and she dug a fresh tissue from her bag.

She wanted to talk about Tommy. He was being nice to her, she said. Calling up, sending flowers. But it just wouldn't do if she made a scene around the office, and he just might have to testify how he spent the night his wife was killed, and he had to keep on the good side of her for the time being.

But he wouldn't see her because it wouldn't look right. Not for a new widower, not for a man who'd been virtually accused of complicity in his wife's death.

'He sends flowers with no card enclosed,' she said. 'He calls me from pay phones. The son of a bitch.'

'Maybe the florist forgot to enclose a card.'

'Oh, Matt. Don't make excuses for him.'

'And he's in a hotel, of course he would use a pay phone.'

'He could call from his room. He as much as said he didn't want the call to go through the hotel switchboard, in case the operator's listening in. There was no card with the flowers because he doesn't want anything in writing. He came to my apartment the other night, but he won't be seen with me, he won't go out with me, and – oh, the hypocrite. The scotch-drinking son of a bitch.'

Billie called me aside. 'I didn't want to put her out,' he said, 'a nice woman like that, shitfaced as she is. But I thought I was gonna have to. You'll see she gets home?'

'Sure.'

First I had to let her buy us another round. She insisted. Then I got her out of there and walked her around the corner to her building. There was rain coming, you could smell it in the air, and when we went from Armstrong's air conditioning into the sultry humidity that heralds a summer storm it took some of the spirit out of her. She held my arm as we walked, gripped it with something on the edge of desperation. In the elevator she sagged against the back panel and braced her feet.

'Oh, God,' she said.

I took the keys from her and unlocked her door. I got her inside. She half sat, half sprawled on the couch. Her eyes were open but I don't know if she saw much through them. I had to use the bathroom, and when I came back her eyes were closed and she was snoring lightly.

I got her shoes off, moved her to a chair, struggled with the couch until I managed to open it into a bed. I put her on it. I figured I ought to loosen her clothing, and while I was at it I undressed her completely. She remained unconscious throughout the operation, and I remembered what a mortician's assistant had told me once about the difficulty of dressing and undressing the dead. My gorge rose at the image and I thought I was going to be sick, but I sat down and my stomach settled itself.

I covered her with the top sheet, sat back down again. There was something else I'd wanted to do but I couldn't think what it was. I tried to think, and I guess I must have dozed off myself. I don't suppose I was out for more than a few minutes, just time enough to lose myself in a dream that fled from me the minute I opened my eyes and blinked it away.

I let myself out. Her door had a spring lock. There was a dead bolt you could engage with the key for extra security, but all I had to do was draw the door shut and it was locked, and reasonably secure. I took the elevator down and went outside.

The rain was holding off. At the corner of Ninth Avenue a jogger passed, running doggedly uptown against what little traffic there was. His T-shirt was gray with sweat and he looked ready to drop. I thought of O'Bannon, Jack Diebold's old partner, getting physically fit before blowing his brains out.

And then I remembered what I'd wanted to do at Carolyn's apartment. I'd been planning on taking away the little gun Tommy had given her. If she was going to drink like that and get depressed like that, she didn't need to have a weapon in the bedside table.

But the door was locked. And she was out cold, she wasn't going to wake up and kill herself.

I crossed the street. The steel gate was drawn most of the way across the front of Armstrong's, and the white globe lights over the front were out, but light showed from within. I walked over to the door, saw that the chairs were on top of the tables, ready for the Dominican kid who came in first thing in the morning to sweep the place out. I didn't see Billie at first, and then I saw him at a stool at the far end of the bar. The door was locked, but he spotted me and came over and let me in.

He locked the door again after I was through it, walked me over to the bar and slipped behind it. Without my saying anything he poured me a glass of bourbon. I curled my hand around it but didn't pick it up from the top of the bar.

'The coffee's all gone,' he said.

'That's all right. I didn't want any more.'

'She all right? Carolyn?'

'Well, she might have a hangover tomorrow.'

'Just about everybody I know might have a hangover tomorrow,' he said. 'I might have a hangover tomorrow. It's gonna pour, I might as well sit in the house and eat aspirin all day.'

Someone banged on the door. Billie shook his head at him, waved him away. The man knocked again. Billie ignored him.

'Can't they see the place is closed?' he complained. 'Put your money away, Matt. We're closed, the register's locked up, it's private-party time.' He held his glass to the light and looked at it. 'Beautiful color,' he said. 'She's a pisser, old Carolyn. A bourbon drinker's a gentleman and a scotch drinker's – what did she say a scotch drinker was?'

'I think a hypocrite.'

'So I gave her the straight line, didn't I? What's it make a man if he drinks Irish whiskey? An Irishman.'

'Well, you asked.'

'What else it makes him is drunk, but in a nice way. I only get drunk in the nicest possible way. Ah, Jesus, Matt, these are the best hours of the day. You can keep your Morrissey's. This is like having your own private after-hours, you know? The joint empty and dark, the music off, the chairs up, one or two people around for company, the rest of the world locked the hell out. Great, huh?'

'It's not bad.'

'No, it's not.'

He was freshening my drink. I didn't remember drinking it. I said, 'You know, my trouble is I can't go home.'

'That's what Thomas Wolfe said, "You Can't Go Home Again." That's everybody's trouble.'

'No, I mean it. My feet keep taking me to a bar instead. I was out in Brooklyn, I got home late, I was tired, I was already half in the bag, I started to walk to my hotel and I turned around and came here instead. And just now I put her to sleep, Carolyn, and I had to drag myself out of there before I fell asleep in her chair, and instead of going home like a sane human being I came back here again like some dim homing pigeon.'

'You're a swallow and this is Capistrano.'

'Is that what I am? I don't know what the hell I am anymore.'

'Oh, bullshit. You're a guy, a human being. Just another poor son of a bitch who doesn't want to be alone when the sacred ginmill closes.'

'The what?' I started to laugh. 'Is that what this place is? The sacred ginmill?'

'Don't you know the song?'

'What song?'

'The Van Ronk song. "And so we've had another night –"' He broke off. 'Hell, I can't sing, I can't even get the tune right. "Last Call," Dave Von Ronk. You don't know it?'

'I don't know what you're talking about.'

'Well, *Christ*,' he said. 'You have got to hear it. You have by Christ got to hear this song. It's what we've been talking about, and on top of that it's the fucking national anthem. Come on.'

'Come on and what?'

'Just come on,' he said. He put a Piedmont Airlines flight bag on top of the bar, rooted around under the back bar and came up with two unopened bottles, one of the twelve-year-old Jameson Irish he favored and one of Jack Daniel's. 'This okay?' he asked me.

519

'Okay for what?'

'For pouring over your head to kill the cooties. Is it okay to drink is my question. You've been drinking Forester, but I can't find an unopened bottle, and there's a law against carrying an opened bottle on the street.'

'There is?'

'There ought to be. I never steal opened bottles. Will you please answer a simple question? Is Jack Black all right?'

'Of course it's all right, but where the hell are we going?'

'My place,' he said. 'You've got to hear this record.'

'Bartenders drink free,' he said. 'Even at home. It's a fringe benefit. Other people get pension plans and dental care. We get all the booze we can steal. You're gonna love this song, Matt.'

We were in his apartment, an L-shaped studio with a parquet floor and a fireplace. He was on the twenty-second floor and his window looked south. He had a good view of the Empire State Building and, farther down on the right, the World Trade Center.

The place was sparsely furnished. There was a white mica platform bed and dresser in the sleeping alcove, a couch and a sling chair in the middle of the room. Books and records overflowed a bookcase and stood around in stacks on the floor. Stereo components were placed here and there – a turntable on an upended milk crate, speakers resting on the floor.

'Where did I put the thing?' Billie wondered.

I walked over to the window, looked out at the city. I was wearing a watch but I purposely didn't look at it because I didn't want to know what time it was. I suppose it must have been somewhere around four o'clock. It still wasn't raining.

'Here,' he said, holding up an album. 'Dave Van Ronk. You know him?'

'Never heard of him.'

'Got a Dutch name, looks like a mick and I swear on the blues numbers he sounds just like a nigger. He's also one bitchin' guitar player but he doesn't play anything on this cut. "Last Call." He sings it al fresco.'

'Okay.'

'*Not* al fresco. I forget the expression. How do you say it when you sing without accompaniment?'

'What difference does it make?'

'How can I forget something like that? I got a mind like a fucking sieve. You're gonna love this song.'

'That's if I ever get to hear it.'

'A cappella. That's what it is, a cappella. As soon as I stopped actively trying to think of it, it popped right into my head. The Zen of Remembering. Where did I put the Irish?'

'Right behind you.'

'Thanks. You all right with the Daniel's? Oh, you got the bottle right there. Okay, listen to this. Ooops, wrong groove. It's the last one on the album. Naturally, you couldn't have anything come after this one. *Listen.*'

> *And so we've had another night*
> *Of poetry and poses*
> *And each man knows he'll be alone*
> *When the sacred ginmill closes.*

The melody sounded like an Irish folk air. The singer did indeed sing without accompaniment, his voice rough but curiously gentle.

'Now listen to this,' Billie said.

> *And so we'll drink the final glass*
> *Each to his joy and sorrow*
> *And hope the numbing drunk will last*
> *Till opening tomorrow*

'Jesus,' Billie said.

> *And when we stumble back again*
> *Like paralytic dancers*
> *Each knows the question he must ask*
> *And each man knows the answer*

I had a bottle in one hand, a glass in the other. I poured from the bottle into the glass. 'Catch this next part,' Billie was saying.

> *And so we'll drink the final drink*
> *That cuts the brain in sections*
> *Where answers do not signify*
> *And there aren't any questions*

Billie was saying something but the words weren't registering. There was only the song.

> *I broke my heart the other day.*
> *It will mend again tomorrow.*
> *If I'd been drunk when I was born*
> *I'd be ignorant of sorrow*

'Play that again,' I said.

'Wait. There's more.'

And so we'll drink the final toast
That never can be spoken:
Here's to the heart that is wise enough
To know when it's better off broken

He said, 'Well?'

'I'd like to hear it again.'

'"Play it again, Sam. You played it for her, you can play it for me. I can take it if she can." Isn't it great?'

'Play it again, will you?'

We listened to it a couple of times through. Finally he took it off and returned it to its jacket and asked me if I understood why he had to drag me up there and play it for me. I just nodded.

'Listen,' he said, 'you're welcome to crash here if you want. That couch is more comfortable than it looks.'

'I can make it home.'

'I don't know. Is it raining yet?' He looked out the window. 'No, but it could start any minute.'

'I'll chance it. I want to be at my place when I wake up.'

'I got to respect a man who can plan that far in the future. You okay to go out on the street? Sure, you're okay. Here, I'll get you a paper bag, you can take the JD home with you. Or here, take the flight bag, they'll think you're a pilot.'

'No, keep it, Billie.'

'What do I want with it? I don't drink bourbon.'

'Well, I've had enough.'

'You might want a nightcap. You might want something in the morning. It's a doggie bag, for Christ's sake. When'd you get so fancy you can't take a doggie bag home with you?'

'Somebody told me it's illegal to carry an opened bottle on the street.'

'Don't worry. It's a first offense, you're odds-on to get probation. Hey, Matt? Thanks for coming by.'

I walked home with the song's phrases echoing in my mind, coming back at me in fragments. 'If I'd been drunk when I was born I'd be ignorant of sorrow.' Jesus.

I got back to my hotel, went straight upstairs without checking the desk for messages. I got out of my clothes, threw them on the chair, took one short pull straight from the bottle and got into bed.

Just as I was drifting off the rain started.

THIRTEEN

The rain kept up all weekend. It was lashing my window when I opened my eyes around noon Friday, but it must have been the phone that woke me. I sat on the edge of the bed and decided not to answer it, and after a few more rings it quit.

My head ached fiercely and my gut felt like it had taken somebody's best shot. I lay down again, got up quickly when the room started to spin. In the bathroom I washed down a couple of aspirin with a half-glass of water, but they came right back up again.

I remembered the bottle Billie had pressed on me. I looked around for it and finally found it in the flight bag. I couldn't remember putting it back after the last drink of the night, but then there were other things I couldn't recall either, like most of the walk home from his apartment. That sort of miniblackout didn't bother me much. When you drove cross-country you didn't remember every billboard, every mile of highway. Why bother recalling every minute of your life?

The bottle was a third gone, and that surprised me. I could recall having had one drink with Billie while we listened to the record, then a short one before I turned the lights out. I didn't want one now, but there are the ones you want and the ones you need, and this came under the latter heading. I poured a short shot into the water glass and shuddered when I swallowed it. It didn't stay down either, but it fixed things so the next one did. And then I could swallow another couple of aspirins with another half-glass of water, and this time they stayed swallowed.

If I'd been drunk when I was born ...

I stayed right there in my room. The weather gave me every reason to remain where I was, but I didn't really need an excuse. I had the sort of hangover I knew enough to treat with respect. If I'd ever felt that bad without having drunk the night before, I'd have gone straight to a hospital. As it was, I stayed put and treated myself like a man with an illness, which in retrospect would seem to have been more than metaphor.

The phone rang again later in the afternoon. I could have had the desk stop my calls, but I didn't feel equal to the conversation that would have required. It seemed easier to let it ring itself out.

It rang a third time in the early evening, and this time I picked it up. It was Skip Devoe.

'I was looking for you,' he said. 'You going to bounce around later?'

'I don't want to go out in this.'

'Yeah, it's coming down again. It was slacking off for a while there and now it's teeming. The weather guy says we're gonna get a lot of it. We saw those guys yesterday.'

'Already?'

'Not the guys in the black hats, not the bad guys. The lawyers and the accountants. Our accountant's armed with what he calls a Jewish revolver. You know what that is?'

'A fountain pen.'

'You heard it, huh? Anyway, they all told us what we already knew, which is terrific, considering they'll bill us for the advice. We got to pay.'

'Well, that's what you figured.'

'Yeah, but it doesn't mean I like it. I spoke to the guy again, Mr Voice on the Phone. I told old Telephone Tommy we needed the weekend to find the money.'

'You told Tillary?'

'Tillary? What are you talking about?'

'You said –'

'Oh, right, I didn't even make the connection. No, not Tillary, I just said Telephone Tommy, I could have said Teddy or any name with a *T*. Which suddenly I can't think of. Name me some names start with *T*.'

'Do I have to?'

There was a pause. 'You don't feel so hot,' he said.

'Keegan had me up till dawn listening to records,' I said. 'I'm not a hundred percent yet.'

'Fucking Keegan,' he said. 'We all hit it pretty good, but he's gonna kill himself with it.'

'He does keep at it.'

'Yeah. Listen, I won't keep you. What I want to know, can you keep Monday open? The day and the night. Because I think that's when we're gonna move on this, and if we have to do it I'd just as soon get it over with.'

'What do you want me to do?'

'We'll talk about that, iron it out. Okay?'

What did I have to do on Monday? I was still working for Tommy Tillary, but I didn't much care what hours I put in. My conversation with Jack Diebold had confirmed my own opinion that I was wasting my time and Tillary's money, that they didn't have a case against him and weren't likely to make one. Carolyn Cheatham's diatribe had left me not greatly inclined to do much for Tommy anyway, or to feel all that guilty about taking his money and giving him small value for it.

I had a couple of things to tell Drew Kaplan next time I talked to him. And I'd dig up a few more along the way. But I might not have to put in too many long hours in Sunset Park's bars and bodegas.

I told Skip Monday was wide open.

Later that evening I called the liquor store across the street. I ordered up two quarts of Early Times and asked them to have the kid stop at the deli and pick up a six-pack of ale and a couple of sandwiches. They knew me and knew I'd make it worth the delivery boy's while to give me special service, and I did. It was worth it to me.

I took it easy with the hard booze, drank a can of ale, and made myself eat half a sandwich. I took a hot shower, and that helped, and then I ate another half-sandwich and drank another can of ale.

I went to sleep, and when I woke up I put the TV on and watched Bogart and Ida Lupino, I guess it was, in *High Sierra*. I didn't pay a whole lot of attention to the movie but it was company. I went over to the window now and then and watched the rain. I ate part of the remaining sandwich, drank some more ale, and nipped a little from the bourbon bottle. When the movie ended I turned the set off and had a couple of aspirins and went back to bed.

Saturday I was a little more mobile. I needed a drink again on awakening but I made it a short one, and the first one stayed down this time. I had a shower, drank the last can of ale, and went downstairs and had breakfast at the Red Flame. I left half of the eggs but ate the potatoes and a double order of rye toast

525

and drank a lot of coffee. I read the paper, or tried to. I couldn't make much sense out of what I read.

After breakfast I stopped in McGovern's for a quick one. Then I went around the corner to St Paul's and sat there in the soft stillness for a half-hour or so.

Then back to the hotel.

I watched a baseball game in my room, and a fight on 'Wide World of Sports,' along with the arm-wrestling championship of the world and some women doing some kind of aquatic mono-ski exhibition. What they were doing was evidently very difficult, but not terribly interesting to look at. I turned them off and left. I dropped in at Armstrong's and talked to a couple of people, then went over to Joey Farrell's for a bowl of three-alarm chili and a couple of Carta Blancas.

I had a brandy with my coffee before returning to the hotel for the night. I had enough bourbon in the room to get me through Sunday but I stopped and picked up some beer because I was almost out and the stores can't sell it before noon on Sunday. Nobody knows why. Maybe the churches are behind it, maybe they want the faithful showing up with their hangovers sharp at the edges, maybe repentance is easier to sell to the severely afflicted.

I sipped and watched TV movies. I slept in front of the set, woke up in the middle of a war movie, had a shower and shaved and sat around in my underwear watching the end of that movie and the start of another, sipping bourbon and beer until I could go back to sleep again.

When I woke up again, it was Sunday afternoon and it was still raining.

Around three-thirty the phone rang. I picked it up on the third ring and said hello.

'Matthew?' It was a woman, and for an instant I thought it was Anita. Then she said, 'I tried you day before yesterday, but there was no answer,' and I heard the Tarheel in her voice.

'I want to thank you,' she said.

'Nothing to thank me for, Carolyn.'

'I want to thank you for being a gentleman,' she said, and her laughter came gently. 'A bourbon-drinking gentleman. I seem to remember having a lot to say on that subject.'

'As I recall, you were reasonably eloquent.'

'And on other subjects as well. I apologized to Billie for being less than a lady and he assured me I was fine, but bartenders always tell you that, don't they? I want to thank you-all for seeing me home.' A pause. 'Uh, did we –'

'No.'

A sigh. 'Well, I'm glad of that, but only 'cause I'd hate to not remember it. I hope I wasn't too disgraceful, Matthew.'

'You were perfectly fine.'

'I was *not* perfectly fine. I remember that much. Matthew, I said some hard things about Tommy. I was bad-mouthing him something awful, and I hope you know that was just the drink talking.'

'I never thought otherwise.'

'He treats me fine, you know. He's a good man. He's got his faults. He's strong, but he has his weaknesses.'

At a fellow police officer's wake, I once heard an Irish woman speak thus of the drink. 'Sure, it's a strong man's weakness,' she had said.

'He cares for me,' Carolyn said. 'Don't you pay any mind to what I said before.'

I told her I'd never doubted he cared for her, and that I wasn't all that clear on what she had or hadn't said, that I'd been hitting it pretty hard that night myself.

Sunday night I walked over to Miss Kitty's. A light rain was falling but it didn't amount to much.

I'd stopped at Armstrong's first, briefly, and Miss Kitty's had the same Sunday-night feel to it. A handful of regulars and neighborhood people rode a mood that was the flip side of Thank God It's Friday. On the jukebox, a girl sang about having a brand-new pair of roller skates. Her voice seemed to slip in between the notes and find sounds that weren't on the scale.

I didn't know the bartender. When I asked for Skip he pointed toward the office in back.

Skip was there, and so was his partner. John Kasabian had a round face, and he wore wire-rimmed glasses with circular lenses that magnified his deep-set dark eyes. He was Skip's age or close to it, but he looked younger, an owlish schoolboy. He had tattoos on both forearms, and he didn't look at all to be the sort of person who got tattooed.

One tattoo was a conventional if garish representation of a snake entwined around a dagger. The snake was ready to strike, and the tip of the dagger dripped blood. The other tattoo was simpler, even tasteful: a chain-link bracelet encircling his right

527

wrist. 'If I'd at least had it on the other wrist,' he had said, 'at least the watch'd cover it.'

I don't know how he really felt about the tattoos. He affected disdain for them, contempt for the young man who'd elected to get himself thus branded, and sometimes he did seem genuinely embarrassed by them. At other times I sensed that he was proud of them.

I didn't really know him all that well. His was a less expansive personality than Skip's. He didn't like to bounce around the bars, worked the early shift and did the marketing before that. And he wasn't the drinker his partner was. He liked his beer, but he didn't hit it the way Skip did.

'Matt,' he said, and pointed to a chair. 'Glad you're going to help us with this.'

'Whatever I can.'

'It's tomorrow night,' Skip said. 'We're supposed to be in this room, eight o'clock sharp, phone's gonna ring.'

'And?'

'We get instructions. I should have a car ready. That's part of the instructions.'

'Have you got a car?'

'I got my car, it's no hassle having it ready.'

'Has John got a car?'

'I'll get it out of the garage,' John said. 'You think we might want to take two cars?'

'I don't know. He told you to have a car and I presume he told you to have the money ready –'

'Yeah, strangely enough he happened to mention it.'

'– but he didn't give any indication of where he's going to want you to drive.'

'None.'

I thought about it. 'What concerns me –'

'Is walking into something.'

'That's right.'

'I got the same concern. It's like walking point, you're out there and they can just bang away at you. It's bad enough paying ransom, but who knows if we're even gonna get what we pay for? It could wind up being a hijack, and they could waste us while they're at it.'

'Why would they do that?'

'I don't know. "Dead men tell no tales." Isn't that what they say?'

'Maybe they do, but murder brings heat.' I was trying to

concentrate, and I wasn't thinking as clearly as I wanted to. I asked if I could have a beer.

'Oh, Jesus, where's my manners? What do you want, bourbon, cup of coffee?'

'I think just a beer.'

Skip went to get it. While he was gone his partner said, 'This is crazy. It's unreal, you know what I mean? Stolen books, extortion, voices over the phone. It has no reality.'

'I guess.'

'The money has no reality. I can't relate to it. The number –'

Skip brought me a bottle of Carlsberg and a bell-shaped glass. I sipped a little beer and frowned in what was supposed to be thought. Skip lit a cigarette, offered the pack to me, then said, 'No, of course you don't want one, you don't smoke,' and put the pack in his pocket.

I said, 'It shouldn't be a hijack. But there's one way it could be.'

'How's that?'

'If they haven't got the books.'

'Of course they got the books. The books are gone and there's this voice on the phone.'

'Suppose someone hasn't got the books, but knows that they're missing. If he doesn't have to prove possession of them, he's got a chance to take a few dollars off you.'

'A few dollars,' John Kasabian said.

Skip said, 'Then who's got the books? The Feds? You mean they could have them all along and be preparing a case and in the meantime we're paying ransom to somebody who hasn't got shit.' He stood up, walked around the desk. 'I fuckin' love it,' he said. 'I love it so much I want to marry it, I want to have babies with it. Jesus.'

'It's just a possibility, but I think we have to guard against it.'

'How? Everything's set for tomorrow.'

'When he calls, you have him read a page from the books.'

He stared at me. 'You just thought of that? Just now? Nobody move.' Kasabian asked him where he was going. 'To get two more of those Carlsbergs,' he said. 'The fucking beer stimulates thought. They should use it in their advertising.'

He brought back two bottles. He sat on the edge of the desk with his feet swinging, sipping his beer straight from the brown bottle. Kasabian stayed in his chair and peeled the label from his bottle. He was in no hurry to drink it. We had our war council, making what plans we could. John and Skip were both coming along, and so of course was I.

'And I was thinking Bobby'd come,' Skip said.

'Ruslander?'

'He's my best friend, he knows what's happening. I don't know if he could do much if the shit hit the fan, but who could? I'm gonna be armed, but if it's a trap I suppose they'll shoot first, so a lot of fucking good a gun's gonna do me. You got anybody you want to bring in on this?'

Kasabian shook his head. 'I thought of my brother,' he said. 'First person I thought of, but what does Zeke need with this shit, you know?'

'What does anybody need with it? Matt, you got anybody you want to bring?'

'No.'

'I was thinking maybe Billie Keegan,' Skip said. 'What do you think?'

'He's good company.'

'Yeah, right. When you think about it, who the hell needs good company? What we need is heavy artillery and air support. Set up the meet and lay down a mortar barrage on their position. John, tell him about the spades with the mortar.'

'Oh,' Kasabian said.

'Tell him.'

'It was just something I saw.'

'Something he saw. Listen to this.'

'It was whenever it was, a month or so ago. I was at my girl's house, she's on West End in the Eighties, I'm supposed to walk her dog, and I come out of the building and diagonally across the street there are these three black guys.'

'So he turns around and goes back in the building,' Skip offered.

'No, they didn't even look in my direction,' Kasabian said. 'They're wearing fatigue jackets, like, and one's got a cap. They look like soldiers.'

'Tell him what they did.'

'Well, it's hard to believe I really saw this,' he said. He took off his glasses, massaged the bridge of his nose. 'They took a look around, and if they saw me they decided I was nothing to worry about –'

'Shrewd judges of character,' Skip put in.

'– and they set up this mortar, like they've done this drill a thousand times before, and one of them drops a shell in, and they lob a round into the Hudson, nice easy shot, they're on the corner and they can see clear to the river, and we all like check it out, and they still don't pay any attention to me, and they nod to each other and strip the mortar down and pack it up and walk off together.'

'Jesus,' I said.

'It happened so fast,' he said, 'and with so little fanfare, I wondered if I imagined it. But it happened.'

'Did the round make a lot of noise?'

'No, not a whole lot. There was the sort of *whump!* sound a mortar makes on firing, and if there was an explosion when the round hit the water I didn't hear it.'

'Probably a blank,' Skip said. 'They were probably, you know, testing the firing mechanism, checking out the trajectory.'

'Yeah, but for what?'

'Well, shit,' he said. 'You never know when you're gonna need a mortar in this town.' He tipped up his beer bottle, drank deeply, and drummed his heels against the side of the desk. 'I don't know,' he said, 'I'm drinking this stuff but I'm not thinking any better than before. Matt, let's talk about money.'

I thought he was referring to the ransom. But he meant money for me, and I was at a loss. I didn't know how to set a price, said something about being a friend.

He said, 'So? This is what you do for a living, right? Do favors for friends?'

'Sure, but –'

'You're doing us a favor. Kasabian and I don't know what the hell we're doing. Am I right, John?'

'Absolutely.'

'I'm not gonna give Bobby anything for coming, he wouldn't take it, and if Keegan comes along it won't be for the money. But you're a professional and a professional gets paid. Tillary's paying you, isn't he?'

'There's a difference.'

'What's the difference?'

'You're a friend of mine.'

'And he isn't?'

'Not in the same way. In fact I like him less and less. He's –'

'He's an asshole,' Skip said. 'No argument. Makes no differ-ence.' He opened a drawer in the desk, counted money, folded the bills, handed them to me. 'Here,' he said. 'That's twenty-five there. Tell me if it's not enough.'

'I don't know,' I said slowly. 'Twenty-five dollars doesn't seem like much, but –'

'It's twenty-five hundred, you dumb fuck.' We all started laughing. '"Twenty-five dollars doesn't seem like much." Johnny, why did we have to hire a comedian? Seriously, Matt, is it okay?'

'Seriously, it seems a little high.'

'You know what the ransom comes to?'

I shook my head. 'Everybody's been careful not to mention it.'

'Well, you don't mention rope in the house of the hanged, do you? We're paying those cocksuckers fifty grand.'

'Jesus Christ,' I said.

'His name came up already,' Kasabian said. 'He a friend of yours, by any chance? Bring him along tomorrow, he's got nothing else on for the evening.'

FOURTEEN

I tried to make it an early night. I went home and went to bed, and somewhere around four I knew I wasn't going to be able to sleep. There was enough bourbon on hand to knock myself out, but I didn't want that, either. I didn't want to be hung over when we dealt with the blackmailers.

I got up and tried sitting around, but I couldn't sit still and there was nothing on television I was willing to watch. I got dressed and went out for a walk, and I was halfway there before I realized my feet were taking me to Morrissey's.

One of the brothers was on the downstairs door. He gave me a bright smile and let me in. Upstairs, another brother sat on a stool opposite the door. His right hand was concealed beneath his white butcher's apron, and I had been given to understand that there was a gun in it. I hadn't been to Morrissey's since Tim Pat had told me of the reward he and his brothers were offering, but I'd heard that the brothers took turns at guard duty, and that anyone who walked in the door was facing a loaded weapon. Opinions differed on the sort of weapon; I'd had various reports, ranging from revolver to automatic pistol to sawed-off shotgun. My thought was that you'd have to be crazy to plan on using a shotgun, sawed-off or otherwise, in a roomful of your own customers, but no one had ever established the Morrisseys' sanity.

I walked in and looked around the room, and Tim Pat saw me and motioned to me, and I took a step toward him when Skip Devoe called my name from a table in the front near the blacked-out window. He was sitting with Bobby Ruslander. I held up a hand, indicating I'd be with them in a minute, and Bobby put his hand to his mouth and a police whistle pierced the room, cutting off all conversation as cleanly as a gunshot. Skip and Bobby laughed, and the other drinkers realized the noise had been a joke, not an official raid, and, after a few people had assured Bobby he was an asshole, conversation resumed. I followed Tim Pat toward the rear of the room, where we stood on opposite sides of an empty table.

'We've not seen you here since we spoke,' he said. 'Do you bring me news?'

I told him I didn't have any news to bring him. 'I just came in for a drink,' I said.

'And you've heard nothing?'

'Not a thing. I went around, I talked to some people. If there were anything in the air I would have had word back by now, I think it must be some kind of Irish thing, Tim Pat.'

'An Irish thing.'

'Political,' I said.

'Then we should have heard tell of it. Some braggart would have let a word slip.' His fingertips caressed his beard. 'They knew right where to go for the money,' he mused. 'And they even took the few dollars from the Norad jar.'

'That's why I thought—'

'If it was Proddies we should have heard tell. Or if it was a faction of our own.' He smiled without humor. 'We have our factional disagreements, don't you know. The Cause has more than one voice speakin' for it.'

'So I've heard.'

'If it were an "Irish thing,"' he said, pronouncing the phrase deliberately, 'there would be other incidents. But there's been only the one.'

'That you know of,' I said.

'Aye,' he said. 'That I know of.'

I went over and joined Skip and Bobby. Bobby was wearing a gray sweat shirt with the sleeves cut off. Around his neck was a blue plastic whistle on one of those lanyards of plastic braid that boys make at summer camp.

'The actor is feeling his way into the role,' Skip said, aiming a thumb at Bobby.

'Oh?'

'I got a call-back on a commercial,' Bobby said. 'I'm a basketball referee, I'm with these kids at a playground. They all tower over me, that's part of the point of it.'

'Everybody towers over you,' Skip said. 'What are they supposed to be selling? Because if it's deodorant, you want to wear a different sweatshirt.'

'It's brotherhood,' Bobby said.

'Brotherhood?'

'Black kids, white kids, Spanish kids, all united in brotherhood as they drive for the fuckin' hoop. It's some public-service
thing, show it during slow spots on the Joe Franklin show.'

'You get paid for this?' Skip demanded.

'Oh! shit, yes. I think the agencies donate their time, and the
TV stations run it free, but the talent gets paid.'

'The talent,' Skip said.

'*Le talent, c'est moi*,' Bobby said.

I ordered a drink. Skip and Bobby stayed with what they had.
Skip lit a cigarette and the smoke hung in the air. My drink
came and I sipped it.

'I thought you were going to make it an early night,' Skip said.
I said I'd been unable to sleep. 'Because of tomorrow?'

I shook my head. 'Just not tired yet. Restless.'

'I get that way. Hey, actor,' he said. 'What time's your
audition?'

'Supposed to be two o'clock.'

'Supposed to be?'

'You can get there and sit around a lot. I'm supposed to be
there at two.'

'You be done in time to give us a hand?'

'Oh, no problem,' he said. 'These agency cats, they got to
catch the five forty-eight to Scarsdale. Couple of pops in the bar
car, then find out how Jason and Tracy did in school today.'

'Jason and Tracy are on summer break, dumbbell.'

'So he's got to see the postcard they sent home from camp.
They go to this fancy camp in Maine, the postcards are already
written by the staff, all they gotta do is sign them.'

My boys would be going to camp in a couple of weeks. One of
them had woven me a lanyard like the one Bobby wore. I had it
somewhere, packed away in a drawer or something. Or was it
still in Syosset? If I were a proper father, I thought, I'd wear the
damned thing, whistle and all.

Skip was telling Bobby that he needed his beauty sleep.

'I'm supposed to look like a jock,' Bobby said.

'We don't get you outta here, you're gonna look more like a
truss.' He looked at his cigarette, dropped it in what was left of
his drink. 'I never want to see you do that,' he told me. 'I never
want to see either of you do that. Disgusting habit.'

The sky was lightening up outside. We walked slowly, not
saying much. Bobby bobbed and weaved a ways ahead of us,
dribbling an imaginary basketball, faking out an invisible
opponent and driving for the hoop. Skip looked at me and

shrugged. 'What can I tell you?' he said. 'The man is my friend. What else is there to say?'

'You're just jealous,' Bobby said. 'You got the height but you haven't got the moves. A good little man can fake you out of your socks.'

'I wept because I had no shoes,' Skip said solemnly, 'and then I met a man who had no socks. What the hell was *that?*'

An explosion echoed half a mile or so to the north of us.

'Kasabian's mortar,' Bobby said.

'Fucking draft-dodger,' Skip said. 'You wouldn't know a mortar from a pessary. I don't mean a pessary. What is it a pharmacist uses?'

'What the fuck are you talking about?'

'A pestle,' Skip said. 'You wouldn't know a mortar from a pestle. That's not what a mortar sounds like.'

'Whatever you say.'

'It sounded like blasting for a foundation,' he said. 'But it's too early, the neighbors would kill anybody started blasting at this hour. I'll tell you, I'm glad it's done raining.'

'Yeah, we had enough of it, didn't we?'

'I suppose we needed it,' he said. 'That's always what they say, isn't it? Every time it rains its ass off, somebody says how we needed it. Because the reservoirs are drying up, or else the farmers need it or something.'

'This is a wonderful conversation,' Bobby said. 'You'd never get a conversation like this in a less sophisticated city.'

'Fuck you,' Skip said. He lit a cigarette and started coughing, got control of the cough and took another puff on the cigarette, this time without a cough. It was like a drink in the morning, I thought. Once you got one to stay down you were all right.

'The air's nice after a storm,' Skip said. 'I think it cleans it.'

'Washes it,' Bobby said.

'Maybe.' He looked around. 'I almost hate to say this,' he said, 'but it ought to be a beautiful day.'

FIFTEEN

At six minutes past eight, the phone on Skip's desk rang. Billie Keegan had been talking about a girl he'd met the previous year on a three-week holiday in the west of Ireland. He stopped his story in midsentence. Skip put his hand on the phone and looked at me, and I reached for the phone that sat on top of the file cabinet. He nodded once, a quick bob of the head, and we lifted the two receivers in unison.

He said, 'Yeah.'

A male voice said, 'Devoe?'

'Yeah.'

'You have the money?'

'All set.'

'Then get a pencil and write this down. You want to get in your car and drive to –'

'Hold on,' Skip said. 'First you got to prove you got what you say you got.'

'What do you mean?'

'Read the entries for the first week of June. That's this June, June of '75.'

There was a pause. Then the voice, taut now, said, 'You don't give us orders, man. We're the ones say frog, you're the ones jump.' Skip straightened up a little in his chair, leaned forward. I held up a hand to stop whatever he was about to say.

I said, 'We want to confirm we're dealing with the right people. We want to buy it as long as we know you've got it to sell. Establish that much and we'll play out the hand.'

'You're not Devoe speaking. Who the hell are you?'

'I'm a friend of Mr Devoe's.'

'You got a name, friend?'

'Scudder.'

'Scudder. You want us to read something?'

Skip told him again what to read.

537

'Get back to you,' the man said, and broke the connection.

Skip looked over at me, the receiver in his hand. I hung up the one I was holding. He passed his own from hand to hand like a hot potato. I had to tell him to hang up.

'Why'd they do that?' he wanted to know.

'Maybe they had to have a conference,' I suggested. 'Or get the books so they can read you what you want to hear.'

'And maybe they never had them in the first place.'

'I don't think so. They'd have tried to stall.'

'Hanging up on somebody's a pretty good way to stall.' He lit a cigarette, shoved the pack back into his shirt pocket. He was wearing a short-sleeved forest-green work shirt with *Alvin's Texaco Service* embroidered in yellow over the breast pocket. 'Why hang up?' he said petulantly.

'Maybe he thought we could trace the call.'

'Could we do that?'

'It's hard even when you've got the cops and the telephone company cooperating on it,' I said. 'It'd be out of the question for us. But they don't necessarily know that.'

'Catch us tracing calls,' John Kasabian put in. 'We had our hands full installing the second phone this afternoon.'

They had done that a few hours earlier, running wires from the terminal on the wall and hooking an extension phone borrowed from Kasabian's girl's apartment into the line so that Skip and I could be on the line at the same time. While Skip and John were doing that, Bobby had been auditioning for the role of referee in the brotherhood commercial and Billie Keegan had been finding someone to fill in for him behind the stick at Armstrong's. I'd used that time to stuff two hundred and fifty dollars into a parish fund box, light a couple of candles, and phone in another meaningless report to Drew Kaplan in Brooklyn. And now we were all five in Miss Kitty's back office, waiting for the phone to ring again.

'Sort of a southern accent,' Skip said. 'You happen to notice?'

'It sounded phony.'

'Think so?'

'When he got angry,' I said. 'Or pretended to get angry, whatever it was. That bit about jump when he says frog.'

'He wasn't the only one got angry just about then.'

'I noticed. But when he first got angry the accent wasn't there, and when he started with the frog shit he was putting it on thicker than before, trying to sound country.'

He frowned, summoning up the memory. 'You're right,' he said shortly.

'Was it the same guy you talked to before?'

'I don't know. His voice sounded phony before, but it wasn't the same as I was hearing tonight. Maybe he's a man of a thousand voices, all of them unconvincing.'

'Guy could do voiceovers,' Bobby suggested, 'in fucking brotherhood commercials.'

The phone rang again.

This time we made less of a thing out of synchronizing our answering, since I'd already made my presence known. When I had the receiver to my ear, Skip said, 'Yeah?' and the voice I'd heard before asked what he was supposed to read. Skip told him and the voice began reading ledger entries. Skip had the fake set of books open on his desk and followed along on the page.

After half a minute the reader stopped and asked if we were satisfied. Skip looked as though he wanted to take exception to the word. Instead he shrugged and nodded, and I spoke up to say we were assured we were dealing with the right people.

'Then here's what you do,' he said, and we both took up pencils and wrote down the directions.

'Two cars,' Skip was saying. 'All they know is me and Matt are coming, so the two of us'll go in my car. John, you take Billie and Bobby. What do you think, Matt, they'll follow us?'

I shook my head. 'Somebody may be watching us leave here,' I said. 'John, why don't you three go ahead now. Your car's handy?'

'I'm parked two blocks from here.'

'The three of you can drive out there now. Bobby, you and Bill walk on ahead and wait at the car. I'd just as soon you all didn't walk out together, just in case somebody's keeping an eye on the front door. You two wait ahead, and John, give them two, three minutes, and then meet them at the car.'

'And then drive out to – where is it, Emmons Avenue?'

'In Sheepshead Bay. You know where that is?'

'Vaguely. I know it's the ass end of Brooklyn. I've gone out on fishing boats there, but somebody else drove and I didn't pay too much attention.'

'You can take the Belt, the Shore Parkway.'

'All right.'

'Get off, let me think, probably the best place is Ocean Avenue. You'll probably see a sign.'

'Hang on,' Skip said. 'I think I got a map someplace, I saw it the other day.'

He found a Hagstrom street map of the borough and the three of us gave it some study. Bobby Ruslander leaned in over Kasabian's shoulder. Billie Keegan picked up a beer somebody had abandoned earlier and took a sip and made a face. We worked out a route, and Skip told John to take the map along with him.

'I can never fold these things right,' Kasabian said.

Skip said, 'Who cares how you fold the fucking thing?' He took the map away from his partner and began tearing it along some of its fold lines, handing a section some eight inches square to Kasabian and dropping the rest to the floor. 'Here's Sheepshead Bay,' he said. 'You want to know where to get off the parkway, right? What do you need with all the rest of fucking Brooklyn?'

'Jesus,' Kasabian said.

'I'm sorry, Johnny. I'm fuckin' twitchy. Johnny, you got a weapon?'

'I don't want anything.'

Skip opened the desk drawer, put a blue-steel automatic pistol on top of the desk. 'We keep it behind the bar,' he told me, 'case we want to blow our brains out when we count up the night's receipts. You don't want it, John?' Kasabian shook his head. 'Matt?'

'I don't think I'll need it.'

'You don't want to carry it?'

'I'd just as soon not.'

He hefted the gun, looked for a place to put it. It was a 45 and it looked like the kind they issue to officers in the army. A big heavy gun, and what they called a forgiving one – its stopping power could compensate for poor aim, bringing a man down with a shoulder wound.

'Weighs a fucking ton,' Skip said. He worked it underneath the waistband of his jeans and frowned at the way it looked. He tugged his shirt free of his belt, let it hang out over the gun. It wasn't the sort of shirt you wear out of your pants and it looked all wrong. 'Jesus,' he complained, 'where am I gonna put the thing?'

'You'll work it out,' Kasabian told him. 'Meanwhile we ought to get going. Don't you think so, Matt?'

I agreed with him. We went over it one more time while Keegan and Ruslander walked on ahead. They would drive to

Sheepshead Bay and park across the street from the restaurant, but not directly across the street. They would wait there, motor off, lights out, and keep an eye on the place and on us when we arrived.

'Don't try and do anything,' I told him. 'If you see anything suspicious, just observe it. Write down license numbers, anything like that.'

'Should I try and follow them?'

'How would you know who you were following?' He shrugged. 'Play it by ear,' I said. 'Mostly just be around, keep an eye open.'

'Got it.'

After he'd left Skip put an attaché case on top of the desk and popped the catches. Banded stacks of used currency filled the case. 'That's what fifty grand looks like,' he said. 'Doesn't look like much, does it?'

'Just paper.'

'It do anything for you, looking at it?'

'Not really.'

'Me either.' He put the .45 on top of the bills, closed the case. It didn't fit right. He rearranged the bills to make a little nest for the gun and closed it again.

'Just until we get in the car,' he said. 'I don't want to walk down the street like Gary Cooper in *High Noon*.' He tucked his shirt back into his pants. On the way to the car he said, 'You'd think people'd be staring at me. I'm dressed like a grease monkey and carrying a case like a banker. Fucking New Yorkers, I could wear a gorilla suit and nobody'd look twice. Remind me, soon as we get in the car, I want to take the gun out of the case.'

'All right.'

'Bad enough if they pull something and shoot us. Be worse if they used my gun to do it.'

His car was garaged on Fifty-fifth Street. He tipped the attendant a buck and drove around the corner, pulled up in front of a hydrant. He opened the attaché case and removed the pistol and checked the clip, then put the gun on the seat between us, thought better of it and wedged it down into the space between the cushion and the seat back.

The car was a Chevy Impala a couple of years old, long and low, loosely sprung. It was white, with a beige and white interior, and it looked as though it hadn't been through a car wash since it left Detroit. The ashtray overflowed with cigarette butts and the floor was deep in litter.

'Car's like my life,' he said as we caught a light at Tenth Avenue.

'A comfortable mess. What do we do, take the same route we worked out for Kasabian?'

'No.'

'You know a better way?'

'Not better, just different. Take the West Side Drive for now, but instead of the Belt we'll take local streets through Brooklyn.'

'Be slower, won't it?'

'Probably. Let them get there ahead of us.'

'Whatever you say. Any particular reason?'

'Might be easier this way to see if we're being followed.'

'You think we are?'

'I don't see the point offhand, not when they know where we're going. But there's no way to know whether we're dealing with one man or an army.'

'That's a point.'

'Take a right the next corner, pick up the Drive at Fifty-sixth Street.'

'Got it. Matt? You want something?'

'What do you mean?'

'You want a pop? Check the glove box, there ought to be something there.'

There was a pint of Black & White in the glove compartment. Actually it wouldn't have been a pint, it would have been a tenth. I remember the bottle, green glass, curved slightly like a hip flask to fit comfortably in a pocket.

'I don't know about you,' he said, 'but I'm kind of wired. I don't want to get sloppy, but it might not hurt to have something to take the edge off.'

'Just a short one,' I agreed, and opened the bottle.

We took the West Side Drive to Canal Street, crossed into Brooklyn via the Manhattan Bridge, and took Flatbush Avenue until it crossed Ocean Avenue. We kept catching red lights, and several times I noticed his gaze fixing on the glove box. But he didn't say anything, and we left the bottle of Black & White untouched after the one short pull each of us had taken earlier.

He drove with his window rolled down all the way and his left elbow out the window, his fingertips resting on the roof,

542

occasionally drumming the metal. Sometimes we made conversation and sometimes we rode along in silence.

At one point he said, 'Matt, I want to know who set this up. It's gotta be inside, don't you think? Somebody saw an opportunity and took it, somebody who took a look at the books and knew what he was looking at. Somebody who used to work for me, except how would they get back in? If I fired some asshole, some drunk bartender or spastic waitress, how do they wind up prancing into my office and waltzing out with my books? Can you figure that?'

'Your office isn't that hard to get into, Skip. Anybody familiar with the layout could head for the bathroom and slip into your office without anybody paying any attention.'

'I suppose. I suppose I'm lucky they didn't piss in the top drawer while they were at it.' He drew a cigarette from the pack in his breast pocket, tapped it against the steering wheel. 'I owe Johnny five grand,' he said.

'How's that?'

'The ransom. He came up with thirty and I put up twenty. His safe-deposit box was in better shape than mine. For all I know he's got another fifty tucked away, or maybe the thirty was enough to tap him.' He braked, letting a gypsy cab change lanes in front of us. 'Look at that asshole,' he said, without rancor. 'Do people drive like that everywhere or is it just Brooklyn? I swear everybody starts driving funny the minute you cross the river. What was I talking about?'

'The money Kasabian put up.'

'Yeah. So he'll cut a few bills extra per week until he makes up the five-grand difference. Matt, I had twenty thousand dollars in a bank vault and now it's all packed up and ready for delivery, and in a few minutes I won't have it anymore, and it's got no reality. You know what I mean?'

'I think so.'

'I don't mean it's just paper. It's more than paper, if it was just paper people wouldn't go so nuts over it. But it wasn't real when it was locked up tight in the bank and it won't be real when it's gone. I have to know who's doing this to me, Matt.'

'Maybe we'll find out.'

'I fucking have to know. I trust Kasabian, you know? This kind of business, you're dead if you can't trust your partner. Two guys in the bar business watching each other all the time, they're gonna go flat fucking nuts in six months. Never make it work, the place'll have the kind of vibe a Bowery bum wouldn't tolerate. On top of which you could watch your partner twenty-three hours a day and he could steal you blind in the hour he's got open. Kasabian does the buying, for Christ's sake. You know how deep you can stick it in when you're doing the buying for a joint?'

'What's your point, Skip?'

'My point is there's a voice in my head saying maybe this is a nice neat way for Johnny to take twenty grand off me, and it doesn't make any sense, Matt. He'd have to split it with a partner, he has to put up a lot of his own cash to do it, and why would he pick this way to steal from me? All aside from the fact that I trust him, I got no reason not to trust him, he's always been straight with me and if he wanted to rip me off there's a thousand easier ways that pay better and I'd never even know I was being taken. But I still get this voice, and I fuckin' bet he gets it, too, because I caught him looking at me a little different earlier, and I probably been looking at him the same way, and who *needs* this shit? I mean this is worse than what it's costing us. This is the kind of thing makes a joint close up overnight.'

'I think that's Ocean Avenue coming up.'

'Yeah? And to think we've only been driving for six days and six nights. I hang a left at Ocean?'

'You want to turn right.'

'You sure?'

'Positive.'

'I'm always lost in Brooklyn,' he said. 'I swear this place was settled by the Ten Lost Tribes. They couldn't find their way back, they broke ground and built houses. Put in sewer lines, ran in electricity. All the comforts of home.'

The restaurants on Emmons Avenue specialized in seafood. One of them, Lundy's, was a great barn of a place where serious eaters would tuck themselves in at big tables for enormous shore dinners. The place we were headed for was two blocks away at a corner. Carlo's Clam House was its name, and its red neon sign winked to show a clam opening and closing.

Kasabian was parked on the other side of the street a few doors up from the restaurant. We pulled up alongside him. Bobby was in the front passenger seat. Billie Keegan sat alone in the back. Kasabian, of course, was behind the wheel. Bobby said, 'Took you long enough. If there's anything going on, you can't see it from here.'

Skip nodded. We drove a half-block farther and he parked next to a hydrant. 'They don't tow you out here,' he said. 'Do they?'

'I don't think so.'

'All we need,' he said. He killed the engine and we exchanged glances, and his eyes moved to the glove compartment.

He said, 'You see Keegan? In the back seat there?'

'Uh-huh.'

'You can bet he's had a couple since they left.'

'Probably.'

'We'll wait, right? Celebrate after.'

'Sure.'

He shoved the gun into the waistband of his pants, draped his shirt to conceal it. 'Probably the style here,' he said, opening the door, hefting the attaché case. 'Sheepshead Bay, home of the flapping shirttail. You nervous, Matt?'

'A little.'

'Good. I don't want to be the only one.'

We walked across the wide street and approached the restaurant. The night was balmy and you could smell the salt water. I wondered for a moment if I should have been the one to take the gun. I wondered if he'd even fire the pistol, or if it was just there for comfort. I wondered if he'd be any good with it. He'd been in the service, but that didn't mean he was proficient with a handgun.

I'd been good with handguns. Barring ricochets, anyway.

'Catch the sign,' he said. 'Clam opening and closing, it's a goddamned obscenity. "C'mere, honey, let's see you open your clam." Place looks empty.'

'It's Monday night and it's getting late.'

'Midmorning's probably late out here. Gun weighs a ton, you ever notice? My pants feel like they're gonna get dragged down around my knees.'

'You want to leave it in the car?'

'Are you kidding? "This is your weapon, soldier. It could save your life." I'm all right, Matt. I'm just running on nerves is all.'

'Sure.'

He reached the door first and held it for me. The place wasn't much more than a glorified diner, all formica and stainless steel, with a long lunch counter on our left and booths on the right and more tables in back. Four boys in their midteens sat at a booth near the front, eating french fries with their fingers from a communal platter. Farther back, a gray-haired woman with a lot of rings on both fingers was reading a hardcover book in a lending library's plastic cover.

The man behind the counter was tall and fat and completely bald. I suppose he shaved his head. Sweat was beaded on his forehead and had soaked through his shirt. The place was cool enough, with the air conditioning running full blast. There were two customers at the counter, one a round-shouldered man in a short-sleeved white shirt who looked like a failed accountant, the other a stolid girl with heavy legs and bad skin. At the rear of the counter the waitress was taking a cigarette break.

We took seats at the counter and ordered coffee. Someone had left that afternoon's *Post* on an adjoining stool. Skip picked it up, paged through it.

He lit a cigarette, smoked it, glancing every few seconds at the door. We both drank our coffee. He picked up a menu and ran his eyes over its listings. 'They got a million different things,' he said. 'Name something, it's probably on here. Why am I looking? I couldn't eat.'

He lit another cigarette, put his pack on the counter. I took one from it and put it between my lips. He raised his eyebrows but didn't say anything, just gave me a light. I took two, three puffs and put out the cigarette.

I must have heard the phone ring, but it didn't register until the waitress had already walked back to answer it and come forward to ask the round-shouldered man if he was Arthur Devoe. He looked astonished at the idea. Skip went to take the call and I tagged along.

He took the phone, listened for a moment, then began motioning for paper and pencil. I got my notebook and wrote down what he repeated to me.

A whoop of laughter came at us from the front of the restaurant. The kids were throwing french fries at each other. The counterman was leaning his bulk onto the formica, saying something to them. I turned my eyes from them and concentrated on writing down what Skip was saying.

SIXTEEN

Skip said, 'Eighteenth and Ovington. You know where that is?'

'I think so. I know Ovington, it runs through Bay Ridge, but Eighteenth Avenue is west of there. I think that would put it in Bensonhurst, a little ways south of Washington Cemetery.'

'How can anybody know all this shit? Did you say Eighteenth *Avenue?* They got avenues up to Eighteen?'

'I think they go up to Twenty-eight, but Twenty-eighth Avenue's only two blocks long. It runs from Cropsey to Stillwell.'

'Where's that?'

'Coney Island. Not all that far from where we are now.'

He waved a hand, dismissing the borough and all its unknowable streets. 'You know where we're going,' he said. 'And we'll get the map from Kasabian. Oh, fuck. Is this going to be on the part of the map they're carrying?'

'Probably not.'

'Fuck. What did I have to go and rip the map for? Jesus.'

We were out of the restaurant by now. We stood in front, with the winking neon in back of us. Skip said, 'Matt, I'm out of my element. Why'd they have us come here first, then call us up and send us to the church?'

'So they can get a look at us first, I guess. And interrupt our lines of communication.'

'You think someone's looking at us right now? How'm I gonna tell Johnny to follow us? Is that what they oughta do, follow us?'

'They probably ought to go home.'

'Why's that?'

'Because they'll be spotted following us, and they'll be spotted anyway when we tell them what's going on.'

'You think we're being watched?'

'It's possible. It's one reason for them to set things up this way.'

'Shit,' he said. 'I can't send Johnny home. If I suspect him, he probably suspects me at the same time, and I can't ... Suppose we all go in one car?'

'Two cars would be better.'

'You just said two cars won't work.'

'We'll try it this way,' I said, and took his arm to steer him. We walked not toward the car where Kasabian and the others were parked but to Skip's Impala. At my direction he started the car up, blinked the lights a couple of times, and drove to the corner, took a right, drove a block and pulled to the curb.

A few minutes later Kasabian's car pulled up beside us.

'You were right,' Skip said to me. To the others he said, 'You guys are smarter than I gave you credit. We got a phone call, they're sending us on a treasure hunt only we got the treasure. We're supposed to go to a church on Eighteenth Avenue and something.'

'Ovington,' I said.

No one knew where that was. 'Follow us,' I told them. 'Stay half a block to a block in back of us, and when we park go around the block and park behind us.'

'Suppose we get lost?' Bobby wanted to know.

'Go home.'

'How?'

'Just follow us,' I said. 'You won't get lost.'

We took Coney Island Avenue and Kings Highway into Bay Parkway, and then we got disoriented and it took me a few blocks to get my bearings. We went across one of the numbered streets, caught Eighteenth Avenue, and found the church we were looking for on the corner of Ovington. In Bay Ridge, Ovington Avenue runs parallel to Bay Ridge Avenue a block to the south of it. Somewhere around Fort Hamilton Parkway it winds up still parallel to Bay Ridge Avenue but a block *north* of it, where Sixty-eighth Street used to be. Even when you know the area, this sort of thing can drive you crazy, and Brooklyn is full of it.

There was a No Parking zone directly across from the church, and Skip pulled the Chevy into it. He cut the lights, killed the engine. We sat in silence until Kasabian's car had moved up, passed us, and turned at the corner.

548

'Did he even see us?' Skip wondered. I said that they had, that was why they'd turned at the corner. 'I guess,' he said.

I turned and watched out the rear window. A couple of minutes later I saw their lights. They found a parking spot half a block back, and their lights went out.

The neighborhood was mostly prewar frame houses, large ones, set on lots with lawns and trees out in front. Skip said, 'It doesn't look like New York out here. You know what I mean? It looks like some normal place in the rest of the country.'

'A lot of Brooklyn is like this.'

'Parts of Queens, too. Not where I grew up, but here and there. You know what this reminds me of? Richmond Hill. You know Richmond Hill?'

'Not well.'

'Track team had a meet out there once. We got the shit kicked out of us. The houses, though, they looked a lot like this.' He dropped his cigarette out the window. 'I guess we might as well do it,' he said. 'Right?'

'I don't like it,' I said.

'*You* don't like it? I haven't liked it since the books disappeared.'

'The other place was public,' I said. I opened my notebook, read what I'd written down. 'There's supposed to be a flight of steps on the left-hand side of the church leading down to the basement. The door's supposed to be open. I don't even see a light on, do you?'

'No.'

'This looks like an awfully easy way to get sandbagged. I think you'd better stay here, Skip.'

'You figure you're safer alone?'

I shook my head. 'I figure we're both safer separated for the moment. The money stays with you. I want to go down there and see what kind of a reception they've got set up for us. If there looks to be a safe way to make the switch, I'll have them blink the lights three times.'

'What lights?'

'Some light that you can see.' I leaned across him, pointed. 'Those are the basement windows down there. There must be lights, and you'll be able to see them.'

'So you wink the lights three times and I bring the money. Suppose you don't like the setup?'

'Then I tell them I have to get you, and I come out and we drive back to Manhattan.'

549

'Assuming we can find it.' He frowned. 'What if – never mind.'
'What?'
'I was gonna say what if you don't come out.'
'You'll find your way home sooner or later.'
'Funny man. What are you doing?'
I'd popped the cover of the dome light and I was unscrewing the bulb. 'In case they're watching,' I said. 'I don't want them to know when I open the door.'
'The man thinks of everything. It's good you're not Polish, we'd need fifteen guys to turn the car while you held onto the bulb. You want the gun, Matt?'
'I don't think so.'
'"Bare-handed, he went up alone against an army." Take the fucking gun, will you?'
'Gimme.'
'And how about a quick one?'
I reached for the glove box.
I got out and stayed low, keeping the car between me and the church basement windows. I walked half a block to the other car and ran down the situation for them. I had Kasabian stay with the car and told him to start the motor when he saw Skip enter the church. I sent the other two around the block on foot. If the other side made their getaway through a rear exit of the church and over a fence and through a yard, Bobby and Billie might be able to spot them. I didn't know that they could do much, but maybe one of them could come up with a license-plate number.
I returned to the Impala and told Skip what I'd done. I put the bulb back in the dome light, and when I opened the door again it went on, lighting up the car's interior. I swung the door shut and crossed the street.
The gun was tucked into the waistband of my slacks, the butt protruding, the whole thing positioned for a draw across the front of my body. I'd have preferred to have it riding in a holster on my hip but I didn't have the choice. It got in the way as I walked, and when I was in the shadows at the side of the church I drew the gun and walked along holding it, but I didn't like that either, and I put it back where I'd had it.
The flight of stairs was steep. Concrete steps with a rusted iron railing that was loosely mounted into the surrounding brick. A bolt or two had evidently worked loose. I walked down the steps and felt myself disappearing into the darkness. There was a door at the bottom. I groped until I found the knob and I

hesitated with my hand on it, listening carefully, trying to hear something within.

Nothing.

I turned the knob, eased the door inward just far enough to be sure that it was unlocked. Then I drew it shut and knocked on it.

Nothing.

I knocked again. This time I heard movement inside, and a voice called out something unintelligible. I turned the knob again and stepped through the doorway.

The time I'd spent in the pitch-dark stairwell had worked to my advantage. A little light filtered into the basement through the windows at the front, and my pupils had dilated enough to make use of it. I was standing in a room that must have measured about thirty by fifty feet. There were chairs and tables scattered around the floor. I pulled the door closed after me and moved into the shadows against one wall.

A voice said, 'Devoe?'

'Scudder,' I said.

'Where's Devoe?'

'In the car.'

'It doesn't matter,' another voice said. I couldn't recognize either of them as the one I'd heard over the phone, but it had been disguised, and for all I knew these voices were disguised, too. They didn't sound like New York but they didn't sound like anyplace else in particular, either.

The first speaker said, 'You bring the money, Scudder?'

'It's in the car.'

'With Devoe.'

'With Devoe,' I agreed.

Still just the two speakers. One was at the far end of the room, the other to his right. I could place them by their voices but the darkness shrouded them, and one of them sounded as if he might be speaking from behind something, some upended table or something of the sort. If they came out where I could see them, I could draw the gun and throw down on them, shoot them if I had to. On the other hand, it was more than possible that they already had guns trained on me and could drop me where I stood before I got the gun out of my pants. And even if I shot first and got them both, there could be another couple of armed men standing in the shadows, and they could shoot me full of holes before I even knew they existed.

551

Besides, I didn't want to shoot anybody. I just wanted to trade the money for the books and get the hell out of there.

'Tell your friend to bring the money,' one of them said. I decided he might have been the voice on the phone, if he were to let his speech soften into a southern accent. 'Unless he wants the books sent to the IRS.'

'He doesn't want that,' I said. 'But he's not going to walk into a blind alley, either.'

'Keep talking.'

'First of all, put a light on. We don't want to do business in the dark.'

There was a whispered conference, then a fair amount of moving around. One of them flicked a wall switch and a fluorescent fixture in the center of the ceiling came on one tube at a time. There was a flickering quality to its light, the way fluorescents get when they're starting to go.

I blinked, as much at what I saw as at the flickering light. For a moment I thought they were hippies or mountain men, some curious breed. Then I realized they were disguised.

There were two of them, shorter than I, slender in build. Both wore full beards and fright wigs that started low on their foreheads and concealed not only their hair but the whole shapes of their heads. Between the low hairline and the beginning of the beard, each wore an oval mask over the eyes and the top half of the nose. The taller of the two, the one who'd turned on the light, had a chrome-yellow wig and a black face mask. The other, half concealed by a table with chairs stacked on it, sported dark brown hair and a white mask. Both had black beards, and the short one had a gun in his hand.

With the light on, I think we all three felt vulnerable, almost naked. I know I did, and there was a tension in their stance that indicated the same feeling. The one with the gun was not exactly training it on me, but neither was he pointing it in another direction altogether. Darkness had protected all three of us, and now we'd flicked it aside.

'The trouble is we're afraid of each other,' I told him. 'You're afraid we'll try to get the books without paying for them. We're afraid you'll rip us off for the money and give us nothing in return, hold us up again with the books or peddle them to somebody else.'

The tall one shook his head. 'This is a one-time deal.'

'For both of us. We pay once and that's all. If you made a copy of the books, get rid of it.'

'No copies.'

'Good,' I said. 'You have the books here?' The short one with the dark wig shoved a navy-blue laundry bag across the room with his foot. His partner hefted it, put it back on the floor. I said it could be anything, it could be laundry, and would they show me what was in the bag.

'When we see money,' the tall one said, 'you get to see the books.'

'I don't want to examine them. Just take them out of the sack before I tell my friend to bring the money.'

They looked at each other. The one with the gun shrugged. He moved the pistol to cover me while the other one worked the drawstring on the laundry bag and withdrew a hinged-post bound ledger similar to the set of fake books I'd seen on Skip's desk.

'All right,' I said. 'Flick the light on and off three times.'

'Who are you signaling?'

'The Coast Guard.'

They exchanged glances, and the one by the light switch worked it up and down three times. The fluorescent fixture winked on and off in ragged fashion. The three of us stood awkwardly and waited what seemed like a long time. I wondered if Skip had seen the signal, wondered if he'd had enough time alone in the car to lose his nerve.

Then I heard him on the stairs and at the door. I called out to him to come in. The door opened and he entered, the attaché case in his left hand.

He looked at me, then caught sight of the two of them in their beards and wigs and masks.

'Jesus,' he said.

I said, 'Each side will have one man to make the exchange and one to cover him. That way nobody will be able to take anybody off and the books and money will pass at the same time.'

The taller one, the one at the light switch, said, 'You sound like an old hand at this.'

'I had time to think about it. Skip, I'll back you up. Bring the case over here, set it down by me. Good. Now you and one of our friends can set up a table in the middle of the room and clear some of the other furniture out from around it.'

The two of them looked at each other, and predictably the taller one kicked the laundry bag over to his partner and came forward. He asked what I wanted him to do and I put him and Skip to work rearranging the furniture.

'I don't know what the union's going to say about this,' he said. The beard hid his mouth, and the mask covered him around the eyes, but I sensed he was smiling.

At my direction, he and Skip positioned a table in the center of the room, almost directly beneath the overhead light fixture. The table was eight feet long and four feet wide, placed to divide their side of the room from ours.

I got down on one knee, crouched behind a nest of chairs. At the far end of the room, the one with the gun was similarly concealing himself. I called Skip back for the case full of money, sent the tall yellow-haired fellow for the books. Moving deliberately, each carried his part of the bargain to one end of the long table. Skip set the case down first, worked the buttons to release the catches. The man in the blond wig slipped the set of books out of the bag and put them down gently, then stepped back, his hands hovering.

I had each of them retreat a few yards, then switch ends of the table. Skip opened the heavy ledger, made sure the books were the ones he'd negotiated for. His opposite number opened the attaché case and took out a banded stack of bills. He riffled through it, put it back, took up another stack.

'Books are okay,' Skip announced. He closed the heavy volume, got it into the laundry bag, hoisted it and started back toward me.

The one with the gun said, 'Hold it.'

'What for?'

'Stay where you are until he counts it.'

'I got to stand here while he counts fifty grand? Be serious.'

'Take a fast count,' the one with the gun told his partner. 'Make sure it's all money. We don't want to go home with a bag full of cut-up newspaper.'

'I'd really do that,' Skip said. 'I'd really walk up into a gun with a case full of fucking Monopoly money. Point that thing somewhere else, will you? It's getting on my nerves.'

There was no answer. Skip held his position, balanced on the balls of his feet. My back was cramping and my knee, the one I was kneeling on, was giving me a little trouble. Time came to a stop while the yellow-haired one flipped through the packets of money, assuring himself that none of it consisted of cut paper or one-dollar bills. He probably did this as quickly as he could but it seemed forever before he was satisfied, closing the case and engaging the clasps.

'All right,' I said. 'Now the two of you –'

Skip said, 'Wait a minute. We get the laundry bag and they get the attaché case, right?'

'So?'

'So it seems uneven. That case was close to a hundred bucks and it's less than two years old, and how much could a laundry bag be worth? A couple of bucks, right?'

'What are you getting at, Devoe?'

'You could throw in something,' he said, his voice tightening. 'You could tell me who set this up.'

They both looked hard at him.

'I don't know you,' he said. 'I don't know either of you. You ripped me off, fine, maybe your kid sister needs an operation or something. I mean everybody's gotta make a living, right?'

No answer.

'But somebody set this up, somebody I know, somebody who knows me. Tell me who. That's all.'

There was a long silence. Then the one with the brown wig said, 'Forget it,' flat, final. Skip's shoulders dropped in resignation.

'We try,' he said.

And he and the man in the yellow wig backed away from the table, one with the attaché case and one with the laundry bag. I called the shots, sending Skip to the door he'd come in, watching the other move not surprisingly through a curtained archway in the rear. Skip had the door open and was backing through it when the one in the dark wig said, 'Hold it.'

His long-barreled pistol had swung around to cover Skip, and for a moment I thought he was going to shoot. I got both hands on the .45 and took a bead on him. Then his gun swung to the side and he raised it and said, 'We leave first. Stay where you are for ten minutes. You got that?'

'All right,' I said.

He pointed the gun at the ceiling, fired twice. The fluorescent tubes exploded overhead, plunging the room into darkness. The gunshots were loud and the exploding tubes were louder, but for some reason neither the noise nor the darkness rattled me. I watched as he moved to the archway, a shadow among shadows, and the .45 stayed centered on him and my finger stayed on the trigger.

We didn't wait ten minutes as instructed. We got out of there in a hurry, Skip lugging the books in the laundry bag, me with the gun still clutched in one hand. Before we could cross the street

555

to the Chevy, Kasabian had put his car in gear and roared down the block, pulling up next to us with a great screech of brakes. We piled into the back seat and told him to go around the block, but the car was already in motion before we got the words out.

We took a left and then another left. On Seventeenth Avenue, we found Bobby Ruslander hanging on to a tree with one hand, struggling to catch his breath. Across the street, Billie Keegan took a few slow steps toward us, then paused to cup his hands around a match and light a cigarette.

Bobby said, 'Oh, Jesus, am I out of shape. They came tearin' out of that driveway, had to be them, they had the case with the money. I was four houses down, I saw 'em but I didn't want to run up on 'em right away, you know? I think one of 'em was carrying a gun.'

'Didn't you hear the shots?'

He hadn't, nor had either of the others. I wasn't surprised. The dark-haired gunman had used a small-caliber pistol, and while the noise was loud enough in a closed room, it wouldn't have been likely to carry very far.

'They jumped into this car,' Bobby said, pointing to where it had been parked, 'and they got out in a hurry and left rubber. I started moving once they were in the car, figuring I could get a look at the plate number, and I chased 'em and the light was rotten and –' He shrugged. 'Nothing,' he said.

Skip said, 'Least you tried.'

'I'm so out of shape,' Bobby said. He slapped himself across the belly. 'No legs, no wind, and my eyes aren't so good, either. I couldn't referee a real basketball game, running up and down the court. I'd fuckin' die.'

'You could have blown your whistle,' Skip suggested.

'Jesus, if I'd had it with me I might have. You think they would have stopped and surrendered?'

'I think they'd probably have shot you,' I said. 'Forget the plate number.'

'At least I tried,' he said. He looked over at Billie. 'Keegan there, he was closer to them and he didn't budge. Just sat under the tree like Ferdinand the bull, smelling the flowers.'

'Smelling the dogshit,' Keegan said. 'We have to work with the materials at hand.'

'Been working on those minibottles, Billie?'

'Just maintaining,' Keegan said.

I asked Bobby if he got the make of the car. He pursed his lips, blew out, shook his head. 'Dark late-model sedan,' he said. 'They all look alike these days anyway.'

'That's the truth,' Kasabian said, and Skip agreed with him. I started to form another question when Billie Keegan announced that the car was a Mercury Marquis, three or four years old, black or navy blue.

We all stopped and looked at him. His face carefully expressionless, he took a scrap of paper from his breast pocket, unfolded it. 'LJK914,' he read. 'Does that mean anything to any of you?' And while we went on staring at him, he said, 'That's the license number. New York plates. I wrote down all the makes and plate numbers earlier to keep from dying of boredom. It seemed easier than chasing cars like a fucking cocker spaniel.'

'Fucking Billie Keegan,' Skip said with wonder, and went over and hugged him.

'You gentlemen will rush to judgment of the man who drinks a bit,' Keegan said. He took a miniature bottle from a pocket, twisted the cap until the seal broke, tipped back his head and drank the whiskey down.

'Maintenance,' he said. 'That's all.'

SEVENTEEN

Bobby couldn't get over it. He seemed almost hurt by Billie's ingenuity. 'Why didn't you say something?' he demanded. 'I could have been writing down numbers the same time, we could have covered more of them.'

Keegan shrugged. 'I figured I'd keep it to myself,' he said. 'So that when they ran past all these cars and caught a bus on Jerome Avenue I wouldn't look like an asshole.'

'Jerome Avenue's in the Bronx,' somebody said. Billie said he knew where Jerome Avenue was, that he had an uncle used to live on Jerome Avenue. I asked if the pair had been wearing their disguises when they emerged from the driveway.

'I don't know,' Bobby said. 'What were they supposed to look like? They had little masks on.' He made twin circles of his thumbs and forefingers, held them to his face in imitation of the masks.

'Were they wearing beards?'

'Of course they were wearing beards. What do you think, they stopped to shave?'

'The beards were fake,' Skip said.

'Oh.'

'They have the wigs on, too? One dark and one light?'

'I guess. I didn't know they were wigs. I – there wasn't a hell of a lot of light, Arthur. Streetlamps there and there, but they came out that driveway and ran to their car, and they didn't exactly pause and hold a press conference, pose for the photographers.'

I said, 'We'd better get out of here.'

'Why's that? I like standing around in the middle of Brooklyn, it reminds me of hanging out on the corner when I was a boy. You're thinking cops?'

'Well, there were gunshots. No point being conspicuous.'

'Makes sense.'

We walked over to Kasabian's car, got in, and circled the block again. We caught a red light, and I gave Kasabian directions back to Manhattan. We had the books in hand, we'd paid the ransom, and we were all alive to tell or not tell the tale. Besides that, we had Keegan's drunken resourcefulness to celebrate. All of this changed our mood for the better, and I was now able to provide clear directions back to the city and Kasabian for his part was able to absorb them.

As we neared the church, we saw a handful of people in front of it, men in undershirts, teenagers, all of them standing around as if waiting for someone. Somewhere in the distance, I heard the undulating siren of a blue-and-white.

I wanted to tell Kasabian to drive us all home, that we could come back tomorrow for Skip's car. But it was parked next to a hydrant, it would stand out. He pulled up – he may not have put the crowd and the siren together – and Skip and I got out. One of the men across the street, balding and beer-gutted, was looking us over.

I called out, asked him what was up. He wanted to know if I was from the precinct. I shook my head.

'Somebody busted into the church,' he said. 'Kids, probably. We got the exits covered, the cops coming.'

'Kids,' I said heavily, and he laughed.

'I think I was more nervous just now than I was in the church basement,' Skip said, after we'd driven a few blocks. 'I'm standing with a laundry bag over my shoulder like I just committed a burglary and you've got a forty-five in your belt. I figured we're in great shape if they see the gun.'

'I forgot it was there.'

'And we just got out of a car full of drunks. Another point in our favor.'

'Keegan was the only one who was drunk.'

'And he was the brilliant one. Figure that out, will you? Speaking of drinking –'

I got the scotch from the glove compartment and uncapped it for him. He took a long pull, handed it to me. We passed it back and forth until it was gone, and Skip said, 'Fuck Brooklyn,' and tossed it out the window. I'd have been just as happy if he hadn't – we had booze on our breath, an unlicensed gun in our possession, and no good way to account for our presence – but I kept it to myself.

'They were pretty professional,' Skip said. 'The disguises, everything. Why did he shoot the light out?'

'To slow us down.'

'I thought he was going to shoot me for a minute there. Matt?'

'What?'

'How come you didn't shoot him?'

'When he was aiming at you? I might have, if I sensed he was about to shoot. I had him covered. As it stood, if I shot him he would shoot you.'

'I mean after that. After he shot the light out. You still had him covered. You were aiming at him when he went out the door.'

I took a moment to answer. I said, 'You decided to pay the ransom to keep the books away from the IRS. What do you think happens if you're tagged to a shooting in a church in Bensonhurst?'

'Jesus, I wasn't thinking.'

'And shooting him wouldn't have recovered the money, anyway. It was already out the back door with the other one.'

'I know. I really wasn't thinking. The thing is, I mighta shot him. Not because it was the right thing to do, but in the heat of the moment.'

'Well,' I said. 'You never know what you'll do in the heat of the moment.'

The next light we caught, I got out my notebook and began sketching. Skip asked me what I was drawing.

'Ears,' I said.

'How's that?'

'Something an instructor told us when I was at the Police Academy. The shapes of people's ears are very distinctive and it's something that's rarely disguised or changed by plastic surgery. There wasn't a hell of a lot to see of these two. I want to make sketches of their ears before I forget.'

'You remember what their ears looked like?'

'Well, I made a point of remembering.'

'Oh, that makes a difference.' He drew on his cigarette. 'I couldn't swear they *had* ears. Didn't the wigs cover them? I guess not, or you wouldn't be drawing pictures. You can't check their ears in some file, can you? Like fingerprints?'

'I just want to have a way to recognize them,' I said. 'I think I might know their voices, if they were using their real ones tonight, and I think they probably were. As far as their height, one was around five-nine or -ten and the other was either a little shorter or it looked that way because he was standing farther back.' I shook my head at my notebook. 'I don't know which set of ears went with which of them. I should have done this right away. That kind of memory fades on you fast.'

'You think it matters, Matt?'

'What their ears look like?' I considered. 'Probably not,' I granted. 'At least ninety percent of what you do in an investigation doesn't lead anywhere. Make that ninety-five percent – the people you talk to, the things you take time to check. But if you do enough things, the one thing that does work is in there.'

'You miss it?'

'Being a cop? Not often.'

'I can see where a person would miss it,' he said. 'Anyway, I didn't mean just ears. I mean is there a point to the whole thing? They did us a dirty and they got away with it. You think the license plate will lead anywhere?'

'No. I think they were smart enough to use a stolen car.'

'That's what I think, too. I didn't want to say anything because I wanted to feel good back there, and I didn't want to piss on Billie's parade, but the trouble they took, disguises, sending us all around the barn before we got to the right place, I don't think they're gonna get tripped up by a license number.'

'Sometimes it happens.'

'I guess. Maybe we're better off if they stole a car.'

'How do you figure that?'

'Maybe they'll get picked up in it, some sharp-eyed patrolman who looked at the hot-car list. Is that what they call it?'

'The hot-car sheet. It takes a while for a car to get on it, though.'

'Maybe they planned in advance. Stole the car a week ago, took it in for a tune-up. What else could they get charged with? Desecrating a church?'

'Oh, Jesus,' I said.

'What's the matter?'

'That church.'

'What about it?'

'Stop the car, Skip.'

'Huh?'

'Stop the car a minute, all right?'

'You serious?' He looked at me. 'You're serious,' he said, and pulled over to the curb.

I closed my eyes, tried to bring things into focus. 'The church,' I said. 'What kind of church was it, did you happen to notice?'

561

'They all look the same to me. It was, I don't know, brick, stone. What the hell's the difference?'

'I mean was it Protestant or Catholic or what?'

'How would I know which it was?'

'There was one of those signs out in front. A glass case with white letters on a black background, tells you when the services are and what the sermon's going to be about.'

'It's always about the same thing. Figure out all the things you like to do and don't do 'em.'

I could close my eyes and see the damn thing but I couldn't bring the letters into focus. 'You didn't notice?'

'I had things on my mind, Matt. What fucking difference does it make?'

'Was it Catholic?'

'*I* don't know. You got something for or against Catholic? The nuns hit you with a ruler when you were a kid? "Impure thoughts, *wham*, take that, you little bastard." You gonna be a while, Matt?' I had my eyes closed, wrestling with memory, and I didn't answer him. 'Because there's a liquor store across the street, and much as I hate to spend money in Brooklyn, I think I'm gonna. All right?'

'Sure.'

'You can pretend it's altar wine,' he said.

He returned with a pint of Teacher's in a brown bag. He cracked the seal and uncapped the bottle without removing it from the bag, took a drink and gave it to me. I held on to it for a moment, then drank.

'We can go now,' I said.

'Go where?'

'Home. Back to Manhattan.'

'We don't have to go back, make a novena or something?'

'The church was some kind of Lutheran.'

'And that means we can go to Manhattan.'

'Right.'

He started the engine, pulled out from the curb. He reached out a hand and I gave him the bottle and he drank and handed it back to me.

He said, 'I don't mean to pry, Detective Scudder, but –'

'But what was all that about?'

'Yeah.'

'I feel silly mentioning it,' I said. 'It's something Tillary told me a few days ago. I don't even know if it was true, but it was supposed to be a church in Bensonhurst.'

'A Catholic one.'

'It would have to be,' I said, and I told him the story Tommy had told me, of the two kids who'd burglarized a Mafia capo's mother's church, and what had supposedly been done to them in return.

Skip said, 'Really? It really happened?'

'I don't know. Neither does Tommy. Stories get around.'

'Hung on meat hooks and fucking skinned alive –'

'It might appeal to Tutto. They call him Dom the Butcher. I think he's got interests in the wholesale meat industry.'

'Jesus. If that was his church –'

'His mother's church.'

'Whatever. You gonna hang on to that bottle until the glass melts?'

'Sorry.'

'If that was his church, or his mother's church, or whatever it was –'

'I wouldn't want him to know we were there tonight while it got shot up. Not that it's the same as burglarizing the premises, but he still might take it personally. Who knows how he'd react?'

'Jesus.'

'But it was definitely a Protestant church and his mother would go to a Catholic one. Even if it was Catholic, there's probably four or five Catholic churches in Bensonhurst. Maybe more, I don't know.'

'Someday we'll have to count 'em.' He drew on his cigarette, coughed, tossed it out the window. 'Why would anybody do something like that?'

'You mean –'

'I mean hang two kids up and fucking skin 'em, that's what I mean. Why would somebody do that, two kids that all they did was stole some shit from a church?'

'I don't know,' I said. 'I know why Tutto probably thought he was doing it.'

'Why?'

'To teach them a lesson.'

He thought about this. 'Well, I bet it worked,' he said. 'I bet those little fuckers never rob another church.'

EIGHTEEN

By the time we were back home the pint of Teacher's was empty. I hadn't had much of it. Skip had kept chipping away at it, finally flipping it empty into the back seat. I guess he only threw them out the window on the other side of the river.

We hadn't talked much since our conversation about Dom the Butcher. The booze was working in him now, showing up a little in his driving. He ran a couple of lights and took a corner a little wildly, but we didn't hit anything or anybody. Nor did we get flagged down by a traffic cop. You just about had to run down a nun to get cited for a moving violation that year in the city of New York.

When we'd pulled up in front of Miss Kitty's he leaned forward and put his elbows on the steering wheel. 'Well, the joint's still open,' he said. 'I got a guy working the bar tonight, he probably took as much off of us as the boys from Bensonhurst. Come on in, I want to put the books away.'

In his office, I suggested he might want to put the ledger in the safe. He gave me a look and worked the combination dial. 'Just overnight,' he said. 'Tomorrow all this shit goes down a couple different incinerators. No more honest books. All you do is leave yourself wide open.'

He put the books in the safe and started to close the big door. I put a hand on his arm to stop him. 'Maybe this should go in there,' I said, and handed him the .45.

'Forgot about that,' he said. 'It doesn't go in the safe. You gonna tell a holdup man, 'Please excuse me a minute, I wanna get the gun from the safe, blow your head off'? We keep it behind the bar.' He took it from me, then looked around for an inconspicuous way to carry it. There was a white paper bag on the desk, stained from the takeout coffee and sandwiches it had once held, and Skip put the gun in it.

'There,' he said. He closed the safe, spun the dial, tugged the

564

handle to make sure the lock had engaged. 'Perfect,' he said. 'Now let me buy you a drink.'

We went out front and he slipped behind the bar, pouring out two drinks of the same scotch we'd had in the car. 'Maybe you wanted bourbon,' he said. 'I didn't think, didn't think when I bought the bottle, either.'

'This is fine.'

'You sure?' He moved off, put the gun somewhere behind the bar. The bartender he had on that night came over and wanted a conference with him, and they walked off and spoke for a few minutes. Skip came back and finished his drink and said he wanted to put his car in the parking garage before somebody towed it, but he'd be back in a few minutes. Or I could come along for the ride.

'You go ahead,' I told him. 'I may go on home myself.'

'Make it an early night?'

'Not the worst idea.'

'No. Well, if you're gone when I get back I'll see you tomorrow.'

I didn't go right home. I hit a few joints first. Not Armstrong's. I didn't want any conversation. I didn't want to get drunk, either. I'm not sure what I wanted.

I was leaving Polly's Cage when I saw a car that looked like Tommy's Buick cruising west on Fifty-seventh. I didn't get a good look at the person behind the wheel. I walked along after it, saw it pull into a parking space in the middle of the next block. By the time the driver got out and locked up, I was close enough to see it was Tommy. He was wearing a jacket and tie and carrying two packages. One, fan-shaped, looked to be flowers.

I watched him enter Carolyn's building.

For some reason I went and stood on the sidewalk across the street from her building. I picked out her window, or what I decided was her window. Her light was on. I stood there for quite a while, until the light went out.

I went to a pay phone, called 411. The Information operator reported to me that she did indeed have a listing for Carolyn Cheatham at the address I gave her, but that the number was unpublished. I called again, got a different operator, and went through the procedure a policeman uses to get an unlisted number. I got it and wrote it down in my notebook, on the same page with my witless little sketch of ears. They were, I thought, rather unremarkable ears. They would pass in a crowd.

I put a dime in the phone and dialed the number. It rang four or five times, and then she picked it up and said hello. I don't know what the hell else I expected. I didn't say anything, and she said hello a second time and broke the connection.

I felt tight across my upper back and in my shoulders. I wanted to go to some bucket of blood and get in a fight. I wanted to hit something.

Where had the anger come from? I wanted to go up there and pull him off of her and hit him in the face, but what the hell had he done? A few days ago I'd been angry with him for neglecting her. Now I was enraged because he wasn't.

Was I jealous? But why? I wasn't interested in her.

Crazy.

I went and looked at her window again. The light was still out. An ambulance from Roosevelt sped down Ninth Avenue, its siren wailing. Rock music blared on the radio of a car waiting for the light to change. Then the car sped away and the ambulance siren faded in the distance, and for a moment the city seemed utterly silent. Then the silence, too, was gone, as I became aware again of all the background noises that never completely disappear.

That song Keegan had played for me came into my mind. Not all of it. I couldn't get the tune right and I only remembered snatches of the lyrics. Something about a night of poetry and poses. Well, you could call it that. And knowing you're all alone when the sacred ginmill closes.

I picked up some beer on the way home.

NINETEEN

The Sixth Precinct is housed on West Tenth Street between Bleecker and Hudson, in the Village. Years before, when I did a tour of duty there, it was in an ornate structure farther west on Charles Street. That building has since been converted into co-op apartments, and named the Gendarme.

The new station house is an ugly modern building that no one will ever carve into apartments. I was there a little before noon on Tuesday and I walked past the front desk and straight to Eddie Koehler's office. I didn't have to ask, I knew where it was.

He looked up from a report he'd been reading, blinked at me. 'Thing about that door,' he said, 'anybody could walk through it.'

'You're looking good, Eddie.'

'Well, you know. Clean living. Sit down, Matt.'

I sat, and we talked a little. We went back a long ways, Eddie and I. When the small talk faded, he said, 'You just happened to be in the neighborhood, right?'

'I just thought of you and figured you needed a new hat.'

'In this weather?'

'Maybe a panama. Nice straw, keep the sun off.'

'Maybe a pith helmet. But in thith neighborhood,' he said, 'Thome of the girlth would make dirty crackth.'

I had my notebook out. 'A license number,' I said. 'I thought maybe you could check it for me.'

'You mean call Motor Vehicles?'

'First check the hot-car sheet.'

'What's it, a hit-and-run? Your client wants to know who hit him, maybe take quiet cash instead of press charges?'

'You've got a great imagination.'

'You got a license number and I should check the hot cars before anything else? Shit. What's the number?'

I read it out to him. He jotted it down and pushed away from his desk. 'Be a minute,' he said.

While he was gone I looked at my ear drawings. Ears really do look different. The thing is you have to train yourself to notice them.

He wasn't gone long. He came back and dropped into his swivel chair. 'Not on the sheet,' he said.

'Could you check the registration with Motor Vehicles?'

'I could, but I don't have to. They don't always get on the sheet so quick. So I called in, and it's hot, all right, it'll be listed on the next sheet. It was phoned in last night, stolen late afternoon or early evening.'

'It figured,' I said.

''Seventy-three Mercury, right? Sedan, dark blue?'

'That's right.'

'That what you wanted?'

'Where was it stolen from?'

'Somewhere in Brooklyn. Ocean Parkway, the high numbers, it must be pretty far out.'

'Makes sense.'

'It does?' he said. 'Why?'

I shook my head. 'It's nothing,' I said. 'I thought the car might be important, but if it's stolen it doesn't lead anywhere.' I took out my wallet, drew out a twenty and a five, the traditional price of a hat in police parlance. I put the bills on his desk. He covered them with his hand but did not pick them up.

'Now I got a question,' he said.

'Oh?'

'Why?'

'That's private,' I said. 'I'm working for someone, I can't –'

He was shaking his head. 'Why spend twenty-five dollars on something you coulda got for nothing over the telephone? Jesus Christ, Matt, how many years did you carry a shield that you don't remember how to get a listing out of the DMV? You call up, you identify yourself, you know the drill, don't you?'

'I thought it was hot.'

'So you want to check hot cars first, you call somebody in the Department. You're a police officer on a stakeout, whatever you want to say, you just spotted a car you think might be hot, and could they check it for you? That saves you running down here and saves you the price of a hat on top of it.'

'That's impersonating an officer,' I said.

'Oh, really?' He patted the money. 'This,' he said, 'is *bribing* an officer, you want to get technical. You pick a funny place to draw the line.'

The conversation was making me uncomfortable. I had impersonated an officer less than twelve hours ago, getting Carolyn Cheatham's unlisted number from Information. I said, 'Maybe I missed the sight of you, Eddie. How's that?'

'Maybe. Maybe your brain's getting rusty.'

'That's possible.'

'Maybe you should lay off the booze and rejoin the human race. Is that possible?'

I stood up. 'Always a pleasure, Eddie.' He had more to say, but I didn't have to stay there and listen to it.

There was a church nearby, Saint Veronica's, a red-brick pile on Christopher Street near the river. A derelict had arranged himself on the steps, an empty bottle of Night Train still clutched in his hand. The thought came to me that Eddie had phoned ahead and had the man placed there, a grim example of what could lie in store for me. I didn't know whether to laugh or to shudder.

I climbed the steps and went inside. The church was cavernous and empty. I found a seat and closed my eyes for a minute. I thought about my two clients, Tommy and Skip, and the ineffectual work I was performing for each of them. Tommy didn't need my help and wasn't getting it. As for Skip, perhaps I'd helped make the exchange go smoothly, but I'd made mistakes. For God's sake, I should have had Billie and Bobby taking down license numbers, I shouldn't have left it for Billie to think of on his own.

I was almost glad the car had turned out to be stolen. So that Keegan's clue wouldn't lead anywhere and my lack of foresight would be less significant.

Stupid. Anyway, I'd posted them there, hadn't I? They wouldn't have seen the car, let alone got the number, if they'd been with Kasabian on the other side of the block.

I went and put a dollar in the slot and lit a candle. A woman was kneeling a few yards to my left. When she rose to her full height I saw she was a transsexual. She stood two inches taller than I. Her features were a mix of Latin and Oriental, her shoulders and upper arms were muscular, and her breasts were the size of cantaloupes, straining the polka-dot sun halter.

'Well, hello,' she said.

'Hello.'

'Have you come to light a candle to Saint Veronica? Do you know anything about her?'

'No.'

'Neither do I. But I prefer to think of her' – She arranged a strand of hair to fall across her forehead – 'as Saint Veronica *Lake*.'

The N train took me to within a few blocks of the church at Ovington and Eighteenth Avenue. A rather scattered woman in paint-spattered jeans and an army shirt pointed me to the pastor's office. There was no one at the desk, just a pudgy young man with an open freckled face. He had one foot on the arm of a chair and was tuning a guitar.

I asked where the pastor was.

'That's me,' he said, straightening up. 'How can I help you?'

I said I understood he'd had some minor vandalism in the basement the previous evening. He grinned at me. 'Is that what it was? Someone seems to have shot up our light fixture. The damage won't amount to much. Would you like to see where it happened?'

We didn't have to use the stairs I'd gone down last night. We walked down an inside staircase and a hallway, entering the room through the curtained archway our wigged and bearded friends had used to make their departure. The room had been straightened since then, the chairs stacked, the tables folded. Daylight filtered in through the windows.

'That's the fixture, of course,' he said, pointing. 'There was glass on the floor but it's been swept up. I suppose you've seen the police report.'

I didn't say anything, just looked around.

'You are with the police, aren't you?'

He wasn't probing. He simply wanted to be reassured. But something stopped me. Maybe the tail end of my conversation with Eddie Koehler.

'No,' I said. 'I'm not.'

'Oh? Then your interest is –'

'I was here last night.'

He looked at me, waiting for me to go on. He was, I thought, a very patient young man. You sensed that he wanted to hear what you had to say, and in your own good time. I suppose that quality would be a useful one for a minister.

I said, 'I used to be a cop. I'm a private detective now.' That was perhaps technically incorrect, but close enough to the truth.

'I was here last night on behalf of a client, seeking to exchange money for some goods of the client's that were being held for ransom.'

'I see.'

'The other parties, the criminals who had stolen my client's goods in the first place, selected this location for the exchange. They were the ones who did the shooting.'

'I see,' he said again. 'Was anyone . . . shot? The police looked for bloodstains. I don't know that all wounds bleed.'

'No one was shot. There were only two shots fired and they both went into the ceiling.'

He sighed. 'That's a relief. Well, Mr. Uh –'

'Scudder. Matthew Scudder.'

'And I'm Nelson Fuhrmann. I guess we missed introducing ourselves earlier.' He ran a hand over a freckled forehead. 'I gather the police don't know about any of this.'

'No, they don't.'

'And you'd rather they didn't.'

'It would certainly be simpler if they didn't.'

He considered, nodded. 'I doubt I'd have occasion to communicate it to them anyway,' he said. 'I don't suppose they'll come around again, do you? It's no major crime.'

'Somebody might follow up. But don't be surprised if you never hear further.'

'They'll file a report,' he said, 'and that will be that.' He sighed again. 'Well, Mr Scudder, you must have had a reason to take the chance that I *would* mention your visit to the police. What is it you're hoping to find out?'

'I'd like to know who they were.'

'The villains?' He laughed. 'I don't know what else to call them. If I were a policeman I suppose I'd call them perpetrators.'

'You could call them sinners.'

'Ah, but we're all that, aren't we?' He smiled at me. 'You don't know their identity?'

'No. And they wore disguises, wigs and false beards, so I don't even know what they looked like.'

'I don't see how I could help you. You don't suppose they're connected with the church, do you?'

'I'm almost certain they're not. But they picked this place, Reverend Fuhrmann, and –'

'Call me Nelson.'

'– and it suggests a familiarity with the church, and with this

571

room in particular. Did the cops find any evidence of forced entry?'

'I don't believe so, no.'

'Mind if I look at the door?' I examined the lock of the door leading to the outside stairs. If it had been tampered with, I couldn't see it. I asked him what other doors led to the outside, and he took me around and we checked, and none of them bore the scars of illegal entry.

'The police said a door must have been left open,' he said.

'That would be a logical guess if this were just a case of vandalism or malicious mischief. A couple of kids happen to find a door left unlocked, go inside, horse around a little. But this was planned and arranged. I don't think our sinners could count on the door being left open. Or is locking up a hit-or-miss business here?'

He shook his head. 'No, we always lock up. We have to, even in a decent neighborhood like this one. Two doors were open when the police arrived last night, this one and the one in the rear. We certainly wouldn't have left both doors unlocked.'

'If one was open, the other could be unlocked from inside without a key.'

'Oh, of course. Still –'

'There must be a lot of keys in circulation, reverend. I'm sure a lot of community groups use the space.'

'Oh, absolutely,' he said. 'We feel it's part of our function to make our space available when we don't require it for our own purposes. And the rent we collect for it is an important part of our income.'

'So the basement is often in use at night.'

'Oh, it certainly is. Let's see, AA meets in this room every Thursday night, and there's an Al-Anon group that uses the room on Tuesdays, they'll be here tonight, come to think of it. And Fridays, who's here Fridays? This space has been put to no end of uses in the few years I've been here. We had a little theater group doing their rehearsals, we have a monthly cub scout meeting when the whole pack assembles together, we have – well, you can see that there are a lot of different groups with access to the premises.'

'But no one meets here on Monday nights.'

'No. There was a women's consciousness-raising group that met here Mondays up until about three months ago, but I believe they decided to meet in one another's homes instead.' He cocked his head. 'You're suggesting that the, uh, sinners would have had to be in a position to know the space would be empty last night.'

'I was thinking that.'

'But they could have called and asked. Anyone could have called and posed as someone interested in the space, and checking on its availability.'

'Did you get any calls like that?'

'Oh, we get them all the time,' he said. 'It's not something anyone here would bother to remember.'

'Why are you comin' around here all the time?' the woman wanted to know. 'Askin' everybody about Mickey Mouse.'

'Who?'

She let out a laugh. 'Miguelito Cruz. Miguelito means Little Michael, you know? Like Mickey. People call him Mickey Mouse. *I* do, anyway.'

We were in a Puerto Rican bar on Fourth Avenue, nestled between a shop that sold botanicals and one that rented formal wear. I'd gotten back on the N train after my visit to the Lutheran church in Bensonhurst, intending to ride it back into the city, but instead I found myself rising abruptly at Fifty-third Street in Sunset Park and leaving the train there. I had nothing else to do with the day, no logical direction to take in Skip's behalf, and I thought I might as well put in some time justifying my fee from Tommy Tillary.

Besides, it was lunchtime, and a plate of black beans and rice sounded good to me.

It tasted as good as it sounded. I washed it down with a bottle of cold beer, then ordered flan for dessert and had a couple of cups of espresso. The Italians give you a thimble of the stuff; the Puerto Ricans pour you a full cup of it.

Then I barhopped, staying with beers and making them last, and now I'd met this woman who wanted to know why I was interested in Mickey Mouse. She was around thirty-five, with dark hair and eyes and a hardness to her face that matched the hardness in her voice. Her voice, scarred by cigarettes and booze and hot food, was the sort that would cut glass.

Her eyes were large and soft, and what showed of her body suggested that it would have a softness to match the eyes. She was wearing a lot of bright colors. Her hair was wrapped up in a hot-pink scarf, her blouse was an electric blue, her hip-hugging slacks canary yellow, her high-heeled shoes Day-Glo orange. The blouse was unbuttoned far enough to reveal the swell of her full breasts. Her skin was like copper, but with a blush to it, as if lighted from within.

I said, 'You know Mickey Mouse?'

'Sure I know him. I see him all the time in the cartoons. He is one funny mouse.'

'I mean Miguelito Cruz. You know that Mickey Mouse?'

'You a cop?'

'No.'

'You look like one, you move like one, you ask questions like one.'

'I used to be a cop.'

'They kick you out for stealin'?' She laughed, showing a couple of gold teeth. 'Takin' bribes?'

I shook my head. 'Shooting kids,' I said.

She laughed louder. 'No way,' she said. 'They don't kick you out for that. They give you a promotion, make you the chief.'

There was no island accent in her speech. She was a Brooklyn girl from the jump. I asked her again if she knew Cruz.

'Why?'

'Forget it.'

'Huh?'

'Forget it,' I said, and turned a shoulder to her and went back to my beer. I didn't figure she'd leave it alone. I watched out of the corner of my eye. She was drinking something colorful through a straw, and as I watched she sucked up the last of it.

'Hey,' she said. 'Buy me a drink?'

I looked at her. The dark eyes didn't waver. I motioned to the bartender, a sullen fat man who gazed on the world with a look of universal disapproval. He made her whatever the hell she was drinking. He needed most of the bottles on the back bar to do it. He put it in front of her and looked at me, and I held my glass aloft to show I was all right.

'I know him pretty good,' she said.

'Yeah? Does he ever smile?'

'I don't mean him, I mean Mickey Mouse.'

'Uh-huh.'

'Whattaya mean, "uh-huh"? He's a baby. When he grows up, then he can come see me. *If* he grows up.'

'Tell me about him.'

'What's to tell?' She sipped her drink. 'He gets in trouble showin' everybody how he's so tough and so smart. But he's not so tough, you know, and he's not so smart either.' Her mouth softened. 'He is nice-lookin', though. Always the nice clothes,

574

always the hair combed neat, always a fresh shave.' Her hand reached to stroke my cheek. 'Smooth, you know? And he's little, and he's cute, and you want to reach out and give him a hug, just wrap him up and take him home.'

'But you never did?'

She laughed again. 'Hey, man, I got all the troubles I need.'

'You figure him for trouble?'

'If I ever took him home,' she said, 'he'd be all the time thinkin', "Now how am I gonna get this bitch to let me put her on the street?"'

'He's a pimp? I never heard that.'

'If you're thinkin' about a pimp with the purple hat and the Eldorado, forget it.' She laughed. 'That's what Mickey Rat wishes he was. One time he hits on this new girl, she's fresh up from Santurce, from a village near Santurce, you know? Very green, and she's not Señorita Einstein to start with, you know? And he gets her to turn tricks for him, you know, workin' outta her apartment, seein' one or two guys a day, guys he finds and brings up to her.'

'"Hey, Joe, you wanna fock my seestair?"'

'You do one lousy PR accent, man. But you got the idea. She works about two weeks, you know, and she gets sick of it, and she takes the plane back to the island. And that's the story of Mickey the pimp.'

By then she needed another drink and I was ready for a beer myself. She had the bartender bring us a little bag of plantain chips and split the side seam so the chips spilled out on the bar between us. They tasted like a cross between potato chips and wood shavings.

Mickey Mouse's trouble, she told me, was how hard he worked trying to prove something. In high school he had proved his toughness by going into Manhattan with a couple of buddies, roaming the crooked streets of the West Village in search of homosexuals to beat up.

She said, 'He was the bait, you know? Small and pretty. And then when they got the guy, he was the guy who went crazy, almost wanted to kill him. Guys who went with him, first time they said he had heart, but later they started to say he had no brains.' She shook her head. 'So I never took him home,' she said. 'He's cute, but cute disappears when you turn the lights out, you know? I don't think he woulda done me much good.' She extended a painted nail, touched my chin. 'You don't want a man that's too cute, you know?'

575

It was an overture, and one I somehow knew I didn't want to follow up on. The realization brought a wave of sadness rolling in on me out of nowhere. I had nothing for this woman and she had nothing for me. I didn't even know her name; if we'd introduced ourselves I couldn't remember it. And I didn't think we had. The only names mentioned had been Miguelito Cruz and Mickey Mouse.

I mentioned another, Angel Herrera's. She didn't want to talk about Herrera. He was nice, she said. He was not so cute and maybe not so smart, but maybe that was better. But she didn't want to talk about Herrera.

I told her I had to go. I put a bill on the bar and instructed the bartender to keep her glass full. She laughed, either mocking me or enjoying the humor of the situation, I don't know which. Her laughter sounded like someone pouring a sack of broken glass down a staircase. It followed me to the door and out.

TWENTY

When I got back to my hotel there was a message from Anita and another from Skip. I called Syosset first, talked with Anita and the boys. I talked with her about money, saying I'd collected a fee and would be sending some soon. I talked with my sons about baseball, and about the camp they'd be going to soon.

I called Skip at Miss Kitty's. Someone else answered the phone and I held while they summoned him.

'I want to get together with you,' he said. 'I'm working tonight. You want to come by afterward?'

'All right.'

'What time is it now? Ten to nine? I've been on less than two hours? Feels like five. Matt, what I'll do, I'll close up around two. Come by then and we'll have a few.'

I watched the Mets. They were out of town. Chicago, I think. I kept my eyes on the screen but I couldn't keep my mind on the game.

There was a beer left over from the night before. I sipped at it during the game, but I couldn't work up much enthusiasm for it, either. After the game ended I watched about half of the newscast, then turned the set off and stretched out on the bed.

I had a paperback edition of *The Lives of the Saints*, and at one point I looked up Saint Veronica. I read that there was no great certainty that she had existed, but that she was supposed to have been a Jerusalem woman who wiped Christ's sweating face with a cloth while he was suffering on his way to Calvary, and that an image of his face remained on the cloth.

I pictured the act that had brought her twenty centuries of fame, and I had to laugh. The woman I was seeing, reaching out to soothe His brow, had the face and hairstyle of Veronica Lake.

*

577

Miss Kitty's was closed when I got there, and for a moment I thought that Skip had said the hell with it and gone home. Then I saw that the iron gates, though drawn, were not secured by a padlock, and that a low-wattage bulb glowed behind the bar. I slid the accordion gates open a foot or so and knocked, and he came and opened up for me, then rearranged the gates and turned the key in the door.

He looked tired. He clapped me on the shoulder, told me it was good to see me, led me to the end of the bar farthest from the door. Without asking he poured me a long drink of Wild Turkey, then topped up his own glass with scotch.

'First of the day,' I said.

'Yeah? I'm impressed. Of course the day's only two hours and ten minutes old.'

I shook my head. 'First since I woke up. I had some beer, but not too much of that, either.' I drank off some of my bourbon. It had a good bite to it.

'Yeah, well, I'm the same way,' he said. 'I have days when I don't drink. I even have days when I don't have so much as a beer. You know what it is? For you and me, drinking's something we choose to do. It's a choice.'

'There's mornings when I don't think it was the most brilliant choice I could have made.'

'Jesus, tell me about it. But even so it's a choice for us. That's the difference between you and me and a guy like Billie Keegan.'

'You think so?'

'Don't you? Matt, the man is always drinking. I mean take last night. All the rest of us, okay, we're pretty heavy drinkers, but we took it easy last night, right? Because it's sometimes appropriate and sometimes not. Am I right?'

'I guess.'

'Afterward, another story. Afterward a man wants to unwind, loosen up. But Keegan was shitfaced before we got there, for God's sake.'

'Then he turned out to be the hero.'

'Yeah, go figure that one. Uh, the plate number, did you –'

'Stolen.'

'Shit. Well, we figured that.'

'Sure.'

He drank some of his drink. 'Keegan,' he said '*has* to drink. For myself, I could stop anytime. I don't, because I happen to like what the stuff does for me. But I could stop anytime, and I figure you're the same.'

'Oh, I would think so.'

'Of course you are. Now Keegan, I don't know. I don't like to call the man an alcoholic –'

'That's a hell of a thing to call a man.'

'I agree with you. I'm not saying that's what he is, and God knows I like the man, but I think he's got a problem.' He straightened up. 'The hell with it. He could be a fucking Bowery bum, I still wish the car hadn't been stolen. C'mon back, we'll spread out and relax a little.'

In the office, with the two whiskey bottles on the desk between us, he leaned back in his chair and put his feet up.

'You checked the license number,' he said. 'So I guess you're already working on it.'

I nodded. 'I went out to Brooklyn, too.'

'Where? Not where we were last night?'

'The church.'

'What did you think you stood to learn there? You figure one of them left his wallet on the floor?'

'You never know what you'll find, Skip. You have to look around.'

'I suppose. I wouldn't know where to start.'

'You start anyplace. And do anything you think of.'

'You learn anything?'

'A few things.'

'Like what? Never mind, I don't want to be sitting on your shoulder while you do all this. You find out anything useful?'

'Maybe. You don't always know until later on what's useful and what isn't. You can look at it that everything you learn is useful. For instance, just knowing that the car was stolen tells me something, even if it doesn't tell me who was driving it.'

'At least you can rule out the owner. Now you know one person out of eight million couldn't have done it. Who was the owner? Some old lady, only drives it to bingo?'

'I don't know, but it was lifted from Ocean Parkway, not far from the clam bar they sent us to first.'

'Means they live out in Brooklyn?'

'Or they drove their own car out there, parked it and stole the one we saw. Or they went out on the subway or took a cab. Or –'

'So we don't know a whole lot.'

'Not yet.'

He leaned back with his hands behind his head. 'Bobby got another call-back on that commercial,' he said. 'The basketball referee in the fight against prejudice? He's got to go in again

579

tomorrow. It's now down to him and four other guys so they want to look at everybody again.'

'That's good, I guess.'

'How can you tell? You believe a profession like that, running your ass off and fighting the competition so you can be on the tube for twenty seconds. You know how many actors it takes to change a light bulb? Nine. One to climb up and replace it and eight others to stand around the ladder and say, 'That should be *me* up there!'

'That's not bad.'

'Well, credit where it's due, it was the actor told me the joke.' He touched up his drink, sat back in his chair. 'Matt, that was strange last night. That was fucking strange last night.'

'In the church basement.'

A nod. 'Those disguises of theirs. What they needed was Groucho noses and moustaches and glasses, you know the kind the kids wear. Because it was like that, the wigs and beards, they didn't even come close to looking real, but they weren't funny. The gun kept it from being funny.'

'Why'd they wear disguises?'

'So we wouldn't recognize them. Why does anybody wear a disguise?'

'Would you have recognized them?'

'I don't know, I didn't get to see them without the disguises. What are we here, Abbott and Costello?'

'I don't think they recognized us,' I said. 'When I went into the basement, one of them called out your name. It was dark, but they'd had time for their eyes to get used to it. You and I don't look alike.'

'I'm the pretty one.' He drew on his cigarette, blew out a great cloud of smoke. 'What are you getting at?'

'I don't know. I'm just wondering why they would bother with disguises if we didn't know them in the first place.'

'To make it harder to find them later, I suppose.'

'I guess. But why should they think we'd bother to look for them? There's not a hell of a lot we can do to them. We made a deal, traded money for your books. What did you wind up doing with the books, incidentally?'

'Burned them, like I said. And what do you mean, there's nothing we could do to them? We could murder them in their beds.'

'Sure.'

'Find the right church, take a shit on the altar, and tell

Dominic Tutto they did it. That has a certain charm, now that I think of it. Fix 'em up, get 'em a date with the Butcher. Maybe they wore disguises for the same reason they stole the car. Because they're pros.'

'They look familiar to you, Skip?'

'You mean looking past the wigs and beards and shit? I don't know that I could *see* past it. I didn't recognize the voices.'

'No.'

'There *was* something familiar about them, but I don't know what it was. The way they moved, maybe. That's it.'

'I think I know what you mean.'

'An economy of motion. You could almost say they were light on their feet.' He laughed. 'Call 'em up, see if they want to go dancing.'

My glass was empty. I poured a little bourbon into it, sat back, and sipped it slowly. Skip drowned his cigarette in a coffee cup and told me, inevitably, that he never wanted to see me do the same. I assured him he wasn't likely to. He lit another cigarette and we sat there in a comfortable silence.

After a while he said, 'You want to explain something to me, forget about disguises. Tell me why they shot the lights out.'

'To cover their exit. Give them a step or two on us.'

'You think they thought we were gonna come stampeding after them? Chase armed men through backyards and driveways?'

'Maybe they wanted it dark, thought they stood a better chance that way.' I frowned. 'All he had to do was take a step and flick the switch. You know the worst thing about the gunshots?'

'Yeah, they scared the shit out of me.'

'They drew heat. One thing a pro knows is you don't do anything that brings the cops. Not if you can help it.'

'Maybe they figured it was worth it. It was a warning: "Don't try to get even."'

'Maybe.'

'A little touch of the dramatic.'

'Maybe.'

'And God knows it was dramatic enough. When the gun was aimed at me I thought I was gonna get shot. I really did. Then when he shot up the ceiling instead I didn't know whether to shit or go blind. What's the matter?'

'Oh, for Christ's sake,' I said.

'What?'

'He pointed the gun at you and then he fired two shots into the ceiling.'

'Is that something we're supposed to have overlooked? What do you think we've been talking about?'

I held up a hand. 'Think a minute,' I said. 'I'd been thinking of him shooting out the lights, that's why I missed it.'

'Missed what? Matt, I don't –'

'Where have you been lately that somebody pointed a gun at someone but didn't shoot him? And fired two bullets into the ceiling?'

'Jesus Christ.'

'Well?'

'Jesus Christ on stilts. Frank and Jesse.'

'What do you think?'

'I don't know what I think. It's such a crazy thought. They didn't sound Irish.'

'How do we know they were Irish at Morrissey's?'

'We don't. I guess I assumed it. Those handkerchief masks, and taking the money for Northern Relief, and the whole sense that it was political. They had that same economy of movement, you know? The way they were so precise, they didn't take extra steps, they moved through that whole robbery like somebody choreographed it.'

'Maybe they're dancers.'

'Right,' he said. '*Ballet Desperadoes of '75*. I'm still trying to wrap my mind around all of this. Two clowns in red hankies take off the Morrissey brothers for fifty grand, and then they jack off me and Kasabian for – hey, it's the same amount. A subtle pattern begins to emerge.'

'We don't know what the Morrisseys lost.'

'No, and they didn't know what was gonna be in the safe, but a pattern's a pattern. I'll take it. What about their ears? You got pictures of their ears from last night. Are those the ears of Frank and Jesse?' He started to laugh. 'I can't believe the lines I'm speaking. "Are those the ears of Frank and Jesse?" Sentence sounds like it was translated from another language. Are they?'

'Skip, I never noticed their ears.'

'I thought you detectives are working all the time.'

'I was trying to figure out how to get out of the line of fire. If I was thinking of anything. They were fair-skinned, Frank and Jesse. And they were fair last night.'

'Fair and warmer. You see their eyes?'

'I didn't see the color.'

'I was close enough to see the eyes of the one who made the trade with me. But if I saw them I wasn't paying attention. Not that it makes any difference. Did either of them speak a word at Morrissey's?'

'I don't think so.'

He closed his eyes. 'I'm trying to remember. I think the whole thing was pantomime. Two gunshots and then silence until they were out the door and down the stairs.'

'That's how I remember it.'

He stood up, paced around the room. 'It's crazy,' he said. 'Hey, maybe we can stop looking for the viper in my bosom. We're not looking at an inside job. We're dealing with a daring gang of two who're specializing in taking off bars in Hell's Kitchen. You don't suppose that local Irish gang, what do they call them –'

'The Westies. No, we'd have heard. Or Morrissey would have heard. That reward of his would have smoked it out in a day if any of them had anything to do with it.' I picked up my glass and drank what was in it. God, it tasted good right now. We had them, I knew we did. I didn't know a single goddamned thing about them I hadn't known an hour ago but now I knew that I was going to bag them.

'That's why they wore disguises,' I said. 'Oh, they might have worn them anyway, but that's why they didn't want us to get a look at them. They made a mistake. We're going to get them.'

'Jesus, look at you, Matt. Like an old firehouse dog when the alarm goes off. How the hell are you going to get them? You still don't know who they are.'

'I know they're Frank and Jesse.'

'So? Morrissey's been trying to find Frank and Jesse for a long time. Fact he tried to get you to go looking for them. What gives you the edge now?'

I poured myself just one more little slug of the Wild Turkey. I said, 'When you plant a bug on a car and then you want to pick it up, you need two cars. One won't do it, but with two you can triangulate on the signal and home in on it.'

'I'm missing something.'

'It's not quite the same thing, but it's close. We've got them at Morrissey's, and we've got them in that church basement in Bensonhurst. That's two points of reference. Now we can home in on them, we can triangulate on their signal. Two bullets in the ceiling – it's their fucking trade-mark. You'd think they wanted to get caught, giving the job a signature like that.'

'Yeah, I feel sorry for 'em,' he said. 'I bet they're really shitting in their pants. So far they only made a hundred grand this month. What they don't realize is Matt 'Bulldog' Scudder is on their trail, and the poor bastards won't get to spend a dime of it.'

TWENTY-ONE

The telephone woke me. I sat up, blinked at daylight. It went on ringing.

I picked it up. Tommy Tillary said, 'Matt, that cop was here. He came here, can you believe it?'

'Where?'

'The office, I'm at my office. You know him. At least he said he knew you. A detective, a very unpleasant man.'

'I don't know who you're talking about, Tommy.'

'I forget his name. He said –'

'What did he say?'

'He said the two of you were in my house together.'

'Jack Diebold.'

'That's it. He was right then? You were in my house together?'

I rubbed my temples, reached over and looked at my watch. It was a few minutes past ten. I tried to figure out when I'd gone to sleep.

'We didn't go there together,' I said. 'I was there, checking the setting, and he turned up. I used to know him years ago.'

It was no use. I couldn't remember anything after I'd assured Skip that Frank and Jesse were living on borrowed time. Maybe I went home right away, maybe I sat drinking with him until dawn. I had no way of knowing.

'Matt? He's been bothering Carolyn.'

'Bothering her?'

My door was bolted. That was a good sign. I couldn't have been in too bad shape if I'd remembered to bolt the door. On the other hand, my pants were tossed over the chair. It would have been better if they'd been hung in the closet. Then again, they weren't in a tangled heap on the floor, nor was I still wearing them. The great detective, sifting clues, trying to find out how bad he'd been last night.

'Bothering her. Called her a couple of times and went over to

585

her place once. Insinuating things, you know, like she's covering for me. Matt, all it's doing is upsetting Carolyn, plus it makes things awkward for me around the office.'

'I can see how it would.'

'Matt, I gather you knew him of old. Do you think you could get him to lay off me?'

'Jesus, Tommy, I don't see how. A cop doesn't ease up on a homicide investigation as a favor to an old friend.'

'Oh, I wouldn't suggest anything out of line, Matt. Don't get me wrong. But a homicide investigation is one thing and harassment's another, don't you agree?' He didn't give me a chance to answer. 'The thing is, the guy's got it in for me. He's got it in his head I'm a lowlife, and if you could just, you know, have a word with him. Tell him I'm good people.'

I tried to remember what I'd told Jack about Tommy. I couldn't recall, but I didn't think it amounted to much in the way of a character reference.

'And touch base with Drew, just as a favor to me, okay? He was asking me just yesterday what I'd heard from you, if you'd come up with anything. I know you're working hard for me, Matt, and we might as well let him know, too. Keep him in the picture, you know what I mean?'

'Sure, Tommy.'

After he hung up I chased two aspirins with a glass of water from the tap. I had a shower and was halfway through with my shave before I realized I'd virtually agreed to try to talk Jack Diebold into letting up on Tommy. For the first time I realized how good the son of a bitch must be at getting people to buy his real-estate syndications, or whatever the hell he was peddling. It was just as everybody said. He was very persuasive over the telephone.

Outside the day was clear, the sun brighter than it needed to be. I stopped at McGovern's for one quick one, just a bracer. I bought a paper from the bag lady on the corner, tossed her a buck and walked away wrapped in a fog of blessings. Well, I'd take her blessing. I could use all the help I could get.

I had coffee and an English muffin at the Red Flame and read the paper. It bothered me that I couldn't remember leaving Skip's office. I told myself I couldn't have been too bad because I didn't have all that bad of a hangover, but there wasn't necessarily any correlation there. Sometimes I awoke clear-headed and physically fit after a night of ugly drinking and a

586

large memory gap. Other times a hangover that kept me in bed all day would follow a night when I hadn't even felt drunk and nothing untoward had taken place, no memory lost.

Never mind. Forget it.

I ordered a refill on the coffee and thought about my discourse on triangulating on the two men we had taken to calling Frank and Jesse. I remembered the confidence I had felt and wondered what had become of it. Maybe I'd had a plan, maybe I'd come up with a brilliant insight and had known just how to track them down. I looked in my notebook on the chance that I'd written down a passing thought that I'd since forgotten. No such luck. There were no entries after I'd left the bar in Sunset Park.

But I did have that entry, notes on Mickey Mouse and his adolescent career as a fag-basher in the Village. So many working-class teenagers take up that sport, sure that they're acting on genuine outrage and confirming their manliness in the process, never realizing they're trying to kill a part of themselves they don't dare acknowledge. Sometimes they overachieve, maiming or killing a gay man. I'd made a couple of arrests in cases like that, and on every occasion the boys had been astonished to find out that they were in genuine trouble, that we cops were not on their side, that they might actually go away for what they'd done.

I started to put my notebook away, then went over and put a dime in the phone instead. I looked up Drew Kaplan's number and dialed it. I thought of the woman who'd told me about Mickey Mouse, glad I didn't have to see her bright clothing on a morning like this one.

'Scudder,' I said, when the girl rang me through to Kaplan. 'I don't know if it helps, but I've got a little more proof that our friends aren't choirboys.'

Afterward I went for a long walk. I walked down Ninth Avenue, stopping at Miss Kitty's to say a quick hello to John Kasabian, but I didn't stay long. I dropped into a church on Forty-second Street, then continued on downtown, past the rear entrance of the Port Authority bus terminal, down through Hell's Kitchen and Chelsea to the Village. I walked through the meatpacking district and stopped at a butchers' bar on the corner of Washington and Thirteenth and stood among men in bloody aprons drinking shots with short beer chasers. I went outside and watched carcasses of beef and lamb suspended on steel hooks, with flies buzzing around them in the heat of the midday sun.

I walked some more and got out of the sun to have a drink at the Corner Bistro on Jane and Fourth and another at the Cookie Bar on Hudson. I sat at a table at the White Horse and ate a hamburger and drank a beer.

Through all of this I kept running things through my mind.

I swear to God I don't know how anybody ever figures anything out, myself included. I'll watch a movie in which someone explains how he figured something out, fitting clues together until a solution appeared, and it will make perfect sense to me as I listen along.

But in my own work it is rarely like that. When I was on the force most of my cases moved toward solution (if they moved that way at all) in one of two ways. Either I didn't know the answer at all until a fresh piece of information made itself instantly evident, or I knew all along who had done whatever had been done, and all that was ever needed was sufficient evidence to prove it in court. In the tiny percentage of cases where I actually worked out a solution, I did so by a process I did not understand then and do not understand now. I took what I had and stared at it and stared at it and stared at it, and all of a sudden I saw the same thing in a new light, and the answer was in my hand.

Have you ever worked a jigsaw puzzle? And have you then been stuck for the moment, and kept taking up pieces and holding them this way and that, until finally you take up a piece you must have already held between thumb and forefinger a hundred times, one you've turned this way and that, fitted here and fitted there? And this time the piece drops neatly into place, it fits where you'd swear you tried it a minute ago, fits perfectly, fits in a way that should have been obvious all along.

I was at a table in the White Horse, a table in which someone had carved his initials, a dark brown table with the varnish wearing thin here and there. I had finished my hamburger, I had finished my beer, I was drinking a cup of coffee with a discreet shot of bourbon in it. Shreds and images flitted through my mind. I heard Nelson Fuhrmann talking about all the people with access to the basement of his church. I saw Billie Keegan draw a record from its jacket and place it on a turntable. I watched Bobby Ruslander put the blue whistle between his lips. I saw the yellow-wigged sinner, Frank or Jesse, grudgingly agree to move furniture. I watched *The Quare Fellow* with Fran the nurse, walked with her and her friends to Miss Kitty's.

There was a moment when I didn't have the answer, and then there was a moment when I did.

I can't say I did anything to make this happen. I didn't work anything out. I kept picking up pieces of the puzzle, I kept turning them this way and that, and all of a sudden I had the whole puzzle, with one piece after another locking effortlessly and infallibly into place.

Had I thought of all this the night before, with all my thoughts unraveled in blackout like Penelope's tapestry? I don't really think so, although such is the nature of blackouts that I shall never be able to say with certainty one way or the other. Yet it almost felt that way. The answers as they came were so obvious – just as with a jigsaw puzzle, once the piece fits you can't believe you didn't see it right away. They were so obvious I felt as though I were discovering something I had known all along.

I called Nelson Fuhrmann. He didn't have the information I wanted, but his secretary gave me a phone number, and I managed to reach a woman who was able to answer some of my questions.

I started to phone Eddie Koehler, then realized I was only a couple of blocks from the Sixth Precinct, I walked over there, found him at his desk, and told him he had a chance to earn the rest of the hat I'd bought him the day before. He made a couple of telephone calls without leaving his desk, and when I left there I had a few more entries in my notebook.

I made phone calls of my own from a booth on the corner, then walked over to Hudson and caught a cab uptown. I got out at the corner of Eleventh Avenue and Fifty-first Street and walked toward the river. I stopped in front of Morissey's, but I didn't bang on the door or ring the bell. Instead I took a moment to read the poster for the theater downstairs. *The Quare Fellow* had finished its brief run. A play by John B. Keane was scheduled to open the following night. *The Man from Clare*, it was called. There was a photograph of the actor who was to play the leading role. He had wiry red hair and a haunted, brooding face.

I tried the door to the theater. It was locked. I knocked on it, and when that brought no response I knocked on it some more. Eventually it opened.

A very short woman in her mid-twenties looked up at me. 'I'm sorry,' she said. 'The box office will be open tomorrow during the afternoon. We're shorthanded right now and we're in final rehearsals and –'

I told her I hadn't come to buy tickets. 'I just need a couple minutes of your time,' I said.

'That's all anybody ever needs, and there's not enough of my time to go around.' She said the line airily, as if a playwright had written it for her. 'I'm sorry,' she said more matter-of-factly. 'It'll have to be some other time.'

'No, it'll have to be now.'

'My god, what is this? You're not the police, are you? What did we do, forget to pay somebody off?'

'I'm working for the fellow upstairs,' I said, gesturing. 'He'd want you to cooperate with me.'

'Mr Morrisey?'

'Call Tim Pat and ask him, if you want. My name is Scudder.'

From the rear of the theater, someone with a rich brogue called out, 'Mary Jean, what in Christ's fucking name is taking you so long?'

She rolled her eyes, sighed, and held the door open for me.

After I left the Irish theater I called Skip at his apartment and looked for him at his saloon. Kasabian suggested I try the gym.

I tried Armstrong's first. He wasn't there, and hadn't been in, but Dennis said someone else had. 'A fellow was looking for you,' he told me.

'Who?'

'He didn't leave his name.'

'What did he look like?'

He considered the question. 'If you were choosing up sides for a game of cops and robbers,' he said thoughtfully, 'you would not pick him to be one of the robbers.'

'Did he leave a message?'

'No. Or a tip.'

I went to Skip's gym, a large open second-floor loft on broadway over a delicatessen. A bowling alley had gone broke there a year or two earlier, and the gym had the air of a place that wouldn't outlast the term of its lease. A couple of men were working out with free weights. A black man, glossy with sweat, struggled with bench presses while a white partner spotted him. On the right, a big man stood flat-footed, working the heavy bag with both hands.

I found Skip doing pulldowns on the lat machine. He was

wearing gray sweat pants and no shirt and he was sweating fiercely. The muscles worked in his back and shoulders and upper arms. I stood a few yards off watching while he finished a set. I called his name, and he turned and saw me and smiled in surprise, then did another set of pulldowns before rising and coming over to take my hand.

He said, 'What's up? How'd you find me here?'

'Your partner's suggestion.'

'Well, your timing's good. I can use a break. Let me get my cigarettes.'

There was an area where you could smoke, a couple of armchairs grouped around a water cooler. He lit up and said, 'It helps, working out. I had a head and a half when I woke up. We kicked it around last night, didn't we? You get home all right?'

'Why, was I in bad shape?'

'No worse'n I was. You were feeling pretty good. The way you were talking, Frank and Jesse had their tits in the wringer and you were ready to start cranking.'

'You think I was a little optimistic?'

'Hey, that's okay.' He drew on his Camel. 'Me, I'm starting to feel human again. You get the blood moving, sweat out some of the poison, it makes a difference. You ever work with weights, Matt?'

'Not in years and years.'

'But you used to?'

'Oh, a hundred years ago I thought I might like to box a little.'

'You serious? You used to duke it out?'

'This was in high school. I started hanging out at the Y gym, lifting a little, training. Then I had a couple of PAL fights and I found out I didn't like getting hit in the face. And I was clumsy in the ring, and I *felt* clumsy, and I didn't like that.'

'So you got a job where they let you carry a gun instead.'

'And a badge and a stick.'

He laughed. 'The runner and the boxer,' he said. 'Look at them now. You came up here for a reason.'

'Uh-huh.'

'And?'

'I know who they are.'

'Frank and Jesse? You're kidding.'

'No.'

'Who are they? And how did you manage it? And –'

'I wondered if we could get the crew together tonight. After closing time, say.'

'The crew? Who do you mean?'

'Everybody we had with us chasing around Brooklyn the other night. We need some manpower, and there's no point involving new people.'

'We need manpower? What are we going to do?'

'Nothing tonight, but I'd like to hold a war council. If that's all right with you.'

He jabbed his cigarette into an ashtray. 'All right with me?' he said. 'Of course it's all right with me. Who do you want, the Magnificent Seven? No, there were five of us. The Magnificent Seven Minus Two. You, me, Kasabian, Keegan and Ruslander. What's tonight, Wednesday? Billie'll close around one-thirty if I ask him nice. I'll call Bobby, I'll talk to John. You really know who they are?'

'I really do.'

'I mean do you know specifically or –'

'The whole thing,' I said. 'Names, addresses, the works.'

'The whole shmear. So who are they?'

'I'll come by your office around two.'

'You fuck. Suppose you get hit by a bus between now and then?'

'Then the secret dies with me.'

'You prick. I'm gonna do some bench presses. You want to try a set of bench presses, just sort of warm up your muscles?'

'No,' I said. 'I want to go have a drink.'

I didn't have the drink. I looked into one bar but it was crowded, and when I got back to my hotel Jack Diebold was sitting in a chair in the lobby.

I said, 'I figured it was you.'

'What, the Chinese bartender describe me?'

'He's Filipino. He said a fat old man who didn't leave a tip.'

'Who tips at bars?'

'Everybody.'

'Are you serious? I tip at tables, I don't tip standing up at a bar. I didn't think anybody did.'

'Oh, come on. Where have you been doing your drinking, the Blarney Stone? The White Rose?'

He looked at me. 'You're in a funny mood,' he said. 'Bouncy, peppy.'

'Well, I'm right in the middle of something.'

'Oh?'

592

'You know how it is when it all falls into place and things break apart for you? I had an afternoon like that.'

'We're not talking about the same case, are we?'

I looked at him. 'You haven't been talking about anything,' I said. 'What case are you – oh, Tommy, Christ. No, I'm not talking about that. There's nothing there to crack.'

'I know.'

I remembered how my day had started. 'He called me this morning,' I said. 'To complain about you.'

'Did he now.'

'You're harassing him, he said.'

'Yeah, and a hot lot of good it's doing me.'

'I'm supposed to give you a character reference, tell you he's really good people.'

'Is that right. Well, is he really good people?'

'No, he's an asshole. But I could be prejudiced.'

'Sure. After all, he's your client.'

'Right.' During all of this he had gotten up from his chair and the two of us had walked to the sidewalk in front of the hotel. At the curb, a cabdriver and the driver of a florist's delivery van were having an argument.

I said, 'Jack, why'd you come looking for me today?'

'Happened to be in the neighborhood and I thought of you.'

'Uh-huh.'

'Oh, hell,' he said. 'I wondered if you had anything.'

'On Tillary? There's not going to be anything on him, and if I found it – he *is* my client.'

'I meant did you find anything on the Spanish kids.' He sighed. 'Because I'm starting to get worried that we're gonna lose that one in court.'

'Seriously? You've got them admitting to the burglary.'

'Yeah, and if they plead to burglary that's the end of it. But the DA's office wants to go for some kind of homicide charge, and if it goes to trial I could see losin' the whole thing.'

'You've got stolen goods ID'd with serial numbers found in their residence, you've got fingerprints, you've –'

'Aw, shit,' he said. 'You know what can happen in a courtroom. All of a sudden the stolen goods isn't evidence anymore because there's some technicality about the search, they found a stolen typewriter when they were only empowered to search for a stolen adding machine, whatever the hell it was. And the fingerprints, well, the one was over there months ago hauling trash for Tillary, that would account for the prints, right? I can see a smart lawyer kicking holes in a solid case. And I just thought, well, if you ran into something good, I'd like to know about it. And it helps your client if it locks up Cruz and Herrera, right?'

'I suppose so. But I haven't got anything.'

'Not a thing?'

'Not as far as I can see.'

I wound up taking him to Armstrong's and buying us both a couple of drinks. I tipped Dennis a pound just for the pleasure of seeing Jack's reaction. Then I went back to my hotel and left a call at the desk for one in the morning, and set my alarm clock for insurance.

I took a shower and sat on the edge of my bed, looking out at the city. The sky was darkening, turning that cobalt blue it shows all too briefly.

I lay down, stretched out, not really expecting to sleep. The next thing I knew the phone was ringing, and I had no sooner answered it and hung it up again than my clock sounded. I put on my clothes, splashed a little cold water on my face, and went out to earn my money.

TWENTY-TWO

When I got there they were still waiting for Keegan. Skip had the top of a file cabinet set up as a bar, with four or five bottles and some mix and a bucket of ice cubes. A Styrofoam ice chest on the floor was full of cold beer. I asked if there was any coffee left. Kasabian said there was probably some in the kitchen, and he came back with an insulated plastic pitcher full of coffee and a mug and some cream and sugar. I poured myself black coffee, and I didn't put any booze in it for the time being.

I took a sip of the coffee and there was a knock on the door out front. Skip answered it and came back with Billie. 'The late Billie Keegan,' Bobby said, and Kasabian fixed him a drink of the same twelve-year-old Irish Billie drank at Armstrong's.

There was a lot of banter, joking back and forth. Then it all died down at once, and before it could start up again I stood up and said, 'Something I wanted to talk to all of you about.'

'Life insurance,' Bobby Ruslander said. 'I mean, have you guys thought about it? I mean, like, really *thought* about it?'

I said, 'Skip and I were talking last night, and we came up with something. The two guys with the wigs and beards, we realized we'd seen them before. A couple of weeks ago, they were the ones who stuck up Morrissey's after-hours.'

'They wore handkerchief masks,' Bobby said. 'And last night they wore wigs and beards *and* masks, so how could you tell?'

'It was them,' Skip said. 'Believe it. Two shots into the ceiling? Remember?'

'I don't know what you're talking about,' Bobby said.

Billie said, 'Bobby and I only saw 'em Monday night from a distance, and you didn't see 'em at all, did you, John? No, of course not, you were around the block. And were you at Morrissey's the night of the holdup? I don't recall seeing you there.'

595

Kasabian said he never went to Morrissey's.

'So the three of us got no opinion,' Billie went on. 'If you say it was the same two guys, I say fine. Is that it? Because unless I missed something, we still don't know who they are.'

'Yes we do.'

Everybody looked at me.

I said, 'I got very cocky last night, telling Skip here that we had them, that once we knew they pulled both jobs it was only a question of zeroing in on them. I think that was mostly some Wild Turkey talking, but there was a certain amount of truth in it, and today I got lucky. I know who they are. Skip and I were right last night, the same pair did pull both jobs, and I know who they are.'

'So where do we go from here?' Bobby wanted to know. 'What do we do now?'

'That comes later,' I said. 'First I'd like to tell you who they are.'

'Let's hear.'

'Their names are Gary Atwood and Lee David Cutler,' I said. 'Skip calls them Frank and Jesse, as in the James brothers, and he may have been picking up on a family resemblance. Atwood and Cutler are cousins. Atwood lives in the East Village, way over in Alphabet City on Ninth Street between B and C. Cutler lives with his girlfriend. She's a schoolteacher and she lives in Washington Heights. Her name is Rita Donegian.'

'An Armenian,' Keegan said. 'She must be a cousin of yours, John. The plot thickens.'

'How'd you find them?' Kasabian wondered. 'Have they done this before? Have they got records?'

'I don't think they have records,' I said. 'That's something I haven't checked yet because it didn't seem important. They probably have Equity cards.'

'Huh?'

'Membership cards in Actors Equity,' I said. 'They're actors.'

Skip said, 'You're kidding.'

'No.'

'I'll be a son of a bitch. It fits. It fucking fits.'

'You see it?'

'Of course I see it,' he said. 'That's why the accents. That's why they seemed Irish when they hit Morrissey's. They didn't make a sound, they didn't *do* anything Irish, but it felt Irish because they were acting.' He turned and glared at Bobby Ruslander. 'Actors,' he said. 'I been robbed by fucking *actors*.'

596

'You were robbed by two actors,' Bobby said. 'Not by the entire profession.'

'Actors,' Skip said. 'John, we paid fifty thousand dollars to a couple of actors.'

'They had real bullets in their guns,' Keegan reminded him.

'Actors,' Skip said. 'We shoulda paid off in stage money.'

I poured out more coffee from the insulated pitcher. I said, 'I don't know what made me think of it. The thought was just there. But once I had it, I could see a lot of places it could have come from. One was a general impression, there was something off about them, some sense that we were getting a performance. And there was the very different performance at Morrissey's compared to the one staged for us Monday night. Once we knew it was the same two men both times, the difference in their manner became noteworthy.'

'I don't see how that makes them actors,' Bobby said. 'It just makes them phonies.'

'There were other things,' I said. 'They moved like people who were professionally conscious of movement. Skip, you commented that they could have been dancers, that their movements might have been choreographed. And there was a line one of them said, and it was so out of character it could only be *in* character – in character for the person if not for the role he was playing.'

Skip said, 'Which line was that? Was I there to hear it?'

'In the church basement. When you and the one in the yellow wig moved the extra furniture out of the way.'

'I remember. What did he say?'

'Something about not knowing whether the union would approve.'

'Yeah, I remember him saying it. It was an odd line but I didn't pay attention.'

'Neither did I, but it registered. And his voice was different when he delivered it, too.'

He closed his eyes, thinking back. 'You're right,' he said.

Bobby said, 'How does that make him an actor? All it makes him is a union member.'

'The stagehands have a very strong union,' I said, 'and they make sure actors don't move scenery or do other similar jobs that would properly employ a stagehand. It was very much an actor's line and the delivery fit with that interpretation.'

'How'd you get on to them in particular?' Kasabian asked.

'Once you got that they were actors, you were still a long way from knowing their names and addresses.'

'Ears,' Skip said.

Everybody looked at him.

'He drew their ears,' he said, pointing to me. 'In his notebook. The ears are the hardest part of the body to disguise. Don't look at me, I got it from the horse's mouth. He made drawings of their ears.'

'And did what?' Bobby demanded. 'Advertised an open audition and looked at everybody's ears?'

'You could go through albums,' Skip said. 'Look at actors' publicity pictures, looking for the right pair of ears.'

'When they take your picture for your passport,' Billie Keegan said, 'it has to show both your ears.'

'Or what?'

'Or they won't give you a passport.'

'Poor Van Gogh,' Skip said. 'The Man Without a Country.'

'How did you find them?' Kasabian still wanted to know. 'It couldn't have been ears.'

'No, of course not,' I said.

'The license number,' Billie said. 'Has everyone forgotten the license number?'

'The license number turned up on the hot-car sheet,' I told him. 'Once I got the idea that they were actors, I took another look at the church. I knew they hadn't just picked that particular church basement at random and broken into it. They had access to it, probably with a key. According to the pastor, there were a lot of community groups with access, and probably a great many keys in circulation. One of the groups he mentioned in passing was an amateur theater group that had used the basement room for auditions and rehearsals.'

'Aha,' someone said.

'I called the church, got the name of someone connected with the theater group. I managed to reach that person and explained that I was trying to contact an actor who had worked with the group within the past several months. I gave a physical description that would have fit either of the two men. Remember, aside from a two-inch difference in height, they were very similar in physical type.'

'And did you get a name?'

'I got a couple of names. One of them was Lee David Cutler.'

'And a bell rang,' Skip said.

598

'What bell?' Kasabian said. 'That was the first the name came up, wasn't it? Or am I missing something?'

'No, you're right,' I told him. 'At this point Cutler was just one of several names in my notebook. What I had to do was tie one of those names to the other crime.'

'What other crime? Oh, Morrissey's. How? He's the one saloonkeeper doesn't hire out-of-work actors as waiters and bartenders. He's got his own family to work with.'

I said, 'What's on the ground floor, Skip?'

'Oh,' he said.

Billie Keegan said, 'That Irish theater. The Donkey Repertory Company or whatever they call it.'

'I went there this afternoon,' I said. 'They were in final rehearsals for a new play, but I managed to drop Tim Pat's name and get a few minutes of one young woman's time. They have display posters in the lobby, individual promotional pictures of each cast member. Head shots, I think they're called. She showed me posters for the various casts of the plays they've staged over the past year. They do short runs, you know, so they've put on quite a few shows.'

'And?'

'Lee David Cutler was in *Donnybrook*, a Brian Friel play that ran the last week of May and the first week of June. I recognized his picture before I saw the name under it. And I recognized his cousin's picture, too. The family resemblance is even stronger when they're not wearing disguises. In fact it's unmistakable. Maybe that helped them get the parts, since they're not regular members of the rep company. But they played two brothers, so the resemblance was a definite asset.'

'Lee David Cutler,' Skip said. 'And what was the other one's name? Something Atwood.'

'Gary Atwood.'

'Actors.'

'Right.'

He tapped a cigarette on the back of his hand, put it in his mouth, lit it. 'Actors. They were in the play on the ground floor and decided to move up in the world, is that it? Being there gave them the idea to hit Morrissey's.'

'Probably.' I took a slug of coffee. The Wild Turkey bottle was right there on the file cabinet, and my eyes were drawn to it, but right now I didn't want anything to take the edge off my perceptions. I was glad I wasn't drinking, and just as glad that everyone else was.

I said, 'They must have had a drink upstairs once or twice in the course of the run of the play. Maybe they heard about the locked wall cupboard, maybe they saw Tim Pat but money into it or take some out of it. One way or another, it must have occurred to them that the place would be easy pickings.'

'If you live to spend it.'

'Maybe they didn't know enough to be afraid of the Morrisseys. That's possible. They probably started planning the job as a lark, making a play out of it, casting themselves as members of some other Irish faction, silent gunmen out of some old play about the Troubles. Then they got carried away with the possibilities of it, went out and got some guns and staged their play.'

'Just like that.'

I shrugged. 'Or maybe they've pulled stickups before. There's no reason to assume Morrissey's was their debut.'

'I suppose it beats walking people's dogs and working office temp,' Bobby said. 'The hell, an actor's got to make a living. Maybe I ought to get myself a mask and a gun.'

'You tend bar sometimes,' Skip said. 'It's the same idea and you don't need props for it.'

'How'd they get on to us?' Kasabian asked. 'Did they start hanging out here while they were working at the Irish theater?'

'Maybe.'

'But that wouldn't explain how they knew about the books,' he said. 'Skip, did they ever work for us? Atwood and Cutler? Do we know those names?'

'I don't think so.'

'I don't either,' I said. 'They may have known the place, but it's not important. They almost certainly didn't work here because they didn't know Skip by sight.'

'That could have been part of the act,' Skip suggested.

'Possibly. As I said, it doesn't really matter. They had an inside man who stole the books and arranged for them to ransom them.'

'An inside man?'

I nodded. 'That's what we figured from the beginning, remember? That's why you hired me, Skip. Partly to see that the exchange went off without a hitch and partly to find out after the fact who it was that set you up.'

'Right.'

'Well, that's how they got the books, and that's how they got on to you in the first place. For all I know they never set foot inside Miss Kitty's. They didn't have to. They had it all set up for them.'

'By an inside man.'

'That's right.'

'And you know who the inside man was?'

'Yes,' I said. 'I know.'

The room got very quiet. I walked around the desk and took the bottle of Wild Turkey from the top of the file cabinet. I poured a couple of ounces into a rocks glass and put the bottle back. I held the glass without tasting the whiskey. I didn't want the drink so much as I wanted to stretch the moment and let the tension build.

I said, 'The inside man had a role to play afterward, too. He had to let Atwood and Cutler know that we got their license number.'

Bobby said, 'I thought the car was stolen.'

'The car was reported stolen. That's how it got on the hot-car sheet. Stolen between five and seven p.m. Monday from an address on Ocean Parkway.'

'So?'

'That was the report, and at the time I let it go at that. This afternoon I did what I probably should have done off the bat, and I got the name of the car's owner. It was Rita Donegian.'

'Atwood's girlfriend,' Skip said.

'Cutler's. Not that it makes a difference.'

'I'm confused,' Kasabian said. 'He stole his girlfriend's car? I don't get it.'

'Everyone picks on the Armenians,' Keegan said.

I said, 'They took her car. Atwood and Cutler took Rita Donegian's car. Afterward they got a call from their accomplice telling them that the plate had been spotted. So they called in then and reported it as having been stolen, and they said it had been taken thus and so many hours earlier, and from an address way out on Ocean Parkway. When I dug a little deeper this afternoon I managed to establish that the report of the theft hadn't been called in until close to midnight.

'I've got things a little out of sequence. The hot-car sheet didn't carry the name of the Mercury's owner as Rita Donegian. It was an Irish name, Flaherty or Farley, I forget, and the address was the one on Ocean Parkway. There was a phone number, but it turned out to be wrong, and I couldn't pick up any listing for the Flaherty or Farley name at that address. So I checked Motor Vehicles, working from the plate number, and the car's owner turned out to be Rita Donegian with an address on Cabrini Boulevard, which is way up in Washington Heights and a long ways from Ocean Parkway or any other part of Brooklyn.'

I drank some of the Wild Turkey.

'I called Rita Donegian,' I said. 'I represented myself as a cop checking the hot-car sheet automatically, making sure what cars have been recovered and what ones are still missing. Oh, yes, she said, they got the car back right away. She didn't think it was really stolen after all; her husband had a few drinks and forgot where he parked it, then found it a couple blocks away after she'd gone and reported it stolen. I said we must have made a clerical error, we had the car listed as stolen in Brooklyn and here she was in upper Manhattan. No, she said, they were visiting her husband's brother in Brooklyn. I said we had an error in the name, too, that it was Flaherty, whatever the hell it was. No, she said, that was no error, that was the brother's name. Then she got a little rattled and explained it was her husband's brother-in-law, actually, that her husband's sister had married a man named Flaherty.'

'A poor Armenian girl,' Keegan said, 'gone to ruination with the Irish. Think of it, Johnny.'

Skip said, 'Was any of what she said true?'

'I asked her if she was Rita Donegian and if she was the owner of a Mercury Marquis with the license number LJK914. She said yes to both of those questions. That was the last time she told me the truth. She told a whole string of lies, and she knew she was covering for them or she'd never have been so inventive. She hasn't got a husband. She might refer to Cutler as her husband but she was calling him Mr Donegian, and the only Mr Donegian is her father. I didn't want to push too hard because I didn't want her to get the idea that my call was anything beyond simple routine.'

Skip said, 'Somebody called them *after* the payoff. To tell them we had the plate number.'

'That's right.'

'So who knew? The five of us and who else? Keegan, did you get waxed and tell a roomful of people how you were the hero and wrote down the plate number? Is that what happened?'

'I went to confession,' Billie said, 'and I told Father O'Houlihan.'

'I'm serious, goddammit.'

'I never did trust the shifty-eyed bastard,' Billie said.

Gently, John Kasabian said, 'Skip, I don't think anybody told anybody. I think that's what Matt's leading up to. It was one of us, wasn't it, Matt?'

Skip said, 'One of us? One of us *here?*'

'Wasn't it, Matt?'

'That's right,' I said. 'It was Bobby.'

TWENTY-THREE

The silence stretched, with everybody looking at Bobby. Then Skip let out a fierce laugh that caromed wildly around the room.

'Matt, you fuck,' he said. 'You had me going there. You just about had me buying it.'

'It's true, Skip.'

'Because I'm an actor, Matt?' Bobby grinned at me. 'You figure all actors know each other, the way Billie figured Kasabian would have to know the schoolteacher. For Christ's sake, there's probably more actors in this town than there are Armenians.'

'Two much-maligned groups,' Keegan intoned. 'Actors and Armenians, both of them much given to starving.'

'I never heard of these guys,' Bobby said. 'Atwood and Cutler? Are those their names? I never heard of either of them.'

I said, 'It won't wash, Bobby. You were in classes with Gary Atwood at the New York Academy of Dramatic Arts. You were in a showcase at the Galinda Theater on Second Avenue last year, and that was one of Lee David Cutler's credits.'

'You're talking about that Strindberg thing? Six performances to a roomful of empty seats and not even the director knew what the play was supposed to be about? Oh, that was Cutler, the thin guy who played Berndt? Is that who you mean?'

I didn't say anything.

'The Lee threw me. Everybody called him Dave. I suppose I remember him but –'

'*Bobby, you son of a bitch, you're lying!*'

He turned, looked at Skip. He said, 'Am I, Arthur? Is that what you think?'

'It's what I fucking know. I know you, I know you all my life. I know when you're lying.'

'The Human Polygraph.' He sighed. 'Happens you're right.'

'I don't believe it.'

'Well, make up your mind, Arthur. You're a hard man to agree with. Either I'm lying or I'm not. Which way do you want it?'

'You robbed me. You stole the books, you sold me down the fucking river. How could you do it? You little fuck, how could you do it?'

Skip was standing up. Bobby was still sitting in his chair, an empty glass in his hand. Keegan and John Kasabian were on either side of Bobby, but they drew a little ways away from him during this exchange, as if to give them room.

I was standing to Skip's right, and I was watching Bobby. He took his time with the question, as if it deserved careful consideration.

'Well, hell,' he said finally. 'Why would anybody do it? I wanted the money.'

'How much did they give you?'

'Not all that much, tell you the truth.'

'How much?'

'I wanted, you know, a third. They laughed. I wanted ten, they said five, we wound up at seven grand.' He spread his hands. 'I'm a lousy negotiator. I'm an actor, I'm not a businessman. What do I know about haggling?'

'You screwed me for seven thousand dollars.'

'Listen, I wish it was more. Believe me.'

'Don't joke with me, you cocksucker.'

'Then don't feed me straight lines, you asshole.'

Skip closed his eyes. The sweat was beading up on his forehead and tendons showed in his neck. His hands knotted into fists, relaxed, knotted up again. He was breathing through his mouth like a fighter between rounds.

He said, 'Why'd you need the money?'

'Well, see, my kid sister needs this operation, and –'

'Bobby, don't clown with me. I'll fucking kill you, I swear it.'

'Yeah? I needed the money, believe it. I was gonna need the operation. I was gonna get my legs broken.'

'What the hell are you talking about?'

'I'm talking about I borrowed five thousand dollars and put it into a cocaine deal and it fell in the shit, and I had to pay back the five because I didn't borrow it from Chase Manhattan. I haven't got that good of a friend there. I borrowed it from a guy out in Woodside who told me my legs were all the collateral I'd need.'

'What the hell were you doing in a coke deal?'

'Trying to make a dollar for a change. Trying to get out from under.'

'You make it sound like the American Dream.'

'It was a fucking nightmare. The deal went in the toilet, I still owed the money, I had to come up with a hundred a week just to keep paying the vig. You know how it works. You pay a hundred a week forever and you still owe the five grand, and I can't cover my expenses to begin with, never mind finding another hundred a week. I was running behind, and there's interest on the interest, and the seven grand I got from Cutler and Atwood, it's fucking *gone*, man. I paid the shy six grand to get him off my back forever. I paid some other debts I owed, I got a couple hundred dollars in my wallet. That's what's left.' He shrugged. 'Easy come, easy go. Right?'

Skip put a cigarette in his mouth and fumbled with his lighter. He dropped it, and when he reached to pick it up he accidentally kicked it under the desk. Kasabian put a hand on his shoulder to steady him, then lit a match and gave him a light. Billie Keegan got down on the floor and looked around until he found the lighter.

Skip said, 'You know what you cost me?'

'I cost you twenty grand. I cost John thirty.'

'You cost us each twenty-five. I owe Johnny five, he knows he'll get it.'

'Whatever you say.'

'You cost us fifty thousand fucking dollars so you could wind up with seven. What am I talking about? You cost us fifty thousand dollars so you could wind up even.'

'I said I got no head for business.'

'You got no head at all, Bobby. You needed money, you could have sold your friends to Tim Pat Morrissey for ten grand. That's the reward he was offering, that's three thousand more than they gave you.'

'I wasn't gonna rat 'em out.'

'No, of course not. But you'd sell me'n John down shit creek, wouldn't you?'

Bobby shrugged.

Skip dropped his cigarette on the floor, stepped on it. 'You needed money,' he said, 'why didn't you come and ask me for it? Will you just tell me that? You coulda come to me before you went to the shy. Or the shy's pushing you, you need money to cover, you could of come to me then.'

'I didn't want to ask you for the money.'

'You didn't want to ask me for it. It's okay to steal it from me, but you didn't want to ask me for it.'

Bobby drew back his head. 'Yeah, that's right, Arrrr-thur. I didn't want to ask you for it.'

'Did I ever refuse you?'

'No.'

'Did I ever make you crawl?'

'Yeah.'

'When?'

'All the time. Let the actor play bartender for a while. Let's put the actor behind the stick, hope he don't give away the whole store. It's a big joke, my acting. I'm your little windup toy, your fucking pet actor.'

'You don't think I take your acting seriously?'

'Of course you don't.'

'I can't believe I'm hearing this. That piece of shit you were in on Second Avenue, fucking Strindberg, how many people did I bring to see that? There was twenty-five people in the house and I brought twenty of them.'

'To see your pet actor. 'That piece of shit you were in.' That's taking my acting seriously, Skippy baby. That's real support.'

'I don't fucking believe this,' Skip said. 'You hate me.' He looked around the room. 'He hates me.'

Bobby just looked at him.

'You did this to screw me. That's all.'

'I did it for the money.'

'*I woulda given you the fucking money!*'

'I didn't want to take it from you.'

'You didn't want to take it from me. Where do you think you did take it from, you cocksucker? You think it came from God? You think it rained outta the sky?'

'I figure I earned it.'

'You what?'

Bobby shrugged. 'Like I said. I figure I earned it. I worked for it. I was with you, I don't know how many times, from the day I took the books. I was along for the ride Monday night, on the scene, everything. And you never had the least suspicion. That's not the worst job of acting anybody ever did.'

'Just an acting job.'

'You could look at it that way.'

'Judas was pretty good, too. He got an Oscar nomination but he couldn't be present at the awards ceremony.'

'You make a funny-looking Jesus, Arthur. You're just not right for the part.'

Skip stared hard at him. 'I don't get it,' he said. 'You're not even ashamed of yourself.'

'Would that make you happy? A little show of shame?'

'You think it's okay, right? Putting your best friend through hell, costing him a lot of money? Stealing from him?'

'You never stole, right, Arthur?'

'What are you talking about?'

'How'd you come up with twenty grand, Arthur? What did you do, save your lunch money?'

'We skimmed it. That's not much of a secret. You mean I stole from the government? Show me anybody with a cash business who doesn't.'

'And how did you get the money to open the joint? How did you and John get started? Did you skim that, too? Tips you didn't declare?'

'So?'

'Bullshit! You worked behind the stick at Jack Balkin's joint and you stole with both hands. You did everything but take the empties to the grocery store for the deposit. You stole so much offa Jack it's a wonder he didn't have to close the place.'

'He made money.'

'Yeah, and so did you. You stole, and Johnny stole where he was working, and lo and behold, the two of you got enough to open a place of your own. Talk about the American Dream, that's the American Dream. Steal from the boss until you can afford to open up in competition with him.'

Skip said something inaudible.

'What's that? I can't hear you, Arthur.'

'I said bartenders steal. It's expected.'

'Makes it honest, right?'

'I didn't screw Balkin. I made money for him. You can twist it all you want, Bobby, you can't make me into what you are.'

'No, you're a fucking saint, Arthur.'

'Jesus,' Skip said. 'I don't know what to do. I don't know what I'm going to do.'

'I do. You're not gonna do anything.'

'I'm not?'

Bobby shook his head. 'What are you gonna do? You gonna get the gun from behind the bar, come back and shoot me with it? You're not gonna do that.'

'I ought to.'

'Yeah, but it's not gonna happen. You want to hit me? You're not even mad anymore, Arthur. You think you oughta be mad but you don't feel it. You don't feel anything.'

'I –'

'Listen, I'm beat,' Bobby said. 'I'm gonna make it an early night if nobody objects. Listen, guys, I'll pay it back one of these days. The whole fifty thousand. When I'm a star, you know? I'm good for it.'

'Bobby –'

'I'll see you,' he said.

After the three of us had walked Skip around the corner and said goodnight to him, after John Kasabian had flagged a cab and headed uptown, I stood on the corner with Billie Keegan and told him I'd made a mistake, that I shouldn't have told Skip what I'd learned.

'No,' he said. 'You had to.'

'Now he knows his best friend hates his guts.' I turned, looked up at the Parc Vendome. 'He lives on a high floor,' I said. 'I hope he doesn't decide to go out a window.'

'He's not the type.'

'I guess not.'

'You had to tell him,' Billie Keegan said. 'What are you gonna do, let him go on thinking Bobby's his friend? That kind of ignorance isn't bliss. What you did, you lanced a boil for him. Right now it hurts like a bastard but it'll heal. You leave it, it just gets worse.'

'I suppose.'

'Count on it. If Bobby got by with this he'd do something else. He'd keep on until Skip knew about it, because it's not enough to screw Skip, Bobby's gotta rub his nose in it while he's at it. You see what I mean?'

'Yeah.'

'Am I right?'

'Probably. Billie? I want to hear that song.'

'Huh?'

'The sacred ginmill, cuts the brain in sections. The one you played for me.'

'"Last Call."'

'You don't mind?'

'Hey, come on up. We'll have a couple.'

We didn't really drink much. I went with him to his apartment and he played the song five, six times for me. We talked a little, but mostly we just listened to the record. When I left he told me again that I'd done the right thing in exposing Bobby Ruslander. I still wasn't sure he was right.

TWENTY-FOUR

I slept late the next day. That night I went out to Sunnyside Gardens in Queens with Danny Boy Bell and two uptown friends of his. There was a middleweight on the card, a Bedford-Stuyvesant kid Danny Boy's friends had an interest in. He won his fight handily, but I didn't think he showed a whole lot.

The following day was Friday, and I was having a late lunch in Armstrong's when Skip came in and had a beer with me. He'd just come from the gym and he was thirsty.

'Jesus, I was strong today,' he said. 'All the anger goes right into the muscles. I could have lifted the roof off the place. Matt? Did I patronize him?'

'What do you mean?'

'All that shit about I made him my pet actor. Was that true?'

'I think he was just looking for a way to justify what he did.'

'I don't know,' he said. 'Maybe I do what he said. Remember you got a hair up your ass when I paid your bar tab?'

'So?'

'Maybe I did that with him. But on a bigger scale.' He lit a cigarette, coughed hard. Recovering, he said, 'Fuck it, the man's a scumbag. That's all. I'm just gonna forget about it.'

'What else can you do?'

'I wish I knew. He'll pay me back when he's rich and famous, I liked that part. Is there any way we can get the money back from those other two fucks? We know who they are.'

'What can you threaten them with?'

'I don't know. Nothing, I guess. The other night you gathered everybody together for a war council, but that was just setting the stage, wasn't it? To have everybody on hand when you put it all on Bobby.'

'It seemed like a good idea.'

'Yeah. But as far as having a war council, or whatever you

611

want to call it, and figuring out a way to sandbag those actors and get the money back –'

'I can't see it.'

'No, neither can I. What am I gonna do, stick up the stickup men? Not really my style. And the thing is, it's only money. I mean that's really all it is. I had this money in the bank, where I wasn't really getting anything out of it, and now I haven't got it, and what difference does it make in my life? You know what I mean?'

'I think so.'

'I just wish I could let go of it,' he said, 'because I go around and around and around with it in my mind. I just wish I could leave it alone.'

I had my sons with me that weekend. It was going to be our last weekend together before they went off to camp. I picked them up at the train station Saturday morning and put them back on the train Sunday night. We saw a movie, I remember, and I think we spent Sunday morning exploring down around Wall Street and the Fulton Fish Market, but that may have been a different weekend. It's hard to distinguish them in memory.

I spent Sunday evening in the Village and didn't get back to my hotel until almost dawn. The telephone woke me out of a frustrating dream, an exercise in acrophobic frustration; I kept trying to descend from a perilous catwalk and kept not reaching the ground.

I picked up the phone. A gruff voice said, 'Well, it's not the way I figured it would go, but at least we don't have to worry about losing it in court.'

'Who is this?'

'Jack Diebold. What's the matter with you? You sound like you're half asleep.'

'I'm up now,' I said. 'What were you talking about?'

'You haven't seen a paper?'

'I was sleeping. What did –'

'You know what time it is? It's almost noon. You're keeping pimp's hours, you son of a bitch.'

'Jesus,' I said.

'Go get yourself a newspaper,' he said. 'I'll call you in an hour.'

The *News* gave it the front page. KILL SUSPECT HANGS SELF IN CELL, with the story on page three.

Miguelito Cruz had torn his clothing into strips, knotted the strips together, stood his iron bedstead on its side, climbed onto it, looped his homemade rope around an overhead pipe, and jumped off the upended bedstead and into the next world.

Jack Diebold never did call me back, but that evening's six o'clock TV news had the rest of the story. Informed of his friend's death, Angel Herrera had recanted his original story and admitted that he and Cruz had conceived and executed the Tillary burglary on their own. It had been Miguelito who heard noises upstairs and picked up a kitchen knife on his way to investigate. He'd stabbed the woman to death while Herrera watched in horror. Miguelito always had a short temper, Herrera said, but they were friends, even cousins, and they had concocted their story to protect Miguelito. But now that Miguelito was dead, Herrera could admit what had really happened.

The funny thing was that I felt like going out to Sunset Park. I was done with the case, everyone was done with the case, but I felt as though I ought to be working my way through the Fourth Avenue bars, buying rum drinks for ladies and eating bags of plantain chips.

Of course I didn't go there. I never really considered it. I just had the feeling that it was something I ought to do.

That night I was in Armstrong's. I wasn't drinking particularly hard or fast, but I was working at it, and then somewhere around ten-thirty or eleven the door opened and I knew who it was before I turned around. Tommy Tillary, all dressed up and freshly barbered, was making his first appearance in Armstrong's since his wife got herself killed.

'Hey, look who's back,' he sang out, and grinned that big grin. People rushed over to shake his hand. Billie was behind the stick, and he'd no sooner set up one on the house for our hero than Tommy insisted on buying a round for the bar. It was an expensive gesture, there must have been thirty or forty people in there, but I don't think he cared if there were three or four hundred.

I stayed where I was, letting the others mob him, but he worked his way over to me and got an arm around my shoulders. 'This is the man,' he announced. 'Best fucking detective ever wore out a pair of shoes. This man's money,' he told Billie, 'is no good at all tonight. He can't buy a drink, he can't buy a cup of coffee, and if you went and put in pay toilets since I was last here, he can't use his own dime.'

'The john's still free,' Billie said, 'but don't go giving Jimmy any ideas.'

'Oh, don't tell me he didn't already think of it,' Tommy said. 'Matt, my boy, I love you. I was in a tight spot, the world was lookin' to fall in on me, and you came through for me.'

What the hell had I done? I hadn't hanged Miguelito Cruz or coaxed a confession out of Angel Herrera. I hadn't even set eyes on either man. But I had taken his money, and now it looked as though I had to let him buy my drinks.

I don't know how long we stayed there. Curiously, my own drinking slowed even as Tommy's picked up speed. I wondered why he hadn't brought Carolyn; I didn't figure he'd care much about appearances now that the case was closed forever. And I wondered if she would walk in. It was, after all, her neighborhood bar, and she'd been known to come to it all by herself.

After a while Tommy was hustling me out of Armstrong's, so maybe I wasn't the only one who realized that Carolyn might turn up. 'This is celebration time,' he told me. 'We don't want to hang around one place until we grow roots. We want to get out and bounce a little.'

He had the Riviera, and I just went along for the ride. We hit a few places. There was a noisy Greek place on the East Side where the waiters all looked like mob hit men. There were a couple of trendy singles joints, including the one Jack Balkin owned, where Skip had reportedly stolen enough money to open Miss Kitty's. There was, finally, a dark beery cave down in the Village; I realized after a while that it reminded me of the Norwegian bar in Sunset Park, the Fjord. I knew the Village bars fairly well in those days, but this place was new to me, and I was never able to find it again. Maybe it wasn't in the Village, maybe it was somewhere in Chelsea. He was doing the driving and I wasn't paying too much attention to the geography.

Wherever the place was, it was quiet for a change and conversation became possible. I found myself asking him what I'd done that deserved such lavish praise. One man had killed himself and another had confessed, and what part had I played in either incident?

'The stuff you came up with,' he said.

'What stuff? I should have brought back fingernail parings, you could have had someone work voodoo on them.'

'About Cruz and the fairies.'

'He was up for murder. He didn't hang himself because he was afraid they'd nail him for fag-bashing when he was a juvenile offender.'

Tommy took a sip of scotch. He said, 'Couple days ago, black guy comes up to Cruz in the chow line. Huge spade, built like the Seagram's Building. "Wait'll you gets up to Green Haven," he tells him. "Every blood there's gwine have you for a girlfriend. Doctor gwine have to cut you a brand-new asshole, time you gets outta there."'

I didn't say anything.

'Kaplan,' he said. 'Talked to somebody who talked to somebody, and that did it. Cruz took a good look at the idea of playin' Drop the Soap for half the jigs in captivity, and the next thing you know the murderous little bastard was dancing on air. And good riddance to him.'

I couldn't seem to catch my breath. I worked on it while Tommy went to the bar for another round. I hadn't touched the one in front of me but I let him buy for both of us.

When he got back I said, 'Herrera.'

'Changed his story. Made a full confession.'

'And pinned the killing on Cruz.'

'Why not? Cruz wasn't around to complain. Cruz probably did it, but who knows which one it really was, and for that matter who cares? The thing is you gave us the lever.'

'For Cruz,' I said. 'To get him to kill himself.'

'And for Herrera. Those kids of his back in Puerto Rico. Drew spoke to Herrera's lawyer and Herrera's lawyer spoke to Herrera, and the message was, look, you're going up for burglary whatever you do, and probably for murder, but if you tell the right story you'll draw shorter time than if you don't, and on top of that, that nice Mr Tillary's gonna let bygones by bygones and every month there's a nice check for your wife and kiddies back home in Santurce.'

At the bar, a couple of old men were reliving the Louis-Schmeling fight. The second one, the one where Louis deliberately punished the German champion. One of the old boys was throwing roundhouse punches in the air, demonstrating.

I said, 'Who killed your wife?'

'One or the other of them. If I had to bet I'd say Cruz. He had those beady little eyes, you looked at him up close and got that he was a killer.'

'When did you look at him close?'

'When they were over to the house. The first time, when they cleaned the basement and the attic. I told you they hauled stuff for me?'

'You told me.'

'Not the second time,' he said, 'when they cleaned me out altogether.'

He smiled broadly, but I kept looking at him until the smile turned uncertain. 'That was Herrera who helped around the house,' I said. 'You never met Cruz.'

'Cruz came along, gave him a hand.'

'You never mentioned that before.'

'I must of, Matt. Or I left it out. What difference does it make, anyway?'

'Cruz wasn't much for manual labor,' I said. 'He wouldn't come along to haul trash. When did you ever get a look at his eyes?'

'Jesus Christ. Maybe it was seeing a picture in the paper, maybe I just have a sense of him as if I saw his eyes. Leave it alone, will you? Whatever kind of eyes he had, they're not seeing anything anymore.'

'Who killed her, Tommy?'

'Hey, didn't I say let it alone?'

'Answer the question.'

'I already answered it.'

'You killed her, didn't you?'

'What are you, crazy? And keep your voice down, for Christ's sake. There's people can hear you.'

'You killed your wife.'

'Cruz killed her and Herrera swore to it. Isn't that enough for you? And your fucking cop friend's been all over my alibi, pickin' at it like a monkey hunting lice. There's no way I coulda killed her.'

'Sure there is.'

'Huh?'

A chair covered in needlepoint, a view of Owl's Head Park. The smell of dust, and layered over it the smell of a spray of little white flowers.

'Lily-of-the-valley,' I said.

'Huh?'

'That's how you did it.'

'What are you talking about?'

'The third floor, the room her aunt used to live in. I smelled her perfume up there. I thought I was just carrying the scent in my nostrils from being in her bedroom earlier, but that wasn't it.

She was up there, and it was traces of her perfume I was smelling. That's why the room held me, I sensed her presence there, the room was trying to tell me something but I couldn't get it.'

'I don't know what you're talking about. You know what you are, Matt? You're a little drunk is all. You'll wake up tomorrow and –'

'You left the office at the end of the day, rushed home to Bay Ridge, and stowed her on the third floor. What did you do, drug her? You probably slipped her a mickey, maybe left her tied up in the room on the third floor. Tied her up, gagged her, left her unconscious. Then you got your ass back to Manhattan and went out to dinner with Carolyn.'

'I'm not listening to this shit.'

'Herrera and Cruz showed up around midnight, just the way you arranged it. They thought they were knocking off an empty house. Your wife was gagged and tucked away on the third floor and they had no reason to go up there. You probably locked the door there anyway just to make sure. They pulled their burglary and went home, figuring it was the safest and easiest illegal buck they ever turned.'

I picked up my glass. Then I remembered he had bought the drink, and I started to put it down. I decided that was ridiculous. Just as money knows no owner, whiskey never remembers who paid for it.

I took a drink.

I said, 'Then a couple hours after that you jumped in your car and raced back to Bay Ridge again. Maybe you slipped something into your girlfriend's drink to keep her out of it. All you had to do was find an hour, hour and a half, and there's room enough in your alibi to find ninety spare minutes. The drive wouldn't take you long, not at that hour. Nobody would see you drive in. You just had to go up to the third floor, carry your wife down a flight, stab her to death, get rid of the knife, and drive back into the city. That's how you did it, Tommy. Isn't it?'

'You're full of shit, you know that?'

'Tell me you didn't kill her.'

'I already told you.'

'Tell me again.'

'I didn't kill her, Matt. I didn't kill anybody.'

'Again.'

'What's the matter with you? I didn't kill her. Jesus, you're the one helped prove it, and now you're trying to twist and turn it back on me. I swear to Christ I didn't kill her.'

'I don't believe you.'

A man at the bar was talking about Rocky Marciano. There was the best fighter ever lived, he said. He wasn't pretty, he wasn't fancy, but it was a funny thing, he was always on his feet at the end of the fight and the other guy wasn't.

'Oh, Jesus,' Tommy said.

He closed his eyes, put his head in his hands. He sighed and looked up and said, 'You know, it's a funny thing with me. Over the phone I'm as good a salesman as Marciano was a fighter. I'm the best you could ever imagine. I swear I could sell sand to the Arabs, I could sell ice in the winter, but face-to-face I'm just no good at all. Wasn't for phones, I'd have trouble making a living selling. Why do you figure that is?'

'You tell me.'

'I swear I don't know. I used to think it was my face, around the eyes and mouth, *I* don't know. Over the phone's a cinch. I'm talkin' to a stranger, I don't know who he is or what he looks like, and he's not lookin' at me, and there's nothing to it. Face-to-face, somebody I know, whole different story.' He looked at me, his eyes not quite meeting mine. 'If we were doin' this over the phone, you'd buy what I'm telling you.'

'It's possible.'

'It's fucking certain. Word for word, you'd buy the package. Matt, suppose for the sake of argument I said I killed her. It was an accident, it was an impulse, we were both upset over the burglary, I was half in the bag, and –'

'You planned the whole thing, Tommy. It was all set up and worked out.'

'The whole story you told, the way you worked it all out, there's not a thing you can prove.'

I didn't say anything.

'And you helped me, don't forget that part of it.'

'I won't.'

'And I wouldn'ta gone away for it anyway, with or without you, Matt. It wouldn'ta got to court, and if it did I'da beat it in court. All you saved is a hassle. And you know something?'

'What?'

'All we got tonight is the booze talking, your booze and my booze, two bottles of whiskey talkin' to each other. That's all. Morning comes, we can forget everything was said here tonight.

I didn't kill anybody, you didn't say I did, everything's cool, we're still buddies. Right? Right?'

I just looked at him.

TWENTY-FIVE

That was Monday night. I don't remember exactly when I talked to Jack Diebold, but it must have been Tuesday or Wednesday. I tried him at the squad room and wound up reaching him at home. We sparred a bit, and then I said, 'You know, I thought of a way he could have done it.'

'Where have you been? We got one dead and one confessed to it, it's history now.'

'I know,' I said, 'but listen to this.' And I explained, just as an exercise in applied logic, how Tommy Tillary could have murdered his wife. I had to go over it a couple of times before he got a handle on it, and even then he wasn't crazy about it.

'I don't know,' he said. 'It sounds pretty complicated. You've got her stuck there in the attic for what, eight, ten hours? That's a long time with no one keeping an eye on her. Suppose she comes to, works herself free? Then he's got his ass in the crack, doesn't he?'

'Not for murder. She can press charges for tying her up, but when's the last time a husband went to jail for that?'

'Yeah, he's not really at risk until he kills her, and by then she's dead. I see what you mean. Even so, Matt, it's pretty farfetched, don't you think?'

'Well, I was just thinking of a way it could have happened.'

'They never happen that way in real life.'

'I guess not.'

'And if they did you couldn't go anywheres with it. Look what you went through explaining it to me, and I'm in the business. You want to try it on a jury, with some prick lawyer interrupting every thirty seconds with an objection? What a jury likes, a jury likes somebody with greasy hair and olive skin and a knife in one hand and blood on his shirt, that's what a jury likes.'

'Yeah.'

'And anyhow, the whole thing's history. You know what I got now? I got that family in Borough Park. You read about it?'

'The Orthodox Jews?'

'Three Orthodox Jews, mother father son, the father's got the beard, the kid's got the earlocks, all sitting at the dinner table, all shot in the back of the head. That's what I got. Far as Tommy Tillary, I don't care right now if he killed Cock Robin and both Kennedys.'

'Well, it was just an idea,' I said.

'And it's a cute one, I'll grant you that. But it's not very realistic, and even if it was, who's got time for it? You know?'

I figured it was time for a drink. My two cases were closed, albeit unsatisfactorily. My sons were on their way to camp. My rent was paid, my bar tabs were all settled, and I had a few dollars in the bank. I had, it seemed to me, every reason in the world to check out for a week or so and stay drunk.

But my body seemed to know there was more to come, and while I did not by any means stay sober, neither did I find myself launched upon the bender to which I felt roundly entitled. And, a day or two later, I was nursing a cup of bourbon-flavored coffee at my table in Armstrong's when Skip Devoe came in.

He gave me a nod from the doorway. Then he went to the bar and had a quick drink, knocking it back while he stood there. And then he came back to my table and pulled out a chair and dropped down into it.

'Here,' he said, and put a brown manila envelope on the table between us. A small envelope, the kind they give you in banks.

I said, 'What's this?'

'For you.'

I opened it. It was full of money. I took out a sheaf of bills and fanned them.

'For Christ's sake,' he said, 'don't do that, you want everybody following you home? Put it in your pocket, count it when you get home.'

'What is it?'

'Your share. Put it away, will you?'

'My share of what?'

He sighed, impatient with me. He had a cigarette going and he dragged angrily on it, turning his head to avoid blowing the smoke in my face. 'Your share of ten grand,' he said. 'You get half. Half of ten grand is five grand, and five grand is what's in the envelope, and whyntcha do us both a favor and put it the hell away?'

'What's this my share of, Skip?'

'The reward.'

'What reward?'

His eyes challenged me. 'Well, I could get something back, couldn't I? No way I owed those cocksuckers anything. Right?'

'I don't know what you're talking about.'

'Atwood and Cutler,' he said. 'I turned 'em in to Tim Pat Morrissey. For the reward.'

I looked at him.

'I couldn't go to them, ask for the money back. I couldn't get a dime from fuckin' Ruslander, he already paid it all out. I went over and sat down with Tim Pat, asked him did he and his brothers still want to pay out that reward. His eyes lit up like fucking stars. I gave him names and addresses and I thought he was gonna kiss me.'

I put the brown envelope on the table between us. I pushed it toward him and he pushed it back. I said, 'This doesn't belong to me, Skip.'

'Yes it does. I already told Tim Pat half of it was yours, that you did all the work. Take it.'

'I don't want it. I already got paid for what I did. The information was yours. You bought it. If you sold it to Tim Pat, you get the reward.'

He drew on his cigarette. 'I already gave half of it to Kasabian. The five grand I owed him. He didn't want to take it either. I told him, listen, you take this and we're, square. He took it. And this here is yours.'

'I don't want it.'

'It's money. What the hell's the matter with it?'

I didn't say anything.

'Look,' he said, 'just take it, will you? You don't want to keep it, don't keep it. Burn it, throw it out, give it away, I don't give a shit what you do with it. Because I cannot keep it. I can't. You understand?'

'Why not?'

'Oh, shit,' he said. 'Oh, fucking shit. I don't know why I did it.'

'What are you talking about?'

'And I'd do it again. That's what's crazy. It's eating me up, but if I had to do it all over again, I'd fucking do it.'

'Do what?'

He looked at me. 'I gave Tim Pat three names,' he said, 'and three addresses.'

He took his cigarette between thumb and forefinger, stared at it. 'I never want to see you do this,' he said, and dropped the butt into my cup of coffee. Then he said, 'Oh, Jesus, what am I doing? You had half a cup of coffee left there. I was thinking it was my cup and I didn't even have a cup. What's the matter with me? I'm sorry, I'll get you another cup of coffee.'

'Forget the coffee.'

'It was just reflex, I wasn't thinking, I –'

'Skip, forget the coffee. Sit down.'

'You sure you don't want –'

'Forget the coffee.'

'Yeah, right,' he said. He took out another cigarette and tapped it against the back of his wrist.

I said, 'You gave Tim Pat three names.'

'Yeah.'

'Atwood and Cutler and –'

'And Bobby,' he said. 'I sold him Bobby Ruslander.'

He put the cigarette in his mouth, took out his lighter and lit it. His eyes half-lidded against the smoke, he said, 'I ratted him out, Matt. My best friend, except it turns out he's not my friend, and now I went and ratted him out. I told Tim Pat how Bobby was the inside man, he set it up.' He looked at me. 'You think I'm a bastard?'

'I don't think anything.'

'It was something I had to do.'

'All right.'

'But you can see I can't keep the money.'

'Yeah, I guess I can see that.'

'He could get out from under, you know. He's pretty good at squirming off the hook. The other night, Christ, he walked outta the office at my joint like he owned the place. The Actor, let's see him act his way outta this, huh?' I didn't say anything.

'It could happen. He could pull it off.'

'Could be.'

He wiped his eyes with the back of his hand. 'I loved the man,' he said. 'I thought, I thought he loved me.' He took a deep breath, let it out. 'From here on in,' he said, 'I don't love nobody.' He stood up. 'I figure he's got a sporting chance, anyway. Maybe he'll get out of it.'

'Maybe.'

*

623

But he didn't. None of them did. By the weekend they had all turned up in the newspapers, Gary Michael Atwood, Lee David Cutler, Robert Joel Ruslander, all three found in different parts of the city, their heads covered with black hoods, their hands secured with wire behind their backs, each shot once in the back of the head with a .25-caliber automatic. Rita Donegian was found with Cutler, similarly hooded and wired and shot. I guess she got in the way.

When I read about it I still had the money in the brown bank envelope. I still hadn't decided what to do with it. I don't know that I ever quite came to a conscious decision, but the following day I tithed five hundred dollars to the poor box at Saint Paul's. I had, after all, a lot of candles to light. And some of the money went to Anita, and some went in the bank, and somewhere along the line it stopped being blood money and became, well, just money.

I figured that was the end of it. But I kept figuring that, and I kept being wrong.

The call came in the middle of the night. I'd been asleep for a couple of hours but the phone woke me and I groped for it. It took me a minute to recognize the voice on the other end.

It was Carolyn Cheatham.

'I had to call you,' she said, 'on account of you're a bourbon drinker and a gentleman. I owed it to you to call you.'

'What's the matter?'

'Our mutual friend ditched me,' she said, 'and he got me fired out of Tannahill & Co. so he won't have to look at me around the office. Once he didn't need me he just went and cut the string, and do you know he did it over the *phone*?'

'Carolyn —'

'It's all in the note,' she said. 'I'm leaving a note.'

'Look, don't do anything yet,' I said. I was out of bed, fumbling for my clothes. 'I'll be right over. We'll sit down and talk about it.'

'You can't stop me, Matthew.'

'I won't try to stop you. We'll talk a little, and then you can do whatever you want to do.'

The phone clicked in my ear.

I threw my clothes on, rushed over there, hoping it would be pills, something that took its time. I broke a small pane of glass in the downstairs door and let myself in, then used an old credit card to slip the bolt of her spring lock. If she had engaged the dead-bolt lock, I would have had to kick it in, but she hadn't, and that made it easier.

I smelled the cordite before I had the door open. Inside, the room reeked of it. She was sprawled on the couch, her head hanging to one side. The gun was still in her hand, limp at her side, and there was a black-rimmed hole in her temple.

There was a note, too, one page torn from a spiral notebook and anchored to the coffee table with an empty bottle of Maker's Mark bourbon. There was an empty glass next to the empty bottle. The booze showed in her handwriting, and in the sullen phrasing of the suicide note.

I read the note. I stood there for a few minutes, not for very long, and then I got a dish towel from the kitchen and wiped the bottle and the glass. I took another matching glass, rinsed it out and wiped it, and put it in the dish strainer on the counter.

I stuffed the note in my pocket. I took the little gun from her fingers, checked routinely for a pulse, then wrapped a sofa pillow around the gun to muffle its report.

I fired one round into the soft tissue below the rib cage, another into her open mouth.

I dropped the gun into a pocket and got out of there.

They found the gun in Tommy Tillary's house on Colonial Road, stuffed between the cushions of the living-room sofa. The outside of the gun had been wiped clean of prints, but they found an identifiable print inside, on the clip, and it turned out to be Tommy's.

Ballistics got a perfect match. Bullets can shatter when they hit bone, but the shot into her abdomen didn't hit any bones and it was recovered intact.

After the story made the papers, I picked up the phone and called Drew Kaplan. 'I don't understand it,' I said. 'He was free and clear, why the hell did he go and kill the girl?'

'Ask him yourself,' Kaplan said. He did not sound happy. 'You want my opinion, he's a lunatic. I honestly didn't think he was. I figured maybe he killed his wife, maybe he didn't, not my job to try him, right? But I didn't figure the son of a bitch for a homicidal maniac.'

'There's no question he killed the girl?'

'No question that I can see. The gun's pretty strong evidence. Talk about finding somebody with the smoking pistol in his hand, here it was in Tommy's couch. The idiot.'

'Funny he kept it.'

'Maybe he had other people he wanted to shoot. Go figure a crazy man. No, the gun's damning evidence, and there was a phone tip, some man called in the shooting, reported a man running out of the building and gave a description that fitted Tommy better than his clothes. In fact his clothes were in the description. Had him wearing that red blazer of his, tacky thing makes him look like an usher at the old Brooklyn Paramount.'

'It sounds tough to square.'

'Well, somebody else'll have to try to do it,' Kaplan said. 'I told him it wouldn't be appropriate for me to defend him this time. What it amounts to, I wash my hands of him.'

I thought of all this when I read that Angel Herrera got out just the other day. He did all ten years of a five-to-ten because he was at least as good at getting into trouble inside the walls as he had been outside.

Somebody killed Tommy Tillary with a homemade knife after he'd served two years and three months of a manslaughter stretch. I wondered at the time if that was Herrera getting even, and I don't suppose I'll ever know. Maybe the checks stopped going to Santurce and Herrera took it the wrong way. Or maybe Tommy made the wrong remark to some other hard case, and did it face-to-face instead of over the phone.

So many things have changed, so many people are gone.

Antares & Spiro's, the Greek bar on the corner, is gone. It's a Korean fruit store now. Polly's Cage is now Cafe 57, changed from sleazy to chic, with the red flocked wallpaper and the neon parrot long gone. The Red Flame is gone, and the Blue Jay. There's a steak house called Desmond's where McGovern's used to be. Miss Kitty's closed about a year and a half after they bought their books back. John and Skip sold the lease and got out. The new owners opened a gay club called Kid Gloves, and two years later it was out and something else was in.

The gym where I watched Skip do lat-machine pulldowns went out of business within the year. A modern-dance studio took over the premises, and then a couple of years ago the whole building came down and a new one went up. Of the two side-by-side French restaurants, the one where I had dinner with Fran is gone, and the latest tenant is a fancy Indian restaurant. The other French place is still there, and I still haven't eaten there.

So many changes.

Jack Diebold is dead. A heart attack. He was dead six months

626

before I even heard about it, but then we didn't have much contact after the Tillary incident.

John Kasabian left the city after he and Skip sold Miss Kitty's. He opened up a similar joint out in the Hamptons, and I heard he got married.

Morrissey's closed late in '77. Tim Pat skipped bail on a federal gunrunning charge and his brothers disappeared. The ground-floor theater is still running, oddly enough.

Skip is dead. He sort of hung around after Miss Kitty's closed, spending more and more of his time by himself in his apartment. Then one day he got an attack of acute pancreatitis and died on the table at Roosevelt.

Billie Keegan left Armstrong's in early '76, if I remember it right. Left Armstrong's and left New York, too. The last I heard he was off the drink entirely, living north of San Francisco and making candles or silk flowers or something equally unlikely. And I ran into Dennis a month or so ago in a bookstore on lower Fifth Avenue, full of odd volumes on yoga and spiritualism and holistic healing.

Eddie Koehler retired from the NYPD a couple of years back. I got cards from him the first two Christmases, mailed from a little fishing village in the Florida panhandle, I didn't hear from him last year, which probably only means that he's dropped me from his list, which is what happens to people who don't send cards in return.

Jesus, where did ten years go? I've got one son in college now, and another in the service. I couldn't tell you the last time we went to a ball game together, let alone a museum.

Anita's remarried. She still lives in Syosset, but I don't send money there anymore.

So many changes, eating away at the world like water dripping on a rock. For God's sake, last summer the sacred ginmill closed, if you want to call it that. The lease on Armstrong's came up for renewal and Jimmy walked away from it, and now there's yet another goddamned Chinese restaurant where the old joint used to be. He reopened a block farther west, at the corner of Fifty-seventh and Tenth, but that's a little out of my way these days.

In more ways than one. Because I don't drink anymore, one day at a time, and thus have no business in ginmills, be they sacred or profane. I spend less of my time lighting candles and more in church basements, drinking my coffee without bourbon, and out of styrofoam cups.

627

So when I look ten years into the past I can say that I would very likely have handled things differently now, but everything is different now. Everything. All changed, changed utterly. I live in the same hotel, I walk the same streets, I go to a fight or a ball game the same as ever, but ten years ago I was always drinking and now I don't drink at all. I don't regret a single one of the drinks I took, and I hope to God I never take another.

Because that, you see, is the less-traveled road on which I find myself these days, and it has made all the difference. Oh, yes. All the difference.